THE 1-800 SERIES

SIX SWEET CONTEMPORARY ROMANCES

JOSIE RIVIERA

DEAR FRIENDS

A heartwarming story is the hallmark of every romance. Savor the magic with all six fun, sweet contemporary romances in:

The 1-800 Series, Six Sweet Contemporary Romances.
The complete series in 1 collection!

Cozy up with your favorite beverage and lose yourself while you read these fun, joyful home-flipping romances.

1-800-CUPID

A house flipper looking for quick profit. A survivor with a dream. Can two broken hearts find a place to call home?

1-800-CHRISTMAS

Taking the high road is a whole lot easier with someone to love …

1-800-IRELAND

Can two determined people separated by years find true love at the end of an Irish rainbow?

1-800-SUMMER

The last thing she can fix is her own life. Until one man's offer changes everything.

1-800-NEW YEAR

Her lost love is back in town. Is he back for a second chance...or closure?

Christmas in the Air

What if you told your innermost secrets to a guy you assumed you'd never see again?

This collection is available in ebook, paperback, and Large Print paperback. Audiobooks for each book sold separately.

USA TODAY BESTSELLING AUTHOR
JOSIE RIVIERA
1•800•CUPID
A SWEET CONTEMPORARY NOVELLA

CHAPTER 1

Twenty thousand dollars.

Click.

Candee Contando licked her dry lips. She'd done it. She'd placed an online bid on a home-auction website for the Victorian mansion on Thompson Lane. Her dream home, her dollhouse. Her dilapidated project.

Two years of savings. Gone.

No matter. Under her guidance, she'd transform the mansion to its former majestic state, painted a mustard-yellow offset by ornamental burnt-sienna "gingerbread" trim. The sounds of children's giggling and music and barking beagles—yes, beagles—would echo across all five acres of the property.

She surveyed her offer and beamed, savoring the moment.

Now if she only could ensure that no one else bid on the property and drove up the price.

She studied the ticking clock on the website. Stay optimistic, she told herself. Deteriorated by age and wear, the Victorian would scare off any prospective buyer.

She pushed away from her desk and surveyed her real estate office. Although only one room, she prided herself on the cheery décor. One wall featured photos of North Carolina—the majestic peaks of the Blue Ridge parkway and scenic waterfalls. Below the photos hung a map of the area with local real estate listings highlighted by pushpins.

She peered out the window into the street below. Since noon, a bright sun had been at odds with January's wind—a wind crazy in its intent to blow the streetlights off their wires.

For the umpteenth time, she checked her nonringing cell phone for messages. Surely the real estate market in Roses, North Carolina, would improve. Didn't prospective home buyers begin looking in January? And wouldn't these buyers call her rather than her competitors? Candee prided herself on her professionalism and up-to-date listings.

Then why hadn't she made a single sale since August?

On the heel of that depressing assessment came a cheerful one. In two hours, she and her older sister, Desiree, planned to enjoy dinner at Desiree's country club.

Candee stepped back to her desk and switched off the computer.

Two single women in their late twenties, she mused, spending Friday night alone and dateless, four weeks before Valentine's Day.

Her cell phone rang, most likely Desiree firming up dinner plans and reminding Candee not to be late. Regardless of what time Candee met her older sister anywhere, Desiree always arrived before her.

Candee clicked on her phone. "1-800-Cupid," she said with a laugh.

"Contando Realty?" a man asked.

"Yes, yes …" So much for professionalism. Candee felt her cheeks color. She hurried to her desk, dropping into the chair and switching her phone to speaker. "Are you looking to buy a home today, sir?"

"I am." The man hesitated. "Is this the correct number?"

She powered on her computer. "Absolutely."

"I'm new to the area and checked into the Roses Hotel last night," he said.

Envisioning the rundown hotel, Candy raised her eyebrows. Although in all fairness, the hotel was the only lodging open in the winter. Roses, North Carolina, was a summer tourist town known for bubbling hot springs and cool mountain temperatures.

Her fingers poised on the keyboard. "I'm more than happy to assist. Your name?"

"Teddy. Teddy Winchester." He had a deep voice, a slight southern drawl.

"What type of home are you searching for, Mr. Winchester?"

"The worst home in the best neighborhood."

Yup. It figured. No significant sales commission to pay the mortgage this month. Fortunately, her part-time job at the local hardware store was stable, although the pay was meager.

She scrolled through the listings. "For yourself, sir?"

"I'm an investor."

"How many bedrooms and baths?"

"Three bedrooms, two baths. Single family and one level."

"Budget?"

"Anything below $50,000."

She rubbed the back of her neck. *Who did he think she was, a miracle worker?*

"Mr. Winchester, the nicer neighborhoods in Roses are priced well above $100,000."

"Nope. Too high."

Certainly a man of few words.

"Perhaps—"

"I'll take another look on the Internet." He seemed to ignore her completely. "Thanks anyway."

She wouldn't lose a potential sale.

"Wait." She feigned checking a non-existent schedule. "I may have an opening this afternoon. I know the area well and I'll find properties to show you. Will three o'clock work?"

"In a half hour? Fine. I admire a realtor who works fast. Should I meet you at your office? The address is listed on the Internet."

Candee verified the street number and ended the phone call with a cheery, "See you at three."

She clicked off and checked her watch. Thirty minutes wasn't enough time to drive to her apartment and change. Her worn jeans and blue flannel shirt would have to suffice.

Immediately, she phoned Desiree. "I may be late for dinner."

"I'm so glad it's you," Desiree said. "Scott, a new lawyer at the firm, asked me out tonight. Barring the fact the invitation was last minute, I said yes. Desperation, right?" She paused. "Can we plan for dinner together tomorrow night instead?"

"Right, sure. The reason I called is because I have a client who's interested in seeing some properties."

"You have a real live client?" Desiree cut immediately to the question.

Candee envisioned her sister, thick blonde hair piled high, sitting behind a mahogany desk in her law firm. Proper, well-dressed, every inch the high-powered attorney. Desiree had proven that, with the right help, a disadvantaged childhood could lead to a successful adulthood. She worked late hours at her law firm advocating justice for low-income families and their children.

"He's an investor," Candee said.

"Maybe he's tall, dark, and handsome?" Desiree said with deceptive casualness. "And rich?"

"Investors are usually short bald men." Candee adjusted her shirt's wrinkled collar, then checked out the frayed hem of her jeans. She let out a frustrated groan and ran a hand through her unruly auburn waves.

"You'll need a rich man if you plan to go through with your insane idea to purchase that Victorian," Desiree said. "The place will eat up all the money you hope to earn in a lifetime."

"I'll handle most of the work myself. Remember, when we lived in foster care, I learned carpentry from the family who took us in."

"How will you offer a quality after-school environment to disadvantaged kids if you're busy driving nails into crumbling walls?"

"Watch me." Briefly, Candee squeezed her eyes shut. It was her turn to pay it forward.

"Well, don't discount short men. They prefer tall, willowy red-heads with green eyes," Desiree said. "Who knows? He might be struck by Cupid's golden arrow when he meets you. This guy might be the one."

Candee drew in a breath. "The one what, exactly?"

"Your partner, your love, your support system. The one who can help pay off the mountainous amount of debt you'll incur if you actually buy the biggest dilapidated disaster in the state."

"Someone supportive? For me? After what happened?"

Desiree's voice grew quieter. "Not every guy pretends to be something he's not."

A lump lodged in Candee's throat. No man was worth having her heart broken again, although she didn't vocalize her feelings. Desiree was an eternal romantic.

With a promise to meet her sister on Saturday evening,

Candee clicked off and bent to pick up a broken pencil lying on the floor. Not once since the ill-fated night two years ago when her long-time boyfriend had walked out had she broken the vow to herself and wept. Life went on, although a sadness she couldn't shake remained precariously close to the surface.

Some lessons were more difficult than others. Her ex had taught her the hardest—she wasn't interesting enough, pretty enough or vivacious enough.

Tears welled and she brushed them away. Standing, she tossed the pencil into a garbage can by the door. While she confirmed two house showings for Mr. Winchester, she cast a critical assessment of her reflection in the mirror by the office door. She pinched her pale cheeks and added a touch of rose lip balm to her lips. Then she gathered her hair into a ponytail, securing the thick curls with an elastic band. With a final glance in the mirror, she pulled on her cream-colored woolen jacket and wound an emerald-green paisley scarf around her neck.

Her suede purse under her arm, she pushed open the exit doors and stepped outside. The sun had buried itself under a formless cloud, and a swirl of wind blew her paisley scarf across her face. She tucked it securely beneath the collar of her jacket. The day was typical January weather for Roses, undecided if it was warm or cold.

CHAPTER 2

Teddy Winchester pondered for the umpteenth time how he'd ended up in Roses, North Carolina. Certainly the town was charming, tucked along a backdrop of the Blue Ridge Mountains. He'd taken a ride around the region before he'd checked into the hotel. The shopping seemed adequate and the town center exuded storybook appeal, retaining a New England quaintness, complete with a bandstand.

Rob, his not-so-silent business partner in Florida, had assured Teddy the North Carolina weather was always cooperative, even pleasant for mid-January. And the area teemed with real estate bargains because Roses, population five thousand, had never fully recovered from the recession.

Rob was wrong on both counts. Relentless gusts battering under the drafty hotel's window had sent a chill through Teddy all morning while he'd sat in his room, and the inventory of low-priced homes on real-estate websites proved nonexistent.

Roses wasn't what he'd hoped for. He needed a quick turnaround investment to help pay for his nephew Joseph's physical therapy. A horrific car accident and the loss of his nephew's father had left Joseph traumatized and weak, and the extensive physical therapy included strength building and stretching.

Teddy took a deep breath, still reeling from his older brother's death. *Christian, we promised to never desert each other. And now you're gone.*

In an effort to keep busy, Teddy perused his email, then texted an abridged list of instructions to his secretary on how to proceed with the sale of his late brother's farm. He assumed Christian retained life insurance, which would help pay for the mountain of medical bills steadily piling up, as well as lawyers' fees. The papers declaring that Teddy was Joseph's legal guardian weren't finalized yet. The courts took their time, although the will guided the court's decision.

With a sigh, he tapped in Rob's business number.

Rob's gruff voice answered on the fifth ring. "Rob's Marvelous Muffins."

"Hi Rob. Is Joseph around?" Teddy asked.

"He's up to his elbows in Valentine muffin ingredients. A four-year-old's favorite activity is making a mess with a cupful of flour, right?" Rob chuckled. "I'll put him on speaker."

"Hi Uncle Teddy!" Joseph's high-pitched voice vibrated through the phone. "Mr. Rob and I are putting a surprise in our muffins and writing something special on each one. Wanna know what's inside?"

Teddy laughed. "Then it wouldn't be a surprise, right?"

The boy hesitated. "Right."

"Is there anything we can do about that?"

"I can save a muffin for you, Uncle Teddy."

"Great idea, buddy. I'll fly to Miami in a couple weeks, and we'll eat muffins together at Mr. Rob's bakery. Okay?"

Joseph giggled. "Okay."

It was the first time he'd heard the boy laugh since his father had died.

"I love you, Joseph," he said softly.

"Love you, too, Uncle Teddy."

Rob got back on the phone. "He's a good kid. You should see how he's mixing the butter and sugar together."

"Maybe he's a born baker like you, Rob."

"Or a farmer like you."

"I was never good at farming." Which was true. It wasn't until he'd met Rob and gone into real estate that he'd discovered his forte.

"Maybe you haven't discovered the right crop. Try tomatoes. Those plants grow regardless of—Hang on a sec." Rob turned away from the phone, but Teddy could still hear him directing one of his employees to be careful attaching the food grinder to the heavy-duty electric mixer he'd recently purchased. His voice returned to normal strength as he inquired how the house hunting was going.

"I'm meeting a local realtor this afternoon."

"Shouldn't take long. It's a buyer's market." He barked another order to one of his employees, then goaded, "You miss slaving over a hot oven?"

Teddy could easily visualize the twinkle in Rob's crystal-blue eyes. "I haven't baked so much as a boxed cake in years," he said, chuckling.

He and Rob had met years earlier at a cooking class for men. Teddy had soon discovered his speciality would never include burning another muffin, but Rob had gone on to build a successful chain of bakeries in the greater Miami area. Teddy could practically inhale the delectable, sugary aromas coming from Rob's spotless commercial kitchen.

"And I'll take Joseph to his equestrian session this weekend," Rob was saying. "The kid has really formed a connection with horses."

"Exactly the reason his therapist advised it," Teddy replied. "She said horseback riding would reduce Joseph's anxiety after the trauma of the accident."

"She's right," Rob said. "And she's such a pretty thing, isn't she?"

"Rob, she's Joseph's therapist."

"Yeah, yeah, I know. And she's a few years younger than me, anyway." Rob gave an exaggerated whistle. "Remember to keep me in the real estate loop."

"Do I have a choice?" Teddy grinned. He was impatient with lawyers and their endless legal jargon and talk of probate court. However, with the man and mentor he owed his real-estate start-up business to, Teddy's patience was limitless.

"Hey, thanks for watching Joseph for me," he added.

"What are oddball friends for? Your job is to snag the best buy in Roses." The usually brash Rob tempered his tone. "And Joseph's no bother, you know. When someone's down and out they need help, right?"

"These past few months … Thank you. For everything." Teddy clicked off and stared at the phone. Sometimes, he didn't know what he would've done if Rob hadn't been there to pick up the pieces after Christian's death.

He checked his watch, then pulled on a gray T-shirt. He was still half-wet from his shower and the T-shirt stuck to his body. He shook his damp hair, threw on a Florida State baseball cap, stuck his wallet in his jeans pocket, and zipped up an olive-green vest. Out in the parking lot, he fired up the engine of his red truck, and at exactly three o'clock arrived at Candee Contando Realty. He needed someone experienced to help him get just the right property, and from the Internet reviews he'd read, Mrs. Contando had been in business over thirty years.

He walked to the entrance of an older brick building

housing various offices and stopped midstep, admiring the beautiful young woman waiting in the doorway. The collar of a cream-colored jacket framed her oval face, along with an absurdly colorful green scarf. A pair of tiny gold cross earrings dangled from her ears. Her features were all high cheekbones and generous lips.

He tipped his baseball hat. "Hello. I'm supposed to meet Mrs. Contando here."

"I'm *Miss* Contando, although please call me Candee." Her smile enhanced her fascinating emerald eyes.

His heartbeat slowed and he had to prompt himself to swallow. "This is *your* realty?"

"Actually, it was said to be my mother's company for a while." She pushed back a stray wisp of auburn hair, handed him a business card, and then extended her hand. "Are you Mr. Winchester?"

"Teddy." Tight jeans emphasized her shapely legs and rounded hips. This woman's stunning good looks could stop traffic.

"I expected someone older," he managed to say.

She let go of his hand, swept her gaze up his six-foot frame, and grinned. "I expected someone shorter."

He met her grin, debating where he should look next.

Her lovely face enhanced by a sprinkle of freckles? Nope, not at all professional to stare. Instead, he gazed at the weathered door behind her and cleared his throat. "Did you find any listings?"

Her mouth curved into a polite smile. "Yes. Ready to see your future house?"

Unexpectedly, he felt drawn to her. She wasn't at all what he'd expected, although his good sense warned him away. He was completely satisfied with being single, having made peace with that reality ever since his one serious relationship with a woman had ended badly. He'd lost his self-reliance once, and once was enough.

He gestured toward his truck. "Should we use my vehicle or yours?"

"Mine." She pointed to a rusted Honda Civic. "I'll drive. I know these roads well."

He opened the car door for her, then came around and settled in the passenger seat.

She buckled her seatbelt. He buckled his, then took in a quick breath. A faint whiff of her scent lingered in the air. Roses. He grinned. Why not?

"So, Candee, have you lived in Roses all your life?"

She glanced at him. "I've lived here and there."

She returned her attention to the road, and an overlong moment passed in silence.

He waited for her to continue. When she didn't elaborate, he asked if he could turn on the radio. The station was set to Classic Rock and "Unchained Melody" by the Righteous Brothers came on, the heartfelt lyrics about "Oh, my love, my darling," filling the little car.

Teddy was about to suggest they try for more upbeat music when she gushed, "I love this song."

Okay, he thought. She must be a romantic.

"How many showings did you schedule?" he asked.

"Two, both in Glenhaven." Flicking on her signal, she turned onto another road. "You want three bedrooms and two baths, correct?"

"The perfect flip house."

"You don't intend to live in the property?"

"Nope. I want an easy fixer-upper that won't take longer than six weeks to renovate. I'm working with another investor, and we intend to make a quick and substantial profit."

"Don't we all," she murmured.

Their gazes met and they shared a grin.

Soon, they were driving past neatly manicured lawns and one-story homes.

She stopped in front of a beige bungalow, parking on the street. "The previous owners relocated, and this house has been on the market over sixty days." They got out and walked toward the house. As you can see—" she gestured to the tidy neighborhood and matching mailboxes—"Glenhaven is lovely."

"The neighborhood is too cookie cutter." He stood on the front porch and studied mismatched shingle patches nailed to the roof. "Needs some work."

"Inside, the home is beautifully decorated."

"The bigger the mess, the bigger the profit." Automatically, he provided the investor's mantra. "What's the asking price?"

"One hundred thousand dollars, although the owners are willing to negotiate."

He shook his head. "Too expensive." *Why did realtors try to sell homes over the buyer's stated limit?*

Noting Candee's downcast expression, he lightened his tone. "Are there any other homes in this town under fifty thousand?"

"There is … one." She paused and pressed a finger to her lips, seeming to search for a reason not to answer.

He overlooked her lack of enthusiasm. "Price?"

"That particular house is listed on an internet auction site and meets none of your criteria." She paused. "It's a rambling Victorian and—"

"Where is this house?"

"On Thompson Lane at the edge of town. It's unoccupied."

"How much land comes with the property?"

"Five acres."

"Can the land be sold off in parcels? Is it zoned commercial or residential?"

"You can get on the website and download the report." She slid into the driver's seat and shut the door.

Had he heard a grunt of disapproval?

"Sorry I can't help you, Teddy," she continued, when he got into the passenger seat. "I'll drive you back to my office to get your truck, and I'll phone if anything in your price range becomes available."

Now he had to beg her to view a property? She might be gorgeous, but she was certainly the world's worst realtor.

"Do you have the lockbox code to this Victorian, Candee?"

She raised her delicate brows. "Yes, but—"

"I assume an appointment isn't necessary if no one lives there."

She inserted the key into the ignition. "My pleasure."

He didn't know why, although he'd bet she was being sarcastic.

A few minutes later she turned onto Thompson Lane. As they passed an elderly man with gray hair and glasses perched on his nose, she waved, explaining he was Mr. Dunworthy, a widower who owned a Queen-Anne-style home two doors away. He'd lived in the neighborhood forever and refused to give up his large home, although it was becoming more and more difficult for him to maintain.

She drove to the end of the road, sped up a circular driveway and parked in front of an imposing three-story house. An octagonal tower soared from the steep multigabled roof. Century-old trees flanked both sides of the property. On one corner of the overgrown front lawn, an oak tree boasted a tire swing. Teddy imagined himself pushing Joseph on that swing. Joseph needed to play more, needed fresh air. He'd been so pale since his father's death.

No, Teddy told himself. Quick and easy sale.

Of course, he could purchase the property for the land and build five new homes, more than tripling his profit. Or build low-income housing. Rob would agree with that decision.

He rounded the car to open the door for her, but she'd already gotten out. They stood side by side and stared at the house. For the first time in many years, he drank in the stillness of a cool winter afternoon, admiring a home he'd only imagined in his dreams—and was well aware of the insane impulse to hold Candee's hand as they walked to the front door.

He extended his hand to her.

She stared at him in surprise, but then she took his hand.

"The home is beautiful, isn't it?" she said as they walked to the front porch together.

It was, although the Victorian sat beneath layers of peeling yellow paint that marred its exterior and several of the windows were boarded up. A covered front porch curved around to the side, and there was also a side entrance. Teddy imagined white wooden rocking chairs, a row of lush Boston ferns, and ceiling fans spinning lazily on a warm summer afternoon.

The land, the land, he reminded himself.

Candee dropped her hand and tapped in the code for the lockbox. She tipped her head toward the purple front door. "In its former glory days, this home reflected the wealth of the owners—the Langrone family. They owned a prosperous knitting mill in Roses."

"And then?"

"And then the mill went out of business. Too much foreign competition. The Langrones declared bankruptcy and moved out shortly afterward. All the owners since then moved in with high expectations until they discovered they weren't able to maintain the upkeep."

What a waste of a beautiful home.

As if she'd read his thoughts she lingered on the porch, a wistfulness in her gaze. "This Victorian was built in 1889 and definitely requires TLC."

An absolute understatement, Teddy decided, when they walked in. The outside needed extensive work, and the hardwood floor of the grand foyer was badly gouged and scratched.

Candee flicked on a light switch. Nothing happened, and she offered an apologetic shrug. With lights not working, they were left in semidarkness. And although the odor in the entrance hall stopped him cold, she didn't miss a beat and continued walking.

"This is the kitchen," she was saying. "The cabinets are an olive color …"

"What's left of them." He eyed the traditional arched raised panel doors and a lone cabinet left on the floor. So much beauty amidst so much neglect.

He stepped onto rusty linoleum. Luxury vinyl it was not because the floor felt soft and spongy beneath his work boots. Water damage, and hopefully not too extensive and requiring a floor joist.

Candee caught the focus of his gaze. "Avocado was a popular color in the 70's when the owners updated the kitchen."

"Avocado is back in style," he replied.

Hadn't Rob uttered the same words when he'd designed his showy corporate office in Miami?

Teddy opened and closed a cabinet door and examined the hinges. "With lots of elbow grease and white paint, these cabinets might work. Better than tossing them in a landfill."

Candee shook her head. "Nothing in this kitchen is

salvageable." She opened the oven door. With a shriek, she slammed it shut.

He inspected the grease-encrusted stove burners. "I'd install stainless steel appliances. The stove can stay. Six burners are a good selling feature, and the microwave can be mounted above the stove. Granite countertops, travertine flooring, a dishwasher, disposal ..." He swung around. "If I open this wall, there'd be an expansive view of the yard, which would be great for kids."

He didn't miss her speculative glance at his ring finger when he mentioned children.

"I'm not married," he said. "It's just me and my four-year-old nephew, Joseph."

She hesitated. "Where is he?"

"He's in Miami spending the next few weeks with my business partner, Rob. Rob's the one who got me started in real estate."

He'd said too much. How could he put into words the way his gut split every time he pondered Christian's death, or the pain Joseph had endured because of his numerous operations, or how Teddy had recently debated selling everything and starting over—somewhere quiet and peaceful—away from the high-pressure lifestyle of fast-paced Miami?

"Every home I take on, I treat as my own," he whispered.

Although this home wouldn't be here, because every bone in his practical body insisted it should be demolished.

He ran the faucet, and rusty water spewed into the chipped porcelain sink.

"City water and sewers," Candee said.

"Good. No septic issues or a dry well save money. What's this house going for?"

"No one knows the final price with an auction."

"Square footage?"

"Over 5500 square feet."

"This house is bigger than I thought." He pressed his lips together. "What's the current bid?"

She paused for a long while. "Twenty thousand dollars. You know you'll pour money into a house this size in order to get it back into shape."

"Did you know you're the exact opposite of a sales-woman, Candee?" With a grin, he stepped forward into what he presumed was the formal living room, appreciatively remarking on the marble fireplace with its updated gas fireplace and the twelve-foot ceilings.

"No use in traipsing through a ramshackle house—" Candee began.

"I noticed there's a dining room and parlor," he interrupted.

"Yes. And an adjacent library. And a music room."

That same wistfulness in her voice again.

He struggled to find the right words, debating whether to ask if she was upset about something. Hesitating, he changed direction. "Is the music room next?"

"You're the buyer." Had she silently inserted the adjective *foolish?*

He assessed the lengthening shadows signaling early nightfall. With no electricity, the house was growing darker by the minute.

As they headed into the music room, the toe of his boot caught on a torn piece of shag carpeting. He heard Candee call out a warning as he lost his footing and fell through the floor.

CHAPTER 3

Candee peered through the hole in the floor into the shadowy basement. Although she heard Teddy's footsteps, she couldn't see him.

"Are you all right?" she called.

"Sure. I wanted to examine the basement, anyway. It appears to be a walk-out."

She leaned over, her eyes adjusting to the darkness. "What's it like down there?"

"I'll let you know in a minute." He switched on his cell phone's flashlight and peeked up at her, waggling his dark eyebrows. "Care to join me?"

He couldn't possibly be flirting.

"Uh no. I'll wait here, thanks."

Teddy pulled himself back up into the music room. "Maybe next time?"

With one hand in his worn jeans pocket, the other wielding a tape measure, he was rugged and impossibly good-looking, his muscled arms straining against a thin gray T shirt. He brushed dirt from his vest and yanked off his baseball cap. His wealth of black hair was mussed, and the late afternoon sun gilded thin strips of golden highlights to the tips. Perhaps he'd stepped right off the cover of the latest men's home improvement magazine without telling her.

Although she'd walked through this house many times, she hadn't ventured into the basement. Desiree often called Candee the opposite of a realist, although what would the world be like, Candee rationalized, without dreamers?

Teddy carried the broken kitchen cabinet from the kitchen and placed it over the hole in the floor.

As they continued through the house, he snapped photos with his cell phone.

"After I see the upstairs, I'll send these pictures to my partner Rob," he said.

She gestured to the sweeping spindle staircase. "This home has five bedrooms, five baths, and five fireplaces. It's the opposite of a perfect flip house."

"Nevertheless, lead the way. There're two more floors to check out."

After he'd inspected the upstairs bathrooms and admired the worn brass hardware on the master suite's mahogany double doors, they made their way downstairs.

When they reached the foyer, he glanced up from his cell phone and said, "I want to make an offer."

She shuffled back two steps. "You're joking … right?" Her gaze shifted to the entrance. She'd made a serious mistake in mentioning this house to him.

"I never joke about real estate."

"This home"—she swept out her hands—"is a money pit."

"Which is why Rob and I will buy the property for the land."

Candee's heart stopped beating.

"We'll demolish the house," he added.

Her house, she wanted to shout. *Her* land for disadvantaged children. She'd envisioned beagle puppies cavorting across the lawn, perhaps an acre set aside for a working farm. Children needed to connect with nature. It was time to get them away from technology and back to values that really mattered.

And music. The music room off the kitchen would reverberate with glorious sounds again.

Teddy faced her. "Anything the matter?"

There was kindness in his gaze, interest on his handsome features. Should she share her ideas with a man she'd known for less than two hours—a man who was bent on destroying those very same ideas? A man who'd held her hand in his strong grip and gazed at the Victorian with the same wonder and appreciation as she had?

Struggling to hold onto her composure, she reminded herself she was a professional. Besides, this house was nothing like what he was looking for.

She lifted her chin. "Not a thing."

Lightly, he touched her cheek, his gesture completely unexpected. "I understand how you feel about a house like this. It's very beautiful, but beyond repair."

Turning away, she quickly dabbed at her eyes. She settled into the tune she'd known the past two years: no matter how sincere, how charming, men couldn't be trusted. Better to hold him at a polite distance and keep her plans to herself. He'd soon be gone back to Miami.

"Are you sure you're okay?" he asked.

She feigned her brightest smile. "Of course."

He waited a beat, then silently followed her, standing on the porch while she locked the front door.

"Any idea what the current bid is? You mentioned under fifty thousand."

Candee rubbed her temples. A quick search on the Internet would spew all the information he'd need to place a bid.

"Twenty thousand dollars," she finally said. "And bidding ends in three weeks."

So many mistakes today, beginning by answering the phone. 1-800-CUPID. Hah!

"Then I'll offer thirty thousand dollars," he said.

An uneasy quiet descended. A cold breeze brushed across her cheeks.

"The auction accepts bids in twenty-thousand dollar-increments," she said.

"Then I'll bid forty thousand, which is still under my fifty-thousand-dollar budget."

"The bank may not accept a lowball offer." Her remark was nonsensical, since she was hoping the bank would accept her offer, because twenty thousand dollars was all she had. She glanced at Teddy's determined stance. Surely there was a way to convince him not to bid. However, thirty years of proper Southern behavior stopped her from saying more.

"I can offer all cash," he said. "Plus, my partner and I can close immediately. On a foreclosure, the bank will take everything into consideration."

"Don't you want to walk the property? If you're interested in the land, there are building requirements and permits—"

He reached into his pocket and handed her a business card. "I do this for a living, Candee. I know all about due diligence." He gave a lazy grin. "And there's another clause, which can either make or break the deal."

She fisted one hand on her hip. "The bank should just hand over the house to you?"

"A definite bonus." He laughed, rich and full. "I'm hoping my lovely realtor will grant me the pleasure of her company at dinner."

"I can't." Her refusal was quick, a knee-jerk reaction. She hadn't dated in two years and wouldn't start now, especially with a tycoon investor who assumed that by flaunting the cash in his pocket, he could take her castle in the air away from her.

"Not even for a slice of pizza? I don't know my way around Roses yet."

She retreated a step. "Tony's Pizza on Main Street is always open. You can spot the red and green awning a mile away."

"Are you saying no, Candee?"

"Is my refusal a deal breaker, Teddy?"

"Not if I can get this property for under fifty thousand dollars."

"If you decide to bid, you'll have to wait three weeks to find out if you've won."

His gaze lingered on her face. "Some things are worth waiting for."

eddy's cell phone buzzed on the nightstand in his hotel room. Awake anyway, he answered it and heard a recognizable woman's voice.

"Teddy?"

"Yvonne?" He peered at the clock on the nightstand. "You realize it's three a.m.?"

"Are you awake?"

He pushed a hand through his hair. "Should I be?"

"It's nine in the morning here in Madrid."

"I'm not in Spain," he countered.

"Such a shame you aren't with me." A long feminine sigh. "I'll never get used to the time difference. Look, my network in the States wants me in Madrid another few weeks to cover the recent drought. Water levels in the reservoirs are abnormally low, and they're aiming for a human-interest story to boost ratings and land a prime-time slot."

Teddy had met Yvonne—an attractive woman with honeyed skin, her thinly arched black brows offset by a pixie cut of platinum-blonde hair—when he'd been offered a weekly television segment featuring tidbits on flipping homes. His fifteen minutes of fame had lasted, well, fifteen minutes. His relationship with Yvonne was going on five months, although he hardly ever saw her. Her job involved a great deal of travel, and he wasn't diligent about keeping in touch with her. He wasn't adaptable to the ever-changing elasticity of dating a woman he saw only twice a month.

He extended the expected congratulatory remarks. Compliments were a prerequisite when dating Yvonne Evette. She was a career woman bent on reaching the top, although what 'the top' was had yet to be determined. Currently, it meant an anchor position on a major American network.

After good-byes, he clicked off his phone and shifted restlessly on his narrow bed. The previous morning when he'd arrived at the Roses Hotel and realized the four-star rating wasn't accurate, he'd debated about sitting on the bed, much less lying on it. Still, he'd pulled back the bedspread, flopped down, and peered at a stain on the ceiling, trying not to ponder how it got there, for it certainly wasn't a water stain.

Now, in the darkened room, he punched a pillow and rolled onto his side.

Night after night since his brother's death, sleep had been elusive.

That's what happened when two brothers grew up together facing the shared futility of scarcity and endless beatings from their drug-addled father. Nothing was left of the Winchester heritage except the old Florida farm, the rundown homestead sitting on two acres of land at the end of a county road. And no matter how wealthy Teddy became, his roots were fixed in poverty.

Fortunately, his brother Christian had held onto the farm after Christian's wife died a year earlier, refurbishing the place and attempting to grow citrus fruit. The crops hadn't produced one grapefruit, as far as Teddy knew. Neither he nor Christian had the knack for farming, and Christian had always struggled when it came to financial success.

Lately, Teddy found himself talking to his late brother: *Christian, should I do this, should I do that? I'm a bachelor. Am I the best choice as Joseph's legal guardian?*

Christian had been an exemplary father. How was Teddy expected to fill those impressive shoes? Perhaps he should marry, he pondered, providing a stable home for Joseph as his brother had done.

Turning onto his back and linking his hands behind his head he thought about Yvonne—her suggestive words, her open invitations, her sultry voice. However, he didn't want Yvonne. His mind traveled instead to *Miss* Candee Contando, the beautiful realtor with the creamy complexion, a mass of red hair framing her face and long legs that went on forever.

Her realty skills were non-existent. When he'd pressed her for details about any property under fifty thousand, she'd hesitated for a lengthy spell before answering. When they'd stood together and stared at the Victorian, he'd had to fight down the impulse to kiss her while holding her hand. She was gorgeous and witty, with a cool no-nonsense façade. And somehow, he knew she'd require a sizable amount of convincing to date him.

He didn't know the reason for his next decision. He only knew he wanted to see her again.

He'd visit her office first thing Monday morning with some excuse, and then invite her to lunch. Perhaps he'd bid on the property with her assistance.

Envisioning Candee's beautiful face, he drifted off to sleep.

* * *

"Pizza?" Desiree repeated. "The guy's taking you out for pizza?"

Candee smoothed the collar of her royal-blue silk blouse. She wore an outfit appropriate for dinner at the fancy country club her sister belonged to—the silk blouse and a black pencil skirt, and black stilettos.

"If you recall," she said, "I'm not going."

"Was he bald?"

Candee sipped her water. "No. His hair is dark and wavy."

"Short?"

"Wrong again. He's at least six feet tall. If anything, he's exceptionally handsome." Her heart gave a peculiar little pitch as she remembered his outrageous smile when he'd asked if she wanted to join him in the basement.

"Married?"

"No, although he talked about his nephew."

Desiree reached for her crystal wineglass filled with a local red wine. "Rich?"

"I checked his business listing on the Internet. R and T Realty in Miami is legit."

A teasing smile tilted Desiree's lips. "Then why would you refuse his offer to go out for pizza?"

Because all her energies were focused on the Victorian house, Candee wanted to say. Because she wasn't ready for a relationship.

"Because he's placing a bid on the Langrone mansion so he can tear it down," she responded aloud.

Desiree beckoned to a waiter who immediately splashed more water into the women's glasses. "Has he lost his mind like you have?"

Candee assessed her perfectly coiffed sister. Desiree was her usual stunning self, her blonde hair caught at the crown of her head with a glittering rhinestone fastener.

Forking a piece of lettuce, she replied, "Perhaps that's how these high-roller investor types go about flips."

"Once the house is torn down, what's he going to do with a vacant five-acre lot?"

"He didn't explain." Candee pushed her half-eaten meal of salad, grilled salmon and roasted red potatoes aside. "Who spends thousands of dollars to tear down a beautiful piece of property which should be preserved, not destroyed?"

Desiree finished her wine and set her glass to the side. "His reasons might be good ones."

"Well, he won't have the opportunity to tell me. I won't be seeing him again."

"Give him a chance. He sounds utterly gorgeous. Call him."

Candee leaned back and crossed her arms. "I've never called a guy in my life."

"Your life, your decision." Desiree's gaze traveled through the expansive dining room. "Did I mention the club is having a Valentine's Day silent auction and dinner dance? I remember how beautifully you helped me decorate the dining room two years ago. We filled champagne glasses with candy hearts—and the chocolate fondue was fabulous!"

Candee faked a glibness she didn't feel. "You're referring to the night my ex walked out on me for another woman."

"You'll be happier if you don't dwell on the past," Desiree said. "Besides, you'd discussed ending your relationship with George two months before the actual breakup. Focus on what's ahead and let the past stay where it belongs."

Before Candee could answer, Desiree trilled a giggle and waved. "Scott's here, the man who took me out last night."

Candee peered over her shoulder. "The guy with the blond crewcut sitting alone at a table near the bar?"

"Yes. I mentioned we were eating here tonight, and he said he might join us for dessert, and then we discussed he might bring a friend … umm … for you. The friend's name is Allen Allen."

"You planned to set me up on a blind date?" Candee half-stood. "Thanks, but no thanks."

"What's wrong with meeting a man for coffee and dessert? Maybe we can double date for the Valentine dance."

"The dance I'm not attending," Candee reminded.

Desiree peered in Scott's direction. "I don't see anyone with him." She frowned, then pulled her vibrating cell phone from her handbag. She flashed Scott a smile and read his text aloud. "Allen heard the weather might take a turn for the worse, so he decided not to come."

"The guy's name really is Allen Allen?"

"He practices law in a neighboring town. He and Scott went to school together."

Candee was no longer listening. She was peering out the nearest window, assessing the weather. The earlier light drizzle was turning to sleet, and she thought it prudent to leave sooner rather than later. Within a few minutes she was pulling on her jacket, a faux fur capelet, and Desiree was sharing Scott's table with him.

As Candee prepared to exit, she walked straight into a tall attractive man wearing navy pants, a striped polo shirt, and a gray sport coat.

"Candee? What are you doing here?" Teddy's gaze slid slowly up her, from her stilettos and slim-fitting skirt to her silk blouse, finally stopping at her face.

She fingered her gold cross earrings. "May I ask you the same question?"

"My partner has a reciprocal agreement with private clubs around the country. Since you refused my pizza offer last night …" He gave an appreciative male smile. "You know, you're a knockout when you're all dressed up."

Heat flushed her cheeks. "Thanks for the … compliment?"

"I mean, you're a beautiful woman whether you're wearing jeans or—"

Now the flush warmed her ears. "Well, thanks again. I was just leaving."

"Me too. I ordered takeout food and forgot forks." He flourished a bag with the country club's logo as proof, then glanced out the window by the front door. "Roses certainly has unpredictable weather."

"It's not usually like this." She attempted to brush past him. "Whereas Florida's weather is predictably hot and sunny."

"Especially Miami." He grinned. "Where are you parked?"

"I came with my sister, Desiree, who's ditched me. She prefers to drink coffee with her latest conquest, a new lawyer at her firm." Candee glanced over her shoulder at the bar area. Desiree was watching her, and she grinned and offered a thumbs-up.

Candee didn't respond, turning back to Teddy. "She and her newest conquest had planned a blind date for me, although Allen Allen, another lawyer, decided I wasn't worth the effort of driving in bad weather."

Teddy's dark eyebrows quirked. "This guy's first and last name are the same?"

"Yes." She surprised herself by adding, "It would have been my first date in two years, although I would've refused."

"His loss is my gain. I'll take you home."

Absolutely not.

"No, no." Candee shook her head while securing her capelet. "I planned to call a taxi."

Teddy gestured toward his pickup truck. "I'm parked at the curb. And your vocabulary might improve if you substituted yes for no once in a while."

"I can't. Really—"

"Say yes."

No use in arguing with him. His references had checked out and he wasn't a total stranger. She smiled. "All right. I don't live far from here."

"Much better."

With his hand on her elbow, he guided her outside to his truck, opening the passenger door and helping her up and in. Her tight skirt didn't allow for much climbing, and she shifted into the seat, hoping her skirt wouldn't ride up her thighs.

It did, and judging from his appreciative smile, he noticed.

"My address is 121 Juniper Street," she said, after she'd adjusted her skirt to a more proper length.

"I'll plug it into my cell phone."

She glanced at his profile as he slid into the driver's seat. Way too attractive, she thought, in a roguish way.

"What about your silverware for the takeout?" she asked.

He flashed a boyish grin, displaying even white teeth. "The club's signature hamburger can be eaten with human fingers, and there's a supply of paper napkins in my truck's glove compartment."

"You're well-equipped."

For a fleeting second, his gaze turned somber. "I try, although sometimes life throws some unexpected curves."

At close range, she noted a scar below his right eye. It certainly didn't affect his good looks, but she wondered if it indicated some of those unexpected curves life had thrown at him.

CHAPTER 5

The sleet came faster, making visibility difficult. Still, Teddy seemed to recognize where they were as they neared the turn-off for Thompson Lane.

"You know the code for the lockbox, right?" Teddy asked.

"Yes, I have it memorized," she said.

"Mind if we stop there first? I'd meant to check the water heater yesterday. In the excitement of falling through the floor, I forgot."

She caught her lower lip with her teeth to stop from blurting out. He wanted to see *her* Victorian again?

"The weather—" She gestured theatrically to the icy roads.

"I have 4-wheel drive."

"Did you offer me a ride tonight in order to get into the house again?"

He slowed the truck, studying her for a couple heartbeats, and she attributed his silence to his interest in the Victorian. "I had no idea you were dining at the country club this evening," he said.

There was enough truth in his statement to make her cheeks burn. Still, she persisted. "But when you did, you seized the opportunity."

He offered a disarming chuckle. "Perhaps that was my second thought."

She couldn't help a reciprocal grin. Truly, the guy was impossible. "And what was your first thought?"

He glanced at her, and for a moment, she was caught in the spell of his irresistible dark eyes. "How lucky I was to see you twice in two days," he said softly.

A faint smile touched her mouth. She stared out the windshield at the falling sleet, trying to decide if he was harmlessly flirting with her or telling the truth.

"There's no electricity at the house, Teddy. It will be freezing and dark."

"There's a gas fireplace in the living room. I called the gas company this morning. The meter is running as the gas was never switched off." The truck slid on the slick road. He reduced his speed again, gripping the steering wheel and focusing on the taillights ahead of them. "And I keep extra flashlights and candles in my truck."

"Are you always prepared, regardless of the circumstances?"

His lips twitched. "I try to think of everything."

When they reached the circular driveway, he inched his truck along it and slid to a stop. At night, the Victorian loomed majestic and mammoth, set against the stormy winter sky. She imagined smoke curling from all five chimneys, the welcoming fireplaces blazing in the enormous hearths.

"This house is a proverbial jewel in the rough," she murmured.

"Yes, it is." Teddy's expression softened. He got out of the truck, hoisted a knapsack over his shoulders, and then opened the passenger door for her.

"I could get used to this," she said.

He assisted her out of the truck and took her hand. "Used to what?"

"Being treated like a lady."

He blinked. "Is there any other way to treat a woman?"

Unfortunately, yes, there were plenty of other ways.

She drew in a sharp breath, remembering the verbal abuse she'd suffered with George. How he'd yell to silence her when she didn't agree with him; his chiding, "Come on, can't you take a joke, Candee?" after he'd made fun of her cooking, or her clothes, or her mannerisms. Their relationship had sent her into a tailspin of self-doubt and self-preservation.

Teddy interrupted her musings. "Shall I carry you up the stairs and over the threshold?"

"I can walk perfectly fine on my own."

She took one step and skated forward.

He slipped an arm around her shoulders. "Just in case, I'll keep you steady."

"Stilettos weren't made for walking," she joked, accepting his embrace and leaning into his solid chest as her heels crunched along the crusty ice.

He chuckled. "I'm not complaining."

They walked to the house under an onslaught of bone-chilling, wind-blown sleet.

Teddy was proving to be a gentleman, she mused, holding her securely and concerned about her welfare, in a fast-paced era where common courtesies were oftentimes forgotten. Gratefully, she smiled up at him.

When they reached the porch, she punched the code into the lockbox, extracted the key and unlocked the door.

He flicked on his phone flashlight and steered them to the living room. "I'll get the gas fireplace running and then we'll have dinner." He pulled a blanket from his knapsack and set it on the floor, gesturing her to sit. Then he placed his gray sport coat beside her.

"You can't light the fireplace and you shouldn't eat in here. The bank owns the house—we don't." She removed her capelet and installed herself on the blanket with her legs straight out, her tight black skirt tucked securely around them. "There are laws, Teddy …"

"If anyone asks, you're my realtor and I'm the man buying the house."

"And as your realtor, may I remind you that you're making a mistake by even thinking about purchasing a home in such poor shape? This isn't a wise investment for a house-flipper."

"I'm tearing it down, remember?" He walked to the fireplace and held the pilot button down for a couple minutes. A flame flickered, and the fire soon glowed, warming the room.

She sighed. "What else is in your knapsack?"

"Soy candles." He brought out a tidy boxed candle set along with a book of matches. He lit the candles and placed them on the fireplace mantel. "The box described these candles as part of the 'jasmine and cedar wood atmosphere collection.'"

"Well then, they're perfect," she said, amused.

He sat beside her, opened his takeout box and held up a massive hamburger. "Ah, dinner by candlelight."

"No dessert? I love caramels coated in chocolate."

"I'll bring caramels next time. Dark or milk chocolate?"

"Dark." She chortled. "Bring those, and how could I refuse?"

"Hopefully, you can't refuse anything I offer." His teasing

laugh was potent, and his affectionate appraisal made her heart rate rise. Along with the aroma of the cedar candles, she inhaled Teddy's clean scent, all male, and the air around them heated.

They fell into companionable silence, as he shared his crispy fries and had a bite of his hamburger. On top of the dinner she'd already eaten, she was consuming more calories than she normally ate in two days.

When they were finished, Teddy picked up the napkins strewn beside them. "What do you do when you're not selling real estate?" he asked.

"I volunteer at the Roses no-kill animal shelter every Sunday." She wiped her fingers on a napkin. "And I work part-time at the hardware store in town, since I like making things out of wood. My foster family's business was working with wood."

His hands stilled. "Your foster family?"

"When we were teenagers, my sister and I were removed from our home and placed into the state welfare system as foster children."

Once she blurted out the words, Candee chided herself. What had compelled her to divulge so much information? If she'd blinked, she would have missed the kind interest clouding Teddy's face before he replaced his expression with a teasing grin.

"And what do you make out of wood? Should I book you a spot on the home improvement channel?" he asked.

"I'd wait about fifty years if I were you. I'm not ready for my own television show." She fixed her stare on the burning gas logs in the fireplace. "I made a detailed dollhouse once with my foster father, complete with a rocking chair measuring three inches." She paused as tears threatened. "I still have that chair."

He kept his gaze on her face. "Care to tell me about your foster family?"

"Which one?"

"There was more than one?"

"We were shuffled to five different families." Her throat tightened as the memories washed over her. "The agency urged each foster family to keep us, and then the family would decide not to adopt."

Two teenage girls with no parents hadn't been worthy of love or a stable home.

Teddy was watching her closely. "Go on," he said quietly.

She swallowed. "The last family Desiree and I were placed with ended up being our 'forever' family." Candee commended herself on her steady tone. "We attended church together, and in the evening we often sang hymns around their old upright piano while I attempted to plunk out the tunes."

"I'm impressed." He considered her with open admiration. "You make dollhouses and play the piano and volunteer at a no-kill animal shelter. That is, when you're not selling real estate."

He'd turned the conversation away from her past, and she was appreciative. Most days, she secured her childhood memories in a protected compartment in her mind. Sitting with Teddy, who seemed so attuned to her, she felt comfortable and safe.

She half smiled. "I don't do any of those things remarkably well, except volunteering at the animal shelter. Animals love you no matter who you are or your background."

He shook his head. "I've never had time for animals."

"Doesn't your four-year-old nephew live with you?"

"Yes, although it's only been for the past few months, and we're still getting used to each other. Rob's watching him now while I'm away. Joseph rides horses on weekends at an equestrian center near Miami, and now he wants a horse."

"He'll probably beg for a dog at some point, too."

Teddy chuckled. "He already has asked."

Get him a rescue dog, preferably a beagle, she wanted to encourage. Although, seeing the closed expression on Teddy's face, she didn't pursue the subject.

"Do you read music?" she asked.

"I'm no Beethoven, although I can keep a steady beat on a timpani drum." He stood and gathered their trash in the carryout bag. "I'd like to go with you to the animal shelter—if I'm properly invited. You volunteer every Sunday?"

"Immediately after church."

He paused, then winked. "I'm waiting for an invite."

She couldn't help laughing. "The shelter needs all the help it can get, although volunteers must first attend an orientation, give references and then commit to a certain length of time."

"Can you vouch for me? I'll be living in Roses for the next few weeks."

"All right."

"Flexible hours?" he asked with amusement.

She grinned. "Absolutely."

"Then I'll assist in any way I can." He pulled a battery-operated transistor radio out of his knapsack. Turning it on, he fiddled with the dial until he found a crackly station playing 80's music. "Would you like to dance, Candee?"

"You want to dance—now?"

"You're still shivering a little." He offered a playful smile. "It's better to move around when you're cold."

"I'm not shivering," she informed him. "And I haven't danced with a man in forever."

Any further protest died on her lips as he pulled her to her feet.

"I can't remember the last time I danced with a woman, either." He placed his arm around her back. "Although I remember I liked it."

Candee silenced another protest. *Why not dance? The entire evening had a one-of-a-kind, storybook quality to it.*

"Unchained Melody" came on.

"I love the Righteous Brothers," she announced.

Teddy smoothed his fingers across her shoulders and pulled her closer. "I noticed when we were riding in your car yesterday."

They swayed in step to the enchanting words of the ballad about lonely rivers flowing and sighing.

The glow of the fireplace, dancing slowly with this strikingly handsome man, made her forget the previous two years of heartache and aloneness and dateless evenings.

"This music is in twelve eight time," she said.

He kept his fingers joined with hers. "It's beautiful."

With a quiet sigh, she submerged herself in the melody of the timeless song. The minutes passed and she lost track of the following medley of classic songs. She simply relaxed against Teddy's chest and allowed herself to experience the reassuring presence of his solid body against hers. His heart thudded in a steady meter and her own heart felt strange, beating oh-so-fast.

"Candee?" He lifted her chin. "If I was that guy with the same first and last names, I'd have rented a snowplow to meet you at the country club tonight."

His deep brown eyes darkened. Her body warmed with anticipation as his hands drifted down her shoulders, pressing her nearer.

It was there, an invisible thread drawing them together.

Her mind warned: It couldn't be, not after knowing him for a day.

But it was.

She knew he was going to kiss her, and she met his insistent lips with an eagerness she'd never known. He kissed her slowly, thoroughly. The strength of his powerful body molded intimately to hers, bringing her to life. The longer the kiss went on, the more she responded, straining to be nearer him.

The doorbell rang.

Teddy broke the kiss. "Are you expecting dinner guests?" He tipped up her chin. Affection and desire smoldered in his gaze as his thumbs stroked her heated cheeks.

Her hands flattened against his polo shirt and she rested her head on his chest. "Not unless they brought chocolate."

He laughed. "It must be the wind."

The odd chime of the doorbell ringing a second time prompted her to pull from his arms.

A moment afterward, the front door opened sending a blast of cold air into the living room.

"Anyone home?" a gruff voice called out.

A pair of heavy footsteps tromped down the hallway, and an elderly man with gray hair appeared in the living room doorway. With one hand, he pushed up a pair of thick glasses. With the other, he raised a sizable wooden baseball bat.

"Who are you two?" he demanded.

Candee retreated a step. "Mr. Dunworthy?"

"Candee Contando? What are you doing here?" The aging man hobbled into the room, using the baseball bat as a cane. "I saw candles flickering and smoke coming from a chimney. I figured it was teenagers up to mischief and decided to walk down here to see for myself."

"Mr. Dunworthy." Teddy came forward. "Candee was showing me the house."

"At this hour?" Up close, the dark age spots on the man's

face showed prominently. He squinted and stared at Teddy. "You live around here?"

"No. I'm from Florida, actually. My name is Teddy Winchester. I live in Miami and I'm an investor." Teddy extended his hand.

Mr. Dunworthy placed the baseball bat on the floor and the men shook hands. "I'm Charles Dunworthy. I live two doors down and I'm your basic nosy neighbor.

CHAPTER 6

The following day, Candee attended church services. Upon returning to her apartment for a quick lunch, she checked her cell phone. Teddy had texted her.

Happy Sunday, his text read. *Planning to volunteer at the animal shelter this afternoon?*

She glanced at her watch—half past noon. *Yes,* she texted back. *On my way now.*

Can I join u?

Teddy was persistent and apparently interested in her. He was so good-looking and not at all arrogant. His manner was compelling, gentle, yet with an aura of control. She so regretted that Mr. Dunworthy had interrupted their one kiss.

She suppressed a grin and texted back. *All hands are welcome.*

She sent him the address and then changed into a plaid flannel shirt, old faded jeans, black leather boots, and a light navy jacket. After pulling her hair into a casual pony tail, she tied the green paisley scarf around her neck. Despite the freezing weather the previous evening, the sky was a brilliant

Carolina blue, the sun efficiently melting any sleet left on the ground.

Candee recognized Teddy's pickup as soon as she drove into the shelter's parking lot. Lounging against his truck, he displayed an easy charm, looking exceedingly handsome wearing dark jeans, his olive-green vest zipped over a black T-shirt. He was ruggedly fit, his arm muscles taut and hard.

He strode to her car, his boots crunching on the graveled parking lot, and had her door open before she'd taken her key out of the ignition.

"Did you attend services this morning?" His slow, lazy smile made her shamelessly wonder how it would feel to kiss him again.

As she got out of the car, she drew a long breath to steady her fluttering pulse and focused on the simple wood-sided entrance door. "Yes, and the sermon was amazing. The pastor spoke about how grace is the way to heaven and faith is the route we choose to take. Do you attend a church?"

His nodded. "A contemporary church in Florida. They stream their services online and I watched on my computer early this morning before I called my nephew."

"How is he?"

"He sounded happy. I'll fly to Miami next weekend to see him. He's having a good time with Rob." He peered past her at the modern concrete and brick building. "How long is our shift?"

"Four hours. And an application is required."

"Done," he said. "I attended the orientation already and used your name as a reference. Was that okay?"

"Of course." She paused. "When you texted me, were you already at the shelter?"

He shifted. "I guess I was."

"You guess? You blithely did nothing while I texted directions?"

He raised a hand. "Guilty as charged. Last night you invited me to join you, remember?" Grinning, he took her hand. "Shall we go inside?"

She liked his easy-going sense of humor. In the spirt of friendly bantering, she teased, "Do you want to clean the crates, walk the dogs or stuff envelopes?"

"I have a choice?"

She chuckled. "It depends on whether you want to sit or stand. I prefer walking the dogs and love being outside."

He gazed down at her and squeezed her hand. "I'll go wherever you go." His words hung significantly in the crisp January breeze.

The next four hours passed amidst amiable sparring and chatter, with Candee teasing Teddy that he was supposed to be walking the dogs—the dogs weren't supposed to be walking him.

Dusk had fallen by the time Teddy was placing the last dog back in its enclosure as Candee explained the shelter's protocol and safety procedures to help limit the transfer of disease. For the next fifteen minutes, they assisted last-minute customers with animal visitations.

As they got ready to leave, Candee called out a jovial good-bye to Agnes, another volunteer.

"Will you and your boyfriend be back here next week?" Agnes asked.

Candee blinked.

She was coming to value Teddy's friendship ... but *boyfriend*? No, no, no. She wasn't ready to open her heart to another relationship—because Teddy would leave, like her parents, like the foster families, like George. Absolutely, she wanted to build a social life for herself again, but not at the expense of another heartbreak.

She took a steadying breath, resolve firmly in control. "Teddy and I met three days ago, Agnes. I'm his ... realtor."

"Oh." The woman studied them. "You two just look like you're together. I assumed you were a couple."

From the corner of her eye, Candee noted Teddy's quirked eyebrow, although he said nothing. She glanced at her hand in the crook of his arm. It felt natural, although she didn't remember placing her hand there.

As they walked away, Teddy whispered in her ear. "Well, that opens up a landslide of potential for us, doesn't it? Now will you join me for dinner?" Leaning over, he opened her car door.

"I'm at my realty office by eight o' clock on Monday morning." She bit her lip, debating his invitation. "In the afternoon, I work at the hardware store."

"I promise to get you home early." His grin was wide, his gaze glinted with merriment. "Say yes, because we're a couple now. Just ask Agnes."

"I never said—"

Lightly, he kissed her forehead. "We've been on our feet for hours. Don't you need nourishment? Eating a few slices of pizza won't take long."

Her hand hovered uncertainly above her car keys before she agreed. "I'm starved, actually."

The sun was descending as they arrived at Tony's pizzeria on Main Street. They parked their cars near the entrance, and Teddy came around to open her car door.

She smiled as he complimented her, citing how magnificent she was with animals and how much he prized her nurturing manner.

He gestured to the entrance of the pizzeria. "I made reservations. I didn't want us to sit around waiting for a pager to go off. Especially since you go to work early in the morning."

The soft tenderness in his deep voice took her breath away.

Was it wrong for her to enjoy being well-treated? she

questioned herself. Teddy made her feel special—listening attentively while she spoke, sensitive to her moods and attuned to her emotions. He obviously cared, showing initiative and planning ahead so she'd have a decent night's rest.

He took her hand as they walked into the pizzeria.

Mouth-watering scents of freshly cooked pasta, pizza, garlic, and oregano drifted through the darkly-lit restaurant. A portly woman, looking just like an Italian grandmother, escorted them to a table near a cheery fireplace. The woman was dressed in pressed black slacks and a turtleneck sweater, with "Tony's" stitched in red on the collar. A spiked-haired pizza maker stood in front of an open brick oven tossing pizza dough in the air and then covering the circle of dough with tomato sauce, pepperoni, and cheese.

Candee took in a deep breath. "Italian is my favorite food in all the world."

"MINE, TOO," Teddy agreed. As he pulled out a chair for Candee, he took in Tony's traditional decor—red and white checkered tablecloths, Italian statues and grapevines, the muted atmospheric lighting enhanced by votive candles at each table.

He took a seat, and they accepted menus from the waitress, a sandy-haired teen who seemed far more interested in the pizza tosser than in her customers.

Teddy perused the menu. "I love anything with the word pizza."

"Tossed salad is a nutritious alternative," she said.

After they were both served, Candee tucked into her salad while Teddy loaded up his plate with three slices of Margherita pizza.

"Do you have a favorite dog?"

He stopped in midchew to consider her unexpected question. "I came across many breeds today and it's hard to say. You?"

She smiled, but there was a hint of sadness to it. "I love beagles."

He was about to ask why when the waitress appeared. "More water? Coffee?"

"Black coffee for me," Candee said.

"Two cups, please," Teddy said.

A few minutes later the waitress set steaming cups of coffee on the table, cleared their empty plates, and encouraged them to order dessert.

"You haven't eaten any pizza yet," Teddy said. "There are two slices left."

"Box up what's left," Candee said to the waitress. "Teddy, you can have the leftovers for a midnight snack."

He laughed. "Since I professed my love for pizza earlier, I therefore have a good excuse for eating most of it." He gazed at Candee, who was twirling the ends of her thick red hair. He knew he was monopolizing her weekend, but she had been utterly enchanting while she'd handled the animals, treating every dog with respect and compassion, sensitive to the different breeds. She'd walked the dogs alongside him, hips swaying, her tall willowy figure provocative, laughing out loud at his knock-knock jokes.

Finally, he'd met someone who appreciated his sense of humor.

He loathed giving her up quite yet, and he planned to ask for a coffee refill when the waitress came back.

As the waitress went around the corner to box up the pizza and flirt with the pizza tosser, Teddy leaned forward. "Why do you love beagles, Candee?"

She broke eye contact and shrugged. "Long story."

"I'm a good listener." He scuffed his chair closer to the

table. "Last night you mentioned your 'forever' family. I'm assuming the two stories go together. Care to elaborate?"

She cupped her hands around her coffee cup as the waitress set the boxed pizza by Teddy. He waited while Candee sipped coffee and fixed her gaze on the crackling fire in the fireplace. Setting the cup down, she said, "The Johnsons encouraged Desiree and me to attend college."

"They sound like good people. Are you still in touch with them?"

"Six years ago, they moved to Chicago. I haven't seen them since I graduated from college. We still email, and I hope to visit them someday."

"What about your other foster families?" he asked gently. "You mentioned there were five families altogether."

She waved a hand dismissively. "Why would you be interested in hearing the sad story of my childhood?"

"Because I'm interested in you and everything about you."

She blushed and slowly exhaled. "Desiree and I encouraged each other every time we moved, assuring each other everything was fine, but it wasn't, you know? Between the ages of twelve and seventeen, we'd lived in four foster homes. New parents were complete strangers to us, and every house had its own set of rules—where to sleep, how to dress, what to eat, chores that had to be done."

Reaching out, he traced his finger along the curve of her cheek. "Those must have been very hard and scary years for two teenage girls."

The smile she offered quickly faded. "I always felt like a misfit. We didn't do anything normal teenagers did. No sleepovers, no driver's licenses—only a continuous series of knowing we were outsiders wherever we went."

She paused and stared down at her coffee. She'd hardly drunk any.

He took her silence as consent that she'd continue, and waited.

She gazed out the window at a cluster of clouds sitting low in the sky, then shifted her gaze to his. "Looking back, the hardest part was the beginning. I can still visualize my sister and me packing all our belongings into green trash bags the day we were taken from our home. I was twelve at the time. Desiree was fourteen."

"May I ask why you were put in foster care?"

She stared past him. "Our parents were declared unfit, and the state deemed it necessary for my sister and me to live in a safer place." She fidgeted with her gold earrings. "Although I didn't understand at the time, in hindsight I see there was no other choice. Our parents died soon after we were removed, and the doctors blamed their deaths on substance abuse."

"I'm sorry." He took her cold, fidgeting hands in his. "And now you've grown into a beautiful young woman. From my brief glimpse of your sister, she seems to be doing well. She's a lawyer?"

"And a good one, advocating for children's rights," Candee responded brightly. "I'm committed to making a difference in children's lives too. I have a plan that includes a rambling property with five acres, where children can safely go after school and learn music and play with dogs and finish their homework and eat healthy snacks ..." Her voice trailed off.

"I applaud you." He grinned approvingly and glided his thumbs over her hands. "What's your plan?"

It was just like her to want to help others, he thought. He imagined her as a kind and caring mother—a perfect mother for Joseph.

Perfect for Joseph and perfect for him. He scowled at himself, surprised the idea had drifted into his mind of its own accord. With a long sigh, he acknowledged the truth. Candee was an extraordinary woman, compassionate and warm-hearted. At thirty-two years old, he'd never felt such an instant attraction to a woman. After knowing her for only a few days, he was already half in love with her.

Perhaps fate had brought them together.

"You might as well know all the facts, Teddy," she was saying.

His thumbs froze on her hands in midstroke. He made himself resume, collecting his thoughts before asking, "What facts?"

She pulled her hands from his. "I should have addressed the situation and told you everything on Friday." Her voice was so low, he strained to hear her.

"Tell me what?" He leaned in closer, promising himself that whatever these facts were, it didn't matter.

For a fleeting moment, she closed her eyes, but then she pushed her shoulders back and squarely met his gaze. "The twenty-thousand dollar bid on the Victorian? It's my bid. I'm planning to live there and renovate the downstairs space, making it an after-school day care for disadvantaged children." Her voice caught. She paused before her words rushed out. "Therefore, I'd appreciate if you took your money elsewhere, preferably Miami, because the Victorian is taken."

Taken? The Victorian was taken?

Teddy jerked off his vest and threw it on the worn oak chair in his hotel room. He approached the window and gazed out at a thick black sky. In the distance, the twinkling lights of shops in the town square beckoned. Somewhere near, a church bell tolled the hour.

He tapped his hands together and spoke softly to his brother. "Really, Christian? Candee bid on the irreparable property in Roses that I'm interested in?"

With a heavy sigh, Teddy shoved his hands into his jean pockets. There were few moments in his life when he recalled being at a loss for words, but he definitely hadn't known what to say when Candee announced her plans. He'd mumbled something about having no idea she'd wanted the property, paid the restaurant bill while acknowledging her 'thank you,' then matched her swift steps as he walked her to her car.

At first, he'd been angry. Why hadn't she simply told him? True, he'd been insistent about seeing the property. However, if the Victorian meant that much to her—which it apparently did—she should have never taken him to see it.

His anger had evaporated on his drive back to the hotel. In retrospect, her intentions explained her hesitancy, her efforts to talk him out of buying it himself. And if he hadn't been so intent on purchasing a bargain, he would have spotted what was clear in hindsight—she loved the house. He'd clearly seen her wistful gaze when she'd held his hand and stared at the property with him.

He shook his head, berating himself. Here he thought she was the world's worst realtor. Instead, she was trying to protect her investment, and perhaps her heart. Her life had been filled with trauma and transience, yet in what he recognized already as true Candee style, her aspiration was to transform the house into a safe environment for disadvantaged children.

His head-strong, courageous Candee.

He recalled the night before, the candlelight living room and her amused, "You want to dance—now?" After the music started, she'd snuggled close, her soft curves pressed against him. She'd felt warm and responsive, and the mere touch of her hands on his shoulders had heated his pulse. Just thinking about the tumultuous highs of the past three days made the short time they'd spent together all the more significant.

He sensed she was beginning to care for him too. Nonetheless, common sense warned that love had no place in his life. He owned a thriving real estate business in Florida and had a nephew who needed him there.

There was no reason he couldn't continue seeing her, though, his heart encouraged. All that stood between them was the house and a distance of over seven hundred miles. Both easily remedied, he assured himself, between phone calls and Skype, although his conscience nagged about how he didn't do well in long-distance relationships.

With a low exhale, he turned away from the window.

Before they'd departed, he'd pressed a kiss to her forehead and informed her he intended to talk further in the morning. She hadn't agreed, although she hadn't disagreed either. Nonetheless, he'd seen the resistance in her green eyes. It had taken the last grain of his self-control not to bring her to his chest and placate that resistance with soft assurances and numerous kisses.

First thing in the morning, he'd arrive at her realty office and check off the first part of what was keeping them apart. He had decided to visit her office on Monday anyway, although now his reasons were different.

He glanced at the clock, dreading the lengthy night awaiting him. At least there were leftovers, he mused.

He uttered a soft curse as he looked around his room. In their quick departure, he'd forgotten the leftover pizza at the restaurant.

More importantly, he'd forgotten to ask Candee why she loved beagles.

Tomorrow. There was always tomorrow. For her sake and for his, he intended to straighten out everything. Tomorrow.

* * *

AFTER CALLING his nephew and speaking briefly to Rob, Teddy arrived at Candee's realty office at nine a.m. His arms were laden with four boxes of chocolate-covered caramels he'd bought at a local supermarket and a carryout bag from the trendy coffee house in town: two espressos topped with steamed milk, a dusting of cinnamon, and dark chocolate curls. A peace offering.

He rapped on Candee's realty door and walked in, smiling his approval at the tastefully decorated sun-lit office.

Candee sat behind an uncluttered desk with her laptop open, clicking rapidly on the keys. It appeared she'd taken extra care with her appearance, wearing a light-pink blouse and tailored black slacks. Her luxurious red hair was pulled back from her face and fastened with a floral-colored barrette, the rest of it falling to curl naturally around her shoulders.

His heart stopped. She was so beautiful.

She didn't seem quite as enraptured to see him. Her greeting consisted of a curt nod.

He held the candy toward her. "These are for you. I realize it's a little early in the morning for chocolate."

"It's never too early for chocolate." A slow smile came across her face as she stood. She accepted the candy and placed the boxes beside her laptop. "Thank you, although I can't eat all this candy."

"I can help you." Encouraged by his success, he pulled up a chair and set the coffees on her desk. "I assume you expected me, and I have four reasons for coming."

She sat back down in her chair. "Teddy, I … The Victorian …If you knew how much the home means to me."

"That's the main reason I'm here." An odd lump formed in his throat at her vulnerable yet unwavering expression. "I have no intention of bidding on the property anymore."

She pressed a palm to her heart. "You don't?"

"Absolutely not. Prompted by the right incentive, of course." He paused. When she didn't respond, he continued, "Besides, I certainly wouldn't want to go against you in a bidding war."

A determined glint shone in her gaze. "Considering you know I'd do anything to win?"

"Considering that fact and everything else, I won't even

try. When you're bent on a course of action, I believe nothing can stop you."

"You've come to know me well in four days." She leaned back in her chair and grinned. "Besides, my twenty-thousand-dollar bid is all the money to my name, and I wouldn't have the funds to bid against you." Without warning, her grin turned into a sob.

He went around her desk and knelt, sliding his arms around her. Turning into his embrace she cried harder, murmuring between sobs about how relieved she was, and how she knew the house could be salvaged with hard work and diligence, and she planned to use the acreage for a small working farm.

When her tears waned, she stayed where she was, her head resting against his chest.

He offered a napkin from the coffee bag. "Everything better?"

Self-consciously, she dabbed at her eyes and composed her features. "I haven't allowed myself to cry in years."

"I haven't cried in a long time either," he admitted. Rising, he skimmed a kiss across her temple.

She offered a rueful grin. "What are the other reasons you're here?'

"Well, the first was to bring you coffee and chocolates, and the second was to inform you I won't be bidding on the Victorian."

"But you mentioned a 'right' incentive. What might that be?"

"I'd like a thank-you kiss in return for preferring to be your ally, not your adversary."

She smiled.

He lifted her from her chair and pulled her into his arms. Gently, he brushed his lips over hers. Her tongue swept across his lips, and he welcomed her, his body shamelessly hungry in its response. His fingers tightened possessively to draw her closer, and an eternity passed before he lifted his mouth.

"The reason you came to Roses was to find a property and now you're giving it up," she murmured. "You would do this for me?"

He gazed into her glistening eyes, brimming with happiness.

"I would do anything for you," he answered thickly, surprised he'd spoken his thoughts aloud. "Although I truly believe the Victorian is beyond renovation."

She pulled out of his arms. "I'm a fairly good carpenter."

His gaze narrowed, although he didn't want to spoil the moment by informing her the house needed at least a dozen carpenters working around the clock—not to mention plumbers, electricians and roofers.

The silence lengthened. His heart gave a lurch at the resolve in her gaze.

"And do you know what I've learned from being a carpenter?" she asked. "Good old-fashioned perseverance and staying power. Even my simple three-inch rocking chair demanded endless hours and a lot of care."

"Making a rocking chair for a dollhouse is a lot different from tackling a five thousand square foot house that's been abandoned for years," he said.

"I'm not impatient. I'll focus on the process and—"

"I'll support you." His quiet tone stopped her from continuing. "However, from my knowledge as a contractor, sometimes you need to move on. Bringing the house up to par with city and code requirements will take a lot of capital."

Adamantly, she shook her head. "I'll never give up my dream."

He noted the guarded hope in her voice and carefully chose his words. "I have an offer for you. Your plan for after-school care is a good one, and I'd like to invest in it. Make me part of your equation." He lifted the coffees from the bag and handed her a cup. "Will you consent to viewing other properties in Roses that might also suit your dream?"

She opened her mouth, presumably to argue.

"Keep an open mind," he reminded.

"I can't accept any money from you, Teddy."

"Consider it a loan, then. I'll even throw in my free expert advice."

She managed a wan smile before sinking into her chair and thoughtfully savoring her coffee.

He glanced around the room. "Your mother owned this business?" He congratulated himself on changing their conversation's direction.

"Those were the days when my mother wasn't drinking. By the time I graduated from college, this office had been boarded up, so I earned my real estate license and opened using her name."

"Which is the reason I called you and not your competitors," he said. "I assumed you'd been in business for many years and knew the area well." Fate again, he thought.

"I wanted to continue my mother's legacy in some way. She wasn't a terrible parent, just terribly misguided." Candee absently touched her gold earrings. "And of course, the drinking and the drugs ..."

"I've noticed you wear those earrings every day. Are they from your mother?"

Sadness flickered across her beautiful face. "It's all I have left as a remembrance. She bought them at a consignment shop for my twelfth birthday. It wasn't long afterward that Desiree and I were moved to our first foster home." A hint of a smile wavered. "Now you've given me three reasons."

He grinned. She didn't miss a thing.

"I'm flying to Miami in a couple weeks to consult with

Rob and see Joseph," he explained. "Joseph's a wonderful kid. I think I mentioned that on weekends, he goes to a horse training therapy facility."

"Do you have custody of your nephew?"

"Hopefully soon." Teddy exhaled a deep breath. "My brother was killed in an automobile accident a few months ago, and I should be granted guardianship of Joseph fairly soon. It's so hard for him right now … For us …" Teddy glanced out the window and knuckled an unexpected tear. She waited in silence while he cleared his throat before turning back to her. "I'd like you to fly down to Florida with me to meet Rob and Joseph. You alluded to a working farm for disadvantaged children and you might want to expand the concept and include animals as therapy."

"It sounds like a wonderful idea, although I can't go. I have too many commitments in Roses."

"We'll be gone from Friday afternoon until Sunday evening and you'd have almost two weeks to prepare for the trip."

"What about my real estate business?"

"Your one client is sitting across from you."

She hesitated. "I've never seen Miami."

"Bring shorts and flip-flops. You can stay at one of Rob's places. He owns apartments above several of his businesses, and one is a five-minute walk from my condo."

"I'd never impose."

"Believe me, Rob owns more properties than he knows what to do with. And didn't you advise me last evening to fly back to Miami? Well, I'm following your advice, except that I want you to join me."

The next two weeks flew by in a pleasant flurry for Candee, as she and Teddy viewed prospective houses and stopped daily at the Victorian home. He'd offered advice on cost-effective strategies to modernize, while staying true to the house's character. Though they'd viewed numerous modest properties more in sync with her nonexistent budget, none came close to matching the Victorian's architectural design, aesthetics, or sheer grandeur.

Together, she and Teddy researched adding a horse farm to the property; and she'd discovered that horses, with their unique nature, were considered mirrors of a person and an excellent choice for therapy. Furthermore, being around horses bolstered a person's self-confidence, as horses were believed to relieve stress.

"You have the acreage," Teddy had encouraged her after they'd exhausted her property search.

On the last afternoon before their departure to Miami, they volunteered at the shelter. When they were about to leave, a pregnant whimpering beagle was brought in. After the veterinarian examination, it was determined the dog was approximately fifty days pregnant and due to give birth to six puppies within the week.

"Where was the dog found?" Teddy asked.

"This poor beagle was left on the side of the road." Candee gazed at the hound-dog look the beagle gave her, and her heart melted. "I may not be able to travel to Miami with you, Teddy, considering how large the beagle's stomach is. I want to be here with her when she gives birth."

He'd assured her they'd technically be gone for one day—traveling to Miami on Friday and returning to Roses on Sunday.

As he knelt beside her, she whispered, "After the beagle has her puppies, I want to keep her."

He raised his eyebrows. "Do you mean her or the puppies?"

"Both. A dog with puppies is costly for a shelter." Lightly, she caressed the dog's black and tan coat, and the dog didn't try to bite. "I'll be a foster mom until the pups can be adopted. All they need is a warm home."

"And food and nursing and a loving caregiver," he murmured, recovering admirably from his shock.

He carefully carried the compact hound dog to her own enclosure with food and water, and Candee placed a worn blanket beneath the dog.

"Try to eat, girl." She offered the beagle a piece of fruit. The dog sniffed and slowly inched toward Candee's outstretched hand.

"Beagles are known to be loving, gentle, and extremely sociable," Candee told Teddy.

Seeing his expression as he brushed a sprinkling of dog hair, which resembled black pepper, from his vest, she assured, "And beagles don't shed, except in the spring when they're ridding themselves of their winter coats."

"You know a lot about these dogs." At the sound of

Teddy's deep voice, the dog keenly watched him and wagged her tail. "Why do you love beagles so much?"

"We owned a dog once, a sweet beagle, and Desiree and I were forced to leave her behind." She hesitated, not trusting her voice to continue. "We called her 'Kisses.'

The pregnant dog stared up at them with wide-set pleading hazel eyes.

"'Kisses.' Your dog's name was Kisses." Apparently weighing his words, Teddy carefully replied, "You're taking on a tremendous amount of work with a monstrous house filled with rubble and weeds and all these dogs."

"I cannot abandon her. And in eight weeks her pups will be adoptable. And yes, I'm naming the beagle Kisses."

She'd been ready to puff up with indignation if he'd tried to discourage her. He didn't. Instead, he smiled and offered his assistance, agreeing that Kisses was a perfect name for a beagle. Stating he wanted to "seal the Kisses decision," he pulled her close, his arms cradling her body as his lips passionately explored hers.

Hours later, Desiree joined them for a festive dinner at a new farm-to-table restaurant in downtown Roses. Although their table had ample room to accommodate the threesome comfortably, his muscled leg had touched Candee's throughout the meal. It seemed like he always made a point to keep her close to him.

Teddy had laughingly concurred with Desiree as she waved a forkful of miniature crab cake and declared, "No one in their right mind places a bid on a property that looks like a tumbledown haunted house. And now my sister is stepping up to take on a pregnant beagle about to give birth to a bunch of puppies?"

"'Kisses needs a home," Candee said staunchly. "And the children at the daycare can teach her and the puppies how to sit and stay and fetch."

"And you'll need to hire a full-time staff," Teddy said while aiming a subtle nod at Desiree. "Although knowing you, Candee, you'll attempt to juggle everything yourself."

"You've offered to help, right?"

He studied her face and replied, "Yes, and I never go back on my word."

She stared up at him, his smiling features, the firm line of his jaw, enveloped by his commanding presence. His gaze locked with hers. Both of them completely disregarded her sister's presence as he lowered his head, his lips hovering close before he kissed her lightly. Her breath caught as his bracing outdoor scent tingled her senses.

When she returned to her apartment that night, she fell into bed, pleasantly exhausted. As she did every night before retiring, she checked the bidding on the Victorian, relieved her twenty-thousand-dollar offer remained the highest.

She courted sleep, although it didn't come. She was too excited, her thoughts humming with elated expectation. Soon she would own her dream house, and she'd be building that dream with Teddy. Yes, he lived in Miami and she lived in Roses, but with Internet and phone calls and airplane travel, their relationship could continue to grow.

Her mood had lightened with each hour she'd spent with him, and life was definitely taking a turn she'd never expected. Perhaps Desiree was right and Cupid's arrow had been aimed directly at Candee and Teddy.

Sighing contentedly, she rolled onto her stomach and drifted to sleep.

CHAPTER 9

The following afternoon, Candee made sure every employee at the shelter knew to call her if Kisses went into labor. Then she and Teddy boarded the plane from Asheville, North Carolina, to Miami, Florida. The trip to the airport took less than an hour, and Teddy did the driving. Their flight was under three hours, and sudden air pockets and strong winds prompted gasps from the passengers in the cabin.

Candee was still recovering from the rough flight when an impish boy, echoing Teddy's good looks, raced to greet her and Teddy while they were retrieving their luggage at baggage claim.

"Uncle Teddy!" the boy called.

"Hey, Joseph!" Teddy squatted, fiercely hugging the boy. As he stood, he hoisted his nephew onto his shoulders.

Pivoting, he motioned to Candee. "Joseph, meet my new friend, Miss Candee Contando."

She extended her hand. "I've heard a lot about you, Joseph."

"Hi." The boy leaned over Teddy's head. "Mr. Rob said Uncle Teddy mentions you every time he calls."

"And I'm Mr. Rob." A short, heavy-set, balding man bent at the waist in an exaggerated bow. Along with a good-natured smile, his blue-eyed gaze was welcoming. He stole Candee's luggage from her and thoughtfully cocked his head. "You're too ravishing to be anyone else. Welcome to Miami, Candee."

Teddy swung Joseph back down to the floor as he offered introductions. He kept one hand possessively around her waist, and as she glanced up at him, he was staring down at her with heartfelt pride.

"No wonder she was one of your main topics when we spoke," Rob said, clapping Teddy on the back. "Everything's certainly coming up Roses, eh?"

The group dissolved into good-natured chuckling.

As they stepped out of the airport, the air of the Miami evening was balmy and inviting. Candee pulled off her paisley scarf and tucked it into her carry-on bag. Teddy walked between her and Joseph, holding their hands. As they walked to Rob's car, they passed an outdoor kiosk brimming with Valentine candy.

"No candy for me," Rob said. "I'm on a diet."

"Again?" Teddy teased.

"I haven't cheated in twenty-four hours. I'm on a roll." He kept his gaze fixed on the sidewalk and whistled an out-of-tune melody.

"We're not dieting." Teddy turned to Candee. "Carmel dark chocolate sound good?"

"I can't. My stomach is reeling from the turbulent airplane ride."

"Dark chocolate helps." He picked up two decorative gold boxes filled with candy, along with a red-foil rose and a jumbo heart swirl lollipop for Joseph.

"Chocolate and more chocolate?" she joked as he handed her the rose and boxed candy.

"Sugar and chocolate is the cure for most maladies."

"Yeah," Rob interjected. "That's been my bakery mantra for years."

She chuckled and eyed the lollipop. "You realize, Teddy, that your nephew will be on a sugar high tonight and you'll only have yourself to blame?"

"Guilty as charged." Teddy held up a hand, then swept a kiss on her lips. "I'll pick you up at Rob's apartment tomorrow at eleven."

He was so wonderfully generous, and when he kissed her, she heartily kissed him back. At least until Rob's raucous throat-clearing broke her and Teddy apart.

* * *

FOLLOWING a leisurely shower in Rob's high-end penthouse Saturday morning, Candee checked her appearance in the bedroom's full-length mirror. The weather was a comfortable seventy degrees, and she was pleased she'd brought a soft royal-blue crepe dress accented by gathered cropped sleeves. She rubbed a drop of her favorite rose fragrance to her wrists, and pulled on black leather ballet flats for walking ease.

She had just knotted the gold tie belt around her waist when she heard a light rap on the penthouse door. Teddy had arrived exactly at eleven a.m.

She smiled as she opened the door. Yes, he was devastatingly handsome, standing in the doorway wearing cotton khaki pants and a slim-fitting gray polo shirt that accented his strong physique. However, it was the little things that drew her to him—his kind actions, how he was true to his word, and the way his eyes lit with boyish enthusiasm when-ever he described the Victorian's renovations.

"Good morning." He took her hands in his and gazed at her with bold dark eyes. "Your beauty lights up this place."

Self-consciously, she laughed. "You must be focusing on the view behind me. You know, the sixteen-foot floor-to-ceiling windows looking out onto Miami beach and 'million-aire's row.'"

He drew her to him. "No, it's you," he whispered. "Only you." His mouth came down on hers for a long passionate kiss, and her heart thumped hard in her chest.

She placed her cell phone in her handbag and slung the bag over her shoulder. Down in the lobby, they encountered a pacing Rob and an exuberant Joseph demonstrating a cart-wheel across the marbled floor.

"About time, you two." Rob pointedly stared at his watch. "What normally takes me five minutes took you ten."

"We were detained," Teddy said, reclaiming Candee's hand. "Shall we all walk to your bakery?"

"Absolutely." Rob patted his round stomach. "Some of us can use the exercise."

In the glittering daylight of the promising morning, Candee tucked her fingers in the crook of Teddy's strong arm. A welcoming breeze lifted her loose hair from her shoulders like a whirlpool.

As the foursome approached Sixty-Fifth Street, Rob's body language punctuated his proud tone. "What's not to like about America's favorite vacation city?" He gestured to the glass skyscrapers on both sides of the street. "Miami boasts a trendy nightlife, boat shows, auto racing, golf, tennis, cruises and deep-sea fishing."

"And we've never done any of those activities," Teddy said dryly.

"We had a lively time on the two-night party cruise a few years back, remember?"

"Lively time?" A knowing grin crossed Teddy's face. "You were seasick the entire forty-eight hours."

They crossed an intersection, and the enticing scent from Rob's bakery beckoned them into the store like a warm embrace. Glazed donuts, masterfully iced rainbow-colored cupcakes, and towering, three-tiered layer cakes frosted with buttercream sat proudly in a row of glass cases.

"I saved your Valentine cupcake for you, Uncle Teddy," Joseph said. And I made one for Miss Candee too. We froze them, and Mr. Rob took them out of the freezer yesterday." Joseph tugged on Teddy's hand. "They're in the kitchen. Come on, I'll show you."

"Save us a table," Teddy said to Candee. "We'll be back shortly."

When half of their group had disbanded, Rob examined a display case for fingerprints while a white-aproned employee boxed an order of cinnamon buns.

Candee hung back, standing behind a parade of customers.

When Rob returned carrying two mugs of coffee and a bag of donuts, he guided her to an inviting seating area adjoining the bakery.

"Freshly baked donuts!" He exclaimed. "Twenty-four hours on a diet is long enough." He set a white bakery bag emblazoned with his Rob's Marvelous Muffins logo and the two mugs on the small round table. "Black coffee, right?"

"Thank you." She inhaled the mouth-watering scent of chocolate iced donuts rolled in sprinkles and the aroma of rich dark coffee. "Your hospitality is generous, and both your places—the penthouse and this bakery—are amazing."

"I don't have any complaints about flattery." He took a large swallow of his coffee. "Keep it coming."

"I'd gain ten pounds in a week if I worked here." She grinned. "A bakery like yours in my hometown would be well-received."

He flashed a smile. "I own a half dozen bakeries in Miami. I haven't considered opening out-of-state, although you never know."

Rob went on to describe the process of running a bakery, embroidering his account of the time he'd changed a hit recipe and used confectioners' sugar instead of granulated, which had resulted in a string of complaints.

Her turquoise and silver bracelets cheerfully clinked against her coffee mug as she drank and listened. He was such a genial man and so talkative, she could imagine him having a conversation without her, chatting non-stop to an empty chair.

"Enough about me." His telescope gaze gave her a measured look. "Let's talk about your grand plans for the Victorian, Candee."

"Hasn't Teddy told you?"

He nodded confirmation. "Now I want to hear it from you."

She blew out an audible breath. "To begin with, every bathroom requires a complete gut job, and the carpeting in each room needs to be pulled up." She paused. "The wood floors are trashed, and Teddy recommended restoring them using four-inch red-oak planks."

"Do you have funds to pay for all these renovations?" Rob flatly asked.

His tone didn't intimidate her in the least. "No. I'll take out loans."

"And how do you intend to pay back these loans? All these restorations will take endless capital."

She let the reality of his words hang in the air between them. She'd learned to stay quiet when she wasn't certain how to answer, and she needed to think before replying. Her foster background, dealing with different people's expectations, had taught her that.

"I'll work extra hours at the hardware store," she said. "And I can wield tools and ladders. There's nothing like carpentry to test a person's patience."

Mentally, she thanked her "forever" foster father for permitting her to work with him in his woodshop.

She met Rob's piercing blue gaze and waved a dismissive hand at herself. "Who knows? Maybe I'll even sell a house or two in the meantime."

"Teddy said your perseverance and goals are admirable."

"I'm going to be the type of caregiver who attends every child's basketball game, every concert …" She forced herself to keep her tone calm and unemotional. "These disadvantaged kids need support."

"I've invested in Teddy's ventures for years, and he's never let me down. He approves of your project and he oversees numerous home-improvement crews."

"We'll give it our best shot."

"The hallmark of a successful baker is self-discipline, and the same goes for real estate." Rob gave a big throaty laugh. "At first, Teddy wanted to raze the house and build low-income housing on the five-acre lot. Our business ethos is to give to those less fortunate."

In the space of seconds, Teddy's ideas collided with hers, and she could see the merit in his plans for the property.

"He never told me," she softly replied.

"You're the best thing that's happened to him in a long time. Has he mentioned his childhood to you?"

She swallowed a deep drink of the exquisitely brewed coffee. "Hardly anything."

"I encouraged him to show you his old homestead," Rob said. "He said he's too embarrassed."

"It can't be any worse than my childhood homes."

Instantly, she was ambushed by scenes from her adolescence. Whenever her birthday had come around, she had waited, hoping for a birthday cake. The cake never came. Neither did the candles, or the balloons, or the birthday gifts.

"Teddy came from nothing," Rob said, "and he and his brother were constantly beaten by his drunken father. When life gets punched out of you, only the outstanding persevere. Unfortunately, after a hard childhood, a person's trust no longer comes easy."

She confirmed his words with a sad smile. Despite his outward bravado, Rob had an astute understanding of people.

"And what about your foster families?" he asked.

She shrugged. "Nothing to say."

He propped his elbows on the table, the gleam in his eyes matching his shiny round face. "Up until now, Teddy's been a confirmed bachelor like me. I'm the furthest a person can get from being a wedding expert, but he genuinely cares about you. He can't stop looking at you whenever you're together."

She stifled a denial as a giggling four-year-old boy raced to the table with Teddy close behind.

"We're back, Miss Candee," Joseph announced. "And we brought your Valentine surprise cupcake." He held up a basket, revealing a red muffin set on a red doily. Piped white icing gel on the muffin read, "Life is butter with you."

Her lips twitched with a grin. Impulsively, she hugged the adorable boy. "Thank you." She turned to Rob. "Clever sentiment, Rob."

Rob laughed. "They're all different. Took me weeks to come up with appropriate Valentine adages that wouldn't offend any customers."

"Taste the muffin and tell me what the surprise is, Miss

Candee," Joseph said. "I'll give you a hint. It has something do with kisses."

"Joseph, you're not supposed to give any hints to Candee, remember?" Teddy hooked his hands in his front pockets. His slow, devastating smile eclipsed all the busyness of the bustling bakery. "It's a taste test and she's supposed to discover the surprise by herself."

Candee bit into the muffin and briefly closed her eyes. The combination of strawberries and butter was delicious. She washed down the muffin with coffee, then took another bite. "There's chocolate inside. Wait ..." she continued around a mouthful of cupcake. "A candy kiss is in the middle?"

"You guessed the surprise!" Joseph jumped up and down. "Like it?"

She laughed. "I love it."

"Me too." Teddy kissed her forehead, then pulled up a wing chair and sat facing her.

"Where's *your* Valentine muffin?" she teased.

"Gone in three bites."

"What was on yours?"

"The Browning quote." He kept his gaze on hers. "'Grow old along with me. The best is yet to be.'"

Positively emanating good cheer, Rob said, "And they all lived long and happily ever after. Long because it was for forty years, and happy for ... two months."

Teddy grinned, glanced at his watch, then back at Candee. "Later today I want to take you to Joseph's horse ranch so you can see him ride his pony."

"I'm looking forward to it."

The cell phone in her purse rang. She pulled out her phone and checked the caller ID. "Please excuse me." She held up an index finger and answered the call.

When she clicked off, she took several quick breaths. Her

gaze flitted to the threesome staring at her before settling on Teddy. "It was one of the volunteers at the shelter. My beagle has gone into labor."

"Kisses?" Teddy's eyebrows drew together. "Don't labors take a long time?"

"For a beagle, anywhere from six to eighteen hours." She matched his stare with a firm one of her own. "I'm sorry. I have to leave this afternoon."

Teddy pressed his lips together and offered a weak smile. "I know how much this beagle means to you." He took his phone from his pocket and began checking the Internet. "There's a direct fight to Asheville leaving at four o'clock and one seat is available."

"Will you book it for me? I'll text Desiree and ask her if she can pick me up at the airport."

After the reservation was made, Teddy set his phone on the table. "Done. I'll keep my return flight to Roses on Sunday night so I can spend more time with Joseph."

"Yes, of course." Looking at the boy, she said, "I'm sorry I can't see you ride your pony."

"That's okay, Miss Candee," Joseph replied. "I ride him every weekend. I love horses! I love every animal in the world!"

She laughed. "Animals and children are very special."

Teddy stroked the auburn curls falling about her shoulders. "You're not even gone yet, and I miss you."

"Okay you two flames, save it for later." Rob cut his gaze to Teddy. Giving him a meaningful look, he lowered his tone. "Your lawyer called this morning. He couldn't reach you and left a message with me. It's about a court date to finalize your guardianship." Rob raised his tone, apparently for Joseph's benefit, who'd been intently watching them. "Hey Teddy, can I talk to you in the back?"

"Sure." Teddy quickly stood. "I wanted to behold the new commercial mixer you purchased for the kitchen, anyway."

"The heavy-duty one? It broke. The grinder lasted a week."

Teddy gave a sharp laugh. "Aren't you glad you came to Miami to meet the special people in my life?" he asked Candee.

She smiled. "Very glad."

He glided his knuckles down her cheek. "Is it all right if I leave Joseph with you for a few minutes?"

"My absolute pleasure."

Teddy grabbed an activity sheet and crayons at the counter and placed them on the table for his nephew. "How about sketching me a horse, buddy?"

"I want to draw the pony I ride at the ranch. His name is Blackjack because he's black."

Candee swallowed a chuckle as the men headed to the kitchen.

"What an excellent name for a pony," she said to Joseph. "I'm sure Blackjack is a beauty." She sat back in her chair, sipping her coffee and watching Joseph color. When Teddy's phone vibrated, she automatically picked it up and scanned the displayed number.

"You can answer it," Joseph said. "Uncle Teddy doesn't mind. I answer his phone all the time."

She debated. The phone number was identified by two initials—YE. A business call, she wondered? Assuming the call might be important, she answered. "Hello?"

"Who's this?" a woman asked.

Candee frowned into the phone. "Candee Contando. And you?"

"Yvonne Evette. Is this Teddy's phone?"

"Yes. May I take a message?"

"Put Teddy on the line," the woman said.

"He's not here."

"Tell him I'll be in Madrid another week and to phone me as soon as he gets this message. That means immediately." The woman hung up.

Candee stared at his phone as she set it on the table. "Who's Yvonne Evette?" she asked aloud, not expecting an answer.

"You mean Miss Yvonne?" Joseph made a face. "She's Uncle Teddy's other girlfriend and she's famous. We watch her on TV."

The shock of Teddy's betrayal knocked the air from Candee's lungs. She swallowed hard.

Unfortunately, Teddy and Rob chose that moment to emerge from the kitchen. They were obviously enjoying themselves, laughing and talking. Rob veered off to speak with an employee. Teddy was still grinning when he approached Candee's table.

He stopped, his probing gaze fixing on her. "What's wrong? You've gone pale."

She pushed back her chair. "Your cell phone rang and I answered it. I shouldn't have—I thought it might be important."

"Who was it?"

"A call from Spain."

Teddy stiffened. "Yvonne?"

"Yes, and she said to call her immediately."

Unnoticed, Rob strolled to the table. "Anything wrong?"

Heartsick from sadness and fury and defeat, Candee shivered and rubbed her arms. "Rob, where's the restroom?"

He pointed to a sign, and she shot past him.

"Candee, wait." Teddy strode purposefully after her. "I can explain."

She inhaled a tortured breath. She'd heard enough explanations from her ex to last a lifetime. And she'd never allow Teddy to see how much his duplicity had hurt her.

"It's not what it seems." He caught her wrist, and she snapped around. "Look," he said, "I've been seeing Yvonne for several months. She travels a lot and I … I don't do long-distance relationships well."

Tears sprang to Candee's eyes. Firmly, determinedly, she held them back. "You don't do any relationship well."

"Please let me explain."

She deliberately stared down at his hand until he released her.

"I'll walk back to the penthouse and call a taxi to the airport," she said. "Please don't follow me. And tell Rob thank you for everything. Kiss Joseph good-bye for me and tell him I love animals too." She pivoted and entered the restroom. Inside, she splashed cold water on her face and peered at her reflection in the mirror above the sink. Her pallid complexion emphasized her emerald-green eyes, giving her a much-too-vulnerable appearance.

Again she was a fool, and she only had herself to blame. How could she have believed it was possible to fall in love with a man after knowing him a few short weeks?

Love. Love happened to other people, not to her. The sooner she came to grips with reality, the simpler her life would become. No more broken hearts, she vowed. Not ever again.

Two hours later she stood alone in the Miami airport, waiting for the boarding to begin.

To pass the time while waiting in line, she checked the foreclosure website. She gasped, almost dropping her phone when the house came on the screen. Her bid was no longer the highest.

She refreshed her phone. Surely, there must be a mistake.

No. The new bid was $40,000, driving the next bid to $60,000—money she didn't have.

This couldn't be happening. Her stomach felt heavy, her heartbeat raced.

Quickly, she texted Desiree. *I logged online at the airport, and the Victorian is now at 40K. Who bid on MY house?*

Online means the Internet, came Desiree's reply. *So that means anyone on the world-wide web. No use worrying. Whatever happened, we'll sort it when u get home. Have a safe flight and see u in Asheville.*

Candee attempted to pull her mind away from one looming fear. She might lose the house.

Another text floated across her screen, this one from Teddy. *Have u boarded the plane?*

He'd texted numerous times since she'd abruptly left Rob's bakery, and she'd ignored him.

However, he'd made and paid for her plane reservation and she knew she should text him.

Soon, she replied.

Can I call you tomorrow?

She hesitated. Her cold, clammy hands clutched the phone tighter.

Something prompted her to ask, although surely his answer would be no.

Did you place a bid on the Victorian house? she texted.

Air stopped entering her lungs as she waited for his response. Time seemed to be slowing down until a single word appeared on her phone.

Yes.

CHAPTER 10

*A*s usual, Desiree had arrived at the country club before Candee. Candee hung her fur capelet by the door and greeted her sister with a hug.

Desiree looked gorgeous in a red velvet figure-hugging pant suit. She went back to arranging a plate of chocolate-covered strawberries on a silver serving tray. The club was empty, save for black-suited waiters setting glass vases of red tulips and rose peonies on every table.

Candee appraised her own outfit—a sleeveless petal-pink lace dress. Unlined along the hem, the dress allowed a peekaboo of her long legs. She'd parted her hair on the side and let the thick curls flow down the opposite shoulder.

Satisfied with the strawberry arrangement, Desiree turned to her. "Finally, I was able to talk you into attending the dinner dance. You can leave those puppies alone for a few hours. Valentine's Day is one of the biggest events at the club. Thanks for coming early to help me finish decorating."

"You insisted you needed help, although there's so much to admire." Candee looked around the room. "The lace

"

ribbons and pom-pom wreaths are glittery and sophisticated, and those smooch balloons are gorgeous."

"White balloons with a stamp of my red lipstick." Desiree puckered her glistening red lips.

Candee smiled and fingered an arrow-toting Cupid on the banquet table. "No use in me sitting in my apartment with Kisses and her six puppies, watching television and hoping that Meg Ryan and Tom Hanks will get me through the evening."

"Her puppies are adorable. So firm and plump."

"And active," Candee replied. "Plus, they've doubled their weight in less than two weeks. Kisses is the best mom in the world. I supply high-quality puppy food and a vitamin mineral tablet, and she does the rest."

Desiree popped a chocolate-covered strawberry into her mouth and smiled. "All is well then."

Was it? The lump in Candee's throat threatened to choke her, and tears burned her eyelids. She swallowed and poured herself a glass of water. She wouldn't cry. She was strong and had made a vow to herself.

Desiree was watching her closely. "Have you heard from Teddy?"

"He's texted me every day and apologized numerous times about Yvonne, although it doesn't matter anymore." Candee forced herself to sound calm and detached. "As far as I know, he hasn't returned to Roses. He said something about being tied up in Miami court because of Joseph's guardianship."

"Did you text him back?"

"Only to tell him I landed safely." She missed him intensely, especially on a night like tonight, Valentine's Day. She squeezed her eyes shut, remembering the feel of his strong calloused hand around her waist while they'd danced, his lips capturing hers.

"If I was that guy with the same first and last names," he'd said. *"I'd have rented a snowplow to meet you at the country club tonight."*

How could he have become so important to her in the short time they'd known each other? Each day that passed, she felt more and more empty without him. She'd even been tempted to answer his texts with an invitation to join her for dinner at Tony's. That night they'd gone there, he'd said that, like her, Italian food was his favorite in all the world.

But Teddy lived in Miami with Yvonne, and Candee lived in Roses with Kisses and her puppies.

Once she allowed them in, her tormenting memories took over. She'd loved listening to his remodeling ideas, the quiet decisiveness in his voice when they'd agreed that horse therapy suited her project perfectly. And then there'd been the comforting reassurance of knowing they were venturing into these daunting tasks side by side.

Hah! Had he played her for a fool the entire time, planning to take her house right out from under her? The auction had just closed, and most likely demolition would begin any day. Candee promised herself she'd never drive down Thompson Lane again. Idly, she wondered if Teddy would manage the project himself, or send one of his many home-improvement crews to demolish the house.

Desiree had advised her to set her sights elsewhere. Perhaps a five-hundred-foot Cape Cod made more sense, considering her budget. Smaller dreams were more realistic.

She opened her eyes.

Her sister's gaze clouded with concern and she clasped Candee's hands. "You know, we tried to raise the funds, but neither Scott nor I had an extra $40,000 hidden under our pillowcases."

"Thank you." Not only was Desiree her sister, but she was also a true friend.

After that, Desiree adeptly changed the subject, resulting in a half hour of setting red candles around the room. But Candee's fragile composure began to slip. Other guests would be arriving soon, and she wasn't sure she could make conversation with anyone. She attempted to bolster herself by remembering she'd agreed to attend the event for only two hours. She eyed an ornate grandfather clock on the opposite wall. An hour and a half left.

Desiree jumped to her feet as two men entered the room. "Scott is here, and he brought … Allen Allen?" she shrieked. Desiree turned so pale, Candee feared the many chocolate-covered strawberries Desiree had eaten had made her ill.

"You're joking, right?" Candee said to her sister. "You invited him?"

Desiree seemed rooted to the floor. "No, actually, I didn't."

Candee threw up her hands. "I'm leaving by seven o'clock," she reminded Desiree.

"Dinner is served at six, leaving you plenty of time." Desiree's gaze narrowed on Scott. Then she grabbed Candee's hand and started toward the two well-dressed men for introductions.

Dusk was streaking pomegranate colors in the darkening sky when Allen seated Candee to his right for dinner. A waiter set glasses of sparkling apple and pear cider at each place setting.

Teddy preferred coffee, she thought, reminding herself that she should be indifferent to his choice of beverage. She frowned. She didn't feel indifferent to anything about him. She missed the bantering they'd shared, the warm strength of his strong muscled body close to hers.

"The first course is a cheese and hazelnut green salad," Desiree declared to the others at the table, rousing Candee from her thoughts of Teddy. "For the entrée, the club is serving chicken in champagne sauce."

"I'm certain the meal will be delicious," Candee replied graciously. She took a long swallow of cider and lapsed into a reflective silence.

* * *

HOLDING HIS NEPHEW'S HAND, Teddy strode into the Roses country club exactly at six o'clock. The flight from Miami to Asheville had been bumpy, and getting his truck from the long-term rental parking lot had taken longer than he'd planned. The Valentine's Day festivities were well underway. A quick assessment of his worn jeans, polo shirt, and vest assured him he was underdressed for the formal occasion.

"Uncle Teddy, where is Miss Candee?" Joseph hopped on one foot. "Look—they have candy hearts in those little glasses by the window. Can I get some?"

Before Teddy could reply, the boy had scurried off. He gazed at him—a bundle of boundless energy and perfection, his dark eyes framed by thick black lashes. His adorable nephew, now his son to raise to the best of his ability.

I can do this, Christian, Teddy thought. Two weeks of endless paperwork had resulted in Teddy being awarded legal guardianship of Joseph.

It had been a difficult two weeks. After Candee had left Miami so abruptly, Teddy had tasted a painful defeat. No matter how much he plunged into his work, or cared for Joseph, or signed papers in the courtroom, he couldn't fully concentrate.

And then he'd made his decision.

His mind told him to stay in Miami. His heart told him otherwise.

"Are you expecting dinner guests?" he'd asked her that night when they'd danced.

Her beautiful green eyes had stared into his. "Not unless they're bringing chocolate," she'd quipped.

She possessed such enthusiasm, such spirit. And he'd hurt her by not being upfront about his relationship with Yvonne. Although in all fairness, he hadn't considered Yvonne a part of his life after he'd met Candee.

"Uncle Teddy! There she is!" Joseph shouted around a mouthful of pink candy hearts.

Teddy's gaze riveted on Candee. She sat at an elegantly decorated table with Desiree and two men. Teddy recognized Scott from the night he'd seen him at the country club. But the other man? He'd better not be that guy with two first names.

He grabbed Joseph's hand and stalked past a group of waiters serving champagne in fluted glasses to the guests.

He stopped Joseph from grabbing a white balloon, and he let a waiter show Joseph where the balloons were stored in an adjoining room.

When he looked at Candee again, she was out of her chair walking toward him.

"Teddy?"

She was exquisite, a glamorous, stunning goddess. Her glossy auburn hair hung to the side, a rosy tint creeping up her flawless cheeks. Her lacy pink dress displayed her alluring figure to full advantage. He was so relieved. Desiree had responded to his texts and told him that she'd finally persuaded Candee to attend this dinner.

He took her hands in his. "You are gorgeous."

She grinned shyly. "Thank you."

His gaze wandered across the crowded dining room, and he was annoyed at their lack of privacy, for all he wanted to do was kiss her inviting lips. Already, the hum of conversation was fading, and several diners were staring at them.

He slipped his arm around her shoulders and guided her into the hallway.

"Why are you here?" she asked.

"Because I missed you."

Her green eyes were soft and tender. "I missed you too."

"Can you leave?" He gestured impatiently around the corner, indicating the threesome at Candee's table.

"Yes, of course. I'll get my capelet."

"Hi, Miss Candee!" Joseph skipped over to them holding three white balloons. "Did you know Uncle Teddy and I flew all the way from Miami today?"

"Joseph, I'm thrilled you're here." Candee affectionately embraced the little boy.

"Uncle Teddy said today is Valentine's Day. I like balloons," Joseph said.

"We've noticed." Chuckling, Teddy put an arm around Candee's waist and held Joseph's hand in the other. He glanced toward the dining room, grinning when he noted Desiree's thumbs-up and conspiratorial smile.

"Where are we going?" Candee asked as they exited the club. Teddy buckled Joseph into the child car seat, then came around and opened the door for her.

"I want to show you the Valentine's gift I bought you." He started the car, and they covered the miles to Thompson Lane in under fifteen minutes.

"I'm still eating the chocolate from two weeks ago," Candee said. She tackled a white balloon that had floated into the front seat and turned to give it back to Joseph. When she turned to face front again, she paled, "Please, Teddy, don't drive down this road."

"How else can you see your Valentine's gift?"

He parked in front of the Victorian, then went around to

unbuckle Joseph. The boy raced to the tire swing, leaving three forgotten white balloons in the car.

Coming swiftly to the passenger side, Teddy opened Candee's door.

In the deepening dusk, she followed his gaze to the large red SOLD sign posted on the front door.

"Congratulations," she said softly.

"The Victorian isn't mine. It's yours."

She flashed him a dubious look, then gazed blindly ahead. "I don't understand."

"Some men buy roses for Valentine's Day, some buy candy. I prefer to buy houses." He paused, continuing in a solemn voice. "And this particular house is for you."

"Me?" She sucked in a breath and her eyes widened. She stared at the house with the same wistfulness he'd seen on her face the first day they'd met.

"Teddy—I ... I can't possibly accept such a gift."

"Yes, you can, under one condition."

"And that is?"

"You allow me to help you renovate."

"How? You're in Miami."

He heard the pain in her voice, and his heart squeezed.

"Not anymore. I'm selling my apartment and moving to Roses, although my realty business will require that I fly to Miami a couple of times a month." He framed her lovely face between his hands and gazed into her shining green eyes. "I'm assuming you'll let Joseph and me adopt one of the beagle pups."

"You can adopt all six," she gladly agreed. Leaning back, she stared lovingly at him. "Will you please tell me the reason you bid against me?"

"I'd intended to bid all along, and your sister knew my plan. Somehow along the way, I managed to mess things up. I never meant to hurt you, and I'm sorry."

She glided her fingers through his hair. "You texted your apology a great many times and you're forgiven." She paused, glancing at the tumbledown Victorian and Joseph skipping up and down the porch steps. "Where will you and your nephew live?"

"I didn't want to stop at one house when I could buy two." Chuckling, Teddy gestured to Mr. Dunworthy's home. "He was more than happy to sell, and he'll be moving into a retirement community so he can be closer to his son."

"You're doing all this for me? Why?"

He hugged her close, breathing in her shiny hair, the scent of sweet and spicy roses.

"Because building a new life often begins with tearing down a few walls." He smiled at the stunning woman nestled in his arms. "Candee Contando, I love you."

"I love you too," she whispered.

And then he kissed her, sealing the most important deal of his life.

THE END

JOSIE RIVIERA

1·800· CHRISTMAS

A SWEET CONTEMPORARY NOVELLA

CHAPTER 1

Desiree Contando had gained weight. Not a lot, although the extra ten pounds on her five-foot-four-inch frame were enough to make her favorite linen skirt fit snugly around her waist. When she was stressed, she ate pumpkin pie. Lately, she'd eaten a lot of pumpkin pie, and she had blamed it on Thanksgiving.

However, it was more than the delicious turkey dinner her sister, Candee, had served. The cause of Desiree's stress was the rundown Queen-Anne style home she'd purchased that morning.

"Your house is beautiful." Candee's voice came from behind her. "Now we both live on Thompson Lane!"

Desiree swallowed hard. "Maybe my house will be beautiful in a thousand years."

She shouldn't have done this. She should have dashed out of the lawyer's office as soon as the closing papers had been handed over for her to sign.

"Mr. Dunworthy, the former owner, never got around to updating the home, and then Teddy didn't have time," Candee said. "Your house won't take long to restore. My dilapidated Victorian is proof that even the most ramshackle house can be renovated."

Teddy and Candee had met in Roses, North Carolina, when Teddy came from Miami searching for a house to flip. They'd married, and together with Teddy's nephew, Joseph, they'd moved into a sprawling Victorian. Teddy had been granted legal guardianship of Joseph a few months earlier.

Desiree pushed out a tight breath. "Your Victorian still needs tons of work."

"Thankfully, it has come a long way." Candee stepped to Desiree's side and flitted her a once-over. She carried a box of pumpkin muffins. "A housewarming token," she'd declared, with a promise of something better coming on Christmas Eve.

"You've accomplished so much this year," Desiree said.

"I'm following your example. Advocating justice for low-income families and children is a daunting task. Fortunately, you're a talented attorney."

"I'm just doing the best job I can."

"You're ensuring the poorest people receive fairness. I respect you." Candee's gaze wandered to the rambling house. "You have more than enough acreage on your property for horses."

"I'll leave horses to your animal expertise. And puppies."

Months earlier, Candee had adopted Kisses, a pregnant beagle, from the local animal shelter. Of the six puppies Kisses had birthed, only one remained, as Candee had sold the rest.

Candee's emerald eyes glowed. "Boomer is adorable—all black and white and tan. And he loves to eat."

"Are you planning to sell him?"

"He'd make a great companion for a special someone."

"I'm sure you'll find a forever home for him."

"I'm sure I will." Candee smirked. "Speaking of animals,

Teddy finished the stable for Joseph's horse therapy. He converted a large shed, and Joseph loves the Haflinger horse. I did my research and the horse is small, with a calm temperament."

"You're wonderful parents. I'm thrilled for all of you." Desiree stared at her house. It seemed to stare back, taunting her. She took a slight step and pressed her lips together. "I don't know if I can do this."

"Of course you can. You're experiencing buyer's remorse." Candee gave Desiree's hand a gentle squeeze. "Everyone panics after buying their first house. Remember, Teddy and I are only two doors away. If you need anything, text me. Better yet, flag me from your driveway."

"Please thank Teddy for selling the house to me at such a bargain price. I'd never have been able to find such a terrific value on my own." Desiree attempted animation, and knew she wavered.

"You have a successful job, and now a home to call your own." Candee kept her hand on Desiree's. "Look how far you've come."

"We," Desiree corrected, keeping her voice light. If she began reminiscing about their miserable childhood, she'd lose it. If she shared her thoughts, they'd both lose it.

The women had been shuffled to five different foster homes in their teens after the state had deemed their parents unfit. Drugs and drink were only part of the issue, as their parents had also struggled with mental health problems. They had died a short time after landing in jail.

Candee broke the somber mood with an encouraging beam. "Just think, you'll pay off the mortgage in thirty years."

"Thirty years." Desiree groaned. "It'll take me forever to find someone with the expertise to fix this house on my limited budget." She paused, willing herself to say her ex-boyfriend's name aloud. "Scott had promised to help."

Not physically, of course, because Scott never got his hands dirty. Nonetheless, he'd agreed to rent the dormer apartment in her attic. In addition, he'd referred his handyman cousin to tackle the house repairs at a reasonable cost.

Some boyfriend. Some *ex*. Desiree had counted on the rental income to help pay her mortgage, and a jack-of-all-trades guy to get the job done. Finally, she had her own house, but no one to share it with. No happily-ever-after.

"Scott is in the past. Forget him," Candee said. "What's worse than a guy who is only around during the good times?"

"I know. It's just . . ."

It was just that it seemed like years had passed since her and Scott's argument, although the breakup had occurred the previous evening when he'd accompanied her to the final walk-through of the house.

"Are you joking? This tumble-down nightmare is your new house?" he'd shouted.

"Well, if you had taken time out of your day before now to see it, you wouldn't be shocked," Desiree had replied. "The owner before Teddy was elderly, and I told you the house needed a facelift."

"A facelift?" Scott had laughed. "Wow, Desiree. The house is a disaster. Is that your smooth-talking attorney jargon kicking into gear?"

"Are you ready to go inside?" Candee asked.

Desiree shifted and checked her shoulder bag for the house key.

Nope. She didn't have it.

"It's better Scott exited before you made a serious commitment to each other." Candee shuffled forward. "Besides, small-town life didn't fit his high-profile aspirations."

"True."

In Roses, life was slower, and people were friendly. A bandstand featured hometown entertainment. Tony's, the local pizzeria, had been there forever. Quaint and charming, the town hadn't given much thought to modernizing.

And now that Thanksgiving was over, the small town was transformed into a magical Christmas wonderland, a virtual postcard. Soon, snow would dust the pine tree branches and outlying mountaintops with a white sheen. Horse-drawn carriages circled the village green every weekend, and scents of gingerbread and cinnamon courtesy of local artisans filled the air. A holiday baking contest was held every year, and Desiree always entered her pistachio cake. She'd never won, although the twenty-five-dollar entry fee was donated to the local animal shelter.

Certainly, the happy Yuletide season and sense of community were reasons Desiree loved Roses and never wanted to leave.

A gust of icy air swept across the house's expansive front lawn, causing the oak tree branches to sway. The chilliness was a firm reminder that winter would soon secure a foothold on their Blue Ridge Mountain town. The wind was like a physical nudge, blowing across Desiree's thin navy suit jacket and bare legs.

She gripped the blue headband holding her thick blond hair in place.

She was out of luck. Her hair had blown into a mass of unmanageable waves.

Willing herself forward, Desiree stared at the various-shaped slate shingles on the roof necessitating repair, and the patterns of varicolored brick laying up the exterior walls. A century ago, the house had been designed to impress. Regardless, did anyone else use green, red, black, blue, and beige on one house?

She shouldered her red tote bag and matched Candee's steps.

This was a moment that Desiree had envisioned sharing with Scott. A life-changing threshold, embarking on their future together. They'd discuss her vision for the house, spend cozy winter evenings thumbing through decorating magazines, and wander paint stores discussing the perfect shade of dove white.

Velvet red ribbons and vibrant green garlands decorating the home's enormous rooms would celebrate Christmas in department-store style, and glittery white lights strung across the expansive front porch would create festive charm.

Now, all these special yet-to-be created memories would be done without Scott, because he was gone.

Her chest tightened, and she told herself to rein in her disappointment. Quietly to herself, she'd even hoped he'd pop the marriage question, bringing their dating arrangement to a happy-ending conclusion. She'd become Mrs. Scott Black, who lived in the beautiful Queen-Anne home on Thompson Lane.

Wow, had she ever been living in a fantasy world.

Between yesterday and today, the dream had disintegrated, and marriage was no longer in the cards. She was reaching thirty years old and every romantic relationship had resulted in a bad breakup. She was beginning to think she would forever be single and relegated to being addressed as Miss Desiree Contando.

Candee was staring at her, apparently wondering about Desiree's peculiar behavior, and why it was taking her so long to enter her new home.

"Desiree?" Candee tucked a strand of auburn hair beneath her faded baseball cap. "I know you're worried about taking on the house repairs, and I understand. When I mentioned to Teddy about your split with Scott, he made inquiries and found a carpenter for you. The guy's relocating here from Atlanta, Georgia. Apparently, Roses is his hometown. He told Teddy he'd like to give back to the community."

"Why would he leave Atlanta with the holidays a few weeks away?" Desiree asked. "Does his family live in the area?"

"Teddy didn't mention anything."

"And this guy's willing to start giving back by renovating my house?" With an overall sweep of her hands, Desiree gestured to the overgrown lawn, the neglected front porch, the weathered slate shingles on the steeply pitched roof.

"Yes. Teddy talked with him, and the guy will be arriving today."

"Does he know how much work my house demands?" Desiree challenged.

"You'll have to ask him yourself. He's reported to be talented and honest."

"Let's hope he's also cheap."

"He'll give you a good price." Candee firmly grasped Desiree's elbow, guiding her up the gravel driveway. "Teddy wanted to make amends for selling you this house when you clearly have reservations. He knows you're in a bind now with Scott gone."

Right. An understatement, to say the least.

Desiree changed her focus from her home's corner tower to Candee. "Who is this carpenter?"

"Keiran O'Malley."

Keiran O'Malley.

His name lodged in her throat. She had to fight down the feelings stirring within her.

"The O'Malleys owned O'Malley's Irish pub, which shut down many years ago," she managed to say.

The image of a tall, green-eyed guy with wavy dark hair came into Desiree's mind. He'd been on the high school football team, his broad chest and strong shoulders emphasized by his well-fitting jersey. He'd been a couple of years ahead of her, and had never given her a passing glance.

She'd glimpsed him at the homecoming game—the only one she and Candee had ever attended. When you lived in as many foster homes as they had, high school socializing was non-existent. Someone had pointed him out as the wealthiest kid in town. From what Desiree had heard, he sometimes helped his parents with their pub, key word being *sometimes*. Usually he was too busy escorting the current prom queen to country club dances, or driving around in his shiny new Ferrari after football practice.

After the game, she'd thought about talking with him, because her heart skipped a beat as she'd watched him. But, he'd been too engrossed in flirting shamelessly with a pretty cheerleader to notice Desiree.

Talk about a guy being off limits. In any event, they had run in completely different social circles. That is, if living in foster care counted as a circle.

"Teddy believes you can benefit from Keiran's carpentry skills," Candee said.

Panic rose inside Desiree. There would be a huge amount of work involved in transforming this house into her dream, and she remembered Keiran as seeming to be the opposite of ambitious.

Was it too late to sell her house back to Teddy and admit she'd made a mistake?

She pressed back her panic and concentrated on the second-story porch—the bracketed columns and neglected ornamental detail.

And the two words the house screamed: money pit.

She grimaced. "How does Teddy know Keiran?" she asked.

"Keiran remodeled a kitchen and bath in Georgia and

someone from Teddy's crew saw his work and recommended him."

Another gust of wind made the women shiver, and Candee jammed one hand into the pocket of her gray hoodie. "Earlier today, Teddy called Keiran and hired him for your project."

Desiree scowled. "Your husband did all this without asking me first?

"The guy's cheap, remember? He's coming back to his hometown and you'll be his—"

Desiree hesitated to finish the sentence. And then she did. "His first client."

"Exactly." Candee cheerfully ignored Desiree's apprehensive glance. "You want to host Christmas Eve dinner in your new house, correct? You can't do that until your kitchen is in working order."

"Regardless, I've never been known for my culinary skills. Except for my pistachio cake."

Candee laughed. "Um, even that's debatable."

The giggles came easier now, and Desiree's mind raced with trying to find a good reason to refuse Keiran's help before he arrived.

"I'd like to see his work. I have a certain design in mind, shabby chic, and I want it to be flawless," she said.

The laughter faded from Candee's face. "Flawlessness isn't the only thing that matters. Sometimes you take what you can get depending on your budget." She extracted Desiree's house key from her purse.

So that was where the key had gone. Desiree had forgotten she'd given it to Candee for safekeeping. Was this a sign she didn't really want the house?

Don't be ridiculous. If it was a sign of anything, it was that she was absentminded.

Candee lifted the key in the air. "Be content."

"Contentment and flawless should always be part of the same sentence."

"Not in our home-flipping world." Candee did a slow whirl, motioning toward the majestic trees, the worn picket fence, the trampled, overgrown bushes. A recent rain had soaked the lawn, and the grass was smeared with clumps of wet clippings. "Every house is a challenge and yours is no exception." She caught Desiree's hand. "C'mon. We've prolonged the inevitable long enough."

Sharing a chuckle, the women stepped onto the porch. Candee inserted the key into the lock, clicked the brass handle, and held the door open. "After you."

They stepped across a straw welcome mat, leaving foot-prints in the layer of dust on the aged parquet floor. Candee switched on the lights and offered a bright smile. "Oh, and there's one more thing about Keiran."

Desiree hesitated. "Only tell me if it's good."

"He planned on renting a place in town until he got on his feet," Candee said. "So Teddy recommended your attic apart-ment. He assumed you wouldn't mind if Keiran lived there for a while. The rent payment will help you with the mortgage."

A light fixture in the hallway swung precariously from an unsightly wire, and Desiree silently grumbled. "Is Keiran also an electrician?"

"Possibly, but he may not be licensed. I'm sure Teddy will know someone who is, though."

"Will a free room equal free labor?" Desiree waved off her sister's assurances. "And will his results be immediate? I want the house presentable by Christmas."

"C'mon, Desiree, don't be impatient. You're obliged to supply him with a salary and money for materials. Celebrate your good fortune because he dropped directly into your lap." Candee checked her watch. "Joseph's school bus will be coming soon. The school has early release because of a teacher planning seminar. I'll text you later."

With a nod signaling agreement, Desiree accepted the muffins and thanked her sister.

She took two paces into the foyer. A bone-deep weariness made her anxious, whereas Candee's enthusiasm was a source of inspiration.

Desiree drew on that inspiration. Taking a deep breath, she marched through the foyer and headed to the living room. The stained gold carpeting was peeling at the edges, and she bent to fold it back. Beneath the carpet were hardwood floors crying out for refinishing.

A large marble fireplace took up half the wall, its wide mantel solid oak. At Christmas, she imagined the mantel transformed, complete with sprigs of holly, miniature tealights and classic quilted stockings.

An unexpected downpour spilled across the bay window, and Desiree hoped that Candee had beaten the rain and reached her house without getting soaked.

She passed her fingers over the mantel, locating several candles and a box of matches, a reminder that Teddy had used the fireplace. He'd mentioned the HVAC unit wasn't operating, which meant no central heating or air conditioning.

The lights in the foyer blinked, then went out.

Already? Desiree massaged her temples. She hadn't been in her new home ten minutes.

Have faith, and everything will fall into place. Practical matters first. The encouraging words from her "forever family" foster mother came to mind.

Certainly, Desiree thought, she should hold fast to that wisdom.

First, deal with the electrical problem. And then the plumbing, then the . . .

The list went on and on.

Whereas now she had Keiran, the playboy turned carpenter who was on some kind of bizarre mission to help the community.

She went to the kitchen and placed the muffin box on the counter. Quickly, she captured her tote bag carrying overnight necessities, climbed the oak staircase to the master bedroom, and changed into an old pair of jeans and a flannel shirt. Although the light would soon fade, she'd begin the first afternoon in her new house by scrubbing the tiled floor.

Fun way to spend a Monday evening, she thought wryly. Fortunately, the plumbing was functional, and Teddy had kept a pail of cleaning supplies beneath the sink.

Although she had a love/hate relationship with scrubbing floors, she rolled up her sleeves and eased into a pair of rubber gloves to protect her hands. She loved the way the floors gleamed after a thorough cleaning, and the fresh lemony smell, barring the exhausting, manual labor that went with it.

Either way, she'd prayed over her decision to purchase the house, and with prayer came peace of mind. So she could do this. And she'd accept Keiran's help, because the financial savings would be tremendous.

That is, as long as he cut her a good deal, stayed in his attic apartment, and they maintained a working relationship.

And if he wasn't happy about that arrangement, he could book a hotel in town.

CHAPTER 2

fter finishing a nitpicky adjustment to a kitchen remodeling project in Atlanta, Keiran O'Malley thanked the customer and gathered his tools as the other crewmen departed.

Done. Finally.

He drove his red pickup truck back to his apartment to finish packing, intentionally shifting his gaze away from the picturesque historic neighborhood of Iredell Park. Trendy and upscale, it had been reported as an up-and-coming neighborhood for young professionals. Many of the apartment buildings featured rooftop terraces, while several others were within walking distance of restaurants and shopping. He'd decided it would be an ideal area to live and raise a family.

And, he'd intended to set up a stand at the annual holiday display and sell his homemade Irish whiskey cake.

That was then, and this was now.

Still, they were everywhere—his shattered dreams. He shook his head, acknowledging that Atlanta held nothing for him anymore.

He slowed for the last turn to his apartment and went over what had happened that morning.

For once, he'd been able to complete a carpentry job on time and wasn't delayed because of Patricia, his ex-girlfriend. When they'd first met, he'd enjoyed her dark, sultry beauty.

Not any longer.

Usually, her compulsions to run in overdrive and make his life difficult were at the top of her priority list. Today she'd seemed preoccupied, although she'd slammed the office door in his face when he told her he was leaving Georgia for good.

Startled, he'd laughed and stared at the door. Really? As if this was all *his* fault?

He'd lifted his hand to knock. And then he'd pivoted and strode away. She was officially gone from his life. It was over. If only he could make peace with the fact that the two people he'd grown closest to—his girlfriend and his best friend, Kyle —had deceived him. They'd found each other and forgotten about him.

He bounded up the last flight of stairs and greeted Georges, his roommate, as he entered their fourth-floor walk-up apartment. They rented a place above a pawn shop, and Georges worked there part time, negotiating prices on the various items. Georges spent the rest of his time attending college online, majoring in international studies.

With a thump, Georges set a pizza box on the kitchen counter.

"I ordered pizza for my new roommate, Oscar." Georges's deep chuckle brought Keiran to the kitchen.

"Glad you found someone to take my place so quickly," Keiran said.

"Yup." Georges snatched a beer from the refrigerator and took a long swallow. "And we're planning to get blindingly drunk tonight."

"I hardly ever drink."

"Fortunately, Oscar drinks all the time. Take heart, *mon ami*. I'll miss your cooking." Georges headed to the living room and Keiran followed.

"That's my takeaway conversation?" Keiran asked.

"Most of it." Chuckling, Georges sank onto an armchair and drained his beer. "Because you're leaving, I'm putting take-out on speed-dial."

"Sorry, I don't deliver. You can always learn how to put together a casserole, or bake potatoes in a crockpot."

"Me? Every kitchen appliance runs when it sees me coming." Georges crooked a grin at the unlikely possibility of preparing a meal. "And I checked. Oscar doesn't even know how to fry an egg. He just drinks."

"Does he work?"

"He works at a law firm in town."

Impressed, Keiran inquired, "Is he a lawyer?"

"Nope. He works outside and struts around with a bill-board advertising their current specials—you know, divorces, insurance claims if you've been in an accident—"

"What kind of a lawyer does that?"

Georges barked a laugh. "The kind you call if you're in a jam. His firm is a one-stop shop kind of place. Oscar said the lawyer is also a locksmith. You've probably seen his advertising on TV. His name is Abraham Realgood and his nick-name is Honest Abe."

Unsuccessfully, Keiran tried to keep his face straight. "Well, thanks for an oversupply of information I'll never need."

"You never know when a lawyer is required, especially one who gets things done in a hurry." Georges lurched to his feet and the men shook hands, Georges joking all the while that he was charging his new roomie a higher rent for their "luxurious" studio apartment in the ancient building.

"You're a good guy, Keiran, and much more forgiving of Patricia and Kyle than I'd ever be," Georges said.

A good guy? Keiran thought.

Not particularly.

Forgiving?

Well, he embraced his faith. But if push came to shove, the answer would be *no*. He wasn't very forgiving.

"Always take the high road, son," his mother had often said.

I'm trying, Mom.

Wouldn't a good Christian man forgive an infidelity, as Georges believed Keiran had done?

Wishing his roommate well, Keiran packed his bags, hoisted his guitar case over his shoulder, and placed his father's precious football card in its plastic case. He tucked the deed to his family's pub, O'Malley's, into his wallet.

He loaded his belongings into his truck alongside the rest of the luggage he'd packed the evening before. Thirty minutes later, he headed east on I-85 through Georgia. He estimated it would take him less than four hours to reach Roses, North Carolina.

This was his opportunity to go back to his roots after leaving his family's pub far behind. He loved to cook and bake, and his father had discouraged him.

"I know the restaurant business," his father had lectured. "It's hard work, and I don't want you tied to a stove night and day, like me and your mother have been all these years. Pursue football. Go pro."

Keiran didn't have the desire, the instinct, or the talent to play football. He really liked the restaurant business. Each night, he'd link his hands behind his head and stare at the ceiling.

He couldn't follow his father's football dreams.

So instead, he'd reacted like an impetuous eighteen-year-old and left town. He'd follow his own road. He'd show his father he'd become a success without his family's support.

In Atlanta, he'd met Patricia. Soon afterward, she'd encouraged him to become a carpenter in her father's construction business, dreaming of million-dollar homes in stellar neighborhoods. Together, they'd climb the ladder of success. He'd learn the carpentry trade while she'd manage his appointments, advertise, and grow his business.

Young and trying to find his way, he'd responded with an enthusiastic "sure," and shelved the idea of opening a restaurant.

Now Patricia was gone and the ladder had been pulled out from under him.

In Roses, he'd be surrounded by the community that had given him an idyllic childhood. And maybe he could find his balance again—reopen the old family pub, visit Ireland for recipe inspirations. The more he thought about this new direction, the more he knew he had planned for the better.

He'd driven thirty minutes when Teddy Winchester phoned, introduced himself as a home flipper, and offered Keiran a job.

Keiran put his cellphone on speaker as Teddy explained that Desiree Contando, his sister-in-law, had purchased a Queen-Anne style home in Roses that was in a desperate state.

"Are you interested?" Teddy asked.

Keiran gripped the steering wheel. "How much repair?"

"I'm estimating a few months' worth. Do you have anything else lined up?"

"Not in the short term." Keiran reminded himself that there was more to life than dreams, and a steady income until he found his footing wasn't a bad idea.

"So will you take the job?"

"Without viewing it? What if your sister-in-law doesn't like my work?"

"She'll like it. Truth is, she's in a jam. The guy overseeing the project bailed, she's moving into 321 Thompson Lane today, and the place is a mess." Teddy paused. "Are you familiar with the road?"

"No, but I can find it."

"It's a definite fixer-upper. Despite that, the house has curb appeal and endless possibilities," Teddy continued in a distinct Southern drawl. "I learned from one of my crewmen that your craftmanship is excellent."

"Roses is my hometown and I'm headed back there as we speak," Keiran replied.

"Yes, so I've heard."

How had Teddy heard? Probably because men gossiped at twice the speed of women.

"As a bonus, I'll offer you an apartment—a remodel in the top dormer of her house. I lived there until my recent marriage and it's in good shape."

"What's the catch?" Keiran asked.

"I'm asking this favor because I sold Desiree the property," Teddy said. "Plus, I live two doors away."

"And you still want your wife speaking to you in the morning," Keiran finished with a laugh.

"Something like that."

"Sure, then," Keiran said. "I've been thinking a lot about making a difference in Roses."

Now why had he said that? Teddy was a stranger who offered employment, not his new buddy.

Serendipity. Fate. A coincidence. Keiran chose to believe the hand of God was bringing him back to his birthplace. A sign to leave his broken heart and Atlanta memories far behind.

Once the carpentry job was finished, he'd reopen his parents' pub. In the meantime, as a favor to Teddy for leading him to his first client, he'd give Desiree an excellent price.

"Thanks. I'll tell her to expect you," Teddy said. "Oh, and by the way, she works full time, so she won't be around much."

"What does she do?"

"She's a lawyer."

Smiling, Keiran clicked off his phone. A lawyer? Really? Two lawyer mentions in one day. He just hoped he never needed one.

He switched on the radio, bypassing the Christmas carols —the cheery "Santa Claus is Coming to Town" sung by a current rap star.

He settled on a classic contemporary station, and his fingers tapped a beat on the steering wheel as an 80's rock song belted, *"Don't stop believin.'"* He knew the lyrics to the Journey hit by heart and sang along.

While sorting his collection of football cards, his father would hum the song after the pub closed for the evening. One particular card had been autographed by a well-known player, a guy he'd met while trying out for a first-pick college draft. His father hadn't made the cut. When Keiran had tried out for high school football, his father had given the prized card to him.

Keiran couldn't imagine his father as young and carefree, full of dreams and aspirations. He only remembered a man with a resigned look on his tired, worn face, his mother cooking diligently by his side.

Keiran glanced at his backpack holding the plastic-encased football card. "Thanks for giving me material things, Dad. I'm sorry I didn't live up to your ambitions. I only wish I had visited Ireland sooner to spend time with you."

But he hadn't.

"Don't stop believin.'"

When the song ended, Keiran clicked off the radio, flicked on his left blinker, and exited the highway leading to Roses. He remembered the area, although he relied on his GPS to locate Thompson Lane.

He admired the natural scenery, the backdrop of the Blue Ridge Mountains, the celebratory way the town center was decked out for the holidays—the streetlights trimmed in decorative red bows, and the garlands strung along every shop's window box. He remembered his parents' love of Christmas had radiated throughout their pub, along with savory scents of homemade relishes, roasted turkeys, and exquisite caraway-seed-filled Irish desserts.

Once upon a time, he'd loved everything about Christmas. Now he was an adult, and the enchantment was gone. The constant arguments with Patricia had cured him of childhood expectations.

He parked at the curb in front of a ramshackle Queen-Anne style home at 321 Thompson Lane. The house stood like a freeze frame of a forgotten time.

"This must be the place," he murmured. He got out of his truck and surveyed the property. "A real fixer-upper, all right."

With his keen eye, Keiran assessed the exterior of the house against the fading afternoon light, grateful he'd arrived in Roses before dark. Patches of spongy moss grew along the slate roof. The window frames bubbled with fading beige paint. All these outdoor repairs would take hours of labor and he hadn't even stepped inside.

Despite the neglected appearance, the house brought back memories, and unexpected emotions rocked him. He recalled his childhood home in Roses, bordered by a white picket fence. The house had been located on the other side of town and was one of the largest in his neighborhood. In his mind, he heard his friends' laughter as they played kickball. He'd had no siblings, but had never felt lonely.

Beams of late afternoon sunshine streamed through the Queen Anne's front bay window. A recent rainfall brought a reflective gleam to the wavy glass. Raindrops trembled and shined along the yellow leaves on thick branches. The house was set in, canopied by four gigantic oak trees that appeared to be over a hundred years old.

Curb appeal, Teddy Winchester had said.

And a whole lot of work.

Keiran hesitated. He was a carpenter, not a demolition crew.

Unlimited possibilities.

Well, that one was negotiable, and depended on how much repair the house required. It certainly exuded charm and a salute to a bygone era. He just had to have faith that the bygone era wasn't so long ago that the home offered no modern comforts.

He didn't blink, hardly moving, debating. A slight drizzle from the tree leaves coated his cheeks and two days' worth of dark stubble. There were no lights on inside the home, although the flicker of candlelight illuminated a window.

He scrubbed a hand over his face, then retrieved his backpack, guitar, and toolbox from his truck. He'd get the rest of his luggage later.

Again, he stared at the house.

He was here, had driven all afternoon, and it seemed foolish not to see if Desiree was home. He went to the front door and knocked once.

No answer.

Twice.

No answer.

He debated about clicking the brass handle to check if the

door was locked. But, even if it was, he couldn't exactly stroll inside.

On the third knock, the door abruptly opened, and he came face to face with a beautiful woman with deep-set blue eyes. She held a lighted candle, sheltering the flickering glow with her small, cupped hand. She could have stepped out of a fairy tale—Cinderella came to mind. Her thick blond hair was piled on top of her head, held precariously by a blue headband. Her fair complexion was smudged with dirt.

"Desiree Contando?" he asked. He thought she flinched, but assumed he was mistaken.

"Just Desiree, please." The expression on her oval-shaped face was calm, and her hair shone in the last rays of daylight. Slender, she wore a pair of worn denims and a plaid flannel shirt with the sleeves rolled up.

A spin of warmth between them sparked an attraction he hadn't expected.

She was drop-dead gorgeous, especially if a guy was drawn to fairytale princesses.

He apparently was. Although he'd tried dating a princess and had failed spectacularly. Patricia had never been happy, despite his attempts to shower her with compliments, expensive meals, and flowers whenever he could afford them.

In the end, it was obvious their values and interests didn't match, and she'd discarded him for his wealthy best friend. Aye, she wanted the castle and the crown. She didn't have time to waste on a guy trying to figure out if he wanted to be a carpenter or a cook.

"Hi, Desiree." Spellbound, he just stared. She had the prettiest golden hair, framing a perfect complexion and generous mouth.

She blinked and took a step back. "Mr. O'Malley?"

"Keiran."

"I've been expecting you." Her tone was dispassionate as

she gestured with her small chin to the home's worn interior. "My brother-in-law said you were driving from Atlanta."

A breeze shifted, the wind carrying the promise of chilly winter nights to come. "Yes, all afternoon."

The weariness in her blue eyes deepened. "Do you realize what you're getting into here?"

"Absolutely." He nodded reassuringly. "I'm a carpenter, more or less."

"With any luck, it's more rather than less. This house warrants an excellent carpenter, plus a whole lot more." Her expression tightened. "Are you also a licensed electrician? I've lost power."

"No," he admitted.

The candle wavered in her hand, vulnerable to the late afternoon breeze.

She shrugged. "Then your services aren't required tonight."

"I was told I had a place to stay when I got here," he said.

"Yes, once you begin working. However, there's nothing for you to do yet, and because it's my first night in my new home, I'd prefer to spend it alone. I'll see you in the morning —and bring an electrician with you." She stepped back and closed the door.

"Well, that's perfect." He stared at the wooden front door, then down at the sagging porch. Evidently, this was his day for women opting to slam the door in his face. "I came all this way, but because I'm not the acceptable tradesman for this evening, I'm supposed to sleep in my truck," he muttered. His earlier enthusiasm at arriving in Roses was quickly waning.

You were planning to come, anyway, a small voice in his head reminded him. *You were going to take a ride by your parents' deserted pub, then find a place to stay in town.*

Aye, before Teddy's phone call.

Nevertheless . . .

He was still muttering when the door opened.

"Mr. O'Malley, are you talking to my porch?" Desiree asked.

"Just enjoying my visit with your broken-down floor. That is, when I'm not having a conversation with the rusty propane grill in the corner." He kept his focus downward. "This porch is unsteady. You'd better hope it doesn't cave in, or you'll be clamoring for a carpenter faster than you can say Queen-Anne disaster."

"Are you saying my house might collapse?" She laughed, and that amazed him. It was unexpected. She seemed so serious, with her slim shoulders and strong posture, her huge eyes speaking of sadness. Slight shadows beneath her eyes gave her an unconscious vulnerability, and one, he guessed, she would never admit to.

Her laugh seemed stilted, though. Just like his had been that morning with Patricia. An ironic laugh of disbelief.

"Minor setbacks. Everything can be fixed." He plastered on a reassuring grin that he didn't quite feel. "We'll bring your house back to her former majestic state."

"For now, she's a good distance from her former crown." Desiree smiled, and this time her smile seemed more genuine. "Why are you still standing on my porch, Mr. O'Malley?"

He studied the lit candle in her hand, and then her. She looked absolutely exquisite, her high cheekbones accentuated by pink color, her classic beauty understated. She wore no makeup, and reminded him of a master painting by Raphael—*Woman with a Veil* came to mind. Alluringly beautiful.

Before answering, he questioned himself. Why *was* he still here? Did he truly belong in Roses? Was he good enough to transform a house in shambles into splendor? Was he good enough to open his parents' pub, a legacy he didn't deserve?

A part of him said aye, although it had nothing to do with the house. Or the pub, for that matter. He wanted to learn more about Desiree Contando.

Not a good idea. Wrong reasons. He was here to work. Besides, he was spinning off of a bad relationship. Better to wall himself off from all women, especially attractive women with enchanting eyes and enticing lips.

He was amazed by his next response, which had nothing to do with his thoughts. "This is my hometown and I haven't been back in ten years. Give me a chance."

"I will, in the morning."

"I would've booked a room in town if I'd known." He pulled out his cell phone. "I'll call Morrison's Hotel on Main Street."

"They closed five years ago."

He didn't think twice. There was Broad Acres, a bed and breakfast on the outskirts. He told her as much.

"They shut down last year," came her cool reply.

He clapped a hand to his forehead. "So here I stand, wondering where I'll be sleeping tonight. Teddy mentioned he lived a couple of doors down. Last name is Winchester?"

"Yes, and … no. I mean, don't call him." Desiree's tone stayed no-nonsense. "He and my sister, Candee, are newly-weds. Plus, they're raising a young boy."

"I'll snooze in my truck for the night, then." Keiran picked up his things. "I've slept in worse places."

"Have you?" Desiree assessed him. "From what I recall, only the finest was good enough for a guy like you."

He grimaced at her evaluation. "Do we know each other, Desiree?"

"I know *of* you. I first saw you at a high school football game. Your nickname was Richie Rich."

Wow, was he ever tired of people assessing him on the basis of his well-to-do background. Sure, his parents had been wealthy and he'd never lacked for anything, although they'd toiled long hours for their success. With the same work ethic, he'd driven himself hard in order to prove himself among the other tradesmen in Atlanta.

He held her gaze. "Rich doesn't mean lazy."

"Not always." Those two words, a slight concession, an assessment of a guy she'd labeled without any facts. Frustration mushroomed inside him.

"Did we talk?" he asked.

"Where?"

"At the football game."

"Are you kidding?" She avoided his gaze. "You were too busy with the pretty cheerleader."

"I can't remember her name."

Desiree started to scowl, but chuckled when he did.

"Do you remember mine?" she asked.

He held out his hand. "I don't think we were ever formally introduced. Let's try this again. I'm Keiran, Desiree."

She accepted his handshake. Her hand was fine and delicate. The idea of living in her house was becoming incredibly appealing.

"So you're an authority about me based on a high school football game?" He still held her hand. She made no move to let go. Neither did he.

Silence reigned for a beat.

Quietly, she shifted her stance and pulled her hand from his. "True. Sometimes one chapter doesn't mean you read the whole book."

"Precisely."

Sure, he'd made bad choices. He'd been foolish and reckless for leaving a town he loved in order to prove he could make it on his own, falling into a profession totally removed from the restaurant scene.

She trained her attention on him, her deep-set eyes considering. "Teddy predicts this house will take several months to complete. I'm hoping he's wrong."

Keiran hoped Teddy was right.

"Hard to tell until I see it." He stamped his feet on the dog-eared welcome mat, a not-so-subtle hint. "May I come in? It's cold out here."

"Why not?" She brushed those gorgeous waves from her face. "After you, Mr. O'Malley." With a graceful turn, she ushered him inside.

CHAPTER 3

esiree led the way through the foyer, pausing to peer at a silvery spider web, an excuse to gain two seconds to compose herself. She'd been totally unprepared. She needed time for this new development she hadn't expected.

And that development was Keiran O'Malley. The handsome, dashing Irish football player. She was certain he was accustomed to plush surroundings, and her house was the farthest one could get from that scenario.

Seeing him, she'd done a double-take, surprised that he surpassed her adolescent daydreams. In high school, she'd heard that he lived on the south side of town, the wealthy side, where tall privacy hedges bordered the homes.

A decade had passed and he'd grown even more striking. His teen body had filled out, and tiny crinkles had formed around his Prince Charming green eyes. The navy-blue parka he wore accentuated his athletic shoulders.

His family had reached financial success owning their profitable pub until it abruptly closed. After Keiran departed (she'd inquired), the pub had gone into a downward slide and never recovered from the economic recession.

The way her heart had thudded when she saw him reminded her that her youthful crush was alive and well. Definitely, she should keep her distance. Difficult to accomplish when she couldn't keep her eyes off him.

She realized his gaze was assessing her, from her messy hair to her disheveled jeans and oversized flannel shirt.

Ten years. During that time she'd earned a bachelor's degree, followed by three years of law school and passed the arduous bar exam on her first try.

Every day since then, she'd had a single-minded vision of creating a picture-perfect life. Her own childhood had been just the opposite. However, she'd learned that as an adult, she could control her destiny. Especially with perseverance and God's generosity.

At present, she focused on the monumental task ahead—transforming a rapidly deteriorating house into the holiday fantasy of her dreams.

"This is lovely," Keiran said.

She swallowed as her gaze shifted to his finely chiseled features. "You're being serious?"

"Aye. The house has good bones. And we'll be able to build on that."

"Speedily, I hope," came her patented reply.

He lifted a dark eyebrow. "In six months this place will be as good as new."

"Six months? I'm hosting Christmas Eve dinner and the kitchen needs to be ready by then."

He gave her a skeptical look. "Does your oven function?" he asked.

"Function? Hah! Fortunately, Christmas Eve isn't tomorrow. I've . . . *we've* got a few weeks."

"To perform a miracle?" He motioned to the mismatched wallpaper in the foyer, the floorboards desperate for major repair, and narrowed his gaze. For a split second, she thought he might turn around and leave.

Purposefully, she didn't meet his stare. "Only God performs miracles."

"Glad we agree on something," he replied. "Six months is a generous estimate and the renovation may take much longer depending on any unforeseen problems once we get started." He set his backpack, guitar, and toolbox in the foyer. "Many times, remodeling goes weeks slower than a customer anticipates. Unexpected delays and spiraling costs are part of the process. When was this house built?"

She rolled her eyes. "Many years ago."

"Please let me know when you find out." He crossed his arms. Tall, athletic, and vital, with his male-model good looks and utterly appealing smile, he was definitely out of place in her shabby interior. He should have been strolling across a Dublin runway wearing designer clothes, not standing in her rundown foyer in worn jeans and a navy-blue parka.

"Surely the age of a home doesn't determine the renovation," she snapped at him, and felt churlish for snapping. Having him stand a few inches away sent unexpected tingles through her nerves. Long ago, she'd secured a place in her heart for him and only him. To have the object of her affection so near made her want to confess her infatuation. Blurt it out and get it over with, so he wouldn't think she was bad mannered for gaping and hesitating and staring.

Whoa. Hold that thought. They'd been together ten minutes and she wanted to tell him how much she'd dreamed about him ten years ago.

No, no, no. She was obviously overtired.

He didn't reply. Instead, he headed for the kitchen. "Other

tradesmen will factor in their estimates and might not cut you the same once-in-a-lifetime deal I'm giving you, and there may be surprises in older homes." He swiped a finger across the double-paneled wainscoting in the adjoining pantry.

That was one of the reasons she loved this house, because of the exquisite detailing not found in cookie-cutter newer homes.

"What kind of surprises?" she asked.

"Termite damage and rotting plumbing, to name a couple."

She winced. Unexpected problems would put a definite crimp in her bank account. "What is your once-in-a-lifetime deal, by the way?"

He paused to check a loose floorboard. "You'll need to trust me."

Easy to say, but words were cheap. She frowned and eyed his strong shoulders.

"Should I start on the renovations tonight?" He pulled off his parka, exposing thick arm muscles bulging from a cream-colored T-shirt. "I feel like I should at least fix that loose wire in your foyer because you're letting me bunk here a day early."

"Sure. Great. Thanks." She had to stop gazing at him.

He'd be sleeping in the attic, which was one floor above her bedroom. She'd hear his footsteps padding across the floor, the water running in the small shower when he bathed. Her heart beat quicker in her chest. This was her teenage dream come true, except the dream was several years too late.

Determined to ignore his desirability, she swallowed hard. Her gaze transferred to the kitchen counter. "Have you eaten?"

"Nope." He peered past her. "Any chance the stove or microwave works?"

"Both appliances are in terrible shape and should be ripped out. Plus, there's no power tonight so you're out of luck." She drew a breath. "Do you cook?"

"My parents owned a pub."

She knew that and waited for him to elaborate. When he didn't, she offered, "My sister brought muffins."

"What kind?"

"Pumpkin. Now you're being selective?" She pointed to the refrigerator. "And there's bottled water in the fridge."

"Any idea when the power will be back on?"

"I checked my phone for an update. A storm hit farther north and affected the lines in this area. The power company estimated everything should be fixed by nightfall."

"Excellent."

Excellent. Excellent would be reporting to her law firm tomorrow morning and coming back home in the evening to a fixed, finished house all decorated for Christmas. Excellent would be keeping her personal life private by living in her own space, far from the gaze of her swoon-worthy new roommate.

She ran a hand through her disheveled curls, wishing she'd pulled a comb through her hair before he'd arrived. And why hadn't she changed back into the proper business suit she'd worn earlier?

Keiran washed his hands in the sink. He slanted a glance at her while grabbing a bottle of water. "You want anything?"

She shook her head, her gaze dropping to her waistline. "After the Thanksgiving holiday, I intend to eat light for the next few weeks."

His gaze did likewise, and he smiled broadly. "You look great to me."

Her heart took a leap.

All day, her emotions had roller-coasted from exhilaration to anxiety. Now, as she stared up at the rugged dark-haired man who seemed sincere in his compliment, unexpected tears sprang to her eyes.

"This has been a difficult week," she admitted. "Usually I can juggle a lot of things with ease—"

"Difficult because of Thanksgiving and working full time? Teddy said you're a lawyer."

His question was so unexpected, so gentle, she smiled despite the tears. "No. Thanksgiving was wonderful. My sister Candee, or rather Teddy, cooked a Thanksgiving feast —a turkey with all the trimmings." She didn't tell him that she and Candee had never experienced a normal Thanksgiving growing up, so they savored every festive get-together. They knew what it was like to go without.

"Holidays are good." Lightly, he covered her hand with his fingers. "They're meant to be enjoyed with loved ones."

Awareness of his masculine presence stirred her pulse. "Mr. O'Malley—"

"Keiran."

She opened her mouth to object, then thought better of it. "Keiran, then."

"Now we're equals, Desiree." Although his tone teased, his expression turned serious.

They were hardly equals. He'd been born with the proverbial silver spoon in his mouth. She'd been born into squalor.

"I . . . I assume your Thanksgiving in Atlanta was pleasant," she offered.

He hesitated, then let out a brief sigh. "I cooked a turkey, a sweet potato casserole, and a round Irish cake filled with caraway seeds for me and my roommate."

"Wow. You'll be a welcome addition to any gathering."

So he'd had a roommate. A woman? she wondered, although she didn't ask.

"I never learned how to fix a proper meal, and now my life is hectic." Despite her shrug, she couldn't quite hold the apology from her voice, although she questioned what she was apologizing for. She hadn't had the opportunity to cook in her foster homes. More often than not, she'd been relegated to a spare room and ignored.

"My favorite pastime is spending afternoons in the kitchen trying new recipes," he said.

"I thought you were a carpenter. I imagined you crafting items out of wood."

He met her gaze. "A guy can do more than one thing, Desiree."

"But can he do more than one thing well?"

"Can you?"

"Absolutely."

"Then so can I." Approval and mirth brightened his face. His hand still covered hers. "Also, I make a mean Irish whiskey cake."

"I bake a pistachio cake that is usually edible, as long as I don't forget it's in the oven."

"How can you forget a cake? Don't you set a kitchen timer?"

"Sometimes." Another shrug. "Believe me, a cake in the oven is easy to forget, especially when I'm immersed in a court case and bring the work home with me. When that happens, I get sidetracked."

He laughed. "When your oven is fixed, we'll set a timer so your cake won't burn, and then I'll challenge you to a baking contest."

"Oh really. Who will be the judge?"

His gaze lit with sharpened interest. "Does Roses still hold a holiday cake contest on the village green?"

"Yes." She acknowledged his question with a smirk. "And always the weekend before Christmas."

"I thought so."

"I'm certain your cake will be a success."

"And so will yours."

She chuckled. "I highly doubt it."

He nodded.

Why was she able to fall into such easy conversation with him when they'd only talked for a short time? He seemed genuinely interested.

Not romantically, though.

No. Guys from his wealthy background didn't give the time of day to women like her.

Still, what was she doing? The peaceful intimacy of his large hand on hers caused her to relax a little too much. However attractive, this man was her employee, and their arrangement was strictly business.

She jerked her hand away.

He didn't seem to notice.

With a flash of white teeth, he offered that devastating grin again. "Do you accept my challenge?" he asked.

"To bake?"

"Aye. I'll make it official. I challenge you to the Roses Christmas baking contest."

"That's not fair. Your parents owned a pub."

"A pub isn't the corner bakery."

"You have more experience in a kitchen than me."

He winked. "I'll teach you all I know."

Cozy evenings baking homemade Christmas treats with him? Immediately, her heart agreed. Her common sense, however, reminded her this wasn't a good idea.

At any rate, she couldn't keep from chuckling and

accepting the challenge. His enthusiasm was contagious, and besides, what was the problem with gaining another ten pounds? Hah! She'd simply buy the next size up in clothes or scope out an elastic waistband.

"We'll schedule oven rights while you're here," she said.

"Sounds good."

Warmth bloomed in her cheeks as she gazed at him. Keiran O'Malley was a strong-featured, devastatingly attractive man who liked to cook and bake. Heads would certainly turn when he strode through town, especially if he toted a cartful of his homemade Irish whiskey cakes.

Opening the bakery box on the counter, he offered her a muffin. She declined and he chose one for himself. The table held a smattering of stoneware, along with boxes of utensils. She intended to arrange the glass-paned cupboards with an artful display of dishes and decided to get started while he ate.

Carefully, she corralled a stack of plates and mounted a chair. At her petite height, she stood on her toes to reach the top shelf of the cupboard.

"Get rid of the doors," he said.

She twisted toward him. "I'm sorry?"

"And lime green isn't trending these days."

"Just like that?" His confident attitude annoyed her. "Doesn't my opinion count? I *am* the owner."

"Of course." He waved a hand around. "Though in the latest designs, kitchens are painted white. And for a more open quality, remove the cupboard doors."

Plates in hand, she remained standing on the chair. "I've already decided to paint the walls dove white. I may want to leave the cupboard doors intact, though, so don't go throwing anything into the junk pile without my permission."

He nodded. "At least wait a few days before you decide."

Digesting his information, she agreed as he helped her off the chair. She loved an open floor plan, and took notes while she watched the home improvement TV shows for modern-day ideas.

While he leaned against the sink, she relit several candles. His gaze assessed her, assessed her kitchen, assessed the flickering candlelight.

She ran warm, sudsy water into the sink and placed several dusty dishes to soak. "You still haven't told me how much the renovation will cost."

Slowly, he bit into the muffin, chewed, swallowed, and took a swig of water. "I haven't seen your house yet."

"You're standing in the main room. Surely you have a rough estimate in your head."

A winning smile lit his features. "A million dollars, give or take a hundred thousand."

"That's not funny."

"I'll know better after you show me around." He strode into the foyer for his toolbox. "First, I'll fix that loose wire hanging from your ceiling."

"You're not an electrician."

"I learned a few things while working on construction sites all these years." He pulled a screwdriver from his toolbox.

"Do you know what you're doing?" She hurried after him. "I don't want you electrocuted before you begin working tomorrow."

He stopped dead and directed a grin at her. "If that happens, your repair list might be delayed a few days."

"You're brimming with not-so-funny jokes today."

"How's this?" he asked. "Providing I'm okay, I'll whip you up an omelet. I noticed you have a dozen eggs in your refrigerator."

"The stove isn't working."

"There's a grill on your front porch. If you have a cast-iron frying pan in one of those boxes, we're all set."

She burst out laughing as mixed reactions filled her. Keiran O'Malley embodied the best qualities in a man. And no matter how much she'd questioned his expertise, he was rapidly becoming a true blessing.

CHAPTER 4

A week passed, bringing the first Friday in December to a close. Along with record-breaking cold temperatures, the promise of snow was in the air, and daylight hours were rapidly becoming shorter.

Despite her desire to snuggle indoors and eat platefuls of carbohydrates, Desiree's over-filled schedule demanded she spend her days at her law firm filing last-minute appeals. Hours, days, had gone by in a blur, and she hadn't devoted as much time as she'd initially earmarked for remodeling her new home. As a lawyer fighting for those who couldn't afford it, she knew her service was critical. Many parents were without the financial means to support themselves or their children, and some spouses were victims of domestic violence. On numerous occasions, she'd provided free legal assistance by working pro bono.

At half past seven in the evening, she eased her car into her gravel driveway. During the day, a number of pickup trucks parked there, although all the tradesmen clocked out by three-thirty. Not Keiran, of course. Keiran worked nonstop.

A light drizzle wet the streets, and she yearned for snow —to sit lightly on her eyelashes, to gift wrap the magical season of Christmas.

She stepped onto the front porch, which Keiran had fixed, and admired the pine-scented, evergreen wreath strung with holly berries and pinecones.

"The first sign of Christmas." He greeted her with a lopsided grin as she opened the front door and smacked into him. Through the thin denim of his shirt, his body was warm, his broad chest hard and toned. She gazed up at his thick midnight-black hair, his well-defined features, and took in a sharp breath.

The smile on his face changed from humor to something else. Something deeper. He gazed at her lips, and she instinctively held her breath. His daily presence in her life was a sweet enticement she refused to acknowledge, and it took all her effort to resist his magnetism.

He dusted off his hands, then took her wool coat and set it on a hallway chair.

The renovation had come an incredibly long way in the short time since he'd arrived, and she peered around approvingly. Although she'd immediately wanted to shop for paint swatches, he'd advised focusing on the practical rather than the aesthetic. The roof, windows, and masonry repairs came first. The house required secure sealing, especially with winter approaching.

She'd approved, and in the course of a few days he'd taken on the role as general contractor, quickly becoming fast friends with Teddy. Keiran relied on Teddy's expertise, as well as his contacts. Once the house was watertight, he'd enlisted a crew to sand and sheetrock the kitchen walls.

As she did every evening upon entering the foyer, she peered at the ceiling and muttered, "Eventually, I'm getting rid of that hideous gold fixture."

"I like it." Keiran came to stand beside her. The harsh light of the open bulbs splayed across his face, and she reached up to brush a trace of sawdust from his cheeks.

He caught her hand, squeezing it warmly. "How was your day?"

"Busy. Yours?"

"The same. And I wouldn't have it any other way."

They'd come to an amiable understanding. He'd maintained a professional, friendly distance and, consequently, they'd built a trusting friendship. Somehow, he'd known intuitively that that was the relationship she wanted, and he'd quickly adapted to her unspoken request.

Her gaze swept the foyer, coming to rest on the hardwood floor. "Can the unevenness be fixed?" she asked.

"Any problem can be fixed. The question is, can you live with an imbalanced floor? I checked with a professional and the house's structure is okay, so I'd leave it and save the money." He gestured toward the bay window in the living room. "Same with the wavy glass. These qualities add character to an older home."

"Beautiful imperfections," she mused. "Like people."

"Perfectly imperfect, my chaplain in Atlanta preached at Sunday services," Keiran replied. "People are setting their sights on happiness, but searching in the wrong places. None of us, and nothing we create, is perfect. We expect a lot of others, though."

"And of ourselves," she said. "It may be that perfection isn't always the best way."

"Better to get over ourselves and think more about serving the people in our lives."

She nodded, reflecting, knowing she was forever striving to create a textbook world for herself, the one she'd read about in fables when she was a child.

Nonetheless, attaining the accomplishments her friends

often displayed on social media brought about exhaustion. Consequently, she didn't enjoy the here and now.

"Wise words," she replied.

And Keiran personified those words. He acted knowledgeably and humbly, and performed his work with a consideration that made her admire the person he was—kind, steadfast, and capable.

Each evening, he'd help her unpack endless boxes and order takeout, with a promise to cook her a proper meal once the stove and oven were installed. In the meantime, he'd rearranged her meager furniture and added a touch she would have expected more from a professional decorator than a carpenter with no formal design training.

"My chaplain is an inspiring person," he went on. "If you're ever free on a weekend, I can bring you to a church service in Atlanta. The drive takes a few hours, although it's doable in one day."

She gazed at him, and pretended she didn't. Her first inclination was to immediately decline his invitation, to maintain their cool, professional relationship.

But how could she?

She could hardly feign disinterest in this six-foot-two man with sparkling green eyes and an utterly masculine appeal. She loved talking with him, laughing with him. And she was impressed by his attention to elements and setup. He had an excellent discernment for arrangement, and was resourceful and creative, keeping her strict budget in mind at all times.

A fun conversationalist, he sported a keen knowledge in topics ranging from child advocacy to football, and, of course, cooking and baking. All in all, she considered him a Renaissance man, a term she'd once heard applied to a man blessed with intellect and proficient in a wide range of areas.

Although the term had originated in Italy, with his mesmerizing charm, Keiran was the epitome of the quick-witted Irish male.

"How's the kitchen coming?" she asked as she set down her briefcase.

"I was waiting for you to ask. Quicker than I anticipated, thanks to Teddy's efficient crew. The walls are painted, and your new appliances were delivered and installed this morning." As always, every sentence he uttered was enhanced by a hand gesture. "Do you want to see it?"

"Of course."

"Close your eyes." Obediently, she squeezed her eyes shut as he led her down the hallway.

He gave her hand a light squeeze. "Open."

She stopped at the kitchen entryway and gasped. Surely, this wasn't the same kitchen that had resembled a demolition area only a few days before.

As she and Keiran had discussed, the walls had been painted a dove white, and shiny new countertops were set in marbled granite. The white freestanding farmhouse sink was a surprise, paired with an old-world style pull-down faucet. A glossy tiled backsplash completed the ambience, along with open cupboards. She'd taken his advice and discarded the doors, giving the space a fluid, chic design.

He gestured to an empty corner. "A base cabinet is on backorder. Once it arrives, I'll install it. Hopefully it will be here in time for Christmas."

She sighed dreamily. "Thank you."

Her kitchen was exactly how she'd envisioned it, and a trendsetter's dream. Natural light spilled inside, thanks to sliding glass doors leading to her two-acre plot of land. A consistent thread of sunny yellow complemented the shelving rims, which were the colors they'd agreed upon. An oversized island in a high-gloss finish created a work triangle between the stove and refrigerator and seamlessly accommodated gleaming stainless-steel appliances. Her kitchen table and chairs had been tucked beneath a set of framed picture windows.

Awestruck, she put her fingers to her mouth. "All you've done in a week is more than most contractors could accomplish in a month."

He laughed. "The credit goes to Teddy's large, efficient crew. I'm merely one person supervising the project and helping wherever warranted."

"Truly, you are a genius."

He gazed down at her with tender amusement. "And while I was overseeing the renovations, you were protecting innocent children. If anyone deserves praise, Desiree, it's you."

Her heart skipped a beat.

Retrieving her coat, he strode to the hallway closet while she kicked off her black leather pumps, pulled on her favorite cardigan, and claimed a stool at the counter. She breathed in the aroma of seafood chowder simmering on the stove, and the sweet, enticing scent of a cake rising in the oven.

"And, in addition to the remodeling, you cooked?" she asked.

"Seafood chowder was my parents' signature dish. During my lunch hour, I shopped for the ingredients. For dessert, I baked an Irish whiskey cake."

"The very same cake you're challenging me with for the baking contest on the village green? It's totally not fair if you get a head start."

"I'll make it up to you."

She crossed her arms. "How?"

"We'll shop for a Christmas tree tomorrow, and I'm

buying. Only a ten-foot spruce will complement your living room's high ceilings. Aye?"

"Aye." How could she refuse a hardworking Irishman? In fascinated admiration, she watched him snap up a wooden spoon and adeptly stir the chowder.

"We'll eat dinner together after I shower and change?" he asked.

"Sure. Everything is wonderful."

He chuckled. "Brilliant."

A jumble of sensations made her pause. No man had ever cooked dinner for her before, inquired about her day, or taken a sincere interest. His consideration went way beyond their work relationship.

She stood and took a bottled water from the refrigerator. "Don't you have anywhere else you'd rather be on a Friday night?"

He studied her face, came closer, then pressed a light kiss on her forehead. "The more time I spend with you, the more time I want to spend with you. Does that make sense?"

There was no reason to offer a blasé answer, so she nodded a yes, because it made perfect sense. That pure attraction for him, a feeling she couldn't shake. Enjoy the moment, she told herself.

The thought made her absurdly pleased.

As he made for the stairs, she paused to take in the splendor of her polished, cheery kitchen. Previously, Keiran had drawn a sketch on his computer and gotten her approval, and his ideas had panned out. Ensuring the interior wall wasn't load-bearing, Teddy's crew had torn down the wall between the kitchen and dining room to make the most of her square footage.

A large communal area for family and friends was ideal for entertaining, Keiran had said.

She hadn't purchased a dining room set, and didn't foresee one in her immediate future.

Smiling, she arranged place settings on the kitchen island using her good china dishes and silver flatware. She'd started a hope chest when she graduated from college. It was silly, and most people had never heard of one. Despite her difficult upbringing, she believed in love and marriage, and a future with a special man. Starry-eyed dreams, she contemplated, while she folded white cloth napkins.

Keiran was down the stairs fifteen minutes later in his favorite pair of lived-in jeans and a T-shirt that revealed his fit physique. His thick jet-black hair was still wet from a shower, and he hadn't bothered to shave. His stubbled chin and prominent cheekbones made her pause. And his scent . . .

Oh, my. Now he even smelled like an Irishman—like early morning and whistle clean.

He raised a questioning dark eyebrow over his teasing gaze. "You own a service of fine crystal and china, your dining area is large enough for a twenty-person feast, and there's no place to sit and enjoy a meal?"

"Pull up a stool, like I did." She nodded to the island. "Or I'll pile cushions on the floor and we'll sit cross-legged. Someday, when I win the lottery, I'll buy dining room furniture."

He regarded the brass flush-mount light above the island. "What type of fixture do you want there?"

"I love French country design." She bent to a stack of magazines she kept in a wicker basket in the corner, and thumbed through one. "I saw a distressed frame fixture with candelabra detailing. See?"

He peered over her shoulder. "Excellent taste. I approve of all you've done." His breath was warm and tickled her ear.

That pull again, drawing her to him.

"You mean, all *you've* done," she corrected.

His lips twitched. Reaching up to the cupboard, he brought out two wine glasses. "I also bought a bottle of sparkling cider for our date."

"You're categorizing eating seafood chowder together at home as kind of a date?"

"Not kind of a date. It is a date."

"Is it a proper date?"

He sobered. "No. But it's here and now and let's embrace the moment."

Her heart did a double-turn in her chest. She didn't want this. Someday . . . maybe . . . when her house was finished and her career was established. And that would take years. Slowly, she was working her way up the ranks, though she owed thousands of dollars in student loans.

Besides, Keiran lived here. Did that count as a date?

At any rate, the man in question strode to the stove and stirred buttery seafood chowder with a wooden spoon.

"Want a taste?" he asked. "I baked a loaf of soda bread to mop up the soup. It's sitting on the table in a wicker bread basket I found in your cupboard."

"Okay, now you're showing off," she teased.

A chuckle tugged at the corners of his mouth. "Do you like the appliances?" As he stirred, he gestured to the six-burner stove and double oven. "Exactly what you ordered."

She kept herself from staring at him by concentrating on slicing the bread.

"It's impressive," she said. "And the low price Teddy's warehouse supplier gave for the cabinets was a relief. A huge thank you."

She'd taken out a home equity loan in addition to her mortgage to cover the improvements. Although she was realistic enough to understand she wasn't financially equipped to afford a total house renovation, she presumed the kitchen and bathrooms were most important. To save money, they'd concentrated on what Keiran labeled "mid-range renovations." He'd upgraded the countertops and changed the lighting.

"You're welcome," he said. "My pleasure, Desiree."

"A modern kitchen has always been my fantasy."

His gaze locked with hers. "Do you have other . . . fantasies?"

You, she almost said aloud. Swallowing, she pushed her gaze to his Irish whiskey cake baking in the oven. She whistled lightly and adeptly changed the subject. "Tell me again how you managed to get all this done, plus bake a cake."

"I delegate." He lifted a clean spoon from a drawer and scooped several spoonfuls of the chowder into a bowl, then brought the bowl to her for a taste. "I learned the skill from my father. When you own a pub, you can't do everything yourself."

She savored the hearty taste of cream, corn and potatoes blended with tender clams and sweet red peppers. "Mmm," she murmured. "This is delicious."

"A secret family recipe."

"Really? You won't share your recipe?"

"It's been handed down through several generations." He watched her, and his gaze shifted to her mouth. Gently, without warning, he kissed her. "Although I can assure you that the chowder isn't nearly as delicious as you."

The oven timer dinged. Reluctantly, he about-faced and gripped a mitt by the stove. He pulled out the cake and set it on a trivet.

"I'll glaze it in a few days. I'm testing a new glaze recipe." He gestured to the sugar and butter glaze, blended with whiskey, and grabbed a spoon so she could taste it.

"More deliciousness," she said softly.

He didn't mention the kiss. It had been quick and light. And memorable.

They'd fallen into a pattern of spending their evenings together, and her first home-cooked meal in her new home proved a mouthwatering delight. After slicing his cake, still warm from the oven, for a "taste test," they washed and dried Desiree's fine china and crystal by hand.

Afterward, Keiran led her into the living room, where he pointed out the detailing on the marble fireplace. Pausing, he got to his knees and inspected the chimney.

"I thought we'd light a fire again tonight," he said. "Eventually, you'll need a chimney sweep. Until then, the fireplace is safe to use."

"Teddy lit the fireplace several times when he lived here," she said.

Still on his knees, Keiran glanced up at her. "So is that a yes? Aye?" When she nodded, he gestured to the matches on the mantel and she handed them to him.

"The crew and I checked your central heating system too," he said, as he lit a match and checked the draft.

"Don't tell me, let me guess. The entire unit died."

"Aye, but don't worry." He offered a reassuring nod. "Fortunately, a reasonably priced HVAC guy stopped over. He's one of Teddy's crewmen."

"How much does a new HVAC cost?"

"Depends on the square footage of the house." Keiran lit the fire and waited for the logs to burn before standing. "I'd estimate your house is around three thousand square feet."

"You're right on target."

"Then your unit will cost six thousand dollars." He gave her the box of matches, his rough fingers brushing against hers. An electric current passed between them, and she felt that insistent magnetism. Not the youthful yearnings of an adolescent. On the contrary, hers were the dreams of a grown woman.

Instinctively, she pulled her hand away and wandered to the bay window. Outside, the vibrant colors of a Carolina winter day had faded, and twilight merged to darkness. The pavement gleamed with the slickness of a wet evening.

Across the street, Mr. Juno, a graduate student with a young family, had decorated his porch with an impressively lit display. Gold, red, and green boxes, wrapped in dazzling silver ribbons and bows, glowed with Christmas color and light.

She wiped unexpected tears from the corners of her eyes. What was it about Christmas that always got to her? Was it because she'd never experienced a real celebration because of her alcoholic parents? Because she'd never had a truly loving home? When life was bleakest, she'd searched for the warmth of faith and community. The Yuletide season was a time of celebration, just never for her and her sister. At least, not until this past year when Candee had married Teddy, and Desiree had purchased her first home.

"Desiree, I realize you're overwhelmed because of the renovations, but everything will evolve into the home of your dreams. I promise." Keiran came to stand behind her. His voice was sincere and deep, and a heat of longing pulsed in her veins. She blamed it on the romance of the candlelight, the flames flickering in the fireplace, the patter of raindrops on the bay window.

With its poignant reminders of the approaching holiday, she hoped that this house was the answer to her prayers. Finally, her days would be filled with the elusive elation everyone around her seemed to experience.

"Will it?" She wrapped her hands around her arms and didn't turn. He'd see the tears shining in her eyes and he'd ask questions—about her, about her past—that she wasn't prepared to answer.

"Aye. You can trust an Irishman's word."

She saw his reassuring smile reflected in the glass. The expression in his eyes, though, was a mirror of her own. Intense and probing.

And she knew what it meant.

He was beginning to fall for her, just as she was falling for him.

He turned her around to face him, his hands resting loosely on her shoulders. "I'm here for you, and I won't leave until this renovation is finished."

"Thanks. It's just—" A wave of emotion choked her voice, and she couldn't get out any words. Strange. She never lost control. After she and her sister had been passed from one foster home to another, she'd learned to keep her feelings securely bound. Not a single person was interested in two teenage girls with no money and no skills. No one had wanted them.

Not even their own mother and father had cared—so why would anyone else?

A ripple of sadness caused tears to stream down her cheeks. Swiftly, she caught the wetness with her fingertips and avoided Keiran's gaze.

"You're a nobody." The harsh words of one of her foster mothers came to the forefront of Desiree's mind. In her early teens, arriving at a brand-new foster family's home, Desiree had broken a dish by mistake. She'd tried to be useful, drying the dishes. Her foster mother had been furious, reprimanding Desiree about having no respect for other people's things, and shouting that Desiree was a useless girl.

Desiree had cried herself to sleep that night. She remembered the loneliness, the sadness, the sense of never belonging. Feasibly, that was the reason she felt inept in the kitchen.

Keiran watched her closely. He seemed unsure what to say next.

Lightly, he kneaded her shoulders. "Are you okay?" he asked quietly.

Grateful, she accepted his silent comfort, his reassuring presence.

"Of course," she murmured. She averted her gaze and thrust her fingers through her hair, attempting to right her curls into a semblance of order. She hadn't bothered to run a comb through her tangles since she'd gotten home, and probably looked a mess.

I'm not a nobody, she reminded herself. *Lift your chin and compose your features. 'Unsophisticated' and 'unimportant' do not belong in your vocabulary anymore. You're a poised, professional, educated woman.*

Although sometimes, oftentimes—she attempted to convince herself more than anyone else.

Gradually, she realized that Keiran was still staring at her, still had his hands on her shoulders.

She raised her gaze to meet his. "What's the matter?" she asked.

"Nothing." He cleared his throat, his face so near that his clear green eyes reminded her of Irish shamrocks, vivid and vital. "I was thinking that I debated about coming back to Roses and starting over. When I first arrived in Atlanta ten years ago, I assumed I was going to live there forever. And now I'm glad—"

Her heart responded in a slow, steady beat. "Glad about what?"

"And now I'm glad I came back. If I hadn't, I wouldn't have met you."

"I'm glad you came too." He was so close she could feel his sweet breath on her cheek. "I would have spent the week trying to find firewood to keep this fireplace burning."

Clearly amused, he said, "I assume you found enough wood."

"Yes, I brought in a few logs the other night, remember? You had stacked a cord behind the fence."

He didn't respond at first. His amusement was replaced by a slow, simmering intensity.

"So you found the firewood." He lowered his head, his lips meeting hers. "And I found you."

CHAPTER 5

Another week went by, marking the fourteenth day until Christmas.

On Friday evening, Keiran experimented with a new dish, mushroom stroganoff, which delighted Desiree. It was heartening to have a simple, unpretentious meal waiting for her when she came home after an exhausting workday.

Following the meal and clean-up, he shadowed her into the living room carrying two glasses of sparkling cider, plates of another Irish whiskey cake he'd baked, and napkins. He stacked kindling over crumpled newspaper in the fireplace, lit the newspaper first, then added large logs. Satisfied, he took a seat beside her on her gray-fabric sofa.

She gazed at the ten-foot spruce tree he'd purchased. Placed in a corner of the large room, the forest-green pine made a majestic statement.

After visiting several Christmas tree sites the previous weekend, Keiran had maintained that the largest tree on the lot was the ideal size to complement her living room's grand design. The tree seller had assisted Keiran in securing the tree to the roof of his truck, and Keiran had driven back to her house slowly with the tree swinging precariously on top.

Between making creamy eggnog and cranking up Yuletide music on a holiday radio station, Desiree and Keiran had decided on traditional red and green lights and a dazzling angel tree topper. Desiree had insisted on sparkly silver tinsel and a popcorn garland, and Keiran had enhanced the glittery embellishments with an array of wooden toy soldier ornaments he'd carved. The result was vibrant, festive, and in Keiran's words, "a masterpiece."

"I might pick up another tree," he casually said.

"One isn't enough? Completely decorated, this tree is practically taking up half my living room."

He grinned impishly, highlighting his boyish features. "I'd like to sprinkle Christmas all through the house. A small tree for the dining room would look festive."

"Especially because I don't own a dining room table or chairs." Desiree picked up the two glasses of sparkling cider from the end table beside her, handed one to him, and beckoned to the fireplace. "You know, everyone at my law firm is encouraging me to convert my fireplace to gas."

"It's your house and you've worked hard to acquire it. You should do what you want." His encouragement was gracious, and a surge of happiness flowed through her that had nothing to do with the delicious meal, the enchantment of a heartening fire on a cold winter's night, or the approaching holidays.

It was him. It was Keiran.

Seeing him like this, relaxed, wearing dark-wash jeans and a sea-green sweater that hugged his wide shoulders to perfection, he lounged beside her on her ten-year-old sofa. How could she remain unaffected when he was so breathtakingly handsome?

"Yes, this house is mine, and I still can't believe it," she replied. "And . . ." She hesitated, trying not to get ahead of herself. This was just the beginning. This was just a house. He was just a man she loved spending every waking hour with.

Just a man.

"And what?" He sipped his cider, set it on the coffee table, and moved nearer. His male presence was compelling, and a quiver of attraction went through her.

Quickly, she pushed the thoughts away, attempting a composure she didn't quite feel.

"I love the smell of a woodburning fireplace, so I'm passing on the gas insert," she said. "Call me outdated."

He pressed a soft kiss to her cheek and murmured agreement.

She gave him a questioning glance. "Can I ask you something?"

"Sure."

"Why did you leave Roses? You had the world at your feet."

"Did I? Tell that to an impulsive teenager." He reached for his glass and drained the cider. "I'll give you the short version, and please don't be sympathetic."

"And if I am?"

He hesitated, his features unreadable. "Don't be."

"Is my question too personal?"

He gave her a look that said it wasn't. "My father and I didn't agree about what I wanted to do for a living," Keiran said. "So, being reckless and headstrong, I decided my way was best."

"Which was?"

"Moving to Atlanta. I planned to become tops in my profession."

"Doing what?"

"Opening my own restaurant."

"And what was your father's way?"

"He wanted me to become an NFL football player. Trouble is, I didn't have the drive, or the interest, or the talent. I was the tallest on the team, but certainly not the fastest."

"I remember seeing you in your football uniform at the homecoming game I attended," she said. "It was the first time I ever saw you."

He offered an indifferent shrug. "Did you actually watch the game?"

"A little, I think. I don't remember you on the playing field."

"You have an awesome memory."

"Why?"

He hesitated. Her question sat in the space between them.

"Because I hardly ever played and frankly, I was relieved, although I knew my father was disappointed." Regret shadowed Keiran's gaze. "The football coach put me on the team to please my father because our pub was one of the sponsors. Soon after that game, I quit."

"I caught glimpses of you in the high school halls. Quitting didn't seem to affect your popularity."

A statement, not a question.

"I suppose." He shrugged. "Although popularity is a difficult word to define, especially when it's used to categorize people."

Wistfully, she gazed at the twinkling tree lights, the shades of red and green belonging to a simpler time, offset by the muted tones of the rustic toy soldiers. Could Christmas be celebrated without glossy bulbs and the sophisticated backdrop of her living room?

Of course.

As a child, well, she had certainly longed for Christmas, although it had never been celebrated at her house. Beer cans littered the floor and food was scarce. Christmas was a luxury her parents couldn't afford, and Santa Claus had never visited.

As an adult, she couldn't imagine life without Christmas. She loved the gift-giving and feasting, the religious celebration, the sacredness of the special holiday.

Profoundly moved by a feeling she couldn't explain, she blinked as her vision blurred. "In my childhood, I wanted a real home so badly—the picket fence, a cute puppy sitting by a welcoming fire burning in the grate, surrounded by people who loved me. When my mother was well and not drinking, she said she envisioned herself as a grand lady living on a beautiful estate." Desiree's lungs and throat felt sore, and she swallowed. "Considering our two-room shack, my mother had quite the imagination."

Tears pricked Desiree's eyes and she wiped them away. She scolded herself for dredging up emotional memories, better kept sealed in a safe corner of her mind. Inhaling, she sat erect. "So what you're saying is that at the end of your senior year, you took off because you didn't get the opportunity to play on the high school team?"

"C'mon, Desiree. Do I seem as shallow as all that? I said I quit football."

"Sorry." She paused. "I mean, you lived in one of the most expensive communities in Roses. I would have given the world to grow up in your shoes."

"It's never just about the stunning home and expensive neighborhood," he said softly. "There's more to a person's story than what's on the surface. I went to Atlanta to pursue my dream, got sidetracked, and failed."

* * *

DESIREE TIPPED her face back to view him. He expected to see disapproval on her beautiful features. After all, he'd had everything and given it all up, while she'd had nothing.

"You're young and can achieve anything you want." A positive smile played on her lips. "Also, you're one of the most talented people I've ever met. But look, we can talk about something else if you're uncomfortable."

"I don't mind our discussion, Desiree." He nodded his assent.

He'd been undecided about what to say, about his past, his future, although being with her lightened his concerns. With Desiree, everything would be okay.

He realized she was watching him, apparently waiting for him to continue.

He put his hands on his knees and focused on the wood sparking in the fireplace, the frosted pine cones and garland adorning the wide wooden mantel. The stylish adornments gave the room a celebratory spirit.

"My father discouraged me from what I wanted to do with my life," he said. "I intended to own a restaurant. Therefore, I rebelled."

"And here I thought you wanted to be a carpenter," she teased.

He pushed out a sigh. "I like woodworking, although my passion is the restaurant business. It's how I grew up. I love the hustle and bustle, the busy dinner hours, the scents of shepherd's pie, potato and leek soup, and thyme complementing my parents' famous corned beef recipe."

She gazed at him, openly interested. "I'm surprised."

"Mind if I ask why?"

Her unpretentious warmth set her apart from any woman he'd ever known. Was that what captivated him about her? Besides her vivaciousness, her sensational figure, and her utterly polished appearance when she came home each evening.

That is, until she pulled her hair from her severe bun and let the blond waves fall down her back. Then she looked irresistible.

She studied his face with a concerned frown. "Because most parents would have been thrilled their kid wanted to follow in their footsteps."

"Mine weren't. They insisted that owning an eating establishment was too difficult because of the long hours, which included early mornings, late evenings, and most holidays." He forked a corner of cake on his plate and chewed around the lump in his throat. "Did you know only one third of all restaurants succeed?"

"I've heard it's one in ten."

He paused, forming his words while he stared at the pile of sheetrock marking the next space in her home to be renovated—the small study attached to the living room via French doors.

"Living in Roses, you probably heard talk that my parents lived beyond their means," he said. "At first they did well and their pub was a huge success. Sadly, they didn't plan for the lean years."

"Yes. I heard." Despite her polite nod, he could tell she knew more than she let on. It was no secret his parents had neglected the pub after his departure, eventually forcing it to close. Even their most loyal customers could no longer endure the erratic schedule and so-so meals.

"They moved to Ireland soon afterward. Dublin," he clarified, briefly closing his eyes. "Although they reached out to me, I never flew across the pond to see them except to attend their funerals years later. They died within a day of each other. In the end, discouragement broke their hearts."

"Keiran."

He opened his eyes. Her gaze held his.

"I'm genuinely sorry. You realize none of this is your fault," she said. "My parents died while serving sentences for several robberies. They were alcoholics."

He felt a twist of sadness in his gut. For her. For him.

She was so sweet, so vulnerable, so totally gorgeous, he was torn between kissing her and commiserating on their losses.

He decided on the latter, and enfolded her into his arms.

Would kissing her mess things up? They got along brilliantly, although he often felt off balance. Could they keep their relationship casual, yet professional, living under the same roof, coming to terms with their attraction? His thoughts scattered, although he already knew the answer.

Nope.

With Desiree, his feelings were too deep to be casual.

He gazed at her mouth and cupped her chin in his hands, forcing her to gaze at him.

What would it be like to kiss her again and again?

Nope, his conscience chimed in a second time. She'd made her intentions known without saying a word. This was a business relationship.

Then why did life with her seem spot-on? Was the universe telling him something—bringing him back to Roses after all this time to open a pub, and bringing him to her? He was at the tail end of one profession, embarking on another. And she was the bridge in between. Or was she more? Perhaps she was the missing link . . . the real reason he was here.

She drew a sharp breath. "Keiran, I—"

He lowered his head and brushed his lips against hers. If she rejected him, he'd deal with it.

She didn't.

With a whisper of acquiescence, she twined her hands around his neck and pressed her delicate body closer.

He shivered. "Do you know how many times I've wanted to kiss you these past two weeks?" His hands slid down her back. "I mean, really kiss you?"

"Then what were you waiting for?" came her teasing reply.

He hadn't planned to spend Friday evening kissing her, he told his intrusive conscience. He'd planned on conversing with her, bantering with her, comparing recipes and paint samples.

Or had he? Because devoting every minute of his free time to her felt like the most natural thing in the world.

Slowly, tenderly, he took her lips in a lingering, passionate kiss.

Her cell phone chirped.

She always had it near in case one of her clients experienced a family emergency. For a second, she hesitated, then drew away from him. She picked up her phone and read the screen. "It's Candee," she said. "She and Teddy and Joseph want to stop over. Candee is helping me plan my Christmas Eve dinner menu."

"Tonight? Christmas isn't for a while yet." Keiran couldn't hide his disappointment. He wanted to spend the evening alone with Desiree. "When? If they've started walking, they'll be here in two minutes."

"They're still at their house." Desiree tapped a text on her phone. "I'll tell her tomorrow is better. Besides, I'm electing you as head preparer for Christmas Eve dinner. You're much better suited to the task, so you should be the one to talk with her."

He brought Desiree back into his arms, fingering the lustrous texture of her hair, breathing in the scent of vanilla and a fresh winter breeze.

"If you'd like," he said, "I'll teach you everything I know."

"Didn't you already offer me that once? Umm, no thanks. You know way too much about too many things—carpentry, decorating, football—"

He laughed. "I'm hardly an expert on anything, especially football."

Her gorgeous eyes sparkled. "Keiran, I hear you play your guitar every night when I'm in bed. You're also an excellent musician."

He'd forgotten her bedroom was directly below his attic apartment. "Do I disturb you?"

"On the contrary. You play really well."

He placed his hand along the curve of her velvety cheek. "Shall I serenade you sometime, my stunning Queen Anne?"

"You sound like a chivalrous knight, although I'm no queen." She grinned. "You're confusing *me* with my Queen-Anne style *home*."

"You're not a queen?" In exaggerated surprise, he splayed his fingers across his chest.

She laughed. "The bay window and spindle work in my home are—"

"Exquisite. Just like you."

"Hardly." The color rose in her cheeks. She didn't meet his gaze, instead looking toward the wavy glass windowpanes splattered with rain. "Most people define me as a workaholic."

"There's nothing wrong with being a workaholic. I prefer the term 'overachiever,' which is an admirable trait."

She shifted and pulled her blue cardigan closer around her shoulders. "Oftentimes, my work gets in the way of the important things in my life—family, friends, and good times."

"I've been accused of the same."

She nodded, agreeing. "I've always believed my career

came first. I've analyzed myself because I've read that understanding the problem is the best way to heal."

"Overachieving isn't a problem, Desiree."

"In some ways it is." Her smooth forehead knit into a pensive frown. "Candee and I have discussed our childhood. More often than not, we were neglected and now we're trying to compensate."

"By buying dilapidated houses?"

"It seems like that, doesn't it?"

"A little." He tried to think of words to encourage her, because he was picturing her as a young girl with fine blond hair and delicate features, helpless and alone. He realized he hadn't spoken for several moments and reminded himself to keep the conversation going. "And what else did your discussion with your sister uncover?" he asked.

Desiree slumped against the couch. "We were parentless children, raising ourselves the best we knew how."

"You had a mother and father."

"They were absent even when they were around. And the parent-child roles were reversed. Candee and I took care of them."

Gently, he slid his arm around her shoulders. "Candee and I spoke one afternoon, and she mentioned your last set of foster parents became your forever family."

"Yes, they're good people." The pensiveness in Desiree's gaze stirred his heart. "They love Candee and me, and email us regularly since they moved away. I'm grateful they came into our lives and offered love and stability."

But still.

She didn't say it, despite the words hanging in the air. She was trying to make up for the negligence in her childhood by . . . by what? Overachieving?

Something about the desolation on her face made him want to do whatever possible to shape her world for the better. She had a successful career, a lovely home, a caring sister.

And she had his heart.

He paused.

His heart?

Aye—and the realization took a firm place in his gut. He'd been half in love with her since the first day they'd met and she'd slammed the front door in his face, then teased him about talking to her porch.

With great effort, he stopped himself from repeating his thoughts aloud, although the shout-in-his-face awareness of their chemistry made him catch his breath. He liked being with her, conversing and comforting her.

No, it was too soon. He wasn't seeking a romance after his breakup with Patricia.

Better to keep things light. Besides, he didn't plan on staying in Desiree's home much longer. As soon as the holidays were over and her house was in better order, he planned to rent an apartment in town.

Move on.

But now, things were different. Fixing her home, spending memorable evenings beside her, anticipating the joyous holiday, and yes, discussing their childhoods—with all the hurts, all the dreams—was the most natural thing in the world. They were content, and he felt as if he'd known her his entire life. She'd given him a peephole into her past, and he'd done the same.

He cradled her face between his fingers, stroking an errant tear from her cheek.

"I'm grateful you came into my life. Or rather, I'm grateful I came into yours."

The tenderness in her soft eyes and lips tore down his defenses. She sparked a yearning in him he barely recognized, reminding him that there was more to life than successful pubs and impeccable carpentry. And these feelings were new. Not even with Patricia had he felt this utter sense of fulfillment.

His mouth descended on hers. She followed his lead, sliding her hands down his shoulders. Her lips were warm and smooth as velvet, tasting of sweet caramel and Irish whiskey cake.

He told himself to go slowly. His lips said otherwise. Their breaths heated the air around them.

An eternity later, the kiss ended.

As they gazed at each other, longing shown from her intense blue eyes.

Along with another emotion.

Wariness?

"You are beautiful," he whispered. "And that was—" How could he find a phrase to describe it?

"Not a good idea," she said.

"You're kidding!" He jerked his head back. "That's what you were thinking?"

"Keiran, we have a business arrangement. Anything else will only complicate things."

He was still searching for an accurate description of their kiss, while she was headed to the other side of the couch.

As usual, she was spot on. They'd only just met.

"Then will you go on a date with me?" he asked.

"After what I just said?"

"I understand you want to take our relationship slowly and I respect your wishes. Let's start with a real date."

She moistened her lips, just enough to captivate him. "A date where? To the kitchen?"

"I was thinking somewhere a little farther." He laughed. "Lunch or dinner in one of the town's restaurants?" His plan was to get to know her. Sure, he was living in her house and familiar with her daily routine, but it wasn't enough. He wanted to learn more.

She spoke what was on her mind, and she was interesting to be around. She was a brave woman. A Christian possessing a kind spirit. Strong, yet gentle. Courageous, yet yielding. Open, yet unassuming.

And these attributes fascinated him.

"Will you play your guitar for me?" she asked.

He widened his eyes at the unexpected question. "Maybe later," he said.

She granted him an audacious smile. "Please, Keiran?"

He knew he could never deny her anything.

Within minutes, he tromped to the attic and reappeared with his father's acoustic guitar. He tuned the strings and strummed a few chords. "What do you want to hear?"

She sat erect, glancing at him, then his guitar. "Something Christmassy."

He plucked the melody of "Jingle Bells" while she sang the lyrics, her voice light and in tune.

When he finished the final refrain, he broke into the beginning of "Don't Stop Believin'."

"That's the song you play in the attic," she said. "I couldn't place the group."

"Journey," he supplied. "Often, my father played the piece after our pub closed for the evening. My mother used to complain it was the only song he knew."

"I read somewhere the composer of that song was inspired by his father's words of encouragement."

"Aye, and the song held special significance for my father, also," Keiran said. "He came to this town disillusioned after he wasn't picked in the NFL draft, and rose to success when he met my mother and they opened the pub. Sadly, the pub closed when he ran out of funds."

"Why, when the pub was so popular at first?" Waiting, she

surveyed him, giving him the kindhearted expression he was coming to know so well.

"Maybe because all along my father was disheartened. Although he worked hard, his initial dreams of becoming a professional football player didn't pan out," Keiran said. "And then, of course, I left."

He shifted, silent for a beat.

"Did this guitar belong to your father?" Desiree asked, breaking the silence.

"Aye. He bequeathed it to me in his will. This and his abandoned Irish pub in town."

"So you own O'Malley's?"

"There's nothing to own. It's my father's broken legacy. This beat-up guitar, an abandoned pub, and a trading card autographed by a famous football player my father met while he was training."

"Hold on. Is the card worth anything?"

"I checked a few years ago because my former roommate, Georges, works at a pawn shop in Atlanta. The card is a 1976 Topps card, and the player didn't sign many, so the estimated worth is around fifteen thousand dollars."

"Certainly, it's a card to treasure and hold on to."

"And it brings back memories, both good and bad." Keiran released a deep breath and set the guitar to the side. "When I attended my parents' funerals in Dublin, I'm ashamed to tell you I was angry and bitter. My cousin William reassured me that although I wasn't there for them, they were always in my heart."

She squeezed his hand. "I know."

"I didn't walk away from my parents because I didn't care. I walked away because I didn't know if I had it in me to live up to my father's expectations. I knew I couldn't be a pro football player, so I disengaged. I found myself in a state of panic."

Caught in the spell of her captivating blue eyes, he placed his arm around her shoulders.

"Go on," she prompted. "You mentioned your cousin William."

He didn't want to spoil their evening by speaking about sadness. Attempting to recover their former gaiety, he replied with an expressive beam. "William lives in Ireland and has the proverbial Irish philosophy. He connects with people and believes forgiveness is most important. It's called Irish craic."

Desiree shot him a quizzical look. "I'm not following."

"Irish craic is fun and good times. William is humorous and witty and earnestly interested in others. You'll like him."

"I'll like him . . . when? I've never visited Ireland nor do I plan to in the future."

"Someday."

Silence lingered between them.

"With my investment in this house, an overseas trip isn't possible," she quietly replied.

"Never say never," Keiran advised. "My father threatened he wouldn't take me back if I ever appeared in Roses again. And here I am, not certain if I'm moving forward or backward, only knowing I was wrong to leave in the first place."

"Don't feel guilty." She touched his arm. "That's life, isn't it? We make mistakes, we brush ourselves off, and we go on."

"Do we ever forgive ourselves?" His voice came as a whisper.

"It's Christmas, the season of forgiveness," she said. "And the answer is an emphatic yes."

CHAPTER 6

"Tomorrow is the bake-off contest," Keiran reminded Desiree as she entered the foyer.

"It's written in bold on my calendar." Desiree set down her briefcase and joked, "How could I ever forget?"

Finally, it was Friday, the last day of another grueling work week.

"I'm glad to see you, gorgeous." He helped her off with her sunny-yellow raincoat and took her in his arms for a long kiss.

He'd been waiting for her at the foot of the stairs, the sparse lighting glinting over his hair. Thick, wavy, and midnight-black. And he looked oh so incredibly handsome.

He was dressed in a cotton chambray shirt unbuttoned at the neckline, showing a deep vee at his throat. His denims were well fitted. Tall, well-built, and confident, he sent her pulse racing. His physique would stop any woman in her tracks.

She linked her fingers around his nape, thinking all the while that he was the type of man she could easily fall in love with.

Wow. Whoa.

Love was the doorway to sorrow, and she'd had enough disappointment to know better than to risk her heart again.

Still, Keiran might be worth the risk. It was pure bliss having his strong, secure arms around her. Love was a quiet, joyous peace with no barriers. Love was exactly that with this man.

For an instant, she squeezed her eyes closed. *No. No. No.*

As much as she cared for him, they could never be together. Although he was talented and creative, he hadn't decided on a career for himself. Cooking or carpentry?

After her chaotic childhood, she knew stability was her primary goal.

Her feelings warred ferociously, and she considered telling him how much she cared, and what she most feared if they were to go forward in their relationship—that he could easily pick up and leave at any time.

Stability. Stability.

Numbly, she pulled from his arms.

He watched her, his gaze penetrating. He was always in tune with her emotions. "Is everything okay?"

"Of course." She dragged her gaze from his and focused on the authentic tin ceiling tile he'd replaced in the foyer. The edges were trimmed neatly and seamlessly overlapped.

Before she could remark on his excellent workmanship, he brushed a kiss across her temple. "Are you ready for an amazing time tomorrow, gorgeous?"

Gorgeous. No one had ever called her gorgeous. Profoundly touched, she brushed away a tear before his perceptive green-eyed gaze leveled on her. She wasn't used to praises, to his unbending good nature, and didn't know how to react.

"I'm ready to win the cake contest." She gave him her best challenging gaze while she shook lingering droplets from her black pencil skirt. Raindrops had chased each other across her car's windshield all the way home. If only it would snow to complete the holiday season.

"We'll see about that." He hung her raincoat in the foyer closet, then laid a callused hand on her cheek. His touch was reassuring. "So how was your day?"

"Demanding, as usual." Without prompting, she lifted her face for a kiss. "I'm delighted I only have one more work week to go before Christmas. You?"

"Hectic. The study off the living room has been sheetrocked and sanded, and the guys left some of their tools there. All you have to do is choose a paint color."

"My specialty."

"That's my girl." He grinned, drawing her to him. "Desiree, I have a confession."

The way he said her name, low and husky, resembled a loving caress.

Her gaze narrowed on his grin. "What is it?" That feeling, that draw, grew stronger each time they were together. That little flip of exhilaration.

"For the first time in a long time, I'm anticipating an amazing holiday." The sentiment in his voice melted her heart. "And it's all because of you."

"I am too." She was helpless to resist him, moving automatically into his arms. "And I'm glad to be home."

"To see me," he clarified.

"Indeed."

"Did you think about me today?"

"Often," she admitted. *Very often.*

"Good. I thought about you too. See how much we are alike? We both love Christmas and we both love—" He bent his head and kissed her deeply, thoroughly.

Both love what?

Each other?

She'd spent far too long trying to figure out men and relationships, and reveled in his kisses instead. She couldn't pull away from him even if she wanted to.

Excuse me, her conscience kicked in. *You're losing your focus.*

Yes, well, because around him she could hardly think. She wasn't good at this—dating—the entire courting process. Her career had always been most important.

Now she wished for more, wished for him.

He'd never mentioned a girlfriend, dismissing Desiree's inquiry with a wave of his hand. He'd explained that he'd dated in Atlanta, although no one worth mentioning. She'd been relieved he hadn't had a serious affair of the heart, although she'd told him about Scott, her ex. She hadn't said much, but apparently just enough, because Keiran had remarked he was sorry she'd been hurt.

His lips twitched as he drew her closer. "I'm glad you're glad to see me."

"Is that proper English?"

His lips moved within an inch of hers. "It is now."

She felt her cheeks flush as she gazed at his ruggedly handsome face.

"Who is judging our cakes?" she asked.

"Excellent change of subject. What cakes?" Smirking, he took her hand and led her to the kitchen. "First, have a cuppa tea with me. I brewed loose leaf tea using a strainer." He pulled out a stool for her, then poured her a steaming cup. "Sugar? Milk?"

"No thanks." She savored a swallow. Loose leaf tea was definitely more flavorful than tea bags. Again, she asked, "So, who is judging our cakes?"

"Several ladies on the town board, and some guy named Rob who owns a chain of bakeries in Florida," Keiran said.

She gasped and set down her cup. "Rob, as in Rob's Marvelous Muffins?"

"Aye." Keiran claimed the seat across from her. "Is he famous or something?"

"He certainly is famous, at least in Miami." Desiree rested her elbows on the island. "Rob is Teddy's mentor and a good friend. He lent Teddy the money for his start-up real estate business. Rob wants to expand his bakeries to another state and is considering Roses because Teddy and Candee are here."

The subject came up again an hour later, after they'd dined on a savory beef and Guinness stew brimming with carrots, potatoes, onions, and chunks of beef.

"I met him when Teddy and Candee got married." Desiree scraped plates while Keiran loaded the dishwasher. "Rob is great fun. You'll like him. Plus, you're both restauranteurs." She paused. "Is that a word?"

An amused gleam lit Keiran's eyes. "Absolutely, and it means the owner or manager of a restaurant. Although technically, I never owned a restaurant. My parents owned the pub."

"Same difference. And you own the pub now."

"True."

She finished wiping down the kitchen counter. "Who else is participating in the baking contest?"

"It's open to everyone. From what I gather, the town will set up tables for our cakes and an awning is being erected in case of bad weather." A lazy smile graced his face. "By the way, Candee is baking a Christmas cake."

"She's participating? To my knowledge, she's never turned on an oven in her life."

"The cake is a surprise. Or rather, it was a surprise until I spilled the beans." A sheepish grin crossed his lips as he gave an apologetic shrug. "Rob flew in from Miami and is staying with Candee and Teddy. Word is that Rob is baking the cake."

Desiree's competitive spirit jumped into true form. "So I'm competing against Rob, who bakes for a living, and you, the guy who's been basting an Irish whiskey cake for four days?"

He chuckled. "The odds are in your favor, though."

"How?"

"You're the prettiest." He stepped behind her and wrapped his arms around her waist. Nuzzling his lips against her neck, he murmured, "Are you certain you have to work next week?"

"Yes, if you want to get paid."

"I work for next to nothing," he joked. "I want a raise."

She laughed, shook her head, and tugged from his grasp. "Not happening."

That morning, she'd driven with a smile on her face all the way to her law firm in the middle of town. Keiran's parents' pub, O'Malley's, was located a few blocks away. Years earlier, the building had been abandoned and boarded up. A "For Lease" sign had hung on the door for ages.

As she'd walked from her car to her office, she'd tried to stop thinking about Keiran.

The more she'd tried, the more she'd failed. And now, another week had passed and Christmas was closing in. So much had happened since he'd arrived. And it was all good. So, so good.

He was a miracle worker, transforming her home into an enchanting, welcoming place. He spent hours in the kitchen after Teddy's crew knocked off for the day, and often sent Candee his baked goods, which she, Teddy, and Joseph enthusiastically praised.

Each evening, Desiree finished her last client's filing with an eye on the clock, counting the minutes until she could see Keiran.

And tomorrow, a week before Christmas, she and Keiran were participating in a baking contest.

She shook her head and added a grin. Her dashing Irishman, her one-of-a-kind Renaissance man, was as equally at home measuring and marking drywall as he was experimenting with a new recipe, or strumming a melody on his guitar.

She closed her eyes and thanked God. During the most blessed season of the year, when she was worried and despondent, He had brought Keiran into her life.

Certainly, she had much to be thankful for. She was no longer stuck in a bad situation with an ex who didn't care about her.

Have faith, her chaplain had preached numerous times.

But how?

She had wondered—as an orphaned teen, as a grown woman with a broken heart.

God had seemed invisible, but He hadn't been. He'd been working for her good all along.

* * *

THE FOLLOWING morning dawned bright and chilly, and sunlight shone through the wavy glass bay window in the living room.

Keiran and Desiree relished their first cup of coffee for the day. Even when their mornings began before dawn, he brewed a fresh pot of coffee and prepared a hearty cooked breakfast. He loved cooking for her.

"You're staring at me again," Desiree said.

"Am I?" He set down his cup. "I can't help it. You're gorgeous." That figure, dressed in flattering faux-leather leggings, suede ankle boots, and a creamy tweed sweater. And those cornflower-blue eyes, even more fascinating than her legs.

Delight quickened inside him. He'd come to Roses to pick up what he'd abandoned ten years before. A timeworn pub. He'd assumed he'd go it alone, far from Atlanta and Patricia.

Except he wasn't alone anymore.

With Desiree, he instinctively felt a sense of coming home and knew that embarking on this journey without her was unthinkable.

He openly admired her as she picked up their empty cups. Her beauty was stunning.

"I'll finish clearing," he offered, coming to his feet.

She held up a hand. "Keiran, I may not be the world's greatest cook, but I certainly know how to keep things tidy. Please let me do a little something to repay all you've done."

"Okay." His gaze shifted to those figure-hugging leggings before doubling back to her face.

She regarded him with her lovely, shiny eyes and smiled.

He thought about her throughout his day while he multi-tasked, installing molding, cutting and sawing wood, and picking up debris after the other crews clocked out.

She'd asked him once if he ever slept, and he'd teased that he obviously didn't require as much sleep as she did.

"Ready for the contest?" he asked, following her to the kitchen where their cakes sat on the counter.

"I feel anything but ready." She set her coffee cup in the sink. "Otherwise, yes, sure."

He helped her on with her cobalt-blue coat. She'd worn her blond hair loose, and she ran her fingers through the ends in that graceful, unassuming way of hers.

They placed their finished cakes on cake boards, then packed them in sturdy, clean covered boxes.

Desiree insisted on them both driving their vehicles to

the event, as she had to pick up a bag of groceries at her favorite green grocer when they were finished. He drove behind her car and parked in an empty parking space. As they got out of their vehicles, Desiree remarked that she felt motivated by seeing all the small-town celebrations.

Her pistachio cake, garnished with powdered sugar and maraschino cherries, presented an eye-catching display. Although Keiran's Irish whiskey cake didn't appear as vibrant, his baking process had taken longer. He'd carefully wrapped the cake, refrigerated it for three days and added a glaze on the fourth.

The first prize for the event was an apron, stamped with a red and green *Kiss Me, It's Christmas* motif.

He and Desiree set their cakes on a long table beneath an expansive white canvas awning on the green. The judges provided cake stands that elevated the cakes to a magnificent new level.

"I'll be wearing that apron when I cook the Christmas Eve dinner you volunteered me to prepare," Keiran baited.

He expected a teasing rejoinder, and she didn't disappoint.

She leaned toward him and joked, "You'll be wearing that apron because I let you *borrow* it. And don't forget we eat dinner at six o'clock sharp."

He gave a shout of laughter as they wended through the crowd and perused the food kiosks. Near the judges' stand she halted in midstep. Spotting Candee and Teddy, Desiree took hold of Keiran's hand and rushed over to them.

As planned, Candee and Teddy were manning a booth distributing free hot chocolate and candy canes to the participants and attendees. Nearby, Joseph skipped and played tag in an adjacent play area with a couple of new friends.

Teddy had confided to Keiran that the boy had changed

significantly since moving to Roses. His demeanor was perky, his gaze gleaming with delight.

"Uncle Teddy, watch me!" the boy called. He'd settled down to working with his playmates to build a sandcastle in the sandbox.

"There's Rob." Desiree waved gaily to an older, bald-headed man, then brought Keiran over to meet him.

"Hello, I'm Keiran O'Malley, Desiree's carpenter." Keiran extended his hand as they met. "I've heard a lot about you."

"I'm Rob the baker." The man beamed good-naturedly. "Although you've got me beat because you're the baker *and* the carpenter. Do you also make candles?"

Keiran blinked.

"You know, the butcher, the baker, and the candlestick—" Rob laughed heartily, gripped Keiran's hand, and vigorously shook it. "An old nursery rhyme. Mother Goose and what-not. Never mind. You're too young for rhymes, and I'm too old to be able to recite them correctly."

Keiran nodded. What was Rob getting at? "Sorry, I'm not following."

He glanced at Desiree, who grinned and shrugged. "Rob's not talking about nursery rhymes," she said. "He means—"

"I've heard about your baking and carpentry skills, Keiran," Rob interrupted. "Teddy expounded at length. You're good at one, exceptional at the other."

"That's a fair assessment," Keiran replied. "Should I ask which one is better?"

Rob checked out Keiran's Irish whiskey cake, set on a white platter and topped with spiced chopped pecans. "Your baking won by a landslide. Can you cook too?"

"Lots of down-home food including corned beef and cabbage and shepherd's pie. Although I like experimenting with new recipes, Guinness stew is my specialty."

"I can attest to that," Desiree said with a Mona Lisa smile.

"Excellent. You can experiment on me anytime. I told Teddy I was going on a diet." Rob patted his protruding stomach. "Though I've decided to wait until the New Year. Maybe my local gym will have a special."

Keiran laughed. He liked Rob's responses. He was a good, honest guy. "My parents owned a pub in town. They served authentic Irish food and homemade desserts."

"Oh?" Rob gave the surrounding streets a once-over. "Which one?"

"Walking distance from here. The pub's been empty a long time, although it was once busy with customers lining up outside the door when we opened for the day."

As Keiran pointed in the pub's direction, Desiree and Rob followed his gaze.

"Is the place available for rent?" Rob asked.

Desiree placed a hand on Keiran's arm. "The pub's been boarded up for years, although Keiran inherited it from his parents."

Keiran shifted. She was telling Rob more than he needed to know.

He and Desiree had visited the pub a few days earlier. Peering through grimy windows, he'd been anxious to assess the place when he'd first arrived, although he'd delayed seeing it, wanting to view the property with her, hesitant about coming to grips with the fact that his parents were no longer alive.

With a tight throat, he'd asked Candee, who was a realtor, to install new door locks. The permit had been provided to him, as the owner, when his parents had passed away. Because the pub was historically significant to the town, O'Malley's had been grandfathered in.

As he'd feared, memories had assailed him when he'd stepped inside—the sticky spilled beer beneath his boots, the heady smell of buttery Irish scones, the pennants from the local sports teams hanging on the timbered walls.

The charm and character of a timeless design.

And he was overwhelmed by his emotions—regret, sadness. And aye, excitement.

Fear of failure, fear of not trying. Was he capable of upholding the legacy of his parents' beloved pub?

Although he didn't have enough capital, should he dare hope he could reopen it? The huge project entailed purchasing inventory, cleaning the place, and passing inspections. Since working for Desiree, he'd saved most of his weekly salary. He'd said goodbye to Atlanta with limited funds, anxious to get away from Patricia.

His Atlanta pastor had once said that if you've gone through a storm, then it was a sure sign that God would be coming. Although Keiran's faith was strong, he'd been skeptical. A storm was difficult. How could it make a person stronger?

More important, was he entitled to success after abandoning his parents? In Roses, in Ireland, they had missed him.

He was selfish. He was undeserving.

He looked past Rob and Desiree. "I own nothing," he said.

"You own a piece of Roses' past." Desiree leaned against him. "Someday, you'll make your pub whole again."

Your pub. *Whole.* Like him, with Desiree by his side.

He knew her well enough to know she'd used the terms on purpose, to give him hope, to support his dream.

"Tell the vendors to start showing up again, and get the word out to former customers that you're planning on reopening," Rob put in. "Then roll up your sleeves and get to work."

Keiran glanced from Rob's firm expression to Desiree's unwavering one.

That day, after viewing the pub, they'd held hands on their way back to his truck.

"I want to make a difference in Roses," he'd said softly.

"So I've heard."

"Once the pub is up and running, I'd like to offer a free meal and worship service every Sunday for the homeless in the community."

"I'll help you." A radiant smile brightened her lovely face as she matched his strong steps. "You're the son who wants to set things right again."

"I feel I must do this."

"Good. This is the place, and this is the time."

The quiet tenderness in her tone was all the reassurance he longed for.

Besides, he loved it here in Roses. The slower pace of life, the sound of children's laughter, the colorful display of twinkling lights around each shop's window.

As Keiran conversed with Rob, gaining insights into running an up-and-coming restaurant, Keiran's questions multiplied.

Desiree gave his hand an encouraging squeeze, excusing herself to go chat with Candee at the hot chocolate stand.

"I have a question," Keiran said to Rob. "Can you guide me?"

"Certainly." Rob's cellphone chirped. "Excuse me. One minute." He held up a hand in apology, pulled out his phone from his colorful plaid jacket, and read the text.

He sent a brief reply. "It's always something in the restaurant business." Rob rolled his eyes and swore under his breath as he clicked off the phone and stuffed it back into his pocket. "One of our customers in Miami complained the service at the bakery was too slow. An employee called in sick and we were short-handed."

"How did you handle it?"

"I'm sending the customer a coupon for a free box of muffins, along with a heartfelt apology. In my opinion, the customer is always right"—he chortled—"even when they aren't."

"Will you hire more employees?" Keiran asked.

"Yes, especially with the busy Christmas season heating up. I own a half-dozen bakeries in the Miami area, so when I think about expanding, I'll employ someone reliable who knows the business." Rob motioned toward Teddy, who was talking with Candee and Desiree while refilling the five-gallon hot chocolate container with water. "I hoped to stay in Roses a couple more days. However, between getting married, formally adopting Joseph, plus renovating his new home, Teddy's got enough to do." He glanced in the direction of the judges' stand. "At any rate, I'll head to Miami tomorrow. What's your question, by the way? Do you need start-up money for your pub?" He dug into his chinos pocket and pulled out his wallet.

"Thank you, but no thank you." Keiran motioned to the wad of hundred-dollar bills Rob extracted, and shook his head.

"Well, from what I hear, you have an excellent work ethic. When the times comes, toss your pride aside and phone me."

"Thanks." Keiran hesitated. "If I ever do, I'll consider it a loan. I'll pay every penny back."

"No worries, as long as your pub becomes a Roses sensation. How's the place looking?"

"Like it's crying out for lots of TLC."

"So, what's your question?" Rob glanced at Desiree, his blue eyes shrewd. "If it concerns a gorgeous blond lawyer who bakes pistachio cakes, then I'm no expert. Inquiries about dating women should be posed to men who have successfully dated them."

"Meaning that, from your experience, women split after the first date?"

"Meaning that, from my experience, women are a full-time job."

"Desiree's not like that." Keiran gazed at her while she and Candee served steaming cups of hot chocolate to a group of teenagers. In the midst of conversation with her sister, she combed the green with her gaze, found him, and gave him a secret smile. He glimpsed the fire smoldering in her eyes and drew a wobbly breath. She was an attraction pulling him to her like a magnet.

Realizing Rob's piercing gaze was fixed on him, Keiran carefully composed his features. "She's brainy and successful and we've become good friends."

"And that's not all." Rob stuffed his wallet back into his pocket and directed a meaningful glance toward her.

"Look, we're taking it slow."

"Uh huh." A skeptical smirk crossed Rob's round face. "Do you want my unasked-for advice?"

Keiran shrugged. "Sure. Why not?"

"If she's anything like her sister Candee, don't let her get away." Rob's smirk widened into a grin. "Besides, I can see that she's already got you smitten. Are you up for the challenge of starting a new life and a new career with a new wife? That's a lot of new."

Rob was dead-on. Aye, Keiran was ready. He embraced challenges and he cared about Desiree. More than cared. He was in love with her. He was in love with her snappy humor, intellect, and especially her openness.

"We'll talk further." Rob hung a left when his name was called at the judging stand. Over his shoulder, he said, "I hope I gave you some food for thought. Get it? Food?" He chuckled at his own joke, then added, "Seriously, I hope I answered your question."

Keiran paused, wondering how he'd started to ask Rob one question—whether Irish whiskey cake could be baked in a jar—and ended up receiving guidance about dating and romance. Although the dating advice Rob had offered was far more significant than a whiskey cake.

Don't let her get away.

Desiree gave Keiran a thoughtful glance as she approached him with two cups of hot chocolate. "Well, you two were deep in conversation."

Keiran accepted a steaming, frothy cup topped with miniature marshmallows. "He's extremely knowledgeable and I'm fortunate to have met him."

"He knows the restaurant business and he can give you lots of excellent tips." She sipped her hot chocolate. "He's a blessing to Teddy and Candee, and stepped in many times to help with Joseph after Teddy's brother Christian died."

"I didn't know."

"The pain of losing Christian was almost Teddy's undoing. Candee helped him begin a new chapter of his life here in Roses."

"Teddy's never talked about it." Keiran was beginning to realize that Desiree's sister and brother-in-law were genuinely good people who cared about others above themselves. He'd also noted the camaraderie between Rob and Teddy as Rob paused in his judging duties to joke with Teddy.

Desiree set her cup down on a tray. "Loss is always hard. Nonetheless, the certainty of a blessed future is guaranteed through faith in God."

With a glance at the holiday festival taking place—the face painter and balloon artist for the children, the four-piece brass band playing Christmas carols—Keiran took heart. Truly, God had brought him to Desiree.

He gazed around, entertained by the small town oozing

with big-time charm. Market stalls along the side streets sold ornaments and nutcrackers, and children mailed their letters to Santa at the corner post office. Historic walking tours were scheduled as soon as the judging finished, and the shops were becoming increasingly crowded with holiday customers.

While a pleasurable morning awaited them, he brought his attention back to the main reason they were here. He slung his arm around Desiree's shoulder and guided her to the colorful array of cakes, lovingly made, and the mouthwatering aromas of butter, sugar, and cherries. The contestants had been instructed to stand behind their respective baked goods to answer questions from the judges.

Delight surged through him. This was perfection. His enchanting birthplace, his exquisite Desiree, and the delight of spending Christmas with her family.

By ten o'clock, the event was finished. Although the contest had been close, the judges announced Desiree had won first place, and Keiran had taken second.

Loud cheering erupted and Desiree blushed gorgeously as a judge tied the red and green *Kiss me, It's Christmas* apron around her cobalt-blue coat. Graciously, she thanked the judges and gave a special mention to Keiran for buying her a kitchen timer.

In a last-minute decision, Candee hadn't entered her Christmas cake. Because Rob had baked it and he was one of the judges, it wouldn't have been fair. Consequently, Rob sat at the judges' stand, along with a plate filled with the cake. At last count, Keiran estimated that Rob had eaten at least three slices, along with a thick wedge of fudge from a food kiosk.

Keiran caught up with Desiree in the middle of the congratulatory crowd. In a laughing voice, she said, "All that powdered sugar paid off."

"Well done." Keiran brought her into his arms for a breathless kiss. Truly, the day couldn't have gone any better.

She hesitated. "You're kissing me here, in front of the entire town?"

"I'm just following directions." He glanced at her apron and grinned.

"It's not Christmas yet."

"I've designated the entire month of December for celebrating Christmas."

Chuckling, she said, "I want to catch up with Candee for a minute."

"Hurry back. There's a Christmassy silk scarf in the front window of one of the boutiques, and I immediately thought of you. You mentioned you wanted a scarf for Christmas."

"I did? When?"

"Well, maybe I just thought you did because I plan to buy it for you."

With a laugh, she pulled off the apron, carefully folded it, then scurried off with it securely tucked under her arm.

Out of the corner of his eye, Keiran noticed Rob speaking to a woman near the judges' stand. Although her back was turned, Keiran felt a wave of familiarity.

The crowd began dispersing and he was facing that same woman a minute later.

A woman he'd assumed he'd never see again. His ex-girlfriend, Patricia.

He gaped. His heartbeat raced.

She stared back at him with a cool smile, her dark hair streaked with blond, and her even white teeth. She was dressed in thigh-high boots, a short pink mini skirt, and a coyote-trimmed puffer jacket. He recognized the expensive jacket, as she'd coveted it the previous year. It had taken all the money he'd set aside, five hundred dollars, but she'd been happy. At least for a little while.

"Patricia?" He said her name and heard the shock in his voice.

"Hi, Keiran. Did you get my text this morning?" Deliberately, she perused Desiree, who'd bounced back to snuggle close to him.

"No. I've been busy," he replied.

He wanted to shout that this was his world, not hers. What was she doing here?

Patricia's gaze slid back to his face. "Well, I arrived."

His stomach plummeted. This couldn't be good. "I see that."

"You two know each other?" Desiree inquired.

Keiran nodded. "Aye," was all he could manage.

"We were practically engaged." Patricia directed her response toward Keiran. "You've been missed."

"Our relationship ended in Atlanta, remember?"

"Maybe our personal relationship." She gave him a heavy stare. "Unfortunately, our business relationship has hit a snag."

Heat flushed through his body. "I left you everything."

Before Patricia could reply, Desiree asked, "Were you two in business together?"

Patricia swept her fingers across Keiran's sleeve, a possessive gesture and decidedly intimate. "He worked for my daddy's company."

The way Patricia had always thrown it up to him twisted Keiran's stomach. In the beginning he had worked for her father, until he'd built his own carpentry business.

"I don't punch a clock for your father anymore," Keiran said.

"True," she rejoined with wry exasperation. "I heard you own a pub in Roses. And I want half the proceeds when you sell." She gestured to the street where O'Malley's was located.

"I'm not selling. And besides, the place hasn't been in business for years."

Her response was a derisive sneer. Few people believed Patricia was anything but a sultry, gorgeous female and ultimate charmer. He knew better. She was a woman who always got what she wanted.

And if she didn't?

Then she'd make life exceedingly unpleasant.

"Everything is for sale for a price." She was talking louder, her shrillness drawing the stares of passing shoppers, as she obviously intended. "Earlier, I went by the pub. It's not worth much, though it's worth something."

He sensed the desperation in her tone and looked her straight in the eye. "So you're here for money?"

"Obviously," she said.

"Where's Kyle?"

"He's long gone."

"And your father?"

"He refused to give me any more money." Her voice lowered to a stage whisper. "Now it's time for you to pay up, Keiran. I get half of everything you earn."

He planned to tread carefully before she went into a fresh fit of anger, although he couldn't contain himself. He just couldn't.

"Our verbal agreement ended." He started to pull his hand away.

"What about our written agreement?" Her grip tightened. Sagely, she shook her head. "You never were good at reading the fine print, darling, were you?"

CHAPTER 7

Laughter burst from the judges' stand, and Desiree jerked at the sound. Keiran shook from Patricia's grip and grabbed Desiree's elbow. He guided her toward the canvas awning, using the excuse he wanted to admire her cake again.

Under her breath, she asked, "What was that about?"

But it didn't matter, because she already knew. And something was shattering deep inside her. Although she tried, she couldn't tear her thoughts away from the lushly provocative Patricia. The woman had the self-confidence of an exceptionally stunning female who commanded attention.

Keiran heaved a sigh. "Her father owns a construction business in Atlanta, and when I met her she got me a job at his company. I learned the trade and became one of his carpentry men."

Desiree felt her face heat, recalling the conversation between Patricia and Keiran. No doubt, they'd been close. Very close. The thought brought a stab of jealousy, along with recalling how the strikingly gorgeous Patricia had ogled Keiran.

Desiree yanked from his grip. "I think this is about a lot more than carpentry."

Neither of them broke the loaded silence as they advanced toward the cake display.

"She's trouble," Keiran said. "Supposedly, she helped me when I was building my carpentry business."

They'd come to the edge of the awning. Desiree leaned against a makeshift pole and crossed her arms. "Supposedly?"

"Aye. We rented an office together. She answered phone calls from customers, scheduled my jobs, and advertised my business. And, I trusted her with all the bookkeeping duties. Now that I look back, though, there were several times that I suspected money was missing."

"Did you confront her?"

"Are you kidding? Of course, although her answer was always the same. She'd nearly bite my head off and her resultant tantrum would last for days."

Desiree glanced at Teddy and Candee near the judges' stand. Teddy had his arm around Candee, and they chatted amiably with Rob.

Oh, to be able to give her heart to a man she could trust, Desiree thought, a man who loved her unconditionally.

She studied Keiran. "And that was okay with you?"

"Unfortunately, aye. I thought she was a prize—pretty, well-heeled, efficient. And then, she cheated on me with Kyle, a moneyed stockbroker."

The tension in the cold air between them crackled.

"You never told me any of this."

"I should have," he admitted. "Except it's demoralizing for a guy to have his girlfriend cheat on him with his best friend. They became a couple and—"

"And you skipped town to land on my doorstep."

"Patricia and I had a rocky relationship from the start. It's odd. Once the truth hit me, I realized I wanted the happily-ever-after ending. Just not with her."

"And yet, you couldn't bring yourself to tell me these revelations."

"I'm sorry. I should have." For a moment, he closed his eyes and breathed aloud. "Teddy said the same thing."

"You told Teddy, yet you wouldn't confide in me?" The surprise that had seized her when she'd realized who Patricia was to Keiran evaporated, along with the belief he actually cared. In a blinding flare of realization, she tore from his hold. "I'm a good listener, I would have understood. Now . . ."

"Nothing's changed."

The lump in her throat was so thick she could hardly manage any words. "Everything's changed."

"Because you're judgmental?"

"You're blaming me?" To stop from splintering into a million pieces, she shielded herself by opposing him. "You're the one who lied by omission."

"I couldn't admit it, okay? I thought I cared about a woman who was nothing more than a liar and a cheat. And then I realized I never cared at all, but wasn't sure how to make a proper exit."

"So your pride got in the way of your decision-making."

"Look, can I show you the silk scarf I saw earlier?" His jaw set with determination. "I think you'll like it."

"Please tell me you're joking."

"I'm completely serious." He laid his hands over one of hers. "We've got something good, Desiree. Surely you realize it too."

He didn't understand. He never could, considering his silver-spoon background. She'd been hurt and disappointed her entire life.

She winced. The only way to protect herself was to stay

away from precarious situations—the risk of heartache was too great.

"You don't get it," she said. "You weren't there when Candee and I were growing up. You didn't live where we lived."

A look of persistence passed across his features. "True, but I'm not to blame."

Angrily, she swiped at a tear running down her cheek.

"This isn't about me." He kept hold of her hands. "Or Patricia. It's about you growing up in the foster care system. You're afraid to open your heart because you might get hurt again. You can trust me, Desiree. I made a mistake and I'm genuinely sorry." He took her in his arms, lovingly stroking her hair. "Let's discuss this in a quiet place. We can have lunch at the new Chinese restaurant near my pub, and designate the occasion as our first real date."

"A date? *Now* we're dating?" Methodically, she removed his hands as Patricia headed toward them with sheer determination planted on her porcelain features.

"I'm back, Keiran," Patricia said, plunking dainty hands on her nonexistent hips while she perused the village green. "Where do you suggest we eat in this single-traffic-light town before we drive back to Atlanta together?"

"How about Chinese?" Desiree indicated the street where the restaurant was located. "It's across from the pub."

Keiran regarded Desiree levelly. "I'm buying you a silk scarf, and then I'm treating you to lunch to celebrate your cake victory."

"I've lost my appetite for eggrolls." Desiree cut her gaze to Patricia. "Although you'll love the food. Try the fried rice too. I've heard it's the best in Roses."

"I will, as long as he's buying. He's a generous guy." Patricia's thin eyebrows lifted in amused mockery. "Keiran, we can visit our pub too." Possessively, she touched his sleeve and beamed up at him.

"Desiree, please listen to me." He edged away from Patricia. "I can make everything right between us."

"You can't," Desiree shot back.

Her retort reverberated in her mind.

Or could he? They'd grown so close that they'd even begun finishing each other's sentences. One emotion bombarded her—hope—but hope would leave her broken-hearted if it didn't work out.

No. She couldn't take the chance.

"Enjoy your lunch, Keiran." For a second, Desiree forced herself to look at him. So handsome, so striking, so utterly appealing—and she faltered.

And then she reminded herself she wouldn't allow any more disappointment into her life. "We're done here," she said.

He met her look. "Really? You won't hear me out?"

She shook her head.

His green-eyed gaze froze to solid ice.

She twisted, trying not to recall the times in his arms, the pleasurable, passionate thrill of his kisses. Blindly, she made her way to the judges' stand, feeling the keenly inquisitive stares of strangers.

"We're not finished. I'll see you as soon as I get things sorted," he called out to her. "Back at the house. Wait for me there."

Drowning in sadness she couldn't control, she struggled to keep her shoulders straight and her gait sure. All around her, cheerful festivities rang out. The boutiques were filled to capacity. Shoppers spilled into the streets, and light-hearted conversation abounded.

"There you are." Candee raced through the throng and hauled Desiree to the side. "Teddy and I want to invite you and Keiran to our house for lunch. By the way, where is Keiran?" She peered around Desiree, shaded her eyes, and scowled. "Who is that woman he's walking with? I've never seen her before. Does she live in Roses?"

"She's from Atlanta."

"Why is she here?"

Why, indeed.

Desiree didn't answer her sister's question, although she agreed to lunch. The trembling that had started in her arms had spread to her legs, and later, she couldn't remember how she managed to get to her car, bypassing the green grocer as she drove home.

One fact she knew for sure. She wouldn't be waiting when Keiran arrived at her house. She couldn't bear the thought of facing him, yet she didn't have the prerogative to confront him. They weren't engaged or even officially dating, unless one counted nightly home-cooked meals as dates.

Sure, she'd presumed he'd told her the truth about his life in Atlanta, but he'd omitted a key point. He'd been seriously dating Patricia.

What did a lie by omission mean? Her lawyer brain clicked into gear. *Leaving out an important fact, thus fostering a misconception,* she automatically supplied. Yes, that described it.

As soon as she arrived home, she dashed off a note telling him to pack his things and leave, and set the note on her kitchen table. Then she planned to stay at Candee's house until midnight. Or longer, if Desiree saw his truck parked in her driveway.

CHAPTER 8

Desiree needn't have worried, because Keiran came and went while she lunched and spent the afternoon with Candee, Teddy, and Joseph.

Keiran had penned his own note and placed it on the kitchen table next to hers, explaining he was driving back to Atlanta with Patricia.

Not sure when I'll return. Will keep you posted, he'd written in his typical bold script.

She crumpled up his note and tossed it on the floor.

A dire, stabbing ache grew as she climbed the stairs to the attic apartment. Hesitating, she slowly opened the door and stared at the room in silence. His bed was neatly made. His scent pervaded the space—raw wood and the outdoors, a hint of sawdust and pine. All related to his job.

And his belongings had vanished.

She inhaled and leaned weakly against the door. Here it was, a week before Christmas, and he'd abandoned her to be with his former girlfriend. For all Desiree knew, Keiran and Patricia planned to return to Roses and renovate O'Malley's as a team.

Her feverish brain refused to accept that scenario, and she seriously considered moving out of her beloved town if that ever occurred. In comparison to Patricia, Desiree felt like an adolescent girl again—ordinary and inexperienced.

Goodbye Keiran, she thought, coming to terms with the fact that they'd gone in opposite directions.

After arriving in Atlanta, he texted and phoned numerous times.

She replied with a brief text: *Don't contact me. No texts, no calls, okay?*

A date when I return? he immediately countered. *It's Christmas, after all.*

And Christmas brought memories of when she was a little kid, feeling alone and deserted while her parents lay drunk on the living room couch. She knew she must come to grips with her emotions in order to move forward. But, oh, this was so hard. Acceptance and forgetting, these were weaknesses in her life she had a hard time acknowledging, although her favorite pastor had assured in a sermon that weakness led to strength.

When, exactly? Had God brought her a Christmas miracle in Keiran? And if so, was she throwing that miracle away with both hands when she refused to speak with him, allowing pride to dictate her lonely path?

She pressed her cell phone to her heart and asked the empty room, "How can I fight you, Keiran, when I'm warring with myself?"

The sparks between them had flamed with his every touch, his every kiss, and she missed his solid strength, calm reassurances, and good humor.

With a deep sigh, she tried to come to terms with the desolation weighing her down. How could she face another day without him when he made her feel so complete? Finally, she'd had a chance to be happy.

But happiness was a funny thing. The fear of being alone stemmed from her childhood, and she'd proven she could succeed on her own.

She reminded herself of all she'd accomplished, that her colleagues had remarked on her spirited, confident nature. With firm determination, she lifted her chin and pushed her thoughts of Keiran aside.

And then she texted him back. A final, single word: *No.*

By Monday of the following week, she knew he'd departed for good. Still, her heart jumped whenever the doorbell rang. Despite her firm reprimands to herself, she'd hurry to the front door, thinking he'd returned for Christmas after all. A secret fantasy come true, despite her conflicting emotions.

Although the opposite prevailed in her real world, and it turned out to be the postman, or an online store delivery.

Very well, then. The next time the doorbell rang, she would take her time answering it.

By the end of the week, she'd established a pattern. No longer did she live in suspended anticipation that Keiran might stride into her foyer. Nonetheless, neither was she able to anticipate the upcoming holiday with delight. She'd thought she'd find the peace she'd been looking for if she bought her own home.

But she hadn't.

Peace had little to do with the most expensive home, the most beautiful neighborhood, she decided. It was who you shared your home with that mattered most. And now that Keiran was gone, despite her attempts to deny it, the truth hit hard.

At six o'clock on the Friday evening before Christmas Eve, Desiree pulled off her black leather boots, hung her jacket in the hall closet, and pulled her blue cardigan over her silk blouse. She was done working for two weeks, and had won a case involving Julie Wallis, a single mother of two children, who was being jailed and fined for a minor offense. When it was clear the mother couldn't afford to pay, Desiree had argued for another solution. The court had accepted a community service plan, and Julie had cried with relief when she was released.

Cause for celebration, Desiree thought, although the day didn't feel at all celebratory.

It felt empty.

Aimlessly, she wandered the spacious rooms of her home, fingering the prominent wooden staircase, the paneled oak walls, the built-in china cabinets.

She barely glanced at her wristwatch as she stepped across the spacious foyer, although her mouth tightened when she realized the time. Candee was coming over in an hour to finalize their Christmas Eve plans.

As much as Desiree liked talking to Candee, she'd avoided her sister's phone calls because she'd been dreading their imminent discussion. Most likely, the topic would center around Keiran and his notable disappearance.

As Desiree headed for the kitchen, Candee phoned, launching into a lengthy monologue regarding the sweet rolls she was bringing for Christmas Eve dinner. Desiree cut her off, making an excuse that a thorough kitchen organization required her attention, and she'd see Candee at seven o'clock.

She poured herself a glass of sparkling cider, sat on a stool, and rehearsed their upcoming exchange in her mind.

"*What happened?*" Candee would ask, referring to Keiran. Most likely, she'd expected to find Desiree and Keiran acting like an official couple by the time Christmas rolled around.

"What happened?" Desiree would repeat. "Keiran lied to me, knowing I was falling in love with him. And then he went off with Patricia."

An unbearable ache pierced her heart. She set down her glass and perused the kitchen. A box of pots and pans required sorting, and her pantry could be more orderly.

As she arranged a variety of spices closer to the stove, a trio of deliverymen knocked on the kitchen's sliding glass doors. Her base cabinet had arrived, they announced, and her contractor had requested they bring the cabinet through the rear door rather than muddying up the new wood floors.

"Is the cabinet heavy?" She invited the men inside to unbox the cabinet in the earmarked corner near the pantry.

"Just awkward, ma'am," the youngest of the three replied, test-fitting the cabinet by what he clarified was dry-fitting. "Do you have a carpenter to install it?" he asked.

She shook her head.

"We're booked until the first of the year, but you're missing the stainless handle for this cabinet. If it's in stock, I'll make a note for a special delivery before Christmas."

"Thank you, and Merry Christmas," she replied.

As the men cheerfully departed, she bid them good-bye with a quiet smile.

She went into the pantry, intending to declutter the shelves by stacking the flat containers on top of one another. Instead, she found herself rummaging in a drawer to retrieve Keiran's note, which she'd salvaged from the floor.

Not sure when I'll return. Will keep you posted, he'd written.

Rereading the simple sentences, she traced the letters with shaking hands, feeling a pang of longing so intense, her knees weakened. He was so magnificent, so unbearably good-looking, she'd taken unabashed pleasure in spending every spare second with him.

If he phoned her even once more, she might cave and answer his call.

Might? Ruefully, she decided that she would answer.

Of course he hadn't, and her phone had sat silent for two days.

"I thought I had everything worked out," she whispered to the quiet pantry.

Apparently not this time. The storybook life she'd planned out hadn't gone the way she'd expected. And despite reaching her goals—her successful career and a home of her own—happiness remained elusive.

Pivoting, she walked into the living room, taking heart in its remarkable transformation, the Christmas tree illuminated in dazzling splendor. She lit a fire in the fireplace, and the flickering light assured her of comfort through the bitter winter ahead.

All week since Keiran's departure, she hadn't allowed herself to cry, and had accomplished her workdays briskly and efficiently. However, now that she didn't have court cases and clients to occupy her mind, the heavy burden of keeping her feelings bottled up threatened to spill over.

As tears welled, she shuffled back to the kitchen. The wintry December wind whistled through a small opening in the sliding glass doors and burned her eyes. She slid the doors closed as tears streamed freely down her cheeks.

She let them come, weeping until there were no tears left to shed—no more sadness or resentment. The picture in her mind's eye of where she was supposed to live, where the man in her life was supposed to stand, and the children she would be blessed with hadn't happened.

She sank onto a chair, her shoulders drooping with desolation. Why had Keiran refrained from telling her about Patricia? And why hadn't he returned to Roses by now? He'd given up so quickly. Wasn't he interested in knowing how Desiree was faring after their break-up?

Her thoughts went back to the previous weekend, and she

visualized Patricia's seductive eyes as she'd gazed intimately up at Keiran.

We were practically engaged, Patricia had said, her words intended to pierce.

Hurt, confused, and angry, Desiree refused to allow that image to dominate her thoughts. Instead, she recalled how Keiran had held her afterwards, murmuring to her, caressing her hair.

You can trust me, Desiree. I made a mistake and I'm genuinely sorry. His voice had been rough with self-reproach.

And later, the guarded hope in his tone as he'd called out, *I'll see you as soon as I get things sorted. Back at the house. Wait for me there.*

A stinging pain punctured her chest with each memory. He'd sounded sincere, and she remembered the despair that had crossed his handsome features.

She half-rose from her chair as a thought struck her. With surprising clarity, she recognized that the pain she felt was more for Keiran than herself.

Angrily, she swiped her wet cheeks and sprang fully to her feet. Surely this proved she was a besotted fool. How could she feel sorry for him when she was the person who'd been deceived?

Surprisingly, with that realization, her mood began to elevate. In fact, by the time she stood by the table and itemized her to-do list for Christmas Eve, she felt better than she had all week. Her sadness began turning into fortitude.

She opened the refrigerator and brought out two bags of fresh cranberries she intended to frost with sugar for a festive centerpiece. She'd also purchased a variety of prepared side dishes including creamy mashed potatoes and a green bean casserole topped with pecans. In the morning, she'd tackle the fresh turkey preparation.

So, the meal was set, and she'd slated her pistachio cake for dessert.

Her gaze travelled to the adjoining dining room.

Where would they all sit—Teddy, Candee, Joseph, and Desiree?

She paused, considered the lack of furniture, then recalled her conversation with Keiran.

You own a service of fine crystal and china, your dining area is large enough for a twenty-people feast, and there's no place to sit and enjoy a meal? he'd teased.

I'll pile cushions on the floor and we'll sit cross-legged, she'd replied.

Dashing back into the living room, she dragged her coffee table into the dining area. Then she draped a red tartan tablecloth over it and arranged colorful throw pillows around the table.

With great care, she set the table with four place settings using her finest china and silver, embellishing the tablespace with shiny silver candle holders and a string of sparkling white lights.

Pleased with the result, she went into the kitchen and sat in the middle of the tiled floor, eyeing the base cabinet waiting to be anchored.

The deliveryman had stated she needed a carpenter. Well, Keiran wasn't here.

However, she was.

On her phone, she searched tutorials on how to install a cabinet, and selected a step-by-step video that assured installation was easy with the proper tools, which included a level, a screw gun, screws, clamps, and a hammer and nails.

"Carefully measure and draw the exact location," the woman in the video instructed. "Drive screws into the wall studs to anchor the cabinet."

Quickly, Desiree changed into jeans and a sweatshirt,

chose the necessary tools from the study where the crewmen kept their supplies, and set to work.

An hour later, she was kneeling on the floor, concentrating intensely on the installation, when Candee entered the kitchen.

"Sorry I'm late," Candee declared as Desiree jerked back, startled by her sister's voice. "Boomer was doing his favorite thing—eating—and then I took him for a quick walk. You didn't hear the doorbell, so I let myself in." Candee's mouth trembled with laughter as she admired the cabinet. "And now I see why. You look remarkably determined."

"Base cabinets aren't difficult to install if the area has been measured accurately and you have the correct tools," Desiree said, parroting the singsong tone of the woman in the video. She finished driving the last nail into the toe kick beneath the cabinet, set the tools on the floor, then stood.

"Bravo!" Candee gave her a high-five. "The place looks great."

She smiled. "Thanks."

"Have you eaten dinner?" Candee's gaze skimmed the kitchen.

"No, and I'm starving." Desiree reminded herself that she needed to set aside a half hour a day for exercise in order to shed the extra ten pounds she'd gained. Appreciating Keiran's magnificent cooking, she hadn't had the opportunity or the inclination to diet.

"Teddy and I are so busy with Joseph and his horse therapy that I haven't eaten, either." Candee peered into the refrigerator and extracted cold cuts and bread, motioning for Desiree to join her. "I'll make us both a sandwich and brew a pot of tea."

The women enjoyed a cozy light supper at the kitchen table.

"You seem much better than I imagined," Candee said as she poured tea. "I mean, after last Saturday."

"I feel better."

"Care to fill me in on what happened between you and Keiran?" Candee fixed Desiree a mug of tea without milk, and added milk and sugar to her own. "Teddy mentioned he and Keiran have been in touch, but when I pressed him for details he was extremely close-lipped."

Desiree debated, opening her mouth to defend her position, then closing it. Today, for the first time in a week, she'd begun to feel purposeful again. A delicate newfound serenity had emerged through her tears. Should she take the risk of talking about it?

But Candee seemed so resolute, Desiree knew holding back was futile. Besides, who was better to confide in than her dear sister?

"Ask away," Desiree said.

"Tell me everything."

"Well," Desiree sat back in her chair, "I suppose our relationship began when he first arrived and began talking to my front porch."

"You mean talking *to you* on your front porch."

"No, I mean talking *to* my front porch," Desiree said with an amused smile. She couldn't explain her attraction to Keiran from that first moment. At night her dreams had been of him. During the day, she'd daydreamed about him. His capable hands as he cooked, or his bass voice as he sang an Irish tune, had awakened her desire for a secure, centered life with the man she loved. Often in the past weeks, she'd told herself that the uniqueness, the unqualified novelty, of having a charismatic Renaissance man living in her house would pass.

Instead, her feelings had intensified.

Noting Candee's raised eyebrows, Desiree set aside her

teacup. "When Keiran arrived, I told him I needed an electrician, not a carpenter, and to return in the morning. So I shut the door on him and when I reopened it, he was still there, muttering to the porch. I invited him to move into the attic because he had nowhere else to stay."

Candee laughed softly. "And then the relationship began."

"A practical relationship."

"A romantic one."

"At night after dinner, we'd go into the living room and he'd light a fire." Desiree drew her legs up in the chair, curling her arms around them. "He'd play his guitar and . . ."

When she finished her story, Candee dabbed at her eyes. "Truly, your entire courtship is enchanting."

"We've never even been out on a formal date."

"In all those hours you spent together you probably know him better than anyone. Teddy said that just because Keiran moved into your house didn't mean a relationship would develop, especially in a short period of time." A satisfied smile wreathed Candee's face. "But I felt certain he was wrong. I heard Keiran talk endlessly about you whenever he came to the house to confer with Teddy. And I watched you two at the cake judging contest, and I knew. He's deeply in love with you."

Desiree stood and wiped her palms on the folds of her sweatshirt. "He has an odd way of showing it, running off to Atlanta with Patricia."

"Has he tried contacting you?"

"He's called and texted many times."

"Have you responded?"

Desiree stared impassively at the glossy white backsplash above the farmhouse sink Keiran had installed. "Only to tell him not to contact me again."

"Well, that's a brilliant way to go about things."

Desiree gave a guilty start. Her heartbeat raced with a

surge of annoyance. Or was it culpability?

Candee crossed the room and took Desiree's cold hands in hers. "Do you love him?"

Understatement. Sweet memories hastened to her mind. With a rush of happiness, she recalled his attentiveness, his patience, the pride she'd felt when he complimented her for fighting court battles against injustice. This broad-shouldered, rugged man gazed at her with such heartfelt tenderness, sometimes words would lodge in her throat.

"Did you think about me today?" he'd asked.

"Often."

"Good. I thought about you too. See how much we are alike? We both love Christmas and we both love—" Then he'd drawn her into his arms and kissed her.

Desiree willed herself to say no, she didn't love him. Instead, she heard herself saying, "Yes. I fell in love with him at a high school football game ten years ago."

Candee tightened her grip on Desiree's hands. "I thought I recognized his name when Teddy first brought him up. Then O'Malley's pub was discussed and I recalled you going on and on about him when we were teenagers. So often, in fact, I suspected you had a crush on him."

"You were right," Desiree said. "But now I'm a grown woman."

"Who loves a grown man. And that man loves you very much."

Desiree shook free and peered out the window at the thick dark night, chilly and moonless.

"He's gone," she said quietly.

"He's not gone." Candee went to the sink and ran soapy hot water over a stack of dishes. "He's just waiting for you to give him the opportunity to make amends. You can't repair a relationship if you avoid him."

"He hasn't texted or called in a couple of days."

"He's probably come to accept that you don't want anything to do with him."

"That's not true."

"Then go to him in Atlanta. And tell him face to face."

Desiree's brain frantically groped for a way to refute Candee's argument. Suppose she failed? He was obviously more interested in Patricia.

"I can't. Tomorrow is Christmas Eve. We're attending church service, and I'm cooking. See?" Desiree gestured to the dining room. "The table's all set."

"Then I'll give you a one-day pass because you admitted you love him."

Her love for him was out of reach, but she knew if she admitted her thoughts to Candee, her sister would argue her point a tad too vehemently.

"Yes, I love him," Desiree said. Desperately loved him. And when he gazed at her as if she were the only person in his universe, her pulse surged with excitement.

"Settled. On Christmas Day, you're driving to Atlanta," Candee said. "Teddy knows where Keiran used to live, and you'll start there. Or, you can phone him."

Desiree hesitated. Would Keiran be angry with her, or coolly polite? Or would he be thrilled to see her, because he still cared?

Desiree blew out a breath. "I'll surprise him."

Although, as she closed the door after Candee's departure, she felt a sickening fear of failure straight to her belly.

Suppose she interrupted Keiran while he was with Patricia?

Suppose he didn't want to see her?

With resolve, she pulled her thoughts away from irrational worry and concentrated on their reunion in Atlanta.

Please love me, my affectionate, gentle Renaissance man, she thought, *as much as I love you.*

Keiran didn't return to Roses in two days, which was the time frame he'd originally planned. Neither did he spend his days with Patricia.

He'd passed on lunching with her in Roses, and hadn't taken her inside O'Malley's. He'd left her in town, driven back to Desiree's home, and read her note with surprised alarm. She wouldn't hear him out.

He'd been raised a gentleman, and quickly packed his bags as she requested and loaded up his truck. It didn't matter who was right or wrong. He'd kept the truth from her, although not intentionally. He'd simply removed Patricia from his heart and mind because Desiree had taken over his thoughts. When he was with her, everything else fell away.

After a silent four-hour drive with Patricia back to Atlanta, he'd dropped her at her apartment. He intended to get to the bottom of her demands, settle any financial score once and for all, and return to Roses, his true home.

And his true love, Desiree.

When Desiree hadn't answered his phone calls or texts in

the ensuing first hours of his departure, he'd tasted a bitter defeat. But not for long. They weren't finished by a long shot.

He bunked in his former apartment, where he discussed his situation with Oscar and Georges. Oscar made a hasty phone call and booked a consultation with Abraham Realgood, Honest Abe, the lawyer he worked for. Although the lawyer wasn't accepting new clients, he'd offer his consultation services as a favor to Oscar.

The following afternoon, Mr. Realgood's receptionist showed Keiran into a dark-paneled office where the lawyer greeted Keiran with a friendly tilt of his head.

"What can I do for you?" He gestured for Keiran to take a seat across from him.

"I'll come directly to the point." Keiran sank into the cushioned chair. "My former girlfriend, Patricia, believes she's entitled to half my earnings, including a pub I inherited."

A pair of astute hazel eyes measured Keiran. "I've heard some of your story, thanks to Oscar and Georges."

"Then can you advise me? I want Patricia out of my life."

"She's requesting money."

"Yes, and more money than I have." With Patricia, it had always been about an extravagant lifestyle, and when she had a goal in mind there was no stopping her.

"Is she entitled to your money?" the lawyer asked.

"When we were together, we had a verbal agreement that we would split half my earnings. I did the work, and she maintained the office and books. However, I've reviewed the paperwork I held on to, because she implied there was some fine print," Keiran said. "I couldn't find anything written down."

"How much does she want?"

"Twenty thousand dollars. I wish it was less. She found out I inherited a pub and she wants me to sell it and she'll take half the proceeds. However, I'm not willing to sell, and besides, the building isn't worth much in its present condition."

"Not functioning?"

"It hasn't been open in many years."

"Is there a possibility she'd take you to court?"

That was a worrisome and infuriating thought. Keiran stretched out his long legs and blew out a sigh. "Knowing Patricia? Aye, although she couldn't possibly win. Could she?"

"Probably not, if your agreement was verbal, but this battle could go on for years. It all depends how badly you want her out of your life."

Furious with himself for getting involved with her in the first place, Keiran glanced out the window at the overcast sky. "I'd like our relationship to be finished, once and for all."

"Then there's a solution because money talks." The lawyer examined the paperwork on his desk and idly pushed it to the side. "Georges mentioned you inherited an autographed football card that might be valuable."

With a nod, Keiran pulled the card from its protective case, as Georges had urged him to bring it to the meeting. He felt a deep, almost agonizing sadness about giving up the card that had meant so much to his father. He'd prayed about it, and realized he needed to get over the sadness and guilt if he sold it. If he reopened the pub, his parents would undoubtedly be grateful and proud. As much as his father's dream had been football, the pub in Roses was his legacy.

Keiran shifted his gaze to the lawyer's sparsely furnished, dimly lit office. He'd expected an oily charmer with a law degree, but Abraham Realgood seemed on the up and up.

"We appraised the card at the pawn shop Georges works for," Keiran said. "The estimate from the pawnbroker is fifteen thousand dollars."

Seemingly impervious to Keiran's emotional state, the lawyer grinned. "I advise you to sell the card and pay the ex. If your past agreement was verbal, you're in the clear, but it's more the matter of guaranteeing she won't be able to badger you for any more money. Otherwise, she may turn up again. More time. More money. Do you want that?"

Keiran shook his head. "I'd like her gone from my life."

"Then I'll draw up a contract, a full and final release stating clearly she's not entitled to anything else after this payment."

"Do you think she'll accept less than she's asking?"

Mr. Realgood rubbed his jaw. "From you and your friends' descriptions, I'm positive she'll jump at it. Fifteen thousand dollars is a lot, especially around Christmas."

"Excellent." It was all Keiran could do not to burst into an Irish song. This was going to work. "How soon can the contract be drafted?"

"By tomorrow. I'll handle everything from here." Slowly, the gray-haired lawyer leaned back in his chair and folded his hands behind his head. "Now I'm not judging, mind you, but if I were you I'd avoid any further correspondence with your ex—verbal or otherwise."

The lawyer *was* judging, Keiran reflected, although he was too relieved to do anything other than watch Mr. Realgood write out a bill and hand it to him.

Keiran looked over the number and gaped.

"Admittedly, my services are costly on account of the short notice and holiday season," the lawyer said. "But your problem is solved. And if you ever need your locks changed, I'll cut you a good deal."

"Thank you." With a deep, relieved breath, Keiran shook hands with the lawyer and left.

By noon the next day, Abe Realgood phoned to report

that Patricia had received the email and accepted via her electronic signature.

Another deep breath of relief.

"The thing is," Keiran told a frowning but somewhat amused Georges and Oscar, "I can't stay to cook Christmas Eve dinner because I'm driving back to Roses."

Georges flashed Keiran a mischievous grin. "What will we eat then, *mon ami?*"

"Why don't you call the local pizzeria? They deliver on Christmas Eve, and pizza goes great with beer." Keiran chuckled as he hoisted his belongings over his shoulder, thanked the men for their help, and wished them a Merry Christmas.

He glanced at his watch. He had two stops to make in Roses, and one important phone call. He hoped he wouldn't be late for Christmas Eve dinner. They ate at six o'clock sharp.

* * *

"YOU BURNED THE TURKEY?" Candee hovered over Desiree, who'd dashed into the kitchen to extract a charred, smoking turkey from the oven. "How can anyone burn a fourteen-pound turkey?"

"Fortunately, it didn't catch fire. When the smoke detector went off, I was worried," Desiree replied. "I went into the living room for a few minutes to start a fire in the fireplace and plug in the Christmas tree lights. Then, while I was lighting the candles on the mantel, I got sidetracked when the radio started playing 'Silent Night' on repeat."

Desiree wore the red and green *Kiss Me, It's Christmas* apron over a red silk blouse and black velvet pants. Christmas Eve was a special occasion, and she planned to slip on suede ankle boots and her cobalt-blue wool coat for midnight church services. To keep her hair away from her face while cooking, she'd pinned it into a chignon secured with a red jeweled clasp.

"I should've helped you with the dinner preparations. Sorry I lost track of time. I love watching Teddy and Joseph play a game of flag football," Candee said. "It's amazing—we haven't gotten any snow this year so the guys are still wearing sweatshirts and jeans."

"The weather forecast predicts a light dusting by midnight." Desiree glanced out the kitchen window at the energetic twosome. They'd decided on another game and were flipping a coin. Then Teddy placed the football in the middle of her large backyard. Starting with a snap, Joseph passed the ball in one fluid motion to a third player.

"Recognize that handsome guy? He looks like he could be a male model." Candee feigned fanning herself as she came to stand by the window with Desiree.

He certainly seemed familiar, with his broad shoulders and midnight-black hair and . . .

Desiree's knees buckled. No, it couldn't be. The guy must be one of the neighborhood men, perhaps Mr. Juno taking a break from his graduate studies.

"I'll try flipping the turkey," Candee suggested. "If I drop it, then we can remember this Christmas as the year you burned the turkey and it fell to the floor."

Desiree laughed. "As long as it doesn't roll into the dining room and—"

The front doorbell rang. The cabinet door handle delivery man, Desiree surmised, because she wasn't expecting any visitors.

Or was she?

She told herself to take her time answering, but scratched the idea as she hastened to the door and swung it open.

It wasn't the delivery man.

He stood on her front porch, tall and lean, his green eyes reminding her of Irish emeralds glimmering in his handsome face. He wore his navy-blue parka, unzipped, accentuating his toned physique. His denim shirt and jeans were rumpled. He was holding a small gift, wrapped in brown paper and tied with a red satin ribbon.

"Keiran." She stepped back and attempted to breathe. Part of her functioning brain reminded her that she should stay calm and composed.

"Merry Christmas, Desiree." He held out the gift.

She kept her hands at her sides. "Why are you here?" Her voice shook. He still offered her the gift, his hands outstretched.

"To finish our discussion from last week. And to tell you what I've wanted to say since we met. Listen—"

"Keiran, you're a little late." Candee approached and gave him a mildly sardonic smile.

"It started to snow in Atlanta and the limited visibility on I-85 slowed traffic," he said. "Plus I stopped in town to buy Desiree's gift, then ducked into my pub. Rob is coming in the morning."

"Rob?" Desiree regarded them both. "Why?"

"Rob and Keiran are reopening the pub. Rob is loaning him the start-up money, much as he did for Teddy when he began his real estate flipping business," Candee said.

"Rob and I will be serving Christmas dinner tomorrow to the homeless in our community," Keiran explained. "Several of the markets in town, including your green grocer, are donating food. We're using the ovens at the local supermarkets to prepare the meals. I hope you'll join us, Desiree."

Blinking, Desiree gaped at Keiran, and then Candee. "And you knew about all this?"

"Only recently," Candee replied. "Teddy and Keiran arranged everything."

"And about Keiran returning here? Tonight?"

Feigning innocence, Candee gushed apologetically. "You wouldn't answer his texts. Tonight, Teddy told me they've been in touch all week. And now I'm going to see to dinner." Candee rolled up the sleeves of her glittery silver blouse and hurried away.

"Keiran." Desiree touched her throat. "I don't know what to say."

His strong fingers were gentle as he pressed them against her lips. "Take my gift and invite me inside."

"Please come in." She accepted his gift. "You didn't need to buy me anything. Thank you."

He stepped inside. "I confess I used the gift as an excuse."

"What? I don't understand."

"I've been working all week to make things right between us. I understand you're hurt and justifiably angry. I met with a lawyer in Atlanta, and Patricia signed a full and final release contract. She's not entitled to half of what I earn anymore. Our former business agreement was verbal, by the way."

Desiree's heart was pounding so hard, he could surely hear each beat. "What do you mean?"

"She was demanding twenty thousand dollars, the estimated proceeds if I sold the pub." He shook his head. "You don't know her the way I do. She would have made our lives miserable. So, I gave her fifteen thousand, and made certain she's out of our life for good."

Desiree's gaze narrowed. "Where did you get the money? Rob?"

"Rob's been great, but no."

She paused for a beat. "Then where?"

"My father's football card. I didn't want to sell it, and I prayed long and hard before agreeing. The pawn shop assured me they'll hold it for a while, in case I can come up with the money to buy it back. I don't see that happening, but you never know. Our pub might become extremely success-ful, just like it once was."

"*Our* pub?"

"I'm hoping you'll help me bring it back to its former glory."

Through tears of happiness, she found her voice. "With you at the helm, how can it fail?"

"And you," he said solemnly. "I hope I'm the man you deserve, and I want to make all my mistakes up to you."

The pain in his voice brought a new swell of tears. "Keiran, please, we all make mistakes and—"

"I'm sorry, Desiree. And I love you."

When she realized he was threading his fingers through her hair, then cupping her face so he could kiss her, she whispered the words bursting from her heart. "I love you too."

All week she'd dreamed of kissing him—the tenderness of his mouth on hers, the elation of being reunited. For a long moment, she felt mesmerized, like she was floating. His kiss was light and sweet, and magnificently poignant.

She snuggled against his warm, hard chest, feeling the solid beat of his heart. There was so much she wanted to tell him—that she'd installed a kitchen cabinet by herself, that she'd won a particularly difficult court case.

Not knowing where to begin, she burst out, "I burned the turkey. But I set a lovely table for dinner and I wasn't going to let a little thing like charred meat stop us from enjoying Christmas."

He chuckled. "Let me survey the damage and see if I can help." He removed his parka and Desiree hung it in the front foyer closet, then placed his gift on a side table in the living room. She crossed to the kitchen, where Keiran was deftly removing the burnt skin from the turkey.

"If everyone likes the legs and thighs, we're golden," he said.

Desiree set out her turkey platter, and Candee artfully arranged sliced lemons and sprigs of rosemary around the carved meat Keiran placed on the platter. He asked Desiree to stir the gravy on the stove.

"You're a little bossy."

His eyes crinkled as a grin touched his lips. "I'm delegating."

Teddy and Joseph joined the group, and they settled, cross-legged, on the cushions Desiree had arranged in the dining room around the makeshift table.

Dinner was a feast that did credit to all of Desiree's preparations. She glanced uncertainly at Keiran as he tasted a slice of turkey. He proclaimed the meat expertly roasted, and she couldn't help but notice he gazed at her with profound pride.

She toyed with the mashed potatoes, wishing she hadn't felt so nervous about entertaining. Keiran assumed the role as host with a casual, gracious elegance.

After her pistachio cake was served for dessert, Joseph turned his attention to her. "We have a present for you, Aunt Desiree!" he burst out. "It's a surprise! Uncle Teddy said we could go back to our house and get him as soon as we were finished." He turned to Candee. "May I be excused?"

Him? Get him? Before Desiree could ask, Candee opened her mouth with the obvious intention of suggesting they wait until Christmas morning, but Teddy forestalled her by grinning at Joseph in agreement.

"This won't take long," Teddy said, as he and Joseph hurried out the door.

They returned ten minutes later holding Boomer, the brown and tan beagle pup.

"Merry Christmas, Desiree!" Candee, Teddy, and Joseph chimed.

The beagle wriggled out of Joseph's arms and lunged for the coffee table laden with food.

"This dog loves to eat, so he must think he's landed in paradise because he can reach the height of this table," Teddy said.

Desiree dissolved with laughter. Her contentment was so real, she thought her chest might burst. This was heaven—a happy home, sharing God's message of joy with the people she loved.

After the meal was cleared, Keiran escorted Desiree to the living room while Candee and her family excused themselves to go back to their house and get ready for church services.

Boomer, apparently full and exhausted, curled up near the fireplace, tail to nose.

"Desiree? There are a few things we need to discuss." Keiran claimed a seat beside her on the sofa. Although he asked gently, she knew by his inquisitive expression that he wanted an explanation for why she refused to accept his phone calls and texts.

She pulled off her apron and smoothed her red silk blouse. Drawing a long breath, she told him her feelings about trust, knowing he'd been correct in surmising her issues had come from early life experiences.

"Trust can be relearned," he said quietly. "It helps if you talk about it. And I'll be here for you, to listen."

"You're moving back in?"

He brushed a wisp of blond hair from her face. "I hope you'll invite me to sleep in your attic. I can't drive back to Atlanta in a blizzard."

"I wouldn't call a few inches of snow a blizzard." She stared out the wavy glass of the front bay window. The snow was starting to fall, its thick wet flakes covering the sidewalks and road in a white blanket.

"You don't want your fiancé to be homeless," he said.

"Fiancé?"

Although his tone was light, she heard the rough tinge in his voice.

Tipping her chin up, he gazed deeply into her eyes. "I love you, Desiree."

She laid a hand on his cheek. "And I love you."

Her Renaissance man. She attempted to smile. "Until now, I felt certain I'd never hear those words from you."

"Desiree, I've loved you since you slammed the door in my face when I first arrived, then berated me for talking to your front porch."

"A bit odd, don't you think? Talking to a porch?"

"Not considering the circumstances." With an arm around her waist, he turned to a side table, picked up his gift and handed it to her.

"I thought about something Christmassy, and it's one of the reasons I stopped in town. Please open it."

She unwrapped the gift and slid a silky scarf between her fingers, admiring the holly design in white and green. "Thank you. It's gorgeous."

"The boutique owner said it's a designer scarf, and the colors will go with everything."

"Ideal for the holidays." She tied the scarf around her throat and smiled. "How does it look?"

"Perfect. Like you." He nodded to the box. "There's something else inside, at the bottom."

"What is it?"

He caught her in a long embrace. "Something special that I hope you'll love."

She unsnapped the lid of a tiny black velvet box and

gasped. An exquisite round-cut diamond ring, styled in yellow gold, reflected sparkling white light across the ceiling.

"I've never seen anything so beautiful," she breathed.

He drew back slightly and regarded her. "Will you marry me?"

From the moment he'd returned, Desiree had known he would ask for an open and honest relationship.

Through tears of bliss, she whispered, "Yes."

His arms closed around her. "Good. Because if you don't mean it, I won't bake any more Irish whiskey cakes."

"Maybe it's better, because I need to lose a few pounds." She laughed through her tears. "Besides, you never shared your secret recipe with me."

He took her hand and led her to the kitchen. "We can start this evening. I promise I'll teach you everything I know."

THE END

CHAPTER 1

hy did I decide to do this? I must've been madder than a box of frogs.

Kathleen Kelly nodded politely while listening to Candee, her Realtor, although she scarcely paid attention. While she tried to come up with an animated reply, her mind spun. She hoped she hadn't made the biggest mistake of her life.

I'm in America. I've done it.

Meanwhile, Candee gushed on and on about Roses, their picture-perfect North Carolina town. Voted one of the best places to live by a national magazine, Roses frequently persuaded travelers passing through to sell their homes and relocate there.

Kathleen grinned, because she was one of those travelers. However, she hadn't passed through Roses. Her Dublin hometown was 3600 miles away.

The internet was a marvelous thing, connecting people from all around the world. Finally, after months of preparation, her dream of owning a business had become a reality.

Cause for celebration?

In truth, she'd been full of starry-eyed dreams and didn't

know what to expect—this being America with its laid-back style. However, she'd found that professionalism and punctuality were respected here, judging by how efficiently Candee had handled the real estate closing.

She eyed the run-down exterior, the broken-down wooden front door that looked like it had once been painted turquoise. Moss flourished beneath the eaves, and numerous shingles were missing. The brick façade was crumbling in several places.

This wasn't Betty's Diner anymore. From here on in, this was her place: Kathleen's Teahouse.

Critically, she assessed her reflection in the smudged plate-glass front window. She'd swept her red-gold hair up at the crown, and pinned the overly long ends back from her face. Tired lines etched the corners of her dark eyes, and the blush of color she'd applied along her cheekbones had disappeared, leaving her complexion pale. Her lips, which she'd always deemed too full, looked a tad solemn.

Despite the sunny day, she'd dressed in a suede skirt, thick black tights and ankle boots.

Budding leaves on the tulip magnolia trees whispered of spring, and buttery-yellow daffodils had begun to open. So different from Ireland, where hawthorn hedges wouldn't bloom until May.

"So, what do you think of your new business on Pine Cone Lane?" Candee asked.

"Everything is brilliant, absolutely brilliant," Kathleen lied effectively. Sometimes white lies were best to hide her reservations because the place wasn't nearly as brilliant as all that.

In its heyday, the former greasy-spoon diner had served countless meals, the floors and countertops spic and span. However, it had been boarded up in recent months, which was why she'd snagged the place at a steal before the building went into foreclosure.

With a silent groan, she estimated the number of weeks it would take to sand and repaint, outfit the kitchen and hire staff, and the numerous unexpected details that would surface.

She came up with months, not weeks, although she reassured herself there was no point in olagonin'—whining and complaining—because it only made things more difficult.

However, since she'd arrived in America, being anxious had become her forte.

The long weeks of anticipation and tension had taken their toll and kept her awake at night, and she could think of nothing she'd like better than a tub soak with the lavender soap she'd brought from Ireland. Followed by a lengthy, leisurely nap.

Resignedly, she knew a nap would be out of the question for a long time.

Perhaps forever.

She paused to stand back, surveying the building. If she thought objectively rather than with her emotions, she understood that she wouldn't be able to accomplish everything by herself, especially within a five-week timeline.

She'd scheduled her grand opening on St. Patrick's Day, deeming the date fitting and appropriate.

She envisioned painting the shingles a serene shade of soft-green, overstated by a burgundy-striped canvas awning, much like the awning gracing The Ground Café, her former employer's coffee shop in Dublin. And she wanted outdoor seating on the patio, allowing customers to dine at wrought iron tables beneath vintage-style Edison light bulbs.

Curb appeal. That's what the place needed.

She focused on which project she would dive into first—the interior or the exterior.

She was weighing the pros and cons when Candee asked,

"You're not having second thoughts about moving to America, are you? I realize it's a huge undertaking."

"Of course not," Kathleen said. "Ireland was getting a little too small for me."

At thirty-five years old, her mantra had become *pursue my dreams or bust*. Besides, it was too late to check out, things being what they were. Her former coworkers knew she was embarking on a refreshingly different chapter in her life, and it would be disheartening to admit defeat.

Kathleen fidgeted with the gold watch on her wrist, a going-away gift from her employer, Danny Brady. "Also," she continued, "baking and the restaurant trade are second nature to me. I've spent half my life managing a coffee shop."

Candee covered Kathleen's hand. "Sometimes a fresh start is as simple as buying a dilapidated building and getting on an airplane."

"Did I say that?"

"Oh, and much more, because you not only said it, you did it," Candee said. "You've created your dream life."

Kathleen shook her head. "I used to be smart and sensible."

"In the present circumstances, you're even smarter," Candee said. "And you're strong and beautiful. The first time we Skyped, I couldn't get over how put together you were. You'd already composed a business plan."

Kathleen offered a brittle smile. "Don't believe everything on your computer screen."

"Positive thinking, plus action, leads to accomplishment. You're a doer."

"Despite what my so-called friends advised," Kathleen replied.

"Weren't they supportive?"

"Aye, in a polite sort of way. They gave me rock-hard, unsolicited advice." For some reason, her thoughts kept darting back to Ireland, and a sense of isolation rolled through her. "They wanted to protect me from making a mistake."

She longed to tell someone about the successful closing of her new property, the deep-blue sky gracing the warm Carolina days, the way the sweetgum tree branches swayed in the pleasant morning breezes.

But there was no one to tell. Danny and his wife, Clara, were busy with their own lives, with a wee one on the way.

"You'll love Roses, and I predict your teahouse will become a tea emporium," Candee said.

"What in the world is that?"

"An emporium is a retail store selling a variety of goods."

"I plan to serve food—Irish tea and scones, sandwiches and cakes. I'm not a chain of fancy shops."

"Well, you should be. Also sell tea and teapots, because you and Roses are poised for success. I can feel it."

Kathleen smiled. Aye, Roses was enchanting. The once sleepy town was thriving, and the lush green grass packed neatly between the brick sidewalks reminded her a wee bit of Ireland.

Except that it wasn't …

Remembrances of lyrical brogues brought a poignant yearning to Kathleen's chest that stopped her cold. She hadn't realized she'd be so homesick. With her accent, she'd already found that oftentimes her words got misheard and misunderstood, and she'd had a hard time communicating even though everyone spoke the same language—English.

"This area will get a lot of foot traffic, especially on warm spring and summer evenings," Candee said. "Here in the Carolinas we enjoy a temperate climate, so don't rule out winter or fall, either."

"Unlike Ireland." Kathleen chuckled.

"Does it truly rain buckets?"

"Our term is bucketing down," Kathleen said, repeating the standard Irish joke. "Although the rain is at least warm in the summer."

Candee laughed. "Is it windy?"

"Not much." Kathleen lifted her shoulders in a teasing shrug. "Except small children and pets are sometimes blown clear away to England."

"Believe me, you'll enjoy the weather here," Candee concluded with a laugh. Gently, she urged Kathleen to the diner's doorway.

Kathleen blinked at the dazzling noon sunlight and realized her stomach was growling. She hadn't eaten anything except a slice of her homemade Irish brown bread when she'd woken at six a.m.

"What do you think of your upstairs apartment?" Candee asked. "Internet photos don't do a place justice, but housing above your teahouse is a money saver. You won't have to pay rent nor commute."

"Aye. Although truth be told, it's all in a little worse shape than I expected."

"Manageable, though, I trust?" Candee's puzzled frown swung from the door to Kathleen. "I realize it needs curtains."

"It lacks a lot more than updated curtains," Kathleen said with a laugh. "And it will take an army of crewmen to get everything in working order by St. Patrick's Day."

"My husband, Teddy, is a contractor. He'll get the place turned around for you in no time." Candee shook back a strand of red hair that had come loose from her braid, exposing a pair of gold cross earrings, the only jewelry she wore except for her wedding rings. Even without an ounce of makeup, the woman was stunning, her green eyes gleaming whenever she discussed her husband and their adopted son, Joseph.

In addition to being a Realtor, Candee had opened an afterschool daycare facility in her home for disadvantaged children in the community. On several occasions, Kathleen wondered how Candee was able to do it all. She'd been inspired to match her stamina and ambition.

"As long as there's running water, a kitchen and a bathroom in my apartment," Kathleen said, "my needs are met."

"Good. Your reference from Danny Brady was excellent, by the way."

"I never missed a day of work."

"And he said your brown bread flew off the shelves whenever it was featured."

"He granted me the option to take my recipe to America, and I ran with it."

"Free and clear?"

"Danny understood I was drained. After countless years as his head assistant, I wanted a change." Kathleen wished the warmth burning her cheeks didn't give her away. Why couldn't she compartmentalize her second thoughts like she did everything else in her life?

Because she was excited.

And mildly terrified.

"I expect he and his wife will come to America and visit me someday," she finished.

Candee studied her. "So, at present, you're alone."

"Aye." Kathleen considered saying more, to explain she always felt lonely despite her attempts to build relationships.

She kept her lips sealed. Some words were better left unsaid.

In a little over two years, she'd been duped by a man not once, but twice. First, by a moneyed Italian she'd met on the internet who had turned out to be, surprise, surprise, a young boy. And then, Alexander, an American businessman, had played her for a muppet—a fool.

Danny Brady and his bodyguard, Ian, had said Alexander was too talkative. Talkative? Hah! What an understatement! Charmer was more like it, and Alexander was so smooth-talking he could sell ya an eye out of your own head. He'd had her believing he was genuinely interested in her. When she'd fallen for him, his charisma had changed to controlling. He'd quickly become domineering and expected her to be subservient.

As Candee continued to study her, Kathleen offered, "The man I believed I loved was actually two different men. He was fine as long as things went his way and I was passive." She shrugged and tried to act unconcerned. "Although being submissive isn't in my nature. As I advanced in my career, our relationship quickly fell apart."

"You said you wanted a fresh start, and you've created it. Here's to new men and extraordinary opportunities." Candee gestured to the doorway.

"I'll take the opportunities minus the men," Kathleen said. Truly, she was done with con men, eejits—idiots—who expected women to take a back seat to them and their opinions. Men who exuded personality while keeping a close watch on their own agendas. Men who fired off derisive comments for no other reason than to feel superior.

She was a woman who had helped Danny Brady's Ground Café achieve fame. Here and now, with determination and hard work, she'd make her teahouse a noteworthy addition to this quaint little town.

"During our Skype sessions, I mentioned that your teahouse will offset Keiran O'Malley's Irish pub nicely." Candee pointed to a side street. "His building isn't far from here."

"Keiran's cousin, William, first spoke of Roses and recommended you as a Realtor, which is why I messaged you,"

Kathleen said. "Fortunately, I zoomed in on this town fairly quickly."

"William lives in Dublin, right?"

"He also knows Sean, my coworker from The Ground Café. Both men wanted to date me, and I turned Sean down flat."

"And William?"

"He frequented the café a couple times a week. We dated for a short while after my breakup with Alexander until I realized I wasn't ready for a romantic involvement." Kathleen swallowed, giving herself a breather before continuing. "Sean still texts me now and then. He wishes to come to America to help me with my new business."

"Is that a good thing or a bad thing?"

"I'm not certain. Sean is competent, but I can't imagine he'd actually fancy working for me. He and I were on the same level as managers." She exhaled. "At any rate, William had told me that Keiran loves it in Roses."

"He's married to my sister, Desiree. They are extremely happy."

"I've heard."

Happy. Such an elusive term.

"Keiran said that life called him back to Roses. Maybe the town called you here too."

Kathleen reflected on Candee's words. She'd read about life's calling in self-help books and tuned in to endless podcasts on the subject. Sometimes, it seemed like she'd waited her entire life for a voice to explain which bend in the road led to happiness.

Nevertheless, if one's calling was a voice whispering in her ear, she hadn't heard a sound. Perhaps a calling was the Lord tapping her on the shoulder. Either way, she'd known in her gut that Roses was the ideal spot, and everything had clicked into place.

"In any case, here I am," she replied.

Candee opened her arms, firmly clasping them around Kathleen. "And this is the dawn of the grandest adventure of your life."

Tears welled in Kathleen's eyes—a mix of joy, fear, and reservations. She'd chosen her destiny, following in the footprints of the Irish immigrant.

Don't be an eejit, her inner voice chided. *You're launching a teahouse, not fleeing from a potato famine.*

"And I can't wait to introduce you to everyone," Candee said. "Desiree and Keiran, my husband Teddy, and our son, Joseph—"

"Aye. When the time comes." Now she was sounding standoffish.

She drew a see-through container from her leather shoulder bag. "Before I forget, I baked a loaf of my brown bread for you this morning."

Candee stepped back. "You haven't been here two days and you're already baking bread in your apartment?"

"I ran the oven before I even unpacked." She handed the container to Candee. "This is a thank-you gift for taking care of the million incidentals that came with an international real-estate transaction. And, for fixing up my apartment before I arrived."

"My pleasure. Decorating is my thing, and you advised me on your likes and dislikes. In fact, you were quite decisive."

"I don't have much of a knack for it."

"Oh, but you do."

Kathleen envisioned the packing boxes strewn throughout her flat's hallway, the luggage and clothes piled by her bed. She should have put away her belongings a while ago. Instead, she'd drawn on a ruffled apron, let a batch of dough rise, and baked.

"Take a bite," she urged.

Candee obliged, closing her eyes as she nibbled. "This bread is one of the best baked goods I've ever tasted. And that's saying a lot, because my friend in Miami owns ..."

"I plan to sell Irish brown bread every day," Kathleen said, grinning broadly at the compliment. "Although I'll need to sell more than bread."

"What about pizza?" Candee asked.

"I'll leave pizza to the pizzeria in town. Presently, I'll turn my energy into outfitting the bakery with delicious Irish desserts and an array of tea selections. In Ireland, people aren't in such a hurry. We savor every moment, and I intend to create the same experience in my teahouse."

"Unlike America," Candee said.

"Comfy couches and free Wi-Fi," Kathleen went on. "Brewed tea in a variety of flavors—chamomile, mint, and a host of exotic herbal leaves."

Her ideas overflowed. Were they too ambitious?

"Have you set your hours?" Candee stooped down at the doorway, muttering about the weather stripping not being sufficiently tight to prevent air leaks.

"I'll open at eleven, and close by nine at night."

"You realize you're describing ten-hour work days?"

"Aye." Like a shot, Kathleen's brain worked rapidly. "I'm still on the lookout for locally sourced ingredients so I can serve healthy salads, sandwiches, and wraps. For dinner, stone-baked pita bread topped with goat cheese and caramelized onions will be a nightly special."

Candee linked arms with Kathleen and walked to the side of the building, where rickety exterior stairs led to the second floor. "What you're describing is enough work for twenty people. And that pita bread sounds a lot like pizza."

"It's Irish pizza, so no competition with the local pizzeria." Deciding on her menu options, Kathleen hardly realized

Candee had come to a determined stop while saying a man's name twice.

Rob. Rob.

"Who is Rob?" Kathleen asked.

"He's a dear friend and owns a string of popular bakeries." For some reason, Candee's pitch heightened. "His chain is called Rob's Marvelous Muffins and is based in the Miami area where he lives. He's delightful and funny and easy-going—"

"Brilliant, I'm sure." Kathleen went back to the menu choices in her mind. Irish bacon and poached eggs, or a traditional Irish breakfast complete with roasted tomatoes and mushrooms? Perhaps beef burgers and cider glazed salmon for lunch.

No. She reined in her thoughts. This wasn't a full-scale restaurant.

"I'll begin advertising for employees soon and start with a modest staff," she said, "Did I tell you I won't be serving alcohol?"

"Yes, and I applaud your decision."

"Thanks. I've had enough of that in Ireland. People going out on the lash and stumbling home in the wee hours." Kathleen waved a dismissive hand. "I'll leave the drinking to the pubs."

She looked back on the intervention Clara Brady had staged for her alcoholic brother, Seamus. Little good that had done. Once a person was addicted, it was often a long road to wellness.

"What are the requisite number of ovens for a bakery?" Candee asked.

"Certainly a small commercial oven, plus a full-size convection oven is necessary. Also, a deck oven for layer cakes and breads." Kathleen frowned as she considered all the equipment yet to purchase. "Where will I buy a mixer and a—"

"You'll need someone knowledgeable to advise you. Fortunately, Rob has extensive retail bakery experience. He studied at a prestigious culinary school in Florida offering lots of hands-on experience." Candee plucked her cell-phone from her purse. The excitement in her voice matched the glow in her eyes. "He was voted Miami's most successful entrepreneur, and he's just the right person to help you."

Whoever this Rob was, he'd be overwhelmed when he saw what needed to be completed in five weeks.

Unless, of course, he was a miracle worker.

CHAPTER 2

"*R*ob's Marvelous Muffins." Realizing both hands were a sticky mess from rolling out pastry dough, Rob Taylor answered his cell-phone, then balanced the phone against his shoulder. His gaze landed on the commercial mixer on the counter. He switched it on to prepare twenty batches of cupcakes.

Mondays weren't usually hectic, but with Valentine's Day over and the forthcoming St. Patrick's Day holiday, baking green cupcakes galore became the blueprint of the day.

Pushing out a sharp breath, he wiped his hands on the white apron tied around his protruding waist, trying to remember how many cupcakes he'd tasted that morning. One. Well, no, at least two. Okay, three, although the third had lacked his bakery's signature Irish Cream liqueur glaze.

He eyed that same liqueur set near several pounds of unsalted butter by the commercial mixer, ticking off the items on his to-do list. Next, dozens of cupcakes needed frosting.

A diet was in order, but he'd made peace with that long ago. A man owning a half-dozen bakery shops couldn't resist the smell of mouth-watering chocolate, succulent blueberry, or tart lemon muffins. At least, *he* couldn't. And there was nothing to do except, well, keep tasting.

"Rob, are you there? Hi. It's Candee."

He grinned. "How's my favorite daughter-in-law?"

"Umm, are we all of a sudden related?"

"Your husband is like a son to me." Rob silently motioned one of the bakers to shut off the timer going off on a convection oven. "So if Teddy is my son, then you're my daughter-in-law."

"I've always loved your logic, Rob." Candee chuckled. "How's the muffin business?"

"Busy. Can't complain." He muffled the phone as an employee wearing a company hat and sporting nonslip clogs ran past looking for the espresso. The featured cupcake was a combination of flour, sugar, espresso, and that Irish Cream liqueur.

"How is everyone in Roses?" Rob asked. "Is the weather warm in the Carolinas? The temperature is in the mid-seventies here in Miami."

"We're all well. It's a pleasant, sunny day and quite typical for February. Teddy sends his love." Candee paused. "Can I ask you something?"

"Anything, my lovely daughter-in-law."

"What are your views on helping a damsel in distress?"

"Like in the original silent movies where the villain wearing a top hat ties the woman to the railroad tracks? What was that guy's name again?"

"Snidely Whiplash. And no, I mean a beautiful woman needs your help."

"Wait. Who in Roses ..." Rob stopped in the middle of his sentence. "I assume you're not referring to yourself."

"Correct."

"Okay then. Who? And why me?" He glanced at his wristwatch. The lunch-hour crowd would be flooding into the bakery soon. Mentally, he estimated the hundreds of cupcakes required to refill the soon-to-be-empty display cases.

"Because you're a professional baker," Candee said. "Plus, you're a perfect gentleman."

"I appreciate the compliments, but where are we going with this conversation?"

"Do you remember my telling you about Kathleen, an Irishwoman from Dublin? She managed The Ground Café."

"Actually, I do," Rob said. "That coffee shop chain recently opened in the States."

"At the time, Kathleen was considering relocating to Roses and starting a teahouse. Well, all that talk became a reality."

Vaguely, he recalled the discussion from a few months earlier. "Congratulations. She made it over the pond okay?"

"Yes, and she's enthusiastic and vivacious and—"

"Good. Wish her luck." He paused to bark instructions to David, a new employee plunging a rack of croissants into a roll-in oven. David had been recommended by a friend of a friend, and Rob had hired him on the spot. High employee turnover and a shortage of staff left him no choice. Too bad the kid hardly looked eighteen, his checkered trousers a size too big for his skinny body, a white torque hat overpowering his small head.

According to his application, David was twenty-something.

Either kids were looking younger, Rob mused, or he was getting older.

"Don't take shortcuts," he directed the newbie. "Check the oven temperature again."

"Yes, Mr. Rob," the newbie acknowledged with a slight bow.

"Do I look like the king of England?" Rob held up a hand, palm up. "Check the temperature, or I'll have you clear out the moat around the bakery."

David gave Rob a blank look and scurried away.

Rob eyed the liqueur. He was inclined to grab the bottle and pour himself a large glass.

Clueless. This next generation was absolutely clueless. Surely the kid realized there was no moat.

The clanging of a pan had him cupping the phone to his ear. "Sorry, Candee. I'd like to chitchat, but it's busier than I anticipated today. Can I call you back tonight? Or better yet, in April."

"Things won't be busy in April?"

"I forgot Easter is in April. Maybe May."

"Isn't Mother's Day in May?"

"June. We'll say June." He ran an irritated hand over his bald head and sighed. "June is the month for weddings. Apparently, a baker's job is never done."

"Coincidentally, Rob, she's a baker too."

"Who?"

"Kathleen. The Irishwoman."

"Right. As we've established, so am I. Tell her cheers, or whatever those Irish people say, and to prepare to never sleep."

"She's lovely."

"Bravo."

"She baked me an Irish brown bread," Candee said. "Her special recipe, and it's delicious."

He slanted over the table to snap off the electric mixer before the over-mixed batter resulted in dense, gummy cupcakes.

"How delicious?" He tried to decide whether he should put the phone on speaker so that he could spoon the batter into tins, or grow a third hand.

"How delicious compared to your cupcakes?" Candee asked.

"Yeah."

"Her bread is the best baked good this side of the Atlantic."

Whoa. Compared to his award-winning cupcakes? Rob frowned and held out a hand to stop an employee from rushing over to him.

"Hold on," he said to Candee. He laid his phone on the counter, yanked off his apron, and stalked to a quiet spot by a window. "Okay, I'm back."

"She is overwhelmed," Candee said. "Relocating to a different country, launching a business from scratch ... I can't imagine how she'll accomplish everything. Do you recall the broken-down diner on Pine Cone Lane? It's been unoccupied for a while."

"The diner is located not far from Keiran's pub, right?"

At his mention of Keiran, Rob rubbed a hand over his eyes. Perhaps he should tell Candee how guilty he felt that he'd been unable to attend the grand re-opening of O'Malley's, the pub Keiran had inherited from his father. Although Keiran and his wife, Desiree, had assured Rob they understood he couldn't leave Miami during the middle of an extensive baking exhibition, he'd missed being in Roses to support them.

"Good memory, Rob," Candee said. "And Kathleen intends to create an old-world teahouse. The problem is the place is screaming for a total remodel. She's experienced, but—"

"What can I do?" Rob conjured up the image of a cherubic, delicate Irishwoman. Slight and fragile, with flaming-red hair and freckles, staring wide-eyed at an undertaking far too large for her.

"You have the expertise and bakery know-how," Candee said.

"Does she need capital and an investor?" Understanding that all new restaurants were under-capitalized, Rob automatically reached for his wallet. A foolish move, he realized, unless cash flew through the phone lines. And even more foolish because he wouldn't see a return on his investment for three to four years.

"She needs advice and support," Candee said. "She's laser-focused on a St. Patrick's Day opening."

"Does she have a business license and sales permit?"

"All set. Fortunately, the diner was already permitted as a restaurant."

"Health and fire department permits?"

"Done."

"Is she making alterations to the building?"

"Major." For the first time, Candee hesitated. "Why?"

He peered out the window. The wrought-iron tables facing his bakery were filled with customers. Between the palm tree border outlining the seating area, low-flowering crepe myrtle trees added pops of vibrant pink blossoms. The effect created a natural arbor, and shade from the bright Florida sun. If customers were comfortable, they tended to stay longer and buy more baked goods.

"She'll need a building permit and possibly a parking permit," he said.

"Good point. I'll check into it."

"Does her business have a name?"

"Kathleen's Teahouse, and the sign is being designed as we speak. She's keeping true to the logo of the old diner. And she's planning to be open ten hours a day and serve break-fast, light lunches, and dinner, as well as tea and baked goods."

"She should add five hours to the beginning and end of

her shift for preparation and clean-up," he said. "Tell her to hire a lot of help, which is forever challenging. Bakery employees find the labor exhausting—both mentally and physically."

"Because of those hot ovens, and they're on their feet so much," Candee commiserated. "Anyway, it's my long-winded way of asking you to come to Roses and give her a hand."

He delayed his response, preparing to launch into a thousand reasons why he couldn't leave his bakeries at such a chaotic time.

"Rob," Candee said, "I know how busy you are."

"You read my mind."

"And I wouldn't phone you if she wasn't in such a bind. The woman is beyond desperate and the place is bleeding money."

Frowning, he strode to the counter and took a sip of the liqueur directly from the bottle. There were plenty of other bottles in the storage room, he rationalized.

"She can email me. No charge for free advice," he said.

Silence on the other end of the phone. Oops. Maybe he'd sounded a little too harsh. A second glance at his watch revealed half past noon. The bakery would be overflowing with people.

He pondered. He hadn't been able to attend the opening of Keiran's pub. However, if he booked a quick trip to Roses, he could be back in Miami by Tuesday.

His bakeries were all closed on Sunday. He'd made the decision since going back to church. It was a religious choice, and a way to honor God.

"You can stay with me and Teddy," Candee pressed. "It will give you an opportunity to see Joseph, the beagles, and Joseph's horse."

The trip made perfect sense. He'd visit with everyone, plus extend his expertise to the Irishwoman. Furthermore,

Roses was absolutely delightful in its slow-paced, countrified way. It would be good to get out of Miami's rat race for three days. Lately, he'd felt exhausted both emotionally and physically.

"Maybe you're right," he murmured.

"Fabulous," Candee said. "You'll love Kathleen. She's all Irish wit and charm. Trust me, you'll want to listen to her brogue all day."

For some reason, Rob felt a little toss of excitement.

Why?

This trip was about a hurried getaway, not meeting an Irishwoman with milky-white skin who brewed perfect cups of tea. She couldn't possibly deal with all that owning a bakery, teahouse, and full-fledged restaurant entailed, so he'd set her straight.

If she was the determined type, she'd remain in Roses, although it was more likely she'd high-tail it back to Ireland before the end of March.

"So when did you say you were arriving?" Candee asked.

"Can Teddy pick me up at the Asheville airport?"

"Absolutely."

Rob took another swig of liqueur. "I'll fly out early Sunday morning, because Saturday is a high-volume day. I'll attend church services on Saturday evening here in Miami."

"Hurray," Candee said with a joyous laugh. "We'll do the same. See you soon."

He started to say more, then stopped, bidding goodbye and clicking off the phone.

How had he been talked into something so quickly?

Truth be told, he was intrigued. This Irishwoman displayed grit by leaving everything behind and coming to America. He guessed she was probably homesick.

He braced a hand on the window sill and stared at the roll-in oven, where smoke was emerging.

"Mr. Rob, do you think the croissants are finished baking?" David, the newbie, asked.

"Did you set the timer?"

"No." David rummaged through a stack of boxes near the oven. "Where is it?

"Do you smell smoke?"

"A little."

"I'd say the entire batch is burned." Rob handed the newbie two oven mitts and snapped a string of instructions. The young man paled and promptly complied, apologizing because it was all his fault.

Rob agreed.

Mitts at the ready, David opened the oven door to a large quantity of burned croissants. He cursed, then swung around. "Are you going to fire me on my first day, Mr. Rob?"

"For cursing?"

"Because … because the croissants are burned."

"I'll give you another chance because I like you."

With that, Rob pushed open the adjoining door to his bustling bakery. Fortunately, no one realized that under his gruff exterior, he was really a marshmallow.

The following Sunday, Rob stepped off the plane at the modern Asheville airport. He and Teddy exchanged greetings with a clap on the back.

Now that he'd arrived, Rob checked his phone for messages. Although his bakeries weren't open, he oversaw a skeleton crew as they prepared products and ingredients for Monday.

Freeze the stock we selected before you punch out, Rob texted his associate manager.

Roger, his manager replied.

Roger? Really? Who said that? Wasn't the term used for radio communication?

Teddy chuckled, eyeing Rob's exasperated sigh. "I don't miss those days."

"Of slaving over a hot oven? I wish I could say neither do I, but I'm still baking after all these years. Sometimes I wonder if I should sell everything and move to Hawaii."

"Or the Carolinas," Teddy suggested.

"You're always trying to convince me to relocate here."

"I'm simply fulfilling my role as your best friend, and

friends like to be near each other. For camaraderie. And support."

The men had been chums for years. A decade earlier, they'd met at a men's cooking class. Rob had discovered he loved baking and pursued a culinary arts degree. Upon graduation, he'd opened a prosperous bakery chain. Teddy decided he didn't want to be in charge of all that dough (he'd quoted the pun from Julia Child), and, with Rob's capital, became a real estate professional and flipped homes.

After Rob retrieved his luggage, he and Teddy settled into Teddy's pickup truck. Morning sun lightened the sky, and the beauty of North Carolina—from the majestic waterfalls to an old-fashioned swimming hole—brought a sense of relaxation.

"Beautiful state, isn't it? Candee and I love it here," Teddy said.

"Yeah. I may rent a car for an afternoon trip tomorrow."

"You won't be able to explore everything in a few hours, so file it under your list of reasons to move here."

"I don't have a list of reasons," Rob said.

"You should." A grin flashed across Teddy's features. "The other day, Candee read a travel brochure advertising outdoor dining by a pool of water in Asheville. She also cited many art galleries tucked away in little towns within an hour's car ride of Roses."

"Sightseeing it is, then."

"I'd go with you, but I'm tied up with renovating the teahouse, plus helping Candee with her daycare facility. And, needless to say, seeing to Joseph. I assume you'll go by yourself?" Teddy asked.

"Who else?" Rob laughed gruffly. "I can't remember when I last toured anywhere with a companion." He drew down the mirrored sun visor for a quick glance at his reflection, keenly studying the lines of fatigue around his mouth. He was closing in on fifty years old, and the strained creases were showing.

"Frankly, you seem like you need an extended vacation, my friend."

"Uh-huh. Thanks for the advice." Rob flipped up the visor, then smoothed the wrinkles on his Rob's Marvelous Muffins T-shirt. He'd worn the shirt under a navy sport jacket paired with khaki pants. A white cotton square handkerchief showed from his breast jacket pocket.

"I thought my age looked good on me, although I don't see as well as I used to." He chuckled. "Get it?"

Teddy grinned. "I can always count on you for the one-liners. I'm glad you're here. I wish you looked more rested."

Dismissing his fatigue with a wave, Rob replied to a sequence of text messages.

Teddy flicked on the blinker and merged onto the road leading to Roses. "Mind if I ask you a question?"

"Not at all," Rob replied, still absorbed in his text messaging. "I'm perfectly willing to listen. I won't guarantee an answer, though."

"When have you ever actually relaxed?"

Not in forever. Rob didn't share that fact with Teddy, as he'd probably encourage Rob to extend his stay. Although he might be tempted, his bakeries could never operate without him.

"It's high time you enjoyed life," Teddy said. "Worrying about every minute decision will only magnify your problems."

Rob paused, reflecting how best to answer. He switched on the radio to the Bee Gees singing "How Deep Is Your Love".

"Since when have you become so philosophical?" Rob asked.

"A wonderful woman changes a man." Lightly, Teddy

tapped the beat of the song on the steering wheel. "Makes him stop and think about what's truly important."

A ping on his cell-phone drew Rob's attention. His manager asked whether to close an hour later in order to customize a cake for a last-minute wedding.

If you need extra time to get the job done, then sure, Rob texted.

You'll be paying the staff overtime, the manager reminded.

What else is new? With that, Rob snapped his phone shut and jammed it into his pocket. He felt his blood pressure rising. A visit with his physician had confirmed that blood pressure medication would soon be a part of Rob's future. For the time being, he'd refused the brigade of medicines his doctor was all too willing to prescribe.

"That nice-looking Irishwoman might make the ideal companion on your sightseeing excursion," Teddy said. "She hasn't explored the area yet, either."

"Not interested. You and Keiran married the last two good women on the planet."

"There's more than two good women in the world, Rob. And a third is waiting for you to sweep her off her feet."

"Based on the number of my failed dates, a successful match for me is probably somewhere on a remote island in the Pacific. And because I'm not vacationing in the Pacific islands anytime soon, I'd say my dating days are over."

"I don't believe that for a minute." Teddy's expression puckered into a pensive frown, and Rob was reminded of Teddy's older brother, Christian, who had died in a horrific car accident. Teddy had stepped in and gained legal custody of his young nephew, Joseph.

Like his brother, Teddy was dark-eyed and tall, and Rob knew Teddy mourned the loss of his brother every day. Teddy and Candee were exemplary parents, raising a child who had been left frail and devastated after the accident.

Fortunately, hours of physical therapy and boundless love had enabled the boy to rebound triumphantly.

"No wonder we never got along," Rob teased. "You're an eternal optimist."

They flew across a bridge, and crushed gravel crackled beneath the truck's tires.

"You'll find your special woman when you least expect it," Teddy said.

Really? Who? He was older now, bald, twenty pounds overweight, and set in his ways. Anyway, bachelor life suited him.

He shifted in his seat. All those long nights in his deluxe Florida condo with a sweeping view of Miami beach had passed in solitude. He filled the void with work, because loneliness only crept up when he had time to think.

He dragged his contemplations away from self-absorption, preferring to stare out the window at the picturesque landscape with a magnificent Blue Ridge mountain backdrop. They traveled past an ancient church, fields of wildflowers, and a garden of violet irises beginning to bloom.

"Candee is preparing a special brunch for us," Teddy said. "Or rather, Keiran is cooking. Desiree hasn't purchased a dining room set yet, so everyone is assembling at my house."

Keiran had met Desiree when he'd been hired to fix up Desiree's Victorian home. They'd married a few months afterward and lived a few doors down from Candee and Teddy.

"Sounds perfect," Rob said. "I'm always up for a delicious meal."

"Be prepared for pandemonium. Our beagle, Kisses, is full grown. Plus, Candee gifted Keiran and Desiree a pup, and the dog goes everywhere with them."

"The more commotion, the better." Rob slanted his head

back, viewing a row of shuttered buildings. "What town are we in?"

"We're going through Hollan Farms. It's a few towns over from Roses."

"Interesting little place." Rob noted mediocre shops and an enormous hotel that dominated the main street. "Someone should give it some TLC. Does anyone live here?"

"At last count there were a few inhabitants. A major factory moved out a while ago, leaving a proverbial ghost town. I heard the entire town is for sale, and the asking price is several million dollars."

Not bad for a place with lots of potential, Rob mused. He was, after all, a businessperson.

A businessperson who could barely handle a half-dozen bakeries in Miami, let alone an entire town.

As they passed through, Teddy indicated the rotted wood on a boarded-up ice cream parlor, then focused a conspiratorial smile on Rob. "Don't even speculate about buying this town to renovate. You have enough on your hands, and should be slowing down to enjoy your wealth."

Rob chuckled. His friend was a mind-reader and knew him like the back of his hand.

"I have absolutely no intention of buying anything," Rob defended brusquely. When skeptical amusement crossed Teddy's face, Rob immediately changed the subject. "How is Keiran's pub?"

"The first few weeks were hectic. At present he's settled in and doing what he loves. Desiree took an extended leave from her law firm to hostess at the pub."

As they entered Roses, Teddy stopped at a crossroads and rounded toward Thompson Lane. The street was lined with trees, large older homes, and plenty of acreage. Window boxes overflowed with velvety purple pansies, ferns, and tulip bulbs, staying true to the traditional origins of the town. Teddy pointed out Keiran and Desiree's Victorian as they drove by.

"Ready to meet Kathleen after brunch?" Teddy eased his truck around the circular driveway and parked in front of his three-story house with its octagonal tower and multi-gabled roof. "Candee has immersed herself in Kathleen's business and vows to make it as popular as Keiran's pub. Too bad the place isn't open yet. Imagine when it is."

"All this Irish charm in one pint-size town," Rob mused. "Sure, I planned on meeting her."

"Excellent." Teddy grinned. "Because she's expecting you."

* * *

THAT AFTERNOON, Kathleen stood on her front stoop and watched a well-dressed bald man wearing a navy sport jacket and khaki pants emerge from Teddy's truck.

Her heart thudded with nervousness. The past few days, endless work had muddled the hours. Today she'd been awake before dawn, baking, attending church, and revising her business plan. She made a mental note to ask Candee if there were any local social media sites where she could advertise.

She'd heard so many stories about the legendary Rob and his marvelous muffins that anticipating his arrival had become an exercise in self-discipline. She flattened the collar of her checkered blouse, critically reviewing her navy-print slacks and sensible leather flats. The mint-green cardigan over her shoulders warded off the midafternoon chill.

She'd half-expected Rob to wear a chef jacket and black trousers, while brandishing a wooden mixing spoon. However, the man confidently striding toward her was solid and broad-shouldered, a warm smile crinkling his face and accentuating his electric-blue eyes. Instead of a wooden spoon, he carried a reflective silver wine bag.

"So you're the lovely Irish rose." He came to the doorstep, stopped within a foot of her, and beamed.

"And you're the famous Rob, who owns bakeries all over Florida."

"Only a half dozen, and they're all located in the Miami area." He grinned. "It saves me from driving all across the state."

"Well, I'll leave you two to get acquainted," Teddy called from his truck. "Rob, when you want a lift back to my place, text me."

"Thanks. Probably in a couple hours." Rob's wave to Teddy was quick before he veered to her. "However, I confess I'm at an impasse."

"A confession already? We just met."

"And an impasse."

She lifted an eyebrow. "Impasse?

"Yes, because I may never want to leave." He extended his hand. "I'm Rob."

"I gathered. Why are you staring at me, Rob?"

"Because you're beautiful, and not at all who I expected."

Near the curb, she heard the purring of Teddy's truck engine.

"Who did you expect?" she asked.

"Not someone who makes me flustered because she's so gorgeous. I get tongue-tied around women like you."

"What?"

"Tongue-tied. At a loss for words."

"For a tongue-tied guy, you're speaking quite well, although I appreciate the compliment." She forced herself to stop and think. "*Was* that a compliment?"

"Absolutely. You remind me of Maureen O'Hara from *Miracle on 34th Street*."

"I love that film. Maureen was originally from Dublin and only twenty-seven years old when she played the role," Kathleen said.

She felt Teddy's gaze on them for another moment before the engine roared and he pulled away from the curb.

"I'm Kathleen, by the way." She accepted Rob's hand. Large and firm, he had the hands of a construction worker with calluses along the base of his fingers. From hours using a rolling pin, she surmised, because she had the same.

"The beautiful Kathleen." He gave a smile, and her heart skipped a beat.

She regarded him, trying to gauge if his words were sincere. She might have given a flippant response, the cool disinterest she employed whenever she suspected men were coming on to her. But wait. Was he—

No, certainly not. Aside from the age difference, he was accomplished and well-educated. She was a country girl who'd grown up in County Galway before moving to Dublin.

He let go of her hand, tugged a bottle out of the bag, and offered it to her. "This is for you. Do you drink Irish liqueur?"

"Tea. I drink tea." She examined the label. "Imported from Ireland?"

"Yes, although this bottle is from Miami. Consider it a housewarming gift. It's a little reminder of your country in case you were homesick."

How did he know she was homesick? A ripple of sadness brought a sting of tears to her eyes that she quickly blinked away.

His gaze fastened on her. "I use the liqueur as an ingredient for a cupcake glaze."

"Thanks."

"I like it," he said.

"Liqueur? Oh, I'm sure." She stuck the bottle in the bag

and set it on the stoop. "Most Irish men love a drink or two." *Or three or four.*

"On special occasions?" Rob asked.

"On any occasion. Many were on the lash."

"Meaning?"

"Irish slang for going out drinking." Ruefully, she laughed. "I've learned to stick with tea, though."

"In that case, so will I." That beam again, flashing charisma, and firing an attraction inside her that took her utterly by surprise.

"And I'll teach you how to create the best buttery glaze on the East Coast," he said.

When, exactly? Candee had told Kathleen that Rob was only in town until Tuesday. He was a wealthy, successful man, setting aside a few days from his busy calendar. Most likely he was overconfident, a tad entitled, and considered his time more valuable than anyone else's.

"Like you, I'm also pressed for any spare hour these days," she said.

"Oh. Sure." He kept his beam. "I understand."

The appeal of his handsome face caused her pulse to leap, and an awkward heartbeat went by. He waited, apparently, for her to elaborate about the host of things she had yet to do.

She didn't respond, just stared at him as if she'd never seen a man before. She should invite him up to her apartment for tea. However, while she was usually neat as a pin, the living room and bedroom were in dusty disarray and boxes were everywhere.

"However, we have a dilemma," he continued.

So do I, she thought. Aloud, she asked, "Which is?"

"How will I prove who is the better baker if we don't bake together?"

There it was. A not-so-silent gauntlet thrown down between two professional chefs.

Or did he propose more than a bake-off contest?

"We're together now," she pointed out.

"We're not baking. I can show you my cupcake recipe, the one crying out for my celebrated buttery glaze. I presume you store flour and sugar in your apartment's pantry?"

"Of course. I raced to the corner grocer as soon as I arrived in Roses."

"Good." He brought levity to the moment with another smile. "I've heard your Irish brown bread is fabulous."

Aye, they could bake, but she preferred to chat. Here, on her front porch, sitting on the two white wicker rocking chairs Candee had restored, enjoying a cheery afternoon.

Debating, she gazed at the park across the way. February in the South was being pushed to an early spring, and the flower bushes near her entryway displayed the first pink buds. Candee had assured Kathleen that a few more warm days and all the trees would be in bloom.

"Actually, I'm shattered," she said.

His thick eyebrows drew together. They were so close, she saw the threads of gray weaving between the dark hair.

"Exhausted," she explained. "More Irish slang. How about we just chat?"

"I'm up for that." He glanced at his watch, a high-priced brand she instantly recognized. "We can exchange classified information."

"This isn't Scotland Yard," she said. "And my commercial ovens haven't been installed yet, so I've been using the oven in my apartment to bake my breads."

"Will you show me around?"

She felt her cheeks heat. Her apartment? The setting was so intimate.

Aye, that was what he'd asked, and what she'd alluded to. The teahouse seemed the better choice, although kitchen equipment wouldn't begin arriving until Monday. And the large dough mixer was on back order. However, the vendor had assured it would arrive in plenty of time for her grand opening.

She shifted. She was fairly good at thinking on her feet and making quick decisions, but since Rob had arrived, the edges of the afternoon had blurred. Perhaps it was because she enjoyed being with him and hoped to impress him. Woefully, her place was the furthest one got from being impressive.

And he thought *he* was tongue-tied?

She rubbed her hands on her slacks, knowing he stared at her.

"Alright, then. Follow me upstairs," she said. "Before you arrived, I pulled loaves of my Irish breads and batches of scones out of the oven. I'd welcome your truthful opinion on the texture."

Rob seemed the kind of fella a woman could talk to. Despite his affluence, he seemed approachable. Who else wore a T-shirt advertising his company beneath a sport jacket?

She noticed there was no wedding band on the fourth finger of his left hand. Candee had offhandedly remarked he had never married. So he was alone in life, reminding Kathleen of herself.

"Lead the way, my beautiful Kathleen." He stepped nearer. "Have you ever sung, 'I'll Take You Home Again, Kathleen'? It's an Irish ballad."

"The song isn't Irish, Rob." She picked up the gift bag and ushered him around the building. "It has German-American origins."

"I memorized all the words. I'll sing it to you if you'd like."

Before she could answer, he belted out the melody in a

smooth tenor voice, slightly out of tune, warbling lyrics about a wild ocean and a bonnie bride.

She laughed out loud, and it felt good to laugh with a friend, with a man.

Somehow, as they ascended the stairs, she knew she'd always remember this afternoon. The soft, promising breeze on her cheeks, the glint of a dipping sun changing her Carolina world to a silky, golden glow.

And the appealing grin on Rob's features that engaged his entire face. Women could be completely charmed by a man whose emotions were so utterly apparent. He literally wore his sentiments on his sleeve, much like the Irish.

They made their way to the top of the stairs, and he took her free hand as if it were the most natural thing in the world. When they reached the landing, he belted out the second verse, *I'll take you to your home again, Kathleen.*

She joined him, and they sang in unison.

CHAPTER 4

When they reached her apartment, they walked directly into her narrow, cozy kitchen as the screen door banged shut behind them. The floorboards creaked as she hung his jacket on a coat rack in the foyer.

The scent of yeast and sugar flavored the air, and Rob sniffed appreciatively. She invited him to sit at a wooden breakfast nook, consisting of corner unit benches and a table polished in a natural white finish and trimmed in yellow.

"Bread lies at the heart of Irish baking," Kathleen said. Efficiently, she sliced Irish soda bread and went to work on a loaf of brown bread. "Before we eat, let's pray a simple thanks to God." She bowed her head, and he did the same. She whispered a blessing, then offered him a portion of each bread.

The brown bread's crust was thick, the texture dense. The soda bread sprinkled with caraway seed tasted like a biscuit. Although hard on the outside, the inside was moist and delectable.

"Wonderful. I like them both." He helped himself to

another two slices and washed them down with a bottle of water she'd pulled from the fridge.

"The trade secret is cooked raisins." She slid onto the bench across from him. "Save and freeze any leftover raisin water for a later batch. It will produce a sweeter flavor in the bread."

"I like trade secrets." *And he liked her.*

"Brown bread is a well-known Irish staple, so what I'm telling you isn't classified information. This bread is a treasured family recipe from my auntie Peggy."

Rob chewed and bobbed his head, encouraging her to continue.

"Auntie lived twenty days shy of her one hundredth birthday." Kathleen dashed tears from her eyes. "She was slim, walked everywhere all her life, and was witty and fun to be around."

"Do you miss her?" he asked quietly.

"Aye. She used to say that without a slab of brown bread every morning, no Irish kitchen is complete. In fact, you can't go into any pub or bakery without brown bread being on the menu."

"I've never visited Ireland." *Perhaps they could go together.*

"You'd love it." Wistfully, she sighed, although she didn't extend an invitation. "After drinking pints in a pub, this bread has saved my stomach at midnight on many occasions. Topped with a sliver of sharp cheddar cheese and heated in the broiler, it's delicious and not too heavy."

He carved another good-sized portion of bread for himself, slathered it with butter, and savored. Awe-inspiring. There were no other words for this woman's baked goods.

"I don't drink, and I'm old enough to admit I've learned a lot through the years," she said. "Giving up alcohol and nights at the pub were two of them. I've witnessed too much heartache. It's been estimated that at least half of all Irish drinkers are problem drinkers."

"Why such a large number?"

"The usual reasons." She looked away. "Affordability, ready availability, and heavy marketing."

"Are you referring to anyone in particular?" Gently cupping her chin in his hand, he directed her to face him.

"My employer, Danny Brady." She eased from Rob's grip, stood and surveyed a decorative ceramic platter in a glass cupboard before reaching for it. "Although not him, because he doesn't drink. His wife, Clara, has a brother who struggles with alcoholism." Kathleen's smoky eyes were remarkably expressive, filled with compassion. "Seamus was a dishwasher for a brief while at The Ground Café. He's been in and out of treatment programs since."

"How is he these days?"

She shrugged casually, a bit too casually considering her shoulders tightened. "Last I heard, he's back in treatment. Success rates for rehab are misleading and aren't as high as people expect."

"If you ever fancy a talk about Ireland, about anything, really, I'm a good listener," Rob said quietly.

"Fancy?" She reached beneath the end bench to a hidden storage unit and retrieved two sage-green place mats. "Is that an American term?"

"I'm trying out your Irish slang."

"*Fancy* is British English." She set the place mats on the table. "And I'll keep your offer in mind."

"Good." He broke the somber mood by gesturing to the counter overflowing with scones. Soon, he'd sampled her blueberry and plain scones baked to a golden-brown, proclaiming them exquisite. As Kathleen directed, he smeared a generous amount of butter and homemade strawberry jam on each.

He grinned. He liked taking directions from her.

Lulled by her lyrical Irish brogue, he listened to her jokes about Ireland's rainy weather and ran his hand down the bench's smooth pine finish. She had a discerning eye for design—it showed in her comfy, appealing kitchen. A leafy English ivy plant hung by the window, a cobalt-blue toaster splashed color on the counter, and a hand-woven rug in a creamy blue weave complemented the tile floor with texture.

"I like your sense of style," he said. "You must enjoy interior decorating."

"Hardly. I find decorating one challenge I prefer to leave to professionals." A smile bloomed on her face. "Tea? I'll put the kettle on."

"Sure."

"You're supposed to say *no, thanks.*"

"I am? Why?"

"Because that's what is expected in an Irish home. No worries. We'll try again." Squarely, she faced him. "Tea?"

"No, thanks."

"Brilliant." She grinned, waited a beat. "Tea?"

"What's the correct answer? Yes?"

She pressed her lips needle thin.

"Aye?"

"Have you suddenly become Irish?" she asked.

"No?"

"Third time's a charm. Let's try once more." She smiled. "Tea?"

"Yes. That would be lovely." He folded his hands on his lap and watched her uncertainly.

"Very good."

"Whew." Dramatically, he wiped his brow. "I feel like I almost failed an algebra exam. Should I have started with a *cheerio?*"

"*Cheerio* is another British term and means farewell. Are you leaving?"

"I just arrived." His gaze flicked to the platter of brown bread and he grabbed another slice. "I sought the magic word, and the word *cheerio* always comes to mind when I think of you Brits."

With a heavy sigh, she bent to pick a crumb from the floor. "I'm from Dublin, which is part of the Republic of Ireland. We're our own country and not part of the UK. Shall I enlighten you on the differences between Northern Ireland and the Republic of Ireland?"

He steepled his fingers. "Certainly. I'm quite interested."

"That's a refreshing change. In the States, this topic doesn't often come up."

"I told you I'm an excellent listener." *Good. Excellent. Same difference.*

She seemed to digest his words before she spoke. "Let's get back to our tea discussion, shall we? In Ireland, it's customary to answer *no thanks* twice when offered tea. It's impolite to say *yes* until the third ask." She took a breath. "Once more for practice. Ready?"

He gave a thumbs-up, considered including the word *aye,* but didn't.

"Tea?" she asked.

He held up one finger, then two, mouthing the numbers. "I assume I'm safe because this is at least the third try."

"It's actually the first because we were trying again," she said. "I'll let it pass, though."

"Then I'd love a cup of tea, thank you."

"Cuppa."

"Cup of."

She laughed. "Soon you'll get the hang of it. Are you ready for more questions?"

"Sure."

"Do you prefer milk and sugar? Or a squeeze of lemon?"

"My choice is black tea with lots of sugar." His mouth twitched in amusement as she approved. "I see you Irish take your tea quite seriously," he added.

"Aye, which is why I'd like to teach Americans how to serve a proper tea." She put water in a kettle and placed it on the stove. While waiting for the water to boil, she retrieved two china cups, saucers, and a matching creamer and sugar bowl embellished with blue flowers. She poured milk into the creamer, added lumps of sugar to the open jar, and arranged china and linen napkins on the table.

He considered telling her that if she spent that long preparing each customer's cup of tea, she'd never earn a profit. Instead, he wisely opted for keeping silent as she poured the boiling water into the teapot and their two teacups.

"This warms the pot and our cups," she explained. She waited a minute before discarding the water from the pot and cups into the sink. Then she added two tea bags into the teapot and poured in boiling water.

While he encouraged her to talk about her vision for the teahouse, they filled their plates with more bread. She kept an eye on her wristwatch in between nibbles. After three minutes, she removed the tea bags to an extra plate, stirred the tea, and glided onto the bench.

"First draw?" she asked, preparing to pour.

"I prefer a dark tea."

"Me too." Quickly, she added the tea bags back to the pot for another minute. "A favorite Irish expression is, *strong enough to trot a mouse in* for dark tea."

"Clever. I suggest you not use that expression around your customers, though."

"Mice in the kitchen. The idea would definitely keep patrons away." Her face lightened with wry laughter. "Did you realize the Irish aren't the world's biggest consumer of tea?"

"Who is? England?"

She shook her head. "Turkey, then Ireland, then the UK."

For the next few minutes, he considered voicing his views on buying and selling, and keeping an eye on profit margin. Because he was a competent entrepreneur, he assumed his advice would be welcomed with enthusiasm.

Painstakingly, she poured the tea.

"Thank you." He relished the rich, deep flavor and smiled. They sat silently for a few minutes, savoring their tea.

"If I opened a teahouse," he said, "I'd insert those attention-grabbing tidbits you shared about tea preparation on the menu. Items of interest will enhance your customers' experience and provide them with something to talk about beyond your delectable desserts."

"Maybe." She stared straight ahead while he sipped. Finally, she said, "I'm glad you like tea."

He hadn't said if he liked tea. In fact, he preferred coffee, even over this exquisite brew. But tea was apparently the Irish way, and he sat back on the wooden bench and warmed his fingers around the fragile china cup. Inhaling the fragrant steam, he plated another sliver of brown bread. "Candee was dead-on. Your baked goods are outstanding. And your scones—"

"Thanks. Coming from you, I'm flattered."

"My cupcakes and muffins aren't anywhere near as exciting as your Irish brown bread." He downed the rest of his tea. "I'm thinking about selling fancier pastries in my bakeries. Every one of them needs a face-lift, and foods not normally experienced in standard American shops might benefit sales. Currently, my blueberry muffins are customer favorites. Mind if I pick your brain for innovative European recipes?"

"Certainly. I'm delighted to share what I know." She placed her teacup on her saucer with a clink. "However, if you're turning a grand profit, which I assume you are judging from what Candee has said, why change anything? My ideas aren't any better than yours."

His instinct was to volley her comment back to her while reciting the adage *two heads are better than one*, or some such sage proverb.

However, that wasn't entirely true. The truth was, he wanted to spend time with her, because he could hardly tear his gaze away from her striking face, her delicate smile. She looked utterly gorgeous, her porcelain complexion flushed from a veil of steamy tea.

Mentally, he went over his flight details, suddenly loathe to leave Roses on Tuesday morning. Maybe he'd stay a few extra days, go sightseeing with her, dine with her at the farm-to-table restaurant Candee and Teddy raved about.

"Would you like to see Asheville with me tomorrow afternoon?" he blurted.

"I can't spare the time, although I'm sure Asheville is splendid." Kathleen busied herself with pouring another round of tea. "After March seventeenth, well, perhaps then. Although you don't live here so timing might be difficult."

"I come to Roses often."

"Do you?"

He'd come more now, even if it meant leaving his precious bakeries in the hands of his assistant managers. And to his amazement, he was okay with that.

"By plane, Miami to Asheville is less than a three-hour flight," he said.

"Rob—"

He couldn't gauge her expression beyond that one sharp word. Was she not interested? Preoccupied?

"I'm just saying," he said. "We can exchange phone

numbers, alright? In case you need to text me about anything."

"Sure." She gave him her cell-phone number.

He sent her a quick text. *Hi. I'm Rob. 1-800-IRELAND.*

Her smile expanded as she scanned his message. "What does that mean?"

"It means you can call me toll free anytime you need my help and never incur a charge."

She grinned. "I'll remember that. In the meantime—" her voice quieted, seeming to soften her refusal—"I want to stand out with an exceptional product so people will flock to my place. What do you judge to be the best …"?

So she sought his opinion after all, although she'd adeptly sidestepped any personal conversation. When they focused on shop talk, her eyes lit with enthusiasm.

And while they faced each other in her inviting kitchen, he realized something extraordinary. His heart, cold for so long, was thawing. He loved a woman with enthusiasm, and her obvious excitement about her business ignited her smile. He saw the evidence in her dark, gleaming eyes and the way she sat straighter, gesturing with her hands. Her grin widened, displaying white, even teeth. She was already striking. When she elaborated on her innovative concepts, she was altogether alluring.

In turn, she fanned a spark in him he thought had been extinguished long ago.

"… vegan baked goods using organic products," she was saying. "What do you think, Rob?"

What did he think about what? He'd been too preoccupied with gazing at her.

"Rob, were you listening?"

"Of course."

"What did I say?"

"You were mentioning using ground flax meal in your …scones."

"Aye, that was ten minutes ago."

"People are opting for a wider variety of choices, so consider customers' lifestyle choices when figuring out your menu." He searched his mind for topics he'd discussed with his managers through the years, and added, "Currently, I'm serving carbohydrates, fats, sugar, and caffeine in my shops, so obviously my menus are on the fattening side."

"It's all a balancing act, isn't it?" she asked.

"Life?"

"I was referring to food, but aye, I suppose life too." Pensively, she regarded him, then fished through a kitchen drawer and came back with two sheets of paper and pencils. "How about we combine taste with nutrition?"

We.

"Don't forget your bottom line," he said. "Otherwise, you'll be out of business within six months."

She seemed not to have heard him, intent on her list-making, mouthing the words as she penned them. "Crave-ability," she wrote with a flourish, then pursed her lips. "Is that a word?"

"It is now. And it's a good one."

"Are you interested in going over my business plan with me step by step?" she asked.

"Can I ask you a question first?"

"Aye."

"Have you begun interviewing applicants?"

"No. I'm running an ad in the local paper soon. If I get stuck, Sean, a coworker in Ireland, has offered to assist me."

"How generous," Rob said sardonically.

"He's a dependable manager, and versed in the restaurant business."

"So he's willing to quit his job in Ireland to fly here to help you?"

"Aye."

"There's plenty of suitable workers here in the US." Rob lifted his pencil off the paper. "Should I start listing my ideas?"

"Aye. Fill up the whole sheet."

A thought struck him. Actually two thoughts.

Without admitting it, she'd concurred that two brains were, in fact, better than one. And any comparing of recipes wouldn't be done that evening. He'd already established that anything baked in her oven came out superb.

He tapped his pencil while she wrote an extensive list in a scholarly penmanship he hadn't seen in ages. Nowadays, everyone typed on their computers.

Soon, her list crammed both sides of the paper.

She nibbled the end of her pencil. "This is too much," she murmured. "I'll never complete all these tasks."

"Have you considered prioritizing?" He skimmed the tasks and numbered them according to importance. "And let's pare down this list. You can do that, right?"

"Aye." She consented, humming a familiar Irish folk song, "Oh Danny Boy", under her breath, as she crossed out a word and added alternates.

Hours later, when he gazed through her sheer white kitchen curtains, a full, round moon sailed high in the sky. He glanced at his wristwatch in amazement. The hours spent with her had been nothing short of delightful.

She was a stunningly attractive woman. A woman who touched something powerful and unfamiliar inside him.

Lifting his cell-phone from his pocket, he texted Teddy.

Pick me up at ten, Rob typed.

Did your two hours change to six? came Teddy's reply. *Glad U R enjoying your evening. We were wondering what happened.*

Worried about me?

Always.

I'm fine, Rob typed.

More than fine.

Across the table, Kathleen smiled at him, and Rob's heart did a little meltdown.

Because she's remarkable.

Rob finished his message to Teddy and clicked send.

CHAPTER 5

Although he tried, Rob couldn't convince Kathleen to play hooky and accompany him to Asheville. She refused, and with good reason considering her opening date of March 17. Instead of sightseeing on his own, he shelved the idea until his next visit, assuring her that he was more than happy to assist her.

While she spent Monday morning securing a line of credit and visiting warehouses, Rob followed breakfasting with Candee and Teddy to lunching at O'Malley's pub, where he assumed head waiter relief for a harried Desiree and Keiran. Pleased the pub appeared busy and profitable, Rob walked the short distance to the teahouse.

Although spring hadn't technically arrived on the calendar, pale lavender crocuses burst through the soil in backyard gardens, and a lazy breeze swept across the grass. Rob plunged his hands into the pockets of his gray windbreaker, delighting in the fresh air against his face. Roses' weather made him feel more animated than he'd felt in ages. February and March were transitional months in Miami, heralding a brief spring before the intense summer heat arrived.

Admittedly, the bounce in his step had more to do with a certain Irishwoman than the temperate weather, his comfortable jeans, or tennis shoes.

As he strolled at a brisk pace, Rob mulled Kathleen's comment from the previous evening.

It's all a balancing act, isn't it?

Yes, he thought. You're so wise. For years, he'd sought to appease thousands of patrons—tweaking recipes, solving every complaint, adhering to the adage "the customer is always right". He'd been so focused on developing his business, he'd pushed aside any notion of personal happiness.

Love? Nope, not even a blip on his radar screen.

Armed with painful past experiences, he struggled to recall why love was so important—why poets wrote sonnets, why it made the world go round.

Because love was everything. Because love mattered above all else.

"Ridiculous notion," he whispered. Besides, he was too old for love. And Kathleen … well, when he calculated their age difference, he came up with fifteen years.

Had it always been so clear, so straightforward, these unspoken rules for dating and romance? Certainly, problematic circumstances occurred, although Candee encouraged his interest in Kathleen. She'd sensed it immediately, sniffed it out like one of her beloved beagles. In fact, he and Candee had discussed Kathleen throughout breakfast while Teddy looked on with amusement.

Before Rob left, Candee suggested that Kathleen join them for an intimate evening get-together at her home.

"Don't forget to tell Kathleen dinner is at six," Candee reminded as Rob ducked out the door and settled into Teddy's pickup for a ride to town. "And, Rob, a May-December romance is just the thing when two people are so attracted to each other."

He'd given a brief nod, neither agreeing nor disagreeing, although he'd googled age-gap couples on the internet. Studies showed these couples were extremely happy despite social disapproval.

Still, he felt as if his searches let him down, as the findings had encouraged dreams he'd catalogued as unattainable. He wasn't about to fall in love with anyone, including the beautiful Kathleen. Anyone who knew him could recite his unsuccessful dating record. Regardless of his wealth and achievements, women left him flat, and it hurt more than he admitted. No woman chose a man with a retreating hairline (he was being kind to himself—the correct term was bald), and a waistline that increased with every passing year. More important, the sting of heartbreak was too steep an expense for a few weeks of happiness.

WHEN HE ROUNDED the last curve to the teahouse, Rob was out of breath from the final rise in the road. Beneath the overhang of the wide front porch, Kathleen paced impatiently, coming to a stop as if she'd sensed his arrival.

"Hi, Rob." She scratched the back of her neck, her shoulders tight. "I'm relieved you're here."

He puffed to a halt. "Anything wrong?"

"I'm waiting for a distributor to ring me about the oven delivery. I admit I'm terribly impatient. And the large dough mixer is still on back order."

"Sometimes things move slower in the South," he said.

"The same holds true for Ireland." She sighed heavily. "I've been known to snap at people if they're late. I don't want a reputation in the States for being rude. Folks in Ireland accused me of bad behavior on more than one occasion, and I was ashamed and apologized."

"You're a person who likes to get things done. I'm the same way."

Her shoulders relaxed. "Thanks for the assurance."

He caught his breath at the sight of her. That smile. Those deep-brown eyes. He knew he'd think about her every minute of his flight back to Florida. Pausing, he remarked favorably on the exterior of the building, the white glossy trim and exposed brick.

"Teddy's crew is painting the interior and exterior," she said. "He provided a generous bid I couldn't refuse. They started this morning and accomplished a lot already."

"What was his bid? Thousands of dollars?"

"He's offering the labor for free. I'm paying for materials."

"Another reason why I always liked him," Rob joked. He chased ideas across his mind. How could he top Teddy's generosity?

"Please, please come in," she said. The screen door groaned on its hinges as she guided him inside. He envisioned how the diner had been situated—the long counter and various booths were still waiting to be removed. The greasy cooktop hadn't been cleaned in years. On the walls were large black square marks where paintings had once hung.

"The place looks … good," he said. He searched for another word and couldn't find it.

She winced. "Surely, you're joking." She meandered, pointing out wet stains on the ceiling, bemoaning the former owner who had left the windows open, subsequently leading to water damage on the ceiling.

They stepped across the linoleum floor, coated in thick layers of dust.

Amidst the constant pounding of hammers, an Irish band played "When Irish Eyes Are Smiling" on a CD player.

Sounding as if the song had been recorded in a pub, the rousing chorus prompted Rob to sing along.

"You recognize this tune?" she asked.

"Doesn't everyone? Irish music is well-known around the world."

She grinned. "I'm proud to be Irish."

"And I'm proud to know you. You're a resourceful entrepreneur."

"You're a grand fella, just like Candee said."

He chuckled.

"Am I turning scarlet this very minute?" she asked. "For complimenting you?"

They stared at each other in comfortable silence. "A little," he admitted.

She burst into laughter. "Well, that's settled then. Crack on."

"Get to work?"

"Aye."

The blue vinyl seating had been torn out and sat in a heap by the back door. Gingerly, they stepped around it.

"I'm baffled about pricing the scones competitively and hope you can brainstorm with me," she said.

"I'll try, but I should warn you. As I grow older, I'm baffled more often than not."

"About scones?"

"About life in general."

She grinned. "Right, well, welcome to my life."

She had twisted her strawberry-blond hair into a semblance of a bun, securing the hairdo with pins and a shiny green ribbon. The pulled-back style accentuated her high cheekbones and dainty chin. Her wide eyes seemed too large for her refined features, and the swingy striped T-shirt and baggy sweatpants reflected her commitment to hard work, not to being a slave to the latest fashion.

Once at an empty booth, Kathleen plunged into ordering kitchen equipment, leaving little time for chitchat save for her sharp questions. He pulled off his windbreaker, rolled up his sleeves, and sat across from her.

"Tea?" she finally asked.

"Oh no. Will it be an all-day process?"

"Only a few minutes, I promise. And I'll take your answer as an *aye*." She climbed the interior steps to her apartment and came back carrying a tray chock full of stoneware—cups, a teapot filled with steaming tea, sugar and creamer, and scones from the previous evening.

Today she wasn't glamorous. Today she was simply breathtaking. Despite her flushed cheeks, her complexion was bone-white, revealing dark shadows under her eyes. Bound by the invisible strands of a strong work ethic, he'd later look back on the afternoon as the best he'd spent in decades.

In between her visiting with suppliers who stopped in and a meeting with a service rep, he inquired about her years as head assistant for Danny Brady. He even pressed for information about her dating past, to be sure no man waited for her in Ireland.

Her responses were vague, although she revealed she'd dated a couple fellas and discovered both were liars. Actually, she used the word *eejit*.

"These days, I'm embarrassed I was a stook for believing them," she said.

"*Stook* is another Irish word for idiot?"

"Aye." She wove her fingers together and glanced at the floor.

By late afternoon one of the ovens had been delivered, and the last of Teddy's crew packed his tools and left. She stepped over to a rusty sink to wash her hands for the umpteenth time, and Rob came beside her.

"I'm leaving tomorrow," he reminded. "I hope you'll join me for dinner tonight at Candee and Teddy's house."

She wrenched the faucet shut. "Is that an invite?"

"A sincere invite."

"I'm sorry." Her expression became pensive. "I wish, but I'm drowning here."

"I'm wishing too." He wished he could stay in Roses. Another day, another two days. She hadn't encouraged him, although he'd dropped several broad hints.

He decided to take matters into his own hands. He couldn't help himself.

Gently, he brought her to face him. Before she could reply, he bent his head and kissed her, a feather-light touch of his lips to hers.

She tasted of tea and sugar, her fragrance the subtle scent of lavender.

At first, she didn't move. When his hand curved around her back and the kiss deepened, she broke free.

"Obviously," she said, "we're not going to start dating."

"Why?"

"Because you live in Miami. And I live in Ire … I mean, Roses."

"That's why they invented airplanes. And cell-phones."

She moved backward. "You, of all people, should know I'm not interested, given you've heard my dating history."

"So you dated a few guys who were rogues. Not all of us are like that."

"*Rogue* is a harsh word." Her reddish-brown eyebrows lifted. "Is the term American?"

"I've never used the word before. I assumed it was British, and I was trying to impress you."

"Irish. I'm Irish." She gazed at him and her smile came slow, lighting her heart-shaped face. She was delightful—part cherub and part tigress. His heart beat in double-time.

"My dating track record wouldn't win any awards, either," he said quietly.

She studied him.

Fearful she might feel sorry for him, an old guy, a desperate bachelor, he waved a hand indifferently. "I'm only telling you so we can commiserate."

"About love and romance?"

"About commonality. We both target accomplishment above all else."

"From the sounds of it, we're both workaholics."

The quiet lasted several beats, punctuated only by the drip, drip, drip of a tarnished faucet.

"You know, I could use someone like you in my bakeries," he said. "Someone energetic and organized."

"*Your* bakeries?" Her Irish brogue thickened. "In Miami?"

"Yes. You'd like Miami. It's—" He'd been about to say it was hot and humid before stopping himself. He certainly couldn't illustrate a Miami travel brochure if those were the only adjectives coming to mind.

She plunked her fists on her hips. "As you are certainly aware, I have my own business right here in Roses."

"How could I forget?" He tugged on his windbreaker. "We've dreamt up a million ideas about it all afternoon."

"Don't you understand? I need to do this on my own."

"I understand that you won't allow me to help you."

"By giving everything up? Why would you ask me such a question?"

Because he didn't want to leave her. And he couldn't just abandon his businesses. Hers was just starting up. Perhaps she could sell the diner. Or the teahouse. Or whatever she preferred to call it.

Thankfully, he kept his opinions to himself, for when he rotated, he confronted narrowed eyes and a stormy expression.

"You'd learn a lot," he said, "and I'd promote you to a manager in my flagship Miami bakery."

"Surely, you're joking. *Flagship* was my middle name in Dublin. Been there, done that."

"You won't earn a decent salary here for months, maybe even years."

Definitely the wrong thing to say, judging by the anger flashing from her dark eyes.

"Haven't you heard a word in all the hours we've spent together? My answer is no. Absolutely not." She spun and gathered up the stoneware, placing cups and teapot on the tray.

"What about this evening's invite?" he asked. "Candee and Teddy are expecting us."

"Tell them I'll probably see them tomorrow." She picked up the tray. "You may not live in Roses, Rob, but I do."

"I can stick around a few more hours. Really. I'll text Teddy and—"

"No. We're done here." Resolutely, she shook her head. "Enjoy the flight back to Miami and thanks for your help."

CHAPTER 6

The following morning, Kathleen was awakened by persistent hammering coming from the floor below her apartment. The sun poured into her bedroom window and she checked the time, knowing she'd overslept.

After a quick shower, she gulped some tea and hastened downstairs.

The five crewmen who greeted her caused her to stop short. All the scene needed was a foreman. As the word came to mind, Teddy appeared. In a lazy southern drawl, he adeptly guided the men to sheetrock, sand and paint. As he joked with them, she could hardly believe he ran such a large construction firm, because he was so laid-back.

Of course, the same held true for Rob. His winning smile was disarming, and he'd been heralded as Miami's most successful entrepreneur.

His dry humor was comfortable, cheerful, and concise. After he'd abruptly left the day before, her reflections continued to revolve around him. Not her business plan, nor her scones, nor a proper cuppa. Just him.

"Good morning, Kathleen." Candee waved from the

doorway of the back room. "Teddy and I came to see how your place is progressing."

Kathleen sucked in her bottom lip. "Good as gold, thanks to Teddy."

"It's a virtual circus around here, but a good sign because it means things are moving quickly."

"Aye." Kathleen fidgeted with the skirt of the apron she'd thrown over her jeans and charcoal-gray sweatshirt. She knew she looked a sight and slanted a glance toward the workers. By way of an explanation, she said, "I was experimenting with a new recipe for scones last night, and went to bed later than I planned."

"You're worn out."

"Knackered is the Irish word."

"Have you eaten breakfast?"

"Black tea."

Candee waved several brown bags in the air. "You must eat a decent meal or you'll fade away. Teddy and I brought you a typical southern breakfast, but I won't take credit for the cooking. Grits and eggs, buttermilk biscuits and sausage swimming in creamy white gravy, compliments of Keiran."

"Thank you. I haven't had the chance to meet him yet."

"As you're aware, he has family in Dublin so you'll have lots to chat about." Candee flashed a sunny grin. "C'mon. Let's eat."

"I won't be able to fit into any of my clothes," Kathleen warned, while Candee led her through the back room, littered with debris. By the window facing the yard, they assembled at a three-legged table salvaged from the diner. A chest of drawers Kathleen had brought from Ireland held some of her personal belongings.

Candee brought out warm food wrapped in foil containers, complete with silverware and cloth napkins. For herself, she set carry-out coffee and sugar packets on the table.

"I assume you drink tea," Candee said as she poured three packets of sugar into her coffee and stirred.

"I've had my fill for now." Kathleen pulled a bottled water from the cooler.

She perched at the end of the booth, gestured for Candee to sit across from her, and said a blessing. Although she'd baked, she hadn't prepared a proper meal for herself since she'd arrived.

"I'm sorry you weren't able to join us last night," Candee said over the rim of her coffee cup.

Kathleen helped herself to another forkful of eggs. Candee had bragged about Keiran's cooking with obvious good reason.

"I'm hoping for a raincheck," she said. "I'd love to see your home."

"Rob missed you."

Kathleen felt her cheeks color. "We had a slight disagreement."

"He was unusually quiet at dinner."

Thinking over his offer tugged hard on Kathleen's mood, and she took a deep breath. "He assumed I'd prefer to work for him rather than run my own business."

"He said that?"

"He suggested I become a manager at his bakery in Miami. Why on earth would—?" Kathleen broke off.

"Only one reason."

"Which is?" After studying Candee's determined features, Kathleen sensed the answer. "You think this was his way of us being together?"

"Are you … together?"

"We met a few days ago. Surely you don't believe we're falling in love."

With a bemused smile, Candee said, "Why do you think people call it falling in love? Love develops quickly and feels like you're losing control. You know—falling, tripping—"

Kathleen dismissed this with a head shake. "I'm not seeking any type of courtship. Too often, I've failed in the dating department. I'm good at business. Strictly business."

She wasn't an obsessed, clingy woman who needed a man.

Nonchalantly, Candee sipped her coffee. "Every person is different. You'll know when the right man comes along."

Like Rob, for instance?

No. Not happening.

Blankly, Kathleen stared at the paneled wall behind Candee. Admittedly, thoughts of Rob consumed her. He made her feel relaxed and encouraged, telling her she could handle the most difficult situation. And he'd made it clear he was available.

She heaved a breath. At this rate, she was focusing more hours and energy on him than her teahouse. How would she ever create a tea emporium if she couldn't even manage to get menus finalized?

"Why don't men ever listen to women?" she asked.

"Because men and women are wired differently," Candee replied. "Knowing Rob, he was only trying to help. He doesn't understand why you should struggle when he can do so much for you."

"He said that?"

"Yes."

"I know he believes in me," Kathleen said. "Now I want him to stand back so I can face the challenges on my own."

"He's a man who looks at a problem and presents a solution. He's practical. Once you learn more about him, you'll understand."

Oh, but she had learned about him. Beneath their light bantering she'd discovered he'd never married and wasn't currently dating. Beneath his laughter, she felt certain he'd been hurt. On their first night, he'd revealed his home life had been filled with rejection. His parents had never responded favorably to his bids for affection and hadn't approved of his profession.

There was more. She knew there was more, although he hadn't spoken of it. Perhaps someday. At present, she wouldn't push, wouldn't pry. Besides, when would she see him again?

Beneath his commanding exterior she sensed an easily bruised sensitivity. And with that insight, she was more attracted to him. Because he was vulnerable, just like her. Sometimes the most prosperous men were the most insecure. Perhaps it was the reason why he was driven to succeed.

She stared out the window. Sunlight exposed floating dust particles. A fluorescent light bulb buzzed overhead, calling attention to the discolored ceiling.

"The thing is," Kathleen said, "Rob is fun to be around. He's well-educated and freely shares his experience."

"When Teddy needed a friend, Rob was there. He's loyal and generous." At Kathleen's inquisitive expression, Candee added, "The next time he comes to Roses, you might see his generosity in action. He's involved in several charitable organizations, including one with Keiran."

"Rob comes to Roses often?"

Candee grinned. "He will now."

Kathleen's heart swelled. When Rob had smiled at her, kissed her, she'd felt a shiny spin of hope. Perhaps here, in America …

No. She refused to dwell on a future that could never be. If she and Rob dated, she knew the ending. Men left her without a care. Every single time.

She concentrated on the last of her biscuit and white

gravy. Some people were meant to live life alone. She was one of them.

"And do you know why?" Candee asked.

"Know why what?" Kathleen glanced up, noting Candee's mischievous grin. "Why Rob will be back? Do you know something I don't?"

"Me?" Candee feigned an expression so innocent, Kathleen burst out laughing. "He talked about you the entire evening and kept looking at his phone," Candee went on. "I think he was hoping you'd reconsidered our invite."

"I couldn't." Kathleen stood and threw open the window to let in some fresh air. "Look around."

"You sent him back to Miami with your rejection." Accusation colored Candee's voice.

Kathleen bristled. "Wasn't he leaving, anyway? He owns a half-dozen bakeries."

"He wanted to stay longer. In fact, he'd been in touch with his Miami assistant manager."

Kathleen knew her cheeks colored. Aye, her refusal had been blunt, but she'd worked for others her entire life. Wasn't sacrificing all those sweat-filled years enough?

"I didn't mean to hurt his feelings, although I doubt he was affected," she said.

"Did you apologize?"

"What?" Kathleen's eyes widened. "He should apologize to me."

Candee settled her elbows on the table and rested her chin on her fists. "Have you heard from him?"

"He texted me last night." Again, Kathleen stared out the window at the post-card perfect sky and shifted on the ripped vinyl seat.

The previous afternoon, she and Rob had tossed designs around. Their conversation had been easy, and she hadn't laughed so hard in years. She'd been impressed with his quick mind, the ease in which he'd presented practical, timely solutions to her questions, writing extensive lists with his bold left-handed scrawl.

"What did he say in his texts?" Candee asked.

"He said he enjoyed his time with me. I wished him a safe flight," Kathleen said.

"Unfortunately, you're both too polite."

Kathleen took note of Candee's set jaw. "Meaning?"

"You didn't discuss what really matters."

"Dating?" Kathleen clenched her hands together. "When I'm drowning in business loan debt?"

"Love is the only thing that matters."

"Maybe in your world. Certainly not in mine. What matters is that I'm starting a brand-new venture and can't concentrate on anything else."

Candee doctored her coffee with another packet of sugar and took a long swallow. "I admit Rob is a little high-handed at times."

"It's because he's skilled and on the ball. And funny and warm-hearted."

Exactly what the other men in her life had lacked. In the short days they'd known each other, Rob had displayed a tenderness she hadn't noticed at first, developing in the course of their hours together. She'd listened as he'd laughingly remarked about his dismal dating history. Although he'd airily portrayed himself as a man who couldn't care less, his admission seemed more heartbreaking than humorous.

"Wow, Kathleen." Candee set down her cup. "You're quick to come to his defense."

"I—" Kathleen rubbed her palms on her sweatshirt.

"I see you're interested in him. It's written all over your face. Admit it."

Kathleen averted her eyes from Candee's attentive gaze. Despite her exhaustion, she hadn't slept well. If she had more time, she might have talked further about Rob, but the sentences wedged in her throat. Unfortunately, time was something she lacked, and life went on.

She dabbed her lips with her napkin. "What interests me is designing this blank space into a charming teahouse in a few short weeks." As she disposed of the containers, Candee wrapped the silverware and napkins.

Through the doorway, Teddy and his crew set up ladders, arranged tools and prepared joint compound.

Kathleen perused the bare walls. She'd never considered interior decorating her strong suit despite Rob's compliments. In any case, he'd only seen her kitchen.

"How can I best utilize every inch of space?" she asked aloud.

"This is where I come in." Candee popped to her feet.

For the next several hours, Candee shared design tips while drawing up a floor plan, adding extra windows and laying out a well-equipped kitchen complete with sinks, a cooler, and oven placement. When Kathleen peered over Candee's shoulder, Candee said, "No worries. I'm keeping in mind the strict health code."

Meanwhile, Kathleen grabbed scrubbing supplies and tackled the shelving.

When they finished, Candee locked arms with Kathleen and yanked her out the front door. "And now, we're going shopping."

"My pantry is stocked with flour and baking soda."

"Good, because we're canvassing all the paint stores for samples. Fun bright colors will look terrific on the interior walls, and I suggest leaving the exposed brick behind the counter. Build a fireplace on the far wall with a wide pine mantel."

"Let's section the rooms to keep them more intimate," Kathleen said. "The smaller room can seat ten to twelve people, the larger up to twenty. I want worn leather couches in the sitting area, a loveseat, and blackboard by the entrance so I can chalk in the soups of the day." A wave of excitement coursed through her as more ideas took hold. "Creamy broccoli or parsnips with apple and curry are favorite soups in Ireland."

"Parsnips?" Candee asked. "What are those?"

"A root vegetable similar to a carrot, only cream-colored."

"When parsnip soup is on your menu, call me," Candee said. "Now, over and above food, let's get back to decorating. Stripping the wood on the sideboards will create an antique feel."

"At some point, I'll need a taste tester for the scones and bread."

Candee paused. "Is that all you think about—food?"

"I own a teahouse, not a bookstore."

Candee gazed at her with an overly satisfied expression. "I know the ideal person for the job."

"Who?"

"Rob."

Kathleen's pulse skipped a beat. The subject, the man she'd avoided talking about all afternoon, brought a smile she couldn't contain.

"Aye," she agreed.

Did her enthusiasm make her look transparent? The twinkle in Candee's eyes gave Kathleen her answer.

Aye.

CHAPTER 7

Rob stood in the backyard of Candee and Teddy's Victorian mansion, gazing at the enclosed pasture. Teddy had converted a large shed into a stable and purchased a Haflinger horse, sturdy and energetic with a flaxen mane, for Joseph's therapy.

When Joseph got off the school bus, Rob was propped against the fence admiring the home's gingerbread trim, which Candee had painted burnt-sienna. The shade nicely offset the mustard color exterior.

"Mr. Rob!" Joseph squealed in delight as he charged down the driveway. "I'm so happy you're back in Roses!" Out of breath, he dropped his bookbag on the ground and launched into Rob's arms. "How long will you stay?"

Rob managed a jovial smile. "A few days, maybe more."

Maybe less. It all depended on how a certain beautiful Irishwoman responded when he showed up at her teahouse.

After Candee had phoned him, breathless with the news that Kathleen had spoken favorably about him, she'd used her finest singsong voice and urged him to return to Roses.

That took some planning, but he'd assembled his managers and arranged the necessary details.

"I'm only a phone call away," he'd assured, with the unspoken hope no one rang.

So here he was, a week later, back in Roses. This time, he vowed not to talk shop with Kathleen. At least, not *his* shop. He was here merely to lend a hand.

As the opening drew nearer, she might fly into a panic. Consequently, he was ready and able to offer his support.

"Mr. Rob, what do you think of my horse?" Joseph tipped his head toward the small horse being led out of the stable by the therapist.

"I think your horse is awesomely pint-sized," Rob said.

"His name is Blackjack," Joseph said with an impish smile.

Nearing seven years old, the little boy had quickly emerged from a preschooler to a thriving second grader. The freckles on his cheeks were disappearing and baby teeth had begun to fall out, leaving a gap-toothed grin.

"Yes, I know. Even though Blackjack is chestnut colored and not at all black."

"Blackjack doesn't mind." Joseph's face shone with happiness. "He likes his name."

Rob touched the boy's chin. "I'm sure he does."

Teddy and Candee's love and affection had strengthened the boy's self-esteem, and he bore little resemblance to the broken child Rob remembered from a few years earlier.

"Rob?" Teddy called from the back porch. "Are you ready? Kathleen's expecting you." Thumbs hooked in his front jean pockets, he grinned indulgently. Whenever he spoke to Rob about Kathleen, he smirked. Just like Candee did.

"Be right there," Rob said.

"I've gotta go too, Mr. Rob." With a breeze tangling his fine hair and an eager smile on his face, Joseph scampered away.

A few minutes later, Rob arrived at the teahouse. In several days, the exterior had been transformed from drab to grand. The old-world appearance Kathleen strived for conveyed a welcoming invitation to passersby. Her signage, Kathleen's Teahouse, stained in lavender and blues and exaggerated by pink teacups, had been fixed high above the entrance.

His gaze roamed enthusiastically over the renovated building. Afternoon had settled, and the windows were aglow with lit electric candles.

A very welcoming place indeed. He just hoped the owner's heart held the same welcome.

WATCHING THROUGH LOWERED LASHES, Kathleen stood on her front porch as Rob got out of Teddy's pickup and waved a thanks. The work crew had retired for the day and the house was empty. They began at seven in the morning and clocked out at three thirty, so without the constant rat-a-tat-tat of hammering, the hollowness echoing through the rooms was oppressive.

"Cheers," she greeted Rob as he approached. "It's good to see you."

"A greeting from a beautiful woman is the best form of welcome," he said.

She smiled. "The Irish are known for their hospitality." As much as she tried, she couldn't tamp down the flurry in her chest at seeing him again.

Should they embrace like great friends, erasing their silly squabble? He had texted an apology and she'd done the same. Since then, the subject of her moving to Miami hadn't been broached. Thankfully, that had been settled.

She kept her hands at her sides while considering what to do next.

"It's good to see you again too." His blue eyes were steady and genial, startlingly intense. His tan golf shirt fit his frame perfectly, and he carried himself as a self-assured man, not a young guy who'd disguised his identity on the internet. Rob's tastes were sophisticated, and he was cultured and witty, an enticing combination.

No doubt about it. No matter how she resisted, she was drawn to him.

An expression of unconcealed admiration touched his handsome face. "I came back for you."

"Because of me, or for me?"

"Both."

"Did you assume I needed help, or did you want to see me?"

"Both."

"So you're not here to sightsee or visit friends?"

"I'm here exclusively for you." Warmly, he appraised her. "And you look gorgeous."

"Gorgeous? Hardly." Self-consciously, she patted her hair and offered a fatigued smile. Then she tugged at the pinstriped blouse and dark-washed jeans she'd changed into after a quick shower. Rob had texted saying when he'd arrive, but, as usual, she hadn't allowed enough time for herself and had settled for braiding her hair and applying pink lip gloss.

"Kathleen." He stepped closer. "I missed you. And I want you to know how much."

"You've only been gone a short while."

"The days were long for me."

The heat in her cheeks became a full-blown fire. Her gaze dropped to the flowers he held.

"I missed you too," she said quietly.

Attraction was a funny thing. It made you forget about feigning disinterest, a game suited for years thankfully well past.

"These are for you." He offered the flowers. "I asked the florist in town for something Irish."

"They're lovely." Kathleen accepted the bouquet of fresh-cut green and white button mums and carnations, the perfumed fragrance reminding her of the bushy plants growing wild in County Galway.

Her beloved Ireland. Nostalgia rushed through her, clogging her throat with emotion.

"Thank you," she managed.

"Are you homesick?"

"A little, although it's childish." Her eyes turned liquid, and a tear streaked down her cheek. "This is what I wanted—America and my own business. Fortunately, I've kept myself so busy my mind doesn't have time to wander."

Gently, he brushed the tear away. "I'm here and not going anywhere. Teddy and Candee said I can stay at their house as long as I'd like."

"What about your bakeries?"

"My marvelous muffins are so marvelous they practically bake themselves."

Despite herself, she chuckled.

He took the flowers from her, set them on the porch's wide railing, and gathered her into his arms.

She'd dreamt of this moment ever since they'd parted, and she didn't resist. Instead, she pressed her cheek along the smooth cotton of his shirt. The steady beating of his heart reassured her that he was here, truly here. And all was well.

He'd texted and emailed nightly since her talk with Candee. Which, he'd admitted, had prompted his return.

His emails were humorous and engaging, often describing a nonsensical situation occurring at work—a customer demanding a slice of huckleberry pie, although his bakery clearly sold only muffins and cupcakes and croissants, or an experimental batch of seaweed muffins everyone refused to eat.

We try to sell healthy selections once in a while, he'd joked.

What did you do with all those wholesome muffins? she'd asked.

I gave them to my skinny employees. Along with the remaining seaweed.

Oftentimes, his solutions to her work-related questions were exceptional. And when she uploaded photos of the daily progress to share with him, he replied instantly. Nothing was too unsettling that Rob couldn't solve with a clever, sensible remedy.

Each evening, when she was too exhausted to decide on another scone recipe or the installation of a gas versus a wood-burning fireplace, she looked forward to the end of her workday. She could finally climb the stairs to her apartment, open her laptop, and eagerly read his email.

When worries about money kept her awake at night, Rob would message her as soon as she logged onto her computer, as if he'd waited up for her. Sometimes, his messages were flirtatious. The actuality that he was eight hundred miles away made their exchanges feel safe and risk-free, and she enjoyed the playful bantering.

"The place looks better in person than in your photos," Rob said as she plucked up the bouquet and they stepped inside. He beamed his approval, sniffing the cedar-scented air and indicating the blazing logs in the stone-faced fireplace. "You decided on wood instead of gas after all."

"Aye." She went to the sink, retrieved a crystal vase, and arranged the flowers. "It's more work, but wood-burning is more authentic. And Teddy's hard-working crew deserves the credit, along with Candee's decorating expertise."

"I love these photographs." He stepped to a white-washed

wall and surveyed the black and white photos of the old diner.

"I chose to pay homage to the diner's legacy. This place is riddled in history and was originally named Betty's Diner."

She'd set a table in Victorian style, complete with an Irish lace tablecloth, bone china cups, and polished silver. She set the vase of flowers in the center.

"Do you like the ambience?" she asked, following his reaction.

"Very, very much." He lifted back a pale-blue wool Oriental rug. "The wide plank oak floors are gleaming and rustic, which was the effect you were going for, right?"

"Absolutely." She tipped up her chin. "The crystal chandeliers will be hung tomorrow. And the paintings depict Ireland's landscapes. I placed them on the wall opposite the photographs, highlighting the old and the new, and two different cultures." She indicated a particularly poignant watercolor of a stone castle atop a hill, the rugged coastline and sea beyond. "I borrowed this concept from Danny Brady. Irish murals grace the walls in The Ground Café."

Rob came beside her. "Kathleen, you are a treasure." His sincere smile melted her heart. He bent his head and kissed her temple, then brushed a butterfly kiss on her lips. Joy surged through her that had nothing to do with his compliment. She couldn't believe this delightful man was interested in her.

And he was. It showed in his avid gaze, his steady eye contact and how he engaged her in endless chats.

"Would you prefer high tea or afternoon tea?" she asked.

"What's the difference?"

She glanced at her wristwatch. "It's around four, so afternoon tea is better."

"Again, what's the difference?"

"Mostly the seating. Afternoon tea is best experienced on low parlor chairs. If it's a high-backed chair, then it's high tea."

"Easy facts to remember," he said. "So these are low chairs."

"Correct."

"Is there a story behind high and low tea you can place on your menus?"

"I'll give you the abridged edition if you're interested."

"If it concerns you, I'm very interested."

"Well, teatime is a British tradition." She steepled her fingers. "Customarily, tea, scones, cakes and sandwiches were served in the nineteenth century. Teatime filled the gap between lunch and dinner, which was usually eaten around eight o'clock."

"I eat muffins every day at four. Should I call my snacks teatime?"

"If you'd like." She chuckled. "Nowadays, obviously, routines have changed. However, teatime is still observed as a civilized tradition. More important, it brings friends and family together and allows everyone the chance to slow down."

His eyes crinkled into a smile. "I'm more than ready to slow down."

Aye, she reasoned, noting the low crease in his forehead. Despite his smile, he looked as exhausted as she felt.

She whisked a glance at a log dropping in the fireplace. The wood sparked and crackled. Knowing his gaze was on her, she donned her prettiest beam. "So, shall we enjoy after-noon tea?"

"Sure. I think."

She laughed out loud at his wary expression. "You think?"

"Mind briefing me on what afternoon tea entails? I

understand the four o'clock part, but is this another no thank you three times discussion?"

"We've done all that." She gestured for him to sit in a flowered parlor chair at the intimate table set for two.

He didn't.

Instead, he pulled out a chair for her before claiming his own. He was a gentleman in numerous ways, opening doors for her, never sitting if she was standing. Always, he was respectful and polite.

She poured the hot tea, which she'd prepared ahead. Gold flatware glinted by the light of tea candles, and metallic gold linen napkins folded in the shape of a crown sat on bone-china plates, the plates so translucent as to be almost see-through. A tiered platter was set with scones, finger sandwiches, clotted cream, and strawberry preserves.

"Is your tea dark enough?" she inquired.

He made a show of examining the brew in his gold-rimmed cup. "Strong enough to trot a mouse in."

"Here, here." She chuckled. "You're learning the Irish sayings quickly."

They bowed their heads and prayed a blessing. When they finished, she presented turkey sandwiches covered in cranberry jelly from the platter.

"I could get used to this," he laughed, taking a bite of a cucumber finger sandwich spread with herbed cream. "How did you make the cream?" he asked.

"It's not difficult. I'll lend you the recipe."

He settled in, slid his teacup closer, and supported his elbows on the table. Tea sloshed over the rim of his cup. "Kathleen, you've made the entire process look easy. You're going to open without a hitch."

The table wobbled, the legs uneven. And with that, the exquisite settings, hot tea, sandwiches, and flower-filled vase clattered to the floor.

Kathleen caught her teacup between her palms, although the brew spilled across her pinstriped blouse, leaving behind a splotchy wet stain. She dabbed at her shirt, her fingertips catching the droplets.

"Aye," she echoed, perching on the edge of her chair. "I'll be opening without a hitch."

CHAPTER 8

To his customers and everyone in Miami who presumed to know him, Rob's bakeries were the epitome of success. To Rob, his bakeries were fast becoming a weight too heavy to carry on his broad shoulders.

And he was seriously considering selling everything.

More and more, Miami had become a place he sought to escape. He was tired of setting aside his personal life for an ever-elusive joy, no matter the vast amount of wealth and accolades he'd accumulated.

He craved laughter and companionship with people he enjoyed.

With Kathleen.

However, he also wanted to make certain their bond was more than a casual exchange between two businesspeople.

The following afternoon, he sat in the back room of Kathleen's teahouse with his cell-phone on speaker. George, his manager, was working in the Miami office, and he'd asked David, the newbie, to be his messenger and relay the bad news to Rob.

Butter prices had substantially risen and were up by 75 percent.

"Tell George to shop around," Rob told David.

"He has, Mr. Rob," David said. "All the local vendors and bulk supply stores have increased their prices."

"Their timing is perfect for the spring baking season. That is, perfect for them," Rob said sardonically. "I'll recalculate our muffin prices so we can stay within profit margins."

"Not possible, sir, unless you're planning to charge five dollars per muffin," David said. "We're currently selling at two dollars apiece."

"And losing money," Rob pointed out. "Although no customer will buy a five-dollar muffin, no matter how marvelous."

"Correct, sir."

"I'm proud of my products. However, I'm not in business to give them away." Impatience thickened Rob's tone. "Tell him."

"Yes, sir." David muffled the phone, and returned a minute later. "George said he's well aware of that, sir."

Heaving a sigh, Rob tipped his head against the back of the chair.

"Rob?" After a light tap on the door, Kathleen's voice floated through the room. "Oh, sorry." She put a hand to her mouth in apology. "I didn't realize you were still on the phone."

The afternoon sun shone through the window, splashing her cheeks with a hint of color. The past three days, she'd worked nonstop from early morning to late evening. Between Teddy's crew and a constant stream of suppliers, organized commotion heralded each new day. Rob had appeared each morning at daybreak, rolled up his sleeves, and worked alongside her.

He smiled at her, stood, and held up an index finger to let her know he was finishing the call.

"Text me later with a better update," he said to David. "Or we'll be churning our own butter."

"No worries. We'll need a cow, though, sir."

Rob stared at his cell-phone in stunned disbelief.

Apparently waiting for a response, David stacked on more assurances. "Actually … we'll probably need two cows, sir."

Frustration reduced Rob's response to a groan. When he did speak, he kept his tone purposefully calm. "Thanks for the helpful tip, David. Goodbye for now." He clicked his phone shut and tossed it across the table.

Kathleen's lips twitched, a twinkle in her sparkling eyes. "You're in the business of buying cows now, are you? I'll take a half dozen. I heard Candee and Teddy own a pasture."

He laughed heartily. With her, every minute was like being in the middle of a splendid dream. She had an aura of exhilaration, a freshness sparking something inside him. Most important, she let him forget his cares, at least for a while.

Strawberry-blond tendrils had worked loose from her high ponytail, which she'd tied back with a teal satin ribbon. She wore a stretchy-knit yellow dress with a pretty V-neckline and tan loafers.

He'd dated beautiful women in his lifetime. No one compared to Kathleen. Perhaps it was her porcelain complexion, or the figure-hugging dress showing off her curves, or her shiny hair glinting in the sunlight. Perhaps it was because, besides being downright striking, she was chic and confident.

And yet she had never married. What was going on in Ireland? Were all the men blind?

Grinning, he placed his hand on his heart. "Kathleen, have

I told you you're gorgeous? I liked the jeans you wore yesterday, but the dress—"

"Aye, you have, and often." She laughed. "And I've thanked
you for your kindness each and every time."

"You're very welcome." He stepped closer and tucked a
silky tendril behind her ear, his fingers brushing across her
high cheekbone. "I applaud your conviction to follow your
dreams. You're a determined, sharp-witted businessperson."

She rubbed her palm against the door which had been
sanded and stained to a satiny oak finish. "Same as you,
aye?"

"Yes, and I don't know if that's a good thing or a bad
thing."

"What do you mean?"

"When you're focused on victory at all costs, it's easy to
forget the important things in life."

A quiet smile, not quite reaching her eyes, lit her fine-
boned face.

He was extremely attracted to her and wondered if it was
a good idea to work so closely. He was caught up in her. She
was caught up in her business.

He knew the feeling. He'd lived that way most of his adult
life. And if he continued analyzing their situation, the
fifteen-year difference between them would clutter things up
even more.

She extended her hands, apparently unaware of his
thoughts. "I hope butter hasn't risen significantly in the
Carolinas," she said.

He took her small hands in his. "I'll check in the morning." He perused her flawless figure before his gaze slid to her
face. "In the meantime, there's something else we can do
besides churn butter."

"What?" She didn't seem to notice the telltale huskiness in
his tone.

He pulled her near and pressed a kiss on her hair, her temple, her cheeks.

"Rob …" She gazed up at him and licked her lips. "Maybe we should—"

He swallowed hard. "Kiss?" He framed her face in his hands, stared at her mouth and bent his head.

From the entrance, a crewman's voice called out. The workers were leaving.

Immediately, she stepped back. "I should see them out."

"Why? They can find their way through the front door. They've worked every day since I've been here."

"Aye, but—"

"Kathleen, are you comfortable with us … with me …" Wow, did he ever sound desperate. Quickly, he closed his mouth before he revealed something he'd regret.

"Surely you understand I didn't come to America to find a man."

"And surely you understand there's a magnetism drawing us together."

"Your businesses will be calling you back soon enough, so we shouldn't get too attached to each other."

He tried his most charming grin. "Why not?"

"It's like giving biscuits to a bear."

There went her Irish slang, and he had no notion of what she was talking about. "Meaning?"

"Our being together is a waste of time. Look at what I've undertaken. I can't manage anything more."

He got it. He'd take it slow. She had mountains of tasks, and it was too soon for a commitment.

"Will you take a wee peek at the kitchen in my apartment?" she asked, her tone shifting to businesslike. "The crewmen have enough to complete down here, and one of my shelves needs an adjustment."

"I'm not a carpenter."

"It isn't a complicated job." She led him through the rooms, separated by brick archways, and paused by the staircase. "If you fix the shelf, I'll best the deal with a warm bowl of colcannon."

At his puzzled expression, she clarified, "Mashed potatoes mixed with kale, scallions, milk and butter. And I'll fry you a pan of sausages on the side."

"Free labor for free food," he said. "How can I refuse when I'm ravenous?"

He was ravenous all right. He wanted to hold her, glide his fingers through her strawberry-blond hair, spend hours chatting with her. Kissing her.

As he accompanied her up the creaky wooden stairs, she remarked, "My father never owned anything he couldn't fix."

Rob grimaced. Aware he didn't immediately respond, and likewise aware she was waiting, he contemplated telling her the truth. He'd never been handy with tools, and if she evaluated a man by his hammer wielding abilities, he'd fail miserably.

"That's the way with most men, isn't it?" she added.

Real men fix things. He visualized the slogan—resembling a television commercial.

The tension in his shoulders tightened with each ascending step. He hoped she wouldn't judge him for not being able to hang cabinets or install crown molding, because his reply would be *I can't*. His affluent parents had deemed carpentry beneath them, and encouraged Rob to perform well in school and play sports.

So he had, excelling at both.

And his father had continued to beat him. They'd kept it hidden, presenting a fake façade to their community. Despite the proper upbringing in the proper home, there was no love; only disinterest, indifference, and cruelty. However, they'd filled their home with material possessions, and Rob never lacked the latest tech toy.

After his father had broken Rob's nose once, he'd whipped out his checkbook and bought Rob a Camaro for his sixteenth birthday.

"I can fix this," his father had said, as if a new Camaro could fix a broken nose.

It had come as no surprise his parents didn't approve of his baking career. Although he became a prosperous businessperson, they'd dismissed his achievements.

And now they were gone. A few years earlier, they'd died within months of each other, both from lung cancer. Rob was an only child, and had tried to accept the fact he had failed them, but he never did.

Ten minutes later, he found himself crouched beneath a loose corner shelf in Kathleen's kitchen.

"Can you hand me a hammer, Kathleen?" he asked with a nail held between his teeth.

"Aye," she obliged.

He pinched a second nail between his thumb and index finger, lined the nails up and gave them several sharp whacks. Two nails hammered at once seemed more efficient. Thankfully, she seemed blissfully unaware of his many misses as he attempted to drive the nails into the board and kept slamming his thumb instead. He held in his colorful curses and tried again. Finally, on the fifth attempt, he succeeded.

He stood and wiped wood particles from his jeans. "All set."

There it was. The shelf was secure. Now he could swing a hammer like any of the burly men on Teddy's construction crew.

Her gracious smile filled with appreciation. "What would I do without all this help?"

He prayed she'd narrow her selection down to one helpful person: him. She simply couldn't accomplish this project without *him.*

She slipped off her loafers. "I have something special for us!"

"A wee bit of whiskey?" He peered at her bare feet. "Will we be stomping the whiskey like the Italians stomp grapes for wine?"

"I don't drink," she reminded, skipping to a CD player on the counter. "And what I planned is indeed better."

A lively jig sounded through the kitchen, played by the traditional Celtic instruments of a fiddle, flute, and tin whistle.

She held out her hands, positioning him to face her. "Dance with me, Rob."

He was almost as inept a dancer as he was a carpenter, and he primed the argument on his tongue. "Kathleen, I'm a baker."

"You've repeated that a number of times. And so am I, but I also can dance." She dropped her hands to her sides, and he followed her lead.

"You're Irish," he said. "You've probably danced a jig your entire life."

She wasn't listening. "First, assume the stance." She bounced with the beat, shoulders back and head held high.

He tried to imitate her and carry out her instructions— cross your feet, point your right toe, do a hop, hop back, and lead with your left.

"Leave it to you Irish to make your dance as complicated as drinking tea," he groaned.

She laughed. "Execute the reel straightaway." She whirled him around in a circle, sending her knit dress flying up and exposing shapely bare legs.

He pulled a handkerchief from his pocket to wipe the

sweat from his forehead. He was dizzy, he was breathless. And he was laughing with an abandonment he hadn't felt since he was little.

She giggled, her deep dimples showing. As the jig ended, she collapsed against him. Tears of laughter streamed down her flushed cheeks. "Not so difficult, aye? You danced grand."

"And you're amazing." He caught her tears with his knuckles. In his arms, she was soft and light and he tightened his grip. He was charmed and totally besotted, and he couldn't recall ever being as in love with a woman.

Whoa. Hold that thought.

"I'll teach you the Irish jig whenever you'd like," she was saying. "There're more steps."

"Uh-huh, I'm sure there's a whole book full. I'll put jigs on a back burner for now, but you're an admirable instructor," he said. "And your cooking—"

"Oh, that reminds me." She tore away. "I'll warm the colcannon. That's part of our deal."

"How about a tour first? I spend most of my life in a kitchen."

She tapped a hand to her forehead. "I forgot you haven't seen the rest of my apartment." A slow smile came across her face. "Although saying it's crying for a complete overhaul is an understatement. I've been too busy to entertain decorating ideas, and I admit it's not my strength."

Evidenced by her charming kitchen, she was more than capable. She obviously set high standards for herself.

They wandered through the half-empty rooms—bathroom, hallway, and bedroom. The bare walls were devoid of mementos—no pictures, no window treatments save for shades, no framed photographs of loved ones. The carpet was bland and tattered, the white paint peeling from the ceiling. A chipped farmhouse stool stood as a table beside a worn plaid couch, a knitted blue blanket draped over an end chair. In the corner, wind whistled through cracks in the walls.

Where were her personal belongings? He considered asking, but didn't. She'd admitted to missing Ireland. Possibly she was hesitant to set down permanent roots in America.

Suppose she decided to leave? He captured the troublesome thought and kept it in the forefront of his mind.

"Lovely," he crooned politely as they reentered the kitchen.

"You're too kind." She removed the mashed potato mixture from the refrigerator and transferred it to a pan on the stove.

He grabbed plates and silverware and set the table before coming to stand beside her. "And you work too hard."

"Not any harder than you. Besides—"

"Therefore, I declare tomorrow afternoon a sightseeing holiday."

"Rob, I can't possibly take off an afternoon. Anyway, I'll be knackered."

He quirked an eyebrow.

"Tired. I'll be tired," she said.

"You'll be more productive afterward. What's more, this town is the size of a postage stamp."

"We'll stay in town?"

"For the most part."

She frowned, crunching her delicate eyebrows together. "What's that supposed to mean?"

"It means I plan to show you something first. Then we'll eat dinner at a farm-to-table restaurant that's drawing glowing reviews. Aren't you interested in your local competition?"

"I'm running a teahouse."

"They serve food. You'll be serving food. Maybe new recipe ideas will inspire you."

Ever the entrepreneur, her face lit up. "I guess I can quit at four o'clock."

"Make it three. Where we're going will require a few hours of daylight." He glanced down at her smoky eyes, placed a kiss on her lips, and added a wink.

"Ooh. Sounds mysterious. We're not staying in Roses, then?"

He shrugged. "There's a surprise first."

"I don't usually like surprises. Is this a good surprise?"

"It's a fun surprise," he corrected. "And one I'd like your opinion on."

She gave the colcannon a quick stir, then twisted. "Alright, then. Brilliant."

He smiled. The main thing was that they were going to enjoy an afternoon outside of work. And, by doing so, he'd show her why she should settle in Roses for good.

CHAPTER 9

The following afternoon, Kathleen hummed "Molly Malone", a favorite tune, as Rob pulled up in his candy-red rental car. The afternoon was balmy, foreshadowing the pleasant weather to come.

They'd stopped working at two o'clock after the power had unexpectedly shut off, leaving the crewmen and teahouse in darkness. Fortunately, the electric company had responded and quickly restored power, giving her the opportunity for a hot shower.

She'd taken care with her appearance, dressing in a royal-blue cotton dress with a flared skirt. She paired the dress with brown leather ankle boots and dark tights, topping the outfit with a twill jacket in a light pink print. She'd scrubbed, blow dried, and brushed her long hair until it crackled and shone. Leaving it to lie in loose ringlets around her shoulders, she donned a jaunty straw hat and pinned it in place.

She called out a cheerful greeting as Rob got out of the car. He was at her door before she'd taken a step.

"My beautiful Kathleen." He kissed her warmly on the lips. "Good to see you again."

"You just left my place an hour ago."

He smirked. "And I missed you the entire time." He opened the passenger door for her, and she settled into the plush leather seats.

"Where are we going?" she asked, buckling her seat belt.

He slid into the driver's seat and did the same. "It's a surprise, remember?"

"Rob, I've never liked surprises and—"

"I'll give you two hints." His teasing voice stilled her protests. "It's a town not far from here and it rhymes with toast."

"We're driving to the coast? But we're near the mountains."

Smiling, he pulled to the curb and turned to face her. "I'll give you another hint."

"Alright."

"Boo!"

She jumped, patting her heart. "What on earth? You scared me."

"Sorry." He planted a kiss on her temple, then eased the car back onto the road.

"So now it's presumed I know where we're going?"

He shrugged, an impish expression on his face. "I assumed my clues were useful."

She smiled. "A town rhyming with toast? Boo?" Her smile widened. "Those are clues? Even Sherlock Holmes would have given up."

Their gazes locked—his filled with mischief, hers with a hint of apprehension.

"The surprise is we're driving to Hollan Farms," he said.

"I've never heard of it."

"Teddy and I passed through when we drove from Asheville to Roses." Rob flicked on his blinker and followed a narrow two-lane road, the only traffic a bicycle rider and a lone scooter. "Hollan Farms is a ghost town."

Images of American cowboys and deserted gold rush cities came to mind. "Here? In the Southeast?"

"Technically, a few inhabitants still live there. Sit back and enjoy the ride." He switched on the radio, and James Taylor sang about seeing fire and rain.

They arrived a half hour later, and Rob parked in a graveled car park at the edge of town. Before she could open the door and reach for her straw clutch handbag, he came around and assisted her.

She linked her hand through his arm, their pleasant banter and discerning observations progressing with each step.

"There's a general belief that ghost towns are creepy and haunted," he said. "From my research, this town is none of these."

"Except it does looks abandoned." She pointed to a string of empty storefronts. "It doesn't take a genius to realize no one has lived here for a while."

"Yes, there's that."

Her cheeks warmed as he regarded her, his gaze moving to her lips before he took her in his arms and kissed her.

She was with him far too often. He was the picture of who and what she'd intended to avoid—a good-looking man sharing precious, remarkable moments with her.

Risky, risky, risky. If she continued along this path, eventually her heart would be broken.

But this was Rob, and he was different.

Aye. Different all right. He was too appealing, too perceptive, too much of a distraction.

Too much of an *attraction.*

A light breeze caused her straw hat to flap, and she placed one hand on top of her head to steady it. Trees on every street corner blossomed, sending tiny white petals floating through the air.

As they wound through a forsaken alleyway, Rob seemed to take in every element of the buildings—the worn scalloped awning on the supermarket, abandoned café tables outside a bistro, an ornamental stone fountain. She imagined water bursting from the basin, children playing around it, street vendors selling bunches of flowers and delectable coffee and desserts.

"This was a boomtown, a resort boasting a healing hot spring, luxurious spa, and top-rate restaurants," Rob said. "The town went belly up because of the economic downturn a few years ago. Sadly, the anticipated clientele—middle America—could no longer afford spa vacations."

She slowed to peer through a dusty café window. Chairs and tables were arranged in the middle of the floor, menus stacked by the receptionist's booth as if frozen in time.

"And the hot spring?" she inquired.

"What about it?"

"Where is it?"

"It still runs through the center of town."

The sky changed to a dove gray, and the sun disappeared. A minute later, a heavy rain shower caught her sleeves with drops of water.

"Hold on to your hat," Rob joked. He grabbed her hand and led her on a race through the streets.

"This happens in Ireland constantly," she said, winded and laughing. "One minute it's sunny, the next, rain is bucketing down."

They ducked beneath the canopied entrance of a once impressive hotel, the windows reflecting a marbled tile entryway and carpet at least ten years old.

"It storms and rains on many hot afternoons in Miami too," Rob said.

Water dripped from the brim of her hat, a puddle forming at their feet. "Except Ireland's weather is a wee bit cooler than Miami, to be sure."

"You think?"

"I know for certain." Her hand was still clasped in his warm one. This close, with his warm blue eyes framed by thick brows and his ever-present smile, he exuded self-assurance. Not arrogant the way some men she'd dated carried themselves, more interested in their lives than anything she had to say.

As she gazed up at Rob, she noticed his nose had been broken at least once. Tenderly, she ran her finger across the bridge. "What happened?" she asked softly.

"He liked whiskey and bourbon and cigarettes."

"Who?"

"My father." Rob was silent for several beats. "The combination was frightening when he was angry."

"Your father." She mulled the two words in her mind. Rob rarely spoke about his family or his past. "Did he … break your nose?"

"Yes."

"So, he beat you?"

"Often."

"Oh, Rob." What could she say? She knew from Clara's brother, Seamus, how alcohol twisted a person's life into a roller-coaster, the ups and downs catching loved ones in a virtual whirlwind of emotions. Inevitably, wreckage and despair followed.

"It happened years ago. Decades, literally." Rob spoke so softly she wasn't sure she heard him. She thought he dabbed at his eyes.

She pictured him as a small boy, chubby, sweet-faced, an infectious beam in his deep-set eyes. "It's alright," she finally said.

"What I remember most is the smell of my father's whiskey and cigarette breath, and the sight of him asleep at the oak desk in his study, an empty liquor bottle lying beside him. I tried to please him, I really did."

The neediness in Rob's voice warmed a secret place in her heart. Perhaps that was why he'd tried so hard all these years to succeed—in his effort to satisfy parents who didn't care. He was a pleaser, thinking of everyone except himself.

"I'm sorry." Something inside prompted her to squeeze his hand and offer reassurance. "The future is what matters."

They stood quiet, the steady rain beating down on the hotel's canopy. He stared at her so long a shiver coursed through her. He trusted her enough to share his heart-breaking memories.

Truly, he cared about her.

And she, in turn, cared about him. Trusted him.

More than cared. More than trusted. She was falling in love with him.

No. Not here. Not now.

Then where, exactly? And when? All she need to do was gaze at him. The confirmation stood directly in front of her —with his every intention, and devotion shining from his brilliant blue eyes. Somehow, in the madness of two different worlds, they'd found each other.

Knowing her rain-dampened cheeks were a hot pink, she broke the spell and spun to peer through the hotel's grimy window. She tented her hands and read the scrawled sign posted in the lobby. "We are open to patrons during the summer months."

"Wow," Rob said. "Business is booming."

She laughed and pivoted. "For who, exactly?"

"I don't know. It might be an old sign."

"Didn't you say a handful of people still live in Hollan Farms?"

"Yes, but they wouldn't stay at the hotel."

"So, where are they?"

He shrugged. Gently, he wiped rain droplets off her chin. "They're probably in Asheville for the day."

"The entire population?"

"The entire population of ten."

The rain stopped as suddenly as it had started. He kept hold of her hand as they continued their exploration, answering her speculative questions with speculative answers. Eventually, they crossed a rickety wooden bridge.

The famed babbling hot spring nestled beside budding trees and shrubs, and Kathleen caught her breath at the exquisite sight. With mountain views in the distance, the scene could have been a page removed from a travel brochure advertising tranquility.

"Beautiful," she murmured. "Like a fairy-tale reproduction of what real life should be."

"Zen."

At her raised eyebrows, he explained, "Zen is Japanese slang for serenity."

She gazed upward and sighed. White, wispy clouds floated above, drifting leisurely. No rush for the clouds. Nature was never in a hurry. If only she could harness that same inner peace.

Directly opposite the sun, a muted band of colors formed an arc. "Look, Rob." She pointed. "A rainbow!"

"I'll snap a photo."

"Quick, before it disappears."

He pulled his cell-phone from his pocket, stepped beside her, and snapped a selfie of them framed by the rainbow.

She was too enchanted by this fascinating town to object.

"You're prettier than any rainbow." Rob hung his arm around her shoulders. "But I can delete the photo if—"

"No, of course not." She wanted to relish the growing

attraction between them, to spend every precious minute with him. Everything about him was appealing—each shared glance, the feel of his callused hand around hers, his agreeable, mellow nature.

She peered at the sky. Already, the rainbow was fading. A homesickness she hadn't felt in a while enveloped her.

"Are you okay?" he asked.

"I'm fine." She brushed her fingers across her eyes. "Oftentimes, the rainbows in Ireland are brilliant."

"Rainbows are brilliant in America too, Kathleen. And Roses is your new home."

Here. With me.

The words dangled between them.

"Do you desire a soak, my lady?" he asked when they reached the edge of the hot spring. "You know, all those healing powers ..."

"I didn't bring my swimsuit," she joked.

"A pity." He moved behind her and wrapped his hands around her waist, nuzzling her neck. She turned, considering, then stood on her tiptoes and kissed him.

He drew an inward breath and folded her in his arms. She wrapped her hands around his nape.

This was decisive.

She was done worrying about dating, or relationships, or whether this was the right time. Because here was Rob, a man she trusted. She loved the way his lips were firm, yet tender and enticing. He was so good to her, polite, calm, respectful.

When the kiss ended, he whispered, "You have no idea how often I think about you."

Likewise. He was in her thoughts every minute.

He beckoned her to dip her hands into the water with him.

"I read that famous actors and actresses who visited here often immersed themselves in the healing waters," he said.

Kathleen splashed water on her face. "Whether the spring is healing or not, this town is delightful."

"I agree." He looked around, pensive, deliberating. "And it's for sale."

"What is?" She aimed her gaze across the street. "The hotel?"

"The town."

Playfully, she swatted him. "A town can't be for sale."

"Sure it can."

The whole town was for sale.

And Rob had a gleam in his eyes she instantly recognized. Once an entrepreneur, always an entrepreneur.

"How much?" she asked.

"I've done some investigating. Plus, Candee's a real estate agent, which is helpful."

"How much?" she repeated.

"Several million dollars."

He might as well have stated several trillion dollars; the amount was so removed from her stratosphere.

"Rob, surely you're not thinking of buying a … town."

He chuckled. "Teddy and Candee voiced the same reservation."

"What about your bakeries?"

"I'm putting them up for sale. I'm retiring."

She touched a hand to her parted lips. "You'd sell Rob's Marvelous Muffins?"

"I'll keep the name and unload the buildings, retail spaces and my condo. I'll start the paperwork when I fly to Miami."

"Is this wise? You've established a wonderful reputation. What about your recipes, your customer base—"

His jaw set. "All too much work."

"Compared to renovating a town?" She couldn't find a

coherent sentence to sputter. "Along with the actual price, it'll take several more millions to fix all the buildings."

"True." Lazily, he stroked a stray ringlet falling across her shoulder.

She stepped back. "Isn't that a lot of money?"

"Yes. However, Hollan Farms has one thing Miami lacks."

His words caught, and she looked up at him. The entire afternoon had followed its own course. And in his explanation, she recognized a deep emotion. Commitment.

"Healing spring water?" she half teased.

"Guess again."

"Rob, I …" She'd forgotten her guesses, anyway. When she was with him, she forgot all her troubles.

She knew he watched her, so she ventured, "The town offers dilapidated cafés just waiting for your marvelous muffins?"

"Nope."

"What could Hollan Farms possibly offer that isn't in Miami?"

"You." He brought her into his arms, bent his head, and thoroughly kissed her. "I'm planning to move to Roses permanently."

WHEN THEIR TOUR of the town ended, the sun hung low in the sky, the beginnings of a sunset casting vivid purple and orange hues that shadowed the derelict buildings. By the time they arrived at the farm-to-table restaurant, stars blanketed a clear night sky.

Rob's admission that he would sell all he'd built in order to be close to her had successfully breached the last of her defenses. Here she'd assumed the wall barricading her heart had been honed to perfection and nothing could penetrate it.

And it had been so, until she'd met this honest, mature gentleman. Until the impossible had occurred.

She'd fallen for him, and there was no turning back.

"Are you hungry?" he inquired.

"I'm starving, actually."

"Next time we go to the hot spring, we'll pack a picnic."

Next time. A promise of shared experiences to come. Celebrations.

Seeing the restaurant's parking lot packed with cars, she remarked, "We may not be eating here tonight."

"I made reservations," he said.

His cell-phone pinged. He darted a glance at the caller ID and scowled. "Sorry, Kathleen, I need to take this. One of my managers—"

She drew in a breath before a sharp retort rolled from her tongue. *Rob,* she wanted to say. *Must your business always come first?*

After a clipped exchange, Rob ended the call.

Scents of smoked bacon and fresh-baked rolls wafted from the doorway as they ascended the restaurant's stairs. Inside, the walls were decorated in cherry-wood paneling. Candlelight and a pianist playing soft background music— well-known Broadway show tunes—completed the under- stated elegance.

As Rob hung her jacket, Kathleen removed her floppy hat and peered at her outfit, grateful she'd worn a dress.

When they were seated, a black-clad waiter brought menus, explaining the food was fresh and locally sourced, while he poured glasses of sparkling water.

She enjoyed an exquisite meal of a seared chicken breast served on a bed of roasted mushrooms and cherry tomatoes, while Rob opted for the grilled beef tenderloin with spinach and spaghetti squash.

For dessert, she ordered black coffee and a cherry fruit

cobbler. She forked a piece of the crust and chewed discerningly.

"How is it?" Rob asked. He'd ordered bread pudding filled with frozen grapes, and raisin rum ice cream on the side.

She placed the fork near her plate and patted her lips with the linen napkin. "Surprisingly mediocre. Yours?"

"The same." He toyed with the pudding, then scooped up a spoonful of ice cream. "Odd, because dinner was delicious. I wonder if they outsource their desserts because I know a certain woman who bakes a heavenly brown bread." A not-so-secret smile appeared on his lips.

Chuckling, she shook her head. "I have enough on my plate baking bread and scones for my patrons-to-be. What about you?"

"I'm retiring, remember?"

Sure, by buying and restoring a ghost town boasting a hot spring, grocery store, hotel, and who knew what else.

As she sipped her coffee, she felt an unexplainable surge of pride for his tenaciousness. Although he'd told her he didn't have a bit of Irish blood in him—his surname, Taylor, being French and Scottish—he was as sharp-witted as any Irishman.

"What's the finest dessert you've ever tasted?" she asked.

In the softness of candlelight, his face appeared younger. He looked rested and happy. "Your brown bread."

She smiled over the rim of her cup. "No, really."

"There's a mom-and-pop restaurant near Asheville. I dined there with Teddy a while back, and the owners specialize in homemade apple cobblers topped with a flaky crust. I'll take you there some time." He leaned in. "What about you?"

"Ah, well, in Ireland, any coffee shop or café will likely serve desserts prepared in-house."

"I'd like to visit Ireland someday," he said quietly.

Don't go there, she thought. A small part of her demanded she stay on track—launching an up-and-coming teahouse in America. That meant no distractions.

But then, she'd already made her decision. With Rob, her world had changed. They could enjoy America and Ireland together, as a team, as a couple, as two people devoted to each other.

She sat back in the tufted chair, moving in time to the pianist's rendition of the upbeat "I Could Have Danced All Night" from *My Fair Lady*.

She tilted back her head, her smile lighthearted. "It would be an honor to show you my country, Rob."

"I can't wait."

She inhaled, treasuring the moment. She'd made the correct choice coming to Roses, and she wanted Rob in her life.

The way he smiled back at her told her everything. It warmed her weary heart, and there was no mistaking the love in his expression.

CHAPTER 10

"I'll depart for Miami tomorrow," Rob told Kathleen a few days after they'd dined at the farm-to-table restaurant. They stood on the front porch of her teahouse on a brisk day in early March. A sharp breeze ruffled the burgundy striped awning that had recently been installed.

She swallowed and avoided his gaze. "Seven days seems like forever."

"I'm merely a few hours away by plane. In the meantime, I have a gift so you won't forget me." He withdrew a silver-foil-wrapped box from his sport jacket and handed it to her.

Solemnly, he watched her open a black velvet box and snap open the lid. Inside was a Victorian heart-shaped skeleton key locket on a cable chain, plated in twenty-four carat gold.

"Thank you," she said. "It's beautiful."

"For a beautiful woman." He secured the chain around her neck. "My Irish queen, you hold the key to my heart. Always remember that."

She laughed. "Fit for a queen, aye?"

"Yes." He nodded. "Open the locket."

She popped the magnetic closure, and all laughter vanished from her face. She studied the miniature photo tucked inside—the one he'd taken of them at Hollan Farms with the stunning rainbow in the background.

"Turn the locket over," he instructed.

On the back was inscribed: 1-800-IRELAND.

Tears welled in her eyes. "Thank you," she said again.

"I hope you will always think of me when you wear it."

"Every day."

"That's what I like to hear." He embraced her in a loving hold. Against her cheek, his chest was warm and comforting, his heartbeat steady and sure. "I'll return well before your grand opening. I promise, and I never go back on my word."

He was considerate and compassionate, intuitive to her feelings.

She acknowledged his promise, although tears burned. "I'll miss you," she said.

"Not as much as I'll miss you."

She declined his pocket handkerchief that he offered, her thoughts scattering.

When he was near, she felt treasured. Now these crucial hours leading up to March 17 would continue without him.

Well, she'd steel her shoulders and deal with it. He had a business to run. So did she. Furthermore, she was a resourceful entrepreneur. Rob had told her so himself.

He pressed a kiss on her lips. "I'll call as soon as I land in Miami." His gaze flicked to the crewmen busily making adjustments to the wood floor in one of the dining rooms. "Teddy, Candee, Keiran, and Desiree are all around, so you won't be alone."

Despite his assurances, a moment of sadness went through her, just long enough to cause her chest to ache. She was truly alone now.

Woodenly, she nodded. "Aye."

And with that, the next day he was gone.

As the week passed, she enlisted Teddy's crew as taste testers while she perfected scones and breads. Happily, they obliged.

Candee designed a high-quality menu, and aprons were ordered to match Kathleen's teahouse logo. At the last minute, the crewmen erected a pergola to the outside seating area, where bottled water, tea, and fruit juices would be sold.

Kathleen stationed a NOW HIRING sign near the entrance of the teahouse, and several applicants immediately responded. Interviewing the bright-faced candidates left her invigorated and hopeful.

However, various decisions still loomed. Would customers prefer high tea or a more casual atmosphere? Parsnips in their soup or a traditional creamy broccoli? Spot-on decisions meant enthusiastic regulars, and she counted on Rob's daily answers to her texts.

As the days flew forward, two catastrophes occurred.

First, the large dough mixer wasn't expected to arrive on time after all.

Forcing herself to sound calm and unemotional, she phoned Rob.

"You have countertop hand mixers, right?" he asked.

"Aye, and a dough proofer and all the bakeware."

"Tell the two assistants you hired to use what's available. They're qualified, correct?"

"Which brings me to my second catastrophe." She could hardly voice the words. "One quit before she started because she said the start-up wage is too low. The other is in university and her work days are limited."

"Keep looking."

"I am. There may be a third applicant. Her name is Nancy, and she's enthusiastic and eager."

"How old is she?"

"Twenty-something. She's willing to work alongside me, doesn't mind long hours, and told me that my teahouse is unique and special."

"She's a keeper. People like that are hard to find, so train her well and take any spare minute to invest in her development. And don't forget to phone Keiran too. He's a block away."

"I did. O'Malley's is busier than ever and he can't spare anyone this close to St. Patrick's Day. Teddy has even bussed a few tables there to help Keiran out."

Rob blew out a sigh. "Unfortunately, being short-staffed is typical in this industry."

"Short-staffed is one thing. No staffed is another."

"Part-time employees aren't dependable. I'd refer a couple of mine, but with my stores for sale, everyone is in an upheaval. Many of my steady workers are seeking employment elsewhere."

"Didn't you assure them that their jobs were secure?"

"I tried, although new owners may bring aboard different people."

She paused. "Rob, can I ask you another question?"

"Certainly."

"Should I urge my customers to place their cell-phones in containers when they walk in? You know, to strengthen community, and encourage family conversations."

Through the phone, she heard a man speaking to Rob.

"Sorry Kathleen, it's David," Rob said.

"The cow guy?"

"Yes, and it's apparently urgent. Hang on." Rob muffled the phone. He addressed David's question, then came back on the line. "This place is like a zoo today. What were you saying?"

"Nothing." Kathleen's grip on her phone tightened. "I'll sort it out myself."

"Sorry," he said softly. "Once this place is sold, we'll be together."

When? Selling a huge commercial operation wouldn't be a matter of a few days. It would take weeks, maybe months. Maybe years.

She'd always found herself cheered after talking with Rob. However, her chin quivered as she felt her safeguards being swept aside. She relied on him, but he had enough on his hands without her constant barrage of questions. In the interim, she needed to trust her own business sense.

She inhaled deeply. "Do you remember Sean, my coworker at The Ground Café?"

"The guy who is supposedly interested in quitting his manager job in Ireland to lend you a hand in America?"

"I wouldn't put it that way, Rob," she corrected. "He isn't *supposedly* interested. He is interested and assured he won't accept a salary from me. Plus, he'd work full-time, so there's no dependability issue."

"You've discussed your last-minute problems with him, plus he'll work for free?" She could almost see Rob's eyes narrowing. "Why?"

"Because he's a friend." She bristled. "He's been nothing but supportive. He rang me again last night."

"And now he's phoning you as well as texting?"

"Only twice since you left. He's as experienced as you are."

"Your brogue is thickening, and you sound defensive, which is never a good sign." There was an inexplicable seriousness in Rob's tone, coupled with frustration. "And what did you tell Mr. Sean?"

"I told him I was handling things well on my own,

although these days I'm thinking I can use his support. He's ringing me tomorrow morning."

"Sounds like you talk with this guy more than you talk with me."

"Don't be ridiculous. You and I chat every day. It's just that you're … preoccupied." She couldn't remember the last time her conversation with Rob hadn't been interrupted at least once. And Sean was 100 percent available—and always sympathizing with her.

"Kathleen." Rob allowed the silence between them to go on for twice as long as she expected. "There's a lot involved here in Miami."

"I know." She squeezed her eyes shut. "And I should be more understanding."

He didn't say yes or no. Instead, he continued, "Several of my managers expressed interest in purchasing the entire business. That's heartening, because they've been with me for years and I trust them to maintain the quality. However, bank loan applications are time-consuming. Not to mention, my bakeries are all still running."

She needed him. Now. Didn't he realize that?

She shook her head. She was being selfish.

"I understand," she said quietly, although she heard the edge in her tone.

"Remember our ghost town. Our life together. Remember us."

Us.

The dovelike caress threading his words caused a delicious shiver up her spine.

"I'll remember." She gave a weary smile into the phone.

Hollan Farms. An empty shell of a town. Despite Rob's assurances, she felt similar to that town. Abandoned.

When her cell-phone rang at dawn, she recognized Sean's

number on the caller ID. And when he asked if she required back-up relief, she answered with one word.

Aye.

He was capable. He was more than eager. And they'd worked closely before.

ON A RAIN-SOAKED afternoon a couple days afterward, Sean appeared in Roses. His flights from Dublin to Asheville were brilliant, he assured. He'd hired an Uber for the final leg to Roses.

"You quit your job at The Ground Café?" Kathleen inquired as he met her under the front awning. Despite the heavy travel he looked well-rested, his olive-camouflage jacket and black pants washed and pressed.

"Aye. Howya." He placed his luggage on the stoop and grasped her in a fierce hug. "I'm tired of working for someone else."

"You'll work for me now."

He didn't answer. A shadow crossed his hard-lined face.

"Well, travel certainly agrees with you." She pondered her statement as she regarded him. "When I flew the transatlantic flight, it took me several days to recover from jet lag."

"Kathleen, I must confess." His gaze darted. "I landed in Boston last week."

"Boston?" With keen effort, she controlled her temper while drawing a slow breath. "I assumed you were in Ireland when you rang me."

"I figured I was off to America, anyway. A few days earlier didn't matter."

"And if I didn't accept your bid to help me?"

"Don't know." He waved his hands airily. His hazel eyes darkened. "I may have stayed in Boston, although I knew you'd come round eventually if I kept badgering."

Typical Sean. He'd always hassled big-hearted Danny Brady at The Ground Café, requesting weekends off or extended paid holidays until Danny agreed.

"You're obviously a pro at badgering," she said.

"I suppose I am."

She couldn't keep from staring at him. His medium-length dark hair had been styled into a kinky perm.

"Any comments?" He finger combed the curls. "A man perm is all the rage."

"It's …" She stopped herself before saying *hysterically funny*, assuming he wouldn't appreciate the humor.

"Foxy?" he questioned.

"Aye, especially combined with your dark beard."

"*Go raibh míle maith agat.*"

Thanks a million. The familiar Irish words brought a rush of tears to her eyes.

"Can you recommend a place in town where I can rent a room?" he asked.

"There's a splendid bed-and-breakfast not far from here."

"And a pub with good craic?" He stepped too close, completely disregarding her personal space. "I'm definitely fond of parties."

She moved backward, remembering the times he'd reported to The Ground Cafe after going out on the lash and drinking. Although she'd often smelled alcohol on his breath, it hadn't seemed to affect his performance.

"If you're in search of lively banter," she pointed down the street, "Keiran O'Malley's pub is walking distance from here. Just don't drink on the days you're working here."

"Wouldn't think of it."

"Do you remember Keiran's cousin William?" she asked.

"I do." His gaze leveled on her. "He won your affection and took you away from me."

"We're all just friends, Sean."

"I'd like us to be more than friends, Kathleen. Surely you must know that."

"Sean. No. Although I'm thankful for your support."

"Gotcha. Loud and clear." He raised his hands in feigned surrender. "As soon as I'm a wee bit settled, I'll visit Keiran's pub on my off days." His small hazel eyes left hers to regard the teahouse's green painted shingles. "Your place looks brilliant. The color reminds me of Ireland."

"Do you think so? Decorating isn't my forte, I just wanted an old European touch. Fortunately, my friend Candee guided me. I couldn't even choose curtains until she carried over several fabric swatches and I finally decided on a jewel-tone floral."

"Candee is your real estate agent?"

"Aye. Her husband, Teddy, is my contractor." Kathleen blew out a breath. "I'm trying hard to resist the impulse to text her every time there's a decorating problem."

"Luckily, here I am to solve everything." He picked up his luggage, and they stepped inside, the front bell tinkling to announce their arrival.

"Thanks for coming. You're an asset, Sean."

"It's because our Irish work ethic is first rate."

She grinned, turning her attention to the shelves teeming with tea. "Today I'm trying to decide how many loose-leaf blends to serve my customers."

"Less is better to keep the quality up."

"Sean, there are over 250 teas to choose from."

"From the looks of it, you've bought them all." He planted his hands on his bony hips. "Stick with a basic selection of twelve."

"I planned a high tea every day at four o'clock. Is that too much?"

"Roses is a little-bitty town," he said. "Compromise and

serve high tea on weekends only. You'll end up failing if you overextend yourself."

"You're right," she said.

His boots clicked across the wood floors, and she glided her hand over a lavish tea service she'd polished until the silver gleamed. "I can't believe you flew such a long way for me."

"My pleasure." Lightly, he brushed a curl coming loose from her pony tail in much the same way when they'd worked double shifts together and were exhausted at the end of the day. "You remember I'm the adventurous sort. Like you."

She also remembered he used to point that out a lot. *Spirited go-getters intent on success,* he'd say. Somehow, the words didn't sound as flattering as they once did.

IN THE ENSUING DAYS, Sean inched his way into becoming an integral part of every decision, from improving providers' terms to mounting a decorative box next to each table for cell-phones.

He was shrewd, often voicing her objectives before she did, or latching on to an idea and expanding it. He repeatedly pointed out that her concepts were comparable to The Ground Café's. Therefore, when she described a problem with the teas or scones, he immediately chimed in with eleventh-hour solutions.

Rob phoned numerous times, and she played phone tag with him. She yearned for his quick grin, the sound of his deep voice, his warm-hearted reassurances. However, immersed in a whirlwind of activity, the hours passed all too quickly.

Another snag, Rob texted the evening after Sean's arrival.

I'm coming, but delayed a few more days. I should be in Roses by Friday.

Understandable, she replied, noting Friday was a week away. *I'll send photos of my new menu.*

Sean watched while she texted Rob and smiled knowingly.

"I'm here for you," was all he said.

The following day, Kathleen went through every nook in her teahouse for elements she might have missed. Lightly, she traced her fingers over the herbal tea baskets, honey dispensers, and a row of clear glass pitchers. Teddy's crew had completed the renovation, and the place was quiet, save for a collection of Irish tunes playing on the CD.

Everything in the teahouse was unique and stylish, a far cry from the greasy, cramped, and gloomy interior she'd first encountered. She knew Rob would be impressed.

Rob.

She'd meant to send him photos of the menu. In the flurry of activity, she'd forgotten, falling into bed at night too weary to think. She'd do it in the morning.

"What will the children drink?" Sean came up behind her and interrupted her thoughts.

"What children?"

"Your customers will bring in their wee ones. You'll want to keep them content and occupied."

"I can serve hot cocoa."

"What about a fun tea experience?" He inclined his head. "Brew decaffeinated tea and give it an unusual name—like cinnamon toast tea served in a cup named Chip."

"A chipped cup?"

"From *Beauty and the Beast,*" he prompted.

"Oh, right." She smiled. "Brilliant. Let's include that name on the chalkboard."

. . .

LATER THE SAME DAY, a $6000 invoice arrived for the double-deck gas convection oven. It was stamped OVERDUE.

Kathleen scanned the bill and gasped.

Sean peered over her shoulder. "Troubles?"

"How can the supplier expect payment if I'm not even open yet?" She set the invoice on the counter and began mixing dough for wheat bread. For her, baking was therapeutic and gave her something to do with her hands. "Financially, I'm stretched to the max."

"You can't apply for another loan?"

"I'm considered an upstart, and banks don't risk their money. I put up my parent's home in County Galway that was deeded to me upon their death as collateral. After $200,000 dollars, I'm tapped out."

He lifted a dark eyebrow, then perused the letter accompanying the invoice. "The company can shut you down if you can't remit."

"Naturally I pay my bills. Just not until the teahouse opens."

"I can help."

She placed the dough into the electric mixer and switched it on. "Sean, I refuse to accept your money. I know you're not a rich man."

The electricity blew out with a snap. The lights switched off, and the mixer stopped.

"Again?" she groaned. "Teddy said we may have an electrical issue if this keeps up, although the power company blames the problem on the new lines being dug in the area. I hope they're right, because I don't have an extra five thousand—"

"At present, it's an easy fix," Sean assured, finding the breaker box and switching the power back on. Once the mixer started running again, he showed up beside her.

"Kathleen, I have a business proposition for you," he said.

"I already had one."

"From your hotshot Miami boyfriend?"

She winced. She'd confided to Sean about Rob's job proposal. She wished she hadn't. A day hadn't gone by when Sean didn't bring up Rob, and his remarks were never flattering.

"I'm not selling my teahouse and setting back to Ireland with my tail between my legs," she declared, "so don't tell me to give up."

"We Irish have more pride than that."

There it was again. *We versus them.* The Irish versus the Americans, the bankers, even Teddy's crewmen if Sean disagreed with their work. He constantly implied the Irish were underdogs and appealed to her sense of patriotism.

She shut off the mixer, wrested the dough from the bowl, and began kneading. "What are you saying?"

"We share a passion for this type of place." He sidled closer. Instinctively, she moved back a step. "You and I worked under brass-hat Brady and watched him make diffi-cult decisions."

"So?"

"So let's face the truth. You can't run a business. You're too emotionally involved." His tone challenged with a hint of mockery. "And there are numerous details, far too many for one person. You're in over your head, luv. Hey, you can't even make a decision about curtains without help."

Luv. She let the word go by.

She kept her head down while she rolled out the dough, then dusted her flour-stained hands along the edges of her apron. "As you obviously guessed, my specialty isn't interior design."

"This isn't about decorating. This is about realizing your strengths and admitting your weaknesses."

Rather than argue, she agreed, because she knew arguing

with him was useless. He was always willing to fight, and she didn't have the energy. Despite the never-ending work hours, her problems continued to mushroom. Somewhere along the way, she'd begun to feel powerless.

Maybe Sean was right. Her corporate sense wasn't strong. Sure, she'd been in positions of management, but that was different from owning a company where every choice meant financial loss and subsequent failure.

She sank onto a high-backed chair. "What are you suggesting?"

"As I said, I'm offering a firm proposition and subsequent solution."

Her eyebrows flicked upward, measuring him. "Which is?"

"I'll buy into your business." He watched her closely as he pulled up a chair. "Your financial worries will end, and you'll be free to bake and serve customers—the services you did best at The Ground Café."

"Your terms …"

He slid his chair closer, then stretched out his legs. "A 60/40 split. In my favor."

"Absolutely not." Firmly, she shook her head. "I did all the groundwork."

"I'll continue your vision going forward, so don't go flashing those blustery eyes at me." With both hands on his knees, he leaned forward. "I'll take over all business aspects, financial and otherwise, and you can concentrate on a successful opening day."

"Sean, this is a difficult conversation." She rubbed the middle of her forehead and closed her eyes. "Give me time to consider."

"Rest assured I have your best interests at heart. In fact, I'll draw up the necessary papers." He lifted her chin. "It's best for everyone, aye?"

A heaviness invaded her body. Quieting, she gazed down at her rumpled apron, her washed-out jeans, and tried not to twist her hands. She was cornered, and her teahouse deserved no less than the best. She surveyed her supply of china cups and saucers stacked neatly on the shelves, the double-deck gas convection oven. What would happen if she lost her oven because of nonpayment? Her teahouse couldn't survive without the main oven and a large dough mixer, and she'd run out of funds.

"I'll think about it," she replied.

But what about Nancy, the new girl she'd hired, who seemed genuinely interested in learning the tea business?

Kathleen's mind whirled in a thousand different directions.

Four more days went by. Four more nights she spent staring at the ceiling in her shabby apartment, seeking the serenity of sleep before it vanished, forcing prolonged hours of insomnia and torturous deliberations.

And somewhere along the way, she stopped communicating with Rob altogether.

CHAPTER 11

On Wednesday of the following week, Rob strode over the tiny white blossoms lacing the front porch of Kathleen's teahouse. He knocked, then opened the wooden door. A tiny bell announced his arrival, though no one acknowledged him.

He'd texted his flight information to Kathleen the night before and she hadn't replied. In fact, he hadn't heard a word from her in several days. A quick query to Candee assured Kathleen was well, albeit "busy beyond words". Still, the silence had prompted him to return to Roses a couple days early.

Despite his focus on Miami and the mountain of paperwork yet to be signed, he congratulated himself. He'd successfully sold his business to a group of managers who'd worked in his bakeries for years. They'd pooled their funds, the bank loans were secured, and the closing was slated in a month.

"Sorry, fella. We're not open until St. Patrick's Day." A pencil-thin man sporting a dark beard and curly hair sat at a round table in the center of the main dining room. He was unmistakably Irish, his dialect quick, his sentences running together. He straightened from his sprawling position and refilled his glass of iced tea. "Come back Saturday for our grand opening."

"I'm aware of when March seventeenth is." Disregarding the man's hostile gaze, Rob strode further into the room.

"You Americans are smarter than people give you credit for."

"Who are you?" Rob demanded.

"Sean."

"Yeah, I figured."

"You?" came Sean's clipped inquiry.

"Rob."

"Aye. Without a doubt." Sean's derisive grin followed his flippant acknowledgement. He lifted his glass. "My only defense against the warm weather. In Ireland, March is a cold, rainy month. Here, the sun shines almost continuously and it's a bit warm for me."

"You'd melt in Miami then," Rob said. "How long have you been in Roses?"

"A few days."

Rob corralled his anger, focusing on the welcoming environment of the teahouse. The stunning renovation was a treasure trove. Orderly shelves displayed simple fruit jellies and preserves, and the counter was stocked with freshly ground coffee and an assortment of loose herbal teas in glass jars. The entire space was airy and bright. On the corner of each table, he noted a container.

Sean followed his gaze. "We added those for cell-phones. Kathleen believes in conversation with no interruptions."

Rob grimaced, recalling the number of times his chats with Kathleen had been cut off by his familiar cell-phone ping.

"Hungry?" Sean raised a silver tray laden with croissants.

"Nope." Rob avoided meeting the man's assessing stare. "Where is she?"

Sunshine eased through the floral curtains, lighting the cozy atmosphere, offset by candles shimmering along an antique sideboard. The cashmere comfort of a welcoming warmth enveloped him. In that instant, Rob saw the realization of Kathleen's remarkable achievement.

Well done, Kathleen.

"She's baking another Keiran O'Malley recipe in her apartment, because she prefers her small oven," Sean was saying. "Keiran has Irish relatives, you see."

"I'm aware."

"He's a decent bloke and has made me feel right at home. His pub is fierce and just the thing after a knackered day in a scorching kitchen."

"And I'm interested in Kathleen, not you." Rob crossed his arms. "I'll wait for her here and you can be on your way."

Since he'd entered, Rob had been struggling with an escalating annoyance, standing by while Sean lazily drank iced tea and tamped up croissant crumbs from his plate with his fingers. He felt like a panhandler waiting to be granted an audience with a queen.

"I'd suggest *you* should be the one on your way." Sean's sharp voice cut through Rob's thoughts. "You're acting like a Holy Joe coming to her rescue, but as you can see, we're ready for our opening and things have gone swimmingly. And we did it all without brainy old you."

"Excuse me?" In three strides, Rob closed the distance between them. "*We're* ready? *Our* opening? What's going on here?"

"I'll blame your questions on poor hearing because of your age and not poor listening. As you Americans speak frankly, I'll frame this so that you understand. Crack on and leave."

"Don't tell me what to do," Rob warned. "This isn't your place." He yanked out his cell-phone and typed Kathleen a text. *Where are you? I'm standing in your dining room.*

"On the contrary, it *is* my place." Sean examined his well-manicured fingernails. "Kathleen has agreed to make me her business partner. I'm here for the long haul."

For a moment, Rob couldn't trust himself to reply, his brain registering disbelief. His narrowed gaze examined Sean's blasé expression.

"I don't believe it. Kathleen is self-reliant."

Sean shrugged. "She's going in a different direction."

"Indeed?" Rob inquired. "Tell me more."

He'd been gone only a short while and Sean had triumphantly wormed his way back into her life. Slowly, something inside Rob began to crumble. While he was working out details and selling everything for her, she was handing over her business to this pompous Irishman.

He recalled his phone call with Kathleen when she'd sprung to Sean's defense.

"Do you remember Sean, my coworker at The Ground Café?" she'd asked.

"The guy who is supposedly interested in quitting his manager job in Ireland to lend you a hand in America?"

"I wouldn't put it that way, Rob. Sean isn't supposedly interested. He is interested and assured he won't accept a salary if he were to come here."

Rob scrubbed a hand over his face. He should've known Sean wouldn't waste a second quitting his job, flying over the Atlantic Ocean and coming to Kathleen's rescue. Nevertheless, she considered Sean a friend, so Rob was willing to endure the rest of the exchange for her sake.

"What are the terms of this offer?" Rob asked. "Because I can make her a better one."

"Can you? Mine is a 60/40 split."

"She'd agree to that?" Rob barked a laugh. "I'm surprised."

"We've always been brilliant together, and I'm her new fella. She's a fine thing, isn't she?"

Rob grappled with a stab of jealousy. "I can afford to give her the world," he said quietly.

"Your wealth doesn't impress me or Kathleen. How dare you flaunt your money around?" Sean enunciated each word in a vicious, thick brogue. "She's thrilled with our recent agreement."

"Oh, am I now, Sean?" Kathleen stormed into the room, her face emanating pure outrage. By the looks of the two steps she'd walked, she'd been in the doorway for some time. The green ribbon tying back her silky hair was askew, and her dark eyes sparked with fury.

Rob's heart thumped in double time, his gaze riveted on her. He trod closer, intending to take her in his embrace. She shrugged him off and marched to within a foot of Sean.

"How are ya, luv?" Sean grinned.

"Luv? Luv? I never decided on any so-called agreement."

"You were earwigging?" Sean shoved his glass aside and rose to his feet. "Eavesdropping on a private chat?"

She stamped her foot. "This is *my* teahouse, not yours."

Her outburst earned her Sean's hangdog expression. "Kathleen, I beg your forgiveness. Just teasing. Obviously, you're a bundle of nerves with St. Paddy's looming. If you'll only—"

"Get out and don't come back."

"What? And go where—" he sputtered.

"Back to Boston, or Ireland. You've ruined it for yourself by your underhandedness." She shook her head and whispered, "I should've realized. Why do I never learn?"

Without so much as picking up his glass or bidding a courteous goodbye, Sean twisted on his heels and blustered through the front door with lengthy, purposeful strides.

"A sound good riddance to him," Rob said as the door slammed. "Now you and I can talk."

Whirling, her glare blasted fury. "As if I'm starving for a chat with you when you're always so preoccupied. I don't need you, and I don't need Sean."

"We've been separated for a while, but now I'm retired. Let's sit down and have a friendly discussion over a cup of tea. Candee mentioned you received an overdue bill for the gas convection oven. I can help by writing out—"

Kathleen's eyes widened, and tears erupted. "How can you be so brilliant and yet think you can buy me? I know what I want, and I can achieve it on my own."

"But I can fix this." He paused. He loathed saying the same words his father had used on him, and it hadn't resolved anything.

Inside his jacket pocket, his cell-phone rang.

She stepped behind a high-backed chair, as if fortifying herself against him. Deliberately, she unclasped the skeleton key locket from her neck and placed it on the chair.

He felt as if his heart was breaking. He rubbed his fist against his chest. His eyes blurred with the effort.

His phone kept ringing.

"Aren't you going to answer?" she asked.

"Later." He came forward and closed his hand over her shoulder. "It's not important."

More tears leaked from her eyes and rolled down her cheeks. He brushed them away, and she flinched.

"Rob, return to Miami where you obviously belong."

They were so close he could see the mix of emotions crossing her face—trembling chin, lips pressed together, the slight freckles dotting her wet cheeks.

"You must know how much I love you," he said.

She drew an inward breath. "Everyone seems to love me

these days." Despite her quaking voice, she remained perfectly still.

"I realize you're joking. I know how you Irish love to—"

"This Irishwoman is deadly serious." Her voice rose. "And another thing, which I'm certain will come as a shocking surprise to you: this business is mine, and mine alone."

CHAPTER 12

At noon a day later, Kathleen sat in a high-backed chair in her teahouse and went through her text messages. Rob hadn't returned since their argument.

Instead, he'd called and left messages, saying he was staying at Candee and Teddy's home if she needed him.

Here's a final idea, he'd texted. *I've partnered with the Roses Chamber of Commerce for a ribbon-cutting ceremony on your official opening day. I know it's late but every bit of advertising helps.*

She hadn't responded.

I've done more market research and can set up a paid advertising media blitz which will coincide with St. Patrick's Day.

No. She'd set up all her online advertising ahead of time. She didn't need to lean on anyone except herself.

Why won't you let me help you? he'd asked again and again. *If you give us half a chance, you will remember how good we r together.*

That dart effectively pierced a nerve, and she'd closed her cell-phone and placed it in her purse.

A soft opening at the teahouse was arranged to begin at

four o'clock. This gave her and Nancy, the new employee, a chance to work out the crimps. Although the public was aware the teahouse was launching, Kathleen hadn't actively publicized it. Candee and Teddy sent their regards, as Joseph was participating in a horse show in Asheville and they couldn't attend. Keiran and Desiree were swamped at O'Malley's. And Sean had fled Roses.

Fortunately, another power outage hadn't occurred while customers dined later that evening, although the lock on the women's bathroom door broke.

Kathleen had also teamed up with Keiran and chalked his mushroom stroganoff as a main dinner entrée, quickly learning that serving the dish at five o'clock was too early and nine too late. Patrons preferred their dinner hour at seven, and she'd soon run out of mushroom stroganoff.

By nine p.m., the teahouse had emptied. After Nancy helped clean, she'd scanned a text message on her phone and departed without an explanation, forgetting her house keys in her haste. Because Nancy lived with her parents on the outskirts of Roses, Kathleen assumed she wouldn't need the keys until morning. Just in case, she put them aside near the herbal tea jars.

Kathleen dreaded the silence that enveloped the unoccupied rooms. It allowed her mind to dwell on all she'd lost. No longer could she hide behind work and busyness. She was forced to confront how much she missed Rob.

She slumped in the loveseat near the foyer and picked up her phone. She planned to make notes about the soft opening, tweaking her original vision. Despite her attempts, she couldn't focus, too intent on the honorable, caring man who had stolen her heart.

He'd been justifiably hurt and angry when he'd returned from Miami to find Sean lounging in her teahouse. And jealous, hiding his emotions by offering her money, hoping it would smooth the rift between them.

Her heart pinched. He'd worked for years to ensure a prosperous business, and desperately wanted her to succeed as well. He was the type of guy who helped people, soft-hearted and obliging. She knew he would never refuse her any favor. Rob was a man she could always count on.

He loved her. He'd told her so.

And what had she done when he'd proclaimed his love?

Why, she'd thrown it in his face.

"You must know how much I love you," he'd said.

"Everyone seems to love me these days," she'd responded coolly.

She read his numerous texts, pleading with her to give them a second chance.

She hadn't replied.

He had inquired about attending her soft opening.

I'd prefer you didn't. Please take my advice and stay in Miami.

And then he'd gone dark and hadn't contacted her since.

Dejectedly, she put her head in her hands and sobbed. Somehow, she'd done it again—succeeded in being involved in a heartbreaking romance with a man.

No. That wasn't true. Rob had given up his life in Miami, his thriving career, *everything* for her. And in the shared hours exploring a ghost town and dancing Irish jigs, amidst toppled tea cups and spilled vases filled with water and flowers, she'd fallen in love with him too.

Restless, she wiped her eyes, stood, and wandered through the vacant, lonely rooms, lighting night light candles and watering the potted green ferns.

Nothing was the same without him. The teahouse wasn't alive. He'd brought laughter, full of ideas, a ready smile on his face. And now he was gone.

She had driven him away, flatly refusing his help. She'd

seen the raw sadness in his blue eyes, the sagging around his mouth, when he'd said goodbye and walked out the door.

She leaned a shoulder on the windowpane and stared out at a cloudless night. Somewhere in the distance, a church bell pealed. When the time neared midnight, she sighted the star-shaped Big Dipper above the northern horizon.

Half-heartedly, she murmured, "Rob, how can you be so quiet after I told you to return to Miami? Did you forget me already?"

With a tattered sigh, she retreated to the back room and burrowed through the chest of drawers. She extracted the skeleton key locket and glided her fingers over the elaborate floral design. He'd confessed she held the key to his heart and requested she wear it always.

"Rainbows are brilliant in America too, Kathleen. And Roses is your new home."

And then the words that had dangled between them.

Here. With me.

She secured the locket, feeling better when it was near her heart, where it belonged.

With trembling hands, she texted him. If he accepted her apology and boarded a plane from Miami in the morning, he might arrive in Roses by midday. There was so much she needed to tell him. She'd been hurt by men countless times in her life and had been afraid to trust again. To love again.

But what was the world without love?

A FEW MINUTES after midnight brought a ping to Rob's cellphone. He'd been sitting by the guest bedroom's window in Candee's home, gazing idly outside at the familiar Big Dipper. The house was quiet, as the family was attending a horse show in Asheville.

"It better not be another manager texting me at this hour," he muttered, yanking the phone from his pocket.

Kathleen's caller ID appeared on the screen.

I miss you. Would you consider flying back from Miami?

And then: *1-800-IRELAND.*

He couldn't contain his excitement. He was already on his feet, his heart pounding with joy.

The drive to Kathleen's teahouse, which normally took under ten minutes, he covered in less than five. He didn't know what he'd say, wasn't sure how she'd respond. All that mattered was she had reached out to him and he was able to see her again.

He knocked once, hesitating only a second outside the teahouse's door, feeling the cool nip in the night air against his heated cheeks. Realizing the door was unlocked, he stepped inside. The tinkling bell announced his arrival.

She sat on a velvet loveseat in the foyer, her back to him, peering at a lengthy list. He recognized the business plan they'd drawn up together.

"Nancy?" Kathleen inquired without glancing up. "I put your keys aside for you. You'll see them by the tea jars on the counter."

He longed to rush to her, to pull her into his arms. She looked vulnerable, her red-gold hair shining in the delicate candlelight. Twice, he'd left her alone when he'd flown to Miami.

"Kathleen," he said.

She twisted and flew to her feet. "Rob?" All color drained from her complexion. "You're here? How?"

"I never left Roses."

"I thought you were in Miami."

"I couldn't leave." He strode to a cell-phone container and slipped his phone inside. "Our life together wasn't finished. It hadn't even started."

She moistened her lips, raced to him, and looped her arms around his neck.

He cradled her and guided her to the loveseat. She wore his locket over a starched white shirt and tailored black pants—the uniform she'd decided on for the teahouse. He traced his fingers along her high cheekbones. Her long dark lashes fluttered.

"I wish you'd been here, for the soft opening," she said.

"I wanted to. I'm here now. How did it go?"

"A few tweaks. Actually more than a few." She snuggled nearer his chest. "I learned people in Roses like to eat dinner at seven o'clock and be home early. The place cleared out by nine."

His lips brushed her forehead. "That's what a little bird told me."

She gazed up at him, this beauty he'd almost lost. "Who?" she asked.

"Nancy."

"My new employee?"

"Lovely woman, and absolutely exceptional. Sorry she'll no longer be working for you."

Rapidly, Kathleen blinked. "Excuse me?"

"Nancy will be working for me. Or rather, for us."

"You can't just walk in and steal my best employee."

"*Our* best employee."

"I'm not following." She frowned, her voice uncertain. "I finally ..."

He pressed a finger to her mouth. "I bought another place. A ghost town, actually."

"You bought ..." Incredulous, she stared at him. "You bought Hollan Farms? Now you'll be busier than ever."

"I didn't buy the town for me." He kissed her lips, softly, sweetly. "I bought the town for David to manage. I'm a silent investor."

She grinned, her face lighting with laughter. "The cow guy?"

"The one and only. And Nancy will help him." Rob twirled a lock of Kathleen's silky hair around his fingers. "Those two are young and ambitious. Hey, maybe it's the start of a budding romance. And you and I can oversee their progress once in a while."

"What will you do in the meantime?" she asked.

"I'm retired." He grinned. "But I'll be around, just in case you need my assistance."

"I do." She sat straighter, meeting his gaze with her own. "And I finally realized that accepting help isn't a sign of weakness, but of strength."

"You'll be far more able to reach your goals."

"Aye. So I've learned."

"Since you're so agreeable," he stood, then got down on one knee. "Will you marry an American man like me?"

"This is really happening," she murmured. "And my answer is, aye. Yes."

His smile reached his ears, and he went back to cuddling her on the loveseat. "After St. Patrick's Day, we'll look for a home in Roses," he said.

"I like the mild weather here. In Ireland, the days get dark quickly in the winter, and it's rainy and cold."

"In Miami, it's too hot most of the year."

Her deep brown eyes brimmed with tears. "Then Roses is perfect." She snuggled into his arms as his lips moved over hers.

"I love you more than anyone in the world," he whispered. "When you told me to leave, I vowed to wait however long it might take. I knew we had something extraordinary together."

"I've always wanted to visit Miami."

"I've always wanted to visit Ireland. I even have their toll-free number."

She laughed. "You don't really think that if you punch in 1-800-IRELAND, someone from Ireland will answer?"

With aching tenderness, he said, "I believe she will."

"I love you," she whispered.

"And I love you."

In the container by a table, his cell-phone rang.

She grinned up at him. "Ireland calling?"

"Toll-free."

"Aren't you going to answer it?"

"Nope. She's already answered all my dreams." He gazed around her comfortable teahouse, then at the exquisite woman in his arms.

A forever love.

THE END

JOSIE RIVIERA

1*800*SUMMER

A SWEET CONTEMPORARY NOVELLA

CHAPTER 1

$\mathcal{B}$elle Boots breathed in the comforting smell of hay and leather and peered around at her beloved stable—the weathered wooden planks, the plastic buckets of water, the wide mirror propped in the corner of the stall …

And, most notably, at Jenkins—her sweet, colorful appaloosa—all one thousand pounds of quirky loyalty and claustrophobia.

"We're leaving, handsome." She fished in her pocket for a carrot. "Off we trot to greener pastures."

Jenkins whinnied and poked his nose through the stall, noisily accepting the carrot and ignoring her quip.

"Why is the pasture greener?" She rubbed his ears. "Because the new landlord of my sorry excuse for an apartment raised the rent." Which meant fewer than five weeks to find another place. She grabbed a water bucket and brush, scrubbing and refilling the bucket. "Maybe this is the ideal opportunity for us to return to Wilmington."

Another crunch of the carrot, and Jenkins pawed the stable floor.

"I can't play right now. I'm sorry. My therapy sessions begin in an hour."

In the past two years, she'd grown fond of the postcard-perfect community of Roses. In fact, she regarded Roses as her hometown.

She blew out a pensive sigh. Or did she?

Sometimes a person needed to leave a place to discover where home truly was. The sense of adventure that had surged through her when she had decided on Roses—the thrill of a different town and untried places—had worn thin. Despite her efforts to stay busy, Belle had never gotten over her loneliness since she had left Wilmington.

Perhaps she was simply homesick. She missed Aunt Lucinda, her mother's older sister and Belle's only living relative. Plus, she missed the ocean—the bracing waves, the salty air rushing across her face, and the sunbeams flashing off the water like silent jewels.

Jenkins stamped his hoof, bringing Belle back to the present.

"I only brought one carrot with me," she said. "I'll return later this afternoon with more."

In the pale-yellow light streaming through the slats, the echoes of a late May morning drifted, and promised a typical North Carolina day. Sunrises were cool and bearable before the humidity and oppressive heat kicked in.

After she mucked the stall and turned out Jenkins to the pasture, Belle's attentions swung back to her dilemma. Wilmington beckoned. Or perhaps Florida or California.

Only one thing was certain. She was moving. Somewhere.

She glanced at her watch. Swiftly, she washed up and sprinted to her pickup truck. In the tangle of the confusing morning, she'd lost track of time.

Her first equine therapy session was with Joseph, a dark-eyed boy whose lean legs raced so quickly he reminded her of a clockwork figure. His adoptive parents, Candee and Teddy, owned a large Victorian home on Thompson Lane and had built a riding ring on their acreage.

The second session was with Megan Bransfield, a chubby, pale girl who wore a bright pink patch over her right eye and rarely smiled.

How could she desert these precious children? Belle's sentiments wrestled between anguish and indecision. At the other side of the spectrum, anticipation welled.

THE DRIVE into Roses went slower than expected, which invariably happened whenever she was in a hurry. When she neared the Thompson Lane turn-off, she took in the scene in front of her—red, white, and blue balloons; the local marching band; and a banner stretching across the main street announcing the Memorial Day parade.

Quietly groaning, she clicked on her right signal, pulled to the curb, and phoned Candee.

"Hi, Belle," came Candee's cheerful response.

"Candee, I apologize." Belle rolled down her window, and a welcoming breeze gusted in, tousling her ponytail. "I'm running late, and traffic is at a standstill."

"No worries," Candee replied. "We'll wait for you."

"If you and your family prefer to attend the parade, it's fine. We can reschedule."

"Joseph wouldn't miss his session with you for anything in the world. Teddy and I appreciate all you've done, because Joseph's transformation is remarkable. He's considerably more outgoing and upbeat."

Belle's compassion squeezed. *Tell Candee gently.*

Belle and Candee had engaged in numerous coffee chats, most of which had centered around Belle's ex-husband, Tyler.

She'd married him at twenty-three years old. He was stoic and impassive and a suitable complement to Belle's over-the-top eagerness to please. And, they had hoped for a large family.

Or so she'd thought.

She yanked her mind back to Candee's enthusiastic, one-sided dialogue regarding her barbecue that evening.

"I have news," Belle blurted.

"What?"

"This session will be Joseph's last, at least with me." Belle fiddled with her truck's side-view mirror as an emptiness hollowed out a pit in her stomach. It wasn't in her nature to abandon her clientele, most notably the children who relied on her.

"Why is this his last session?" Candee asked.

"I'm moving." *So much for gently.* "Soon."

"So sudden?"

"My rent was raised to an astronomical amount. The new landlord said his parents are relocating to a retirement community, and he is taking over the property."

"Astronomical?"

"He didn't exactly use the word astronomical, but he offered a marathon explanation and got his point across."

"Can't you find somewhere else close by to live? Teddy and I have extra bedrooms on the third floor. What's more, Desiree and Kieran are hardly ever home. I'm certain they wouldn't mind if you lived with them for a while, either."

Desiree was Candee's sister, and she and her husband lived a few houses away from Candee. Kieran had opened O'Malley's, an Irish restaurant which had become tremendously well-liked. Desiree had set her profession as a lawyer on hold in order to assist Kieran.

"I refuse to inconvenience anyone," Belle replied.

"You're no inconvenience, and your horse can stable here."

"Jenkins? One never can predict how he'll behave."

"We're currently only boarding Joseph's and Megan's horses. Besides, Jenkins is a sweetie—despite his behavioral issues."

Belle chuckled. "He'll figure out a way to get out of his stall and invite the other horses to slip away with him."

"He did that once, right? When he was a racehorse?"

"He was tired of being a racehorse and has adapted to becoming a riding horse." Although Jenkins was notorious for bucking off a forceful advanced rider by stopping fast ensuring the unsuspecting rider sailed over him.

"At present, Jenkins is happy," Candee said.

"As long as everything goes his way. Though I'm thinking practically, and any arrangements in Roses would be merely temporary." Belle added a smile to her words to soften her refusal. "Thank you for your offer, though."

"Roses is home."

"For you." Belle shifted her attention back to the road. "Not for me. My home is in Wilmington, where my roots are."

Wilmington? Roots? She'd made a decision?

Apparently yes, at least in her subconscious.

"Teddy has contacts in Wilmington," Candee was saying. "Besides, I'm a Realtor ... are you looking for anyplace special?

"I'd like to live near the ocean. We'll talk more when I arrive."

The women said their goodbyes and hung up.

As Belle merged into traffic, the slam of a door broke her concentration. A man strode onto a second-floor balcony and leaned over the railing. His broad shoulders were starkly outlined in a crisp white shirt. His breaths were slow and deliberate.

And then he did something completely out of character—considering the elegant house, his tailored silhouette, and the passing motorists who could witness his despair.

He placed his head in his hands.

Belle craned her neck. Was he weeping? Should she offer support?

Behind her, a car horn beeped, and she twisted back to the policewoman directing traffic. Caught in the uneasy silence of indecision, Belle followed the policewoman's signals and kept moving.

One last time, she turned. Just as the cars picked up speed, the man raised his head. For an instant, their gazes met.

He was incredibly handsome, in a Kevin Costner sort of way. His hair was dark with a hint of crimson, layered and expertly cut. His lips were firmly drawn.

And Belle couldn't help noticing that his cheeks were wet with tears. Swiftly, he mopped his eyes with a handkerchief, and the vulnerable gesture touched her heart.

AN HOUR LATER, she pulled her truck into the driveway of Candee's Victorian style home.

On the lush, expansive front yard, Joseph swung on a rope swing tied to the limb of an enormous oak tree. His thin legs kicked vigorously and the tree branch bent in an arc as Candee pushed him back and forth.

As soon as he spotted Belle, Joseph jumped off the swing and scurried to her. "Miss Belle!" He reached up and quickly hugged her. "Did you get to see the parade?"

"You are more important than a parade." Belle pressed back tears, reminding herself there were other excellent horse therapists in the area.

She slung her backpack over her shoulder and kneeled. Joseph's brown eyes sparkled with mischief, his complexion glowed healthy and tanned. After his father had died in a horrific car accident, Candee and Teddy had steered him through several difficult years. Teddy was Joseph's uncle, and he and Candee had legally adopted the little boy.

Belle scrubbed a hand over his dark wavy hair. "Let's get started, shall we?"

An irresistible giggle lit his expression. With an "okay," he tore down the driveway as Candee fell in step beside Belle.

"Teddy is in the stable and will help Joseph saddle up the horse," Candee said. "I informed him about your move."

Because of his home-flipping and construction dealings, Teddy teamed up with workers across the state. Along with Rob, his partner—who also resided in Roses with his wife, Kathleen—their supportive network of crewmen was substantial.

"What did Teddy say?" Belle prompted.

"He provided several leads, and I found a Wilmington rental available at a reasonable price. The landlords are a young couple." Candee tucked a strand of red hair behind her ear. "The apartment is located a few blocks from the beach and is situated on a modest amount of acreage. The couple is giving up farming, but keeping their house and barn and outbuildings. They'll allow you to use their stable and grounds, because they're both taking full-time jobs in Wilmington."

"What is the rental amount?" Belle asked.

"Three hundred dollars a month."

"Perfect. The situation sounds ideal."

"*Almost* ideal," Candee hedged. "The property needs work, judging from the description and photos."

"Do you have any information?" Belle asked.

"All on my phone. Let's review everything tonight when

you attend my barbecue. Rob and Kathleen are coming, and Rob is baking a batch of his marvelous muffins. Kieran and Desiree are bringing Irish pub food from their restaurant." Candee laughed. "A traditional, all-American buffet with a dash of Irish flavor and delectable desserts."

Belle pushed out a sigh. "I'd love to attend, but I can't. I need to start packing."

Candee pulled out her cellphone. "Then I'll text you the information."

There was a recognizable whoosh followed by a ping as photos appeared on Belle's phone. She scrolled through, scrutinizing each one.

"I like the apartment," she murmured.

Candee peered over Belle's shoulder. "It has charm and character."

"Is that your Realtor's way of describing the paint that's peeling off the ceiling?" Belle enlarged the kitchen photo. "I'll help clean."

"You won't need to, because Teddy will provide a crew and charge a nominal fee for repairs." Candee placed a hand on Belle's arm. "I know you're going to object, but please don't because we insist."

The first shred of optimism broke through Belle's concerns. Candee was a true friend, and her relocation might go easier than she anticipated. She extended a heartfelt thank you.

"Are you done talking to my Mom?" Joseph called out while Teddy led Blackjack, Joseph's sleek black horse, from the stable.

"Yes. I'm coming." Belle placed her backpack near the fence and hastened toward them. Later, she'd ask Candee for another referral, just in case this rental didn't work out. Then again, perhaps the apartment was fate.

But fate, Belle would later realize, was a funny thing.

.   .   .

AFTER JOSEPH'S SESSION ENDED, Megan appeared at the riding ring, the familiar pink patch covering her right eye. Her crimson-colored hair fell to her shoulders in slight curls, a startling contrast to her fair complexion and freckled features.

"Hi, Megan!" Belle enthusiastically greeted.

While Candee, Joseph and Teddy tended to Blackjack, Belle saddled Megan's pony, Honeycrisp, and led the solid Haflinger out of the stable, securing the pony to the fence with a halter rope.

A nanny normally brought Megan to her sessions, but today a man brought her.

A man with dark hair, enhanced by a hint of crimson.

An incredibly handsome man.

An incredibly familiar man.

He strode to the fence with Megan clinging tightly to his hand. As always, her riding boots were sturdy, her jeans washed and pressed.

"Hi, Miss Belle," the child said.

"Megan, you look so pretty." Belle bent to greet her. "If it's Monday morning, then it's time for your session with Honeycrisp."

Eagerly, Megan nodded.

As Belle straightened, the man eyed Belle, and then Honeycrisp. He wiped a hand along his pinstriped suit coat and stepped backward.

"I'm Andrew Bransfield," he said. "Are you the instructor?"

"Daddy." Megan giggled, her dimpled cheeks expanding in a wide grin as she handed Belle her riding bag. "Miss Belle teaches me every week."

His expression held no glimmer of recognition. He

merely stared at Belle while her own pulse gave a leap of acknowledgment.

"Hello, Mr. Bransfield," she managed. "It's a pleasure to meet you."

She accepted Megan's bag and dug through it until she found the riding helmet. She crouched to fasten the helmet under Megan's chin.

"Andrew."

"I'm sorry?" Belle glanced up.

"Please, call me Andrew."

"Andrew," Belle repeated. She stood, tightened her ponytail, and extended a friendly grin. Wow, up close he was even handsomer than she'd thought. And she couldn't determine from his clear, emerald-colored eyes whether he'd actually wept on the balcony. Perhaps she'd imagined the entire scenario.

Or perhaps he'd experienced a moment of desolation he couldn't contain.

Desolation was completely acceptable, wasn't it? She'd suffered through it, especially after her divorce.

She kept her grin. "I'm glad you're here so I can speak with you, Mr. Bransfield."

"Andrew." He returned her grin with one of his own. "Is anything wrong?"

She pressed her lips together, grappling to find the right words. "Megan is making excellent progress."

Coward. Tell him you're leaving and this will be his daughter's last session with you.

"She is, isn't she?" He gazed at Megan. "And she's adorable in her pink riding helmet."

"She certainly is. And we believe in safety first."

Brilliant, Belle. As if a father wouldn't understand the importance of safety for his little girl.

Andrew regarded his daughter with unabashed pride.

"The doctor said that the patch therapy for her lazy eye made a difference. Her eyes are beginning to work together."

"That's such good news," Belle replied.

Still wearing his shiny blue helmet, Joseph ran up to them. "My parents are in the stable," he assured, as he and Megan skipped away hand in hand. Amused and impressed by their easy camaraderie, Belle smiled. While Joseph often giggled during his sessions, Megan's lips usually never spared a curve.

"I'll be along shortly," Belle called after them.

"So, I'm finally meeting the famous Belle." A lyrical Scottish accent enhanced Andrew's baritone voice. She pictured him wearing a kilt, knee socks, and a clan badge, rather than a business suit.

"I can assure that I lead a quiet, uneventful life."

"In these parts, you are remarkable."

"Hardly." Compared to his voice, hers sounded fluttery and breathy.

His presence was commanding, partly because of his six-foot tall frame, and partly because of the self-confidence he exuded. And his smile. Oh, his smile did funny things to her pulse. Gone was the bleak man from the balcony.

She studied him. In his pinstriped suit and carrying a leather briefcase, he was completely out of his element in the dusty surroundings of a riding ring. He belonged in an uptown high-rise office on Wall Street.

Yet, despite his buttoned-up appearance, a lock of that crimson-colored hair fell across his temple, giving him a slightly disheveled appeal.

In any event, he was far too fine looking for his own good. And from her limited experience with men, he was probably well aware of his charisma.

"Here in Roses, your skill is renowned," he said. "Megan's

physician recommended equine therapy. I checked numerous references before I chose you."

"Horses have the best hearts and are excellent listeners."

"I was referring to you, not the horses." He rubbed the back of his neck and eyed Honeycrisp.

"Horses are awesome."

"Sure." His jaw set. That is, until he smiled. "Your compassionate skills are highly regarded."

"Thank you." He didn't provide her the opportunity to refute his obvious dislike of horses. "I love these kids. I love my job." Belle ignored Candee's scrutiny as she and Megan emerged from the stable. Teddy, with a wave, strode to the house with Joseph.

"How about a proper hello?"

"We've been talking for several minutes."

"But a proper handshake comes first." He reached out his hand, sending an unexpected quiver through her as their fingers touched.

Oh, my. What on earth?

She kept her hand in his, although she should let go. Shouldn't she?

As she ended their handshake, she focused on the ground.

The ensuing silence between them was interrupted only by chirping birds and chattering squirrels.

"Are you captivated by dirt?" he inquired.

"Candee made certain the ground was ideal for a ring. You see ... clay-based soil is the best for riding because ..." She was babbling. She never babbled. To her chagrin, her cheeks overheated.

No, no. This was absurd. She wasn't a woman who melted because a man shook her hand.

Candee called out and Belle performed a smooth turn.

"I'm coming," she replied, then turned. "Mr. Bransfield ..."

"Andrew."

He backed up, keeping a watchful eye on Honeycrisp.

On several occasions, Megan had confided that her father didn't like horses.

Or was he afraid of them?

With a knowing grin, Belle nodded in Honeycrisp's direction, admiring the horse's flaxen blond mane and tail. "You purchased a stunning horse for your daughter."

"Right."

Belle hurried to Megan as she climbed up on the mounting block. The child put her small foot in the stirrup, grabbed the saddle horn, and swung onto the horse.

"I promise there's nothing to fear," Belle called out. "Horses are gentle."

"In your opinion," he returned. "In mine, horses are large and awkward."

"Honeycrisp is small. A pony, actually. She's only thirteen hands."

"That's a lot of hands," came his quick reply.

WHEN MEGAN'S SESSION ENDED, Belle became distinctly aware of the laughing conversation between Mr. Bransfield and Candee as they stood outside the fence.

She extended a professional smile as Candee entered the ring.

"I'll tend to the horses while you and Andrew talk." Candee snatched Honeycrisp's halter rope and, with Megan, led the pony's return to the stable.

"Miss Belle? May I have a word with you?" Mr. Bransfield unlocked the gate and cautiously stepped into the riding ring. "It is *Miss* Belle, isn't it?"

"Yes." She wondered how he'd learned she wasn't married. Most likely, Candee had told him. And, Belle didn't wear a wedding band. Angling toward him, she glimpsed his ring finger. No wedding band, either. "But may I ask *you* something first?"

He scowled.

Belle glanced over her shoulder to be certain Candee had let the horses out into the adjoining pasture to graze and drink at the creek. When she faced him again, he watched her with quiet contemplation.

"I saw you in town," Belle began. "In any event, I believe it was you."

"Because it *was* me."

He muttered in a Gaelic dialect she didn't understand. Nonetheless, she drew a breath and forged ahead. "Whatever happened that made you so upset on the balcony?"

CHAPTER 2

ndrew kept his expression carefully bland. "What led you to believe that was my house?"

His challenge was an excuse to pause while he fitted his response into a plausible answer. He wouldn't admit he was prone to tears. Nor would he discuss his former wife's behavior regarding her interest in their daughter.

Or rather, her disinterest.

His divorce had induced him to frustration, anger, and heartache. Megan deserved her mother's love. Weren't mothers supposed to be devoted to their children?

"That was you on the balcony, wasn't it?" Belle asked.

"Yes, we've established that."

"We have?"

"We have now."

"You looked … distressed. I considered stopping my truck to come help you."

"Were you planning on rushing up to rescue me?"

Okay, that snappish reply was uncalled for. He softened his response with a quiet "sorry."

"I like to help." She sighed. "Were you rattled about a

business deal that went wrong?"

"Rattled?" *Another question, another deflection, another ploy to delay responding.*

"Distressed … troubled …." She glanced sideways. "I was concerned."

"No need. I can take care of myself." He sent an indifferent shrug.

Nonetheless, she was obviously worried and there was no disdain in her voice. Again, his reaction had been uncalled for. "Are you normally this inquisitive, Miss Belle?"

"No." A hint of embarrassment crept into her gentle voice, along with a pink blush on her cheeks. And those incredible eyes. At first, he'd thought her eyes were blue. At closer range, they were a gorgeous, smoky gray.

"I'm a fixer."

"I don't require fixing, but thanks." He suppressed a smile at the trace of rebelliousness and curiosity warring across her attractive features. Her slender fingers fluttered, and she bent to tug on the hem of her snug fitting jeans. They enhanced the slim curves he'd been admiring for the past hour.

"A business problem is easy to resolve," he continued. "Mine is personal and heart-wrenching."

"Men don't often use the word heart-wrenching."

"I believe heart-wrenching is two words."

She laughed. "It's a relief to meet a sensitive man who is comfortable describing his emotions."

He nodded to the stable. "I'm not all that comfortable."

"Will I have a weeping man at my feet because of a horse?"

His gaze shifted to her. "Nope, although you may have a man sprinting away from a charging horse."

"You harbor many misconceptions about horses."

"Realities," he corrected.

"Yet you allow your daughter to ride."

"Honeycrisp is a pony as you've kindly explained, and Megan's sessions are the result of our doctor's recommendation."

"Well, you enlisted the expertise of a wise doctor." Belle shuffled her feet. She was petite and trim, reminding him of a nimble gymnast. "At any rate, I'm sorry for prying."

"You're young," he said.

She blinked. "What does that have to do with—" Her chin lifted. "I'm almost thirty."

"You're not married."

"I was, for a brief spell."

"Therefore, you're divorced?"

"Yes. He …he left me."

"Why would a man leave a beautiful, empathetic woman like you?"

She shook her head. "Wow. Mr. Bransfield … Andrew … our conversation is becoming too personal."

"I'm forty."

"Thanks for the information, but I don't remember asking your age."

"I'm also divorced. Thus, I have a decade of experience on you."

She pulled blue-rimmed sunglasses from her denim pocket and wiped off the dust. "Perhaps in years."

"But not wisdom?" He waited for a reaction and was rewarded with her tinkling laugh.

"Because you're older, you assume you're more knowledgeable?"

"That's the way it usually works."

"What can you fix, Mr. Knowledgeable?"

"Personally or professionally?"

"Personally."

"Evidently, not much." His gaze rested on her face. "The

Scots have a saying, 'Ye'ill dee a thousand deaths ye'ill never see.'"

She quirked a delicate eyebrow. "Please explain the meaning?"

"Don't concern yourself with fixing others."

"Are you sharing your older, better informed advice?"

Something about her teasing voice and pure gray eyes stirred the ashes of his loneliness.

"Yes."

"Mr. Bransfield, not only is our conversation becoming too philosophical for such a lovely day, but you're beginning to sound a lot like my Aunt Lucinda."

"I hope I don't look like her."

"You don't." She chuckled. "My aunt wears a cobalt-blue beret, and her white hair hangs to her shoulders." Belle fidgeted with her sunglasses. "In any event, I've had an upsetting morning and didn't intend to take it out on you."

A breeze ruffled dark-brown wisps from her ponytail. In the shimmering sunlight, she brushed a fine strand from her cheeks. He had the urge to stroke her hair gently, as if she were a precious bird.

Because he felt something. And so did she. He'd felt it in town when they'd locked gazes. And he felt it now.

"Your apology is accepted, though you deserve clarification about my circumstances." He folded his hands together. "Rowena, my ex-wife, never returns my phone calls. As usual, I'd left several messages for her."

"She must be busy."

"She's not busy. She's selfish."

"It's not my place, but perhaps you'd feel better if you didn't judge her."

"Now *you're* becoming too philosophical. When you saw me, I had walked onto my balcony to breathe in some fresh air."

"I crave fresh air when I'm upset too," Belle said softly.

As if on cue, a delicate breeze rustled the leaves of a nearby Elm tree. More strands flew across her cheeks, and he resisted the urge to brush them away by keeping his hands at his sides.

"I had phoned my ex to inform her that Megan wouldn't be needing surgery," he said.

"Such wonderful news."

He'd conversed with Belle for fifteen minutes, but there was something about her easy-going nature that gave him comfort. She seemed genuinely interested in Megan.

"The patch will come off within a few weeks," he said. "Then she'll be fitted with eyeglasses. When she gets older, she can wear contact lenses if she prefers."

"I've prayed for her full recovery."

"Prayers are always appreciated."

Their gazes stayed connected, and Belle wiped a bead of sweat from her forehead. Scents of sunshine and leather, with an undertone of interest, held them together. Or rather, it held him, for Belle had turned toward the stable.

He wavered. Should he call out to her?

Earlier, when he'd pulled into Candee's driveway, he'd intended to drop off Megan at the riding ring, say hello to Candee and Teddy, and return to his SUV to resume a lengthy list of important business calls to secure new clients.

Besides, horses weren't his thing. They were, as he'd remarked, big. As a rule, he didn't like animals in general.

After he'd met and talked with Belle, though, he'd leaned against the fence and set down his briefcase.

He'd been impressed by her in action. Her silky hair was pulled back into a severe ponytail, and her worn jeans and denim shirt showed off her flawless curves.

She'd walked quietly beside his daughter as she completed the therapy session, talking encouragingly, and he'd hardly noticed when Candee had come to stand beside him. Often when Belle spoke, Megan had giggled. And his heart had swelled. Since his ex-wife's abrupt departure, laughter had been infrequent in the Bransfield household.

He'd been overly involved with dwelling on the hurt she'd caused him and their daughter. As a result, he'd concentrated on his work, allotting precious few occasions for fun. Or joy. Resentment was more comfortable.

"Is there anything else, Mr. Bransfield?" Belle glanced at him. "Megan likes to spend time with Honeycrisp after her therapy sessions, and I left a few treats for the horses."

He still stood in the ring, staring at Belle like a besotted fool.

"Andrew," he reminded with a sardonic smile. "And there is no hurry."

Except for that lengthy list of business calls, though he'd forgotten why they were so important.

Yes, he wanted something else from Belle. He wanted to get to know her better, although why that particular thought floated through his mind was beyond him. The petite dark-haired beauty—who couldn't be any taller than five feet, nor weigh more than a hundred pounds—was stunning. How did she manage those one thousand-pound horses with such ease?

"Miss Belle … I'm not sure how to address you."

She came around to face him. "Just call me Belle."

"What is your last name?" He studied her delicate hands as she plucked a package of what resembled baby wipes from a backpack, then wiped the dust and grime from a saddle.

"Leather wipes," she explained at his questioning gaze.

He nodded. "Your last name?" he inquired again.

She coupled her hesitation with an awkward, indrawn breath. "Boots."

Andrew lifted his eyebrows. "Your name is Belle Boots?"

A telltale flush heightened her high cheekbones, and she smiled. "I know, I know. It's a ridiculous name for a woman in the equine therapy profession. Belle Boots."

"It's my turn to apologize." He chuckled—he couldn't help it—and was grateful when she joined in. "It's just that you work with horses—"

Her smiled widened, enhancing full, heart-shaped lips. Another attractive feature. "What if my parents had named me Bronco?"

"Bronco Boots," he said easily, "has a nice ring."

"Or Bridle Boots."

"Or Bucking Boots."

She laughed. She had a wry sense of humor, coupled with the ability to joke about herself. Few people were prepared to do that.

"Please accept my compliments on the fine job you're doing with Megan. Did I tell you that already?" He motioned Belle to the railing again. He wished to continue conversing with her, although he was keeping her from her tasks.

"Not in so many words," she replied. "But thank you."

"My daughter has blossomed these past few months." He slipped behind the gate—one never knew when a horse might bound in from the pasture.

"Any credit goes to Megan and Honeycrisp. Their hard work and effort paid off." Belle made a show of shaking the dirt off her brown Western boots—first one boot, then the other. "Megan's face lights up whenever she's riding, which brings me tremendous satisfaction."

In an instant, Andrew relived his daughter's appointments and the trauma she'd undergone—the lighted magnifying glass the doctor had used, the eye drops to blur the vision of the strong eye, the pictures and letter exams when she'd been younger.

"Me too." He swallowed the lump in his throat. He always choked up when he spoke of her welfare.

Certainly, society deemed it acceptable for a man to cry, he'd often told himself.

But was it acceptable?

He'd never seen a grown man cry. None … except himself.

Surely not his overbearing father.

Rowena had seized on Andrew's perceived weakness and found endless opportunities to chide him. He'd always felt like he was on the outside looking in, anyway.

"Mr. Bransfield," Belle began.

"Andrew."

"Your nanny has referred to you as Mr. Bransfield so often that it's difficult for me to make the transition."

"I'll correct you every time."

"Considerate of you," Belle said wryly.

He smiled. "Although I'm biased because I'm her father, Megan is a delight. Her mother doted on Megan—until she drove off with the delivery man."

Belle's thoughtful expression changed to surprise. "You're joking."

His gaze restlessly shifted to the pasture, then Belle. "Such a cliché, but it's true."

Although he and Rowena had reached a divorce agreement before she'd left because fidelity had never been Rowena's strong suit. He grimaced at the understatement.

That was the thing about a woman as pampered and beautiful as Rowena. She'd demanded only the best, which included a red sports car easily reaching eighty miles an hour in mere seconds. Fast cars and a fast life that had ended with a fast departure.

He trained his gaze on Belle's small hands; she was clutching such an enormous horse's saddle.

"Andrew." Another hesitation. "I'm glad I finally met you."

"We've established this."

"Normally your daughter's nanny brings her to the sessions."

"Nancy, and I'm aware of that fact because I pay her."

"Yes, Nancy," Belle agreed. "Anyway, Megan's sessions with me are coming to an end."

"Really? Why?"

"I'm moving."

He jerked back. The stable, the focal point of his gaze while he stared past Belle, was not lost on her.

"When were you planning on sharing this little tidbit of information?" he asked.

"I didn't intend to withhold anything. I considered emailing you since I just found out this morning. In all fairness, I'm still reeling from the news myself."

"Isn't the decision to move yours?"

"Yes and no. Circumstances happened without warning and prompted me to make a hasty decision." Belle hung the saddle on the fence railing with quick, efficient movements. "I'm relocating to Wilmington. Candee found me an apartment near the beach, on a small farm with a stable. I thought she may have told you when you two were talking."

"Nope. We discussed other things."

"Her barbecue this evening?"

"Yes. Are you going?"

"I can't spare the evening." She sighed. "Unfortunately, I have a bag of potatoes that will go to waste."

"Neither can I." With a dry grin, he added, "No potatoes, though."

Those 'other things' had centered around Megan before he'd asked about Belle. The conversation had ended when the therapy session finished, which was sooner than he'd anticipated.

"Naturally, I will miss your daughter desperately," Belle was saying.

"Then why leave?"

"It's time." Conflicting reactions flickered across her lovely face. "However, my stable in Wilmington needs extensive renovation."

"As well as your apartment?"

"Yes, if the photos are any indication. Fortunately, Candee insisted that Teddy's crew will repair everything for a nominal fee."

He shook his head. "This is a lot to take in."

"Teddy is more than generous."

"I wasn't referring to Teddy's generosity. We've been acquainted for years through our business connections, and he's reliable and honest." Andrew displayed an engaging smile while he assembled a plan. "Exactly when are you leaving?"

"By the end of the month. I'll transport my horse, Jenkins, who is quite nervous. Hopefully, he won't fly into a sweaty panic when he's trailered and—"

"Miss Belle, you're moving?" Megan raced up to them. Wide-eyed, she lifted her freckled face to Belle.

"Yes, and I'm sorry, Megan," Belle said. "I'll miss you very, very much."

"Why are you moving?" The little girl's bottom lip trembled. His daughter's pink cherubic lips were a clear indicator of her distress. As Andrew gazed down at her, timeworn anxieties clustered in his mind. She was still a child, and he intended to shield her from life's disappointments.

"My landlord raised my rent to a rate higher than I can manage," Belle said. "Plus, Wilmington is my hometown, and my aunt lives there."

Megan's shoulders crumpled. "You mean I won't ever see you again?"

"We'll only live a few hours apart. I promise I'll visit Roses whenever possible."

The child balled her tiny hands into fists. She did that, Andrew noted, not in anger, but in frustration whenever she was upset. Now, with Rowena gone, Megan's frustration level had escalated. Again, Andrew was thankful for the equine therapy.

"What about Honeycrisp?" Megan asked.

"I'm certain Honeycrisp can continue to board here," Belle said. "There's no reason why not—"

"As it so happens, Belle," Andrew broke in, "I'll renovate your stable at no charge."

She was a bargain-hunter, right? Anyone who fretted about wasting a bag of potatoes wouldn't be able to resist his offer.

"Thank you, but Teddy's crewmen will provide the repairs," she replied.

"Yes, so you mentioned." He greeted her reply with all the enthusiasm of a root canal. "How's this?"

"How's what?"

"I'll renovate at *no* charge, including the work on your apartment." His competitiveness kicked in. Why not? The trait had contributed to his company's significant success. However, he was in the business of making money, not losing it. Therefore, providing a service and materials without payment was not a keen business practice.

Nonetheless, he was significantly more interested in Belle Boots than any monetary gain. Surely she couldn't resist the rock-bottom offer of a lifetime. Nothing beat free.

"Thank you." Belle looked away. "Still, I can't accept your kindness. We are hardly acquainted, and it wouldn't be right."

Her response only encouraged him.

Lightly, he placed his hand on her shoulder. "Considering all you've done for my daughter, most definitely you can consent. I'm expanding my company, Bransfield Designs, to Wilmington. Moreover, I've considered purchasing a beach house and residing near the sea with Megan in a calm, relaxing little place. Maybe I'll rent the house when we're not there."

He did? Since when? He didn't have a second to cavort on a beach or deal with renters—not with his schedule.

"We're moving to be near Miss Belle, Daddy?" Megan perked up as she tugged on his shirtsleeve.

"We're flitting to live closer to the ocean."

"Flitting?" Belle inquired.

"A Scottish term for moving. We'll use the house on holidays." He lifted Megan onto his shoulders. "You like the beach, don't you?"

She clapped her hands together. "I love the beach!"

He swung toward Belle. "What say you, Miss Belle Boots?"

"I've never been the object of a bidding war. Are you certain Teddy won't mind?"

"I'll tell him myself. No worries."

Belle smiled. "What about you, Andrew?"

"What about me?"

"Do *you* like the beach?"

"Doesn't everyone?" His lips twitched. "Oceanside living, dining on fresh caught fish, surfing ..."

"You fish?"

"Nope."

"Surf?"

"Never."

They shared a chuckle.

Quiet walks on the sand with Belle accompanied by a chirpy Megan gathering seashells. He grinned inwardly at the agreeable prospect.

"Megan and I will appreciate a change of scenery and an

opportunity to escape the sweltering summers in town. A beach house where we can savor sunsets and watch the tide roll in."

"Savor sunsets?" Belle chuckled. "You are a remarkably poetic man."

"Sensitive," he corrected, planting a kiss on Megan's chubby leg. "Blame it on my Scottish ancestry. We Scots are a thoughtful people."

"Don't forget stubborn," Belle quipped.

He laughed. "You've been watching too much Braveheart."

"I've never seen the movie."

"Someday, we'll watch it together."

"The movie is about Scotland's history, right?"

"Somewhat." He combined his shrug with a grin and his shoulders relaxed. The pleasant mood was a respite from his usual tenseness "The cinematography is stunning."

He and Megan deserved peace and closure, he rationalized. A beach house was the ticket, along with the opportunity to see the lovely Belle. Yet, actually finding the perfect house would involve an experienced Realtor who acted quickly.

As he set Megan down, she turned her face to his. "Daddy, can Honeycrisp move with us to Wilmington?"

"Absolutely. Perhaps we can board Honeycrisp at Miss Belle's new stable." He smiled and met Belle's gaze. "Obviously, I'll pay the usual boarding rate."

"Do you have any idea what that is, Andrew?"

"Candee charges six hundred dollars a month. I expect you'll charge me a fair price as well."

"Rest assured, considering your free labor." Warily, she regarded him.

"So." He displayed his most charismatic smile, "I assume everything is agreed, then, right?"

CHAPTER 3

Somehow, this entire situation seemed mildly unethical, Belle mused, as she gazed at the two horses in her newly renovated stable in Wilmington. In record time, Andrew had enlisted a crew. They'd completely gutted the stable—replacing the tack, feed rooms, and wash stalls. After installing the latest lighting and a septic system, she'd opted for sliding stall doors and a concrete floor. The damaged fence lines had been repaired, as well as the post gate's hinge.

She might be a bargain hunter, but when it came to her horses, she never scrimped.

Straightaway, Andrew had notified Teddy that he was taking over "Belle's Project." From her conversation with Candee, Belle learned that Andrew and Megan had moved into a two-story oceanfront beach house.

In the month since, Andrew's crewmen had transported Honeycrisp to Belle's stable, and the gentle pony now had the finicky Jenkins as a neighboring stall mate.

Belle had ensured that a bag of Honeycrisp's feed was available, and hand walked the horse around the fence line in an effort to ease her into the different environment. Systematically, she familiarized Honeycrisp with the pasture. Once she was stalled, Honeycrisp and Jenkins eyed each other at a distance. After a few days, Belle turned them out together in the pasture, placing their feed over a large space with ample room around the water source. Sure, there'd been some biting and chasing—mostly by Jenkins, because he hadn't been thrilled with the situation.

Fortunately, both horses had ultimately settled into a contented routine.

In a flurry of busyness, Belle had moved her belongings into her sunlit and welcoming new apartment. Boasting a wide, fully equipped breakfast area, an adjoining living room with a pull-out couch, and a small bedroom with an attached bathroom, it was upscale and chic. She was impressed by the renovation, scarcely believing the home was now hers.

Through numerous texts, Andrew had inquired about her vision for a dream kitchen and she had described espresso cabinets, stainless steel appliances and wood-style flooring. After hand-sketching the design and emailing her for approval, he'd taken her words to heart and delivered to the letter.

Thrilled to discover her place was a mere six blocks from the ocean, she jogged on the beach every morning and again at sundown.

As always she woke at dawn, showered, dressed and went to the stable. She opened the door, and both horses stuck their heads out of their stalls to greet her. She fed them grain in a bucket, distributed the hay, and cleaned and refilled the water buckets. After brushing their coats and applying fly spray, she haltered and walked the horses to the pasture.

Chores came next, which began with sweeping the stalls.

Once finished, she hiked through an overgrown shortcut to the beach, removed her waterproof muck boots and jogged barefoot along the shore. The soothing splash of water on her toes brought her spirits up. Surely, she'd made the right decision in relocating to Wilmington.

Her eccentric Aunt Lucinda had been thrilled Belle was back in their hometown, and Belle visited her often. Her aunt had never married, spouting that a man would tie her down. Nevertheless, there had been one man in her life, she'd confessed. A man she'd loved, although she'd never divulged his name.

Men were too much of a bother, she'd stated on numerous occasions.

After her divorce from Tyler, Belle had agreed. Nevertheless, after numerous hours talking and texting with Andrew, she'd changed her mind. He displayed a kindness, courteousness, and indisputable attentiveness that proved both disarming and heartening.

With a tremulous smile, she recalled their initial meeting. Apprehension had been written across his handsome features when he'd surveyed Blackjack and Honeycrisp. Just wait until he came face-to-face with the cantankerous Jenkins. She'd need to introduce them gently.

After her jog, Belle returned to the stable. She intended to clean the hay out of the stalls, replace old tack, and carry out the million other chores awaiting her.

Tires crunching on gravel prompted her to shade her eyes and peer toward the road, as Andrew drove into the driveway in his shiny silver SUV.

He got out of the SUV and strode to her with a decidedly mischievous grin. He wore slim jeans, a white T-shirt that clung to his broad shoulders and work boots. In one hand, he carried a toolbox.

Her heart did a thump.

He looked entirely different from the fine-looking professional of a few weeks ago.

Because today, wearing jeans and a T-shirt?

Oh, my.

The morning at Candee's stable he'd been pin-striped proper, and Belle couldn't choose which look she preferred.

The jeans, she decided. Definitely the jeans.

"Hi, Andrew." She smiled as he neared.

"Greetings, Belle." He withdrew a bouquet of slightly wilted yellow flowers from his toolbox.

To discount the treacherous jump of her heart, she tried to think of something to say. "Tools and flowers," she observed. *Just brilliant, Belle.*

"Do you like flowers?" he asked.

"I love flowers, and the color reminds me of a burst of sunshine."

"I like flowers too. However, the tools aren't for you. Only the flowers. When I passed by the florist in town, I thought, 'Beautiful flowers for a beautiful woman' and I couldn't resist. What's more, they were on sale, so I knew you'd approve."

"I hope they were at least fifty percent off?"

"Try a dollar off."

"What was the original price?"

"Fifty dollars."

"What?" Raising a hand, she checked him from continuing. "You paid forty-nine dollars for a bouquet?"

He bent to nuzzle her ear and whispered, "For you, I would have paid a hundred dollars."

She couldn't contain her grin.

He liked flowers. He liked *her.* And he was a wonderful father. Contrary to his rugged exterior, he possessed a sensitive nature. She wondered if he wrote poetry.

Probably.

"Thank you." She accepted the bouquet and sniffed.

"Flowers as pretty as dahlias should have a strong, fragrant scent, but they don't."

"We think alike. I told the florist the same thing."

"They're gorgeous."

"They're a house-warming gift."

"You didn't have to do this."

"I wanted to."

Her cheeks heated beneath his steady, admiring gaze. "You've done too much already."

"You've heard the familiar adage." He finger quoted. "'It's better to give than to receive.'"

"You mean, there's no Scottish saying?"

"'Don't judge each day by the harvest you reap, but by the seeds you plant.'"

She plucked a petal from the dahlia's stem. "That's Scottish?"

"By Scotland's very own novelist, Robert Louis Stevenson."

"Which I assume means, 'It's better to give than to get?'"

"Nope." Unabashed, he chuckled. "Sadly, it's the best I can come up with."

She placed the bouquet in a shady area. "You knew my favorite flower?"

"I asked Candee, and she mentioned your former apartment was painted yellow. Thus, I selected dahlias."

"Most people think of daisies for a yellow flower."

"I studied the meanings of both. In our situation, dahlias were more appropriate."

She made a mental note to research the meanings. "Andrew Bransfield, you're an extraordinarily thoughtful man."

He nodded. "I also was compelled to see if the stable area begs for my finishing touches."

"No begging is required." She gestured to the fencing. "Thanks to you, every inch is repaired."

He eyed the pasture where the two horses sunbathed. "Are they safe?"

"Do you mean, are we safe from them?"

"Both."

"We are all safe and secure," she said.

He set down the toolbox. "Just in case, I'll keep a safe and secure distance from them."

"Why are you afraid of horses?"

"When I was young, I was attacked by a large dog and required stitches."

"I'm sorry." She paused, picked up a rake and piled dry straw into mounds. "That must have been frightening."

"It was traumatic for a ten-year-old kid who loved animals."

"Past tense?" she inquired. "*Loved* animals?"

He shrugged. "I suppose."

She let the comment pass. It wasn't the time to analyze him. "What type of dog attacked you?"

"If you're suspecting a mean, vicious dog, you're wrong. The day was scorching, the hottest on record, and I ran up to the dog to pet him. His name was Rusty, and he belonged to a neighbor. Apparently, I startled him, and he bit me." Andrew pointed to a thin white line on his forearm. "Consequently, animals aren't my number one love."

What was his number one love?

Without a doubt, it was Megan. His devotion to his daughter was undeniable.

"I guarantee you're safe from any galloping horses," Belle said.

"Whew!" He forced a larger-than-life wipe at his forehead, but his posture tensed as his gaze canvassed the pasture. "Are you certain?"

"Totally." She decided to hold off telling him that a stray tabby had found his way to her front yard and she'd immediately adopted and dubbed him Ginger. Or about the two white goats, Hester and Hilda, who were already members of the farm when she'd showed up.

Andrew would find out soon enough.

He paused and gazed at her. "You are gorgeous, Belle," he said quietly.

Donned in a pair of military-green cropped pants and a striped crewneck shirt, she highly doubted it. She opened her mouth to dispute him, but he forestalled her by leaning over the fence and gently sliding a finger across her lips.

His touch was casual and friendly and brought an unexpected tingle. Dumbstruck, she shook her head at the strong attraction.

"Sorry." He dropped his hand. "Did I invade your personal space?"

Not a bit, she wished to tell him, but refrained from speaking.

She returned to tackling the raking with outward efficiency, though her fingers trembled so significantly she could hardly hold the rake. She gave up, set the rake down and glanced at her watch. "Are you on a lunch break, Andrew?"

He gestured to his jeans. "Does it look like I am?"

"No, but it's Friday. We've texted often enough for me to be aware of your grueling schedule."

His green eyes sparkled with laughing speculation. "What might my grueling schedule entail?"

"At seven a.m. you eat breakfast with Megan. Once her nanny arrives, you report to your office by eight. You allot a half hour for lunch and leave work by six in order to spend an hour with Megan before her bedtime."

"If I'm lucky. I wish I had more time," came his frustrated reply.

"Oftentimes you take your computer home," she went on. "And I know you're up at all hours of the night, because I've received texts from you at three a.m. asking which flooring style I prefer."

"You've memorized my schedule in only a few short weeks."

"You're easy because your routine is always the same. Work, work, work." She tried a lame attempt at sternness. "Any robber could watch you for a couple days and then fleece you blind."

He grinned, but his eyes darkened, reminding her of pine trees in the subdued light of a summer sunset.

"Are you planning to rob me, Belle? Of my senses, perhaps? Because I lose track of time when I'm with you. In fact, I'm not certain of anything since we met."

Surely he joked. They were business acquaintances. Yet he sounded surprisingly off balance. Seeking to lighten the strangely intimate mood, she said, "You certainly lost your senses when you offered your services for free."

"Let's not forget my phone and text consultations."

"Is there an added fee?"

"Certainly."

"We talked about other matters," she reminded.

The way he watched her filled her with compassion and affection. Although business had dominated their exchanges, he'd spoken about his daughter and the challenges he'd encountered upon becoming a single parent. His intent was to make everything right in his daughter's world, he'd said. Or rather, it seemed, he was bent on make everything right in the *entire* world.

When silence had rung out, he'd encouraged Belle to discuss her reservations regarding her relocation and leaving behind her clients. She felt as though she had abandoned them.

Andrew had immediately corrected her when she had used the term "abandon," and she could almost see him visibly flinch. "You're a kind, caring woman," he'd declared, and her refutes were no match against his thoughtful assurances.

Belle grabbed the rake again and swirled the dry grass round and round. She concentrated on the areas near the gate that got the highest traffic. When Andrew stayed silent, she motioned to the stable. "Are your rates generally expensive, then?"

His dark eyebrows rose in a teasing challenge. "Extremely."

"Could I afford you if you charged me your regular fee?"

"Highly doubtful."

Their laughing gazes joined.

"In truth, helping you was my pleasure," Andrew said softly.

She slanted him a glance and yanked up a garden hose to water the riding ring.

Andrew held up his hands. "Do you intend to spray me, Belle?"

Hmm. No. Or maybe?

"Push the notion from your mind." He retreated a step. "We are both adults, and a prank like the one you're thinking would be extremely childish."

"How do you know what I'm thinking?"

"I just know."

"And why should I obey you?"

"Because I asked politely."

"Politeness only goes so far, Andrew." She inched closer to him and unlatched the gate. Sunlight glinted through his hair, lightening the shade to a shiny copper penny.

He refused to retreat any further. Her beating heart brought a knot of longing and indescribable attraction. Now? Yes, now. It had been years since her divorce. Although she wasn't actively searching for a relationship, she appreciated the company of a good-hearted, kind man. A man who laughed at silly pranks. A man with substance and confidence.

"The hose?" he reminded. "You're aiming at me rather than the ground."

"What's more, I'll continue aiming at you until you admit you lead a highly regimented life."

"Where did that come from?" She expected him to take flight, but he held his ground. "Is this truth or dare?"

"Possibly," she hedged.

"I'm a businessman." He shrugged with an indifference Belle suspected was partly feigned. "Need I explain more?"

"Yes." With an innocent smile, she turned the hose on him.

CHAPTER 4

ndrew toppled backwards and landed on the grass while Belle's chuckle pealed through the air.

He peered at his wet shirt then up at her. "Was that necessary?"

She dropped the hose and hurried over, taking stock of him sprawled on the ground. "Was it necessary for you to display such an ambitious dramatization?"

"I was startled."

"Uh huh. You're hardly wet."

"I'm wet enough."

Her gaze narrowed. "Aren't you getting up?"

"Maybe."

She came to stand over him. "Time to get up," she repeated.

"Why?" he countered. "Are you standing by to spray me again?"

"Maybe." She repaid his question with uncharacteristic sarcasm. Belatedly registering his frown, she guardedly asked, "Are you hurt?"

"Only my pride. Fortunately, I have a thick skin in my

business." His tone sounded forced despite his assertion, bringing an ache to her throat. She considered his wet shirt, and regretted spraying him. What had seemed like a fun, playful idea a few seconds earlier now wasn't quite as humorous.

He was under obvious emotional strain, trying to keep his architectural firm prosperous while spending considerable time with his daughter. Which was the very reason why she'd injected light-heartedness into their morning. That, and the fact he'd given her the idea. Why, he'd practically goaded her.

Now, seeing him defenseless, the solemn expression on his ruggedly handsome face caused her pulse to quiver. He had a mysterious effect on her she couldn't shake, whether he was upright or on the ground.

Her memory of him when he'd strode onto his balcony flashed through her mind. She remembered thinking how pleasingly male he looked, so urbane in his sophisticated home. The fact that his ex-wife had brought such sorrow to him and his little girl prompted Belle's empathy.

His skin might be thick in business, but he was an exceptional breed—emotional and vulnerable while exuding a tough exterior.

He continued to lie in the grass. He was either milking the situation or trying to tug at her heart strings. He accomplished both quite successfully.

If, indeed, the force of the water had knocked him off his feet.

"I apologize," she began offering him the benefit of the doubt. "You're right. That was childish of me."

"I accept." He squinted up at her, shielding his eyes from the sun. "That is, unless you're planning to hose me again?"

She held out a hand to help him to his feet. "I hardly call dampening your shirt hosing you down."

With an overstated sigh, he stood and brushed the grass

sticking to his white shirt. He'd have grass stains, which were difficult to wash out, but she didn't tell him that.

"I brought no change of clothes," he said.

"With the hot July sun beating down, your shirt will dry in five minutes," she assured.

Together, they walked back to the riding ring holding hands.

There, she paused to consider the fencing. "Thank you for combining wire mesh along with the wood. As I explained, otherwise horses might catch their legs. Plus the fence is more resilient."

"Are you always this conscientious, Belle?" he asked.

"I've lived around horses and pastures since I was a teen. Fencing and barns come with the territory."

"Both are alien territories to me."

"Because you sit in an office all day."

"You're a master at describing me, but could you toss in a few descriptions other than businessman now and then? I'm an architect and work outdoors often. While we're discussing the subject, let's not forget *you're* a businesswoman."

"I'm proud of the distinction." Her dignified reproof brought a grin to his lips. "Studies prove professional women are more emotionally intelligent than men."

His steady, green-eyed gaze met hers. "Please continue."

They still held hands. He didn't seem to want to let go. Neither did she.

"Well," she adopted a formidable instructor's manner, "a woman values a person's well-being."

"And I don't?"

"You're taking my words personally. I was comparing men to women—not all men in general."

They reached the spot where she'd dropped the hose. He

released her hand, eyed the hose and grinned. Quietness billowed between them.

"Therefore, I'm not necessarily referring to you," she clarified.

"It's important to spell out the difference."

"I did." She tilted her head and granted a genuine smile. "Furthermore, women aren't as ego-driven as men."

"I agree that men like to win." Still grinning, Andrew grabbed the hose, held steady, and aimed at her.

She gaped, steering away from the sudden stream of gushing water. "You, Mr. Bransfield, are incorrigible," she shouted.

He shut the hose. "Did I win?"

"Definitely not. And because of you, my hair will stick out straight the rest of the day."

"Your hair will dry in a few minutes. Remember? The hot sun and all that …" He gestured upward to the airy white clouds floating in a blue sky.

She ran a hand through her hair, squeezing the ends with her fingers. Helplessly, she laughed. "If you even consider turning that hose on me again …"

In three quick strides, he reached her. "Do you give up easily?"

"Never." With a cool dose of spitfire, she included, "Unless this is a water fight."

"It may yet become one."

"Andrew … don't you dare …"

"Now I'm Andrew again? Which is it, Belle? Mr. Bransfield or Andrew?"

"I told you already. Because your nanny referred to you as Mr. Bransfield so often—"

"You and I have progressed to a first name basis since then."

"Are you asking a question?" She shied backward. She was

ready for the game to end, especially while he still held the hose.

"It's a statement." He looked positively boyish, a sparkling gleam in his eyes as he set down the hose. "And I promise I won't spray you again under one condition."

"Now there's a condition?"

In reply, his laughter was deep and intimate. His gaze fell to her lips.

She drew a shaky inhale. They stood within inches of each other.

"What is the condition?" she asked again.

"This." Tenderly, he brushed his knuckles across her cheek, outlined her lips with his fingertips. The rhythm in her veins accelerated, taking on a mind of its own as he bent his head and kissed her.

She melted, responding to the radiant heat of his mouth as he drew her into his arms. Her heart beat much too fast, but in that moment she was aware of only one thing.

She'd been waiting for his kiss, anticipating it. He'd been waiting too. She had seen the desire in his gaze, heard the underlying huskiness.

When had their magnetism begun? In Roses?

Or here? In Wilmington?

He framed her face and deepened the kiss.

No, no, no.

But she couldn't surface from the delicious pleasure of his lips.

She slid her hands around his neck and kissed him back, reacting to the instinctive tightening of his arms as he brought her tightly against him. So close, she felt the beating of his heart.

When he loosened his hold, she leaned against the fence until their breathing slowed. After a lingering silence, he said softly, "I've had an urge to kiss you ever since we met."

"You evidently have no objections to personal space," she half-joked.

"None at all." His voice quieted. "Not when it comes to you."

How should she respond? Start with the truth. Confess she had the same feelings.

Absolutely not, that would never do. A woman shouldn't wear her heart on her sleeve.

She swallowed. When she was with him, she was vaguely aware that she was negotiating a land mine, with no relationship experience to guide her except for a degrading ex and a marriage that never should have happened.

Andrew, on the other hand, with his charisma-plus charm and velvety Scottish lilt, left her no choice but to examine each of her words, because to say exactly what she thought and describe her emotions would expose her. She was attracted to him, very attracted, but it was too soon in their friendship for those thoughts.

This was merely a kiss between a man and a woman who had worked together the past few weeks and had become close.

Andrew appeared to take the change in their relationship with an easy-going stride. His face was calm, his features neutral.

"You're getting off the hook easily with your personal space reply, if that sums up your explanation," she said shakily.

"With you, all bets are off." He chuckled when she frowned. "Belle, you are beautiful and desirable. Be proud of that." When she continued frowning, he chuckled louder. "You know, there is simply no substitute for a smart, perceptive businesswoman."

With a self-conscious laugh, she didn't refute him. Unfortunately, her conscience deemed this as the appropriate time for an admonition.

Remember? Andrew was the father of one of her clients.

Should she have accepted his help so willingly? Or kissed him? Their association was professional, not personal.

Yet, Andrew had done more for her than anyone.

How could she repay him? Everything—materials and labor—is free of charge, he'd insisted. In the short weeks they'd been acquainted, he'd proven a wonderful friend.

Friend, she reminded herself.

He had the resources, restating that this was his opportunity to repay the kindness, patience, and understanding she'd shown his daughter.

She stood motionless. Hesitant to speak, hesitant not to speak.

Andrew broke the silence by fixing his thumbs in his pockets and stepping away. "Back to business," he remarked.

No beat was missed. He bent to inspect the fence, tugged on the gate, and began measuring the replaced wood.

He hadn't dismissed her, had he?

"Business as usual," she echoed. She wished her voice sounded as unshaken as his. "Are you resuming duty as my project foreman?"

"I never went off duty."

Sure he had, when he'd kissed her a moment earlier, but some thoughts weren't meant to be shared.

He cleared his throat. "Is everything falling into place the way you imagined?"

At the stable? Unquestionably.

In the heart department? She wasn't so certain.

He pulled a hammer and nails from the toolbox and secured a piece of wire mesh to the fencing.

"I love this area. It's my hometown," she began answering

his question. She stifled the urge to gush on and on about herself. "How about you and *your* new place?"

"Couldn't be better. I'm delighted with the house now that Megan and I are mostly unpacked."

"Where is Megan? I meant to inquire when you arrived."

"Her nanny took her to play on the beach."

"Nancy?"

"I hired Adella, a new nanny, and I'll rehire Nancy if Megan and I return to Roses."

If.

Was he thinking of settling in Wilmington indefinitely?

"I mentioned Adella to you the other day," he was saying.

He had, she admitted to him. In the torrent of activity, she'd forgotten.

"Megan will begin again soon, right?" he asked.

"I scheduled her on Monday. I'm looking forward to our weekly sessions because I've missed her."

"Excellent." His mouth tilted up whenever he spoke of his daughter. "She misses you too and mentions you constantly."

During Belle's move, Andrew had texted or phoned often. There was an easiness about conversing with him behind a safe screen which had served as a safety net. However, communicating in person was something else entirely. Suddenly feeling awkward, she drew up the rake and concentrated on a rutted area.

"Do you like your new home?" she inquired.

"Very much. Thanks to our super Realtor friend, Candee, my house is in a secluded area by the ocean. Megan and I will invite you for dinner some night. Our evenings are quiet and lonely."

Somehow, watching this undeniably compelling man, she sincerely doubted he spent his evenings alone.

"You cook?" she asked.

"My housekeeper does. She is from Scotland."

"I'm not familiar with Scottish food."

"Have you ever eaten haggis?"

"I've never heard of haggis. Is it a variety of sausage?"

"A little more." He chuckled. "My sister, Kate, who lives in Scotland, used to prepare authentic haggis."

"Used to? How long since you've last seen her?"

His features shuttered. "Many years."

"Why? Don't you ever visit Scotland?"

"Kate retained the rights to our ancestral home with my blessings." He crossed his arms over his chest. "Scotland is dead to me."

"You aren't keen on visiting?"

He stepped away, his posture rigid. "Nope."

"How many sisters do you have?"

"Only Kate. As a young boy, I was surrounded by femininity—my mother and several maids, and a wee elipel."

"Meaning?"

"Kate was a tattle-tale."

"You're holding a juvenile grudge against her because of that?"

"I'm not shallow, and this is an adult feud." He propped his elbows on the fence. "You?"

She shook her head. "I'm an only child. Do you have any brothers?"

"No other males aside from my father who was too busy womanizing to take care of his business properly. He couldn't be trusted with holding on to the family fortune."

In the wake of Andrew's unemotional attitude, Belle floundered.

"Both of my parents were domineering and opinionated," she finally said. "Fortunately, my Aunt Lucinda doesn't subscribe to artificiality. She's my mother's sister—spry and wiry and a hoot."

"She lives in Wilmington?"

"Yes. She lives alone, although she traveled the country on a Harley in her younger years. Finally she retired, boasts numerous friends and enjoys entertaining. She is free with her jokes … and her colorful phrases."

"I'd like to meet her. Her experience and wisdom must span decades."

"It does. Fair warning, though. She narrates her adventures with a larger-than-life laugh." Belle paused to study him. "I wager she'd like to meet you too."

"Thus, we have a date." Before she refuted, he grabbed a handful of nails. "I'll ensure the other side of the fence is solid."

Wait. There was more to discuss, beginning with … he had an overbearing father?

She counted on Andrew to elaborate, but he apparently didn't wish to discuss his family any further. Only hers. Only work. He had a way of doing that.

After he strode away, Belle pulled out her cellphone.

She discovered that haggis was a national Scottish dish comprised of the liver, heart, and lungs of a sheep. The recipe got better, or worse—depending on a person's appetite—because the mixture was boiled in a sheep's stomach. If haggis was ever on a menu, she'd stick with a more appetizing entrée, such as mashed potatoes and turnips.

She then texted Candee to inquire about Andrew's new house.

Five bedrooms and five bathrooms, including an in-ground pool, came Candee's immediate text. *From the photos, it's spectacular and even boasts an elevator. The address is One Carolina Way.*

Why would he rent such a large home? Belle texted.

The inventory for oceanfront is sparse, and hardly any are available. And he liked the lines.

What does that mean?

Architectural talk, LOL, and the house has an option to buy.

Belle paused. *He's considering purchasing a home in Wilmington?*

Do you realize who he is? He owns Bransfield Designs, the most profitable architectural firm in the Carolinas. Also, he's been praised in numerous magazines as being a creative genius.

No, Belle hadn't realized, although Megan's nanny had mentioned Andrew's firm on occasion.

The creative genius description fit him, though.

"I honestly don't care what people think about me," he'd once said.

And he kept odd hours, sometimes texting her in the middle of the night. When she'd asked when he slept, he'd replied that his mind was always racing.

When it came to his wealth, he paid the monthly invoices for Megan's sessions quickly, which marked the extent of Belle's knowledge regarding Andrew's finances. He owned a grand home in Roses and now rented in Wilmington and employed a nanny and housekeeper.

Thanks, she texted.

Andrew stood at the other end of the fence, scrutinizing and hammering, looking as if he would happily spend the entire afternoon repairing fences.

When she typed his name on the Internet, her jaw literally dropped. He came from a notable line of aristocrats who had resided in the Scottish Highlands. His biography detailed the family's relocation to the United States when Andrew was young because his father's investment business had gone under.

Andrew had attended public schools and there was no mention of college.

A quick scan detailed his propensity for architecture and how he'd begun Bransfield Designs with little capital. Nowadays, he didn't work for professional gain. He was compelled by something else.

A driving force within him he couldn't quell, perhaps? She admired him for making it on his own resolve.

Impressive. Very impressive. That explained his refined jaw, his straight, regal bearing, and her realization that he wasn't a millionaire. Because, in actuality, he was a billionaire.

With a quick mapping she learned he lived a short distance from her apartment, his home located on a private stretch of beach.

She looked up as he ducked into the stable, then quickly exited.

As he advanced toward her, she snapped her cellphone shut and jammed it into her pocket.

"There's a mirror in the horse stall," he said.

"Right."

"Why?"

"Years ago, I rescued Jenkins from a racetrack because he'd been mistreated. Sadly, he fretted about being closed off. Thus I brought in the acrylic mirror for companionship. He's high strung."

"Not only is Jenkins a horse, but he's a high strung horse?"

"He can't help being a horse, and he's rewarded my rescue with affection and loyalty." She gestured at the fencing. "All set?"

"The fence will hold for years. I'm pleased with the workmanship."

"Because you and your crew were responsible for the repairs."

"Something like that." He gave a short laugh. "Nonetheless, there are always improvements—even for my spectacular crewmen."

"Always the perfectionist."

"Does it show?" A sardonic smile tugged at his lips. "By the way, there's another reason I'm here today. I hope to take you to lunch."

And to kiss her.

"I'm flattered," she replied. "I had wondered why you stopped by unexpectedly. I assumed it wasn't solely to bring me flowers."

"A man needs no excuse to gift flowers to a stunning woman. Do you accept my offer?"

"For lunch?" She considered her appearance—jean shorts and a T-shirt, and promptly shook her head. "Unfortunately, I can't."

"Why not?"

"Look around," she averred. *Just look at me.* Her hair was still damp and plastered to her forehead. Any makeup she'd applied that morning, a light peach gloss, had surely disappeared hours ago.

"Can we reschedule?" he asked.

"Feasibly." He looked so disappointed, she supplied, "Although I can whip you up an exquisite omelette. A French omelette, not your run-of-the-mill American-style scrambled eggs."

"What's the difference?"

"Basically the way the eggs are rolled."

"You cook?"

"Not gourmet, but I get by. I'm pretty much an amateur."

"Are you inviting me to lunch?"

"I snagged a great deal on a dozen eggs. What's more, you can inspect the remodel on my apartment. All you've seen up till now are photos."

He smiled. "That being the case, I gladly accept." He gathered his hammer and nails and placed them neatly in his toolbox.

He was clearly a man who didn't object to rolling up his sleeves, working alongside his crewmen, and getting calluses on his hands. He was also equally comfortable in a board room wearing a fine woolen suit.

He directed his gaze toward the pasture. "Are the horses okay if we go inside?"

"On a nice day when the humidity isn't high and there's no rain or bad weather in the forecast, grazing in a pasture is ideal for horses." She lifted an eyebrow. "Why, are you concerned about them?"

"Just wondering."

"One might say you actually like horses."

"One might say you're wrong."

"Despite your reservations, I applaud you for placing the well-being of your daughter before your fears," Belle said. "You allow her to experience the joys of riding. Someday you'll realize that horses are like family. Speaking of Megan, how does she like Wilmington?"

"She met a girl her age who lives nearby. She loves inviting friends over for play dates. She used to be a fun-loving kid. Hopefully, she will again ..." He fell silent, but Belle heard the catch in his voice.

He was a father who loved his child.

She nodded. "Are you ready to taste my delectable omelette?"

"More than ready." He bent to pick up his toolbox when Hester bleated, drawing Belle's attention. And, unfortunately, Andrew's as well.

Andrew paused. "What's that?"

Belle slanted him a wry glance. "A goat."

"You mean while I was fixing the fence, that goat was hiding?"

"He wasn't hiding. Hester and Hilda were preoccupied in the patch of woods beyond the stable."

"So while I was feeling safe and secure, I truly wasn't." Cautiously, Andrew peered around. "Hilda? There's a Hilda?"

"A male and a female. Hilda is Hester's sister. To alleviate your concerns, goats are intelligent, gentle creatures."

He scratched his head. "Goats as in plural?"

"I have a little herd of two. Or rather, the farm does. Goats don't like being alone."

Andrew retreated as Hester and Hilda rounded the stable. "What type of goats are they?"

"They're referred to as myotonic goats."

"Will they charge at us?"

"Hester never has. I doubt Hilda will." The air stilled apart from Andrew's quiet, indrawn breath as he suspiciously eyed the two white goats.

"Should I walk carefully?" he asked.

"Definitely, as running or a loud noise will startle them. They might faint."

"Seriously?"

"I couldn't be more serious."

Gingerly, he stepped to his SUV, opened the door, and placed the toolbox on the back seat.

Belle nodded her approval and placed a forefinger to her lips. "We'll walk quietly to my apartment," she whispered.

With a nod, Andrew lifted his foot to close the door. It slammed shut.

Belle jumped.

And the goats fainted.

CHAPTER 5

Comfortably sitting on a stool in Belle's cozy kitchen ten minutes later, Andrew favorably assessed the improvements. The walls were now painted the color of butter, and despite the small size, the breakfast area was expansive. A brilliant yellow cuckoo clock, sporting a bird and leaf motif, recapped the hour with a dual chime.

A sizable granite countertop island separated the kitchen from the living room. Barn-style doors led to the hallway, bathroom, and Belle's bedroom. Wide-plank oak flooring, stainless steel appliances, and a glass tile accent wall enhanced the espresso cabinets.

Once they entered her apartment, they stepped out of their boots. She padded to the kitchen and filled a plain white vase with water, setting the dahlias in the center of the island. Quickly, she'd shown him the apartment.

He pointed to a stain on the hallway ceiling. "There's a roof leak? I presumed we fixed everything."

"Me too. The other day it rained, and I quickly grabbed a bucket. I alerted my landlords, Abby and Felix, but they're a young couple and struggle financially."

"I'll take care of it," Andrew said.

"Thanks." She pinned back her hair and washed her hands at the kitchen sink, requesting he do the same. She tied an apron embossed with lemons around her waist while Andrew texted Adella.

He was reassured that Megan was enjoying a delightful afternoon building a sandcastle in front of their home.

Are you using lots of sunscreen? he asked. He always kept Megan's fair, freckled skin in mind.

She is plastered from head to toe, came the nanny's reply. *Her playmate has joined us.*

Good. He smiled and snapped his phone shut. Yes, a move to Wilmington was definitely in his daughter's best interests.

He gazed at Belle. And his interests, too.

"Is Megan having fun at the beach?" Belle inquired.

"Her nanny said she's loving it."

"Did they go to a Wilmington beach?"

"They're closer to my home."

"Your home is near the beach?"

"It's beachfront."

When she responded with silence, he upbraided himself. He certainly hadn't intended to flaunt his wealth, but in all fairness, Belle was also within walking distance of the beach. His place happened to be oceanfront.

She spread her arms wide. "Your house must cost two thousand dollars a month in rent."

The lease was more like five thousand, but he didn't share that information.

Belle pulled a frying pan from the cabinet and added a pat of butter to the pan to sizzle on the stove while she cracked and beat a half dozen eggs into a mixing bowl.

"Is a cheese omelette okay?" She poured him a glass of her "famous" southern style iced tea from the refrigerator.

"What exactly is southern style iced tea?" he asked.

She set the pitcher on the table. "You live in the south. Don't you know?"

"I'm originally from Scotland."

"You moved to America when you were eighteen."

"Where did you hear that?"

She flushed, which prompted his grin. She'd done her due diligence—perhaps gleaning her information about him from Candee.

"Anyhow, with your Scottish brogue, how can I forget where you're originally from?" She smiled. "Southern iced tea requires heaps of sugar and freshly squeezed lemons. Also, the lemons were on sale."

He grinned and reclaimed the stool. He drained his glass and concluded that sugar was the gateway to happiness. He set down his glass and Belle quickly tipped the pitcher and refilled.

"Did the grocery store offer a deal on cheese this week too, when you went for your messages?" he asked.

"What messages?"

"The Scottish term for groceries."

"You Scots have such interesting words."

He lifted his glass as a salute. "So do you Americans."

"I assume you're American too."

"Yes, I claim dual citizenship, although I haven't been back to Scotland for many years." He surveyed the stove and its contents. "Will your French creation ooze with Camembert and fresh lavender?"

"I can't afford Camembert." Her lips curved easily as she headed for the cheese board. "Swiss cheese was only two dollars a pound this week, and I asked the woman at the deli to slice the cheese extra thin."

"Did she oblige?"

"Indeed." Belle returned to the stove and glanced at him over her shoulder. "The clerks recognize me. For your information, coupons and specials can result in substantial grocery savings."

He savored another sip of the refreshing tea, allowing the flavors of sweet and sour to linger on his tongue. "Is this a fact?"

"From first-hand experience."

He gave an overstated groan. "Are you one of those customers who hold up the entire grocery line so that the clerk can scan your fifty cent coupon?"

"That's me."

She was so serious he chuckled. His ex-wife had never clipped a coupon in her life.

For several minutes he sat silently, allowing his luncheon hostess an opportunity to prepare the omelet, correction *omelette,* without interruption.

He used the minutes to contemplate the next phase of his firm's expansion, but soon chose to reflect on his surprising good fortune.

Belle Boots stood five feet away from him at her shiny, stainless steel stove.

And he liked that—being with her, sharing lunch.

During the never-ending evenings he'd spent alone since his divorce—he'd never envisioned himself living in any other manner other than as a single man. Absorbed in his business and raising his daughter, he'd convinced himself that he was better off alone.

For starters, just look what he'd accomplished since his divorce. Why, his firm had doubled in size. Imagine if he had a demanding wife to please, as during the seven years of marriage to Rowena.

Therefore, he'd be happier if he remained unattached, apart from an occasional, impersonal date. Any free time was earmarked for his precious daughter.

After weeks of texting and phoning Belle, he was inclined

to remain on the same course. Belle had encouraged him to examine aspects of life he'd overlooked—the outdoors, nature, and humorous banter—and that made him uncomfortable. However, not so uncomfortable he'd give up his frenetic work pace.

Besides, by Sunday evening he'd be on the road again, continuing his commitment to excellent design over cheap construction, connecting with Megan through Skype, while reassured that the nanny provided excellent care.

He and his firm fought for projects to be completed without politics interfering. That was all well and good, but left little time for laughing conversations with Belle, or water fights with a hose, or heartfelt discussions concerning his daughter.

Or, he amended with a smile, any fainting goats.

Whenever he mentioned Megan, compassion and concern would immediately touch Belle's features.

As he lifted his glass, Belle flipped the omelette as adeptly as any French chef. She shook the pan constantly over the gas stove's flame.

When she slanted him a glance, he made a show of applause. She flamboyantly bowed, then turned back to the stove to flick dashes of black pepper and basil on the eggs.

His heart skipped a beat at her exuberance, her enthusiasm. He sat back, indulging himself by staring at her slim profile and exquisite features. She was a natural beauty.

What if he'd met her soon after his divorce? Would she have been able to teach him how to forgive, to assuage his jaded heart? Would she have encouraged him to seek ambitions more gratifying than wealth and influence and acknowledgment—motivations that had molded his childhood and adulthood? He was, after all, a Bransfield, and well aware of his illustrious legacy.

The improbability of ever meeting Belle when he was at

an earlier age surfaced, and he checked himself. At what cocktail party would they have connected? His life had revolved around affluence before his father had lost everything because of laziness and indifference. To be successful, a business required continuous monitoring and long business hours.

Sure, monetary and societal advantages had been a given in Scotland, and Andrew and his sister's seats among the elite were secured.

During those years, an equine therapist named Belle would never have entered his sphere of aristocratic friends.

Even if they'd met, would he have been interested? More than likely not, for she would have been overshadowed by the fashionable and ostentatious women. Belle wouldn't have been comfortable if he had escorted her to an exclusive country club dinner.

Or would she? No doubt, she was as gorgeous in a fancy ball gown as in jeans.

Distractedly, he envisioned her in an elegant green silk, her dark hair combed to the side and secured with a glittering diamond pin.

He rolled his glass between his palms, striving to be completely truthful with himself while Belle focused on her skillet creation.

When he was younger, he would have respected her intelligence and openness, her kind-heartedness, her pure, fresh nature.

But he wouldn't have asked her out.

However, that was then. This was now.

"Watch, Andrew." Belle signaled him over as she tilted the pan, added a generous sprinkling of cheese and slid it onto a plate. "This is what makes a French omelette different from an American-style. It's all in the rolling. See? The omelette is in the shape of an oval, whereas an American omelet is folded in half."

"Thus, you produced a perfect omelet," he said.

"*Omelette*." She held up the plate. "Voila!"

Laughing, he pressed a kiss on her forehead.

He couldn't help himself. She was a woman who needed to be appreciated and kissed.

"Belle Boots, you are priceless." He chucked her beneath her chin. "Thank you for helping me to laugh again."

"It's good to laugh, isn't it?"

Her assertion called for another kiss. "I haven't enjoyed myself this much in eons."

"Eons?"

"Months … years."

"I haven't laughed this much in eons, either." She reached for napkins, plates, and forks, then arranged two settings on the kitchen island.

"Did you study cooking in college?" He waited for her to sit before taking his place across from her.

She shrugged and looked away. "Most of my college courses were related to equine therapy.

"Is that a bad thing? Equine therapy?"

"Not at all."

"What courses did you study?"

"I earned an undergraduate degree in counseling. Afterward, I completed a certification program, focusing on equine interaction."

"Which is?"

"To treat patients, particularly children, with emotional or physical disabilities through a mutual affection for horses."

"You're obviously passionate about your work."

"I am. Except …" She grimaced and shifted in her seat.

"Except?"

"Except my parents expected me to become a doctor like my father. I might have satisfied them if I had pursued a veterinarian degree." Belle sighed. "I considered it …"

"And then?"

"I love animals but also aspired to help people. My major seemed a suitable way to incorporate both."

"Did you? Please your parents?" he asked.

"No. They tried to steer my aspirations to match theirs. Obviously they didn't succeed." A sheen of tears shimmered in her velvety gray eyes, and she concentrated on a circle of copper pots hanging from the ceiling.

"Embrace your profession." He grabbed her hand. "You're improving lives and helping your students overcome emotional and physical trauma."

"Am I? Truly?"

"I speak from experience because you changed Megan's life." Reassuringly, he squeezed her fingers. "Most definitely."

She kept her focus on the pots. "Or maybe I studied equine therapy to become something my parents didn't want me to be."

Had she suppressed those contemplations, or silently contemplated them all these years? She'd spoken quickly, then seemed to regret her outburst.

"We are all rebellious once in a while," he said. "I was certainly unmanageable when I first moved to America."

"Why?"

"Because going from affluence to poverty, especially in an unfamiliar country, was disheartening." Andrew rubbed his forehead. "My mother never forgave my father for his poor business decisions."

"And you?"

"I did my own thing, made my own way."

"Your sister?"

"In Kate's opinion, my father could do no wrong." He

drew a long breath and curled his fingers around hers. "Tell me something, Belle. Are you content?"

"Undeniably."

"Then stay true to who you are and be happy with your choice. My grandfather in Scotland used to say, "You're a long time deid.'"

"Dead? That goes without saying?"

"Once you're dead, you're dead for a long time, so enjoy life."

"Not the most heartening of Scottish sayings," she muttered.

"But true, nonetheless."

The thought flitted through his mind that he should take the saying to heart. He was committed to a continuous strive for perfection and success, pushing too fast on a narrow lane, but he couldn't help himself.

He remembered what it was like to lose everything.

Never again.

Belle eyed their plates. "Our food is getting cold."

"We can't let your creation go to waste. I'm impressed by your expertise."

"I watch numerous demonstrations on television, and you can learn a lot from YouTube."

"I'm sure, and we mustn't waste all those eggs."

She bowed her head and said grace, something Andrew had never done, although his demeanor was suitably prayerful. When she finished, he forked a mouthful of omelette and closed his eyes, savoring the delectable combination of finely cooked eggs combined with the velvety smoothness of milky sweet cheese.

"Pure dead brilliant," he said, and Belle smiled at the compliment.

He washed down the omelette with another glass of iced tea.

After lunch was over, he helped her clear and rinse the plates.

When the kitchen was tidied to her satisfaction, she brewed a pot of coffee and arranged a set of glass mugs on the island.

Over steaming coffee, he said, "Again, I'm sorry the goats fainted. My habit is to shut the door with my foot because I usually carry papers or tools—"

"No explanation is necessary, Andrew." Lightly, she touched his hand. "The goats are healthy, and actually, they didn't faint. Myotonic goats just stiffen and fall over, appearing to faint."

"I felt like I should rush over to splash cold water on their faces to revive them." He hadn't, because he didn't care to be near two stiff goats, especially one as ornery looking as Hester. "But they were up again in a few seconds and didn't seem hurt."

Belle's eyes sparkled. "No negative consequences."

A radiant sun lit the kitchen, and tiny silver hoops glinted from her ears.

Beyond the expansive window over the sink, vibrant purple zinnias blossomed beneath carefully trimmed hedging and a white oak tree. Belle had mentioned that Abby and Felix were avid gardeners.

Belle smoothed the napkin on her lap. Her movements were elegant, and he admired her aura of kindness. Despite the hard manual exertion in the stalls, her fingers were long and slender and diligently clean. Poignantly, he recalled her adjusting Megan's horse helmet, ensuring that his daughter was safe and protected.

"To put your mind at ease," she continued, "fainting doesn't hurt a goat nor cause any pain."

He gazed at her and smiled. He couldn't get enough of seeing her, being with her. She was naturally sophisticated, humorous, and captivating. She'd been forced to move from Roses quickly, and the sadness she felt at leaving her precious students was real. Despite her optimism, the move hadn't been easy.

And the attention she showed her animals was diligent and caring.

He was a decade older, and a hundred times more world-weary. Yet, every minute with her put another chink in his inflexible armor toward life.

Where Belle was concerned, things weren't all business, and her empathy softened him.

"I leave on Sunday to work in Roses for a couple days. Adella will care for Megan." He glanced at his watch. They were scheduled to return to the house so Megan could take her afternoon nap.

"If you see Candee in Roses, tell her how much I miss her and her family," Belle replied. "With the blur of moving, I haven't had time to phone, except for a quick text to refer Joseph to another therapist."

"How is he doing?"

"The therapist is excellent, although I miss Joseph."

"I'm sure he misses you too." Andrew pushed back his stool. Belle did the same. "I'll return to Wilmington by midweek. Thank you for a delicious lunch."

She walked him to the entryway. "Thank *you* for the gorgeous flowers."

"My pleasure. I'm a romantic at heart.

He was? Well, with Belle he was becoming a regular Romeo.

"You're a sensitive and kind man."

"And princely?"

"Sure."

"And you're a wonderful woman. A princess." More than wonderful. More than a princess. That prickle of awareness whenever she was near flooded his senses.

Out of the corner of his eye he spotted an orange tabby. The cat shot from the hallway and skirted around his legs before disappearing.

"Ginger," Belle supplied.

"Ginger. Right. Okay. Will Ginger bite?"

"Not that I'm aware."

"Does Ginger have a sister or brother?"

Belle elbowed him. "No."

"I'm starting to think you live in a glorified petting zoo."

She burst out laughing. "Don't tell me you're going to make a scene whenever you see one of my animals?"

"Never." He tugged her close. "But I'll show you what a scene looks like."

He didn't give her time to catch her breath nor fire a snappy rejoinder, because he kissed her, long and deep.

"That's quite a scene," she murmured between his kisses. "An extremely romantic one."

"It's from a Scottish movie."

"Which is?"

"Braveheart."

"You mean the movie with the stunning camera work?"

"The very same." He nuzzled her neck. "I'll text you while I'm gone. Will you miss me?"

She pulled back and brushed stray blades of dried grass from his shirt, giving him a tender look with those gorgeous gray eyes. "I'm a pushover for a man who shows up at my riding ring bearing flowers. Especially flowers he snagged at a great sale." She granted him one of her heart-stopping smiles.

Thus, she offered all the proof he needed. He kissed her again and would have continued. Unfortunately, his cell-phone chirped, jerking him back to reality.

He snatched the phone from his pocket while muttering a

string of colorful Scottish phrases. As Belle stepped away, he scanned the text message from his foreman.

Problem with a work site in Camden, SC, boss.

Which site? Andrew texted.

The healthcare renovation at the senior living facility. Construction debris containment, and an extremely vocal town board who are concerned about infection control. They're demanding a meeting with you at eight a.m. on Monday morning or they're shutting the project down.

He pushed out a sigh.

"Troubles with Megan?" Belle asked.

"Thankfully, Megan is fine. An addition to an existing building I've designed is more complex than anticipated, and the board insists the healthcare facility remain in operation while the addition is completed."

"Is it possible to keep the facility open?"

"Not easily, but necessary because the logistics of moving senior citizens to another facility would be difficult." He shoved a hand through his hair. "Part of the problem is economics. The city paid for the renovation. The crew isn't as fastidious about debris as they should be, which leads to a cleanliness issue. The town requires a meeting with me or construction ceases."

"Is a solution possible?"

He slipped on his boots. "Anything is possible."

He insisted on a standard of excellence, not adapting lightly to changes. He thrust his cellphone into his pocket after replying to his foreman. *I'll arrive in Camden by Sunday afternoon so we can talk this over before the Monday meeting.*

This issue would push back his trip to Roses, and consequently, his return to Wilmington.

And this newest demand reminded him that what had happened in Belle's apartment would never happen again.

His work was a part of himself he wouldn't relinquish. Through his designs, his visions became realities.

In truth, being recognized by pleased customers motivated him. Consequently, he would carry out whatever orders were enforced in order to satisfy the requirements for the Camden, SC, town board.

CHAPTER 6

Summer visitors flooded Wilmington, and the intense heat of a southern July eased on.

Belle began offering equine therapy sessions and hadn't seen Andrew since he'd departed for Camden. His texts to her were short and concise.

The first arrived on Sunday.

Hi Belle. I'm in Camden. Here is Adella's cellphone number. Store it in your contacts and text her directly regarding Megan's sessions.

In other words, no communication with him.

Will do. And your drive to Camden was ...? Belle texted.

She grimaced. She'd never been good at texting. She was literally all thumbs.

Uneventful, came his reply. *What did you do this weekend?*

I was busy. Still unpacking. Plus, I visited my Aunt Lucinda.

Her aunt had remarked that she was pleased Belle had begun a new chapter in her life, grinning when Belle mentioned Andrew numerous times. With each recounting of the services he provided, Aunt Lucinda had stretched her hand across the porch swing to pat Belle's arm. "You found someone special. Don't throw love away, like I did."

"Didn't you once say men were a bother?"

"A woman has the prerogative to change her mind and admit her mistakes. If the right man comes along—"

"Andrew and I aren't serious," Belle had protested.

"You will be."

Belle had a swift, unbidden thought that Aunt Lucinda might be correct.

With a sigh, she batted away the contemplation. Sure, she felt special when she was with him, and they chatted about everything because he was easy to talk to. But she'd given her heart to someone only to have her dreams broken.

How is your aunt? Andrew texted.

Eccentric, as usual. She insisted on wearing green gloves and an Indiana Jones hat when we shopped at the Farmer's Market.

Did anyone remark on her appearance?

After all these years, they're accustomed to her.

Does she use coupons too? he asked.

LOL, no. What about you?

No coupons.

I mean, how was your weekend?

More unpacking, same as you. Spent hours with Megan before I drove to Camden. Look, I gotta go. My foreman is pounding on my hotel door.

Good luck with the meeting.

Thanks. Hope your week goes well.

You too.

Impersonal, affable, informal. Hurried. No mention of their lunch together. No mention of French omelettes or tabby cats. This wasn't the teasing, good-natured man who had kissed her by the fence, or in the entryway of her apartment.

This was a different Andrew. The entrepreneur. The billionaire. The man firmly out of reach.

When her cellphone pinged the following week, her heart stopped when his name crossed her screen.

Crazy busy here, Andrew texted. *How are you?*

Fine. You?

Overloaded in work.

The project is taking longer than anticipated?

Much longer.

She waited for him to continue. When he didn't, she asked, *Are you there?*

Sorry, Belle. I'm preoccupied. A local crew was hired, and it's up to me to maintain a high benchmark. Safety is our first priority.

Lots of details?

Yes. I've divided off part of the construction with barriers and stay on site to ensure the crew is complying with town regulations.

Numerous problems waiting for only you to solve?

Okay, that was edgy, but it was too late to take it back. Another long hesitation, and she watched her phone screen for the telltale bubbles indicating that he was texting.

Architects like solving problems, Belle. BTW, Megan is loving her sessions with you.

She's a pleasure. Belle's fingers hovered over her phone's keyboard. Should she inquire when he planned on returning to Wilmington? She typed the question, quickly deleting it. Too needy.

Take care of yourself, she typed in its place. *Don't work too hard.* Ugh. Such a cliché. She pulled at the collar of her sleeveless denim shirt.

That's my job, Belle.

That's your life, she wanted to fire back. Instead, she said nothing.

. . .

Several days afterward, she claimed a stool at her kitchen island and examined the bouquet of dahlias—the petals brown and curling, the stalks drooping.

Nonetheless, a slight yellow tint remained. A sign of hope.

She re-cut the stems, changed the old water to fresh and returned them to the vase.

What is the meaning of yellow flowers? she typed into her cellphone.

Daisies mean cheerfulness and innocence. Dahlias represent a forever commitment between two persons.

She sucked in a breath. She couldn't focus on any words with tears flooding her eyes.

"I looked up the meanings of the flowers," Andrew had told her. *"Dahlias seemed more appropriate."*

Slowly, her annoyance at him for being preoccupied in Camden gave way to regret that he wasn't with her in Wilmington. Unfortunately, her practical brain reminded, that same romantic man had forgotten all about her only in a matter of days.

On a leisurely walk a week later, Belle came upon a street sign that read Carolina Way. Andrew was in Camden, she rationalized, and she was more than a little curious to see his house. Besides, she enjoyed viewing real estate, assuming that someday she'd have a home of her own.

As she strolled the shore, she relished the slap of ocean water against the rocks, the Atlantic-blue churning surf. All familiar. All soothing. She loved living in Wilmington again.

She neared a secluded mansion and verified the location using the map on her cellphone. One Carolina Way. Andrew's house.

Her lips parted. She stood silent in mute confusion.

His "little" place? Painted a vivid turquoise blue, the spectacular home sat directly on the ocean and claimed a broad, sandy beach.

This was his rental—with the outsized swimming pool flanked by elegant Roman columns, complemented by faultlessly groomed shrubs? Really?

Yes, really, because, clutching a cellphone, he waved to her from the second-floor balcony.

Her legs froze in place. Wasn't he supposed to be in Camden? He'd caught her spying on him.

At any rate, he'd returned and had obviously neglected to phone her.

And what was it with this man and balconies?

Despite her compulsion to flee, she gathered her courage and feigned a smile. "Hi." She enhanced her smile with a high-spirited wave. "I took a walk and—" *Happened to be strolling along Carolina Way? Why were her thoughts so muddled?* "This is private property, correct?"

He clicked off his cellphone. "It's *my* private property, Belle, and you're always welcome. Adella just left, and Megan is in bed."

Belle's hands curled. "I assumed you were out of town." Okay, she was incriminating herself further. Not to mention that she was shouting and had no right to question his whereabouts.

"The problems in Camden are resolved, and I arrived home an hour ago. I showered and read Megan a story before her bedtime. I planned to phone you when I finished this last business call and here you are. C'mon over." He waved her forward.

"I can't." She peered at her cut-off shorts. Her hair must look a sight, and sand had taken up permanent residence in her sandals. "Thanks for the invite, but I'll take a raincheck." She hastened her steps and backed away from the house.

"Belle, please. I'll meet you on the deck." That Scottish lilt, affirming an unpretentious warmth, both enchanting and entrancing. He slid his cellphone into the pocket of his gray polo shirt. "We can watch the sunset together."

Ever the romantic.

She swallowed her protest, slowly starting up the lush expanse of emerald lawn. He was sensitive and seemed sincere, she conceded, and the combination was irresistible.

As she approached, she took in the inviting scene. Candles were lit on a teak credenza, and a Mozart piano sonata played from an invisible speaker. The dancing flames from a rectangular fire pit beckoned, and potted red zinnias brought radiant color to the deck.

He finished arranging two white Adirondack chairs on either side of a wooden table, set a child monitor nearby, then surveyed Belle from head to toe. Striding forward, he grasped her hands in his. "Miss Belle Boots, you are adorable."

"Adorable?"

"You always remind me of a poster woman for ... I don't know ... small-town goodness."

"Is that a Scottish compliment?"

"American." He laughed. "In any event, you're gorgeous and a perfect package."

Promptly recognizing that after two weeks on the road, any woman would undoubtedly be a perfect package, she took a guarded step backward.

"How are you?" A Scottish burr laced his words, trilling the 'r.'

"I'm fine. You?" She gazed up at his impossibly attractive face. Would he welcome her into his arms?

He didn't, murmuring he was also fine and gesturing for her to sit. "Can I offer you anything to drink?" he asked. "You name it, I have it."

"Iced tea."

"Ah, sweet iced tea. My beverage of choice is non-alcoholic Scottish ginger beer this evening. Adella picked up a six-pack at a local specialty store. Are you up to trying it?"

"Sure. Was the beer on sale?"

"We're just glad the store carries it." He grabbed two bottles from a free-standing mini fridge tucked in the corner of the deck. "Adella would have paid any price, especially because it's on my tab." He grinned and Belle reciprocated.

He gazed at her as he poured beer into her glass. "You are lovely."

"A minute ago, your choice phrases were adorable and small-town goodness."

"Pure dead brilliant also comes to mind and beautiful and I—" His words rushed together. "Sorry. Scots don't give praise well."

She studied the glass as he continued pouring. "You're spilling the beer," she noted.

He muttered a lively Gaelic phrase, reached for a linen napkin to mop the overflow, then handed her an overflowing glass.

She sniffed, then tasted, rewarded with a sampling of spicy ginger and citrus.

He set the bottle upright and waited for her to sit, then claimed the chair beside hers. "Good?"

She lifted her glass. "Delicious."

Judging from his reddish beard stubble, he hadn't shaved in several days. His hair was still damp from the shower and his shirt, open at the throat, was tucked into olive-colored shorts. Involuntarily, she memorized the way he looked, the rigid planes of his chest, the strong profile—every inch the charismatic male. She also noted the fixed lines of fatigue around his eyes and mouth, which she hadn't noticed when she'd last seen him.

He smiled and leaned back. "Do I meet with your approval?"

"Sorry. I was staring, wasn't I?"

"Don't be sorry. You meet with my approval too." There was no mistaking his quiet assertion. Despite his laid-back teasing, her pulse doubled.

She shifted. Swallowed. Even if she had the courage to ask him why he'd texted her only twice, she couldn't be certain whether her question wouldn't come with an answer she wasn't prepared to hear.

"Thanks for repairing my leaky roof," she said. "Abby and Felix gratefully appreciated your generosity."

"My pleasure." Andrew stretched out his long legs, picked up his glass and watched the fire's cheery blaze leaping and flickering. "I, too, fix things, except my specialty is buildings."

She sat straighter. "You remember I'm a fixer?"

"There's nothing about you I ever forget." A warmhearted gleam shone from his eyes. "Did Candee mention I visited her when I was in Roses?"

Belle placed her glass aside. "Briefly, yes."

"Did she say who we discussed?"

Recalling their phone conversation, Belle replied in a cool voice, "She was evasive." And that had made Belle uncomfortable. "I assume you two discussed Joseph's new horse therapist, or Megan, or Bransfield Designs." Noting the rigidity in his jaw, Belle ended with a short laugh. "Correct?"

ANDREW SET down his glass and reached for Belle, although she drew away and planted her hands on her lap. Despite her off-the-cuff response, he had the uneasy impression he'd unintentionally upset her. Determining their conversation required a clearer explanation, he began, "Candee and I discussed you."

"Me?" Belle tilted her head. "Why?"

"I was eager to learn more about you. After considerable prodding, Candee was kind enough to share the details of your marriage with me."

"You mean my divorce?"

"From what I understand, you were married to a guy named Tyler who didn't appreciate you."

Slender eyebrows snapped together. "Why were you two discussing my personal life?"

He caught the resentment lacing her tone. "I explained why. I'm interested in you, Belle. Surely you realize that."

Well, that wasn't the entire truth. He was *more* than interested.

In Camden, he hadn't been able to think clearly, which had put him in a state he wasn't accustomed to, causing the job to take twice as long. He'd been certain when he'd left Wilmington that a relationship with Belle was too emotionally harrowing to contemplate. However, sitting next to her now played havoc with his sentiments.

She kept her gaze on the ocean. Her fingers toyed with the silky hair at her temple.

"Look at me." He touched his lips to her restless fingers. "Talk to me."

"About my failed marriage? About Tyler?"

"If you wish."

"Hasn't Candee regaled you with all the tragic, pathetic details?"

"They're not pathetic," he said. "And I'd like to hear them from you."

Her gaze darted to his. "We're friends, aren't we?"

"Without question."

"Alright then." She plucked up her glass. "To begin with, Tyler was in my life for several years. I believed I loved him."

Despite the irrationality of it, a surge of jealousy went through Andrew.

The air became unnaturally quiet.

"When I first met him, he asked if I could keep a secret. He'd been hurt by several unpleasant relationships and had lost faith in women. I felt bad for him and privileged that he confided in me. He was such a stoic man. He was a professional accountant, you know."

Andrew gave a bitter laugh. "I heard."

"A string of unfortunate luck, Tyler told me." Belle's heel incessantly tapped on the wooden deck. "His sad stories inspired me to prove to him that he shouldn't lose faith in women and love."

"Did you succeed?"

Belle choked on her beer. "A month after we were married he verbally degraded me after a horse competition, mocking that I smelled like a barn."

The sadness, the humiliation brimming from her gray eyes, drew a dawning of compassion within him. That frozen ocean of deep uncertainty—to care for a woman again—to care for anyone save his precious daughter; began to crack.

He laid a palm on Belle's cheek. He longed to embrace her, to hold on to the intense emotions gripping him, the first real emotions he'd felt in years. He wanted to share more than a moment with her. He anticipated sharing a lifetime.

The knowledge surprised him, but only for an instant. He embraced it for what it was. The truth.

A tear ran down her face and he kissed her there, sampling the saltiness. He rifled through his intentions to continue the conversation, half-heartedly rejecting the subject of her beauty, her mesmerizing smile, her declaration that they were friends.

They were more than friends. Much more.

"Go on," he said tenderly.

She fixed her glass on the table. "Six months into our marriage, Tyler screamed at me for not keeping myself up to his excessive standards. He scolded me for always wearing informal clothes." She bit down on her bottom lip as it quivered. "I tried to reason with him. Jeans were, after all, what a therapist wore when around horses all day. But he merely yelled louder. His profession required a well-dressed woman he could escort to corporate dinners." She gazed up at Andrew with tear-filled eyes. "I didn't provide a proper fit for him."

Andrew kept his features neutral, although his insides churned with fury. "Your beauty rivals any of the prettiest starlets."

"I'm adorable, if I remember your words correctly."

"And lovely," he emphasized.

She waved an airy hand, dismissing his compliments. "The next day Tyler apologized for his outburst. Nonetheless, a few days afterward he filed for divorce. He told me I couldn't compare to his glamorous ex-girlfriends if I tried."

"He told you he'd dated glamorous women?"

Her chin lowered. "Often."

Andrew recalled Belle's hands gently fastening Megan's helmet, her soothing, encouraging voice, their shared giggles when his daughter rode Honeycrisp.

He marveled at her kindness, suppressing a frown because now she was assiduously avoiding his stare. For all her dauntless independence, wit, and spirit, she became hesitant and withdrawn when talking about Tyler.

"The papers from his lawyer decreed irreconcilable differences," Belle was saying.

"You should have been glad to get rid of him." Andrew evened out his voice, seeking to reassure her while tamping down the impulse to physically strangle her ex.

"My aunt said the same. So did Candee. I should've known by the way Jenkins reacted the first time Tyler entered his stall."

"Your horse, you mean?"

"Yes, I believe animals have a sixth sense." Briefly, Belle closed her eyes. "I keenly remember Jenkins' soft brown eyes going hard, and his ears pinned back. That marked the last time Tyler ever entered his stall."

"Tyler never tried again?"

"Once, but Jenkins threatened to kick him."

"So Tyler got the memo?"

"Loud and clear." She grinned, but her expression swiftly turned sober. "But you know what?" She picked up her glass. Her hand shook. "When the divorce documents arrived, I accepted and signed while my heart broke."

"Why? You clearly were abused."

"In my mind I was a failure—trying to fix Tyler, trying to fix my marriage, and ultimately not gratifying my parents' wishes."

"You chose to follow your own professional path, and for that I commend you." Andrew raised his glass for a toast.

She clinked her glass against his. "True."

They exchanged congratulatory glances.

Her thick hair gleamed in the firelight, spilling forward across her face. Her lashes, dark and lush, cast the hint of a shadow across her unblemished cheeks.

"I'm wondering if you ever really loved Tyler." Andrew voiced his thoughts aloud. Although perhaps he shouldn't have because her eyebrows pulled together and she frowned.

"Maybe. Maybe not." She stood, and he admired her pure loveliness, the subtle finesse in the way she wore her clothes, no matter how casual.

She peered at the sun setting on the horizon, the sky a brilliant brush of vivid rose and intense orange, the waves shimmering like diamonds as an unflinching moon cast silvery beams on the water.

He came behind her and enfolded her in his arms, tracing the curve of her ear with his mouth. She trembled. He hoped she would turn to gaze at him so he could see her face.

When she didn't turn, he brushed his knuckles against her cheek and delicately kissed her shoulders, her nape, her hair.

"Andrew, I—"

"Don't, Belle."

"Don't what?"

He drew in a slow, leaden breath. "Don't ever change."

Because he was falling in love with her.

She brought him a quiet sense of joy. In quick-thinking texts, emotional moments, and dazzling smiles, she'd stolen his heart.

His words wrung a hesitant chuckle from her. "Don't ever change what? My profession?"

"Anything about you."

"Are you saying that you're beginning to like horses?"

"Fortunately, you're not a horse."

"I'm around them all week."

He smirked. "I'll manage."

"You haven't met Jenkins face to face yet." She threw a rueful smile over her shoulder, and he set his sights on her alluring lips.

He laughed, deep and throaty, steadying himself, marveling at her bewitching effect on him. Impulsively, he tightened his arms around her. He couldn't get enough of her, and this was a unique experience. Yes, women had been a social duty all his adult life, but certainly not his entire world. He'd never been preoccupied with a woman before.

"Andrew?"

He closed his eyes. "Hmm?"

"Are you interested in hearing the rest of my story?"

Even with his eyes closed, he felt her gaze on him as she turned and rested her soft cheek against his chest.

The simple affection of her movements plunged his spirits. Effectively, it reminded him that if he stopped seeing her, there would be no further tender moments.

He should let her go. He was committed to his work, to his daughter. There was no room in his life for another relationship. Another failure.

Not in business. Not personally. He'd learned that hard lesson from experience.

But he *couldn't* let Belle go.

"Yes. Tell me everything." He opened his eyes. "Under one condition."

"What's that?"

Huskily, he murmured, "I can keep my arms around you."

For a beat she was silent, followed by a quiet sigh.

"I'd love that," she whispered.

He tipped up her head, prompting her with an over bright smile. "I'm listening."

"Right …well … " She inhaled. "When I rationalized my situation, I attributed my divorce to a marriage gone wrong at an early age and a manipulative husband. I shouldn't have tried to fix his problems."

"Fixers place other people's needs before their own," Andrew said.

"I have an overwhelming urge to support folks, and try to come up with a solution to make things better. Sometimes, I can't help myself."

"Sometimes?"

"Oftentimes," she conceded.

Her eyes reminded him of the color of dove feathers, soft and gentle, which perfectly described his selfless, caring Belle.

The last beams of sunlight streamed down, enhancing her shiny hair with golden highlights.

She interrupted his delightful contemplation by rhapsodizing, "Isn't the sky picturesque? The sun sets over the ocean in so many colors. It resembles a portrait."

"Or a painting on canvas." He cradled her close to his chest. "Sometimes I forget to appreciate the precious things in life."

Like love.

He'd never known what love felt like. Now he did.

The exhilaration, the joy. The feeling that every last breath had been taken from his lungs.

Love wasn't planned. It never was.

And love was the only thing in life that truly mattered.

CHAPTER 7

The night Belle had watched the sunset with Andrew, she'd agreed to text him the minute she returned to her apartment. Touched and flattered when he'd insisted, she'd happily obliged.

Twenty-four hours later, he suggested dinner with him and Megan when he came back to Wilmington the following weekend.

She accepted.

He canceled soon afterward. Problems in Camden.

The days merged into another week before he arrived back in Wilmington.

When can I see you again? he texted. *My foreman told me there are wild horses on a beach in the Outer Banks.*

You mean in Corolla? she asked.

Yes.

Megan will love this, Belle replied.

I missed you while I was away.

Audibly, she swallowed, processing Andrew's comment.

And you? he pressed. *You love horses.*

A given. But he'd been gone. Now he assumed she was at his beck and call.

Wild horses will be a grand adventure, she hedged.

I agree. BTW, Megan's eye patch was removed this week.

I know. I saw her when she came for her session. How wonderful.

I wasn't around. I relied on Adella to bring Megan for her eyeglass fitting, because work necessitated that I stay in Camden. Still, I should have been there.

I would have enthusiastically joined them, Belle responded.

Really?

Without question. I love Megan.

Thank you. A hesitation filled the space between them. *That means a lot.*

Wait ...The horses at the Outer Banks wander freely, Belle texted. *What if a horse gallops near you?*

I'd jump into the ocean.

She laughed out loud. *Sounds like a plan.*

Not a particularly good plan, but a plan, nonetheless.

Are you aware Corolla is four hours away from Wilmington by car? she added.

It is?

Aren't you aware of the distance?

I've been so preoccupied lately.

Perhaps a beach trip somewhere a bit closer?

I missed you, he texted a second time. *Will you come to the beach with us?*

She squeezed her cellphone, briefly closing her eyes while her heartbeat soared.

"You missed me," she whispered to the phone screen, visualizing his handsome face.

She'd missed him too, but she wouldn't tell him that.

You work too much, she typed instead.

No, no, too bossy.

She deleted it. He'd just arrived after several nonstop workdays.

I'm trying to change, he texted, as if he had read her mind. *I tuned in to a bunch of self-help audiobooks during the long drive. How to balance work with everyday life.*

Were the books helpful?

Interesting. Thought-provoking.

Perhaps he should practice what he listened to.

Still, a much-needed beach respite would allow Andrew a renewed and refreshed outlook.

Don't mention anything else on this subject, she warned herself before her fingers touched the keypad. She had no right trying to fix him.

Shall I pack a lunch? she inquired.

No. You have enough to do. There's a certain colonel who makes a delicious fried chicken.

I thought you loved fresh seafood?

Who said that? Me?

Uh, huh. Fresh caught fish for dinner…

Hmm. We'll order seafood when we get closer to the beach. Pan-fried scallops and fried pickles are my favorite. Megan likes chicken strips.

Scallops sound good. Undecided on the pickles. Which beach?

The beach in front of my house.

You just went from a four-hour car ride to a one minute car ride. Have you considered Carolina Beach?

Is it far?

About twenty minutes away.

She loved the sun-drenched feel of the modest town and hadn't had the opportunity to visit since landing in Wilmington.

Excellent. I'll pick you up at ten on Saturday morning.

. . .

TWO DAYS LATER, Andrew and Megan arrived at Belle's apartment exactly as her cuckoo clock chimed ten a.m. Punctuality was a trait Belle admired about him.

What did it cost him to juggle a multi-million-dollar business while single parenting? Sure, he had the means and domestic help, but it still required resourcefulness and a perseverance she seldom witnessed in men. Certainly not Tyler. Certainly not any she'd dated since her divorce.

Of course, she and Andrew weren't dating. They were friends who shared a common interest in his daughter's happiness and security.

And horses.

Well, not horses, exactly. Goats. Nope. Tabby cats. Umm, no.

Nonetheless, they got along splendidly.

AS WAS HIS CUSTOM, Andrew got out of his SUV as soon as Belle emerged from her apartment.

He opened the passenger door for her. "You are stunning," he said.

"Thank you, but hardly." She glanced down at the khaki shorts and red ribbed tank top she'd worn over her swimsuit. "I appreciate your earlier home-town goodness compliment, though."

"Small-town goodness," he corrected. "Here's another compliment. 'A pretty face suits the dish-cloth.'"

"Now I look like a dish-cloth?" She hung her hands on her hips. "Is that a step up or down from small-town goodness?"

"It's Scottish flattery. You are stunning in anything you wear." He chucked her under the chin. "So it's a step up."

"Well, perhaps if you said it in Scottish …"

"English will do." He grabbed her raffia bag and feigned a groan as he fixed it in the trunk. "What's in this? Lead?"

"All the necessary supplies. Sunscreen, towels, water bottles and my script." Belle displayed a tablet from her tote bag, settled into the SUV's plush leather upholstery and greeted Megan with a jovial smile.

The child sat securely buckled in her car seat. Her emerald-colored eyes, enhanced by raspberry eyeglass frames, twinkled with excitement.

"Hi, Miss Belle." Megan lifted her terry cloth cover-up with exaggerated flair. "Do you like my bathing suit?"

"I love pink unicorns," Belle replied. "And you are utterly adorable."

"Daddy helped dress me, but I picked out my own clothes."

"Kudos to you and daddy." Belle grinned as Andrew winked at her.

"A script, Belle?" He slipped into the driver's seat. "As in a movie script?"

"Not quite Hollywood, I'm afraid, but yes."

"You act as well as offer equine therapy? I'm impressed."

"Thanks. The Little Theater in Wilmington put out a casting call for The Lion, The Witch, and The Wardrobe." She glanced at her tablet before embarking on details.

"C.S. Lewis?"

"Very good."

"Daddy, you read that story to me," Megan said. "I like the part when the four kids go into the wardrobe and all the animals talk."

"Their world is magical." Belle grinned at Megan over her shoulder, then gazed ahead. "The story's message focuses on faith and courage."

"Don't forget love," Andrew said. For a split-second he

watched her, the heat in his tone igniting his words. "Because in the end, it's all about love."

His deep voice, that Scottish brogue, his green, fathomless eyes, had an alarming effect on Belle's heart rate. The remark was so typical of his romantic nature that she smiled.

"Is it?" she asked.

"What the world needs now … All you need is … you've heard the lyrics to these popular songs, correct?"

"Of course."

"I wasn't certain, because you're younger than me."

"By only a few years." She rolled her eyes in amused exasperation. "You're certainly brimming with all sorts of sayings this morning."

He wore a pair of swim trunks in a dashing pattern of tropical leaves, and a royal-blue T-shirt that read *Bransfield Designs*. He was drop-dead handsome, and his debonair attitude mesmerized her. Another Andrew she was beginning to know better—this one playful and humorous.

When he rolled down the windows, a breeze grabbed her hair. Deeply, she breathed in, delighting in the scents of fish and salt, the promise of the ocean.

He switched on the radio to a station with kid-safe lyrics and transferred it to the back speakers. Immediately, Megan and Belle hummed along to a familiar tune.

"Belle, are you auditioning for the role of Mrs. Beaver?" Andrew asked.

"Mr. Beaver's wife?" Belle stopped humming, glancing at him as he concentrated on the road. "The obsessive, overly careful woman?"

"If I remember correctly, Mrs. Beaver is kind-hearted."

"I'll need to audition first before I'm cast in one of the bigger roles. Fortunately, there's always a place in the supporting cast for a forest squirrel or chipmunk."

"That's the part where the animals turn to stone," Megan chimed in.

"Little ears hear everything," he whispered.

With a chuckle, Belle twisted, brushing her hand reassuringly up and down Megan's bare, freckled leg. Lovably innocent, she presented an endearing picture in an oversized nautical bucket hat, and Belle found herself wanting to protect her, similar to Andrew's instincts.

"In Narnia," Belle assured Megan, "everything works out for the best."

Leaning back in her seat, Belle recalled that in the play, the children were separated from their mother. Some animals died, as well.

"Megan and I will attend your performance, providing it's a mild version," Andrew was saying.

"It might not be," Belle replied.

He frowned. Belle could see his brilliant mind turning, reviewing the tale.

"In any event," he continued, "I'll be the one clapping the loudest when you take your final bow."

She grinned. "Good to know."

"I enjoy live plays." He brightened. "I especially liked *My Fair Lady.*"

"*My Fair Lady* is a musical, not a play."

"Same difference."

"Hardly." Her lips quirked. "But you haven't seen me act yet. You may snatch up your program and dash from the theater at intermission."

"I'll support you no matter what. Good, bad …" He squeezed her hand. "Exactly as you supported my daughter through her rough times."

THEY REACHED Carolina Beach a half hour later.

"It's illegal to intentionally come within fifty feet of the horses at Corolla," Belle informed Andrew as he opened her door. "We wouldn't have been permitted to feed or pet the horses, anyway."

He gave a thumbs-up. "Best news I've heard all day."

"Daddy!" Megan admonished as he unbuckled her seat belt. "Horses are nice."

"These horses are different, Megan," Belle explained. "Think of them as Honeycrisp's wild cousins."

"They don't faint, do they?" Andrew muttered.

Belle smiled, then drew a wobbly breath. She and Andrew already shared a history of memories and fun, private jokes.

Years earlier, when she'd first acted in minor roles, she'd waited for the director to give her cues. Now, with Andrew, she felt as if she were exactly where she was supposed to be. With him and his daughter. No direction was needed. She just *knew*.

When it came to finding a man she could genuinely love, she hadn't been looking.

But here he was.

A single father. A man of principle. A man who felt real emotions and wasn't ashamed to show them. And she was falling in love with him with a ferocity she could hardly explain.

She brushed her hand against his. "Wild horses don't faint. Only goats. Or women who haven't eaten lunch."

She grinned at his perplexed intake of breath.

"We are grabbing fried scallops later," he said. "Shall we find a place to eat first?"

"Lunch is this afternoon," Belle reminded.

"But we can snack anytime, right, Daddy?" Megan asked. "Didn't you pack corn curls?"

At Belle's lifted eyebrows, he explained, "I'm better with packaged food requiring no preparation."

"Sliced carrots and hummus are nutritious and easy to pack."

"Special days merit special treats."

At his affectionate gaze, her cheeks heated.

Fifteen minutes later, Megan was thoroughly drenched in sunscreen and their beach chairs, towels, and a portable cooler were arranged beside them. Belle and Andrew dug a moat around a castle Megan erected, tamping down wet sand with oversized shovels.

The sky, a brilliant Carolina-blue, mirrored the sunlight and a briny wind whipped across Belle's cheeks. Oftentimes, she'd visualized living near the beach again. Walking barefoot while the waves lapped at her ankles, the golden sand warm and comforting.

And here she was.

"Daddy, can we dive in the water?" Megan, apparently tiring of filling buckets, yanked on Andrew's arm. He held out his hand to Belle although she declined, preferring to lounge on a reclining chair.

She adjusted her sunglasses and easily spotted father and daughter as they splashed in the surf. Andrew's tall, trim body dripped with water, and his drenched swim trunks slicked against his powerful thighs. He had an indisputable magnetism, and she tracked him with her gaze.

Her cellphone pinged, and a text message from her Aunt Lucinda slid across Belle's screen.

How's it going? her aunt inquired.

Alarm prompted Belle to waver. *Are you okay?*

Perfectly fine. I'm sixty, not six hundred.

We're enjoying a day at the beach.

We're?

Andrew and I and Megan.

His daughter? You mention her frequently.

She's precious, Belle responded.

You always wanted children.

Belle touched her throat. Aunt Lucinda invariably stated whatever was on her mind. She had no filter.

Yes, but— Belle began.

I predict you and Andrew will have a big family.

Belle pulled the phone close to her chest. *We've hardly—*

In the meantime, I'm still waiting to meet him.

Dear aunt, I'll arrange something soon. I love you.

I love you. I also love the idea of finding your true partner. Someone to share your joy and sorrow. Do you agree?

Belle nodded, recalling Andrew's song lyric comments. On a promising day like this, love definitely made the world a brighter place.

She snapped her phone shut and shook the sand from her sandals, intending to join Andrew and Megan along the water's edge.

He met her before she'd taken ten steps. She paused, the water fizzing and bubbling at her feet.

"Take a swim," he said. "We'll watch from the shore."

"I'll go in later." With a smile, Belle followed them back to their chairs.

Megan rubbed her eyes, her rosy-red mouth set in a cherubic smile. "Am I a good swimmer?"

Belle gave her a high-five. "The finest on the entire Wilmington shore."

"Sun and water wear her out, although she fights nap time," Andrew mouthed. He wrapped his daughter in a beach towel and tucked her into a chair with an umbrella overhead. Within minutes, the child was asleep.

He slung a towel over his shoulders. Grabbing two water bottles from the cooler, he offered one to Belle. He took a swig of the other and landed on a lounge chair beside her. Their bare feet were so close they almost touched.

"Beach living is the best," he announced.

"You said something similar before. You mentioned surfing—"

He slipped his hand through hers and chuckled. "Do you remember everything I say?"

"Absolutely not." She hid her lie behind an amicable smile and quickly bent her head, concentrating on the water bottle.

"A pity, because I remember everything about you," he murmured.

She reminded herself that Andrew was part of an imaginary life, similar to this brilliant beach day—bold, dazzling and memorable, yet transitory.

He gazed at the ocean. He still held her hand as if he craved her near, craved her touch. She liked that, liked that about him.

"Did I ever tell you about my ex?" he asked.

His serious tone conveyed the importance of the subject.

"A little," she ventured. "You cited the delivery man." She waited for him to offer a Scottish proverb or witty jibe. When he didn't reply, she said softly, "It helps to talk about our concerns."

He nodded. "After Rowena's abrupt departure, Megan was devastated."

"It's only natural. It must have been difficult."

His laugh was brief and grim.

"Rowena didn't give any notice?" Belle asked.

"None. She taped a note to the front door and drove off. We haven't seen her since." Andrew tossed down his water and rested his gaze on Megan.

"How long has Rowena been gone?"

He shifted positions. For several minutes, he focused on the vast expanse of sparkling water reaching the horizon, the sunlight reflecting an intensity of colors.

"Then what happened?" she finally inquired.

Andrew glanced at Belle as if he'd forgotten she sat next

to him. "These past two years she's missed Megan's birthdays and Christmases. I'm the primary custodial parent, and Rowena hasn't contested the lawyer's papers."

"Although I'm sorry for everything, be grateful Megan is in your life." Belle tried to sound untroubled by Rowena's startling lack of interest. "Your daughter adores you and she's happy."

Belle studied the bleak expression on Andrew's face, sensed the somber mood that had descended. Despite his mumble of agreement, he wasn't at peace.

"Don't be sorry for me," he said. "It sounds like this happened all of a sudden, but breakups don't occur in a vacuum. Rowena and I were headed for divorce court several years beforehand." His tone took on a sharp edge. "I can't forgive her."

Belle touched his hand. "Surely, Rowena has attempted to see Megan."

"No," he said shortly. "And selfish is too kind a word to describe her."

Sea gulls cried in the distance, the ocean waves foamy and white. Near them, a group of giggling children made angels in the sand. Carolina Beach was a favorite of Belle's. As a child she'd spent hours wading in the sea spray, and loved the unique, family flavor of the beach and adjacent boardwalk.

She searched her mind for a pleasanter topic rather than dwelling on Andrew's divorce details.

"Ask me anything about Wilmington, and I can answer," she declared with a bright smile.

He wrinkled an eyebrow. "Anything?"

"For instance, the rare Venus flytrap grows here in the wild."

Although his lips were pressed together, a grin slipped through. "I'll keep a look out for it."

"And the flytrap flourishes in a sixty-mile radius around

Wilmington." Belle bobbed her head, delighted and thankful her subject change had worked so swiftly.

"At the risk of dispelling any Venus flytrap myths, if a fly just sits in the trap and doesn't resist, the plant will open, and the fly can leave in the morning," he replied.

"Did you pick up that specific scientific fact from your audiobooks? You are an architect and study ... building structures."

"I am. I do. I learned about the Venus flytrap from science *class* in secondary school."

Belle grinned.

She intended to ask more questions—about the bitterness he harbored toward his sister and ex-wife, because she believed she could help him heal.

However, sensitive to the quiet mood, the way it had changed for the better, she held onto the comfortable silence.

The tautness in his jaw relaxed, and she almost missed the genuine affection in his eyes when he smiled at her, because she'd gazed down at their hands, still entwined.

CHAPTER 8

$\mathcal{A}$ couple days afterward, Belle stood in her riding ring and announced to Megan, "If it's Monday, it's time for …"

"Equine therapy!" the little girl chortled as she raced from Andrew's SUV.

"Hurray!" Belle dragged the mounting block to the center of the ring, then bent to secure Megan's pink helmet.

"What about me?" Andrew baited indignantly as he reached the fence.

"Are you wanting a horseback ride?" Belle met his grin with a teasing one beneath her lashes. "Jenkins is in the stable along with Honeycrisp and Felix, my landlord."

"Can I see the horses?" Megan asked.

"Sure," Belle replied, "they're expecting you."

Andrew considered the surroundings. "Where are the goats today?"

"Around."

"Around is a little too vague. I'll stay here." He reached for Belle's arm and shifted her to face him. "First, I'm here to confess that I missed you."

"You confess that a lot."

"Because I think it a lot."

"If you recall, we spent last evening together. Adella watched Megan at your house while we strolled the boardwalk." Belle well remembered the sticky blue blobs of cotton candy she and Andrew had fed each other, the windswept sand dunes, the noisy arcade games lining the two-mile boardwalk. Inside a quaint shop, Andrew had purchased Megan a handmade shell bracelet.

'I like Wilmington,' he'd said to Belle. *'I appreciate the feeling of normality. I tend to forget how valuable leisure time is to a person's health.'*

Belle had agreed in a matter-of-fact voice.

They proceeded, beaming at couples who passed them with affable nods.

"Happily, I finally met your Aunt Lucinda," Andrew was saying.

"Finally." Belle smiled at him. "She prefers living near the boardwalk, so it was an easy walk for us."

"Does she like living close to all these stomach-churning rides?"

"No rides," Belle replied. "Although every Sunday, the Farmer's Market is her chosen spot for homegrown kale. She also shops the adjacent booth for chocolate-covered bacon."

"I suppose healthy cancels out unhealthy when you're sixty years old."

"She buys me bacon too," Belle said. "And I'm not sixty."

He laughed. "So, you like chocolate-covered bacon too?"

"No, but I won't hurt her feelings."

"Let me guess—the bacon is on sale."

"It depends," Belle replied. "I figured out that the man who owns the bacon booth is attracted to her. He becomes all animated when he sees her."

"Vice versa?"

"If I know Aunt Lucinda, it will take more than a pound of chocolate-covered bacon to court her." Belle muffled a laugh. "In any event, you two got along famously when we arrived at her bungalow unannounced."

"She is everything you described and more."

"How much more?"

"Shall I begin with her outfit?" Andrew stifled a grin. "I admit I'm not up-to-date on women's fashion—"

"You object to her Indiana Jones hat?"

"I was prepared for the hat. For her remarks, not so much."

Belle paused. "Aunt Lucinda doesn't mince words."

"I noticed."

"She likes you."

"I like her too. I especially like what she suggested."

"Who's Aunt Lucinda?" Megan bounded up to them. "What did she say, daddy?"

Belle's cheeks burned as Andrew extended a helpless smile. Aunt Lucinda had given Andrew the once-over and candidly declared he was exactly the man Belle was destined to marry.

Andrew had agreed, pulling Belle into his arms and kissing her. Belle had returned his kiss with all the love brimming in her heart.

Because Andrew had agreed.

"Aunt Lucinda is Miss Belle's aunt. Soon, you'll meet her." He kissed Megan on the cheek and looped an arm around Belle's waist.

A HALF HOUR LATER, Megan finished her therapy session, and Felix offered to bring Megan to the stable to unsaddle Honeycrisp, then turn the horses out to pasture.

"I'm in town all week," Andrew said, when Belle met him

at the fence. "Will dinner and a movie at my place suffice for a date?"

"More than suffice."

"I can stream Braveheart."

"So you're in a sentimental mood and reminiscing about Scotland." Belle opened the gate and stepped over to him. "Are you serving haggis?"

"Are you brave enough to sample a plate?"

"You mentioned your sister makes the best haggis. Next, you'll probably charter a private jet to Scotland to see her."

He rubbed his hands over his face. "Nope."

"Potatoes and turnips will do, then. Both are favorite Scottish dishes."

"You've done your Scottish homework." His mouth tilted at the corners. "I assume it's because you were eager to learn more about me?"

Thinking of an excuse to refute his claim, she ended up simply nodding. There was no sense hiding her feelings. He knew she was interested.

He just didn't know how much, because she was unquestionably, unequivocally falling in love with him.

"I'll ask Adella to prepare a Scottish meal for us." He rubbed his palm against Belle's cheek and grinned. "When we watch Braveheart, be prepared to see some of the most gorgeous scenery you'll ever witness."

The ache of longing in his voice for his homeland tugged at her. She squeezed her eyes shut as his fingers wandered to stroke her hair.

He missed Scotland. He should resolve the issues with his sister. There was no purpose in holding onto a grudge. What was the Scottish phrase?

"You're a long time deid," she murmured.

The grin vanished from his features. "What did you say?" He dropped his hand and stared at her.

"Nothing."

"You're parroting one of my Scottish sayings?"

"They're not *your* sayings, they're your country's sayings, and you should embrace them. Life is short. Forgive your ex. Forgive your sister."

"Why?"

"It's obvious. Forgiveness will set you free."

He glanced toward the stable before fixing his gaze on Belle. "Sometimes there are too many wrongs to right."

"Forgiving the people who may have wronged you will provide peace of mind."

"I am at peace."

"Are you?"

"You're an equine therapist, Belle, not a human therapist." His brief smile didn't reach his eyes. "If I need advice, I'll check a self-help book out of the library."

She recoiled, but pushed on. "Begin the process of healing. Do it for yourself."

Instead of agreeing, he stared past her.

"Furthermore, Andrew," she touched his arm, "you work too much."

"Thanks for the advice. Unfortunately, this isn't a good time for a psychological discussion."

"When? When is a good time?"

He brought up a hand, interrupting her with utter finality. "Let's put this conversation behind us."

Belle held her tongue, quelling her reflexive reaction to offer more suggestions.

His cellphone buzzed. He read the text and frowned.

"What is it?" she asked.

"There is trouble in Camden. A resident was hurt, and they're blaming the accident on the worksite not being properly secured and safe." He blew out a breath as Megan emerged from the stable. "Let's take a raincheck, okay?"

Belle didn't respond, and he hardly noticed as he signaled to Megan that they were leaving. He brushed a kiss on Belle's forehead as he passed, murmuring an assurance that he would text her as soon as he arrived in Camden.

She waited. Surely he would turn back to her, so she could suggest that he stay.

Maybe he would ponder his quick decision. Maybe he would declare that his foreman could easily handle any problems.

But he didn't, and neither did she, swallowing her protests because they were futile.

Knowing he would refuse, anyway.

CHAPTER 9

elle braced a hand on the window frame over her kitchen sink, and admired the purple zinnias flowering in the garden, the whitish-gray bark of an oak tree, the sun setting on another September day.

Summer was over, and so was her romance with Andrew.

That is, if it had ever begun.

Andrew. First in her thoughts, first in her heart.

They'd been friends before their relationship had deepened to romance. Good friends, confidantes, really. She could tell him anything.

But love was elusive. Yes, there were moments made just for them—the boardwalk, the sunsets, the shared laughter.

Followed by longer moments, like today, when she felt utterly alone.

The beautiful dahlias he'd gifted had died, and she'd replaced the flowers with a ceramic bowl of fake oranges.

Andrew. With him, she believed she'd found a genuine love. A deep connection, both large and small. In his arms, she was beloved and cherished.

She shook her head. She'd been so wrong.

She suppressed her heart's disloyal leap whenever she envisioned Andrew's striking features, his enthralling smile, his endearing Scottish brogue.

Forcibly reminding herself that he was gone, she brewed peppermint tea in a glass mug and claimed a kitchen chair.

Andrew was content expanding his architecture firm and raising his daughter. What more did he need?

When he Skyped Belle from Camden a few minutes later, Belle told him as much.

"That's your version of a hello?" His features sharpened beneath the brash overhead light of his hotel room.

"You left the riding ring quickly the other day," she answered.

"Belle, there is a lot going on here. I can't deal with any more guilt—if that's where this conversation is headed." Although his words were firm, there was no harshness. His tone with her and his daughter was always kind, gentle and respectful.

By now, however, Belle understood the rules, his rules. He'd made them clear. Don't discuss his life, his choices, his priorities.

"In any case, will you heed my advice?" she pressed.

"Which is?"

"Appreciate your life. You employ a large staff and shouldn't do everything yourself." She took a deep breath. "Not to mention you carry a heavy burden you should confront."

Immediately, she regretted her outburst when his features became firm and unbending.

"Are you trying to fix me?" he asked.

"No. Well, yes, maybe. I can't understand your unreasonable work ethic. You love your daughter, yet you leave her alone constantly."

"I've provided a magnificent home, enrolled Megan in an exclusive private school, and bought her a horse. Aside from that, Adella is an excellent caretaker."

"Still, you should—"

"I need … I should…" He shot her a wearied look. "I am who I am."

She stared at the phone screen as he looked away. When she caught his gaze again, his eyes glistened. With frustration? Unshed tears? Now she wasn't certain he'd handled their discussion as dismissively as she'd assumed.

I love you, which is why I'm trying to help you, she wanted to tell him, but his manner became patronizing when he inserted, "I'm older than you, remember? Be a good equine therapist and don't worry about fixing a jaded architect like me."

"You're right, then. I won't." Her chin came up. "And it's time I resume my quiet life with my animals."

"What are you saying?"

"I'm ending our discussion, Andrew. The horses need to come in from the pasture."

Her wounded pride wouldn't permit her to say anymore.

"Right now?" he asked irritably. "All day I looked forward to talking to you. It was what got me through a very wearying meeting with the Camden town council."

"Sorry, but you'll need to conduct both ends of our conversation because I'm clicking off."

"I'll phone you tomorrow night."

"Rehearsals are beginning for The Lion, The Witch, and the Wardrobe."

"So you got a role? Are you Mrs. Beaver?"

"I'm a forest animal."

"Which one?"

"A squirrel."

"That's nuts. Get it?"

She couldn't suppress her grin, though her heart was breaking. She'd miss his wit and Scottish phrases, but she'd made up her mind. A long-distance relationship that relied on his unpredictable work schedule would never be successful.

"I'll be back in Wilmington on Saturday," he said. "Dinner at my place?"

His simple request almost brought her to tears. She tugged her gaze from the cellphone screen, grappling with the desolate mood settling over her. It took all her limited acting skills to summon a spirited attitude as she uttered a final goodbye.

When he clicked off, her breath pushed out in a rush. She'd never see his home again, never watch a sunset with him, never experience his tender kisses.

She struggled to control the agonizing tug in her heart.

But she failed, put her head in her hands, and wept.

In typical Andrew fashion, he texted daily, updating her on his work progress before declaring the problem in Camden was solved and he would return to Wilmington by the weekend.

He didn't, and one week became two, then three. Days merged into weeks, and the end of September loomed. The weather remained sticky-hot as the final days of torrid temperatures descended on the Southern beachfront town.

Although Belle continued seeing Megan, and Adella briefed her on Andrew's whereabouts, the sessions weren't the same.

With a wobbly smile, Belle responded to Adella's updates with a cheerful acknowledgement.

To Andrew's credit, he communicated with her often, although she continuously cut him off. Instead of wasting the hours alone, she immersed herself in caring for the horses, her clients' therapy sessions, and nightly play rehearsals.

Aunt Lucinda had little doubt behind the reasons for Belle's ceaseless round of activity, but as their afternoon at the Sunday Farmer's Market faded into twilight, her worried glances whenever Belle became teary-eyed when Andrew's name was mentioned came less often. And even her aunt wasn't bold enough to continue asking why Belle no longer would discuss the man she loved.

There were mornings when Belle didn't contemplate how her life would have been with Andrew, evenings when she didn't revisit his texts, and dawns when she didn't lie awake staring listlessly out the window, recalling his Scottish brogue as he whispered loving words to her.

Nevertheless, those days were few.

"How is Andrew?" Candee inquired when she phoned Belle one evening.

Belle settled on the living room couch with the cat stretched out beside her. "He's still in Camden, I think."

"You *think* he's in Camden? Where else would he be? Don't you trust him?"

"Of course. It's just—"

"There isn't a man who works harder, except for my husband Teddy, or Rob, or Kieran."

Belle murmured a concession at Candee's fierce protectiveness of Andrew, as well as all the other men in her life. Teddy worked alongside his crewmen on job sites, plus flipped homes. Rob assisted his wife, Kathleen, at her teahouse. Beforehand, he'd owned several bakeries, Rob's Marvelous Muffins, in Florida. Kieran, who had married Candee's sister, Desiree, ran an Irish pub in Roses. In all three cases, the wives were supportive of their husbands' endeavors.

Why couldn't Belle do the same?

To begin with, she and Andrew weren't married, much less engaged. He'd never declared his love for her, not in so many words.

"Andrew is consumed with his business and when he isn't, he deserves to spend any precious free hours with his daughter," Belle responded. "Which is, of course, as it should be."

"Should it be? Why?"

Belle sighed. "I don't know if he loves me enough to spend time with me, anyway."

"You're being absurd. From what I understand, he spends every spare moment with you when he's in Wilmington. Has he texted you?"

"Constantly."

"And?"

"I hardly respond. What's the use? I can't depend on him, because, well, he's never here."

Candee cleared her throat. "First, I can assure you that he's in love with you. The look on his face when he visited me in Roses a few weeks ago ... well ... he's completely enamored with you, Belle."

"Candee, you're a true friend, but you're wrong."

"Andrew keeps to himself. Did you know his family moved to America with literally nothing?"

Belle didn't respond.

"Give him a chance. Accept his phone calls and texts. He's a complex man."

And brilliant, Belle thought. And sensitive, honest, and attentive.

Still ...

"I can't." A quiet dignity firmed Belle's assertion. "I don't understand his intense drive to succeed. What is he proving? He's accumulated a fortune already."

"It's not about the money, Belle. His father lost his business, his wealth, and that left an impression on Andrew. Teddy and I have discussed him at length."

"Someone should tell Andrew to stop working so much."

"A Type A personality rarely listens to good advice, or any advice, for that matter."

With a ragged laugh, Belle agreed. "Even if he heeded our suggestions, I won't take him away from his daughter."

"He has enough love for both you and Megan, just as I love Teddy and Joseph."

Belle tried not to listen to Candee's words. She'd continue to push Andrew Bransfield out of her heart, out of her life, by ignoring him.

And by doing so, she had never felt as forlorn.

"By the way," Candee was saying, "Andrew purchased the Wilmington house he was renting."

Disregarding the lump in her throat at the realization he would live only a few blocks away, Belle sat up. "He did? When?"

"A week ago. Sorry. He may have intended to spill the news as a surprise."

Through a sheen of tears, Belle pulled her knees to her chest.

Firmly, she repeated to herself that she had no reason to be angry just because Andrew Bransfield was moving forward with his life, while her life had stalled.

So, she continued to ride her finicky horse, nurture the animals, and treat her therapy clients with fastidious care. She'd put herself in neutral; an emotional balance she maintained, ensuring she'd shed no more tears over him. It was better this way, ending the relationship slowly, with no confrontation.

. . .

WHEN ANDREW RETURNED to Wilmington the following Friday evening, he texted Belle and invited her to his home for takeout dinner and a movie.

She declined.

He suggested a Saturday boardwalk date, but she declined, citing the excuse of busyness.

"Right. Okay." She visualized his frown as he accepted her refusal. "Shall we try for Sunday? There's a Mexican restaurant serving the best—"

Before he finished, she made up an explanation about studying her script, although they both knew her part in The Lion, The Witch, and The Wardrobe had no words.

It hardly mattered, because he texted her on Monday. He was leaving for another job site in the Carolinas.

A PATTERN FORMED as the days drifted through the month of October. He'd text her, and she'd respond with quick one-sentences.

How are you? he'd ask.

Good. You?

The same. Equine therapy still on for Monday? I will finally be in town for a while. Can we have dinner together? There's a new Italian place in town.

Sorry. Too busy, she texted. *Opening night is next Friday.*

Finally. These play rehearsals have gone on forever. Did you nail your infamous role as a squirrel?

Soundly. Complete with a white vinyl tail and furry gray mitts.

Can't wait to see you.

Perform? Visit her? He knew where she lived. She didn't touch that one, instead replying with, *Can't. Rehearsals are till ten PM.*

Through the weeks of correspondence, he'd finish his

texts with smiling emojis, flashing red or pink hearts. Tonight he concluded with a questioning face.

455

What was more exciting, more intoxicating, more nerve-wracking, than opening night at a theater? It hardly mattered if the production was professional or amateur, the thrill, the rush, was the same.

Belle adjusted the tail on her squirrel costume and peeked at the audience as the curtain raised. The Lion, The Witch, and The Wardrobe had sold out for both weekend nights, and the crowded community theater shifted with anticipation. Posters hung in various businesses, in addition to the announcements on local radio stations, and the advertisements had proved beneficial. The director insisted on staying true to the book, incessantly occupied with the imaginative sets and choreography.

Belle searched the rows for Aunt Lucinda, who had arranged to meet her backstage afterwards, but didn't spot her. In many instances, her aunt had made a late grand entrance, so not seeing her wasn't cause for alarm.

Aunt Lucinda had mentioned bringing a surprise. Perhaps the right man for her had come along after all … perhaps the man from the Farmer's Market?

Belle ducked into the hallway, the canned music began, and the narrator intoned:

"Once there were ..."

THE TWO-AND-A-HALF HOURS of the play passed in an exhilarating blur. Afterwards, Belle hugged and congratulated the actors and actresses, then reported to her makeshift dressing room. Settled on a stool in front of a mirror, she yanked off her mitts and scrubbed away her face make-up while she waited for her aunt.

Muted voices made her pause. Aunt Lucinda's voice, followed by her larger-than-life laugh, announced she was near.

But it was the other voice, a rich Scottish brogue, that forced Belle slowly to her feet. This man was not the bacon shopkeeper, nor the suave, sophisticated Andrew of her dreams. This Andrew was an irresistible force. As he rounded the corner, his rugged features were torn between distress and tenderness.

He was real. He was here.

ANDREW DIDN'T HEAR Aunt Lucinda, nor the performers they passed in the hallway. He was already striding into a cramped dressing room, packed with discarded water bottles, headphones and a clothes rack jammed with costumes.

Belle stood by a mirror, holding a cloth in one hand, a pair of furry gray mitts in the other.

Entranced, he remained by the doorway, observing her radiant smile as her aunt scurried forward, holding her arms wide for a congratulatory hug.

He advanced, standing five feet away from Belle. He kept

his hands at his sides, clutching the flowers he'd brought. He was uncertain what to say, how to move.

He stared at her freshly scrubbed face, devoid of make-up, her dove-gray eyes filled with tears. The eyes that had gripped his nightly dreams and consumed his daytime thoughts.

He hadn't the slightest notion if she still cared for him. Or worse, had she forgotten all about him? He hadn't known what kind of reception he would receive from her when he'd phoned her aunt, requesting a ticket to the production.

Or, if he could now prove to Belle that he was worthy of sharing her life.

Her aunt gave them both a look of profound satisfaction. "Say what you came here for, Andrew, before Belle starts to cry."

His gaze trained on Belle's delicate face as he set down the flowers and wiped his eyes. "I'll cry with her."

"Men don't cry." Aunt Lucinda clucked her tongue. "Especially strong Scottish men."

"Dear aunt, you've been watching too much Braveheart," Belle said, as she rushed into his arms.

He cradled her, shielding her from her aunt's observant stare.

"I missed you," he whispered, knowing Aunt Lucinda heard every word, and not caring.

"You always say that," Belle replied.

"I couldn't figure out any other way to see you. Adella agreed to watch Megan, although Megan wanted to come. I wasn't sure about this production, though."

"It's okay. Next time. Andrew, I love your little girl."

He smiled. Belle carried enough love for everyone.

"If I asked you out again," he continued, "I assumed you would make up another excuse to avoid me."

She gazed up at him. "What's better than tonight, coupled

with my triumph as a squirrel?" She grinned, but then her shoulders shook with sobs as she glided her hands around his neck, and snuggled her tear-stained face close to his chest.

Her aunt's sing-song voice made them both jump. "I'm grabbing a bite to eat and headed home. Well done, Belle. Your performance did me proud."

"All thirty seconds of my debut."

"You were the prettiest squirrel on stage," came Aunt Lucinda's reply.

Belle brought her head up and offered her aunt a dry smile. "I was also the *only* squirrel on stage."

Andrew grinned. "Thank you, Aunt Lucinda." He hesitated. "May I call you my aunt?"

"You're welcome. And now that you've finally come to your senses, then yes."

He kept Belle firmly in his arms. Desperate to be alone with her, he speculated how to politely ask her aunt to leave without being blunt.

Aunt Lucinda caught his uneasy gaze. "It's a jubilant day when two people find true partners to share their lives." At the far end of the room, she switched the lights to dim, and was gone.

Belle stepped back and regarded him. "I still can't believe you're here. An hour earlier, I felt so desolate and—"

"Hollow?" he provided. "Unfulfilled?"

"And yet, you came to my performance."

"Because musicals are my favorite."

"The Lion, The Witch, and the Wardrobe is a play."

"Right." He picked up the flowers. "I bought these dahlias for you. They're a bit wilted."

She accepted, sniffed, and clutched the bouquet to her chest. "They're beautiful. Thank you."

"Why are you crying again?"

"Because I know … I know what they mean."

"A commitment shared forever by two persons." He took her slender hand in his. "Belle Boots, I love you."

She answered with her lips, parting them as he stroked her luxurious hair. She responded with the same ardor as when they'd kissed at his home, the night of the sunset.

Then she pulled away. "Can we talk?" she asked, her gaze honest and direct.

"Now?"

"Now is the best time."

"I forgot you're as blunt as your aunt."

"Andrew, I love you, but you're always working."

"Not anymore." Somehow, he managed to control his tone, recalling the weight that had been lifted from him when he'd come to his decision. "I offered my main foreman more responsibility, and he accepted. We've worked together for years, and I trust him."

"That's so encouraging. But there's more, Andrew. For your sake, can you find it in your heart to forgive your sister?"

"I can't."

"You can, with me standing beside you."

"What is it about you that brings out the best in me?"

Her hand tightened on his arm. "So you might reach out to Kate?"

"These things take time, but I will try."

"Thank you." Her infectious laugh that had lightened his days conveyed a trace of innocence. "And there's one more thing."

"More?"

"What about horses?"

"What about them?" Distracted, he kissed her, relishing the delicious combination of joy and love she brought to his heart.

"Will you venture into the riding ring with me, when the horses are there?"

"Under one condition."

"Which is?"

"Will you marry me?"

"You're bartering horses with an offer of marriage?"

"Exactly."

"Then yes." She nodded, replying with the response he'd waited for.

"I can't guarantee I'll stay in the ring for more than a minute," he warned. "But I expect our marriage will last a lifetime."

"I know it will." She lifted her delicate eyebrows in a challenge. "I also know that you and Jenkins will get along. He's an excellent judge of character."

"Does that mean he'll like me?"

"If you're a beginning rider, then yes."

"How did we go from entering a ring, to actually riding a horse?"

She stood on her toes and kissed him. "We'll take it slow."

He reached into his pocket and handed her a program. "I wrote a poem." On the back of the program, he'd written in large letters, "You're the woman I want, you're the woman I need."

She scanned the words. "You write poems," she said quietly. "Why am I not surprised?"

"Not very good ones because they don't rhyme, but yes." He held her close, reciting the last two lines of his poem with her:

"Because in the end, it's all about love."

And he sealed his words in Scottish Gaelic.

"Tha-mi-gad-ghradh."

I love you.

THE END

JOSIE RIVIERA

1-800-NEW YEAR

A Sweet Contemporary Romance

CHAPTER 1

I think I fancy you.

Shanice Williams sat in her rustic farmhouse kitchen, absorbed by the text flashing across the dating app on her cell phone.

She'd received a private message from Todd.

She kneaded her forehead and sighed.

Todd who?

And he *fancied* her? How? He'd never even met her.

She winced. Surely there were better pickup lines.

While she searched her brain for a suitable response, she peered out the window over the sink. The early morning sun rose higher in the sky, illuminating the fields. The timbered barn was located on the hill beyond, its green metal roof gleaming. A khaki-colored stone firepit sat nearby. Feathery snow powdered the grass, confirming the December wintry weather.

Still there? Todd inquired.

She didn't reply.

At the suggestion of Candee Winchester, her friend and Realtor, Shanice had joined Cupid Aplenty, a dating website, and uploaded a selfie. In the photo, her dark skin glowed, enhanced by a brush of deep-pink blusher, and her headful of black hair peeked from beneath her trademark white beanie. The words, "A Patch of Heaven," the name of her landscaping company, were embroidered on the brim in vivid green.

"I'm a professional landscaper. Consequently, I appreciate the outdoors," she'd described herself. "Faith in God is important, as well as family, friends, and old-fashioned morals. I own a super cute cat who is often erratic and reckless, and I'm an animal lover. Oh, and my ideal match is a knight in shining armor with scruples and ethics."

Still there? Todd asked again.

Unsure how to respond, she scanned his profile.

Todd Herring. A normal-looking fellow flashing a mouthful of dazzling white teeth. His shaggy blond hair glistened with platinum highlights.

Did he dye his hair? She speculated on that while another of his texts rolled in.

I bet my new kitten would really like your cat.

She wasn't certain whether to laugh or cry.

Do you have a favorite indoor restaurant, or are you the outdoorsy type? he asked.

Huh?

Twice, she reread his question. Apparently, Todd had zeroed in on her cat and ignored her profession.

Outdoorsy, she typed.

Wanna go on a date sometime?

Her fingers hovered over the phone's keyboard. Why, oh why, had she joined an online dating service? Was she that desperate?

The recent breakup with her on-again, off-again boyfriend, Brian, had been difficult. They'd grown apart, and she'd never felt as if he actually listened to her or valued what she'd accomplished. Besides, he wasn't the type of guy who liked to stay in one place. He preferred to travel, whereas she was a homebody.

Candee insisted Shanice was a romantic at heart—pointing out her fondness for reading sweet romance books.

People took solace in different things. For some, it was eating comfort food, such as meat loaf and mashed potatoes, or chocolate, or wintergreen puff candy. Shanice favored the optimism, promise and happy outcomes of romantic novels.

"Online dating eliminates awkward first dates," Candee had encouraged.

Shanice preferred face-to-face interaction rather than communicating through a phone or computer screen. In addition, she always deferred to her gut reaction.

She gazed at Todd's photo grinning up at her and went with her gut.

I can't commit, but thanks for the invite, she replied.

Polite and done.

Then she hit the delete button, blocking Todd from contacting her again.

Well, that was quite an adventure, and it wasn't even seven o'clock in the morning.

She padded to the refrigerator and poured a glass of sweet iced tea.

She hadn't mastered the art of refusal. In fact, dating in general had never been her forte. Not since she'd attended community college fifteen years earlier and met the most wonderful man imaginable.

"A girl never gets over her first love," Granny had once declared. "Especially a smart, handsome guy like Lincoln Reid. Shanice, that boy is clearly in love with you."

Shanice ran a hand across her brow. Everyone knew Jasmine Williams was an authority on most everything. A widow at twenty-six, Jasmine had managed to purchase several acres and a rundown farm, hired farmhands, and eventually turned a profit. She was tenacious, independent, and more than a little impulsive. As a black woman living alone in a sleepy Blue Ridge Mountain town, those qualities had served her well.

Only after Jasmine's second husband died unexpectedly did her health decline. Sadness had taken its toll on Shanice's eighty-five-year-old grandmother.

"Of course a person gets over their first love, Granny," Shanice said aloud.

Wasn't she proof? She'd carried on, hadn't she?

Admittedly, she'd combed for Lincoln on the internet, always regretting her searches afterwards because she could never find him.

It was high time to get over him, she told herself. In any case, she'd come to the conclusion he didn't use social media.

She set down her glass and softly sang "Go Tell It on the Mountain." She'd committed every word of the song to memory. She'd attempted to teach the lyrics to Lincoln, though he'd invariably mixed up the words, changing "over the hills," to "over the mountains."

"No, Lincoln. It's a hill, not a mountain. There's a difference." At his grimace and half-shrug, they'd laugh. Christmas had held so much fun, so much joy.

So much anticipation.

Up until the day she died, Granny had sung hymns. In years past, Shanice had embraced Christmas celebrations, but this December was different—lonelier and sadder with Granny gone.

They'd always been a dynamic twosome.

Wherever Shanice went on the farm, every room smelled like Granny's fragrance—fragrant gardenias—in the kitchen, the bedrooms and even the outdoor gardens.

Perhaps that was why Lincoln was in her thoughts today.

She was emotional amidst all the festivities and no one to share it with.

"Go tell it on …" The hymn stalled on her lips. "Granny, I'm sorry, but I need to sell the farmhouse. Jasmine's Joy is a splendid name for a house with a proud legacy, though I'm not the person to carry the legacy into the next generation. All the labor and money needed for restoration are beyond my expertise and limited funds."

Shanice ran her hands across the plaid curtains hanging over the sink, and then the plate racks displaying chipped, flowered blue china dishes. Her sad excuse for holiday decorations—a gingerbread cookie jar, circa 1970—occupied a space on the enamel kitchen table.

According to Candee, selling and then closing on the farmhouse by New Year's Day allowed enough time for the paperwork to be signed and a check issued, enabling Shanice to pay for her next loan installment.

Due January 30.

Her hands fell to her sides. Her landscaping business wasn't bringing in sufficient funds to provide for everyday expenses, let alone cover loan payments.

She sat back down. Her tortoiseshell cat, a "tortie" she'd adopted from a pet rescue center years ago, jumped on her lap.

"What can we do, Duchess?" Shanice stroked the cat's patch-colored fur and a throaty purring rewarded her. "I'm in a hurry and forced to sell the house 'as is.'"

Fortunately, there was no mortgage and minimal property taxes. Her grandmother's will had only stipulated she live in the house for three months before deciding whether she'd sell.

A rather odd request.

Still, she'd agreed, because three months flew by quickly. Moreover, she'd often called the farmhouse her "castle in the air," because the ramble of rooms resembled a miniature castle. Add the intricate woodwork and stone tile, and all the house needed was a Prince Charming.

Subleasing her rather boring apartment in Huntington, an adjacent town, she'd honored her grandmother's final request and moved to Roses, North Carolina. She'd intended to modernize the house in her free time.

Hah! Shanice soon discovered she had none. She managed to update one bathroom—an absolute necessity— and painted the upstairs room she'd chosen for her bedroom a lovely light blue. The extra seven rooms were closed off to conserve on the utility bills. She hadn't gotten around to staining the wood trim, nor did she have the means to fix the old radiators that struggled to keep the place warm.

Her cell phone rang.

"Hi," Candee said before Shanice uttered a greeting. "I haven't heard from the potential buyer scheduled to view your house today."

"The showing is for ten o'clock, correct?"

"Precisely. He's a last-minute buyer."

"Is he dependable?" Shanice asked.

"I don't know. He was supposed to drive from Hilton Head Island early this morning. Plus, we've never met."

"Does he live on Hilton Head?"

"I believe so."

"Why is he interested in a house a few hours away?"

"He claims he used to live here. However, with this unexpected cold snap and being the day after Christmas, I suspect he'll cancel."

"Fingers crossed he'll make an offer."

"He'll need to see the house first." Candee chuckled. "May I remind you that you refused two offers last month?"

"Because both were insultingly low." Shanice cuddled her cat closer to her chest. "I want a fair price because this house meant the world to Granny. In addition, my finances are nonexistent."

"But you said your landscaping business is profitable. That'll help."

"Fall cleanups were a blessing, but winter is the slow season."

"The right buyer will come along." Candee hesitated. "How was your Christmas?"

"Quiet. I attended church, then volunteered at the food bank in town serving roasted turkey with all the trimmings."

"Teddy and I hoped you'd reconsidered our invite to share Christmas dinner with us. Joseph has a new horse he wants to show you—a Shetland pony, and we have beagles running all over the place. Plus, I have landscaping questions. I want to redo my front lawn, and I'd appreciate an estimate."

Candee had met her husband, Teddy, when he visited Roses searching for a real estate investment. They'd married and adopted Joseph, Teddy's nephew. Joseph's father had died in a horrific car accident. His mother had died a year earlier.

"I'll provide a landscaping quote when I visit," Shanice replied. "Lawns in the south are best overhauled in the spring or fall."

"Desiree and Keiran stopped by yesterday and brought their infamous pistachio cake," Candee added. "They still act as if they're newlyweds."

"They're adorable together," Shanice said.

"Love and romance are in the air during the holidays."

Shanice winced. Maybe for other people. Certainly not for her.

She glanced toward the living room. Besides the cookie jar, her only other attempt at festive decorations was a one-foot potted fir tree, which she'd trimmed with African-themed ornaments she found in the attic. Likewise, she'd decorated her sponsored tree for Roses' annual Festival of Trees event. The tree was sparse, though Candee had assured her it looked effortlessly chic, which was all the rage.

Shanice also observed Kwanzaa, a cultural holiday celebrated along with her Christian Christmas. Today, December twenty-sixth, marked the beginning of that week-long celebration.

She'd placed an African cloth, a mat, an ear of corn, pieces of fruit, and seven candles on a bureau. The corn represented fertility, the fruit brought happiness and perseverance. She planned on lighting the first candle later in the evening.

Granny had used those same trimmings and Kwanzaa decorations year after year.

"No use in buying new when old is just as good," she would declare, tossing her gray braids over her shoulders. "Cash is better spent on farm equipment and keeping Jasmine's Joy afloat."

Granny was an expert on pinching a dollar. She'd taught Shanice how to shop at thrift stores for the best bargains.

I haven't changed a thing, she silently told her grandmother, *although I did purchase seven new candles. Candles don't expire, but there wasn't enough wax in the old ones to melt and reuse.*

Her cat leapt from her arms, spotting a bird by the living room window. She'd set up a birdwatching station in the yard, and Duchess spent hours watching cardinals and chickadees fly to the feeders.

"I'll continue to schedule showings while you're at work," Candee was saying, bringing Shanice back to the present.

"I'm stopping by the Festival of Trees to view my tree before the event is dismantled."

"Your tree is gorgeous," Candee continued. "The zebra ornaments and African American angel topper are so elegant."

"The decorations were Granny's, and I donated the six-foot artificial balsam fir. This was my way to honor her legacy."

"She would've been proud," Candee said. "Your tree commanded the highest bid at the online auction."

"Really? Who bought the tree?"

"A mysterious bidder from out of town."

"Hmm." Shanice paused. "I wonder who."

"Don't know."

"Most important, the funds go toward the town's senior food program," Shanice said.

Granny had relied on that program, which provided a daily healthy hot meal. At first, she'd protested, declaring her independence, but Shanice had insisted and arranged the service. It brought her peace of mind because she'd discouraged her grandmother from using the stove or microwave. In the final weeks, she'd hired full-time care since she wasn't always able to get to town.

Her grandmother had refused to move from the farmhouse and live with Shanice.

As the year had passed, the corn crop went unplanted. The sheep and goats had eventually been sold. All that remained were four chickens. Granny would sit for hours by the fireplace, an afghan pulled snugly to her chin.

"I'm getting another call," Candee said.

"Any likelihood it's the Hilton Head buyer? Feel free to bring him and a conga line of other prospective purchasers around. I'm eager for a quick closing and cash is best."

Candee laughed. "My job and my pleasure."

Shanice clicked off as another call rang through. She recognized the caller ID of MaryEllen, an elderly woman and Granny's dearest friend.

"May I ask a favor?" MaryEllen inquired. "Can you stop

by my place and throw down ice melt so I can get to my Monday lunch at the women's club this afternoon?"

"I'll be over within the hour."

As Shanice disconnected, Duchess jumped onto her favorite perch, a worn green sofa. The sofa was serviceable, though it had faded and bleached after forty years of service.

Shanice shrugged on a cream-colored Sherpa parka, gloves, her knitted white beanie, and tucked her jeans into sturdy work boots. She snatched a handful of wintergreen peppermint puffs from a glass jar. No holiday was complete without a sweet candy that melted in your mouth.

A minute later, she started her blue pickup truck and drove several miles to MaryEllen's apartment complex. When Shanice arrived, she responded to calls from other customers requesting the same service, breathing a sense of relief for the extra money the jobs brought in.

If only she could sell her house for a fair price, secure her business loan, and return to her Huntington apartment.

At noon, her hands shaking from exhaustion, she pulled her truck to the rear of the farmhouse and worked off her gloves. She hadn't mustered the energy to visit the Festival of Trees, and assured herself she had until tomorrow to see her exquisitely decorated tree before it was claimed and taken away by the winning bidder.

She rubbed her jeans, damp with snow, and bit back a groan. How could she have slipped and fallen on the icy sidewalk at MaryEllen's house? A peril from outdoor tasks, she supposed.

Since then, her hip and knee smarted. She stepped onto the back entrance that led to the kitchen, envisioning a warm Epsom-salt soak in the antique, cast-iron bathtub.

As she opened the door, a man's voice gave her pause.

"I'm thinking of building apartments here," he said. "Maybe condominiums. There's plenty of land."

Her fingers stilled on the doorknob.

His voice, *that* voice, sounded heartbreakingly familiar.

She put a hand to her throat. No. It couldn't be.

"Do you want to check out the upstairs?" Candee asked.

"There's only one bathroom, right?"

"Right, and there's admittedly a lack of closet space," Candee said. "Naturally, all these updates are possible, though a character-laden house like this is special."

He chuckled. "Character-laden? I like that."

"We Realtors try our best, Lincoln."

Lincoln Reid. Here? In Roses?

She closed her eyes. Lincoln's voice, the voice of the guy she'd once dated, once been head-over-heels in love with, whispered through her mind.

She often intended to bring closure to her past. But not here. Not today. She needed more than a minute to prepare.

"No matter what, Shay, we'll tackle life together," he'd once declared. Everyone else called her by her legal name. Not him. He'd given her the nickname Shay—*his* nickname for her. "We'll give each other courage to fight any obstacles and come out together on the other side."

They'd come out on the other side, all right. Though not together.

She struggled for several seconds to compose herself. Her fingers clung to the doorknob.

"This house is in a time warp and hasn't changed," Lincoln was saying. "I never noticed that there are no countertops in the kitchen. Plus, the floor slopes."

"A century-old home offers loads of appeal," Candee said. "Especially a home boasting its own name."

"Jasmine's Joy. *Jasmine* means a gift from God," he said. "Granny Jasmine always considered this farm to be her little piece of heaven."

"Wait." Candee hesitated. "Have you seen the house already?"

"On many occasions. The owner died recently, correct?"

"Three months ago. The current title-holder is temporarily residing here."

"Temporarily?"

"Shanice moved in after her grandmother died."

He didn't reply.

"This home belonged to Jasmine Williams," Candee went on after a brief pause. "Old Jasmine was a legend around these parts."

He chuckled. "I know."

As they climbed the stairs, their voices faded, and Shanice scurried out the back door. She wasn't prepared to face him. This wasn't the occasion to trample into the rubble of a long-ago relationship.

Furthermore, she didn't appreciate Lincoln's disapproval of Granny's kitchen, and could hardly swallow her outrage. In more instances than she could count, he'd busied himself around that same enamel table, the focal point of the household and the place where everyone gathered.

An accomplished cook, Lincoln embraced new recipes, mixing flour, paprika and salt, and forking fresh perch into the grease sizzling from Granny's cast-iron skillet.

His high-falutin' family would've disapproved if they'd known how often he'd visited Shanice and Granny at the farmhouse.

But they hadn't known. Because dating Lincoln had ended several months after they'd met. It was a universe ago and the circumstances that followed had forced her to start over.

She hurried down the gravel driveway, her thoughts unraveling.

However, hearing Lincoln's words prompted her to think fairly. He was right about the lack of kitchen countertops.

But then, he was always right, except when it came to insisting their love would carry them through the difficult times.

Then, he'd been wrong.

SHANICE CLIMBED into her truck and headed downtown. Roses was a storybook town, reminding her of a quaint New England community, even boasting a bandstand.

She slowed to view the depressed-looking decorations lining the quaint streets. Why did everything look so sad after Christmas? The drooping and sagging pine trees were a reminder the holidays were ending soon.

For that part, she was grateful. She was more than ready to put these difficult months behind her—most notably the large farmhouse and continuous labor the rambling acreage entailed.

If only she found a buyer.

Her memories reverted to the front yard of the farmhouse, where she'd often tossed sticks to Henry, the family's golden retriever. Granny would burst out laughing at their antics while she repotted zinnias on the wide wraparound porch. She delighted in the ordinary and encouraged the dog's joyful dashes. Through Shanice's childhood, Granny supported her while her parents traveled for eight to twelve months at a time, on the road as geologists.

Her breath caught at the wonderful remembrances and she debated.

Should she sell?

Yes.

No.

Yes, she said firmly, resolving to be practical.

Only sentimentality kept her attached to the house. Jasmine's Joy was too big for a single person and Lincoln was spot-on about the kitchen. Although it boasted an oversized pantry, countertops were a necessity. How had Granny tolerated the inconveniences—buckling, squeaky stairs, single-pane windows, and narrow doorways? Not to mention the twenty-minute drive to town for groceries.

Sentimentality aside, the idea of the well-worn farmhouse and its acres of land being converted into an apartment complex brought a sickness to Shanice's stomach. Her emotions swung in every direction. Building apartments on the property was bad enough, but the idea carried out by Lincoln Reid made it a thousand times worse.

Several minutes later, she pulled up to Kathleen's Teahouse, an outstanding restaurant in Roses. She stepped beneath the burgundy awning, opened the wooden door, and a tiny silver bell signaled her arrival. She seated herself at a corner table.

Though her wristwatch showed past noon, she ordered a full Irish breakfast—bacon, sausage, eggs, and potatoes fried in creamery butter, a cup of black tea, and orange juice.

Kathleen Taylor, the owner, set the glass of juice and the steaming hot tea on Shanice's table.

"Cold out there today, aye?" Kathleen's sparkling eyes heightened her fair complexion. "Were you out aiding icebound customers since the blush of dawn?"

Shanice smiled. "MaryEllen and several of the tenants in her complex wanted the ice and snow cleared from the sidewalks."

Behind Kathleen, a pretty red-haired waitress, who appeared to be in her twenties, scurried around tables and poured coffee. The scent of yeasty rolls topped with cream cheese and sugar permeated the air.

"I marvel at how well you manage to service all your

clients, no matter the weather. You are absolutely brilliant." Kathleen pushed up the sleeves of her emerald-green blouse. "You're juggling customers in Huntington too."

"I'm grateful for any winter jobs." Shanice savored the steaming mug of Irish tea. Although she loved sweets, she took her tea without cream or sugar.

She tipped down her chin and winced, refusing to give in to the pain in her knee and hip. "Thankfully, you're open today. Many restaurants shut down for the holidays."

"We were closed yesterday for Christmas, but back to regular hours today. As you know, Rob is an expert on operating an eatery." Kathleen gestured to the celebratory home blessings. Shamrock ornaments on a tabletop tree enhanced the tasteful Irish décor.

Kathleen's husband, Rob, came to stand beside her. He patted his protruding waistline and took a bite of Irish soda bread he held in his hand. "How's the sale of your house going? Any prospective buyers?"

That was the thing about postage-sized towns. Everyone knew everyone else's business.

Shanice pushed the juice glass nearer her cloth napkin. "No one yet."

"You'll find a buyer." Kathleen gave Shanice's forearm a squeeze. "Although we'll miss you here when you move back to Huntington."

It was a thoughtful assurance from Kathleen, though it left Shanice feeling sadder than she already felt. It was strange. The more time she spent in Roses, the more the prospect of leaving brought a sorrow all the way to the pit of her stomach.

She reminded herself she was here to honor Granny's wishes.

"My apartment is less than two hours away," she

prompted, half to herself. "I'm back and forth between Huntington and Roses more often than not."

"A commute isn't the same as actually living here," Kathleen replied. She excused herself to welcome a couple entering the restaurant, while laughter radiated from behind the counter. Shanice reached for her juice glass as Kathleen ushered Candee and a tall, dark-haired man to a booth in a far corner.

A tall, dark-haired *familiar* man.

She'd recognize him anywhere.

Lincoln.

Her chest tightened. Her hand stopped short. She resisted the urge to dash from the restaurant.

Of course, no such luck, because Rob still stood near her table, regaling her with stories of the special Christmas he and Kathleen had shared.

"Next year we're flying over the Atlantic Ocean to Ireland." Rob shot an appreciative glance toward his wife. "Kathleen is originally from a county near Dublin and intends to show me the sights."

"Sounds marvelous," Shanice mumbled, though she hardly heard him because the walls were quickly closing in. She caught Lincoln's profile as he helped Candee off with her coat.

He smiled at something Candee said, and Shanice's pulse accelerated as she admired his devastating good looks. How was it possible? As a man in his thirties, he was even more handsome now than when he was a teen. More appealing. More George Clooneyish.

Would Lincoln have brought Shanice to dine at Kathleen's Teahouse when they dated? Probably, if the restaurant had existed. Lincoln had always been generous, although he preferred quiet weekend afternoons on the farm, tending to the animals or playfully splashing her at the creek that wound through the property.

On Granny's acreage, fields rolled to hills, with no neighbors or homes for miles. You might think life would always turn out the way you wanted if you stared at the vast blue sky long enough.

"Once we're in Ireland," Rob went on, "Kathleen intends to introduce me to Danny Brady and his wife, Clara, the owners of The Ground Café, where she once worked. And did I ever tell you about the ghost town I bought?"

"Kathleen mentioned it. Hollan Farms?"

Rob brightened. "I'm revitalizing the entire town and recently put in a spa."

Shanice nodded, grateful when a waitress came over to serve her. Rob excused himself to assist the wait staff.

After a prayer of grace, she placed a napkin on her lap and soaked up creamy, buttery eggs with homemade brown bread. From the corner of her eye, she watched as Candee invited Kathleen to join her and Lincoln.

Shanice leaned in.

What were they discussing?

Her dilapidated farmhouse, she supposed.

The high-pitched perkiness of the hostess, who poured more tea, cut through her disquiet like a dull blade. She reached for her cup and sipped.

As she continued to gaze at Lincoln, her cheeks heated.

His grin was quick, his gestures elegant. He was confident and controlled, just as he'd been at the age of nineteen.

She hadn't laid eyes on him in years and wasn't prepared for her heart deciding to stop every second she glanced at him. Time hadn't eased her sorrow and regrets.

His thick hair still held a telltale wave, and a dark bristle of a beard brought shadowed maturity to his features. His jaw was square, the cleft in his chin prominent. His fine wool coat, casually draped over the back of his chair, probably cost more than her entire outfit.

He'd been rich. She'd been poor.

Today he wore tailored navy-blue pants that fit his muscular thighs perfectly and a trim blue button-down shirt.

She glanced down at her clothes and released a sigh.

Nothing had changed.

He was still rich. She was still poor.

Landscaping chic, she often referred to her everyday attire, defined by denim bib overalls over a long-sleeved cotton turtleneck. Her parka had a heavy lining with pockets for the tools a landscaper used—snips, leather gloves, and safety glasses.

Kathleen excused herself from Lincoln's table and scurried to the kitchen, and Shanice's gaze stole back to Lincoln. She never could help herself from staring at him.

Stop. Mad crushes are for teenagers, not grown women.

Finishing her breakfast quicker than she intended, she laid cash on the table to cover her bill plus a tip, pulled on her wool cap, and grabbed her parka. With any luck, no one would notice her speedy departure as she slipped past the other patrons.

"Shanice!" Candee called out. "Where are you headed? Aren't you going to come over and say hello?"

CHAPTER 2

*L*incoln Reid wasn't certain what to make of the feigned smile and abrupt nod of recognition that Shay granted to him when she stepped to their table.

"Hi, Shanice." Candee gestured to Lincoln. "He's the buyer I mentioned this morning. This is Lincoln."

He placed his napkin on the table and got to his feet—his manners too entrenched to do otherwise. Candee stayed seated and drank her coffee.

Shay's deep-set brown eyes regarded him under sweeping dark eyebrows. Sweet yet fearless, she met his stare. She'd once given him a welcoming smile. Now her entire expression was replaced by caution.

Wisps of springy ebony hair escaped from her wool beanie, and he resisted the urge to tuck her hair behind her ear. just as he once had. It wouldn't matter, though. The wisps would only spring back.

He swallowed. She was a fresh-faced beauty.

"Shay." Unsure of his voice, he cleared his throat and extended a hand. "What a wonderful treat to see you."

Her lips pursed. He'd used her nickname, and she didn't look pleased.

"Hello, Lincoln." She peered over her shoulder at the door.

"You're more beautiful than ever, Shay."

"Shanice."

The subtle reminder was clear. She wasn't his Shay anymore, and his nickname for her was clearly unappreciated. He wasn't sure what to say, his sadness taking over. Once, he'd dreamed of her being part of his family, carrying his surname, bearing his children.

His hand was still extended. He was vaguely aware that between coffee sips, Candee's eyebrows had shot up.

"You two are already acquainted?" Candee tacked on a grin, her gaze flickering to his outstretched hand.

"Yes," he and Shay replied together. They'd often echoed each other's thoughts.

He cleared his head of the poignant memories as a red-haired waitress bustled by hoisting a tray, and he inhaled the essence of the restaurant—freshly roasted coffee, buttered flaky biscuits and a traditional Irish whiskey cake.

Candee flagged down the waitress and snagged a slice of cake. The woman gave Lincoln a flirtatious wink and guaranteed that if he needed anything, she was available.

He murmured a thank you, keeping his gaze glued to Shay.

With a diplomatic dip of her head, Candee leaned on her elbow and slanted her chair toward a plump, middle-aged woman at the table behind them. She immediately began chatting about the holidays.

"We haven't seen each other in fifteen years," Shay murmured.

Was she talking to him or Candee? Or the waitress who had sashayed away?

Or herself?

She finally accepted his handshake, her callused fingers brushing his. Her touch restored him, creating a recognizable fluttering in his heart.

The years had been kind to her, but of course they had. She was a natural beauty, more gorgeous now than when they'd attended the same community college. He told her as much.

She murmured a thank you.

She'd been a freshman, he a sophomore. Eighteen and nineteen years old, respectively.

They'd met at an interest-sharing bulletin board on campus. He remembered the exact date and time. September first, four o'clock in the afternoon, when classes had ended for the day. Both elected to join the same Habitat for Humanity team and exchanged phone numbers.

One day each weekend that semester, they labored side by side on neighborhood revitalization, reviewing the instructions provided on their professor's notecards. She taught inner-city residents how to plant gardens—beans, carrots and squash—and he lent his labor to framing and sheet rocking, all life skills that had served him well. He liked getting to know her. At the end of their day, they'd celebrated with a hip bump, high fives, and over-the-top accolades.

Afterwards, they'd rock on worn rockers on Granny's front porch, viewing the sunset or playing checkers on the red and black checkerboard. Sometimes, they'd watch old black-and-white TV sitcoms on cable networks, like *The Honeymooners* or *I Love Lucy*, laughing at the funny slapstick comedy.

How long had it been since he'd played checkers? Old-time nostalgia for a less complicated life served a lump to his throat.

"Sixteen years, Shay," he corrected her. "We haven't seen each other in sixteen years." He tried to focus on her face, though his appreciative gaze slid over her worn overalls. The fabric skimmed her body and long legs. Never a slave to the latest fashion, she'd preferred plain clothes, her outfits consisting of denim jeans and a brightly colored blouse or turtleneck sweater.

She dropped her hand and stood straighter. Her smile was positively wintry. "Why are you here, Lincoln?"

She wasn't a woman to sidestep an issue.

"First, my sincere sympathies for your loss," he said. "Jasmine was a remarkable lady."

"You're here to offer condolences?"

He tapped his fingers on his leg, a nervous habit he'd never been able to break. "It's one of the reasons."

"The rooms are quiet without Granny."

"I remember how she used to fuss over her chickens. And that she always had four of them."

"You remember she had four?"

"Tootsie, Twizzle, Tweetie and Trixie."

"Your memory is outstanding."

"For some things. This was easy because it's all T's. She kept the chicks in a corner of the barn. When I saw the farmhouse this morning, there were no chickens."

"You inspected the barn?"

"I walked through it."

"I sold the hens."

"Does that mean no more fresh eggs?"

She scratched her cheek. "If I remember correctly, you're allergic to eggs."

"I outgrew the allergy in my twenties. Usually, a person outgrows an egg allergy by sixteen. I was late."

She wavered, no doubt chasing questions in her mind. "Therefore, Candee showed you the farmhouse."

She stated her response as a fact, not a question.

"Yes. Our out-of-town prospective buyer." Candee did a quick turnaround and answered for him, then resumed chatting with the middle-aged woman.

Shay evidently expected an explanation as to why Lincoln was in Roses and why he was with a Realtor. She couldn't imagine she was the main draw.

He fumbled in his pants pocket and extracted an envelope neatly typed with his name and address. "I received a letter from your grandmother through her attorney, although it's dated three months ago." He plucked the letter from the envelope.

Shay gave a short, dubious laugh. "My grandmother sent you a letter?"

"Her attorney forwarded it to me upon her request." Lincoln held up the letter and waved it as proof. "It was typewritten and dated several days before she died. Somehow, it was delivered to the wrong address and ended up at my business instead of my home address, then it got misplaced under a pile of bookkeeping."

"Why did she send you a letter after all these years? What did she say?"

"That she was leaving the farmhouse for you as your inheritance." In the next second, Lincoln made a decision. "Imagine my surprise when I checked the listings in Roses and noticed the house was for sale."

He folded the letter, placed it back in the envelope, and pocketed it. "Your grandmother and I were in touch often."

"Often?"

"Special occasions—Christmas and her birthday."

"She never spoke of any correspondence with you." She tapped her chin. "So now you're interested in buying a house in Roses?"

"Why not?"

"*Her* house?"

"Maybe."

Her jaw set, her gaze steely. "Granny mentioned that you and your family moved away many years ago."

"We relocated our toy business to Hilton Head Island. Because of the Christmas holiday, I decided to take a road trip and visit my sister, her husband, and son in Virginia."

Shay peered at their table, where a waitress topped off steaming coffee for Candee and her friend. "I remember Penny. She always laughed at her own jokes. So, she's married?"

"Married to Roy Schoner for several years. He's a guy she met at grad school in Virginia." Lincoln drew a long breath. "Although from what she has mentioned, he isn't home often, and uses the excuse that his travels are work-related."

"Excuse?"

"My opinion." He shrugged. "They have an eight-year-old son, my nephew, Evan."

"So why are you here again?" Shay asked.

"Because of business."

"Utterly mysterious, Lincoln."

"Me? I'm an open book."

He could see her mind processing the information, trying to decide if she trusted him. She blinked, though her gaze seemed mighty sharp. "You live on Hilton Head Island?"

"On a houseboat docked at a marina near Palmetto Junction. Roses is practically on the road to Virginia."

It wasn't, and this trip had nothing to do with convenience. He knew it. Shay knew it.

"Checking on random homes along the way?"

"Only fixer-uppers."

"I can't wrap my head around your interest in Roses and in Granny's house in particular."

"Jasmine's Joy is your house now."

"It'll always be Granny's house."

"As silly as it sounds, I couldn't resist stopping in Roses." He tried for a grin before his words broke off. "I missed the chickens."

In truth, he missed *her.*

"Uh-huh." A ghost of a smile played on her exquisitely full lips.

"They happily cheeped in the chicken coop whenever I collected eggs. Sometimes, I glimpsed an owl in the barn roosting in the eaves."

On rainy days, he'd listened to the raindrops pounding on the barn's metal roof; on sunny days, he'd admire the sunlight streaming in from the holes in the aged wooden planks. In the back of his mind, he wondered how their conversation had veered to chickens and owls.

She smiled and glanced at his half-eaten corned beef sandwich, the water glass nearby. "Alleged by the guy who broke out in hives whenever an omelet was placed within two feet of him."

Her smile brought images of their shared adventures. He adored her high cheekbones, her stoic carriage. Shay never bent to adversity. She was strong. Stronger than him by miles. She seemed to carry a veil of armor around her. For what? Protection from him? From life?

It took a resilient woman to leave a man with only a hurried "Dear John" explanation scribbled on a notecard. An explanation that prompted more questions than answers.

"You?" he asked.

"Me?"

"You're living in Roses?"

She shifted from one foot to the other. "I'm subletting my apartment in Huntington and staying here until I get the right price for the farmhouse."

"What is the right price?"

"A fair market value."

His thoughts traveled in every direction. Why was she selling? She'd felt at home in Roses. So had he. When he had followed Candee up the drive to the farmhouse that morning, he'd found himself slowing his Jeep. He'd gazed out his window and recognized the barn, worn from years of neglect, and the stone firepit beyond. He breathed in, imagining whiffs of sun-soaked grass and wildflowers growing by the creek. As his Jeep climbed the hill, the dirt road narrowed. The rambling farmhouse stood in full view as he rounded the last curve.

Jasmine's Joy. Shay's castle in the air.

He'd shut off the engine and stepped out.

His heart had skipped a beat as he surveyed the sprawling farmhouse for the first time in years. It was no longer painted blue, but a cottony white, although the paint had weathered. The roofline flashed slightly uneven, and he knew that when he strode inside, the floor would sag beneath his feet. A double oven would never fit through the tight doorways.

Still, he had smiled. He'd forgotten the old-fashioned appeal, the beauty of a solid home built to last generations. Even in disrepair, he visualized how it would look if restored to its original grandeur. With funds and foresight, the house could stand impressive and striking once again.

Beside a row of potted plants, two wooden rocking chairs sat on the spacious front porch, and his fingers grazed the carved initials as he passed.

Still there, after all these years.

L.R. loves S.W. engraved in a heart, symbolizing their love. A love that would last forever.

He leaned against a post, barely holding up one side of the porch roof. The farm's acreage spread before him and he visualized rows of thick pointed corn stalks, heard the vibrato-like baas of sheep grazing in the fields. Twenty feet from the barn stood the two-tiered, wood-burning firepit he and Shay had built from stones. They'd dug a spot where the grass grew thin and checked for high and low spots in the dirt. He had preferred to use a shovel, though she had insisted they use their hands, then jumped on the dirt to level it. He'd chosen a leveler before distributing the stones. She'd insisted on eyeballing the entire process.

"We're building a firepit, Lincoln," she'd informed him. "We're not constructing the Empire State Building."

Typical Shay. Her simplistic, environment-loving instincts invariably proved correct. Goodness emanated from her. She was wholesome and uncorrupted, preferring to tend to her gardens or explore a stone path. Similar to her parents, she was engaged in the earth and wildlife, though her interests led her toward landscaping rather than geology.

That picture of long ago, stunningly serene and poignant, brought a dull thud to his chest.

Candee had slammed her car door shut, jolting him from his memories, and she'd joined him on the front porch. He'd opened the wooden door and accompanied her inside the farmhouse.

He kept these reflections to himself, ran a hand through his hair, and met Shay's inquisitive stare.

"I have several clients in Roses," she continued. "Therefore, my time between Roses and Huntington is productive."

He regarded her beanie. "You're a landscaper."

Brilliant, Lincoln.

She opened her mouth, and he expected her to tease him. Instead, she cut him off with a brisk, "I am."

"You always were a wizard with plants."

"Thanks."

"You own the company?"

"Finally. After several years of saving money, I bought the

business from my former employer. Now I don't work for anyone but myself."

He winced. Her intended jab met its mark.

He wasn't about to enter into a rebuttal about when she'd worked at his parents' toy shop or why she suddenly quit, certainly not in full view of the patrons in Kathleen's Teahouse. Most notably, Candee, who had scooted her chair back toward them.

"Your thumb was decidedly green, Shay," he replied.

She frowned.

He'd used her nickname again, but he couldn't help himself.

"Is that what they call it?" she asked. "A green thumb?"

"I believe so. Whoever *they* are." He wouldn't let on to her, or anyone, that she'd trampled his heart to bits when she broke up with him and then disappeared from his life. Or that he'd gone a little crazy and rebelled against his inflexible father, consequently making some decidedly bad choices.

An impossibly beautiful woman like Shay normally wouldn't have given him a second glance. He'd been lucky in those few short months they'd had together. They clicked. He made her laugh.

Or perhaps she'd been lonely. Her parents were never around and she had no siblings. He was a buffer, a companion, a friend.

More than a friend.

And he? Well, he and his sister had punched the proverbial clock from sunup to sundown, while his father pressured Lincoln to assume only masculine roles. No creative side for Lincoln—that role was best assigned to the women.

Nevertheless, Lincoln had persevered. Now he and his sister owned one of the most successful toy shops in the country. He fought for a deep breath. How successful was he, though, if he didn't share that achievement with the woman who mattered most?

Behind Shay, two families herding a group of noisy young children streamed into the packed restaurant. Cold air whooshed inside with them. A grateful distraction.

An Irish folk song from piped-in music echoed, a Celtic tune sung by a man accompanied by a fiddle. Kathleen encouraged the patrons to sing the familiar tune.

"'That time of year was coming round,'" she sang.

Lincoln didn't participate in the singalong, although he enjoyed Kathleen's lilting Irish brogue. Shay didn't sing, either. Neither did Candee.

Instead, Candee rhapsodized the numerous benefits of small-town living.

Meanwhile, Shay sidestepped the entire discussion and peeked at her watch. "Sorry. Gotta run, I forgot to buy mulch at the garden center and want to get there before they close."

Lincoln doubted the center closed before five o'clock. Before he refuted her, she zipped up her parka and headed for the door.

Or rather, she limped. After several paces, her leg buckled beneath her and she grasped a chair.

Lincoln's heart plummeted.

He and Candee rushed to assist Shay before she fell, though he was faster. He grabbed her shoulders and supported her as she dropped into a seat. Lincoln asked Rob to bring a bucket of ice, and the threesome—Lincoln, Candee, and Rob—gathered near.

"Are you all right?" Lincoln wound a cloth napkin around the ice and realized his hands were shaking.

"I'm fine. I fell earlier today." Shay braced her hands on the arms of the chair to stand, though Lincoln held down her shoulders. He was determined she rest.

He looked down at her. "What happened?"

"I slipped." She waved off his question. "The perils of icy winter sidewalks."

"Don't get up." He seized another chair and instructed her to stretch out her leg. "Where does it hurt?"

"My right knee, mostly, and my hip."

He knelt in front of her and applied the cold compress to her knee. His fingers brushed her leg, and the slight contact lit a fire in his veins in direct contrast to the ice. He caught a whiff of peppermint, a reminder of the holiday candy Shay adored. She'd always had a voracious sweet tooth.

"They're made from pure cane sugar, right here in the South," she'd once declared to him as they sat at the farmhouse's kitchen table. She'd unwrapped the candy and popped two into his mouth. He'd agreed they were heavenly and had snatched another handful.

And then he'd kissed her, a sugary mingling of peppermint candy and sweet kisses.

He remembered her quiet sigh before she returned his kiss, and he had longed to kiss her again and again. Ironic that the fresh scent of peppermint carried such bittersweet memories.

A hollowness struck him squarely in the chest. His silent pause hung heavy.

No, he instructed himself. He couldn't remain stuck in the past. He was here in the present, and Shay's gaze was on him. In fact, she was glaring at him as he began to massage her knee.

He willed his hand to move away, although it stayed there of its own accord.

"Is your knee bruised?" He focused on listening to her and moved his hand away.

"I haven't checked, though it's nothing serious, I assure you." She wiggled in her seat and glanced at the door.

"Forget any ideas of dashing out of here." He dragged up a

chair, intending to sit beside her. "You're not going anywhere."

"I'm busy. I don't have time to just sit here." She slipped a rebellious strand of thick, dense hair beneath her beanie. "I haven't stopped at the Festival of Trees to check on my tree yet."

"Weren't you in a hurry to get to the garden center?"

"Well, yes. That too."

"The Festival ended on Christmas Day," he said.

Her chocolate-brown eyes scrutinized him. "Don't you live in Hilton Head?"

"You know I do."

"So why are you keeping up on events in Roses?"

"I like Roses. You know, the cool mountain air, the concerts in the park during the summer ..."

"You're not answering my question."

He smiled and held up his hands. "Busted."

"Lincoln, honestly. You still haven't answered my question." She exhaled. "Not everything in life is a joke."

He hadn't been joking, although he didn't admit it. He'd subscribed to the *Roses Daily Sentinel* ever since he'd relocated to Hilton Head Island. She looked up at Rob and Candee, who both watched them expectantly. "Please folks. I'm fine."

With a concerned nod, Candee excused herself to answer her buzzing phone, and Rob produced menus for a waiting couple by the door. For the most part, the restaurant patrons went back to finishing their meals.

Shay had landed by a table insulated behind a wall. A side cupboard played host to a variety of Irish cookbooks.

"You have a particular knack for trying to do the work of three people," Lincoln said.

She rewarded him with an irresistible smile. "Thank you."

"I may not be complimenting you."

"I'll assume you are."

He grinned at their verbal volleyball. How quickly sixteen years melted away.

"Well, I've rested long enough. Time to get on with things." She placed the compress on the table. Before he could stop her, she stood and hobbled a couple of steps toward the exit.

"Why are you limping?" Lincoln asked as he followed. "What happened to you, exactly?"

"I told you. A hazard of the job." She winced with each tentative yet determined step.

He gripped his fingers around her arm to steady her. "You intend to hurry off without an explanation?"

"I gave you an explanation."

"It wasn't a good enough excuse to leave."

He couldn't let go of her. Not again. And he'd been referring to her long-ago departure, using the past tense.

Had she noticed?

She bristled.

Yep, she'd noticed.

"*Isn't* a good enough excuse to leave," he corrected.

"My mind is made up and you can't stop me. I'm going."

He scowled. "Why are you so headstrong, Shay?"

"*I'm* headstrong?" She froze. She looked past him, focusing on the wooden door.

He couldn't gather enough thoughts to respond. *He* wasn't the person who had ended their relationship so abruptly.

She shrugged off his hand. "I don't need anyone's assistance, Lincoln. Don't you understand that by now?" Her pointed words punctuated the air as she hobbled out the door.

He stood in the entryway. She paused by a rusty blue truck parked at the curb and gazed straight at him. That same profound tingling flooded his veins, just as it always had when they locked gazes. But the moment was fleeting, because she soon backed her truck out of the parking space and sped away.

He closed his eyes.

Shay.

He hadn't realized how much he missed her. For so long, he'd scrolled through his memories using a soft-focused lens. Surely he couldn't have loved her for season after season. Surely there were bad times as well as good.

Nonetheless, he didn't recall the bad times. Only the good —the laughter, the joy when they were together. The undeniable attraction. He'd imagined their dream life, experiencing everyday events as if each were an animated adventure.

Alas, there'd been no dream life together.

He had tried to forget her and dated other women. A quick marriage had ended in an even quicker divorce when he realized that Pamela, his ex-wife, had married him for his wealth. He'd assumed Pamela cared for him. In reality, she'd anticipated sailing the world on a yacht, from one expensive port to another, not living on a houseboat and stocking shelves in a toy shop.

A long-suffering sigh from a waitress hoisting a heavy tray returned him to the present.

The Celtic music had ended, underscoring the silence.

Lincoln glanced around. When had the restaurant gotten so quiet?

He stepped outside and inhaled a breath of cold air.

Returning to Roses wasn't about the past, though the letter he'd received from Jasmine Williams had roused a hope in his chest he couldn't deny.

Spending long ago hours at Jasmine's Joy, he'd been connected to a loving family—Shay and her doting, fearless grandmother. Jasmine was completely unlike his parents—

his overachieving father, whom Lincoln had once put on a pedestal, and his quiet mother—a bit more of a free spirit. His sister, Penny, was several years older. Although they were close, his childhood had been spent without her.

For almost two decades, he had assured himself he didn't miss Roses. The isolation of a quirky farm, the absence of artistic experiences—professional concerts and literary events by prominent speakers—was lacking.

Even after the heartbreak, he'd debated whether to build a life in Roses, as he and Shay had once planned, or move with his parents when they relocated.

Hilton Head Island was scenic, and a houseboat on the sea all he could have ever imagined.

Still, the air in Roses was clean, the grass and wheat swaying in an unseen breeze forever in his thoughts. There was gladness in the birdsong, the endless cluck of the chickens, the white puffs of clouds in a cobalt-blue sky.

Shay had been a balm to his soul and brought steadiness to his heartbeat.

He opened the door and stepped back inside the restaurant.

"Shanice's landscaping company is very successful in the spring and summer," Candee said as he rejoined her at their table. "In fact, her business is considered the best in three counties."

"I'm not surprised. Her work ethic is impeccable." Slowly, he nodded. "That explains the mounds of crushed stone and mulch I saw at the farm."

"It's convenient for her to utilize the land for her vehicles and supplies while she's living here. Normally, she's back and forth between her apartment in Huntington and Roses."

"Huntington isn't far."

"A couple hours away, depending on traffic and weather conditions."

So why is she selling? The property meant the world to her.

He kept the question to himself.

Candee peered at him over the rim of her coffee cup. "If you decide to buy in Roses, I recommend you hire Shanice to design any gardens and walkways for your condominiums. Of course, I don't know why I'm saying this. You seem better acquainted with her than I am."

He didn't take the bait to explain how and why he knew Shay. He felt hurt she'd never mentioned him to Candee.

Then again, why would she?

"I'm not certain landscaping will be a major part of my building designs," he responded. "I plan to build affordable housing, particularly for midrange salary workers."

"Here? Why?"

"For my employees. Although my sister and I now own several stores throughout the country, Roses is where the toy shop originated. My parents started the business before I was born." Lincoln stretched out his legs. "Penny and I inherited the business and share ownership. Therefore, any decision is a joint one."

"So, are you intending to get back to your roots by restarting your original shop?" Candee asked.

"No time is better than the present." The notion had settled around him like a beloved blanket, although his decision had been made only days ago—after he'd received Jasmine Williams's letter. He'd then relayed his idea to Penny.

"Besides horses, a visit to a toy store is always a special treat for my son," Candee said.

"I've never ridden a horse."

"My son is a horse lover. My friends, Belle and Andrew, who live in Wilmington, bought him a Shetland pony recently." She smiled. "But this conversation isn't about me. It's about you and your toy shop expansion."

"My mother was the creative force and all of our toys are

made with recycled materials. My father handled the business side of things."

"What a marvelous concept." Candee took a last sip of coffee. "What's the name of your business?"

"New Beginnings Toys."

"Wow." She gasped out loud and set down her cup. "Your company is the leading toy manufacturer in the country."

He polished off his sandwich, nodding. "We're best recognized for our hand-carved wooden rocking horses, which started right here in Roses."

"Thus, a once modest beginning led to phenomenal growth?"

He tapped his fingers on his leg. He'd never been comfortable discussing his wealth. Sometimes, he believed he existed between two worlds—an affluent world that he could afford to enter and a world of incessant struggle during the toy shop's early years. Often, he wasn't contented in either world, for neither delivered a sense of peace.

Financial security and donating to charities brought their own rewards. A prosperous business, the freedom to travel, and a relaxed lifestyle on the sea.

What else could he want?

His purpose in life. What was it, exactly?

The ever-alert Candee was watching him and he cast about for a change of subject.

"Shay is asking a substantial price for a home that clearly needs renovation," he said.

"There's a large amount of land that comes with the property. Ideal for building condos."

"Right."

"Is the farmhouse more important than any business expansion?"

Truth be told, yes. He glanced at Candee. Had he expressed his thoughts aloud? He couldn't be certain.

"Let me get this clear about your—" She faltered in midsentence. "You won't renovate the farmhouse by turning it into a manufacturing center for toys."

"I won't." His business sense kicked in. "Though the house is large enough to be converted into two, possibly three, apartments."

"For …?"

"As I mentioned, for my employees. It's a long story." He washed down the rest of his sandwich with a swig of water.

Candee took a last bite of whiskey cake. "I have another showing scheduled for tomorrow and an earlier potential buyer is expressing interest in the farmhouse. Apologies. I shouldn't push you."

"I don't mind."

"You're saying Shanice's property would be utilized for housing your employees?"

"Exactly."

"How many employees do you anticipate hiring?"

"Thirty."

"You'll need more than three apartments."

He reached for his coat. "We still own the building in Roses that housed the original toy shop. It's located on the outskirts of town and stands at the intersection of highways 9 and 21."

"I can pinpoint exactly where the building is located. I wondered who owned it." She perched her chin on her hands. "Roses will benefit from good-paying jobs, plus reasonable housing."

He'd considered that possibility, which was another reason to move forward on his decision. After all, he'd been born in Roses and the charming community was his hometown. He wanted to contribute to the town's prosperity.

He'd discovered another home on the internet a few days earlier that came with a higher price tag than Shay's farmhouse, though it didn't matter. He was using Shay's property as a grand excuse to see *her.* He'd never build condos on her beloved property.

Candee steadily observed him, but he had no intention of divulging his plans yet. Nonetheless, he vowed to give Candee his business for any real estate he purchased in the area.

He shoved back his chair. "I'll discuss any acquisitions with Penny and get back to you."

Candee retrieved her purse. "I'm surprised your sister doesn't live in Hilton Head where your shop is located."

Lincoln stood, helped Candee on with her coat, then pulled on his own. "Her husband has a high-powered job in Virginia. She's in charge of the toy shop's strategy, organization, and building our teams to succeed. Nowadays, much of her work is done remotely."

The familiar lyrics of "I Will Always Love You," sung by Whitney Houston, rang out, and Lincoln stopped short, recognizing the tune immediately. Once, that particular song was his and Shay's special refrain, defining their relationship after they'd watched the movie, *The Bodyguard.*

They'd held hands afterward, strolling the farmhouse grounds. The picturesque scenery melted away as he twirled her around in an impromptu slow dance to the silent rhythm of the music.

Shay, they're playing our song was the first sentence that popped into his mind. That extraordinary ballad had expressed their love. Forever and always.

The song continued, and everyone in the restaurant looked around, wondering where it was coming from. It sounded like a ringtone, he thought, wondering at the coincidence, the heartfelt words belted out by Whitney Houston when his emotions were high. He spotted a cell phone on

Shay's table as Kathleen emerged through the swinging kitchen door.

He strode to the table and retrieved the phone. "Evidently, this is Shay's?" he asked no one on particular.

"Shanice never forgets anything," Candee said. "I'm surprised she didn't realize she left it here." She cast a sideways glance at Lincoln and smiled mischievously. "However, she needs her phone."

"I can't leave the restaurant." Kathleen lowered an elaborate silver tray laden with tiny sandwiches stuffed with cream cheese and cucumbers to an empty table.

"I'd love to help. Regrettably, I have another appointment." Candee's sly gleam landed on Lincoln. "Will you …?"

"Will I what?" He bit down on his grin. Things were definitely improving by the hour.

Call it fate. Call it good fortune. He called it the hand of an all-giving God.

"Bring Shanice her cell phone?"

The question wasn't out of Candee's mouth before he agreed.

"Sure." He kept his fingers around the phone, promised Candee he'd be in touch and left money for the check and a generous tip on the table. He turned to Kathleen. "Thank you for your flexibility in allowing my sister and I to celebrate our company's New Year's Eve party at your restaurant. I realize I phoned you last-minute."

"No worries. The teahouse closes to the public at eight o'clock and your private party afterwards will finish up the evening brilliantly. Rob is planning on shooting fireworks outside at midnight." She beamed. "What are you celebrating?"

"An opportunity to make amends. A fresh start for our company. Another new location. Or rather, an old location. Let's say we're honoring our humble beginnings. My grandparents, my mother's parents, kept their noses to the grind. They approved of my father because his views were exactly like theirs—conventional, workaholic values."

"What about your mother?" Kathleen asked.

"She was the creative parent."

"Do you take after your father or your mother?"

"Both, I imagine. Mostly my mother."

Kathleen was quiet for a moment. "I also come from modest beginnings. My family in Ireland worked hard to succeed. This holiday is special in numerous ways."

"Indeed," he reaffirmed.

He'd made the right decision to come to Roses.

Business and pleasure. People advised not to mix the two. He disagreed.

A company expansion and the opportunity to see Shay. What could be better?

For a brief second, he pictured her smiling with delight when she saw him standing at the front door of her farmhouse, her big brown eyes gazing up at him.

Well, maybe not exactly *delight* at seeing him. At any rate, she would be delighted at the sight of her cell phone, and he looked forward to her reaction.

Naturally, his wisest choice would be to leave the phone for someone else to bring to her. Or to disregard her presence altogether, the way she'd disregarded him. However, he'd never been sensible where she was concerned, and rational thought often deserted him.

Like now, for example.

With a hasty goodbye, he pocketed Shay's phone and strode to his car.

CHAPTER 3

A half hour later, after soaking in a warm Epsom-salt bath, Shanice sat at her antique desk in the living room. She'd delayed her trip to the garden center and Festival of Trees. There was always tomorrow.

Her encounter with Lincoln left her restless. Having laid eyes on him, she was reminded that he was a likable man—polite, witty and compassionate to animals. She'd observed him when he'd collected eggs, and his easygoing crooning soothed the nervous chicks.

She changed into clean jeans, a green and blue tartan shirt, wool socks, and cozy faux-leopard slippers. She drew her hair up into a high ponytail and stepped to the kitchen.

On impulse, she decided to bake a sweet potato pie, using MaryEllen's tried-and-true recipe. She kept sweet potato pulp frozen, and used a refrigerated store-bought crust, a tremendous time-saver. Soon, the wholesome scents of butter, vanilla, and pumpkin spice wafted throughout the house.

Back at her laptop computer while the pie baked, she scanned the desk and mound of paperwork. There were bills demanding to be paid and customer invoices, some of them second notices.

"Why can't people pay their statements when they're due?" she asked her cat. Duchess sniffed, jumped on the sofa, and cuddled on an embroidered pillow. "If they did, I'd actually be able to make my payments on time."

Nevertheless, it was year-end and her suppliers required payment or they'd stop extending credit. If that happened, she wouldn't have the money to purchase the supplies she needed for her already contracted early-spring jobs: two major garden renovations and building a retaining wall.

She pushed out an overwhelmed sigh and scrubbed her hands along her forearms. A draft constantly seeped through the windows.

No defeatism, she scolded herself. Except the glaring awareness that owning and operating a business marked all her decisions.

She snapped her computer shut and regarded the massive stone fireplace. Lush displays of pink and white poinsettias flanked the mantel. Birthday photos of her and Granny, a candid shot of Shanice with her parents in the kitchen, and a tangerine-orange sky captured once at sunset.

On a recent afternoon, she'd spent hours in the attic sorting her grandmother's artifacts organized in antique crates and cartons. She'd sneezed as the dust flew everywhere and poked through a box labeled "N.B.'s Boat Books."

Boat books? She'd scrunched her eyebrows into a frown. Her grandmother had loved sweet romance novels and passed that appreciation on to Shanice.

Like her grandmother, she was a romantic. She believed in happily ever after. Reading the novels, she escaped reality, immersed in the integrity of the characters. She laughed and cried with them. Sometimes fate carried their love, sometimes good fortune.

But boat books for children?

She lifted the books from the box and sorted them. Each was forty pages long and featured imaginative, colorful artwork. Each featured the same hero: a sturdy little blue tugboat, sailing the ocean on thrilling adventures.

Each book had a similar title.

Tuggy the Tugboat Goes To Sea, Tuggy the Tugboat Meets Mr. Whale, and so on.

All promoted kindness, and a powerful lesson resonated throughout: sailing on a voyage was fun, and the tugboat was always searching, searching, searching. Invariably, the books encouraged the same theme—that children stay true to themselves.

Clever and insightful, she thought, after she'd read each book from cover to cover. *Don't allow people to push you into doing things that don't resonate with your true values.*

The author was listed by four initials: N. B. L. R.

A TRADITIONAL WOODEN checkerboard set from the attic sat positioned on the coffee table. Shanice well-remembered sitting with Lincoln on the braided rug, a blazing fire in the fireplace, and deliberating over their checker games for hours.

"Kinged pieces can move in both directions," Lincoln had instructed as he threatened one of her pieces.

"I'm double-jumping and capturing two of your kings," she countered. She scrutinized the checkerboard and grinned. "In fact, I won."

"No way." He quirked a dark eyebrow. "You cheated."

"Absolutely not."

"Then why do you always win?"

She laughed. "Talent."

"Someday, Shay, I intend to study checker strategy and will beat you."

"There's such a thing as checker strategy?"

"There must be."

"I'm waiting," she teased.

He never beat her, because she'd left Roses a month later. On a brisk January day, frost had settled on the farm as she trooped across the grass with her luggage in tow to a waiting taxi. Her teeth chattered, and she'd pulled on her gloves. The cold chilled her numbed fingers.

Granny had stood by the living room window and waved. She smiled back, though there was no joy in it. They'd argued for days about Shanice's decision beforehand.

Shanice had flown to Rome, where her parents temporarily resided. Modern construction projects sought archaeologists and geologists to survey and study the ground before building began.

Much to Granny's disappointment, Shanice had lived abroad for her remaining university years.

Shanice turned away and sighed. The checkerboard game was forgotten, though the memories lingered. The same loneliness brimmed hot in her chest when her thoughts gravitated to Lincoln.

She dashed away the tears blurring her vision. Selling the house was her last chance.

But what if Jasmine's Joy didn't sell? How much longer could she put up a brave front that everything was fine? Less than a week remained before she'd be reduced to giving up all she had built and starting over. To do what? Landscaping was the only life she'd known and the profession she loved.

Love.

Her thoughts looped back to Lincoln and their former days together.

After a Saturday afternoon working with Habitat for

Humanity, they'd sit on the living room floor, their backs against the worn sofa, their legs outstretched. His arm often slung casually around her while she'd talked about her day. On one occasion, when she described the buckets of soil she had moved, he scolded her.

"As usual, you're overexerting yourself." He massaged her shoulders. "Why didn't you call me over to assist you when you moved those buckets of soil?"

"You were on a ladder installing windows on the second floor."

He'd been wearing paint-splattered jeans and a white T-shirt, the tanned muscles in his forearms glistening in the hot sun.

"I would've hurried down," he said.

"You might've fallen."

"I've already fallen … in love." He rained kisses on her cheeks, her nose, her mouth. Slow, delicate and exquisite. "What's another fall?"

The word *fall* forced her back to the present, and she absently rubbed her hip and knee.

Why hadn't Candee phoned to update her on Lincoln's decision regarding the house? Even if he disliked the kitchen, maybe he'd make an offer. Even better, a substantial offer.

Though the reason why he was interested in her house wasn't clear.

He didn't even live here. And speaking of living—who lived on a houseboat, anyway? She'd envisioned him on a yacht. Or a Manhattan penthouse. Yet she remembered him as an ordinary, modest guy, despite his buttoned-up father.

Shanice leaned back in her chair. Perhaps she should call Candee. She reached for her cell phone in the pocket of her jeans and her breath hitched. The phone wasn't there.

She bolted upright. Of course it wasn't. She'd changed her clothes.

She fished in her purse while mentally retracing her steps. She hadn't recalled seeing her phone since she'd returned from Kathleen's Teahouse.

She checked her parka, fearing she may have missed some important phone calls. Tamping down her panic, she dashed upstairs and scoured the pockets of the overalls she'd worn earlier. No trace of a cell phone anyplace.

Ugh.

Without a phone, she couldn't call the teahouse. Thus, she was forced to drive back to town. She glanced toward the kitchen. Bad enough she hadn't intended to go anywhere. She needed to wait a half hour until the pie finished baking.

In the uncertain silence, she switched on Granny's vintage radio to her preferred contemporary station. This station, and many others, continued with Christmas music through the end of the year, and "All I Want For Christmas Is You," was being crooned by Mariah Carey.

Shanice spun the dial. Though she prized Mariah's voice, her amazing high and low notes, the song brought emotions that she wasn't ready to face after seeing Lincoln. Thankfully, a rendition of "Silent Night" on another station, in the Temptations' faultless harmony, proved soothing and peaceful and the DJ promised more holiday hits to follow.

Her gaze swept the living room. A rustling in the kitchen suggested the cat was sniffing and exploring. She'd noticed a collection of bottle caps under the sink, and discovered that Duchess hoarded them.

She smirked. Her cat had a secret stash.

Shanice put her hands behind her head and scrutinized the sag in the ceiling. Was she imagining the cracks? Probably not. More often than not, the ceiling leaked.

"Fixer-upper," she reminded herself. She was selling the farmhouse "as is."

Candee had mentioned another showing with prospective buyers in the morning, a couple in their twenties with a baby who were relocating to the area. With any luck, the couple would offer a generous amount over the asking price.

She envisioned a bidding war between the couple and Lincoln.

Hah! Not in today's market, and certainly not happening the week after Christmas. The optimal season to buy and sell real estate was typically in the spring and summer.

Her contemplations swung again to her prospective buyer—Lincoln Reid. At the teahouse, she'd admired him from a safe distance—his self-assured stance, his easy smile, his jaw-dropping good looks.

Emotion welled in her chest.

At the touch of his hand on her knee, a jolt had flown through her, a chemistry that occurred whenever they were close. When they'd met her first semester of college, she had assumed that as the wealthy kid on the Habitat for Humanity team, he was unaccustomed to hard work. She'd soon discovered he was strong and muscular and embraced physical labor.

At the teahouse, he'd regarded her from head to toe, giving her more than a once-over and her cheeks had heated.

After introductions and they'd done a bit of reminiscing, a loaded silence had fallen between them. Unnerving and burdened with questions neither dared to broach.

She wasn't the reason he was in Roses, thus there was no sense in examining the subject with any detail. Still, who could have imagined he'd land here the day after Christmas? And why did Granny send him a letter?

An abrupt knock followed by the doorbell brought Shanice upright. The cat appeared and trailed her to the front foyer.

She opened the door and was hit with a blast of wintry air.

And something else. Or rather, someone else. Lincoln.

With a gasp, she stepped back.

He smiled, his lips desirable and firm. He was so tall and masculine, his form filled the doorway. He still wore his expensive gray wool coat over navy-blue pants and a blue shirt. Evidently, he hadn't changed since their exchange at Kathleen's Teahouse.

He held out a bouquet—Christmas red roses, stark-white lilies and green hydrangeas, offset by Douglas fir branches and tied with a red satin bow.

"Hi, beautiful. These are for you."

"Hi, Lincoln." She surveyed the bouquet in his outstretched hand. "Why?"

She caught his hurt stare and immediately apologized.

"Because it's Christmas, Shay," he replied.

Shay.

His special nickname for her. He spoke her name so easily; it flowed from his tongue without a thought. He'd always used her nickname before they kissed.

She met his warm gaze. He remembered too.

Shivers of anticipation traveled up her spine. He was such a fine, rugged man. Masculinity oozed from him, and she felt the unmistakable draw right down to her toes.

"Thank you." She lifted an unsteady hand and accepted the bouquet. "I wasn't expecting you." *That* was the understatement of the year. She'd been dreaming about him and suddenly he appeared.

"Surprised?" Amusement colored his voice.

"A … a little."

"I stopped by the florist on my way over. I realize you're a landscaper and constantly around plants, but—"

"Thanks." She buried her nose in the thick, velvety roses and inhaled the heady fragrance, the sharp scent of pine.

"They're gorgeous. What brings you to the farmhouse again today?"

"Again?"

"You were here earlier with Candee."

"True." He altered his stance, keeping his gaze on her. "For a variety of reasons."

"Such as?"

"Certain qualities which are difficult to describe."

Qualities?

Shanice inclined her head, an acknowledgement she'd heard him, although a *quality* was quite different from a *reason.* She kept her posture straight, exhaled, and reined in her thoughts.

She peered around him. The sun had melted the snow, and leafless trees swayed in a gust of wind.

This was winter in the south. Some days were humid and pleasant, others cold and biting, with temperatures below freezing. Today was one of those cooler days, when the weather couldn't determine which season December belonged in.

The sky boasted silvery streaks of clouds. The temperature on the outdoor thermometer showed the low thirties, and daylight hours were still short. A flash of red caught her eye as a cardinal flew by and headed to the bird feeder.

Duchess wound through Shanice's legs and rubbed her body against Lincoln. In response, he bent to stroke the cat. Duchess head-bunted his calf, making her mark, then strutted to her roost by the window.

"Is this your cat?" he asked.

"Yes. Her name is Duchess. I adopted her from a no-kill shelter when I learned she'd been abandoned on the side of a highway."

He grimaced. He was an animal lover, and the remembrance of his kindness filled her with a pleasing shiver. He'd owned a dog, a sturdy brown and white beagle named Lucky. Sometimes, he brought Lucky to campus, going on leisurely strolls with him after classes. He'd often bake homemade treats for Lucky and showered him with attention and affection.

He motioned toward the cat. "She's a beauty like her owner."

"Thanks." The man had a thing for complimenting her. "When I saw Duchess advertised on the shelter's website, I made an appointment and it was love at first sight."

"I know the feeling, Shay." He smiled, crossed his arms over his broad chest and leaned against the doorjamb. This close, his black lashes were long and spiky, the dimples on his cheeks prominent. He looked younger when he smiled, reminding her of the nineteen-year-old boy she'd loved.

Whoa. Don't go there. Before you realize it, you'll be mesmerized by him again.

It took all her willpower to take a mental step back from him.

"May I come in?" He gestured toward the foyer.

For some reason, she found it difficult to collect her thoughts.

She regarded the sharp planes of his face, his deep-set blue eyes, the shadow of a beard darkening his jaw. Afternoon sunlight highlighted his thick dark hair, trimmed sleek and clean-cut, a little longer on top. In the back, his hair curled over his collar.

He looked like a man straight off the cover of an island living magazine, and so heart-stoppingly gorgeous.

"Is Candee here too?" Shanice answered with a question of her own.

"Nope. Just me." He tightened the gray wool scarf around his neck and stamped his boots on the welcome mat, a subtle reminder of the raw weather.

He waited. She debated, but couldn't hold back her laughter. "Is this the part where I'm supposed to invite you inside?"

"Precisely. In fact, it's past the part. It's freezing out here."

"Come in." She swung the door wider, and he entered. "But, I need to go out soon, because I lost something and need to find it."

He nodded. "Ah."

She lifted a quizzical eyebrow. "Why did you drive to the farmhouse twice today? Besides the flowers, I mean."

He seemed to read her thoughts, her expectation that he was here to make an offer on her house. Gently, he settled his hand on her shoulder and gave a companionable squeeze. "I'm not here because of the farmhouse."

A minute stretched to two. The implication of his announcement brought a shadow to her contemplations, to the porch where sun had shone a moment earlier.

Confused, she swallowed hard. "Then why?"

"Is this what you lost?" He reached in his pocket. "You forgot your cell phone at Kathleen's Teahouse. Your ring tone sang out to us from your table."

"All the patrons heard?" Warmth crept up her neck, an embarrassment she couldn't hide. "I Will Always Love You," sung by the incomparable Whitney Houston, had blasted for all to hear.

His fathomless gaze met hers. Naturally, he'd recognized the tune. Despite her protests to the contrary, how could she deny she'd clung to the past when the proof was displayed in her ringtone?

"I hadn't realized my phone was missing until a few minutes ago." She transferred her weight from one foot to the other, favoring the leg that didn't ache. "I searched everywhere."

"Your phone sang my favorite song." His tone was quiet. His gaze never left hers.

She didn't spout a frivolous excuse for the ringtone. Instead, she opted for honesty.

"Me too," she replied. "Of course, you already know that."

He cupped her chin in his hand, a light caress, his thumb moving across her skin. "Together forever, Shay."

Their motto. Hurray for the Three Musketeers, although she and Lincoln were only two. One for all, all for one.

She'd listened to the lyrics of "I Will Always Love You" a million times. Lincoln had sung the melody to her a million times. He'd never mixed up the words to *that* particular tune.

The verses were all about love, but upon deeper examination, the chorus described letting go.

Letting go.

Lincoln's father had insisted she let Lincoln go. He'd hurled his demands at her.

And so she had. Dub the heartbroken soundtrack.

"Am I correct in assuming you no longer need to search for your phone?" Lincoln asked with a laugh. Consistently easy-going and relaxed, humor suited him and his personality. He invariably put people at ease.

She raised a nonchalant shoulder and pocketed her phone.

"Excellent. I'll take that as an affirmative." He leaned around her and sniffed. "Mmm. Something smells good."

"Me?" She tossed him a radiant smile. She couldn't resist bantering with him.

The corner of his mouth quirked. "Well, yes, of course. But something else. Something sugary and cinnamon."

"Sweet potato pie is baking in the oven. Granny's friend's famous recipe."

"I love freshly baked sweet potato pie."

"Thanks for the broad hint, but I intend to bring the pie to the homeless shelter tomorrow."

"Can you spare a slice for a guy who has been standing in the cold and came all this way to deliver your phone?"

She laughed. "When you describe yourself in those terms, I can't say no."

"Did you cut the shortening in the crust until it was crumbly? That's my secret."

"My secret is using a refrigerated crust from the supermarket to save work and ensure an easy cleanup."

He put a hand to his chest. "You didn't roll out a homemade crust?"

"Nope. No messy kitchen on my watch." She threw him a satisfied grin. "For your information, Mr. Accomplished Cook, a homemade crust doesn't make a snap of difference in a pie's flavor or texture."

"I beg to disagree."

She flung a fist to her hip. "You're insulting my pie?"

"Never. I'll be the elected taste-tester to ensure your theory is correct."

"You?"

"I'm the 'accomplished cook.'" He air-quoted with his fingers. "And I prefer tea with my sweet potato pie."

In a feigned British accent, she replied, "I don't serve high tea, though I'll heat a pan of mulled apple cider. The pie won't be ready for a while."

He brought her hand to his lips and delicately kissed her knuckles. The essence of a well-mannered gentleman. His eyes sparkled with mirth. "I'm happy to wait for the pie, under one condition."

"There's a condition now?"

"Absolutely." His gaze drifted to the hallway leading to the kitchen. "Let's eat the pie in your living room."

"Why?"

"The living room is my favorite room. It's homey." He spent the next couple minutes pointing out the furnishings—

the dish of peppermint candy on a sideboard, the flowered wallpaper covering the walls and rows of framed cross stitch designs with Bible verse quotes.

She studied him, then pulled away her hand. "Let's not forget that you don't like the kitchen."

He shed his coat and hung it on a wooden hanger near the door. His movements came slow and deliberate, his look speculative. "Why do you say that?"

Gone were the freckles on his tanned face. His well-cut clothes—tailored pants emphasizing long, lean legs and the fitted, casual shirt—spoke of ease and elegance.

She was out of her league with him. He'd never spend one night in a tired, dilapidated farmhouse. Lincoln was accustomed to five-star hotels, watching super-size flat screen TV's, and jetting around the world on a whim.

At least, that's the life his father had decided for him.

She took in Lincoln's scent. He'd always smelled like he'd just gotten out of the shower. Clean, invigorating, and a subtle whiff of lemon. Or was it lime?

"I have a confession," she said.

Expectantly, he watched her. "Which is?"

She couldn't bear to reveal why she'd left Roses. Why she'd left *him.* She had reasoned that if she stayed, it would have hurt his relationship with his family too much. He had held his father in high esteem—a larger-than-life, formidable man—who towered over Lincoln's six-foot frame by several inches. His father was interested in honor and position above all else.

Shanice, at an average height, had felt small in Lincoln's father's presence.

As Lincoln concentrated on her, her mouth went dry, her mind flooded with opposing thoughts. Even now, she couldn't work up the nerve to state the truth about the warning his father had issued, nor the money he'd tried to bribe her with.

"While Candee was showing you my house this morning," she said, "I heard you remarking about Granny's counter space. Or rather, the *lack* of counter space."

He frowned. "I also remarked on the discolored ceiling in the living room. There must be a leak somewhere, probably coming from the upstairs bathroom."

"I didn't hear that part of the conversation."

"You must've left by then."

"I didn't want to interrupt anything."

"You could've stayed. The house is yours." He shot her an apologetic glance. "I didn't intend my negative comment the way it must have sounded. My recollections of this house are fond, as well as your grandmother's cooking lessons. We had a system for homemade biscuits—I stirred the flour, milk and sugar, and she kneaded the dough."

"You ate half the biscuits as soon as they came out of the oven," Shanice reminded.

He chucked her under the chin. "I couldn't resist."

While he waited for the biscuits to bake, she remembered him gripping the door frame and doing pull ups. Invariably, that earned him a scolding from Granny.

Those fun, laid-back memories. Tears stung and clung to her lashes. Before her emotions completely derailed, she spun and called out for Duchess, a means to sidestep the conversation.

As usual, the cat didn't respond. Duchess only reacted to the sound of the can opener when Shanice was in the kitchen.

"Your cat darted by so rapidly this morning, I wasn't sure if she was yours," Lincoln was saying.

Shanice wiped at her eyes, though a tear escaped. "It's one of my best skills."

He grinned and brought an index finger to her cheek, capturing her tear. "Owning a darting cat?"

"A cat who disappears whenever she feels like it." At his encouraging grin, she found herself smiling again. Only Lincoln could change her feelings from sad to happy in a flash.

"Is disappearing a skill?" he asked.

That hit home. Shanice jerked up her head in surprise and nearly dropped the bouquet. Was he referring to their past and her abrupt departure?

She clutched the bouquet closer to her chest. "Excuse me while I find a vase for the flowers and check the pie."

No one could blame her for beating a hasty retreat. All her life, cutting a difficult conversation short and vanishing had been her approach to dealing with challenging emotional situations.

Not that their past mattered any longer. She scarcely needed a recap on how she'd let them both down, how she hadn't been tough enough to stand up for their love. In the end, both their hearts had been broken.

She hurried to the kitchen. From a glass cabinet, she selected a stoneware vase. She trimmed the flower stems with kitchen scissors and pruned the extra leaves. Filling the vase with water, she placed the flowers in the middle of the enamel table.

On to the mulled cider. She sliced an orange and proceeded to mix apple cider with the orange slices, cinnamon sticks and cloves in a pan, heating it to a near boil.

She caught a glimpse of herself in the mirror over the stove and patted her hair. There was nothing she could do about her tired-looking face and the exhausted lines creasing her forehead. She could hardly run upstairs and style the wispy tangles escaping from her ponytail or apply a dab of blush and lipstick.

Once the cider warmed, she set china cups, saucers and napkins on a silver tray and poured the mulled cider into an ornate silver teapot. Humming to herself, she carried the tray into the living room. The idea that Lincoln was waiting for her tightened her stomach, bringing an expectation of happiness.

He was kneeling by the fireplace and peering inside. "Shay, have you started a fire lately?" he asked.

"The fireplace was cleaned a month ago, and I haven't used it since Thanksgiving." She set the tray on the coffee table. "The chimney sweep said the smoke ducts and flue are safe."

"May I start a fire?"

He'd already started one, a slow burn of attraction, that made her heart race. How was she supposed to respond coherently when he was in the same room?

Her cat's insistent meowing at a cardinal flying past the window returned Shanice to the present. "Sure, Lincoln. A fire would be great."

"Guess the matches are in here?" He dug through a drawer near the fireplace and retrieved them, answering his own question.

He piled several dry, split logs and lit the match, and soon flames glowed from the fireplace. The wood scent lent a coziness to the air, a comforting atmosphere, and she gravitated toward it. And toward the man who had started the fire.

He rose and indicated the radio playing a festive tune hummed by the Ten Tenors. He joined in, his baritone voice belting out the lyrics to "The Little Drummer Boy" and completely messing up the second verse. When the song was over, he gestured to the tray. "Very fancy, Shay. I recognize the poinsettia flowered teacups. Your grandmother used different seasonal sets depending on the holiday. Weren't there brown and gold cups for the fall?"

"And blue-flowered sets for summer."

"Bone china, right?"

"For special occasions."

He stepped closer. "Is this a special occasion?"

He must stop being so charming. Their past attraction was over. Done.

"I rarely have company." She raised her hand in a weak protest, chastising herself inwardly for the admittance. She sounded pathetic. Good thing he wasn't aware of the online dating website she'd joined.

Sometimes it seemed like all the best guys were taken. Except for the man standing in front of her, studying her with a decided glint of interest in his eyes.

"Thank you for allowing me to stay," he said.

She chuckled. "Did I have a choice?"

"I can be very persuasive." He nodded. Smiled. "You create a festive mood wherever you go."

Her mouth twitched. "Regretfully, I haven't created an abundance of festivity this year since I'm in the process of moving."

He scanned the room. "Now that you mention it, there aren't many holiday decorations, except for Kwanzaa."

"Kwanzaa begins tonight. The first night celebrates unity."

"I'd like to stay for the ceremony."

"After you eat?"

He winked. "You're reading my mind."

His gaze fixed on the bowl of fruit—bananas and red, ripe apples—and the seven candles in the candleholder positioned on the bureau, particularly the black candle in the center. "Your grandmother once remarked that Kwanzaa is the occasion for reflection and gratefulness."

"She repeatedly stressed honoring our African-American heritage."

"She was the wisest woman I ever knew," he said. "Extraordinary in every regard, besides being feisty and shrewd."

"*Average* wasn't in her vocabulary. Her focus was on building relationships and continually stretching herself."

He chuckled, twisted in a circle and picked up the potted fir tree. "Where are all the ornaments?"

"I donated most of them to the Festival of Trees. The event is held every year and is for a worthy cause."

"The senior citizen nutrition program."

"How do you know?"

He raised his hands, palms up. "Busted, remember?"

She assumed he'd been joking in Kathleen's Teahouse, but apparently he wasn't.

She rearranged the tray, and he waited for her to pour the cider.

As was his custom, he remained standing. Forever the gentleman—coming to his feet when a woman entered the room, pulling out chairs, opening car doors.

He always remembered how she took her tea, her coffee. He often picked up a candy bar at the corner store in town and surprised her. Lincoln was continually polite, respectful and thoughtful of other people's feelings, especially hers.

He peered toward the kitchen. "When is the pie done?"

"Probably another five or ten minutes."

"Did you lower the oven temperature?"

"No."

"The crust will burn." He was already striding toward the kitchen. "Same oven, correct?" he called over his shoulder.

"Two decades old and counting."

He reappeared several minutes later. "The crust partially

burned, but is edible. I set the pie on the stovetop to cool. I estimate another hour before our taste test."

"*Our* taste test?"

"I'm generous." He beamed. "I'll let you have a slice."

He picked up a delicate china cup and handed it to her, then held his own. Quickly, he glanced at his watch before he clinked her cup with his. "Any ideas for what we can do to pass the next hour besides drinking mulled cider?" he challenged with a grin.

CHAPTER 4

*L*incoln helped himself to another cup of cider and gestured toward the checkerboard set. "I recognize your grandmother's old wooden set. Does it still work?"

Shay shook her head in teasing confusion. "As you are well aware, you don't wind up a checker set. No batteries allowed."

"Just good old-fashioned fun." He took a hearty swallow of cider before setting his cup down. "Is this the board we always used?" He slid the cover off the set and peered inside.

"Unchanged, and the rules are the same." She bit back a laugh. "Twelve black pieces, twelve red pieces, and an eight-by-eight-inch square board."

He placed the board in front of the fireplace, sat on the floor, and began extracting red and black checkers. He invited her to sit across from him. "Are you up for a round?"

She settled with the checkerboard between them. "I'll bet you five dollars I'll win."

"Ah … So confident you're playing for money now?"

"Absolutely. Especially when the odds are in my favor."

"Oh, they are, are they? Why is that?"

She rested her chin on her hands. "I always beat you."

"You're in for a surprise, because I've honed my skills."

"Oh, really? Do tell."

"I refuse to give away all my secrets at once."

"Just give away one then."

"Alright." He gave a theatrical sigh. "I often play checkers with my nephew."

A smile curved her beautiful lips. "Evan? Penny's son? How old is he?"

"Eight."

Shay dipped her head to hide her grin. "Aren't you going to set up your black checkers?" Choosing red, she positioned her pieces on the board.

"Checkers?" he asked absently. He was paying too close attention to Shay and the way her eyes glistened with laughter. Her lips were rosy from the warm cider, and the minor detail that they were a few feet apart didn't stop him. He leaned over and pressed a casual, spontaneous peck on her cheek.

For the next half hour, the house was quiet, save for a medley of familiar Christmas tunes from the radio playing in the background. He hummed in harmony to songs he knew, and, to Shay's amusement, songs he didn't know, making up funny, silly lyrics.

"On the first day of Christmas, my server gave to me, a lonely burger covered with cheese." Followed with, "On the second day of Christmas, my server gave to me, two French fries, and a lonely burger covered in cheese."

By the time he'd finished the twelfth verse, Shay had dissolved into laughter, pleading for him to stop singing so she could concentrate on the checker game. Her spontaneous delight emanated from within. Her dark-brown eyes changed to the color of sweet melted chocolate. He stared at her, immersing himself in her eyes, in her smile.

"That's the idea," he said. "I'm trying to deter you from concentrating on our checker game."

"Don't you want me to win?"

"Absolutely not."

When "Go Tell It on the Mountain" sounded from the radio, he pleaded innocence when he mixed up the lyrics.

"You still haven't learned the correct words?" With a gratified snicker, she reached the end of his board, raised a red checker and declared, "King me."

He paused to analyze his mistake, deliberating on his next approach. He needed to play a better offense and move his pieces together. That stray checker might cost him the game. He reminded himself to focus on her kings and improve his strategies. But how could he concentrate when this exquisite woman sat across from him and distracted him?

"I should learn the correct words, right?" he asked.

Playfully, she swatted his forearm. "Uh, right." She jumped his final piece and removed it.

A quick scan of the checker board reminded him that he was losing. No, take that back. He'd lost the game. Just as he'd lost his heart years ago to a stunning, vivacious woman who had regularly beaten him at checkers.

She laughed triumphantly, and he congratulated her on a game well played with a genial high-five.

He caught her hand and held it. "Did I ever tell you I had a thing for landscapers?"

She beamed. "Not that I recall."

He kissed her again, his mouth feathery-light, trailing kisses down her throat. He caressed her cheek, his fingers grazing her smooth skin. Her cheekbones were high, her bearing fine and elegant. And her lips, soft and tempting.

Her eyelashes fluttered closed. He slid his hand behind

her nape and drew her flush to him. Silently, he willed the checkerboard between them to move so he could cuddle her.

She drew back and opened her eyes. "'Go Tell It on the Mountain'" is my favorite hymn. The words aren't difficult. You could've learned them by now."

I didn't have the heart to learn the words after you left. Had he said that aloud? He wasn't sure.

But now she was here, in his arms. He jotted a mental note to study the lyrics and sing the hymn to her soon.

In a flash, another song came to mind.

"I Will Always Love You."

His heartbeat slowed, and he envisioned being totally honest.

I've loved you for years, Shay. I've never gotten over you. I was devastated after you left me and not a pleasant person to be around. I was moody and temperamental and alcohol became my drug of choice. It didn't help. Nothing helped until I sought counseling and finally got my head on straight. Then I immersed myself in my work.

"'I Will Always Love You' will forever be my favorite song," he said aloud.

He left it at that.

Her eyes widened. She considered him, although he couldn't read her expression. She grazed her fingers across her lips, collected herself, and stood. "The pie should be cool enough to slice now."

Her manner had switched from playful to formal. What had upset her? His admission about their song? His kiss?

"I'll help you get the forks." He stood. If she could be cool and collected, he could too.

He followed her into the kitchen. By habit, he scanned the ceiling, half envisioning lavender hung upside down from the rafters to dry. Shay's grandmother invariably declared that lavender-scented linens kept insects away.

"The forks aren't on the ceiling, Lincoln," Shay said.

He grinned and rummaged through the drawers. She smacked his hand with the back of a fork when he tried to sneak a piece of crust.

"You caught me," he joked as he plated pie for each of them.

"It wasn't difficult. You did it right in front of my eyes."

He laughed. The fragrant smells of sweet potatoes, sugar, and a hint of cinnamon filled the entire kitchen.

"Do you have any whipped topping?"

"There's whipped cream in the refrigerator," she was saying. "Before you interrogate me, I didn't haul out the electric mixer and whip heavy cream and sugar. The whipped cream is store bought and sold in a plastic tube."

He sprayed a dollop of whipped cream on their pie slices, then carried plates, forks, and napkins into the living room.

She seated herself on the sofa and he sank down beside her. Any unease between them had evaporated while they'd joked, and he was grateful for her mood change.

Before she took a bite of pie, she bowed her head to offer a prayer of grace. He murmured the words with her.

Then he placed a napkin on his lap and she did the same. They both sampled and savored. The pie tasted similar to pumpkin, a bit creamier, and exactly how he remembered it. He told Shay as much.

"Are you still a churchgoer?" he asked.

She dabbed at her lips with a napkin. "I've been remiss of late, although I attended church service yesterday in Roses."

"I've been remiss too." He volunteered the information without her asking. "I missed the Christmas service because I was traveling. Truthfully, I haven't visited a church in a while. I've been busy." He set down his plate and held up a hand. "I know. Excuses, excuses."

"No use in tripping over how to justify it. Have confidence God will work it out. He always listens."

Religion was an integral part of Shay's life. She embraced her Christian belief and lived by conviction. In the spirit of harmony, her first reaction was one of faith.

She sat back. "I have to ask you something."

"Go ahead."

"Do you truly live on a houseboat?"

"Yes. It's docked at a marina on the far end of Hilton Head Island."

"Why?"

"Because the island is surrounded by water."

She laughed. "What I meant was, why live on a houseboat? It seems so … modest."

"My boat is 2000 square feet and more than adequate. The size is ideal. There's lots of glass and the views are magnificent." He took a sip of cider and placed the cup on the saucer. "You can't beat waking up and drinking coffee while looking out onto the Atlantic Ocean. The scenery is water and sky. Nothing beats it."

"Do you ever get seasick?"

"Good question. The boat sways now and again, though it's stable for the most part. The dock is my sidewalk."

She pushed out a sigh, as if living on a houseboat was the oddest idea ever.

"What's the name of your houseboat?"

He didn't reply.

"Can you go far with it?"

"My boat is moored and tethered to the land so I can access utilities. It's my home and not motorized. I'll take you to Hilton Head sometime if you'd like to see where I live."

"I can't commit." She gazed at him through lowered lashes. "I'm tied here until I sell the house. Plus, the wintry weather is unpredictable for travel."

"Hilton Head is only a few hours away, and Southern weather is typically mild."

He'd drive her to Hilton Head in the middle of a blizzard if it meant she'd actually accompany him to see his home.

Leave it to Shay to be practical, though. One thing at a time and the house was her top priority.

She was such a refreshing change from the glamorous women he'd dated in his twenties and early thirties, most notably his ex-wife. She'd never been satisfied, no matter how many sparkly necklaces and earrings he'd showered her with. And shoes. That woman adored expensive designer shoes. A gold digger was how his sister had described her. Boy, had Penny been spot-on.

"How fares the toy business these days?" Shay was asking.

He brushed his fingers over his neatly trimmed beard. "Busy." He rested his back against the sofa cushion, reflecting, relishing the glow of the fire. "We strive to ensure customer satisfaction, requiring our dedication and patience. Toys made with recycled materials cost more to construct than mass produced toys, and the demand isn't as high. Our marketing emphasizes that our toys are hand-me-downs for future generations."

"Spoken like a true businessman."

He chuckled. "In addition, we make wooden toys free of chemical risks, which our loyal consumers appreciate."

"Your toys are top-quality. The wooden rocking horses are pieces of art."

He gave a thumbs-up, though she didn't see him, because she'd glanced down to take another bite of pie. When she looked up at him, she said, "Your parents were adamant about focusing on quality. How are they?"

"Sadly, they're both deceased."

"I wasn't aware." Her voice softened. "Please accept my sincere condolences."

"Thank you. I'm sorry about your parents too. They died in Europe several years ago, correct?"

"Yes, within months of each other. First my father and then my mother three months later. How did you—" She arched a delicate eyebrow. "Oh, right. Granny probably wrote you."

"She did. She even referred to their deaths as the widowhood effect."

"Granny and I discussed that too. My parents were inseparable, and she swore that my mother died from a broken heart."

"I've read articles on the subject and broken heart syndrome is real." Unable to stop himself, Lincoln draped his arm around her and offered a tender squeeze of reassurance.

Duchess announced her presence and jumped on Shay's lap. She stroked the cat's head until the cat decided she'd had enough and went on to more exciting activities. Tail up, she strutted away and resumed her perch by the window.

Shay stared at the logs of wood popping and snapping in the fireplace. "Duchess has a lazy life," she murmured.

"I can see that."

"Your dog, Lucky, enjoyed a good life. He was seven years old when I met him."

"He was the best dog. Devoted and loyal and a wonderful companion. I could do no wrong in his eyes."

"That's the nature of man's best friend. Dogs love us unconditionally."

"He lived until the age of fifteen." Lincoln couldn't say more because he always choked up about losing Lucky.

"Your grief is valid," Shay said sincerely.

"Even after all these years? I haven't owned another dog since."

"You'll know if and when the time is right again."

They traded glances. She invariably sensed what to say to make him feel better. Tenderness was a part of her.

After giving him time to regroup, she said, "I remember family dinners at your house. I was unsure which fork or spoon to use. Why were there three utensils on each side of the dinner plate? And all the glassware, the endless courses—"

"I didn't notice."

"You were used to the formality. You lived there. I was uncomfortable."

"At every meal, your charisma and intelligence lit up the dining room."

She laughed. "Uh-huh. Right beneath the crystal chandelier."

He picked up his plate and polished off the pie, then set the empty plate on the tray. "You adapted like a pro. No one in my family ever mentioned your confusion."

She showed a small smile. "Are you sure? I felt so clumsy and that your father's expectations were impossible for me to attain."

"He never said a word to me."

All things considered, he would've recognized his father's disapproval by his discouraging, offhand remarks. Right? But then, he avoided meaningful conversations at all costs. Instead, he used more subtle tactics, such as an eyebrow shooting up at the dinner table. Nothing like that had ever happened.

And his mother went along with his father's decisions. They all did.

He'd informed them that Shay lived with her grandmother and they often struggled to make ends meet. Not everyone had the advantage of wealthy grandparents. Lincoln's paternal grandparents had given Lincoln's parents the funds to establish their toy business once it had gotten underway.

"You must have realized there was a tremendous economic difference between us," Shay said.

Her statement wasn't completely lost on him. Many folks in Roses regarded his family as upper class and, indeed, stuck-up. In a brief conversation with him, Shay's grandmother had once implied that although he and Shay were clearly in love, they might be better off with people who matched their life experiences.

A sigh escaped him. "My father expected everyone involved in the business to work nonstop to maintain the shop's success."

Shay busied herself with folding and refolding the napkin on her lap. "In the short time I worked there during the busy holiday season, I remember giving up my breaks in order to serve customers."

"Under my father's watchful eye, I bet?" Lincoln said.

She nodded. "Very much so."

Had his father worked Shay *too* hard before their break-up? Toys were a seasonal business, and December was their busiest month. Is that why she'd abruptly quit and disappeared from his life soon afterwards?

He picked up his cup and downed the last of his cider. "Pamela was never happy working in a toy—"

Shay's gaze narrowed. "Pamela?"

Grimacing, he scrubbed a hand over his face. He stopped himself from continuing and hoped Shay wouldn't pursue the subject of his ex-wife.

Judging from her expression, that wasn't going to happen.

"I thought your houseboat was ideal for one person," she noted.

"It is."

She shifted a few inches away from him. "Then who is Pamela?"

He crossed his legs at the ankles, then uncrossed them. "My ex-wife."

"Oh." She took in the information with a stiff nod, and he almost felt guilty, as if he'd cheated on her. As if he was supposed to miss Shay forever and never move on.

Which was exactly what had happened.

Her eyebrows furrowed, and she leaned forward. "Naturally, you have women in your past."

"Not many." He attempted a chuckle. "My father scared most of them off. His standards and beliefs were excessive."

The air topped with tension. "He was blatant about expressing his opinion about the women you dated?" she asked.

A flare of frustration went through him. "Very."

"Are there women in your present, also?"

"Shay—"

She tucked a strand of hair behind her ear. "Sorry. It's none of my business."

"Go ahead. Ask away." His heart caught at her apology.

She raised an eyebrow, and he answered her unspoken question. "I was married to

Pamela for less than eight months, divorced for years, never had children and currently not dating anyone."

She didn't speak. Instead, she blew out a shallow breath.

"What about you?" he prompted.

"I dated a guy for a while. His name was Brian. I was under the impression our relationship might get serious, though he told me in no uncertain terms that seeing two women at once was perfectly acceptable in his book. Maybe it was in his book, but it wasn't in mine. Obviously, we never married." She glanced at the fourth finger of her left hand as confirmation, then folded her arms in a defensive stance, as if she dared Lincoln to challenge her.

"I'd never date two women at once." He winked. "One is more than enough for any guy to handle."

She ran a hand along her jeans. "And vice versa. The thought of dating two guys at once makes my head explode."

"You're going to be an incredible mother."

"It's too late."

"No, it's not."

It's never too late, Shay. We're both in our thirties.

"Your grandmother was an amazing role model," he said. "She put everyone before herself, exactly like you do."

He met her gaze. He wished they could rewind the clock, though it wasn't possible. For now, he put their current moment on pause and visualized their future and a promise of optimism.

Her eyes dampened. She looked vulnerable, and he pushed back the inclination to enfold her in his arms and assure her that the universe was in harmony. He was here, and they were finally together again.

That might scare her away, though, and he vowed to take it slow. However, the realization she was as single as he was brought a gladness to his chest.

Brylcreem's loss, or whatever that guy's name was. Lincoln's gain.

"Why didn't a stunning woman like you ever get married?" he asked aloud.

She shrugged. "Busy."

There was a simpler answer. Brylcreem was an idiot.

"So, why are you looking at buying a house in Roses?" she asked.

"Long, sad story."

"I'm listening."

He gazed into her dark eyes, searching for genuine

compassion. He found it. Shay's grace and tenderness extended to others.

"Several of our employees lived in an apartment complex near the manufacturing facility on Hilton Head Island," he said. "A fire broke out on Thanksgiving Day and swept through the complex. Thankfully, no one was hurt." He shuddered at the memory of the alarming, devastating phone call he'd received.

"Was the building a complete loss?"

"Not totally. But while it was being repaired, our employees had to scramble to find places to stay. My sister and I found housing, but we were appalled at the few, affordable options available. Neither of us planned to be in the construction trade, but it made sense to take some of our capital and build our own apartments. And make a complex large enough to house other renters, thus enabling us to recoup our investment."

She studied his face. "So why purchase property here?"

"We're expanding our toy business by reopening the original shop in Roses."

"I hadn't heard any news about it."

"Penny and I decided only a few days ago."

Okay, it was a small lie. Actually, *he* had decided. Now he needed to persuade Penny to agree.

Shay managed a slight nod. "I appreciate what you're doing for your employees. However, throwing cinder block apartment buildings up on my grandmother's land will destroy the property's scenic beauty."

He hadn't intended to mislead her or Candee, though he saw no recourse other than to keep up the facade. True, he was looking for suitable housing for his employees. Then again, he hadn't thought his plan through. He'd hastily arranged to visit Roses after receiving Granny's letter.

I'm sorry, she'd written at the end of the letter.

Why had she felt the need to apologize? She had been the epitome of kindness. Moreover, her meaning wasn't clear. She never hand wrote anything, preferring to use her vintage black typewriter. All in all, her obvious regret had spurred him into action.

He hooked a leg over his knee. "Your land might be better utilized for affordable housing. In addition, may I point out that you're selling the house and land, anyway? You have no say or control over what a new owner will do with it."

She set her napkin down. "You'd need the town's permission to build apartments."

"I've already talked with members of the planning board. I'll have to submit a proposal but no one made any serious objections."

"You were able to reach people during the holidays?"

"I was in touch before the Christmas recess."

"About my house? A special phone call to the board about my house?"

"Among other issues."

"Money sure talks, Lincoln."

"I don't appreciate the insinuation, Shay. This isn't all about money. It's about good planning and a few simple phone calls."

She appeared to accept his reply, and he forged ahead. "When the board meets in January, my petition is the first item on the agenda."

"So you intend to buy my farmhouse?"

"I haven't decided for certain." He had, but she didn't need to know yet.

"Will you tear it down?"

"I haven't decided for certain," he repeated.

"Oh, but you have." Her back straightened. "From the sounds of it, you won't close until the second week of

January at the earliest. That is, if the board approves. However, your time frame isn't mine."

"Why are you in such a rush? You don't really want to sell the farmhouse, do you? This house means the world to you."

A castle in the sky. For her. For them both.

"What I want and what I need are entirely different, Lincoln."

He heard the resignation in her voice. Her sadness ran deep. This rambling house was her home.

He gripped her hand. "Shay, what can I do to help?"

"Sometimes I wonder if you're part of this world, Lincoln." She paused, seeming to consider his question. "Many people, normal, middle-class, working citizens, have financial concerns. You'll either need to buy my property before the new year, or I'll reject your bid altogether."

"Wait a minute. You're in charge now?"

"Absolutely." She sent him an offended look and shook off his hand. "It's my house."

"You're refusing to sell me a property I haven't even put in an offer on yet? Is that what you're suggesting?"

"Exactly."

He pushed off the sofa and stood. "Well, I won't be manipulated into buying your house."

They were arguing over an offer on her house, a house he intended to buy.

Shay might never forgive him when she learned the truth. She might accuse him of being a manipulator. A guy who planned their future to a fault.

An irritating voice inside his head chided, *Let's examine how far that planning has gotten you thus far.*

Despite his teenage plans, Shay had disappeared without a trace. He'd been too pushy, too bold, too vocal when he described their future. He'd scared her away.

This time, he wanted to do it his way and control the

situation. This time, he'd do whatever was in his power to reignite their lost love before she vanished again.

Still, what if he merely explained the main reason why he was here?

He came to Roses for her. Not for the toy business. Not for the farmhouse.

Her.

Call it providence, but Granny's letter had been the catalyst. If he missed this opportunity with Shay, he'd only have himself to blame.

He'd made up his mind. Explaining complicated the matter. He knew by Shay's

tentative smiles that she wasn't ready to resume their past relationship. Not yet. To date her again would take time, patience, and an extraordinary amount of wooing on his part.

Torn about what to say, what not to say, he collected their dishes onto the tray and carried the tray into the kitchen.

She fell into step beside him. "What are you doing?"

"I'm helping you clean up."

"I don't need any assistance."

"Of course you don't."

He placed the dishes in the sink and began running the water to wash them.

"I'm perfectly capable of washing my own dishes, Lincoln."

"Independent as always," he muttered. He pressed down the frustration welling in his chest. "Have a pleasant evening, Shay."

"You're leaving?"

He made his way into the living room and peered out the front window. "It's getting dark."

"It's been dark for an hour. What about Kwanzaa?"

"Some other time." Ludicrous. Kwanzaa celebrations didn't wait for Lincoln Reid.

He started for the doorway, but his feet refused to move. *What are you doing, Lincoln? This is the opposite of wooing her.* There went that irritating voice again—spouting an opinion when he hadn't asked for one.

Nope. No. No. If he stayed, he'd only antagonize the situation further.

Seizing on a kernel of truth, he turned to her. "I'm meeting my sister here in Roses tomorrow."

Shay caught up with him in the doorway. Her hand brushed his. "I thought you were on your way to see your sister in Virginia?"

That was the trouble with a lie. Once you started, it was difficult to dig yourself out. Why couldn't Shay be a little less sweet, a little less alluring? A little less astute? Then his hand wouldn't tingle each time their fingers touched. Then he wouldn't want to kiss her whenever he studied her tempting lips.

"There's a change of plans." He grabbed his coat and opened the door. "Thank you for the pie."

Tomorrow, he'd start anew. He'd phone her. He'd invite her to dinner. He'd explain why he was really here and suffer the consequences if she rejected him.

She once loved him as much as he loved her.

The key word was *once*.

He stepped outside. As the cool night air skimmed his cheeks, he encouraged himself. A new year. A fresh start. There was nothing like an exciting, promising beginning.

CHAPTER 5

The front door clicking shut was the only sound a minute later.

Shanice stood in the living room of her farmhouse, her hands on her hips, and glared at the door.

"Thank you for the pie?" Is that your polite way of ending the conversation, Lincoln?

The words tumbled over her. Her heart hammered.

She should've thrown the pie at him, then watched as he wiped whipped cream from his face, like those familiar TV sitcoms they'd enjoyed.

Black and white television instead of high-definition color TV—where the characters were likable, outcomes foreseeable and real peril non-existent.

She yearned for those days. Days spent with Lincoln, brimming with enthusiasm. In the evenings spent with Granny, they discussed topics ranging from their favorite foods to the latest best-selling books. Lincoln bought mystery novels and he teased her about her sweet romances.

Often, if someone didn't finish speaking their views within the first few minutes, Granny happily headed off the conversation with her own opinions. These cheery yesterdays. She remembered every image.

When would she be capable of shaking off the past? Nearly impossible now that Lincoln was in town.

She peered at the fruit, corn and candles on the bureau, resigned to the fact she'd light the first Kwanzaa candle alone tonight. The house felt empty without him, and the painful, overwhelming reality resonated that he was gone for good.

"No matter." She measured her words and steadied her voice. "I've celebrated Kwanzaa for fifteen years with Lincoln nowhere in sight."

But he was always in her mind, constantly in her thoughts.

"Sixteen years, Shay," he'd corrected her. "We haven't seen each other in sixteen years."

She drew a sharp breath. His scent, citrus and tangy, lingered in the air, enveloping her like a warm bear hug.

She collapsed on the sofa and patted the seat beside her when Duchess looked up from her perch. "Sit with me," she invited the cat.

Duchess debated, then complied in her usual haughty fashion.

THE FOLLOWING DAY, Candee confirmed another showing of the farmhouse at ten o'clock. After Shanice showered, she chose stretchy dark-washed jeans and a navy-blue sweatshirt with "Merry Christmas" embroidered on it.

She dropped off slices of the pie to the homeless shelter, then devoted the remaining morning hours to the local garden nursery. A few customers had already asked her to refresh their gardens come spring, and she wanted to get ideas. The ache in her hip and knee had eased, and she wandered comfortably from aisle to aisle, examining the plants, poring over their tags, taking notes.

Although the outdoor ground was cold and firm, within a few months, azaleas and tulips would be blooming and her landscaping business would pick up again.

She checked her cell phone from time to time, expecting to hear from Candee. Nevertheless, by lunchtime, she hadn't heard a word. Desperate for any news, she drove her truck to Candee's real estate office and parked at the curb.

The door was open and with a quick knock, Shanice stepped inside. Candee sat behind her desk with a cell phone attached to her ear. She waved and clicked off her phone.

"Hi, Shanice." Candee leaned back in her chair. "What's up?"

"How did the showing go this morning?" Shanice closed the door. "Have you heard anything?"

"The buyers are lovely."

"Lovely. Well, most people are lovely. What about Lincoln Reid?"

"Nothing from him."

Shanice quietly moaned. "I'm not surprised."

"Why do you say that?"

"We had an argument." At Candee's raised eyebrows, Shanice pulled up a chair and sat across from her. "Yesterday, he came by my house to return my cell phone, which I'd forgotten at Kathleen's Teahouse."

"I'm aware." Candee tossed Shanice a conspiratorial smile. "I left him no choice."

"You coerced him?"

"I wanted to encourage your relationship, and he was more than happy to oblige. I didn't realize you two shared such a romantic past."

"We did, once upon a time."

"And now?"

"And now we don't. When we were teens, we were foolishly in love."

"Why foolishly?"

"Our world was picture-perfect and carefree. Lincoln swept me off my feet. He was so handsome and witty."

"He still is."

"And we never fought," Shanice murmured.

"Good for you. Couples usually fight at least once in a while."

"Now that I think back, we weren't together long enough to fight. His father didn't seem thrilled with our relationship, although Lincoln and I found plenty of opportunities to spend time together. Lincoln Reid Senior and Lincoln Reid Junior were as different as night and day."

"And then?"

Shanice twisted, determined not to cry. "I realized we should go our separate ways."

"Who made you realize that?"

"His father."

"Lincoln had no say in the matter?" Candee asked.

"No, and history can't be changed." Realizing she wasn't going to win this dispute, Shanice took a firm grip on her reflections. She'd shared enough with her friend, she told herself.

An awkward silence followed.

Candee sat forward. "Love happens at any age. Perfect love doesn't exist, but if you two give yourselves another chance, things may turn out different." Candee was obviously intrigued by the subject of romance. "He couldn't take his eyes off you at Kathleen's. He's besotted with you."

"Our past is ancient history, and your imagination is astounding." Shanice went over the last minutes with Lincoln at her house and scratched her temple. Surely Candee was mistaken.

"Don't you believe in second chances?" Candee asked.

"Hardly. A couple hours after he arrived, we got into an argument."

"You said you two never argued."

"Now we do."

"Hmm. He stayed at your house for a couple of hours?"

"We played checkers and ate pie."

Candee's gaze grew shrewd, her smile significant. "Don't stop now."

Reluctantly, Shanice smiled back. She scraped her thoughts for any tidbit of information to satisfy her inquisitive and entirely too starry-eyed friend.

"Obviously, the argument wasn't professional on my part," Shanice said. "As you might imagine, the disagreement centered around my house."

"Why?"

"He said he's meeting with the town planning board about building apartments on my property. I told him if he decided to make an offer on the house, it would need to be made before January first."

"He made an offer?" There was no missing Candee's narrowed stare. As Lincoln's Realtor, this announcement came as an unwelcome surprise.

"No." Shanice offered a hasty reassurance. "I said if he *decided* to make an offer."

"You issued him an ultimatum on a non-offer?"

Shanice raked her hair from her face. "I have to sell the house before January first in order to secure the funds to pay my business loan."

"I'm fully informed regarding your situation. Is he?"

"I'd never divulge such information. It's too personal."

Plus, she'd sound pitiable.

"You've declined other offers." Candee allowed her statement to hang out in the open. "You can't be picky much longer."

"Without a firm and fair offer, I have no choice. At the peril of losing my business, I didn't *want* to turn the offers down. I *needed* to turn them down."

"I realize you're in a financial predicament." Candee's worried expression revealed her concern. "Did you and Lincoln resolve the argument?"

"Considering he grabbed his coat and walked out, I'd say no. He's my best prospect for a quick sale, although I'm fairly certain he's no longer interested."

"There are other buyers." Candee came to her feet and picked up a candy bar and two bottles of water from a shelf. "As I mentioned, this morning's showing went well."

Relief coursed through Shanice. "Go on."

"The couple is young. They have a one-year-old with another baby on the way. They want a country property where their family has room to grow. In spite of this, they're daunted by the amount of renovation and upkeep your house requires, and uncertain whether they can meet the asking price."

Shanice nodded. She understood.

"I admit, Shanice, I'm surprised."

Shanice quirked an eyebrow. "By my asking price?"

"No. I priced your house, and it's fair, bearing in mind the home's size and acreage. I'm surprised you argued with Lincoln." Candee reclaimed her seat and placed the candy and water between them. "That isn't like you, especially considering your history together."

Shanice gave a self-depreciating laugh. "My never-ending cash woes are worrisome."

Candee handed her a bottle of water. "Maybe you quarreled because he unsettles you."

"With good reason, considering he's opinionated and overbearing."

"In the short time I've known him, I found him gracious and considerate." Candee split the candy bar and offered Shanice half. "Have you eaten lunch yet?"

Shanice declined the candy. "I'll fix soup and a sandwich when I get home. Water is fine."

"Water isn't enough."

"I'll be home within the hour."

Candee grabbed her cell phone and quickly sent a text, ignoring Shanice's quizzical stare. Then she treated herself to the candy. "You haven't devoted much time to dating anyone since your breakup with Brian."

Shanice sat back. Clearly, their conversation wasn't over. "There's no place in town to meet men and I don't patronize bars."

"There are church and social groups." Candee's observation sounded like a criticism, as if Shanice wasn't trying hard enough.

"I joined the dating website you recommended."

"How's it going?"

Shanice uncapped her water bottle. "It's not."

In the end, Brian had broken things off. Just like her parents did when they went off to study the latest earth process—an earthquake or volcanic eruption. They chose their professions instead of their daughter. Without her grandmother, Shay might have been forced to raise herself.

Candee grabbed the candy bar and leisurely chewed. "On the other hand, Lincoln is an attractive and eligible man."

"*Attractive* has nothing to do with my romantic interests. He's not my type."

Talk about a statement that wasn't true. With his strong, angular features and mesmerizing blue eyes, Lincoln was incredible. He was every woman's type.

"You two share a past." Candee fairly twinkled with excitement. "Maybe you're both being granted a second chance at love."

The fact that Shanice didn't argue encouraged Candee to press her point. She took three gulps of water, then leaned forward. "I assume he's quite wealthy."

"Believe me, wealth is a hindrance." Rather than surrender to more reasons and rationale, Shanice concluded, "Besides, men aren't on my radar at the moment."

That was partly true. She was focused on her business right now. But she fantasized about having a household, nurturing her children, and a devoted, loving husband. The commitment of marriage was the basis of a family unit. She wanted real love, true love, as her parents had, the way her grandmother had loved her husbands.

"Yet," Candee corrected. "Men aren't on your radar *yet*."

"I'm committed to getting back on my feet financially and growing my landscaping business."

"Growing?" Candee smirked. "Pun intended?"

Shanice bit back a smile. "Let's just say I have no room in my life for love. Not with Lincoln, not with anyone."

A knock on Candee's office door prompted Shanice to turn, although Candee was quickly up and opening the door. Her delighted smile beamed. "Hi, Lincoln! Please come in."

"I'm early for our appointment," Lincoln said as she showed him inside.

"Actually, you're right on time."

Shanice choked on a disbelieving laugh. Had Candee purposefully been delaying her until Lincoln showed up?

"I wanted to talk with you about the property I'm—" He broke off, seeming to just notice Shanice, and greeted her with a blend of cordiality and eagerness.

"How are you feeling?" His gaze searched hers, as if he attempted to assess her reaction to seeing him again.

He shrugged off his jacket, and the creamy cotton fabric of his vee neck shirt stretched over his commanding shoulders and revealed every contour of his muscular forearms. He was all chiseled jaw and rugged angles, and entirely too masculine.

"Better, thanks." She tamped down the curious burst of elation in her heart, and turned away to drink from her water bottle.

"Oh, my!" Candee inspected her watch and slapped a palm to her forehead. "I have another showing at a bungalow in town in five minutes. I forgot all about it."

"You do?" Lincoln blinked, and Shanice almost spit out her water.

Candee reached for her coat, seeming to take great effort in keeping her face straight. "The showing slipped my mind."

Candee forget a showing? Shanice had to smile. Candee was prompt and punctual to a fault.

Shanice stood. "I'm leaving too."

"Everyone's leaving?" Lincoln cut his gaze to Shanice and a lazy white grin appeared.

She tried to counter with a clever comeback, but nothing came to mind.

"I'll call you later," Candee said to Lincoln.

"Much appreciated." He kept his grin and focused on Shanice. "I need to talk to Kathleen about final arrangements for my New Year's Eve party. Can you direct me to her teahouse? I walked here from my hotel."

"Where are you staying?" she asked.

"The Roses Hotel."

"Oh." Candee frowned. "How are the accommodations? The owners are hardly ever around."

"The rooms are okay, a polite way of saying the hotel is screaming for an update. The baseboards and picture frames look as if they haven't been dusted in over a year." He provided a short laugh. "Correction. The owners are *never* around."

"Keep on walking, Lincoln." Shanice shouldered past him. "Kathleen's Teahouse is a mere two blocks away."

"I've gotta run or I'll be late." Candee glanced at Shanice, probably gauging how she was processing the situation. "Luckily, Shanice will show you, won't you, Shanice? You can walk Lincoln to the teahouse."

"I drove here," Shanice replied. "My truck is parked outside."

"Even better. You can drive him. You haven't eaten, and I bet Lincoln hasn't, either."

"I already—" Lincoln gave Candee an odd look, before awareness dawned in his eyes. "You read my mind. I'm starving."

At the risk of charging them both with conspiring to force her and Lincoln together, Shanice eyed them with veiled amusement. Whatever their strategy, she wasn't buying. She'd refuse any invitation Lincoln might extend.

She followed Candee out the door with Lincoln on her heels. Did she imagine he lightly placed his hand on her elbow to steer her toward her truck?

When Candee was out of sight, Shanice whirled on him. "Is there any chance you recognized my truck while taking your stroll?"

His grin was positively boyish. "Maybe." He opened the driver's door for her. Once she slid inside, he strode around to the passenger side with a decided spring in his step and settled beside her.

"Don't you dare raise your hands and say *busted*," she said.

His response was another grin.

"Will you join me for lunch?" he asked once she found a parking space near the teahouse.

"Sorry, I can't stay."

"A pity." His insightful blue eyes regarded her. "Kathleen's specialty is Irish coffee, and I've heard the sandwich of the day is delicious."

Her stomach growled loud enough for him to hear. "What is the sandwich of the day?"

"I have no idea." He was already out of the truck and had her door open before she'd unbuckled her seatbelt. "I hope you'll join me."

"I can't." He frowned at her emphatic rejection. She drew a fortifying breath and firmly explained, "The last time we ate together—"

"Didn't turn out well. Fortunately, I have a solution."

She let the truck's engine idle. "Our discussions lead to an argument, Lincoln."

He leaned against the half-open door. "Only when we talk about real estate. So, we won't."

"What will we talk about?"

"Let's concentrate on the present."

And our future. He didn't say the words, yet they hung in the air between them.

Relenting, Shanice shut off the engine and agreed. So much for her refusal. Besides, after early morning devotions, her quick breakfast had consisted of a cup of yogurt and a mug of strong coffee. "What's our first topic?"

"Toys. The ideal subject for the holidays." He provided an easy smile. "Would you like to hear more about my business expansion and getting back to my New Beginnings roots here in Roses?"

His persuasive question had her laughing out loud. "Sure."

"Then let's go inside."

"I can't stay long. I planned on stopping at the Festival of Trees."

"The trees have all been claimed."

His remark surprised her, and she cocked her head. "You're an expert on the Festival of Trees?"

"This year I am." Casually, he placed a hand on the small of her back and opened the teahouse door for her. "After you."

He'd always done that. Opened doors for her and insisted she enter first.

The heavy aroma of coffee filled the air as he waved a greeting at Kathleen. The red-haired waitress was also there, and she sent him a broad smile of acknowledgement that Lincoln politely reciprocated.

Afterward, Shanice would recall that he'd never replied to her question about the Festival of Trees.

"I also plan to stop at the thrift store this afternoon for a pair of gloves," she said, after she and Lincoln were seated at an intimate table in the corner.

Before Lincoln could respond, Kathleen came over. The two of them discussed last-minute party plans, and then she smiled at them both and headed back to the kitchen.

Lincoln turned to Shanice. "I've never shopped at a thrift store."

"Because you shop in fancy stores."

He gave a throaty laugh. "Actually, whatever I need, I purchase online."

"I don't do well in huge department stores."

"Can I go with you to the thrift store?"

"Fair warning. You're in for an exciting adventure."

He opened a menu. "Lunch first?"

"Of course."

"My treat."

Her pride kicked in. "I can pay for myself."

"It's the least I can do to repay you for driving me here."

She raised an eyebrow. "Two blocks?"

He gave her hand a gentle squeeze. "I appreciate you,

Shay. You're friendly and giving, and you've always been my girl." He leaned across the table and brushed a gentle kiss on her cheek. His fingers lingered, tightening around her hand.

Her face grew hot. *His girl?*

And who knew a sweet, unexpected kiss could raise such a tumult of emotions? She'd responded immediately to his touch. Good thing she was sitting, because otherwise her legs might have given way, sending her tumbling to the floor.

LINCOLN RECIPROCATED Shay's smile with one of his own, and then sat back in his seat and stared at her.

Her eyes sparkled. Vivid, animated and full of perception. Their rich brown color reminded him of deep, lush velvet, offset by inky-black eyebrows. Wow, she was gorgeous.

Reluctantly, he released her hand. Years ago, she'd captivated him. She still did. Her dark-lashed gaze examined him with wariness, though he also read desire.

What was she thinking when he kissed her? Attraction? Denial?

When they were in their teens, he'd considered proposing. He was impossibly drawn to her. She was a beacon of light, and he couldn't lose her again.

She broke eye contact and remarked on the upbeat shamrock-green paint accenting the walls. They both chuckled at the tiny Santa-like leprechauns that served as salt and pepper shakers.

Once they had deliberated over the menu and ordered their sandwiches and coffees, a basket of complimentary Irish soda bread was provided. Shay bowed her head to say grace. He murmured the prayer with her.

She focused on the sandwich, a toastie, which Kathleen described as an Irish specialty. A toasted sandwich featuring two slices of bread stuffed with cheese, lettuce, tomato and sliced meat. He opted for ham and Shanice chose the same.

"Tell me more about your toy company," she prompted.

He dragged his gaze from her entrancing face and took a bite of his sandwich. "I share ownership with my sister, Penny. If you recall, she lives in Virginia, although our manufacturing plant and headquarters are located on Hilton Head Island."

"Speaking of Penny, where is she? Wasn't she headed to Roses today?"

"Right." He avoided her stare and shifted in his seat.

Shay was intelligent and resourceful, and she seldom forgot anything.

After a restless night's sleep, he'd decided he needed more time courting her before his boisterous sister appeared on the scene. He'd phoned Penny and requested she and her family delay their trip. Thanks to Candee's brief text, lunching with Shay was the ideal opportunity to begin another day in Roses.

"Penny and my nephew are heading here tomorrow instead," he replied.

"Is her husband coming too?"

"He was called out of town for a work project. He should be here for New Year's." The explanations for Penny's husband's frequent disappearances were not at all to Lincoln's liking, though he decided not to interfere. In fact, the state of their marriage depressed him. That wasn't the way a marriage was supposed to be.

He drained his coffee. "I'm convinced that Roses is the best place for our shop's growth," he continued. "Now I need to convince Penny."

"I was under the impression your expansion in Roses was a done deal."

"I'm only half of the decision-making process."

Shay's forehead creased in thought. "Roses was once Penny's home as well."

"Until she moved to Virginia after college graduation and settled there with her husband. Naturally, she prefers any new business development to take place in her city."

"Weigh the benefits of both locations, Lincoln. Roses versus Virginia."

"Exactly my sentiments."

Despite his casual manner, he had seriously weighed the pros and cons. The pros were that Shay lived in Roses … at least for now. He couldn't see any con, except possibly his sister's objections.

He stole another admiring glance at Shay's profile as she swung around to wave hello to Rob. Today, she had a particularly engaging smile. He hoped she was enjoying their lunch.

"My sister and her son will also stay at the Roses Hotel when they arrive here," he said.

"I remember when the hotel was the grand dame of Roses." Shay tossed him a jaunty grin. "As you noted, the place now needs a major overhaul."

"To put it mildly." He gave a laugh at her summation of the run-down building, then lapsed into contemplation. Feasibly, the hotel was another option for employee housing. Was the hotel for sale? He hadn't met the owners and would ask Candee to do some digging.

"How long are you planning on staying in Roses, Lincoln?" Shay smiled at the waitress refilling their water glasses, then turned her attention back to him.

He was about to take another bite of his toastie. Her question took him by surprise and the toastie hung in midair. "I haven't decided. At least until after New Year's."

"And then?"

"And then … we'll see."

"Is this conversation shifting to real estate?"

The smile she granted was generous and teasing, filled with a promise he might be imagining. But then again, maybe not. He warned himself that she didn't intend to entrance him with her melting gaze, it just happened naturally. Furthermore, the teahouse was an inappropriate place to take her in his arms and kiss her.

He switched the conversation to a safer subject.

"What have you been doing all these years?" he asked. "Any landscaping adventures?"

"I'd hardly call them adventures."

Though soon, she began regaling him with entertaining stories, especially about clients who spent outrageous amounts of money on their front lawns and gardens to outdo their neighbors.

"I had an eighty-year-old client who walked with a limp. Everyone worried about him—his friends, his family. Everyone." Shay nibbled on her sandwich. "Whenever I showed up to mow his lawn, I rang the doorbell first. One afternoon, he didn't answer and his door was locked. I peeked in the windows and didn't see him anywhere. I remembered I had passed an ambulance on the way over and began to worry."

"Please don't say he died."

She wiped her lips on her napkin. "On the contrary, he was alive and fit. He'd gone down the street to assist the paramedics. Afterward, he gave me a speech that everyone needed to stop fussing over him. He was a healthy, self-reliant senior citizen who could fend for himself."

Her laughter was infectious, and Lincoln laughed with her.

"All's well that ends well," he replied.

Her expression changed, becoming more serious. She glanced at the half-eaten sandwich on her plate. "Are you referring to us?"

"Did we end well?"

"I don't know. I—"

At her frown, he chided himself for his insinuation, reminding himself it was too soon. "If it sets your mind at ease, I was referring to the toy shop."

He was lying outright. He assured himself this was for her benefit, so as not to scare her off. The smile dawning on her lovely face was his reward.

She helped herself to another cup of coffee when the waitress came round. "I want to know more about your business."

He told himself this was a milestone already, just being with her.

However, this conversation was a mistake. He couldn't concentrate on anything but her. She was poise and grace personified and he couldn't focus on business when he was with her.

"From my parents, I learned that innovation and diligence are the keys to success," he finally replied.

"Sound advice."

"What about you? What did you learn from your parents?"

Her spine straightened. "I learned reliance."

"Reliance on your parents?" He'd never met her parents. He'd learned from Shay's grandmother that they were gone for months on end, often in Europe. They were geologists.

"Hardly. They were never around." Shay's lips tightened, confirming his suspicions. "I relied on myself because no one else could be trusted. That is, no one except Granny."

He read the disappointment in her expression, the grief over the woman who had offered a solid rock of insight and a firm foundation. No one beat Granny's wisdom.

He curved his fingers around hers. "I'm sorry."

"Don't be." Sadness shone in her eyes, though she held her head high. "Worthy life lessons are oftentimes difficult."

"From my perspective, not trusting others sounds mighty lonely."

Before she responded, Kathleen dashed over. "Lincoln, before I forget, Rob and I were going over more details for your New Year's party, and an Irish flair might be fun. Plus, your suggestion for a silent auction is excellent, especially the grand prize."

"Which is?" Shay asked.

"His shop's famous wooden rocking horse."

Lincoln chuckled. "Famous?"

"I looked it up on your website," Kathleen said. "The rocking horse will command a minimum bid of at least ten thousand dollars."

"I'm donating the proceeds to the local charities," he said.

"Thank you. You've already donated a truckload of toys. Your generosity is appreciated."

"My pleasure. Christmas is a time for children."

"For children of all ages." Shay clasped her hands. "I wasn't aware you gave so generously to our community, Lincoln."

He grinned. "Only wooden rocking horses."

"Don't lie."

"Okay."

"Do you carve the horses yourself?" she asked.

He sat back. "I'm still learning."

"Still? After all these years?"

"It's an art to shape a block of wood into something."

"That's what you used to say all the time when you were learning the woodworking trade. What type of wood do you use again?"

"Butternut has an excellent grain. The color is light, and the wood carves easily. In addition, it polishes up beautifully.

Basswood and pine are excellent choices too. Depends on the grain and the knots in the wood. The secret to carving is to peel back the layers."

"Sounds like the secret to life."

He shrugged. "Perhaps it is."

She picked up her coffee cup. "Do you hide all your good deeds, Lincoln?"

In a playful motion, he placed his hand on his heart. "Always."

"The invite list for your party is twenty people, correct?" Kathleen, who had patiently waited on the sidelines, hopped in.

"Yes," he replied. "Including my sister, her family, and several employees from our Hilton Head location." He gazed at Shay. "Regrettably, I don't have a date."

"How calamitous."

"Are you available?"

Her eyes grew wide. "Me?"

"Do you two want dessert?" Kathleen inquired, successfully changing the subject. "Our specialty today is bread pudding with butterscotch sauce."

"Bread pudding is my favorite." Shay pressed a hand to her stomach. "Sadly, I can't eat another bite."

"You only ate half your sandwich," Lincoln pointed out.

"Do you want the other half?"

"Absolutely." He gave an outrageous smile.

"This is my hint to disappear." Kathleen scooped up a handful of menus from a nearby table. "Here's to an Irish goodbye."

After she scurried away, Shay asked him, "What's an Irish good-bye?"

"I'm guessing it's a way to exit an awkward conversation." She laughed, and he leaned forward, grazing his thumb along her palm. "Well?"

"Well, what?" She studied her watch. "I didn't realize how late it is. The thrift store closes at four o'clock."

She'd skipped over his New Year's invitation, but he went along with her.

"Two hours is plenty of time to find a pair of gloves," he said.

She chuckled. "A proper thrift-store hunt takes patience and stamina."

"For gloves?"

"Thrifting is a sport. I can easily spend hours in a thrift store."

"I've never spent more than two minutes buying gloves."

"Be prepared to rummage through racks and piles of clothes."

"For a pair of gloves?" he repeated.

"Consider this a warning. The process is exhausting."

"Are you trying to talk me out of going with you?"

"I wouldn't dream of it after you've treated me to such a delicious lunch."

"I'll make a deal." His throat thickened with emotion. "I'll accompany you if you'll be my date for the party."

"I don't usually go out on New Year's Eve. All the venues are too busy and I don't drink."

"Me, neither. However, this is a special occasion."

"Why?"

"Because we've known each other a long time." *Because I'm still in love with you.*

He caught a glimpse of her anxious features, forced that thought away, and kept his tone low and casual. "Decided?"

"You're bargaining with me? I didn't ask you to accompany me to the store. You invited yourself."

"I did?"

"I think so." She paused. "Considering you might be

purchasing my farmhouse, being your date at the party isn't at all appropriate."

"We vowed not to bring up the R word."

"What R word?"

"Real estate."

Her eyes flashed with humor. "Real estate is two words."

"Not if you say them fast."

She laughed. "I'll keep you posted about New Year's."

CHAPTER 6

$\mathcal{E}$arly the following morning, Shanice took a relaxing soak in her antique clawfoot bathtub. She was relieved that the muscle soreness in her knee and hip had subsided. Based on her health history, she healed quickly.

After her bath, she dressed in casual jeans and a green fleece sweatshirt, then padded downstairs barefoot. There, she slipped into her cozy faux-leopard slippers.

For much of the morning, she found herself staring into space. Mentally, she reprimanded herself because she should have accomplished something. Anything.

There were dishes to wash, laundry, and a myriad of outdoor chores calling for attention. Nevertheless, all she achieved was landing on the living room sofa with her cat and immersing herself in her latest sweet romance e-book. She swore she'd only read a couple of chapters. But soon, she was in the thick of the scene where the hero and heroine first kiss, and two hours flew by.

She rooted for the heroine's optimistic, capable nature to prevail, and counted on the hero's affection and undeniable interest. If only they'd recognize their stubbornness and realize they were made for each other.

With a dreamy sigh, Shanice roused herself and clicked out of the e-reader, then stared at the blank screen. What woman wouldn't want to hear the voice of the man she loved, his reassurance she was safe, and share precious smiles with him?

She closed her eyes and lost herself in images of Lincoln. He was a hero in every sense of the word. He was genuine, a man of conviction, determined to have a shake at creating a perfect world. He was helpful and creative, playful and humorous. He liked to laugh. He liked to make other people laugh.

Furthermore, he shared her values of family and faith.

Okay, the circumstances of their romance hadn't been ideal at first. They had been young and inexperienced and torn apart by his judgmental father.

Yet, an attraction she couldn't deny had held steadfast.

She set her e-reader on the coffee table and wandered to the kitchen. As she washed the breakfast dishes, she contemplated the two wooden rocking chairs on the porch. The chairs had withstood the passing of years and all kinds of weather, yet they stayed intact and sturdy, carrying a wealth of memories.

Just like her.

Just like Lincoln.

Since taking ownership of Granny's house, Shanice hadn't sat in the chairs. The remembrances were too vivid.

Even so, they shot through her mind with stunning clarity.

At the age of nineteen, Lincoln had stood on the front porch on a sunny October afternoon, intent on carving their initials on the back of one of the chairs. He'd been wearing jeans and a gray T-shirt that defined the muscles in his arms, and his freckled face had been tanned from hours of laboring in the sun for Habitat for Humanity.

Their conversation on that calm, crisp day still rang in her ears.

With a satisfied expression, he'd set down his carving knife and grinned at her, inviting her to look.

L.R. loves *S.W.* had been enclosed with a heart.

"You're extraordinarily talented." Her gaze dropped to the chair. "Soon, you'll become a master carver."

"Thank you. Your compliments mean a lot to me." He skimmed a kiss along her temple. "What better way to hone my skills as a creative than carving initials?"

"What about your writing? You never let me even peek at any of your books."

"I write for my own enjoyment. And they're manuscripts, not books."

"Which means?"

"They're not published and in the early draft stages. They're short books, not long novels."

"When do you write?"

"Late at night when I can't sleep."

She hesitated, digesting the information. "And in your spare time, you're learning how to carve toys out of wood?"

"Whenever I can, I work outside the shop in a side yard with a skilled carpenter. As you can imagine, dust goes everywhere."

"Congratulations on learning a remarkable trade."

"I'm not learning as quickly as my father would like." Lincoln reacted with a ragged sigh. "Hand carving toys is a slow, laborious process."

She pondered that. "New Beginnings doesn't hand carve all their toys, do they?"

He stroked his fingers across their initials. "Electricity

and machines are our friends, although hand-carved rocking horses are our biggest seller."

At his invitation, she sat in the rocker and he took the chair beside her.

Slowly, she rocked. "Children love rocking horses," she mused.

"I love children." He offered a broad smile. Affection shown from his brilliant blue eyes and promised her the world.

She heartily matched his enthusiasm. "Me too."

He stood, grabbed her hands, and drew her to her feet. "Someday, I'll carve a rocking horse for our kids. We can paint it white or brown, pink or blue, or whatever color they choose. By then, I should be an expert."

"Kids? As in, more than one?"

"Indeed." His smile was a tad wicked and her heart leapt in her chest. "After we're married, I want six children."

"Six?" She rolled her eyes. "How about we'll see how it goes?"

"How about we seal the deal with a kiss?"

"I didn't say it was a deal."

"I'll try to persuade you." He caught her chin and held her for a long kiss. He was solid and male; and when he hugged her, the sensation of his powerful chest against her cheek, the firm assurance of his arms, promised her that their love was a forever love.

When he released her, he stood back, his hands trailing to her sides. Then he pointed to their carved initials with unhidden pride. A testament to their affection, he proclaimed with a dramatic flourish.

The memories faded, and Shanice shook her head.

How quickly events had changed. A few short months afterward, their relationship would end, and the storybook finale they envisioned would be extinguished.

She peeked at the avocado-green wall clock in the kitchen. Less than twenty-four hours earlier, she'd been with Lincoln, so she couldn't possibly be missing him. Nonetheless, any day without him seemed infinitely long.

She wiped her hands on a kitchen towel and checked her cell phone. He hadn't called or texted.

Shaking off thoughts of him, she returned to the living room and sat at her computer to review her customers' overdue invoices. Several had paid. Several more still had not.

With a groan, she buried her face in her hands. Through her fingers, she squinted at the Kwanzaa candles set on the bureau. The night before, she'd lit the red candle to honor self-determination. Red represented expressing yourself and creating. She'd elected to use the mindset in a positive way and enrolled in an online training program to further her expertise in landscape design. Education was a never-ending learning process and fed her innovation.

Out of pure habit, she switched on the radio to a contemporary station and sang the opening bars of *Believe,* with Josh Groban. The ballad was from *Polar Express,* which was a top pick for holiday viewing. She'd watched the movie alone on Christmas Eve.

As she clicked through the invoices, her singing trailed off when she reached her own outstanding invoice. She didn't have the funds to pay the five hundred dollars she'd charged in November for landscaping supplies. Why hadn't she anticipated the financial crisis she would face during the slow winter season and planned ahead? She should've put Granny's house up for sale sooner, though she'd held out hope that an opportunity would surface—a last-minute solution to save her beloved farmhouse.

In the end, no magic solution had appeared.

She forced the disheartening thought away and singled

out an unpaid invoice from a long-standing customer. That particular client usually paid promptly, but the husband had recently been laid off from his factory job. In good conscience, how could Shanice send them a second notice—especially right after Christmas?

Unsettled, she closed her computer and focused on cheerier events—beginning with her recent outing with Lincoln.

She'd expected him to duck out of the thrift store after a few minutes with the excuse he had business to attend to. She hadn't expected the mischievous twitch of his lips as he scoured the store shelves and piled one treasure after another into his cart.

She smirked at the number of high-fives he'd extended with each find. He'd spent a long while considering castoff paintings and glassware, and rummaged through bins while complaining about the low quality of plastic toys.

After that, she lost track of time while she hunted through stacks of gloves. When he rejoined her, he crouched beside her to survey the five pairs she'd spread on the floor.

"Have you finally come to a decision?" he asked.

"I can't decide between the black or brown gloves," she replied. "Fortunately, I've narrowed it down."

"Let's place the green, blue and purple gloves here." He scooped up the gloves and set them on top of his overflowing cart. "What's the price for the others?"

"Three dollars. They cost more because they're new. The original price tag is attached and they retail for twenty dollars each."

"I'll make the choice easy for you." She smiled at the humor in his tone. "You purchase one pair, and I'll buy the other pair for you."

"You spent too much money on me already," she protested.

"A toastie and a cup of coffee? I insist on splurging today. Besides, the pleasure is all mine."

He took her hand and led her to a jewelry display case, where he pointed at a vintage ruby-red and emerald-green gemstone necklace. "Do you like it?" he asked.

"It's beautiful."

"I'd like to buy you something for Christmas."

"Lincoln, there's no need, and Christmas has passed."

"Please." He summoned a clerk to fetch the necklace from the case, checked the solid clasp, and held the necklace up for Shanice to appreciate. A ruby stone had come loose. The clerk assured the stone could easily be glued back, then excused herself, saying she needed to check with the manager about the necklace. Returning, she explained that the necklace was a one of a kind piece and an heirloom.

Necklace in hand, Lincoln spun to Shanice with an expectant smile. "Well?"

"Aren't you going to ask how much it costs?"

He surveyed her as if she was the most remarkable woman in the store. "Nope."

How could she refuse his kindness and generosity? How could she refuse *him*?

Nearby, conversations from customers broke off, and several people stared at them.

Shanice glanced at the clerk, then back at Lincoln, and uttered the first words that came to mind. "Thank you."

"I'm glad you approve." Lincoln paid for the necklace, the five pairs of gloves, and all the items in his cart, which included used textbooks, a snow globe, a paint-by-number piece of artwork, and a wooden tray.

She surveyed his armload of bags as they exited the store. "What on earth do you possibly want with all those items?"

"I'm preparing for the holidays."

"Christmas has passed," she reminded.

"Why cram all that happiness into one day when there's more to celebrate?"

"Like what?"

"Like you and me. Here. Together in our hometown sharing the best season of the year." He set down the bags and enveloped her in his arms. "May I put in a request?"

She twined her fingers around his neck and fingered the fine dark hairs at his nape. "After your generosity this afternoon, I can hardly refuse."

He kissed her cheek. "Please wear the necklace to my New Year's party."

She tried to pull back. After all, they were kissing in full view of anyone who passed on the public street.

His lips reclaimed hers, his mouth steady and warm, and her protests disappeared.

"I didn't say for certain whether I was attending," she murmured between kisses.

Every minute she was with him, he was ever more appealing. She tried to draw back a second time, but then decided … no. She wanted him to continue kissing her, and there was little use in denying it.

Lincoln broke the kiss. "Will you attend my New Year's party?" His blue eyes sparkled down at her.

"Do I have a choice?" She didn't, considering her balance was unstable and she was clinging to his arms.

"The choice is always yours, Shay."

She searched his face for any hint of teasing and saw only sincerity and guarded hope. Her response was an unabashed smile. She'd wear her red crepe sheath dress—slim-fitting and ideal for the festive occasion. On a whim, she'd purchased the dress at a bargain price and never had the opportunity to show it off.

"In truth, I'm looking forward to the party," she said. "I love Kathleen's Teahouse."

More significant, she was beginning to realize more and more that she loved *him.*

Afterward, she'd driven him to the Roses Hotel. They'd exchanged a giggle at the condition of the neglected lobby and the cobwebs dangling from the ceiling.

Several more kisses ensued.

"I'll call you tomorrow," Lincoln promised. He enfolded her in a huge hug and declared she was the best of everything in his life. She believed him because his gaze was so earnest, his voice so romantic, that a shiver of delight crept up her spine. Going forward, she had a good feeling about where their relationship was headed. Her heart filled with hope.

She cordoned off her thoughts, and returned to the present. The clock showed past noon and she hadn't received any messages from him. But then she remembered his sister was driving in with her son from Virginia, and he was probably too busy to phone.

Surely he would soon.

Without warning, a curious sense of uneasiness troubled her, though she couldn't pinpoint the reason. She wasn't lonely or tired.

Money worries, she supposed.

Or was it more?

Because as surely as the sun rose each morning, she missed Lincoln.

As the afternoon wore on, Shanice headed to the greenhouse on the edge of her property. The snow had melted, and the walkway was lined with fragrant evergreen trees and brilliant-red holly berries.

She'd built the greenhouse a decade earlier—constructed out of plastic on a stark frame and designed to maximize natural light. She'd invested in an extensive variety of popular annuals to replant in her customers' flower beds in the spring. Cheaper to grow plants herself rather than purchasing from a garden center.

Upon entering the greenhouse, she immersed herself in the feel and aroma of the fertile soil, the sultry mugginess, and the satisfaction of bringing precious plants to life. She switched on her cell phone to her favorite music playlist, and Whitney Houston's lyrical voice began singing, "Do You Hear What I Hear?"

"'Said the shepherd boy,'" she sang along. She attempted not to think about her property and prospective buyers and house showings that resulted in minimal offers.

And so, her mind gravitated to Lincoln—his good-looking face, his linebacker shoulders, the dimple on his strong chin.

"He always liked flowers," she said aloud. All those years ago, he'd admired the various flowers she'd planted in front of numerous Habitat for Humanity houses.

She grabbed a packet of seeds and a terra cotta pot, intending to plant impatiens next.

"Shanice?" Lincoln's deep voice flooded her senses.

She dropped the packet and pot with a clatter and sent him an exasperated look as he entered the greenhouse.

"Lincoln, why do you always do that?"

He swung her into his arms for a slow dance, a teasing rendition of a tango, his black leather boots shuffling along the dirt floor.

Gracefully, he whirled her around. "Do what?"

A greenhouse wasn't her first choice in the world to dance, considering they knocked over a pile of clay pots. Nor was "Do You Hear What I Hear?" considered a tango.

She laughed and skipped out of his arms. "You catch me off guard and appear out of nowhere!" Whenever she thought about him, he appeared. Which, if she was honest, was often.

Shanice took in his athletic form, dressed in jeans and a blue flannel shirt that brought out the blue in his eyes. A definite looker, he displayed a devastating smile, and the pairing of those eyes with his smile sent her pulse racing. He bent to pick up the pots and seed packet and deposited them on a shelf.

"Sorry, Shay. I should've texted you first."

"No problem," she replied in what she hoped was a dismissive tone. There was no reason to confess she'd been on edge while she waited all day for his text. She clicked out of the playlist and tucked the cell phone in her jean pocket.

"I assume you remember my sister, Penny." He ushered a short, dark-haired, heavy-set woman inside the greenhouse. Penny was older than Lincoln by a number of years. Despite her height, she had a stately presence, along with a cheery disposition and laugh lines at the corners of her mouth and eyes. Shanice had looked up to her as an older sister and sensed that Penny was continually in her corner.

"Hi, Shanice." Dressed in a gray wool sweater and black slacks, Penny shouldered her fine leather tote bag and spoke in a cultured voice. Yet Shanice well remembered Penny's amiable nature blended with drollness. "Is my little brother wooing you again? As soon as I arrived, I was hardly able to unpack before he insisted we drive to your farm."

Shanice's shoulders shook with laughter. "I assume he was his usual charming self when he insisted."

Lincoln tapped his fingers on his leg. "Thanks, big sister, for exposing any weakness I might wish to hide."

"Truth is paramount, and my older age proves I'm smarter."

"What can I say?" Lincoln replied with a chuckle. "I was a surprise baby."

"You won't admit I'm smarter?"

"Mum's the word." He issued a confident smile.

Shanice and Penny shook hands. The well-mannered handshake became a firm clasp of reassurance that lasted seconds longer than mere politeness dictated. Their handshake led to an embrace. When they stepped back from each other, both were self-conscious at their unexpected emotional display. Their friendship had been reignited, recognized, and reestablished.

"Shanice, you never gain an ounce of weight." Penny splayed her hands around her waistline. "When you turn to the side, you practically disappear."

"Oh, right. Hardly."

"My problem is I love carbs. And cheese and Christmas cookies." Penny patted her round stomach. "Have you heard of the latest weight loss plan where all you eat is greens?"

"No. Are you on a diet?"

"I'm always on a diet, except around food."

Shanice met Penny's laughing gaze with one of her own. "I spend a lot of time in a greenhouse. Does that count?"

"Green. Clever," Lincoln and Penny chorused.

The greenhouse filled with the pleasant laughter of friends who had known each other for years. Or was it more? Shanice wondered. Perhaps this was a family. The kind of family she had yearned for. The kind Lincoln took for granted.

Two parents and a kind, caring sibling, while Shanice had none of those. What would she have done without Granny to wipe her tears, encourage her to be proud, and embrace her strengths?

When their laughter subsided, Shanice asked Penny, "Where is your son? Wasn't he traveling with you?"

"Evan is with my husband, Roy, in Virginia." Penny glanced at Lincoln. "Roy's business meeting was canceled."

"That's probably for the best." Lincoln sighed heavily. "It gives him an opportunity to spend a few days with Evan. He's not around often."

"When I left, Evan and Roy were playing with the toys Evan got for Christmas."

"That seems a suitable pastime for Roy," Lincoln muttered.

Penny threw him a warning scowl. "What are you insinuating?"

"I wouldn't dream of insinuating anything."

"Your business is toys." Aware of the tension between the siblings, Shanice forged into the conversation. "All sorts of toys must be at Evan's disposal."

Penny shook her head. "I don't believe in excess for children, or adults for that matter, although Roy prefers a fancier lifestyle than I do."

"Like fancy watches and expensive cars," Lincoln said.

His light sarcasm didn't go unnoticed. "You're judging my husband?"

"The thought never crossed my mind."

Penny rejected Lincoln's remark with a wave of her hand. "I try to run our household simply and donate to many causes that are meaningful to me. Evan plays with a few preferred toys—wooden percussion instruments are his current preferences. Roy declared that maybe Evan will become the next Ringo Starr."

Shanice smiled. "Maybe."

"In any event, they'll be here soon. After Lincoln's description of the Roses Hotel, I thought it wise to delay them."

"Can't you stay anywhere else in town?" Shanice asked.

"Lincoln insisted I see the hotel, your place, and our parents' shop. He set up an ambitious agenda for us."

"I wanted Penny's opinion on your house and land," Lincoln put in.

Cheered by the evidence of a possible sale, Shanice beamed. "Is Candee with you?"

"I phoned her and left a voice mail," Lincoln said. "May we look around your property without her?"

"Sure. You're the prospective buyers." She started for the greenhouse door. "I know the home better than anyone and can answer all your questions."

Lincoln and Penny followed Shanice. After an hour of touring the entire property, they headed to the front porch. The sun was beginning to set, and a rich golden hue filled the sky. In a distant field, cows grazed, the stillness interrupted only by a slow moving tractor.

"A person can see for miles," Penny remarked as they stood on the porch. "Fresh air and no smog or pollution. The peace and quiet are calming yet invigorating. In the city, traffic is a challenge and car horns are an integral part of the experience."

"What kind of experience?" Shanice asked.

"The sensory overload kind."

"On a happier note," Lincoln said, "you can see the stars out here in the evening when there are no clouds." He inhaled a breath of air and motioned toward the edge of the land. "Shay, our firepit is still standing."

"Our?"

"I helped built it, remember?"

"Landscape adhesive did the trick," she replied. "That's why it hasn't collapsed."

"Impressive! You built a firepit." Penny joined the discussion. "It looks like it always belonged there."

"*We* built it sixteen years ago." Lincoln shot Shanice a sideways smile. "Literally with our own two hands."

Shanice overruled his statement with a shake of her head. "Four hands."

"We dug the pit, laid the stone."

She raised an eyebrow. "*We?*"

"Well, mostly you. Your grandmother added the sand and pea pebbles. Shay, the landscape expert, used a portion of wood to level out the pieces." Lincoln broke into a grin. "A professional job all around."

Penny smirked. "Thanks for the stroll down memory lane."

"I'm not finished." Lincoln's gaze brightened. "Afterward, we roasted marshmallows and shared s'mores with each other."

He was reliving her memories, Shanice thought, feeling a pang of longing in her chest. In their teens, they'd taken a blanket and lay on the grass in these very same fields on mild autumn nights. She still smelled the wood bonfire, tasted sweet graham crackers topped with melted chocolate and gooey marshmallows.

"The number of stars was limitless," she said.

"The stars are still there. And the sight will take your breath away." He pinned his gaze to hers. She saw the flame of desire, felt the unspoken connection between them.

Out of the corner of her eye, Shanice was also aware of the perceptive gleam in Penny's stare.

Lincoln excused himself to inspect the house's interior. Shanice assumed he was examining the second-floor bathroom to pinpoint the location of the water leak that had stained the living room ceiling. He suspected the leak might be in the drain trap.

"You've never been to the farm," she said to Penny as Lincoln strode off.

"No. You visited my parents' home every Sunday while

you and Lincoln dated." Penny laid a hand on Shanice's forearm. "I bet you'll never forget those formal dinners."

"The meals were superb, though I was always nervous." Shanice carefully controlled her voice. "Your father was a formidable presence, and your mother was disengaged, which made me ill at ease."

To Shanice's surprise, Penny didn't seem offended.

"Be grateful you weren't their daughter." Penny let out a stormy sigh. "Rest assured, my father's expectations were excessive, most noticeably with Lincoln. He constantly goaded him to fulfill the masculine role in the family."

"Lincoln did so admirably."

In fact, he exemplified self-assurance and strength, though Shanice kept her thoughts to herself.

Penny gave her a feisty nudge. "My brother also has a creative side."

"He hand carves rocking horses."

"Oh, he does much more than that. Ask him about it sometime."

Shanice tucked that remark away for future reference. "Your mother seemed approachable, although I kept my distance. Lofty standards are lofty standards."

"Mom laughed a lot and didn't worry as much as Dad. She preferred her alone time and none of us took it personally. She needed space for herself."

Penny's reassurance put Shanice at ease. "Your family was in a different social sphere than mine, though I doubt Lincoln ever noticed. As for me, I was fine with it." Her indifference was a facade to cover up her hurt, and Shanice hoped Penny wouldn't detect it.

"He was so smitten with you," Penny said, "he couldn't see anyone or anything else. Let's make that present tense. He *is* smitten with you."

"That's ridiculous."

"Clearly you are meant for each other." Penny wiggled her eyebrows. "I want you for my sister-in-law. I always have, and I'm prepared to undo any damage that led to your breakup."

Shanice pulled back, worried she might display more emotion than she wanted to exhibit. She was also worried she might spill information that would only hurt Penny's opinion of her father.

"Don't you wish you and Lincoln were together again?" Penny asked.

"I don't know how to answer that."

"Sure you do. I mean, I'm confident living the single life is fabulous. You can go wherever you want. What woman in her right mind wants a lasting relationship with a man who clearly loves her?" In typical Penny style, she laughed at her own tongue-in-cheek jokes.

Astonished, Shanice chuckled. "You definitely have a flair with words."

"I'm trying to get you to see things the way they were meant to be and cajoling apparently doesn't help."

"Oh, I think you're doing a fine job."

"My specialty." Penny sat in one of the porch rockers and, with a sidewise smile, gestured toward the house. "I trust your home holds a bunch of memories."

Grateful for the subject change, Shanice replied, "I spent most of my childhood here on the farm with Granny. As an adult, I visited often." Restless, Shanice wandered over to the window and leaned against the pane.

Penny hoisted one ankle over her knee. "You aren't keen on selling?"

"I have no choice. Financial worries are a part of my life."

"Lincoln is looking for a way to supply housing for our employees. That is, if we reopen the former toy shop in

Roses. I voted for our second location to be located in Virginia for purely selfish reasons."

"You're still debating between the two locations?"

Penny's sharp blue eyes, identical to her brother's, darted past Shanice and landed on the sprawling acreage. "Lincoln and I usually are able to come to an understanding."

"I heard about what happened in Hilton Head and I'm sorry about the fire."

"Fortunately, no one was injured." Penny fished in her tote bag and withdrew a stack of drawings. "Here are the architect's plans for the apartment buildings if we buy your property."

"*If* we go that route." The front door opened, and Lincoln peeked his head out. Shanice's cat also appeared. To prove her arrival, the cat glided through Shanice's legs, then chased after a bird she spotted in the meadow.

Penny patted to the other rocker, gesturing for Shanice to sit beside her. She smoothed out the drawings on her lap. "Clearly, the buildings are attractive."

Before Shanice nodded, Penny's cell phone rang, and she examined the caller ID. "It's Roy. I'll take the call inside." She rolled up the drawings and disappeared into the house.

Lincoln took up the rocker Penny had vacated and scooted closer to Shanice. "Just like old times," he said quietly.

"I haven't sat in these rockers in years."

"Really?" He lifted her chin. "Why not?"

She met his inquiring gaze. "Because of the memories."

He peered behind her and ran his fingers up and down the carvings. "The initials and heart are still there."

She nodded. She was too choked up to respond.

He brushed a wayward lock of hair from her forehead. "Will you have dinner with me tonight? We can make it easy and go for pizza. Tony's Pizzeria has been on Main Street forever. We ate there a number of times."

"I remember, though I can't go."

"Don't tell me you're dieting too?"

"No. I love pizza, but you treated me to lunch yesterday. Besides, what will your sister do?"

"Knowing Penny, she'll keep herself occupied. She mentioned stopping by the old toy shop and looking up some childhood friends she hasn't seen in ages."

"Lincoln, I haven't started to pack all of Granny's belongings yet."

"Why are you packing?"

"I'm moving, remember?"

He responded with a dismissive smile. "After dinner, I'll drive you back here and we'll celebrate Kwanzaa."

"You're not listening."

"I am, but we're both aware you won't get much done this evening. I'll send professional packers to your house when the time comes."

She sputtered. "I don't need your—"

"Tonight is night three, correct?"

"Kwanzaa?" Momentarily sidetracked, she asked, "You're keeping track?"

"Absolutely. This evening, another candle is lit."

"Which means?"

"The third principle. Cooperative effort and responsibility." He bent his head, their faces so close she could feel his warm breath on her cheek, smell the citrus scent on his skin. "Just you and me, and no discussion of the R word. No talking about property or business or employee housing."

"Promise?"

"Promise. This is our first formal date in sixteen years."

"We've had other dates."

"I'm considering this our first."

His sincere response made her heart lurch. "What about yesterday's lunch at the teahouse?"

"The lunch was spontaneous. Impromptu. Pick your reason. Tonight is official and therefore more special." Their gazes locked. His eyes darkened. Surely, he wasn't intending to kiss her.

"Wow, you two are such an attractive couple." Penny emerged from the house and loudly stomped her feet. "Obviously I'm interrupting. However, I'm more than happy to disappear inside again if you're busy kissing."

Lincoln frowned up at her as if she had, indeed, interrupted them. "We haven't kissed yet."

"You will, though. No worries. I can practice my … my yoga."

"You do yoga?" Lincoln asked.

"Oh yes. Yoga reduces stress. It's beneficial for people who work all the time." Penny brightened. "People like us! We should all take a yoga class."

Shanice grabbed onto Penny's arm. "The same class together?"

"That will never happen," Lincoln solemnly pronounced, then smiled at Penny. "Incidentally, how is my favorite nephew?"

"Evan is your only nephew, and he is excited to see you. If you recall, you were supposed to visit my family in Virginia for the holidays before the events got turned around and you changed all our plans."

"Me?" Lincoln's feigned innocence was rewarded by the women's chuckling.

"Yes, you. Roy and Evan will drive here to help prepare for the party at the Irish teahouse. How European, although I'll need to lose ten pounds by then."

"New Year's Eve is in a few days," Lincoln reminded her.

"The sparkly silver dress I planned to wear is too small on me."

"There are several shops in town if you care to buy another," Shanice said.

"There's that, though you don't do much at a New Year's party. People just stand around holding a cocktail. I must remember to hold in my stomach and not move my arms." Penny twisted to Shanice. "We'd be thrilled if you joined us. Roy has a business meeting in San Francisco on January first, so he won't be able to stay long since he's flying out early the next day."

"Isn't New Year's Day considered a holiday?" Lincoln tipped his head to the side. "Roy seems to have a lot of meetings in California lately."

Penny flinched and averted her gaze. "He's an excellent salesman."

"In any case, I already invited Shay to the party, and she accepted." Lincoln smiled. "She picked out a lovely piece of jewelry for the occasion."

"Actually," Shanice corrected, "Lincoln insisted on buying the necklace for me."

He slid his arm around her shoulders. "Did you glue the red stone on more securely?"

"I used superglue."

"Okay, now I'm definitely going back inside." Penny swatted at an imaginary insect. "Lincoln, you purchased a broken necklace for Shanice? Bring it back to the jewelry store at once and buy her another one—preferably more expensive."

"The thrift store doesn't accept returns. She's stuck with the necklace." His gaze found Shanice's and held it. "And she's stuck with me."

Shanice took in a short, startled intake of air. As she

restrained the urge to question him, Penny tossed Lincoln a scathing look.

"Thrift store, you cheapskate?" Penny glowered. "You haven't seen this woman in sixteen years and you bought her a necklace at a second-hand store?"

"The necklace is perfectly fine," Shanice began, "and thrift stores are—"

"Awesome," Lincoln interrupted. "What's more, Shay is single."

Penny leveled Lincoln with a steady gaze. "What's that got to do with anything?"

He plucked at a piece of lint on his jeans. "She and Brylcreem called it quits. Now I can buy things for her and take her to dinner without feeling like I'm intruding."

"Brylcreem?" Shanice wondered if all that living on a swaying houseboat had made Lincoln forgetful. "You mean my former boyfriend, Brian?"

"Close enough."

Penny turned to Shanice. "Ignore my obviously jealous little brother. He doesn't want to think about any other man dating you, and he hides it by teasing." She gave his forearm a frisky punch. "Sometimes I can't tell if he's joking or serious, and I've known him all my life."

That seemed to be the case with the entire Reid family, Shanice thought, the exception being Mr. Lincoln Reid Senior. He'd proven unsmiling and serious.

CHAPTER 7

*D*inner with Shay at Tony's Pizzeria proved exactly like Lincoln remembered when they'd dated. He picked her up at the farmhouse at six o'clock and insisted on driving. Once in town, he parked his Jeep near the restaurant, opened Shay's door, and took her hand as he escorted her inside.

This was one of the things Lincoln loved most about Roses.

Nothing changed and time stood still. Nostalgia reminded him of where he'd once been and where he was going. Nostalgia reeled him back to the "good old days." He missed those days. He missed sharing them with Shay.

The familiar mouthwatering scents of oregano, basil, and rich tomato sauce floated through the dimly lit restaurant, already packed with patrons. A roaring wood fire provided a welcoming glow and a decided warmness to a December evening.

A spiky-haired hostess, with "Tony's" stitched in red on her black turtleneck sweater, showed Lincoln and Shay to a corner table covered with a checkered tablecloth. Identical

Italian statues, faux grapevines, and a resident pizza maker tossing dough beside a brick oven roused a wistful longing in him for the way life had once been.

They stopped to admire oversized glass vases stuffed with candy canes displayed on the fireplace mantel, as well as the festive garland.

Lincoln noted a group of businessmen seated by the bar. Several of the men eyed Shay with appreciative smiles as she passed. Lincoln wasn't surprised, considering how beautiful she looked.

When she'd opened the front door of her farmhouse, his chest had burst with pride at her stunning appearance. She'd combed her hair off her forehead with an emerald-green headband, enhancing her dark, clear complexion. Her almond-shaped eyes, that seemed to reach clear down to his soul, mesmerized him, and he marveled at how they sparkled when she was happy. For their date, she'd chosen black corduroy jeans, brown knee-high boots, a blue cashmere sweater, and turquoise stud earrings. To ward off the chill of a Southern evening, she'd tossed a camel wool coat over her shoulders.

Seeing her, he'd been thankful that he'd decided to dress up, somewhat, wearing dark-wash jeans and a plaid button-up shirt. His black leather jacket completed the extent of what he considered his formal clothes.

He planted his hand under Shay's elbow and drew her away from the businessmen's interested stares.

"You look gorgeous," he said.

"You already complimented me."

He grinned. "This is only the beginning."

He collected their coats and handed them to the hostess to bring to the coat check. His pleasant contemplation of the evening was considerably diminished because the businessmen still stared at her. He scowled toward them, a broad hint that Shay was taken, then showered her with a brilliant smile.

She held out her hands to him in unrestrained delight.

He moved closer and gallantly kissed her fingers. "This is a special occasion."

"Why?"

"Because it's official."

"Official …?"

"First date." He congratulated himself for his quick thinking and pulled out a chair for her. This night was the first rekindling of their relationship.

"Do you eat here often?" he asked.

"Mostly for takeout pizza. Dining in a restaurant is a treat, certainly for me." She swayed to the background holiday music. Her upturned face radiated her happiness. "I imagine you eat in fancy eateries all over the country."

He seated himself across from her and frowned. "Why do you say that? I hardly ever travel."

"Because I'm aware of your background and upbringing."

"Do I come across as pretentious in any way?"

"No. If anything, you're down to earth." She gazed down at her hands. "It's just that you were born with a proverbial silver spoon in your mouth, Lincoln. In this town, you're practically British aristocracy." Aware of his frown, she amended, "Granny always described your family in certain terms."

"I'm afraid to ask what those certain terms were."

"Pompous. Presumptuous."

"Huh." His frown deepened. "I suppose Granny knows best." He reached for his empty water glass and realized the waitress hadn't filled it yet.

Shanice's gaze narrowed. "You're being sarcastic?"

His tone sharpened. "A tad."

They were interrupted by a chorus of waitresses singing

"Happy Birthday" as they set a huge portion of chocolate cake topped with lit candles in front of an elderly woman sitting across the room.

"Sorry. I apologize." He searched for the right words. "In many ways, your grandmother was my confidante and her opinion mattered. My father was rigid, my mother a free spirit, and my sister years older than me."

In truth, Jasmine Williams's typewritten letters had been his lifeline to Shay. She was the woman who had read his manuscripts and became his cheerleader to carry on with his writing.

"Money changes perspectives," Shay said. "If you've never encountered financial struggle, then you don't understand."

"All of a sudden, you're upset with me because I'm wealthy?" He scrutinized her lovely face. Her remark didn't make sense. She'd never held his wealth against him. At least, not that he was aware.

"Granny also bragged about your good qualities," she went on, her voice slow and thoughtful. "You dream big, you're optimistic and you persevere."

"That's better." He edged his chair closer to the table and couldn't repress his grin. "Don't forget creative."

A teenage waitress brought menus and poured water into their glasses. Lincoln and Shay both refused glasses of the house wine, an Italian merlot. Smiling, Lincoln announced they were splurging on warm mugs of gingerbread-flavored lattes instead.

"During the holidays, a celebration is in order." He clinked mugs with Shay after the lattes were delivered. "We're back together and all is well."

The waitress came over and took their order—a Margherita cheese pizza and two caprese salads—then promptly disappeared.

Shay set her white napkin on her lap. "You mentioned creativity, Lincoln."

"Creativity is essential for running a toy shop."

"Your sister told me to ask you about your creativity."

"Did she?" He kept his expression bland, grabbed for the water glass, but decided to snatch up the latte instead.

"Yes. So, I'm asking."

Another server set a basket of piping-hot Italian bread on the table, describing the bread as the best in Roses. The crust was thin, the inside soft and absorbent. When she brought their salads, she explained the tomatoes were doused in an olive oil and vinegar based dressing.

"The better to mop up the tomatoes." A face-framing strand of blond highlighted hair fell over her forehead, and she shook it back. "Of course, the mozzarella is the delicious factor."

Grateful for the interlude, Lincoln thanked the server, then bowed his head and murmured a prayer of grace with Shay.

"You're creative too," he said when they finished praying.

"Thanks." She forked a tomato slice and chewed. "Though we were chatting about you, not me."

He'd never been comfortable talking about himself and drew back. With his fork, he pushed the salad around on his plate. "The truth is, I'm also a published writer."

Shay gasped. "You are?"

"You're acting like you're shocked."

"I'm not acting. I *am* shocked." She took a generous gulp of water. "I remember you used to write. I assumed nothing came of it."

"Thanks."

"I didn't mean it as an insult. Your writing was a hobby. Don't forget, after we lost touch, you disappeared."

"*I* disappeared?"

"Right. Well, I did at the onset. Later on, *you* disappeared."

"In what way?"

"You're not active on any social media accounts. And I never considered asking Granny."

She'd checked up on him on the internet. Heat radiated through his chest with the knowledge. She'd never forgotten him.

"Your grandmother read all my books."

"Impressive! All these secrets, and she never breathed a word."

"I didn't have confidence in my writing and she was my kind, yet truthful, editor." He tapped a fist lightly against his heart. "She encouraged me and believed I had talent."

"I never doubted you. I just didn't know." Shay leaned her chin on her hands. "Keep talking."

"I pursued my dream to write children's books. The toy shop remained my key priority, but in any spare time I wrote until after midnight. After several rejections, a publisher finally took notice."

"*Tuggy the Tugboat Goes to Sea,*" she murmured.

"My first book. How did you know the title?"

She nudged her salad to the side, suddenly preoccupied with studying her short, buffed nails. Her downcast eyes hidden beneath her dark lashes, she replied, "All your books are in a box in the attic. Not long ago, I came across them. I just wondered about the author initials. N. B. L. R."

"New Beginnings Lincoln Reid."

"New Beginnings Lincoln Reid." She repeated his response slowly, as if mulling it around in her mind. "Of course. Your toy shop's initials and yours. That makes sense."

He chucked her under the chin. "You read my books?"

"Each one. They are all amazing, especially the last book, *Tuggy the Tugboat Saves a Friend.* Such a lovely sentiment. Tuggy is a hero."

"Thank you."

"Though it seems as if Tuggy is always searching for something."

"I suppose he is." Lincoln stretched out the words. He paused, then began eating his salad and dunked a wedge of bread in olive oil. Shay echoed his movements.

The young waitress appeared again. "Your pizza will be out shortly," she promised as she whisked away their plates and headed for the kitchen.

"Did you hire a publicist for your books?" Shay asked.

"As a matter of fact, I did. I was nameless in the publishing world, and the tugboat books garnered unexpected success."

"Your money helped," she said quietly. "Publicists are no doubt expensive."

He bristled. Her comment hurt. He'd clocked in more hours on his manuscripts than working at the toy shop and carving rocking horses combined.

He'd donated all his book profits to projects of deep interest—first and foremost Habitat for Humanity. He didn't physically build or refurbish homes anymore, although his philanthropic contributions had enabled several rundown communities to flourish.

The waitress deposited a steaming hot pizza in the center of the table, along with clean plates and flatware.

Neither Lincoln nor Shay grabbed a slice of pizza.

Still stinging from Shay's insinuations, he leaned back, his body rigid.

As if money were a ticket to success. In many instances, money helped when combined with perseverance and initiative. But then, awareness of Shay's cash struggles surged, bringing empathy, and he mentally berated himself.

"I noticed your books have the same theme," she said into the lengthening silence.

"Which is?"

"Stand up for what you believe in."

He nodded. "I learned the lesson the hard way."

"I don't understand."

His jaw tightened. "As you're no doubt aware, my father was a tough taskmaster."

"Taskmaster." The skin bunched around her eyes. "A neutral term."

"May I be truthful?"

"Of course."

"After you were gone, each day proved harder than the previous one. Your departure left a literal hole in my heart that never healed. For a while, I didn't believe in God anymore." He ran a thumb across his glass. "Eventually I realized you'd made my life wonderful, even if only for a short time, and I shouldn't undervalue that joy, that sense of wonder."

Tears sprang to her eyes. "We've traveled a long road from when we first met."

"I remember when you stood by the college's bulletin board going on and on about the benefits of Habitat for Humanity. From that day forward, I was smitten with you."

"You didn't act very smitten," she replied. "In fact, I was positive you never once looked in my direction."

"I peeked when you weren't aware." He laughed. "You volunteered to tackle all the outdoor landscaping jobs by yourself. A crazy, monumental undertaking."

"Meanwhile, you asked me a million questions every time we were together. I assumed you were interested in plants."

"Plants? Not a chance." He shook his head. "I was interested in *you*."

"That's why you often switched the topic from plants to any guy I might be dating?"

"There was that annoying dude. Zack Canning."

Theatrically, she groaned. "He was constantly around."

"That's because he followed you everywhere. I pegged him as a stalker."

"He was a nice guy."

"Take my word for it. He was anything but nice." Lincoln grazed his fingers along her palm. "All in all, I figured I needed to know my competition, because I wanted to be *the one*."

"And you were," she said softly.

"Past tense."

She didn't reply.

Silence meant she understood—that indefinable communication without words.

He stretched out his legs and relaxed.

When they dated, she'd merely have to glance at him and he would know what she was thinking.

"Lincoln, let's have a picnic," she would say, linking her arm through his and pulling him forward. "Look, I packed a blanket and a thermos." They would sit by the creek, and he'd roll onto his side and kiss her.

Every week, she read aloud a brief letter from her parents. They told her little to nothing about their lives and never asked about hers.

"Lincoln, please hold me." Her eyes would fill with tears.

He talked to his sister about Shay, soliciting advice. He'd doodle Shay's name on his textbooks, on napkins. How else could he rationalize that the minute he met her, he knew he'd found the woman he wanted to spend the rest of his life with?

Providence? Luck? Both words seemed inadequate. He likened his meeting Shay to finding a compass that led him to a place he didn't know he was searching for. A special place, a place where he belonged. A blessing.

"Didn't you receive my note?" she asked.

"Yes." He tried to swallow and found it difficult. "After reading it, I had more questions than answers."

"I flew to Europe."

His gaze fixed on her. "I stayed in Roses. My father pushed me at every turn. I tried to be the son he wanted and ended up botching everything." He pursed his lips and didn't meet her gaze. "I failed on all accounts and made disastrous choices."

She laced her slim fingers through his. "Lincoln, I had no idea."

"Your grandmother never mentioned anything?"

"Never. I'm so sorry."

"None of this is your fault." He squeezed her hand reassuringly. "My personal challenge was to man up and accept the outcome of your decision. I became obsessed with staying out late and partying with friends. In time, I brought women home to meet my parents, but my father scared them all off."

He caught Shay's expression, wounded and wary, as she pulled from his grasp.

He finished his latte and set down the mug. "My father approved of only one woman because she was in our same social class. I'm assuming you can guess who?"

"Pamela."

"Correct. After enormous pressure from my father, I married her and soon discovered she didn't recognize the difference between love and hate."

"Your family accepted her?"

"My father did, with open arms. Sadly, he was the only person who mattered, considering that his word was law. In her defense, Penny never liked Pamela long before the official dinner at our house."

"So Pamela was your new dinner guest?"

"Something like that."

Shay bit back a wan smile. "I expect your ex was able to distinguish the proper fork from the proper spoon."

Lincoln waved a hand, indicating how unimportant that was. "What Pamela knew was how to play the rules, and she was a pro at the dating game. Too bad she couldn't distinguish a person's true worth from a pencil. She mixed up wealth with character and sized me up as her personal walking credit card." Idly, he rubbed his hands together. "Once I got my head on straight after the divorce, I immersed myself in my writing."

"Your books are heartwarming. Be who you are and be your authentic self. What an encouraging premise for children of all ages."

"And for adults." He leaned over the table and kissed her.

Their pizza went untouched, and he asked the waitress to box it. He paid the bill with cash, leaving a generous tip on the table, and collected their coats.

"A midnight snack for you," he said, as they left the pizzeria, carrying two boxes of pizza.

"Or for breakfast," Shay said.

His cell phone buzzed. He checked it, frowning as he read the text. "That's odd. Penny wants to talk to me about something significant and insists it can't wait."

Shay glanced up at him. They stood on the sidewalk in front of the pizzeria, under the red awning. The air was frigid, the night clear. Her cheeks had pinkened from the cold.

"My day was exhausting, and yours was even longer," she said. "Your sister is important. I pray everything is okay."

"Penny is a drama queen." He fidgeted with his coat sleeves and feigned a smile.

Shay scrutinized his expression. "This isn't a joke, is it?"

She knew him so well.

"Probably not." His strained voice revealed his frustration. "I wanted to celebrate Kwanzaa with you tonight."

"There are other nights."

He leaned in, their mouths close. "Tomorrow?"

"Sure."

He guided her out from the awning. On sunny days, the awning shaded the sidewalk from the sun. On a frosty winter evening, it shielded customers from snow and ice. As if on cue, thick snowflakes began to fall.

He brushed the snowflakes from her coat. "Kwanzaa's theme tomorrow is cooperative economics."

"Your memory is outstanding."

"The year we dated, I celebrated every night with you and your grandmother." He texted Penny and assured he would return to the hotel shortly, then clicked his phone shut. "We'll light a bonfire in our fire pit, make s'mores, and then observe Kwanzaa."

"*Our* firepit?"

"I'm fairly certain we've already had this conversation. I helped build the pit, remember? Tomorrow night, I'll bring the marshmallows, graham crackers and chocolate bars."

"Since you're the accomplished cook?" She wiggled her eyebrows. "There's an art to roasting marshmallows."

"Exactly." He offered a bemused smile. "Is seven o'clock okay?"

"Perfect."

The snowflakes fell harder, and they both peered up at the sky.

"What is that scar on your jaw?" She ran her fingers along it. "I never noticed anything before."

"It's nothing." He dismissed the inquiry with a shrug. He didn't want to burden her with his foolish past actions, a template of his past. Actions he'd repeatedly apologized for.

A sheen of white, glistening snow covered the top of her

hair, peeking out from the green headband. He brushed the damp flakes away before they melted.

The evening felt intimate and magical, and nothing was going to ruin it. He compared the fresh snow to their relationship. Fairylike and enchanted.

"I'll provide leftover pizza tomorrow night," she said.

"If there's any left to share."

Her soft eyes glinted with mischief. "I'll save mine if you save yours."

"I can't make any promises."

"Neither can I."

He chuckled, placed the pizza boxes on the ground, then kissed her, long and hard. Her lips were cold, and he warmed them with his mouth.

"I've wanted to kiss you like that all evening," he said.

She wound her arms around him and returned his kiss, weaving her fingers through his hair. The night proved as extraordinary as he'd anticipated, and his love for her increased tenfold.

Whenever she was near, he couldn't pull his gaze away. If they were alone, he couldn't resist kissing her. When they weren't together, his thoughts centered around her.

She was attracted to him too. From the very first day, he'd sensed the magnetism. Her love for him hadn't changed, no matter how hard she tried to act as if they were merely friends. She melted in his embrace each time he held her, kissed her.

Those non-responses were answer enough. His resolution to resume their relationship was tangible. His heart held no reservations.

His hands slid up her back, his fingers insistently stroking her hair. He pressed his mouth tightly to hers. He wanted to guard her heart, to cherish her. He'd missed her so very much.

CHAPTER 8

The following day, Shanice decided to take a break from her endless tasks. She'd eaten leftover pizza for breakfast, and she'd eaten leftover pizza for lunch.

She brewed a giant mug of green tea, snatched the last slice of pizza from the refrigerator and placed it on a napkin, then snuggled with her cat on the living room sofa.

She'd busied herself all morning with outdoor chores and replaced the annuals in the porch pots with evergreens. Though she hoped to move soon, she couldn't resist. She took pride in the hearty low-maintenance shrubs she'd planted years before. Granny had requested her flower beds include pink hydrangeas, white gardenias and scarlet crape myrtles, and Shanice had gladly obliged. On a side yard, a massive oak canopy grew majestically and enhanced the natural surroundings.

She glanced toward the bureau and Kwanzaa candles. Loneliness swirled and reached into her throat. She swallowed sadness as the memories flooded back of Lincoln observing Kwanzaa with her and Granny. All those celebrations they'd missed when they might've been together. Her heart ached at the knowledge that she'd made a mistake and should've stood her ground with his father.

"Lincoln deserves a woman in the same economic class." While she stroked her cat's silky fur, she spoke aloud his father's last words to her. She remembered his every sentence, every intonation. A deep scowl had creased his lined face, the gray hair at his temples lending an air of power.

Duchess took the stroking as her cue to burrow closer and Shanice teared up. Animals gave so much comfort and kept solitude at bay.

Despite the encouragement of her cat's keen purring, reality lingered. Another night had passed, and she'd celebrated Kwanzaa alone.

Once more, she checked her cell phone. Lincoln hadn't called or texted. Had he forgotten about their promised evening together?

She tossed her napkin on the coffee table and slipped from the sofa. The front hedges screamed for a clipping, and a batch of clothes needed to be washed. It was time to move on and not wallow in self-pity. It was time to dismiss her warring emotions. After all, her relationship with Lincoln had ended sixteen years earlier.

"You have an offer on your house!"

Shanice answered her cell phone on speaker, and didn't have the opportunity to say hello before Candee's enthusiastic words filled the living room.

"Who made the offer?" Shanice gave herself a mental shake. "Lincoln Reid?"

"No. The young couple with the toddler," Candee replied. "They're thrilled about all the room at the farmhouse and the acreage."

Not Lincoln?

Shanice's mouth fell open. She'd been certain he'd offer a generous price. Hadn't he said he loved everything about the farm?

Well, he hadn't, and the disappointment settled in her stomach like a heavy weight. For a moment, she couldn't speak. She drank a mouthful of tepid green tea and squared her shoulders. Under no circumstance would she dwell on this frustration or resulting setback.

But still ...

She pressed a finger to her lips, reliving Lincoln's warm kisses outside the pizzeria.

No. She refused to relive his kisses, his smiles, his stunning manner that made her heart stall.

Thoroughly dismayed with herself for doing exactly what she instructed herself not to do, she asked, "Is the couple's offer a fair one?"

"It's higher than your previous two offers."

"Both of those were low. Did they meet the asking price?"

"They're offering one hundred thousand dollars."

"Okay."

"Okay? I thought you were anxious to sell your home. Your January deadline is fast approaching."

"Their offer is nowhere near the asking price. Plus, it doesn't even meet the minimal amount required to pay my bills. What about Lincoln?"

"I left him a voice mail and haven't heard back. Frankly, I'm concerned that he and his sister found a better property elsewhere. If their company is worth what my husband believes, Lincoln could buy the entire town of Roses."

"He was concerned about his sister last night." Shanice kept her tone conversational and refused to comment on Lincoln's millionaire status.

"You saw him?"

"Twice. They stopped by the farm yesterday afternoon. They didn't stay overly long, and I haven't heard from him today."

"That's once. You said you saw him twice."

As Shanice expected, Candee's romantic antenna had gone up. She visualized the impish gleam that must be dancing in her friend's eyes.

"Lincoln and I dined out at Tony's for dinner. I'm supposed to see him tonight too." Momentarily forgetting she'd denied any romantic involvement with him, Shanice checked herself from saying more.

"Ah-ha! Dining out with him are the magic words. Dining out means you're dating again."

Shanice lowered herself onto the sofa. "Lincoln and I are friends."

"A little more than friends, yes?" Candee enhanced her response by a dramatic pause. "I'll draw up the purchase offer and email the documents to you. Study the figures, make changes, and send everything back to me."

"I need a minimum of one hundred and fifty thousand dollars. My asking price is near double what this couple is offering."

"We'll start with your counter and wait for their response. Before any documents are signed, I'll text Lincoln to remind him he'll lose out on a pastoral country farmhouse and acreage with loads of potential if he doesn't act quick."

"Spoken like a true Realtor."

Candee laughed. "Perhaps you'll have a bidding war on your house!"

That optimistic conclusion had also occurred to Shanice. She only hoped Lincoln was thinking the same.

.   .   .

SHANICE RESUMED her tasks and called it quits as darkness approached.

Her moods were a shifting contrast that changed minute by minute.

She'd begun to make headway in packing. Nevertheless, her confidence regarding Lincoln's offer waned as the seconds ticked by with no word from him. Perhaps she'd imagined his interest in her.

But no, she couldn't have. His eyes glinted with attentiveness whenever he gazed at her. He'd asked her to be his date for the New Year's party. A dashing, intelligent man had his pick of any woman, yet he'd reached out to her. He'd even bought her a necklace to wear to the event—a necklace that meant more to her than she'd let on.

The evening before, he'd held her in his arms as if he wanted to stay near the pizzeria's awning and kiss her forever.

Nevertheless, her traitorous mind envisioned his ex-wife, Pamela, who came from the right family, attended the right schools, and knew the right people. Most likely, she was fashionable and hip too, which only contributed to Shanice's feelings of inadequacy.

After inhaling a last breath of outdoor air, she clicked on the documents on her computer, carried out the changes, and emailed the attachments to Candee. *Please let me know when you receive*, she typed.

At five o'clock, Lincoln's text appeared, and a delighted thrill washed over her. He hadn't forgotten her.

Sorry I didn't have an opportunity to text you sooner. I should be at your farmhouse in a couple hours. See you at seven.

She hesitated. Should she chide him with an, *I assumed I'd have heard from you before now*. Refusing to appear needy and controlling, she lifted her hand from her phone. He'd said he was coming and never went back on his word. Still, he'd waited until the last minute to contact her.

How should she reply?

She found it difficult to express her frustration, to cave in to the reality that she'd missed him without revealing the hollowness in her life. The hollowness in her heart.

Did you have a busy day? she asked conversationally.

Quite. I'll tell you all about it when I see you.

Curiosity nudged her to inquire about Penny. Nonetheless, she kept silent, assuming it best to wait and ask him in person.

With her newfound information regarding the house offer, she also considered questioning whether Candee had communicated with him.

Her hand wavered. She nixed the idea and texted, *Don't expect dinner.*

Yes, it was a bit snide, but he'd kept her waiting all day.

I won't. LOL. Did you eat all your pizza?

Yes. You?

Penny ate mine. As you might expect, no mini fridges here at the Roses Hotel, and she refused to allow the pizza to sit on the windowsill and spoil.

No microwaves there, either?

You've got to be kidding. Not a one.

You never even tried the pizza?

Nope. Penny ate it all.

She chuckled, remembering Penny's diet.

I'm looking forward to sharing dessert with you, Shay, he continued. *In truth, I'm looking forward to seeing you. More than you'll ever know.*

To her utter chagrin, she typed, *Me too,* and pressed send before realizing she was wearing her heart on her sleeve.

She showered and dressed in jeans and a Scotch plaid

flannel shirt as a nod to the holidays. If they planned on roasting s'mores outdoors, the night could prove chilly.

Punctual to a tee, Lincoln rang her doorbell at seven o'clock. When she opened the door, he appraised her from head to toe, and a smile of approval crept across his face. He wore a navy-blue wool sweater, jeans, and a gray fleece jacket. Life wasn't fair, she decided, to allow a man to be that good-looking.

"How is my most special woman tonight?" A full moon shone down, highlighting his chiseled features. "You look gorgeous, as always."

Self-conscious, she patted down a riotous curl that had sprung over her eyes. "Thank you. You're looking fine yourself."

He grinned. "Much appreciated."

She motioned to the entryway. "Please come in."

He carried a canvas bag and tailed her inside. "I packed all the ingredients for our s'mores—marshmallows, graham crackers and milk chocolate bars. Are you ready to venture out into the cold?"

"Absolutely." She grabbed her Sherpa parka by the doorway. Her white beanie followed.

He covered her hand with his. "Not so fast. You forgot something."

"You packed chocolate and—"

"You forgot to greet me with a proper hello." Without waiting for a reply, he pulled her into his arms and smoothed his lips over hers.

The butterflies in her stomach fluttered a quick, light rhythm. She accepted the familiar stir that took place whenever she was around him. More and more, she welcomed the sensation.

"How could I forget something so important?" she teased.

His amazing blue eyes met hers, and he brought her closer for a series of toe-curling kisses.

Her cell phone pinged.

His gaze flicked upward. "Now?"

"I'm expecting a message." Shanice stepped from his embrace, withdrew the phone from her pocket, and skimmed Candee's confirmation. She'd received the returned documents and would discuss Shanice's changes with the couple.

Lincoln shifted his weight. "Is everything all right?"

"Fine and dandy."

Bundled up, they walked hand in hand along a pine tree-lined path. The moon directed their steps, and Lincoln pulled out his cell phone to use as a flashlight. The stars provided a sparkling framework to the coal-black sky.

Snowflakes clung to the fir branches. The scent of fresh earth, the lingering trace of grass and woods, filled her every breath.

With the toe of his leather boot, Lincoln kicked a rock from their path and claimed a firm grip on her hand. "After your recent injury, I don't want you to slip and fall again."

"I'm grand," she replied. "And I'm careful."

"I intend for you to stay that way." His gaze grew reflective, his voice husky with emotion. "I'm always here for you, Shay."

Her protector. Her knight in shining armor.

"It's more than I ever did for you."

"We all have reasons for our actions," he said. "Don't ever believe for a minute that I'm perfect."

"Ah, so you're not perfect." She grinned and tipped her head back to gaze up at him.

He feigned an insulted look. "Thanks. You're easy to convince."

She couldn't help staring at him, reflecting on his handsome face—the shadow of a dark beard enhancing his features.

"You're smart, witty and supportive of my career and independence." She granted an irrepressible smile. "However, we're not discussing perfection here."

"Aren't we? You are perfection." He cradled her face in his hands and lowered his lips to hers. A modest kiss didn't seem to be enough for him, and he deepened the kiss.

An owl hooted, and she jumped back.

Lincoln let her go quickly.

Whether he was aware or not, he sometimes sent her mixed signals. Was he interested in her or her house? Or both? Or neither? The questions took her off guard. As desperately as she wished to believe his interest was all about her, she was sensible enough to confront the truth. If push came to shove, Lincoln was a businessman, and his father's son.

He grabbed her hand, and they continued walking.

"How is your sister?" she asked. "I was worried after her text last evening."

"She needed to bounce some ideas off me. At noon today, she returned to Virginia."

"Why?" Shanice stopped in her tracks. "I thought Roy and Evan were driving to Roses."

"She received upsetting news regarding her husband."

Mentally, Shanice ticked off the reasons in her mind— Roy was sick or injured. "Is he okay?"

"They're having marital problems."

She raised her eyebrows in disbelief. "Penny is always so jovial. She never let on anything was wrong."

"Penny is a proud woman and jokes to hide her inner feelings. Outward appearances rarely reveal the full truth."

"She seemed content in her marriage and loves living in Virginia."

"Situations change. Roy is difficult. He and Penny have gone through the motions of marriage for quite some time." Lincoln scratched his jaw. "Believe me, I recognize the signs."

"You speak from experience?"

"Quite."

"Your ex was difficult?"

"Pamela was beyond difficult." He talked with his hands, something he rarely did. "In fact, she was a full-fledged pain in the … side."

Shanice couldn't help but laugh, then quickly sobered. "Is there a chance your sister and her husband can fix their problems?"

"They tried marriage therapy once, but infidelity is difficult to forgive. Roy has been seeing another woman in San Francisco."

"Unfaithfulness." The ground seemed to spin beneath Shanice's feet, thinking about how Penny would react. "She must be devastated."

"She is seeking to come to grips with the facts after being in denial. For the next couple of days, she'll stay in Virginia and try to resolve their differences. She intends to return to Roses for New Year's, so you'll get a chance to meet her son —who is truly the love of her life."

"With her husband?"

Lincoln laced his hand through hers. "From overhearing her phone conversation to Roy, my understanding is that she's trying to piece together a reconciliation."

They reached the firepit, where Lincoln had already deposited dry logs, newspaper and matches. He gestured to a bucket of water, which he'd apparently filled beforehand from a hose near the barn. He drew a thick waterproof plaid blanket from another wide canvas bag and spread the blanket on the damp grass.

She patted his hand as he smoothed out the blanket. "Your organizational skills are top-notch."

A charismatic grin spread across his face. "I stopped here first before driving to your house."

"What can I do? It looks like you've thought of everything."

"Make yourself comfortable and continue to look gorgeous." He beckoned her to sit on the blanket, and she obliged. He leaned over and threaded his fingers through the ends of her hair. "You're more beautiful now than you were at the farmhouse."

"I grew prettier in fifteen minutes?"

He pressed a soft kiss on her lips. "Absolutely."

"Uh-huh. You are such a tease. Lincoln, I truly can help you do something."

His lips trailed to her cheek. "You work too hard already."

"So do you. Your successful business is the end product of blood, sweat and tears."

"Blood, sweat, and tears?" His eyes danced. "Isn't that a song?"

"It's a group."

"This group?" He hummed the opening measures of "You've Made Me So Very Happy," one of Blood, Sweat & Tears' greatest hits. "In any case, we can compliment each other for the rest of the evening."

She quirked an eyebrow. "Or?"

"Or we can kiss."

"Is that all you ever think about?"

"Kissing you? Definitely." He laughed, held out his arms, and inhaled. "The air on the farm is invigorating. Sometimes in my houseboat, I feel cooped up."

"Looking out at that big, expansive Atlantic Ocean?"

"True. Nonetheless, spending time with you—here, there, wherever—is the highlight of my day." He piled the logs and newspaper into the firepit and lit a match. Soon, a smoldering fire sparked and crackled.

She inhaled the heartwarming scent while he plucked wipes and a thermos of hot chocolate from the bag. She'd always appreciated this considerate side of him and he'd never changed. Her heart had squeezed at his acts of kindness when they'd dated—consistently offering to lend a hand around the farm, or cook Granny's favorite meal— which invariably consisted of baked chicken, mashed potatoes, and fried okra.

"Do you like my mashed potatoes?" he often asked her.

"Excellent." She scooped up a buttery bite and joked, "Remember, young man, I don't like you just for your mashed potatoes. I like you because you're good to my granddaughter. You're dependable and there for her whenever she needs anything."

Lincoln eased down behind Shanice. Fishing into the canvas bag, he drew out a graham cracker. He popped half into her mouth, the other half in his.

She chewed, swallowed, and leaned back against his hard chest. "No one has ever fed me before. You're spoiling me."

"I intend to spoil you a whole lot more." He dipped into the bag for another graham cracker and held it up. "There's a condition, though."

"For a graham cracker?"

"The condition is simple." He tapped the cracker on the tip of her nose, then kissed the crumbs. "Let's stay like this forever."

"That's not exactly a condition."

"Sure it is."

A comforting fantasy. She wanted to correct him. Instead, she replied, "You and I are adults with responsibilities. You rewind the years as if we were carefree teenagers again."

In truth, this was the exact same scene she'd daydreamed

about. Years ago, they'd sit like this for hours, with his arms wrapped securely around her. Once, she'd visualized their wedding, settling on the farm and having a family of their own. Lately, she'd even imagined living on his houseboat while they viewed the sparkling Atlantic Ocean. Both scenarios portrayed a happily ever after. Both were far cries from her everyday life.

He leaned closer and whispered in her ear, "I have something to tell you."

His offer on her house. A generous, full-priced offer.

She looked heavenward and pressed a palm to her heart. With a shaky laugh, she whirled to face him. "What is it?"

"I learned the words." Whether he was teasing or serious, there was no hint in his expression.

She blinked. "The words to …"

"An important Christmas song."

"All Christmas songs are important. Any one in particular?"

"Go Tell It on the Mountain."

"Oh." He'd remembered his promise, and she murmured a delighted, "Why is that song important?"

"Because it's important to you."

To demonstrate his newfound expertise, he cleared his throat and sang the first verse of "Go Tell It on the Mountain" in a rich baritone voice, expertly in tune. When he reached the second verse, she provided harmony.

When he finished the third verse, she applauded.

Sheepishly, he held up his hands. "I'm sixteen years late, but I never forget."

Never forget. Her heart lurched. Never forget the wondrous memories they'd created. A love that had lasted throughout years of separation.

Love. The word permeated her brain, yet it had been there all along. She loved Lincoln. She always had.

He hadn't made an offer on her house, though in many respects the song represented a value far more important. She would continue to struggle financially, but he cared for her, enough to make good on a promise from ages ago.

Her self-esteem and happiness intact, she tucked up her legs and hung her hands around her knees. Their attraction was always at play, though her interest in him went far beyond. She longed to learn more about the man and the details of what she'd missed since they'd separated.

"You never told me the name of your houseboat," she prompted.

"Didn't I?"

"You're hedging. Again."

"Am I?" He brushed a strand of hair from her face. She burrowed her cheek into his broad chest and whispered, "Is the name a secret?"

"Perhaps."

She peeked up at him. He'd been smiling. Now his smile faltered.

"It's okay. Don't tell me. I don't want you to feel uncomfortable."

"No, no, I don't mind. In fact, it's high time. The name of my houseboat is …" His chin dipped down. He cleared his throat. "*Shay's Secret.*"

His admittance stole the air from her lungs. All these years he'd lived on a houseboat he'd named after her.

He believed she had a secret. And she did. The realization settled, chilling her. She prided herself on honesty, though she'd been a coward when it came to Lincoln.

"My turn." She adjusted her clothes, rubbed her hands. "Are you wondering why I left so abruptly?"

He hesitated. His arms fit around her waist. "Yes." He whispered the word so softly, she didn't hear him.

She glanced at him inquiringly.

"Yes," he repeated.

Guilt impelled her to swivel. She couldn't meet his gaze and focused on the fizzle and pop of the bonfire. "I wanted to help you. I left for you."

"For me? As if you were doing me a favor?"

"I'm sorry. I never meant to hurt you." She sucked in a lungful of air. "Your father wanted your family's wealth to remain intact and he'd already planned for you to marry Pamela—an arrangement that benefitted both your families. I blocked the road to your success and happiness."

"What's my father got to do with this?"

"Your father told me to leave."

Beneath his jacket, Lincoln's muscles tensed. "When? How?"

"One January afternoon, he drove to the farmhouse and requested I take a walk with him. When we neared the barn, he outlined your future, which is a gracious way of saying he issued a command. He described the Ivy League college you'd attend when your credits transferred, and also informed me about your upcoming marriage. In addition, he explained that you were only attending a community college for two years in order to learn the woodcarving trade. He'd delayed the better school until you excelled at the craft."

Lincoln blew out a noisy breath. "All these grand plans I wasn't aware of."

"You were whip-smart. You took your studies seriously and maintained a high average."

"After you left, I dropped out of college." He made a sweeping motion with his hands. "In fact, I never finished."

The sadness of his situation hit her, and her stomach clenched. Was she so lacking in compassion and trust that she'd failed to realize that Lincoln was owed a proper explanation? She wished she'd handled the situation better, but the reality was, she hadn't.

"What did you do instead of attending college?" she asked.

"I partied and fell in with the wrong crowd." He shrugged and spoke quickly. "Eventually, my parents sent me out of state for counseling and enrolled me in a detox program."

"Is that where you got your scar?" She touched his jawline.

His expression shuttered. A muscle throbbed in his cheek.

"Sorry. I'm prying."

"I don't mind." His tone was steady and low-pitched. "I got my scar when I lived in Roses. One night I was out with a group of friends drinking beer at a local bar, and that stalker, Zach, wandered in. He talked nonstop about you and began badgering me, insinuating I'd gotten you pregnant and that was the reason you rushed out of town."

"Oh, no." Her mouth went dry. She went to reach for Lincoln but her arms felt heavy. "What happened?"

"I wouldn't allow him to gossip and ruin your reputation, so I did what any guy who loved his girl would do."

Something about the restrained way Lincoln answered made her look up quickly. "Which was?"

"I slugged him. Hard."

She tipped her head. "And then?"

"His fist came at me and almost broke my jaw. My friends tore us apart, though the police were called to the scene. Needless to report, my father wasn't pleased when he saw my beat-up face and bleeding lips. He was even less pleased when the bar fight was headlined on the front page of the local newspaper the following day."

Tears burned the back of Shanice's eyes. He'd endured a great deal for her while nursing a broken heart. Upset by what she'd learned, she peered up at the sky to ask God for forgiveness. "Lincoln, I'm so sorry any of this had to happen."

"There's a happy ending, Shay. I repaired my life, resumed my job in Roses and plunged into a stellar performance at the toy shop. Ultimately, my parents were delighted. When they moved the business to Hilton Head Island, I went along."

"What about Penny?"

"She was in Virginia and chose to stay there." He straightened and regarded her with a mixture of sadness and irritation. "Now it's my turn to ask some questions. Why would you, of all people, bend to my father's wishes? You're a strong, self-supporting woman with a backbone. A woman who sticks up for herself."

His candid compliment caused her heartbeat to double. "Your father gave me little choice. I was a teen. I obeyed."

"Why didn't you confide in me?" Sadness underlined his voice. "Wasn't our love worth fighting for?"

"After he drove away that afternoon, I confided to Granny." Her spirits plummeted as she retold the memory. "In the end, she reaffirmed your father's arguments and declared that a breakup was for the best. Only heartache was ahead for you and me if I remained in Roses. I couldn't let that happen. I wanted you to be happy."

"Instead, I was miserable. Hah. That's an understatement. More like devastated."

She shut her eyes tightly. If only she'd listened to her heart.

His breath was warm on her neck. "Where did you go?"

"I lived with my parents in Rome."

"Were they happy to see you?"

"They were accommodating. I wasn't with them long because I attended university in Milan."

"All this happened." His jaw went slack. He was obviously shocked by all her information. "Your grandmother never uttered a word."

"Granny was tight-lipped."

"I suspected you were somewhere in the States—you

mentioned attending college in South Carolina. I researched the number of colleges in the state."

"How many are there?"

"At last count, sixty one."

He'd moved heaven and earth trying to find her. Feelings of regret and recrimination hit her from all sides, along with an emotion she couldn't identify at first.

But of course. The feeling was love. For him, for all he'd endured for her.

She rested her head on his shoulder. She'd redirected their paths, and they'd carried on. But their lives hadn't been complete or joyful. "I've unburdened myself, but I can't change the past."

"Shay, I care for you more now than when we were teens, if that's possible," Lincoln said. "Though you didn't do either of us any favors by obeying my father."

"Twenty-twenty hindsight. Lincoln, I—"

"When I pressed your grandmother, she insisted you'd gone far away and couldn't be reached." He spoke as if he hadn't heard her. "I scoured nearby towns. I called your friends so often they began to avoid me. I even begged Penny to help me. Her advice was to hire a private detective. That is, after she scolded me."

"What did she say?"

"Too little, too late. Leave it to Penny to offer real words of advice." A wry smile touched his mouth. "I must've written your grandmother the same request at the end of every letter I sent her."

"Which was?"

"Please tell Shay I miss her and I love her. Ask her to come back to me."

"Your pleas wouldn't have changed my mind."

"Yeah, well ..." He stroked his chin. She expected him to finish by saying, "Thanks for nothing." Instead, he continued in a voice that gave little away. "I had obligations, I realized that. However, I had no idea my father had my future all planned. That realization came much later."

Shanice's throat clogged, helpless in her remorse. *I love you,* she wanted to say. *I made a mistake. Our lives could've been so different.*

Be honest, she scolded herself. Had his father's visit been the only reason prompting her to flee? Had she bolted because their emotional attachment was so strong it scared her?

She tried to speak. Her voice cracked.

Did she fear the same disinterest from Lincoln that her parents displayed? They'd rejected putting their careers on hold for her, and Lincoln would have been put in a similar predicament if she stayed in Roses. She never wanted to keep him from reaching his full potential.

In the same vein, he might grow tired of her. She was plain and unworldly, as his father pointed out. Lincoln deserved more.

Nonetheless, these past few days, fate had intervened and offered a second chance. Destiny. Sometimes events happened beyond a person's control. Perhaps they were two star-crossed lovers, similar to the heroes and heroines in the romance books she adored.

Destiny. The word swam through her mind. Or was their reunion caused because of Granny? She'd written Lincoln a final letter, as if she envisioned creating their second chance.

Silence surrounded them. The bonfire burned slow and rhythmic. The owl's hooting ceased, and the nighttime still-ness was swallowed by a slight breeze.

Lincoln held her close, his masculine scent enfolding her. He cupped her chin, urging her to gaze into his eyes. "Let's not ruin our night together by discussing the past anymore. Our future is what's more important."

She studied him with a slight smile. "You're an astute man."

His lips grazed hers. His kiss was light and quick, causing her pulse to kick up. Maybe that was what he intended—to remind her she craved more.

To shatter the spell, she busied herself with rummaging through the bag and brought out the sleeve of graham crackers, a package of marshmallows, and two chocolate bars.

She waved the chocolate in the air. "Only two?"

"You can eat half of my s'more if—"

"You can eat half of mine?" She rubbed her hands along the edges of her parka. "Hmm. You are always bargaining, Lincoln. You probably wanted both mine and yours."

"Me? Bargain?" He covered her chilled fingers with his and lowered his forehead to her shoulder. "You're mixing me up with my father. Let's base our future relationship on honesty."

"Settled."

"Our foundation is strong, Shay."

She grew thoughtful and tugged her hands away. "I need to ask you a question."

"I'm listening."

She had difficulty breathing. She took in a gulp of air and hugged herself to keep warm.

Now or never, she told herself.

"Did Candee text you this afternoon?" she asked.

"Yes."

"Therefore, you realize I received an offer on the farmhouse."

"Yes."

He answered in monosyllables, his features expressionless.

"Do I have to spell it out, Lincoln?" Her voice was low as she tried to determine her next sentence. Her cheeks burned with humiliation. He put her in an awkward predicament. "Will you make a counteroffer?"

He placed a gentle hand on her shoulder. "I bought the Roses Hotel today. I contacted the owners and asked if they were willing to sell their property. I quoted them a fair cash offer, and they accepted."

She shook off his hand and shot back, "You're buying the hotel—for cash—and not my farmhouse?" Surely he was aware of her dire financial straits. Her embarrassment knew no bounds. Was she supposed to beg him?

His gaze veered to the bonfire. "I never said that."

"The couple's offer was lowball." She cringed, knowing her voice was too high, and she sounded desperate.

His hand hovered again over her shoulder, apparently debating whether he should touch her or not. "Candee filled me in on all the details. They're offering half of your asking price."

"Wow! You're a man in the know." Shanice stood so quickly, the crackers spilled onto the grass. "Money is certainly a powerful tool, isn't it?"

"What's that supposed to mean?"

"You millionaires think you can crook your little finger and the universe will bow to your demands. You're more concerned with your bank account than anything else."

He was only interested in wooing her to get what he wanted—probably waiting to offer a few thousand dollars more than the young couple—so he could flip her house and make a profit. Even if he paid full asking price, the house was a tremendous value.

He rose to his feet. "You're not making any sense."

"Oh, but I am." She plunged her hands in her pockets. "You and your father are cut from the same cloth. I bent to his will, but I'm not bending to yours."

"What am I asking for?" His deep voice edged with pain.

"Nothing."

Everything. Her self-respect. Her dignity.

She stared at him, waiting for his next question. The air shifted between them. Wasn't he aware of her pathetic finances?

A painful lump settled in her throat.

"Shay … listen. I can clarify the situation—"

"The fact that you're holding your offer over my head? Is this your way of getting back at me for leaving you?"

A flare of exasperation lit his eyes. "You know me better than that."

"Do I? Sixteen years is a long time."

He grasped her elbow. "I'm the same person. You are too."

She backed away, stumbling, not wanting him to see her pain and disappointment. "We're not the same, save for one glaring example."

He reached for her. "Which is?"

She leaned away, her posture strong. "You're still rich and I'm still poor. And you know what? There's nothing wrong with living on a reduced income." Mentally, she ran through what she must say, what she must do.

This was farewell. The real truth. His father was right. She and Lincoln were galaxies apart in economic statuses. "I don't need your offer, nor would I accept it."

He held his hands behind his back and gave a heavy sigh. "If you can be patient for once in your life, I promise your circumstances will change after the new year."

"Patient?" She sucked in her cheeks. "I'm the epitome of patience."

"I hate to be the one to tell you this, but you're the opposite of patient."

She sputtered, gaped. "I'm going back to the farmhouse. Alone. By January first, I anticipate the couple's offer is accepted, signed and sealed."

He searched the stars, apparently looking for answers, then met her gaze. Longing shone from his deep blue eyes. "Really? Can you live with your decision to leave me a second time?"

"Absolutely." She shivered. The temperature must've plummeted ten degrees. "Don't try to follow me."

"I won't." His voice raised. "I'm not that foolish."

"Good." Gathering steam, she spun toward the path. She grabbed her cell phone and switched on the flashlight, though she could find the path blindfolded.

Lincoln's sharp intake of breath from behind was like a metal sword to her chest. She must have hurt him, but she refused to allow his hurt to deter her.

"What about our s'mores?" he called out.

One pivot and she confronted him. "I'm not hungry anymore."

He shot a glance at the bonfire. "This blaze will go on for hours."

"Just … just douse the fire out." She pointed to the bucket and began walking backward. Her hands were shaking. Her eyes were a blurry haze.

"Tonight is another night of Kwanzaa." He opened his mouth, closed it, opened it again, as if he had a hundred more words he wished to say. "The principle is cooperative economics."

"Yes, yes, so you've stated. Ironic considering our circumstances, isn't it?" Before she lost control of her remaining composure, she wheeled around and swiped at her wet eyes. "Please don't concern yourself. I'm used to celebrating Kwanzaa alone."

CHAPTER 9

The following morning, Lincoln peered out the grimy window of the Roses Hotel and stared at the pavement, covered with frost. The weather had shifted, promising swollen gray clouds and a hard arctic rain.

He drew a breath, tapped his fingers together. Everything was cold and flat today—the world, the town, and his raw emotions.

Here's what he knew for sure. The holidays ended soon. He'd bought a bunch of items at the thrift store that had overtaken his hotel room, and Shay wasn't by his side, where she belonged.

He ran his fingers along the glass, absorbed in his thoughts. The chair scraped across the linoleum floor as he rose to his feet. He lifted a water bottle to his lips, then set it down. He couldn't swallow. The tension in the tiny room was too strained.

What on earth had he said to upset her?

She pushed him away whenever he tried to get too close. During her childhood, her parents were gone more often than not, and she had suffered. Their absence had stung. As a defense mechanism, her protective shields were often fully deployed.

She feared being abandoned again, hurt again. If she let her shields down, she'd be too vulnerable and exposed. Can't have that, she'd probably decided. She'd push away first before someone pushed *her* away.

Was she truly afraid of getting hurt—of *him* leaving *her*? Surely she realized that would never happen.

Minute by minute, he dissected their argument. Why had she become so prickly when the conversation had turned to money? He and his father didn't share the same views on wealth, on life. On love …

He sent a prayer heavenward and didn't receive a response. God must be tired of hearing from him when he needed help. His parents had fostered no relationship with God, although Shay and her grandmother prayed often. Granny insisted that God met every need, and a person found healing in faith during troublesome seasons.

Since returning to Roses, Lincoln's religious convictions had been restored, and he had started praying more.

He swallowed against the pain in the back of his throat. He knew Shay's financial struggles, and he believed the outcome he'd arranged for her was positive. Nevertheless, knowing her abhorrence to wealth and the fact that she wouldn't accept any house offer from him, he doubted she'd be pleased.

Definitely, the joke was on him. The young couple's offer had resulted in a bidding war, and he'd ended up paying twice the amount he'd expected to pay for the farmhouse. He trusted Candee would be as tight-lipped as Shay's grandmother. He'd sworn her to secrecy.

The clock on the nightstand blinked eleven o'clock. Precious minutes he could have been spending with Shay were ticking away.

He texted her for the third time since dawn. As usual, his text was met with silence.

"Ghosting," Penny explained when he'd phoned her. "The term means withdrawing from all communication. Shanice is ghosting you."

"Why would—?" He almost tripped over his inquiry.

"Allow her another day," Penny interrupted. "Reflect on your argument and the reason why it occurred."

"What should I do in the meantime?" He paced, changing direction midstride. "It's difficult to do nothing."

"Tomorrow is New Year's Eve," Penny replied. "I'll be back in Roses. If you haven't heard from her by then, I'll contact her."

"How?"

Penny offered a half-hearted explanation. Her particulars were sketchy at best.

He frowned. He didn't like the sound of any plan when the details weren't specific.

"She is my date." Carefully, he controlled his tone.

"Don't count on it."

"Thanks for the encouragement, Penny. And your unsuccessful attempt to cheer me up."

"You asked for my advice."

He glared at his cell phone. "Did I?"

"I'm brutally frank to keep you on your toes, little brother. You sound frantic, so chill out. Go visit our old toy shop this afternoon. It'll bring back fond memories."

The last thing he needed was more memories.

"There's no understanding a woman, is there, Penny?"

"Nope. I'm living proof."

After a few parting words, he wished her a safe trip. At the last second, he asked if Roy was coming with her.

"I'll be driving alone with Evan." Her tone changed, as brisk as the weather. "Roy moved out. He phoned a while ago and tried to give excuses for why he cheated. I'm not feeling morally correct about what I did, but I hung up on him in midsentence."

"Understandable," Lincoln said.

Their conversation lagged. She didn't crack any jokes and Lincoln feared he'd overstepped his bounds.

"Another thing," she finally continued after she'd stayed quiet for a beat. "I approve of our toy business expanding to Roses."

He flopped back on the chair. "I'm glad to hear that. You don't want a toy shop built in Virginia, then?"

"Roses is my hometown."

Lincoln smiled. Her agreement was important. He'd expected she'd go along with his plans. Nevertheless, having her full-fledged commitment was a relief.

"I'm thinking the welcoming community in Roses is ideal for Evan," Penny said. "He needs a change, needs new friends. We both do."

"Sounds like you've decided your marriage is over."

"Sounds that way, doesn't it?"

After exchanging polite pleasantries, they clicked off.

He muttered under his breath as he buttoned his canvas jacket. He wasn't especially enthusiastic about getting on with his day without Shay. However, an afternoon at the toy shop would lift his spirits, plus give her the space she desired. He checked with a couple contractors in the area to begin renovations, and managed to set up an appointment with one.

He wanted to protect her from pain—whether hurt, disappointment, or financial.

"Lean on me, Shay," he said aloud. "I'm here. I've always been here for you."

He loved her. Certainly, she knew that. He hadn't told her lately—not in so many words. He'd been cautious, taking it slow. Nonetheless, his actions spoke for themselves.

He marveled at her fierce determination to become a self-sufficient entrepreneur. She answered to no one and fiercely held onto her independence.

"Your successful business proves the end product of blood, sweat and tears." Her dark eyes had glowed with pride as she spoke.

His heart lurched at the memory.

He didn't deserve her admiration. He'd done exactly what his father intended. He'd poured himself into sixty-hour work weeks at the toy shop and married Pamela.

Lincoln strode to the hotel's parking lot and started up his Jeep. He drove to the toy shop, his fingers tightly gripped around the steering wheel.

As he parked at the curb, he surveyed the old building. The shop sat on a corner, shuttered and neglected. Once, it had been flanked by a sandwich delicatessen and a hardware store. Both had closed. However, the old-fashioned pharmacy and soda fountain that stood kitty-corner from the toy shop was still open. When he'd dated Shay, they'd duck inside for root beer floats. He vowed to do it again soon.

Hesitating, he took it all in—the memories of his parents, the delightful customers—enthusiastic parents and excited toddlers. He had often stepped in to work last-minute, say, if an employee had to stay home with a sick child.

He'd met with vendors, ordered supplies, and managed the company finances.

Moving quickly, he reached the shop's entrance. He hadn't been inside in years. Cars whizzed by, though he hardly heard them.

He rattled the doorknob, inserted the key, and stepped inside. The shop had been cleared, save for an ageless rocking horse poster. A glass counter remained where he and his parents had served customers. Display shelves stood intact, and Lincoln visualized the shelves in former years, packed with wooden puzzles, soft stuffed dolls and educational games.

He peered behind the counter. Fragments of cedar, as well as a hammer, saw, and file had been left. An idea emerged, a project, bringing a light-hearted feeling to his limbs.

He smiled. All he lacked was a drill and an assortment of rainbow-colored paint. He'd rectify things by gifting Shay with a meaningful present. Or two.

He climbed the three floors of stairs in semidarkness, avoiding the holes in the floorboards.

He recalled that in the short time Shay had worked at the shop, she had devoted an entire section to intricate wooden trains. She'd piled the latest deliveries in every spare corner.

After a leaky roof had ruined several boxes, her eyes had brimmed with tears.

Penny had walked into the store, her greeting trailing off when she saw Shay and the ruined boxes.

It wasn't her fault, Lincoln had assured Shay, offering a smile, although she'd darted an apprehensive glimpse toward his father. So had Lincoln. So had Penny.

His father had cut Penny off when she tried to speak. He'd flashed a stony smile, and then excused himself.

Discouragement gave Lincoln pause. Shay should be with him right now. Right this very minute—giving him ideas for refurbishment, outlining her plans for the exterior and the plants she would use.

During one of their formal Sunday dinners years ago, she'd suggested red and white flowers at the entrance of the toy shop for an inviting cheeriness, plus feathered grass and shrubs. Lincoln's father had ignored her designs with a polite, though dismissive gesture.

Silence had fallen over the meal. The subject was

dropped, never to be brought up again. Looking back, Lincoln regretted that he hadn't intervened. Those dinners must have been excruciating and awkward for Shay.

He blamed his age, his immaturity. His cowardice. He pulled at the collar of his jacket and breathed slowly. If only there was a way to wash away his remorse.

"Please, Shay," he murmured. "Let me make up to you all that you lost. All that *we* lost."

From the ground floor of the shop, the contractor called out to him.

"Right on time," Lincoln shouted as he descended the stairs.

Tomorrow, he'd call her. Text her. For tomorrow was New Year's Eve.

SHANICE HAD CELEBRATED another night of Kwanzaa alone. The story of her life, this lack of companionship, and she had held back tears of weariness and desolation. When Lincoln's voice mail messages pleaded with her to pick up the phone, she detected his dejection. His desperation. Conceivably, she was so despondent herself that her emotions had been reflected in his voice.

He also texted numerous times, that night and the next day. She didn't reply, *couldn't* reply.

"God resolves every provision in my life," she stated to the empty living room. "Nothing is beyond His strength." Her throat clogged as she prayed for wisdom. She believed God delivered blessings in mysterious ways.

Still, the heaviness in her chest refused to go away. Her house was so lonely without Lincoln. All she did was think about him—whether in the kitchen, outdoors, or repotting plants in the greenhouse. He was always on her mind.

On the other hand, Candee had neither called nor texted,

and Shanice hadn't determined if that was good news or bad news. If the young couple really loved the house, it made sense they would up their offer to a fair price.

Because of the holidays, she decided to wait and contact Candee after New Year's.

THE NEXT DAY, she climbed the rickety wooden stairs to the attic and separated Granny's artifacts—stroking the pages of treasured paperback romances, vintage small appliances, and an old-fashioned typewriter. She wondered if Granny had used the typewriter each time she typed a letter to Lincoln. She'd certainly typed often while Shanice was growing up, and had refused to even touch a computer, though Shanice had offered to teach her.

"Too new-fangled and complicated," Granny had declared.

In its place, she'd typed letters to their congressman on issues affecting the community, compiled notes for errands, and tried her hand at poetry for a while. She'd written weekly letters to Shanice's parents.

Shanice's breathing slowed as she reflected on how much she missed her. Granny sensed whenever she was sad and knew exactly the right words to cheer her up.

"You are loved, Shanice. Never forget that."

She closed her eyes to bring the memories back more clearly.

Often, when she wrote a letter to her parents, she grew teary-eyed and fretful. Why hadn't they been able to fly back to the farmhouse for her birthday, or for Christmas? Why were their professions more important than their daughter?

Granny would help her, spelling words and inserting the correct punctuation. However, she never gave an opinion, never instructed Shanice on what to write.

When Shanice read the letters her parents sent her, she'd cry for hours, and Granny would scoop up the mountain of tissues on her bed and throw them in the wastebasket.

"My parents leave me constantly," she complained one night, frustrated and angry, sitting huddled on her bedroom rug in her favorite pink unicorn pajamas.

"They did us a kindness," Granny replied in a lyrical, comforting voice.

"A kindness?" Shanice looked into her grandmother's chocolate-brown eyes, searching for an answer to ease her sadness. "How? By sending us money to sustain the farm?"

"Money helps, though it's not what's most important. What's important is that I can watch you grow up to become a fine young woman. If your parents were here, you and I wouldn't be spending these precious hours together."

Shanice recalled the optimistic books of her childhood: *Mufaro's Beautiful Daughters* and *Beauty and the Beast.* In her youth, she stayed by the farmhouse's living room window, watching and waiting for her parents to drive up, sweep her into their arms, and promise to live on the farm forever with her.

She sniffed back tears. This was proof of her innocent childhood illusions.

Similar to a future with Lincoln.

She'd run from the security he offered. Suppose he left her? she had worried. She needed to control the situation.

She distanced herself from her emotions and refused to probe any deeper into her feelings. Everyday life was difficult enough. Him showing up in Roses now had complicated her concerns in ways she never imagined.

After she was done in the attic, she soaked in a sudsy, lavender-scented bath and washed her hair, then pulled on a snug pair of jogging pants, a fleecy sweatshirt, heavy wool socks, and her leopard slippers.

At her desk in the living room, she scribbled a list and titled it: Tasks to accomplish. Her pen poised over the paper, motionless. She couldn't focus.

"Concentrate!" she scolded herself. She crumpled the paper and tossed it to the floor.

She glanced at Lincoln's children's books. She'd placed them in a wicker basket by the fireplace. The illustrations were vibrant, the script eye-catching. The message simple yet profound.

Be yourself. Stand up for your beliefs.

Breathing a long, low sigh, Shanice walked over to the window. Daylight was fading, the sky a blush of vivid rose. She could hardly make out the barn to the right of the house. Beyond, the hills were dotted with a dusting of snow.

Her cherished farm stood resplendent on a December evening, and she dreaded leaving the cherished memories behind. All this nostalgia rewound the clock to a simpler era.

She glimpsed her phone on the bureau. She wanted to be furious at Lincoln—for his disinterest in her house, his vague promises urging her to look beyond December. Easy for him to say; his finances weren't an issue.

Though somehow, she wasn't angry anymore. If anything, she was touched by his unfailing patience and consideration, and the realization sent a flood of tears so hard, her shoulders quaked. If only he cared for her as much as she cared for him.

She rubbed her eyes, recalling his concern at the teahouse.

"Forget any ideas of dashing out the door," he'd said as he pulled up a chair near her. *"You're not going anywhere."*

Or when he'd spread a blanket on the wintry ground.

"Make yourself comfortable and continue to look gorgeous."

Her heart thrummed with affection. He continually overindulged her.

She sat on the sofa, stroked her cat, and reflected on the routineness of her days. Calm. Quiet. Mundane. Since seeing Lincoln, she sensed that every minute brought her closer to the edge of a momentous decision. A decision she was free to choose.

But if she fell headfirst into loving him again, she might get her heart broken and never recover. Who would be there to extend a helping hand?

No, she argued with herself. She didn't need anyone. She was self-reliant and independent.

Though she was tired. Tired of being strong, intrepid, and courageous.

Lincoln's solid, handsome image emerged, and she rubbed a hand over her heart.

He *was* her helping hand, her lifeline. He'd been there for her all along. She could share her hopes and dreams with him. She could be vulnerable with him.

She studied her phone. She should return his texts. She'd hurt him deeply.

No, no, no. Her gaze darted to his books by the fireplace, then to the Kwanzaa candles standing strong and proud, an invite for tonight's celebration.

She refused to be derailed by self-reproach. She'd apologized. Time to accept the evidence that destiny and reality were on the opposite ends of her spectrum.

Tonight was New Year's Eve. Another New Year's spent alone watching television, waiting for the ball to drop at midnight in Times Square and polishing off an entire bag of potato chips. Meanwhile, Lincoln would usher in the new year at Kathleen's Teahouse with family and employees.

Shanice's throat constricted, the upsurge of envy magnified. Her arms curled around herself. Would he miss her when she didn't show for his party? She was supposed to be his date.

Hmm. She pinched her bottom lip. Be that as it may, she wasn't going.

As she marched to the pantry for a bag of chips, the wall clock chimed the hour. Six o'clock. The party began at eight.

It didn't matter. How could she blithely waltz into the teahouse by herself?

Lincoln might act cool and distant when he saw her. Even worse, he might ignore her completely, preferring to flirt with the pretty red-haired waitress.

Nope. Not again. Jealousy over Lincoln? Absurd.

An insistent ringing of the doorbell cut into her musings.

She opened the door, surprised to see Penny standing there with an adorable, dark-haired boy. Penny wore a sparkly silver dress emphasizing her curvy figure and a matching glittery silk capelet.

"Hi. Happy New Year." Penny kept her hand on the slim boy's shoulder. The child's expression was somber, though his bright blue eyes revealed a mischievous gleam. "This is my son, Evan. May we come in?"

"Of course." Shanice stepped aside and opened the door wider.

"First, I gotta yank off these stiletto heels. They're killing my feet and the party hasn't even begun." She winked as if Shanice was an accomplice to a mysterious crime. "My shapewear will follow shortly."

"You're wearing shapewear?"

"How do you think I fit into this tight dress? I hoped either the dress would expand or I would shrink." Penny hung her capelet by the door, plunked down on the sofa, and kicked off her shoes. "Neither miracle occurred. Now I'm squished."

Duchess blinked up at Penny, obviously affronted for taking up her space. Issuing a high-pitched trill, the cat jumped off the sofa.

Evan followed her, declaring that he'd been promised a pet once he and his mother relocated to Roses.

"I'd like a cat," he informed Shanice. "Or a dog. Or a hamster."

"Let's start with a hamster," Penny said. Despite her firm tone, she added a smile, and Shanice suspected that any pet Evan asked for he would probably receive.

Shanice placed the bag of chips on the coffee table. "You're leaving Virginia?"

"I'm returning to my roots." Penny plucked up the potato chip bag. "May I?"

"Please help yourself.

Penny offered some chips to Evan. When he refused, she popped open the bag, grabbed a handful of chips and crunched. "This small town is ideal to raise a child. People are friendly and the schools are outstanding."

"Is Roy with you?"

"No." Penny glanced at Evan and set down the chips. In a hushed tone, she confided, "We decided to try a separation."

"I hope you can resolve your differences."

"We'll see. It might be time for me to make a change."

"In husbands?"

"Husbands, home, lifestyle. I'll look at what's best for my son." Penny shifted slightly to make room for Shanice to sit beside her.

"May I offer you anything to drink?" Shanice asked.

"A glass of champagne at the teahouse will cap off the evening for me. We're serving an Irish buffet. On the menu are mini shepherd pies, Guinness cheese pretzels and corned beef and cabbage."

"I see."

"What do you mean, 'I see'?"

Shanice twisted her fingers.

"Aren't you a fan of Irish food?" Penny asked.

"I love Irish food."

"Then why aren't you dressed for the party?" Penny placed a firm hand on Shanice's arm. "Don't you want to see Lincoln?"

"Yes, but—"

"Look, if you don't want to talk to him, there will be plenty of other guests there."

"True." Shanice closed her eyes, rubbed the middle of her forehead.

She'd made a savvy financial decision by countering the couple's bid in order to preserve her business. That was more than a lot of people accomplished.

Why had she imagined all her problems would magically disappear just because Lincoln Reid had reentered her life? She didn't want him to buy Granny's house and erect apartments. What she truly wanted was the chance to maintain a connection with him.

Somewhere inside, hope blossomed. "I suppose I could attend, although—"

Penny wagged her index finger. "No excuses allowed on New Year's Eve. Fresh starts and all that."

"I've dreamed enough happy endings to last a lifetime." Shanice stood, stepped back to the window and looked out. "I'm an adult and my story is real life."

"You're spouting nonsense. Do you love my brother?"

Shanice stared into the twilight. Off to her right, Evan had discovered the crumpled paper. Much to the cat's delight, Evan rolled it on the floor for the cat to chase.

"Do you love him?" Penny repeated.

"Yes," Shanice replied softly.

"Then give your love a chance. It may be none of my business, but my possessive sisterly love is kicking in. Please don't hurt him again."

Shanice turned. "I have no intention of ever hurting him."

"He's a wonderful guy."

Try as she might, Shanice couldn't avoid Penny's laser-sharp gaze. "Have you been appointed to sing Lincoln's virtues to me?"

"I'll sing it, I'll say it. I'll do whatever it takes." Penny brushed aside Shanice's objections. "You must realize how much he loves you. If not, you're a foolish woman."

Shanice struggled against her immediate response. This didn't seem the best moment to remind Penny that, in spotlighting Shanice's foolishness, she'd apparently forgotten that her husband had been unfaithful for years. She'd denied his constant travel and made excuses.

But weren't all women foolish when it came to the men they loved? They couldn't see their faults. Or perhaps they overlooked them. Shanice should accept any perceived flaws in Lincoln. After all, she had countless flaws of her own.

"Go get dressed in your New Year's Eve outfit," Penny said. "No pressure."

"Huh?"

"You're going to the party if I have to throw you over my shoulder and carry you there myself."

Some part of Shanice wanted to leap over the coffee table and hug Penny for her perception and forcefulness. The other part wanted to dig in her heels and refuse.

She vacillated.

"Give me twenty minutes," she finally said.

Penny's eyes crinkled. "That'll give me a chance to wiggle out of this shapewear that's cutting off my air supply."

Shanice chuckled and hurried up the stairs, just as Penny's shapewear flew across the room—black lacy spandex that looked too small for even a Barbie doll.

Still chuckling as she entered her bedroom, she selected her red crepe dress, black patent leather heels, and Lincoln's necklace which she'd placed on her nightstand. She was surprised the red stone on the necklace was missing again. She reached under the bed, but nope, no stone.

She stood and lifted her gaze to her reflection in the full-length mirror. She smiled in approval at the glowing, pretty woman staring back at her. Lovingly, she ran her finger over the necklace, then clasped it around her throat. She completed the festive outfit with faux diamond chandelier earrings. Her makeup consisted of blusher, eyeliner, and thick black mascara, and she styled her hair in loose ringlets. Smoothing out her dress, she descended the stairs.

Stiletto heels in hand, Penny stood at the bottom. A smile emerged on her rosy face, though she didn't speak.

Shanice braced herself. "I wish you would say something."

"You are dazzling," Penny replied. "I want to grab your arm and drag you out of here."

"I'm ready."

"Unfortunately, I have bad news."

"What is it?"

"Your cat is missing. We think she slipped out the front door."

"How?"

"The door must've been left ajar after we walked in. We called her but there's no sight of her anywhere."

Evan's face reddened. His eyes filled with tears. "It's dark outside. Is she lost?"

"Cats have night vision." Shanice overruled his concerns with a shake of her head. "Duchess is an indoor and outdoor cat. Please don't worry."

"Well, it's time to go." Penny eyed her cell phone, made an unusual sound in her throat, and began typing madly.

"I'll hop in with you, if that's okay," Shanice said.

"I'm sorry. That won't work." Penny slipped on her shoes and snatched her capelet.

"I thought you wanted to grab my arm and drag—"

"Some other time."

Shanice watched the rapid rise and fall of Penny's large chest. "Huh?"

"By the way, I like your necklace. Too bad about the missing stone."

"You noticed?"

"I knew what to look for. Tell my brother to buy you another one. He can well afford it." Penny scanned Shanice's entire outfit. "Lincoln will be tongue-tied when he sees you."

"Let's hope not." Shanice stretched out her arms. "We have a lot to discuss."

"First, you need to find your cat."

"I told you—"

"See you at the party." Penny rushed Evan out, acting as if the matter was settled and promptly ending the conversation.

CHAPTER 10

ell, that was odd.

Shanice was half of the opinion that Penny had lost her mind. Possibly her tight dress had affected her oxygen intake.

She retrieved the empty bag of chips, the crumpled paper from the floor, and Penny's lacy shapewear.

Uh, she'd forgotten it?

She stepped into the kitchen to throw the paper and chip bag in the wastebasket and draped the shapewear over a chair.

On the enamel table stood the bouquet Lincoln had given her—fragrant red roses and pure-white lilies. They had survived beautifully, hardly wilted, and the faint scent of Douglas fir persisted.

She changed the water in the vase and retrimmed the stems. With any luck, the flowers would last through January first.

She fingered the velvety petals. Something of Lincoln's remained. The thought should've soothed her emotions, yet everything about this evening seemed strained.

Conceivably, her decision to attend the party might lead to disaster and a broken heart. It was foolish to expect otherwise. Kathleen and Rob would welcome her, but Lincoln might be the uncomfortable exception, and it was his party.

The doorbell rang, and she looked up sharply. No doubt, Penny realized she'd forgotten her shapewear. Firmly, she'd tell her that she had changed her mind and wouldn't attend the party.

She wiped her hands on a dishtowel and weighed her conflicting emotions.

Yes. No. Yes.

No.

Her decision had nothing to do with Penny. Her conflict was Lincoln. She missed him, and the prospect of spending another New Year's Eve alone carried an undefinable sadness to her chest.

She mumbled her despondency aloud, and stared down at her empty hands.

A sharp knock followed by the doorbell again. Her wall clock chimed seven o'clock.

She grabbed the shapewear, trooped to the entry and swung open the door. "Forget something?" she asked.

"Umm, I don't think so." Lincoln stood in the doorway, a fine wool jacket over his shoulders, holding a whirling wrath of fur. Her cat. Duchess tolerated being held, but only on her terms.

Lincoln's gaze shifted from the shapewear to Shanice's face. No doubt he was registering the heightened color of her cheeks.

"Happy New Year, Shay." Duchess blinked at her, smacking her tail against his arm. "Isn't this your cat? She was sitting near the porch."

"Lincoln, Lincoln!" Honestly, the man materialized when

she least expected. "Duchess! We wondered where you were off to."

"We?"

"Penny was just here."

"Ah." He squirmed.

"Did you know?"

"Maybe." His words said one thing. His smile said another.

She wanted to touch his arm and welcome him. She didn't. "Don't you have a party to attend?"

He stopped halfway in the process of setting the cat down. With a tail swish and a loud meow, the cat reminded him she was still in his arms and clearly displeased.

"Don't you?" he asked.

That pull between them. There was no refuting it. She stepped backward. "I'm not going."

He set the cat on the floor and Duchess skirted toward the kitchen.

Lincoln edged closer. "Why not? Parties are enjoyable."

"It's your party, not mine."

"Yet you're dressed for a party." He arched a dark eyebrow and waited for an answer that didn't come. His appreciative gaze roamed over her, lingering at the necklace at her throat. He smiled, subtle but meaningful. "You look stunning."

"Thank you."

"I love your necklace."

She chuckled. Consistently charming. "Thanks."

His hand stroked the necklace. "It's missing that ruby stone again."

"I glued it on. I told you. I don't know where it went."

"Regardless, you're still wearing it."

"Yes." How could she not? It meant so much to her.

He studied her expression. He could always read her mood. "May I come in?"

She tossed the shapewear onto her shoulder. She couldn't look more awkward. She tried not to grin, but couldn't help herself. "I assume you're in a hurry. I didn't expect—"

She didn't finish her thoughts because she was gaping at him, as if she'd never seen his face before. He was impeccably dressed in tailored black pants and a crisp white shirt open at the throat. In contrast, dark shadows underlined his brilliant blue eyes.

"I'm not in a hurry. Not at all. Stay right there." He strode to his Jeep parked at the front of the house, and returned with a covered platter of food. He set the food on the rocking chair.

"One more thing." He dashed to the side of the porch, then carried a six foot balsam fir to her front door. It was bedecked with zebra ornaments and an African-American angel topper. Somehow, the tree looked fuller. *Her tree.*

Breathless, she swallowed a laugh of disbelief. "How did you ever—"

"Very, very carefully." He reached down and handed her the platter of food.

She could hardly speak. "Now what's this?" There was too much to take in.

"Bread pudding with butterscotch sauce. All the way from Kathleen's Teahouse in County Derry, Ireland … I mean, Roses."

She peeled back the cover. "Ten servings. Who are they all for?"

"You. And me. I remember you liked bread pudding and included it on the buffet menu."

"I like pudding. But I'm only one person. If I ate all that pudding—"

"Together we're two people, Shay."

Two. Together, we're two.

His tone was a meaningful, captivating drawl that turned her limbs to liquid.

She leaned against the doorjamb, the platter in one hand, the shapewear on her shoulder. "Which means?"

He seemed to consider where to begin and kissed her lightly on the forehead. "I'd like to celebrate New Year's with you. Here. At the farm."

"What about your party at the teahouse?"

"They'll never miss me. Penny will keep the party lively and explain our absences."

"*Our?*"

"You're my date, remember?"

Her voice hitched with the realization of his words, of his actions. "But why shouldn't *you* go?"

"I'd prefer to spend a quiet New Year's here with you. I hope you feel the same. We'll honor Kwanzaa ... watch sitcoms ... play a round of checkers."

"I'll beat you."

He laughed. "Is that an invitation?"

"Sure." She pressed her lips together to keep from grinning. "A marathon of *I Love Lucy* is playing from nine o'clock till midnight."

"Excellent." He eyed the shapewear. "Should I ask what that is, exactly?"

"It belongs to your sister."

"Figures."

"Don't knock it." She hung the garment on the coat rack. He placed his coat beside it. "For many women, it's a miracle worker."

The cat whizzed by her feet as she set the platter on the coffee table. Lincoln picked up the tree and arranged the balsam beside the fireplace. Her tree. The six-foot artificial fir was so familiar when she'd decorated it for the Festival of Trees, yet now looked so different.

"Do you want to see your tree up close?" he asked.

She moved forward, her heart hammering in anticipation. The zebra ornaments and angel topper were still there. On closer inspection, colorful wooden rocking horses hung from several branches.

"You made these?"

"Yep."

"When?"

"In my spare time at the old toy shop yesterday."

"They're beautiful."

He smiled. Actually, he hummed. "Thanks."

She gaped at him. "You were the mysterious bidder who placed the winning bid on the tree?"

"Yep.

"The money went for a good cause—the senior nutrition program in town."

"Yep."

Seriously, the man was exasperating. When she wanted him to communicate and explain, he'd decided he was a man of few words.

She marched to the coffee table and retrieved the platter. Even from this distance, she felt his presence. The magnetism was real, and also transitory. True, he made her smile, and each minute she spent with him brought a feeling of breathless anticipation. She could chat with him for hours. They never ran out of subjects to discuss. Thanks to him, these past few days were a holiday she'd treasure forever.

Now, though, it was over, and him being here merely compounded a heartbreaking situation.

She glanced at him. "What's wrong with us?"

He muffled a laugh. "Nothing. Absolutely nothing. We are a man and a woman who are attracted to each other. More than attracted ..."

Intending to get spoons and napkins, she dashed to the

kitchen. His footsteps followed behind her, steady and sure. When he entered, he propped his shoulder against the opposite wall and asked, "Do you need any help?"

"I can manage sorting a couple dishes of pudding by myself."

"Are you forgetting I'm the accomplished cook?"

She stood across from him, her back to the refrigerator, and gave a thumbs up.

"I feared you wouldn't let me in," he continued. "I planned to call you first, or text you, but decided because of your nonresponse, that in person was better." His feet were braced slightly apart. Idly, he tapped his fingers on his leg. His nervous habit.

For a split second, her limbs refused to move. She grabbed for the spoons. "You're always welcome."

"Am I? I'm hopeful because I have an offer for you."

"The farmhouse is already sold."

"I'm well aware, Shay, because I bought it, though that wasn't the offer I was referring to."

"You bought the farmhouse?" Her heartbeat drummed in her chest. She pondered throwing the spoons up into the air. "You bought the farmhouse?" She pressed her hand to her mouth in disbelief.

A brief spurt of happiness flowed through her before she realized he must be lying. "No you didn't. The young couple bought my house."

"They tried, though I outbid them." He gave a short laugh. "I must've set a record, buying three properties in a day. Your Realtor is quite happy with her hefty commissions."

"What—" Shanice's voice broke as the full meaning of his admittance sank in. "What properties did you buy?"

"First, the Roses Hotel. Then, as soon as Candee informed me about the couple's offer on your house, I jumped in."

"You didn't tell me."

"I wanted to. I encouraged you to be patient because I hoped to surprise you."

"Encouraged? That's not quite the term I'd use. You were downright secretive."

He shrugged. "What are surprises for?"

She tried to understand all he was saying, though her thoughts scattered. She was too elated to think clearly. "So now you own my house."

"Correction. *We* own your house, Shay."

She walked toward him and he met her halfway by the enamel kitchen table. Her steps were light. Surely, he heard the loud banging of her heart.

His arms closed around her. "I want to be *the one*. The only one. I missed you so very much."

"And I've missed you."

Exquisite and emotional, his kisses were tender and sweet. Filled with happiness and awe, she gazed up at him. He was so handsome, resembling a man from her romance books—all solid planes and rock-hard muscle.

With a quiet groan, he broke away and caught her wrist. "I have some things to show you."

He led her to the tree and gestured to a purple velvet box hanging from an upper branch.

"It's not what you think," he warned as she flipped the box open.

In all honesty, she expected a diamond ring, a proposal of marriage. Instead, she peered inside and lifted out a gold key.

She held the key up and inspected it. "Is this an official key to my farmhouse?"

"No. It's the key to my houseboat. I'm hoping you'll come and live with me." Before she replied, he fished in his pocket. "I also have something else. Actually, two things." Two additional velvet boxes appeared. One red and one black.

"Which should I open first?"

"The red box."

She complied and pulled out another key. "What's this?"

"The key to your apartment complex."

"In Huntington?" She processed his remarks. "Not only my apartment? The entire apartment complex?"

"Eventually, I might expand the toy business to Huntington too, and the complex will give new employees an option for housing. In the meantime, I'll keep renting it."

"Therefore, you own two places where I live."

"No. *You* own two places." He brushed a stubborn curl from her cheek. "Now open the black velvet box."

He waited, studying the expression on her face. A tiny diamond sparkled up at her.

"Do you like it?" He pressed his hands lightly to her cheeks.

Joy spread through her, so intensely that she ached. "I love it." Her fingers tingled as she withdrew the diamond and held it up to the light. It glittered and sparkled with shining promise.

"I bought that ring for you sixteen years ago. I held out a confidence you'd return to me, and here you are. Or rather, here I am." He slid his hands up her arms, gazing directly into her eyes. "The diamond is small, but it's all a nineteen-year-old guy could afford. I promise I'll buy you a bigger ring, a better one."

"No, no, it's perfect."

He slipped it on the fourth finger of her left hand. "Shay, will you marry me?"

"Yes." She nodded, though the streaming tears made it difficult to speak. "Yes, yes, I'll marry you."

"I love you." He cradled her face and thumbed the tears from her eyes. "I'm waiting to hear three exquisite words. I'm willing to wait until you're ready to say them."

Duchess strutted into the room, interrupting as she foraged beneath the sink.

"Her secret stash," Shanice said. Reluctantly, she pulled from Lincoln's arms and bent to examine the bottle caps. A glittering red stone snagged her attention. "Ah-hah. I found the criminal."

"And I found you. Again." He kissed her as if he'd never let go.

"Am I in your way?" she asked paraphrasing the lyrics of their favorite song.

"Never." He held her close, gazing into her eyes. They fell into a soundless cadence to the Whitney Houston love song they knew so well. "I will always love you, Shay."

She understood. His fingers tightened around her, and she turned her face up as he brushed kisses on her temple, her chin, her nape. This was happening. This was reality.

She recognized the love, the tenderness, on his handsome face. "And I will always love you."

EPILOGUE

 ight Months Later

LINCOLN WALKED ONTO HIS HOUSEBOAT, moored and tethered on Hilton Head Island. The boat rocked when he came on board. He was used to it, and hoped his beautiful wife hadn't suffered morning sickness because of it.

She hadn't complained. But then, Shay never complained.

He was pleased to see her soaking up the sun on the upper deck.

Hmm. On closer look, she wasn't soaking up the sun. A laptop computer was balanced on her legs and she was studying. A bowl of wintergreen peppermint puff candy sat on a patio table beside her.

"Hello, gorgeous." He climbed the stairs and planted a kiss on her lips. "You're supposed to be resting."

"I'm trying to finish this online landscape-design course before the baby comes."

"You have three months left." He sat beside her and

glanced at his watch. The date was September first. The time was four o'clock. The day and time when they first met all those years ago.

A coincidence? He doubted it. He didn't believe in coincidences anymore. He believed in fate. And one discerning and perceptive grandmother.

"Thank you, Granny," he whispered.

"After we move into the farmhouse next month, I want to get a dog," he said aloud.

Shay shaded her eyes and peered up at him. "And chickens?"

"Definitely chickens."

She grinned. "I won't need to balance along a narrow dock to borrow a cup of sugar from a neighbor anymore."

"You've never borrowed any sugar." He laughed. "Besides, I'm the accomplished cook."

"I don't know if Duchess will approve."

"You're referring to your cat's reaction to my imaginary dog?"

"Yes."

"Lucky is a good name, don't you think?"

"For a dog, yes."

He trailed a kiss up to her ear. "What about for a child?"

"We don't know if our baby is a boy or a girl. You refused to find out ahead of time."

He lifted her hair and kissed her nape. "I like surprises."

He gazed out at the Atlantic Ocean. So much had changed in a few short months. Soon after he'd proposed, they'd been married in a small chapel on the island. Penny was the only attendant and the matron of honor. His nephew, Evan, was the ring bearer.

Since then, Penny had divorced Roy and taken over the supervision of the toy shop's renovations in Roses.

"You need to spend time with your wife," she had

declared. She was also dieting and kept a running diary of her weight loss. So far, she'd lost ten pounds.

His wife looked up from her laptop. "How is your new children's book coming? I hope Tuggy the Tugboat is going on a new adventure and will find what he's been looking for."

Lincoln placed his arm around her shoulders. "I promise he'll sail the high seas, though this is Tuggy's last book."

"Why?"

"His search is over because *my* search is over."

"Have you thought of a title yet?"

He had. The title had come before he finished the book.

Tuggy the Tugboat Is Finally Home.

Lincoln added a P.S. to himself.

And married the woman he loved. The woman of his dreams.

THE END

USA TODAY BESTSELLING AUTHOR
JOSIE RIVIERA
Christmas in the Air
PUPPIES FOR CHRISTMAS

PROLOGUE

*P*enelope Reid sat glued to her seat.

Breathe in. There's nothing to be nervous about. Flying in an airplane is routine for many businesspeople.

And she, unfortunately, was a businessperson.

She attempted to smile at the flight attendant who walked past, before resuming her pep talk to herself.

Virginia to Hilton Head Island is a short flight.

She considered texting her brother, Lincoln, with a 'mission accomplished' message, though he wouldn't get the message until she had cell service again. He'd encouraged her to take the flight to secure a toy shop location. She'd complied, albeit reluctantly, though she'd been successful with the negotiations and closed on the deal. Nonetheless, when she finally arrived home, she intended to wring his neck. He knew how much she dreaded flying.

She cut a glance at her handsome seatmate's profile. She'd admired the angle of his face—his sharp jawline and straight nose—throughout most of the flight. Framed by the afternoon sunlight streaming in the window, he seemed relaxed.

Of course, he seemed relaxed because he was sleeping. In fact, he'd slept almost non-stop.

She coughed and nudged him with her elbow. She needed someone to talk to and take her mind off the flight. She'd already breezed through every magazine in the seat pocket.

"Hmm?" He took off his aviator sunglasses and turned toward her. His eyes were a deep shade of brown, warm and mesmerizing, rimmed with black eyelashes. His skin exuded a healthy golden glow. "Have we arrived?"

"Hardly."

He peered out the window. "Cloudy day."

"The weather forecaster called for rain."

"He was probably right."

"*She* was probably right," Penelope corrected.

He grinned. "Touché."

Penelope sat up straighter. "Before you fell asleep, we were discussing our jobs."

"Were we?"

"We were about to." Her seatbelt tightened as she leaned toward him. "I've managed a toy shop business ever since I was a teenager."

"Sounds fun."

"I hate it."

His dark eyebrows curved upward. "Why?"

"Do you want the truth?"

"By all means."

"I shouldn't be telling you this, but I've never been good at deception."

"Bravo." He gave her a thumbs-up. "So, do tell."

"I'd like to do something else."

"Nothing wrong with that. I'll keep your secret." He flashed her a positively magnetic smile.

Her heart stilled. Here sat a good-looking man who had listened to her rattle on about her life whenever he opened his eyes. At least, she assumed he listened. She'd held him captive because he couldn't escape. They were seated next to each other in first class. Still, she'd begun to assume they were friends, and he was an attentive guy.

At his assessing gaze, a flush warmed her cheeks. "I'm bored with my job. I want to create, not manage."

"Create what?"

"I'm not cut out for left-brained, logical analysis anymore. Let's call it a midlife crisis."

"Let's." Another smile. "Do you have another job lined up?"

"No."

"Is your job difficult?" His tone lowered. Thick, wavy hair fell across his forehead, and he pushed back the strands with his hand. His features were a bit weathered, his jawline and cheekbones prominent. A rugged man who apparently spent time outdoors if appearances were any indication.

The thump of attraction in her chest surprised her. She hadn't felt an interest in any guy since her divorce.

"No, my job isn't difficult," she said. "Just repetitive."

"Playing with toys can't be all bad."

She stiffened at his off-hand remark. If he was teasing, he wasn't funny.

"I don't play with toys and they're not mine," she clarified. "I *manage* the business and we sell toys."

He cocked an eyebrow. "We?"

"My brother and I."

"No husband?" He sounded as if he accused her of something—she wasn't sure what—because of her marital status.

"No husband."

"So, you're in the family firm. Come on, mate. Toys are heaps of fun."

Mate? Inwardly, she shook her head.

"Bloody tough, then?"

Bloody? Who used these terms?

"I've done the same job forever." She gave herself a second to regroup. "Since I was a teen."

"When you decide what you want in life, focus on it and let go of the old ways," he replied. "Embrace your creativity."

"At my age?"

"At any age."

He scratched a finger along the shadowy bristles on his jaw. Wasn't it time he shaved? Come to think of it, he looked as if he hadn't slept soundly in a week. His jeans were clean, though his green cotton shirt was rumpled.

He paused to consider her—regarding her cream-colored crepe blouse, which she'd managed to spill coffee on that morning—and her stretchy brown slacks. She hadn't had an extra minute to put on an ounce of makeup before rushing through the Richmond, Virginia, airport to catch the plane to Hilton Head Island. In her hotel room, she'd only showered and added a light spritz of her favorite lavender-scented perfume.

She hardly traveled anywhere anymore, and a commute to Virginia was a last-minute meeting she couldn't avoid. She didn't even like going to Virginia, because it reminded her of her old life and her ex.

To make matters worse, she'd overslept. The evening before, she'd overindulged in fried food and two glasses of celebratory wine.

Conversation was easy when her seatmate didn't stare at her. But now that he was wide awake, she was unprepared for his assessing gaze.

She brushed nonexistent lint from her slacks. "What should I do for a living? Any suggestions?"

Mr. Too Handsome for his own good, she added to herself.

"There are heaps of books on the subject. Whatever suits

your skill level and interests." He gave a short nod, turned back toward the window, and slipped on his sunglasses.

"I'm excellent at parenting, although my son disagrees," she said. "I'm a single mother of a soon-to-be teenager and life isn't easy."

"No matter the age of the child, parenting calls for patience."

"Do you speak from experience?" she asked.

"Nope."

"Do you have kids?"

"Nope. Never will."

Why? she wondered. She grabbed a candy bar from her purse and took a nibble, debating on whether to ask him to explain. However, he kept his face turned toward the window. In under two minutes, she detected soft breathing. Most likely, he was asleep again.

"I'm divorced and my ex has remarried," she said. "His twenty-something wife was a coworker, and she is decades younger than me." Penelope added another fact that continually gnawed at her. "They're blissfully happy and expecting a baby."

"Are congratulations in order?" her seatmate mumbled.

"Not on my end." She tried to push down her snide comment and found she couldn't. "I find it all a bit odd, considering my ex's age." Resentment boiled inside her when she least expected. "He'll be in his seventies by the time their child graduates from college."

"What's your ex's name?"

"Roy."

"Mmm."

She stopped speaking for a second to gain control of her voice. "He moved to another state, making our shared custody agreement for our son trickier than ever."

Her seatmate nodded slightly.

"You know what else?"

He still faced the window. "Hmm?"

She bit off a piece of candy, chewed, and swallowed. "All the guys I've seen since my divorce are cads. I subscribed to an online dating website, but my first date proved an embarrassing bust." She didn't elaborate, and he didn't ask. She'd also dated an art teacher at her son's school until the man gave up. He was a pleasant guy, but her feelings for him had been absent. Plus, he'd acted as if her son didn't exist.

She'd resolved herself to the fact that she wouldn't commit to anyone ever again. Her heart couldn't recover from another broken relationship. Living inside the cocoon of a quiet, safe environment was preferable and assured no one got hurt.

"In summary," she finished, "I've decided to stop dating altogether."

"An archaic term," he replied.

"Dating?"

"Cad."

She waved a dismissive hand. "I refuse to be forced into any more awkward conversations at the local pizza joint."

"You don't like pizza?"

"I like all food."

"Then never say never."

"What's that supposed to—"

The plane jerked. Several shrieks from passengers rang throughout the plane.

Penelope joined in the shrieking, louder than the rest. Her half-eaten candy bar dropped to the floor.

Her seatmate swiveled to her and pocketed his sunglasses. "Are you all right?" His gaze darted about the plane's cabin before landing on her.

"Didn't you feel the plane?" she asked.

"It's just a bump."

"I'm afraid of heights."

"You're on a plane," he reminded.

"I had no choice. I was forced to close on a business deal." She hadn't had a spare moment for anxiety to grab hold when her brother had booked the last-minute flight, and hindsight did little good. She'd assured herself there was nothing to fear.

Envision floating above pearly fluffy clouds while drinking a glass of sparkling water, she told herself.

What was it about reality that proved so different from your imaginings?

She indicated the window—they were flying above *gray* clouds, not pearly, and they weren't at all fluffy.

"To keep my mind off of the fact we're thirty-five thousand feet in the air, I've babbled constantly," she said.

"You talked. You haven't babbled. Talk all you want." He reached into his pocket and handed her a clean white handkerchief. Despite the plane's cold temperature, she was sweating. He'd noticed the sweat beads on her forehead before she had.

"You haven't told me anything about yourself," she prompted.

"What would you like to know?"

She glanced at his left hand. No ring. He wasn't married, although the lack of a wedding ring didn't mean anything.

Regardless, she asked, "Are you married?"

"Absolutely not. Once was enough."

"You're divorced?"

"Thankfully divorced. Marriage isn't for me."

"Why not?"

He shrugged. "My career is important and all-consuming. Romance, women, and marriage got in the way."

She took several seconds to digest his information.

Got in the way of what? she wanted to ask.

"Planes are remarkable if you stop to analyze the mechanics," he said.

"Now is not the time to analyze how planes stay in the air." She dabbed at her forehead with his handkerchief. Her hands were clammy. "Never again," she muttered.

"You won't ever fly again?"

She twisted her wristwatch. "I'll drive or take a bus or a train."

"Have you always been afraid of flying?"

"No. Only the past few years."

"Suppose you're traveling overseas?" he asked.

"Are you kidding? I'll never fly overseas."

When the plane bounced from side to side, she grabbed hold of his arm. Her throat went dry. A fresh start of panic stunned her as the fasten seat belts sign flashed.

Flight attendants buzzed through the cabin, reminding the passengers to buckle up, before scurrying to their own seats. The captain came on the intercom and assured that the plane was flying outside of a thunderstorm, and the occurrence was brief and passing.

Penelope tugged at her seatbelt, ensuring she was secure. Her seatmate patted her shoulder, making no attempt to move away or disentangle his arm from her death grip.

He was tuned in to her fear.

Maybe he was attracted to her—despite the deepening lines around her mouth and the dark circles under her eyes. She didn't need to peer at herself in a mirror to realize she looked a sight. She never seemed to get a sound night's sleep anymore and blamed her restless, worried thoughts on her son for keeping her awake at two a.m.

She dropped her hand and passed him his handkerchief. "Is Hilton Head Island your final destination?"

"No. You?"

"I'm staying overnight on my brother's houseboat, then

driving on to Roses in North Carolina," she said. "You may have heard of the town."

Roses combined small-town charm with big-city conveniences. The tidy homes blended with the landscape of the scenic mountains. In the summer, the town was renowned for bubbling hot springs and comfortable mountain temperatures.

A look she couldn't read flickered across his tanned face. "You're staying on a houseboat?"

"Southern summers are intense, and the ocean breeze is a welcome respite, especially at night."

"Houseboat living is … different; I'll grant you that. As for me, I'll stay on land, thank you very much."

"Or in the air," she reminded.

He laughed out loud. "You live in Roses?'

She nodded. "Roses is my childhood home. I moved away after college and got married, then returned after my divorce. Since then, I haven't made many friends."

At first, familiarity had enfolded her like a generous hug. Now, things had changed.

"Why not?" he asked.

"Friendships are difficult. The women at my son's school have a close circle reaching back to when their kids were in kindergarten. I missed all that." She cast a glance at him. His expression was unreadable. "Don't get me wrong. Roses is lovely. The main street is lined with local shops, and the park boasts a bandstand for outdoor concerts."

"I prefer big cities. I like all the restaurant options and public transportation."

"Roses is unique and has loads of restaurants."

"I'm sure the town is a beaut." His gaze lingered on her face. "Care for a cold one?"

"I don't drink," she said. "Correction. I don't drink often."

"I used to say that."

"And *now* you drink?"

"Depends on the circumstances."

"The flight attendants are buckled in." She indicated them with her chin.

"They'll be up and about soon."

"You fly a lot?"

"Sometimes," he said. "I've experienced turbulence, though flying is safer than any other form of transportation."

"A quote from …?"

"Me." He smiled. "In all fairness, I read the statistic in *Popular Science* magazine."

"Are you trying to reassure me with a magazine quote?"

"I'm a pro. My job is all about counseling and prevention."

He opted for a caffeinated soda when the flight attendants came to their feet and began serving passengers one last time. He picked up Penelope's candy bar, murmuring, "Your sweet fell on the floor," and handed the candy to the attendant to discard.

"No cold one?" she asked him.

He raised his glass. "I'm a fan of America's free refills."

She'd noted his accent. Probably Australian.

Penelope ordered a low-calorie lemon-lime sparkling water.

"I prefer coffee," she informed him. "In fact, I'm obsessed, and drink six cups a day."

"You didn't order coffee."

"I take my coffee with loads of cream and sugar. Low-calorie soda has no calories, while sugar and cream add hundreds. It's clear sailing for healthy eating now since the fourth of July is safely behind me."

He regarded her with a quizzical frown. "The fourth of July is a problem?"

"If you love hot dogs, hamburgers, and potato salad." She

extended her hand. "Introductions are a little late, but I'm Penelope Reid."

"Jacob." He shook her hand. His fingers were strong. She wondered what he did for a living—his all-consuming profession. Perhaps he was a professor of some sort—teaching psychology courses or counseling. He projected an air of professionalism, despite his casual appearance.

"Here's to the next holiday, Penelope."

"And will-power." She slipped her hand from his. "Fortunately, there are no holidays until my birthday in November."

Her fiftieth birthday. She left that noteworthy detail out, although she guessed this guy's age close to hers. A few threads of silver in his dark-brown hair caught a sliver of sunlight, and subtle lines were etched on his forehead. Men's ages were often difficult to determine. Many men grew handsomer with age. Jacob was apparently one of them.

"What kind of cake do you like?" he asked.

She paused. No one had ever posed that question to her before. "Carrot cake is my favorite."

"Me too. With cream cheese frosting?"

She gave a thumbs-up. "The best."

After her birthday, and much worse, came Christmas. These past few years, her saddest memories were at Christmas. She struggled hard not to think about her ex's unexplained absences when he'd begun having his affair. They were lonely. And now, with Evan readying to visit his father in Florida by flying there by himself, the days preceding Christmas would be lonelier still.

In truth, she couldn't wait for the holiday to be over. Silently, she shook her head, guilty about her lack of Christmas spirit.

By the time they landed, she realized she had told him the month of her birthday, her hometown, her parenting situation, and her single status.

When the plane stopped at the terminal, Jacob hoisted her carry-on luggage down from the overhead compartment. All Aussie charm, if Australia was indeed his homeland, and chivalrous to a fault.

He followed behind her as they exited the plane, and a blast of sultry air greeted them. A reminder that summer still held a firm hold on the Carolinas.

"A pleasure meeting you, Penelope Reid," he said.

She met his gaze as they stepped into the bustling terminal. "The feeling is mutual, Jacob."

"Safe travels to Roses."

"Thanks. You, too." For wherever he was going. She slung her handbag over her shoulder and grabbed her carry-on bag.

He walked backwards a few steps. "Penelope?"

"Yes?"

He drew out his cell phone. "May I take your picture?"

"Why?"

"Truth?"

"By all means."

"You're a lovely woman."

She hesitated. "Okay."

"More than okay. Perfect." He snapped a photo and pocketed his phone. "Well, cheerio."

"Goodbye, Jacob."

She watched as he departed. Broad shouldered, he held himself tall, self-assured as he disappeared into the swarm of passengers.

Somewhere in her gut, she regretted the fact she wouldn't see him again.

After two hours of non-stop conversation, admittedly one-sided and except for when he was sleeping, she'd only learned his first name.

CHAPTER 1

What a way for her son to start the second month of seventh grade.

Penelope studied herself in the tall gold mirror propped in her bedroom. She'd dressed professionally—a bohemian style midi dress and strappy sandals, because she planned to head to work after seeing to Evan.

She suspected he had strep throat. Again. What twelve-year-old boy got strep throat every other week?

She'd been surprised the previous evening when he hadn't finished the chocolate ice cream she'd brought to soothe his throat. She'd finished it instead because she couldn't let the ice cream go to waste. She'd used a clean spoon, assuring herself that whatever virus he had wasn't contagious.

"I'm not sick, Mom. Everyone gets sore throats." Evan stood in the living room of their eighteenth-century Victorian home wearing his customary saggy jeans. He shrugged on his black leather jacket and crossed his chubby arms. His cheeks shone a bright red, a sprinkling of freckles across his nose. His stout build reminded Penelope of herself, though his legs were too long for his body—a promise—if her ex's height was any indication, of the tall man Evan would someday become.

Her thoughts swerved to Jacob and his muscular, sturdy physique. She scolded herself to stop thinking about him—yet he remained in her thoughts. He was a curve in the road, a curve in her life she could ill afford. She didn't know why she'd told him so much about herself.

"Did you hear me, Mom?" Her son interrupted her musings.

The humidity of a Southern October afternoon should have deterred him from wearing a jacket. And what was it about dark colors these days? A kind of rebellion, she supposed. She kept her opinions to herself. No use fighting over small battles like a black jacket.

She placed her hand on his warm forehead. "You have a fever."

He pulled back as if she'd branded him with her touch. Where had her apple-cheeked, angelic son gone? Once Evan hit twelve years old, he'd turned into a mini monster.

"Are you driving me to the doctor's office?" he asked.

Did he try to avoid being seen with her, or was this all her imagination? He sure didn't act like a kid who wanted to go places with his mother. "We can't walk from the outskirts of town. Besides, my throat is sore, too."

"You made two appointments?" He groaned. "We'll be there forever."

"Just one. I'm hoping the doctor will recommend an over-the-counter medicine for me."

"I'll ask him for you." Evan jutted out his chin in defiance. "Then I can go by myself."

"Dr. Williams' office is past the Roses' recreation center." She vacillated, remembering the numerous swim meets Evan had once participated in.

"So?"

"You used to love to swim." Happy memories flooded her thoughts. "The coach said you were a natural at the butterfly stroke."

"I guess the butterflies flew away," Evan muttered.

"Swimming is a lifelong sport. Exercise builds endurance and will keep you healthy and slim." That last bit slipped out, and her son frowned. She hadn't meant any inference to his weight gain over the past year.

"I like ocean swimming," he said quietly. "The rec center's indoor pool is too closed in."

She wondered how their conversation had gone from strep throat to swimming, but a dialogue, any dialogue, with Evan, was welcome.

"We never lived near the ocean, but we'll visit during the summer." A thought came to mind; overseeing the Hilton Head toy headquarters instead of the shop in Roses, commuting if she was needed in the office. "I'll homeschool you next semester and we can live on Uncle Lincoln's houseboat."

"How will I be able to spend spring break with Dad and Victoria?"

"Your stepmother will be absorbed with the newborn baby, and I'm sure your father and I can work out a congenial solution."

"Oh, right. Like that would ever happen."

A solution might be possible, if her ex was even remotely agreeable, and they didn't get into an argument whenever they discussed custody. Only Roy would move clear to another state to please his young wife, forsaking the needs of his son.

"A houseboat in a harbor is a fishbowl, like living here," Evan said.

"Well, we can rent a cottage farther out. How about

Daufuskie? The island is only a short ferry ride from Hilton Head's mainland and surrounded by the Atlantic Ocean."

"Oh, great. Then everyone at school will call me a freak."

She sighed. There was no pleasing Evan, though she tried and tried. "You're a freak for living on a houseboat?"

"For being home schooled."

She faltered. "Have your classmates called you a freak before?"

"Try every day, Mom. I just want to swim where no one is staring at me. Especially my teammates from the swim team."

"Why on earth would they stare at you?"

"Because I'm fat and ugly and a slow swimmer."

"That's ridiculous."

"Don't say it's not true, because we both know it is. The popular kids don't want anything to do with me." His shoulders hunched, yet his gaze was astute. "You competed in championship competitions. Uncle Lincoln showed me the newspaper clipping when you won first place in freestyle."

"Perseverance pays off."

"You always say swimming is a lifetime sport, but you never swim anymore."

That was her life eons ago, before her college years, her failed marriage. In high school, she'd immersed herself in competitions.

Everything had changed after her marriage.

But not at first. Blissful happiness came first.

And then she'd begun to suspect her husband was unfaithful, though Roy had denied her suspicions. If she ignored the signs, perhaps his affair would go away, she told herself.

It hadn't.

Since the betrayal, heartbreak, and subsequent divorce, she'd fortified herself with an impenetrable barricade. She was serene and no-nonsense. In her youth, she'd been known for her sense of humor, but hardly anything made her laugh anymore.

She breathed in. Nothing was going to topple her hard-earned and sensible equilibrium.

She recalled the comradery with her teammates and the late-night swim meets. She loved belonging to a tight-knit group of friends she relied on. Was Evan missing out on those same memories because he'd abruptly quit the team?

Why hadn't she realized his withdrawal from all extracurricular activities since her divorce and their move to Roses? The signs were clearly there if she'd only taken the time to notice.

You're a bad mom, her conscience reprimanded.

I try my best.

Still, she should've encouraged him more. Instead, she'd become more involved in the business and neglected her son in the bargain.

She took in Evan's appearance—sandy-brown hair and vivid blue eyes, and her heart squeezed. His heavy-set build would thin out as he grew, and his resemblance to her good-looking brother, Lincoln, was striking. Someday, Evan would become a young man with more girlfriends than he could count.

He wasn't aware of that yet and didn't care. He was interested in the present. She prided herself on identifying issues at the toy shop and fixing them. Now she needed to focus on her vulnerable son and fix whatever was causing his problems. She hoped she wasn't too late.

"Make sure your hamster's cage is secure," she said. "Yesterday, he got out and ran all over the house."

"Giblet is a girl, Mom," Evan replied. "Besides, I want a puppy."

"Let's see how well you care for your hamster first. Last week I rescued her from behind a shelf where she got stuck."

Evan obeyed while muttering under his breath for having to do chores when he was sick, and they walked out the front door.

"Won't you be late for work?" he asked.

"Are you still trying to get rid of me?"

He stooped to pick up a loose stone and sent it hurtling across the lawn. "Maybe."

"It hurts when you speak to me like that."

"Sorry, Mom," he muttered.

"I phoned Uncle Lincoln and told him to expect me by midmorning." Penelope kept her voice calm. "He and the staff can easily handle my absence. Besides, I make my own hours."

Penelope and Lincoln shared ownership of New Beginnings Toys, a well-known toy company noted for producing heirloom wooden rocking horses and organic toys. In addition to the Roses shop and headquarters on Hilton Head, the business distributed toys across the United States. Her flight to Virginia had been to finalize the acquisition of another property for expansion.

Since the plane trip, she'd pushed aside her confession to Jacob that she hated her job. Just keep on living and working in a no longer challenging career, was her motto. She led an isolated life, the fate of soon turning fifty, and had come to accept the sad truth.

As a pastime, she'd begun making wooden dolls that children seemed to love, but the craft, though easy and enjoyable, was time-consuming.

"I'll be late for school," Evan said.

"All this concern about lateness. You don't even like school," she said.

Throughout his elementary days, Evan had aced classes and scored straight A report cards. The past couple of years, his grades had slipped. He had no friends, at least none who came over to their house anymore. He stayed in his room, munching on bags of potato chips, and played video games for hours.

Her once athletic son.

"I'll get behind in school if I don't go," he protested. A last-ditch effort, she supposed.

"You'll catch up. This is the only appointment available with the new doctor in town. Emphasis on the word new. Everyone is raving about how gentle and patient he is. The mothers at your school say he's excellent with kids and won't rush us. He'll answer all our questions."

"You mean *my* questions, Mom, not *our*. The appointment is mine. I'm not a kid anymore."

True. He was turning into an adolescent, and she doubted she could live through the next few years.

"Why aren't we seeing Dr. Damian?" Evan asked as he slipped into the front seat of their truck and buckled his seat belt. "I'm used to him."

"For one thing, Uncle Lincoln and I remember Dr. Damian treating us, which goes back decades. For another, Dr. Damian has thankfully retired. I was beginning to question whether he was thorough enough."

"I liked him."

"I was comfortable with him, too. However, I assume Dr. Williams is up on the latest medical techniques."

"Aunt Shanice said he is good-looking."

Shanice was Lincoln's wife. They'd been wed a few years and still displayed a delightful newlywed affection for each other.

Penelope grinned. She'd heard an earful about the handsome Dr. Williams, but romance was the last thing on her mind. He was probably fresh out of medical school, married, with a couple of kids.

When she found a spot in the crowded parking lot, she

parked a distance from the entrance, declaring the walk was beneficial for both her and Evan.

Once they stepped inside the office, the receptionist, clearly flustered, greeted them with a distracted hello and ushered them to a packed waiting room.

"We're behind at least forty-five minutes," she explained. "Dr. Williams was called in for an emergency at the free clinic he established in town. He has returned and is seeing patients, and we apologize for the delay."

Considering the time, Penelope surmised that Dr. Williams kept early hours. Unlike her. She was the opposite of a morning person.

She'd read about the clinic. He'd secured a donated warehouse facility near the hospital and solicited donations from businesses and additional funding through a state grant. He provided free health care to patients who couldn't afford otherwise. Open on weekdays and weekends, the word was spreading, and evening hours were being extended.

After filing their paperwork, the nurse called Evan's name.

Penelope stood, and Evan stuffed his hands into his pockets. Much to Evan's frowning dismay, she followed him into the examining room.

She pointed to her throat, her excuse to accompany him. "You'll get the swab done and tested, and we'll leave with a prescription for your antibiotics in hand. Couldn't be easier."

CHAPTER 2

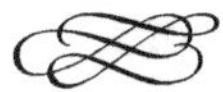

 van plunked onto the examination table and yanked his phone from his pocket.

"Why are you constantly absorbed with your cell phone?" Penelope seated herself on an empty chair across from him.

"Everything is on the internet, Mom. Everyone famous, and whatever is going on in the world."

Penelope pulled out her own cell phone and gestured toward the window. "Isn't the world happening outside and all around us? Your screen doesn't tell the truth."

"You're on *your* phone."

"I intend to get some work done."

He stared straight ahead, his features impassive. "Then why are you always watching me?"

"I don't mean to. I'm worried about you."

"I've had strep throat four times."

"Exactly." In fact, her nerves were frayed. Evan had never been a sickly child, but this year, things were different, beginning with his unhealthy diet. She vowed to make changes in her grocery shopping and eliminate the candy and chips they'd both grown so fond of.

The door opened abruptly, and Penelope reminded Evan to put his phone away.

"G' day, mate. Evan, is it?" A tall man stepped inside, his deep male greeting filling the tiny room.

His voice. That accent. She'd recognize him anywhere.

Penelope snapped her phone shut and slowly rose to her feet. An email she'd been typing to an employee was halted in midsentence.

Evan swung his legs back and forth, clearly impatient, still wearing his black leather jacket. He glanced up from the latest video on his phone, a tower defense game he'd tried to explain to her once. At her stern frown and second sharp reminder, he shoved the phone into his pocket.

"I'm Dr. Williams." This attractive doctor, wearing a white coat and khaki pants, exuded competence as he closed the door behind him. A stethoscope hung from around his neck. He looked up from the chart on his clipboard, gave Evan a sincere smile, then turned to Penelope.

Her heart did a double flip.

"You. Here?" she asked.

A beat of silence passed.

"Penelope Reid." He smiled. "I recognized the last name."

"What are you doing in Roses?" She found herself staring. Why couldn't she shake off this attraction to him? Since they'd met on the plane, she continued to envision his slow, discerning smile. His voice had been gentle when he'd leaned close and assured her that he didn't mind her babbling.

He set down the chart. "I bought the practice from Dr. Damian."

"I thought you preferred big cities."

"I changed my mind."

Whoa. Not because of her. No, of course not.

"You never mentioned anything on the plane," she said.

"What plane?" Evan asked.

"Dr. Williams and I met a while ago when I … we … flew back from Virginia."

"I visited several physicians' practices before making my final decision." Jacob studied her. "I interviewed in Virginia, then planned to fly on to Florida. I made a detour in Hilton Head."

"A detour," she echoed. "To Roses. You never mentioned any interviews."

Why would an older doctor buy another doctor's practice? Had Jacob lost his own practice due to incompetence?

He offered a half smile. "I believe you did most of the talking on the plane."

He was hardly the young, recently out-of-medical school doctor she'd anticipated.

He turned to Evan, who assessed their conversation with a peculiar, thoughtful scowl.

"Anything you'd like to talk to me about, Evan?" Jacob asked. "How's it hangin'?"

"My throat hurts."

"You're how old?" Jacob scanned Evan's chart.

"I'm twelve."

"Almost an adult, mate. Shall we ask your mum to leave?"

"No." Evan shot a glance toward Penelope. "She can stay. She has a sore throat, too."

"I'm fine." She waved off his remark. She didn't want to discuss any illness of hers with Jacob Williams. She intended to keep her replies brief and avoid any personal connection. "My sore throat went away."

"Did it?" Jacob pressed the back of his hand to her forehead. His touch was warm and firm. Her cheeks heated.

"She wants you to recommend an over-the-counter medicine for her," Evan chimed in.

Jacob quirked an eyebrow. "Does she now?"

"If a recommendation isn't too much trouble," she said.

Jacob dropped his hand. "No trouble at all. Let's have a look at your son first." He lifted his stethoscope and listened to Evan's heart and lungs. "Nothing of concern there." He flipped a page on his chart and made a note. Then he produced a swab and instructed Evan to say "ah." Much to Penelope's surprise, Evan didn't gag. His usual sullen expression vanished. In fact, he urged Jacob to explain the test.

"Evan is tossing around becoming a physician or a veterinarian when he gets older," Penelope explained.

Evan crossed his arms. "I want a puppy."

"Do you like dogs?" Jacob asked.

"I love dogs."

"Is that why you're interested in becoming a vet?"

Evan shrugged. "Maybe."

"I'm encouraging him." Penelope turned to Jacob. "What mother doesn't hope her son will someday become a doctor?"

"I can name one." Jacob looked away before meeting her gaze. "You're a sweet and caring mum, Penelope Reid."

"I don't know about the sweet part." Evan was scowling at her again. Flustered, she groped for a subject change. "Evan loves all animals."

People ... well, not so much.

"The medical profession needs bright young minds," Jacob said.

They returned to the waiting room while awaiting the results, then were summoned back to the examining room. As Penelope suspected, the test confirmed strep throat.

Evan's eyes widened. "I've got strep for the fifth time?"

"You're obviously susceptible to strep," she replied. "Does your throat still hurt?"

"Are you kidding? Yes."

She turned to Jacob. "Our previous doctor recommended a tonsillectomy for Evan."

"Weigh the pros and cons of a tonsillectomy at Evan's age," Jacob said. "There's always a risk of complications from the surgery. A recent study suggests patients are more prone to long-term respiratory disease afterwards."

"I don't want an operation," Evan said.

"I agree, at least for now." Jacob extended a hand to Evan and shook. "Have a good one. I'll send a prescription for antibiotics to the local pharmacy, and you should start feeling better in two or three days. And this is my recommendation for your mom." He scribbled on a sheet of paper and handed it to her.

She scanned the instructions. "Tea with honey and lemon and loads of rest?"

"Works like a charm."

"When should Evan return to school?"

"I'd advise he stay home for at least forty-eight hours after he starts the antibiotics."

"Good," Evan said. "If I don't ever have to go to school again, my life will be a lot better."

"Quitting isn't an option, Evan," she broke in. "You'll never be a doctor if you can't finish junior high."

Evan opened his mouth.

The last thing she needed was her son spilling more of their personal affairs. Jacob Williams knew enough about her already.

She cut Evan off with an abrupt nod.

"Thank you, Doctor," she said.

"Please call me Jacob."

She felt torn. She really wanted to keep up the formality in a doctor's office, but she really, really liked calling Jacob by his first name.

She nodded. "Okay."

"Thanks, Dr. Jacob," Evan chimed in.

"Not you," she replied. "To you, he's Dr. Williams."

"Why? That's not fair."

"Life isn't always fair. We're adults. You're a kid, and you must be respectful."

"Why would your life be better if you didn't attend school?" Jacob's gaze swayed to Evan.

"Because all the kids hate me, and I hate them."

"I could use some help in my clinic. Do you ever volunteer?"

Evan lifted his shoulders. "Not much, unless I go with my mom."

"Oh, where do you go?"

"She and Uncle Lincoln donate toys to the homeless center in town."

"Several of the families I see are refugees from other countries," Jacob said. "They come into my clinic for free health care."

"We hang out with the kids at the shelter and help them with homework and stuff," Evan continued. "Mom was bringing in the wooden dolls she made, but not anymore."

"I'm tied up at work," she murmured.

"Admirable, and very creative. I encourage you to get back to it." Jacob shot Penelope an approving glance, then turned to Evan. "Would you like to lend a hand in the clinic, mate?"

Evan fixed his gaze on the tile floor. "Doing what?"

"Whatever the moment requires because the patients' needs change minute by minute. How are your phone skills?"

"Okay."

"We need more beds and chairs. I'll give you a list of the other clinics in the area," Jacob said. "Do you speak Spanish?"

"He doesn't, but Evan took a signing class last year," Penelope put in.

"I'm in seventh grade." Evan rolled his eyes. "I can communicate all by myself, Mom."

Jacob concentrated on Evan. "Signing will be helpful for my deaf patients."

"Okay," Evan mumbled.

Penelope's eyebrows raised. *I can't believe my son agreed so easily.*

"Excellent." Jacob patted Evan on the back, and she caught Jacob's smirk as he winked at her. "I'll ask the nurse to provide the details. She volunteers at the clinic every Saturday morning. Will Saturday work for you, Evan?"

"I guess."

"Can you arrive by seven?"

Evan blinked. "A.M.?"

"Yep."

"Evan doesn't usually get up until—" Penelope tried to keep her voice neutral.

Jacob made eye contact with her and gave a subtle shake of his head.

His silent message, to allow Evan to answer for himself, stopped her. She knew what Jacob surmised. She was an overprotective, hovering parent.

Evan broke the ensuing silence. "All right. I'll get up early."

"Let's plan on a week from this upcoming Saturday, so you have several days to recuperate."

As they exited, Penelope's chest filled with encouragement over the conversation. Jacob Williams had accomplished a great deal during their short office visit. Whether he realized or not, and she had a sneaking suspicion he did, he'd given her son a purpose.

At the pharmacy, Evan waited in the car. Penelope hastened inside and collided with Candee Winchester, a local realtor. Candee was a striking woman with wavy auburn hair and an amiable personality. She'd married Teddy, one of her clients and a real estate investor. They'd adopted his nephew, Joseph, who loved horses.

"What brings you to the pharmacy on a weekday morning?" Candee slung her handbag over her shoulder and juggled a bag filled with cleaning supplies. She explained that she and Teddy were redoing her office.

"I'm picking up a prescription for Evan," Penelope said. "He has strep throat again."

"Did you see the handsome new doctor?"

"The guy everyone is fixated on?"

"Who else?" Candee had made a name for herself as the town matchmaker, and Penelope recognized her cupid grin from a mile away. "I'm working to find him a house here. In the meantime, he's renting an apartment at the old Roses Hotel."

"Lincoln never mentioned anything."

Lincoln and Penelope had purchased the rundown hotel and renovated it. Besides an investment, the hotel provided housing for their toy shop employees. A couple of years ago, though, they'd sold the hotel, preferring to concentrate on their business rather than real estate.

"I've shown Dr. Williams numerous properties, though he's very particular." Candee fingered the gold cross earrings she always wore. "He wants what he wants, all wrapped up in a certain low-price range."

"I assumed a doctor's salary was more than ample."

"For whatever reason, not in his case."

Penelope picked up the prescription. Before she headed out the door, she bought three chocolate candy bars. She earned them, she decided, foreseeing a challenging week ahead while caring for her cranky son.

CHAPTER 3

The following day, Jacob grinned at the remembrance of his brief conversation with Penelope and her son in his office. He'd never met a teen who liked to get up early, and Evan proved no exception. He admired the boy's commitment when agreeing to volunteer at the clinic. Of course, the real test was yet to come. Would Evan show up at the assigned hour?

Jacob scanned his mile-long to-do list for the evening. More house-hunting with Candee Winchester can wait, he concluded, as he closed his office.

He looked up Penelope's address, discovered she lived on the edge of town, and decided to drive to her home. He'd purchased a ten-year-old yellow four-door Volkswagen when he'd moved to Roses. Driving wasn't his thing, and he'd never gotten used to seeing cars on the wrong side of the road in America. He'd relied on big-city transportation in Atlanta, and Roses didn't boast subways. Fortunately, traffic here was minimal.

He didn't make house calls, and strep throat wasn't usually a cause for concern. However, Evan was a new patient, and, for lack of any other reason, rational or otherwise, why not? He was attracted to Penelope and wanted to get to know her better.

Reservations stirred. He'd vowed to keep his life simple ever since his niece's death. He'd vowed to prioritize what was important. He'd vowed to devote his career to serving people.

Eighteen-hour workdays had worked well throughout his successful career. He had shouldered all responsibility with unrestrained energy, though he had never achieved his goal.

Success and kudos aren't necessary anymore, he reminded himself.

He'd quit his job; walked away to reassess and refocus, searching for more simplistic goals.

His thoughts gravitated to Penelope.

From what he'd learned from their plane conversation, she was anything but simple. However, she was unassuming and vivacious. In fact, she was a stunner.

Penelope revealed that Evan's father didn't see his son much anymore. Although he didn't intend to become a surrogate father, Jacob made a mental note to engage with Evan, and volunteering at the clinic proved a positive beginning.

He located Penelope's home and parked at the curb, viewing the expansive driveway, and surrounding half acre of land. Inhaling, he breathed in freshly mowed grass and the honeyed scent of late-blooming flowers.

Her home was a beaut. A splendid, old-fashioned Victorian, classic, with a rectangular shaped, sloping roof, and boasting a veranda.

He got out of his car and scanned the property. This was the house he envisioned for himself. This was exactly the type of house he was looking for.

The few Candee had shown him were out of his price

range. He'd poured a lot of money into helping his sister, Kylie, rebuild her life after his niece's death, and even more money setting up his clinic.

He paused to study Penelope's home. He wasn't certain what to expect when he stepped inside, but based on the exterior, he assumed the interior was gorgeous.

All the homes he'd viewed in Roses had lacked one specific requirement. He wanted to have a medical practice in his home, and most weren't big enough. This home, painted in colors of vivid blue with gold trim, resembled a doll house. Standing two stories, with a stained-glass window facing the street and a rounded turret, the architecture was a reminder of the historic Victorian era, where nothing came cheap.

He surveyed the area. The house was located at the end of a main road leading to town.

Penelope hadn't exaggerated when she'd described Roses. Storybook wasn't an adequate description. The town was idyllic, a scene straight out of a Norman Rockwell painting. In addition, from his early morning jogs, he'd discovered something even better than a wholesome culture. He'd observed the heart.

The people.

Young and old alike were kind, interested in others, and respectful. Honest and polite and middle America at its best, where church was at the center.

He scanned the block. Other homes and businesses were located nearby Penelope's house. Surely the area was zoned for both business and residential properties.

Not only would a home office reduce his overhead, but he could treat more patients on evenings and weekends. He liked the idea of a short commute from his kitchen to his office instead of driving to town.

Trouble was, this house was hers, not his.

You'll never be able to afford anything on this scale. Occasionally, his mother's voice echoed in his ears, and his chest tightened. He allowed the mental numbness to take hold and shook away his contemplation.

He *could* afford a lovely home.

Eventually.

He stepped onto the porch. After seeing patients at his office all day, he'd stopped at his rental apartment at the Roses Hotel to shower and change into dark jeans and a clean T-shirt.

He rang the doorbell. From inside, a squeal sounded.

"Giblet, get into your cage this instant." The sound of rushing footsteps. "There, I've got you. Come with me, it's probably the postman with a late toy delivery." She opened the front door with a tiny hamster nestled in her hands.

She gaped. "Jacob?"

"Hello, Penelope." He caught his breath. He'd forgotten what she'd been wearing on the plane, or in his office, but it wasn't a stunning striped dress that flared at the waist.

That generous figure. Her bare toes peeked out from a pair of beige sandals. He'd be thinking about her for the rest of the evening. Oddly, her sharp blue eyes, focused on him, were even more captivating.

Her gaze narrowed. "Why are you here?"

"I'm not delivering any toys."

"I can see that. Is Evan supposed to report to your clinic tonight?"

"I hope not, unless he intended to expose my patients to strep throat."

"Then why?" A slight breeze lifted her dark hair, shaped in a short bob style. Classy and elegant silver highlights framed her round face. He wanted to tuck one of the stray strands behind her ears. He wanted—

He cleared his throat. "You drink coffee, right?"

"Every day."

He held out a bag of ground coffee he'd picked up at the local shop in town. "Did you reach your quota for today?"

"That will never happen."

"Care to brew us a cup?"

Fearing she might protest, he held up a hand to hold her off.

"You like coffee, too?" she asked.

"Very much." He had her compete attention.

"You didn't mention anything about coffee on the plane."

"No?"

Her delicate eyebrows came together. "All you said was that you liked to drink."

"I do, especially ginger beer."

She tilted her head. "What is ginger beer?"

"A beverage made from ginger, sugar, and water."

"Is the beer alcoholic?"

"Sometimes. Where I come from, ginger beer is a local favorite."

"Australia?"

"Yea. Down under."

"I suspected you were from Australia but couldn't place your accent for certain." She peered out the door. "You drove here?"

"I didn't ride my kangaroo. In fact, riding a kangaroo is forbidden in Australia."

"Probably in America, too."

"Why did you suspect I was Australian?"

She offered a half-smile. "Your accent is a dead giveaway."

"I've never been able to shake it."

"You've lived in America a long time?"

He stroked his fingers over the hamster's caramel-colored fur. "Uh-huh."

"A man's foreign accent is usually appealing to a woman." She stared at him while holding the wriggling hamster.

"Usually?"

She didn't reply and pushed the door open wider with her hip. "Would you like to come in?"

"I was hoping you'd ask."

"I don't have any ginger beer."

He shook the bag. "I'll provide the coffee."

She ushered him inside and cradled the hamster. "Are you afraid of hamsters?"

"Is he going to race about?"

"Not if I can help it, and I've been informed that Giblet is a she. Evan refilled her water bowl a while ago and didn't secure the cage." Penelope placed the hamster in a cage situated on a table in the hallway and secured the latch. "Are you comfortable with animals?"

"Animals are my passion." Jacob closed the door behind him. The gorgeous Penelope was becoming his passion, too. "My family owned a dog, a golden retriever."

"In Australia?"

"We moved to the States when I entered primary school and gave the dog to a friend. My mum and dad announced that our dog was too old for a big trip and a bigger change."

"Didn't your parents like Australia?"

"Australia is awesome, from what I remembered, and they both grew up near Melbourne, where I was raised. Unfortunately, my father went bankrupt."

"I'm sorry," she said quietly.

He shifted. Alrighty, then. If he was trying to make a good impression, blurting out his family's descent into poverty wasn't the best way to go about it.

"We struggled, but we landed on our feet," he replied.

"What happened?"

"The bankruptcy? Long story. My father packed up my

mum, my sister, Kylie, and me and then found a job in Maryland. We've lived in the States ever since."

"Do you see your parents often?"

"My mum, on occasion. My sister lives near her but is considering moving back to Australia."

"Do you visit your mother?"

"Not as often as I should."

"Is your sister older or younger?"

"Kylie is younger than me. She and her husband split soon after ..." He swallowed the lump in his throat. The expected tears came to his eyes.

Penelope studied him, giving him no place to look but straight at her. She didn't press him for any more details, and he didn't offer an explanation.

"I'm sorry," she said simply.

"Thanks." He couldn't say more. After a difficult and uncomfortable minute with no words, he relaxed. That was extraordinary. He never relaxed when he spoke about his adorable niece, Linda, and her tragic death. Normally, he tensed and felt worse.

"If you ever need to talk with someone." Penelope offered a tentative smile. "I'm a good listener. I don't usually babble on and on. Honest." She attempted to lighten the mood with a disparaging wave at herself. She'd noted his sadness and responded with empathy.

He moved from one foot to the other. "I won't be discussing the subject again but thank you."

"I talked nonstop on the plane."

He couldn't help his smile. Quiet filled the air, spun with kindness and understanding. He recognized the whiff of lavender, her scent.

"I liked your stories." He kept his expression neutral. "Do you want to hear a truth?"

"This truth business again?" Her lips twitched. "Sure."

"You're a remarkable woman." His observation surprised himself. He truly was interested in her. In fact, he planned to learn everything about her.

He surveyed the expansive living room, the cushioned window seat overlooking the side yard. A cherry-wood coffee table and armchairs were cluttered with books. People called him a neatnik. Maybe so. He pressed down the inclination to straighten the stacks, so all the book edges aligned.

"Gorgeous home." He peered up at the high ceilings, the gold-carved wooden mirror hanging over the marble fireplace. The room was painted a rich hue of chocolate brown. He assumed to his left was the music room, judging by the ebony-black grand piano. No white or beige walls anywhere.

"You play piano?" he asked.

"I tried. I struggled. I couldn't get the hang of reading the notes in the bass clef, so I quit."

"On the plane, you mentioned you wanted to create something."

The corners of her eyes crinkled. "If you ask my piano teacher, she'll assure you it wasn't a Mozart sonata."

He gestured toward the wooden beads, paint, sharpies, newspaper, and glue on a separate table. Several beads were painted in various neutral shades and stood upright. "Are these the dolls you're making?"

She shrugged. "I've put the craft aside."

He stepped into the room and picked up a miniature doll. Her black hair and blue eyes were intricately drawn, her hands clasped together. Two yellow silk hair bows were glued on either side of her head above her ears.

"She is precious." He fingered the hair bows.

"I name all my dolls after spices. Hers is Cinnamon."

"Nice name."

"Our business has a large amount of scrap wood I can use."

"Right." He'd looked up her toy shop on the internet.

"I brought the dolls to the homeless shelter Evan mentioned. My brother Lincoln donated several rocking horses, but I decided each child needed something simple."

Simple. There was that word again.

"Congrats on a worthwhile project," he said. "I'm learning simple is best."

"Me too. Life is all about balance. So many material things are relatively useless."

"Like big expensive cars."

She grinned. "And designer purses."

"You're an inspiration, Penelope."

She picked up a tiny blue silk scarf and handed it to him. "I love this craft. Of course, you're familiar with my story."

"Some parts. Remember, I'm an excellent listener, so keep talking."

"When you're not sleeping," she reminded. "I prefer to keep my story to the parts you've probably memorized, so don't press me, okay?"

"Apologies." He draped the tiny scarf over the doll's shoulders. "Sometimes I lose my finesse around beautiful women. Women who have survived hardships and heartbreak are even more ..."

She snatched the doll from him, readjusting the scarf before setting the doll back on the table. "You should've stopped when you were ahead with the word 'beautiful.'"

"You're also fun and creative."

"I'll brew your coffee, and you can tell me the reason you're here." She breezed down the hallway, and he followed. The wooden floor creaked as they stepped into the kitchen.

"I dropped by to see Evan," Jacob said. "How is he feeling?"

"So, this is a house call?"

Truth? Well, he wasn't ready for the blatant truth, because he hadn't come to terms with it yet himself.

"You can call it a house call," he replied.

"Evan is resting." Penelope surveyed the hallway, as if Evan might materialize at any moment. "Correction. He's playing video games. Do you want to go upstairs and check on him?"

"You're his mum." Jacob moved beside her. "What do you suggest?"

"Stay down here." She nudged him, a lighthearted nudge. "He'd probably prefer to run a 5K race than see you. He's a bit prickly when he's interrogated." Though she joked, her face beamed whenever she mentioned her son. Her delight exposed a wide-open fracture in his own defenses and his attraction to her. Again, he questioned himself. What was he really doing here?

"I blame his change in disposition on the rough road to adolescence," she finished.

When she opened the bag, Jacob inhaled the scent of fresh ground coffee.

"Is the antibiotic working?" he asked.

"Antibiotics are a miracle drug." She scrutinized him, peeling away more and more layers of his resistance. "You realize, Jacob, that not many doctors make personal house calls anymore."

"I'm new in town." Same old excuse, and he debated whether he should elaborate. "This is a way for me to get to know my patients better."

"Do you make calls often?"

"Not very often." In fact, he never had.

She spooned four scoops of coffee, then measured filtered water into the coffeepot. "Your interest means a lot. Most physicians won't take the time."

"My patients are the reason I'm a doctor."

"You look like a doctor." She switched on the coffee machine, then appraised him from head to toe. "I should've realized that on the plane. I imagined you—"

He stepped closer to the counter. Why was he so fascinated with her?

A difficult remembrance of his marriage and subsequent divorce resurfaced.

"I'm having a baby," his wife, Janet, had declared. Tears had poured down her cheeks. He'd assumed they were tears of joy, and he joined in with ecstatic tears of his own. Before he could bring out the champagne glasses, she'd added, "The baby isn't yours." And thus, the marriage had ended.

Her unfaithfulness had killed his pride and left him stunned.

"Where did you go, Doctor?" Penelope's steady voice drew him back from the devastating remembrance.

"Down memory lane," he said.

"Joyful times?"

He tapped his chin. "No. I was thinking about my ex-wife."

"You mentioned you were married."

"A decade ago, and for a couple of years. She's an anchor-woman on a national network. You'd probably recognize her. In fact, she was awarded an honor for investigative journalism."

"I'm impressed."

"Don't be." He blinked. "Let's discuss something else. You were in the middle of imagining me."

"I'd like to hear more about you."

He'd severed all recollections of Janet from his mind, though when he caught a glimpse of her on a cable television show, a slight pinch of awareness went through him. Thankfully, nothing more. He'd made peace with the hurt she'd caused and resolved never to get his heart all twisted up again. He dated women casually, and the women knew not to demand any emotional entanglement from him.

So, for the umpteenth bloody time, what on earth was he doing in Penelope's kitchen?

As a concerned physician, I'm here for Evan.

"I'm a doctor," he said aloud.

"At first, I imagined you as a professor who worked in academia."

"Why?"

"You cited statistics about airplanes."

He stepped back as she reached around him to grab two mugs from a high glass cabinet. She handed them to him, one by one.

He set the mugs on the wooden kitchen table. "A single offhand remark, and you pegged me as Professor Jacob."

"Now that I think of it, you don't fit the stereotype."

"Which is?"

"Shirt, tie, and tweed jacket."

"Another cliché." He folded cloth napkins she handed him and placed the napkins next to the mugs. "Are you interested in how I pictured you, Penelope?"

"After we went our separate ways?"

"While you were working at your job."

"Probably sitting on the floor and playing with tiny toy trucks."

"Gorgeous blue eyes, brown hair, and drop-dead gorgeous." He followed her back to the counter and grabbed two spoons. "I checked your website and saw your photo. You own New Beginnings Toys."

"The photo is old." She pushed back her hair, the hint of silver strands. Her cheeks turned crimson. "How did you realize I was one of the owners of the toy shop?"

"I asked Candee to verify for certain. The custom, hand-made rocking horses are ..."

"Our specialty."

"Right. And now you can sell your charming wooden dolls there."

"Hardly a specialty, and I don't sell them. If I had my way, I'd gift them to every child in the world." Her gaze shifted to the stairway. "Evan is returning to school in a couple of days. He's not thrilled about going back."

"Why doesn't he like school?"

"Peer pressure. Twelve years old is a challenging age." She placed sugar and a creamer on the table and poured steaming coffee into two mugs. Once she sat, he claimed the chair across from her.

"I met one of Evan's friends at the office today," he said. "He came in for a checkup."

"Oh?"

"A polite kid named Zack. He mentioned he was in seventh grade, and I asked him if he knew Evan."

"Zack was once Evan's best friend."

"Not anymore?"

She cupped her hands around her mug. "Not anymore."

"Zack inquired about volunteering at the clinic, and I encouraged him. He seems an ambitious chap. He is trying out for the high school swim team." Jacob spooned sugar into his coffee and stirred. "The coach accepts students in junior high."

"If the swimmer is good enough. A big *if.*"

"Is Evan trying out?"

"He'd rather wash dinner dishes for a week." Penelope circled the rim of her mug with her forefinger. "A couple of years ago, he was the star of the team. Now he doesn't seem to belong anywhere, and I have no idea how to help him."

Let Evan find his own way. The consideration came to Jacob's mind, and he quickly dismissed it. He had no right to tell Penelope how to raise her child.

An hour passed quicker than anticipated—an easy hour, filled with friendly conversation. She discussed the toy business and explained that everything had to be worth the cost of the retail value. Business was business. However, toys were unique and personal to each child. Discerning parents chose specialty toys for their children, believing in the value when cheap plastic toys were readily available at every big box store.

The perfect toy was designed as an heirloom for the child and family, Penelope went on, though she and her brother were businesspeople, and profit was a consideration. Excited parents gushed to their friends that they were being mindful of what they bought for their children, so everyone was satisfied.

Success meant Penelope's employees continued to work, and the toy shops remained open. It also meant that Penelope and her brother could continue to enjoy a comfortable lifestyle.

When Jacob stood, she walked him to the front door. "As usual, I did all the talking."

He smiled. "I always liked making house calls."

Evan never materialized, and Jacob didn't press the issue. After all, Penelope assured him that Evan was getting better.

"Thanks for the coffee," she said.

"You're welcome. I like your home. It's exactly the type of place I'm looking for."

"I met Candee in the pharmacy. If anyone can find your dream house, she's your realtor."

"Considering my hectic schedule," he said, "I've had only a few hours to scope out Roses and the surrounding area, and my house-hunting is hindered."

"I've lived here most of my life."

He knew that from their conversation on the plane.

"Where is the best place to find a home?" he asked. "Any suggestions?"

"Well, I—"

At the doorway, he turned to her. "May I call you?"

"Why? I don't need another prescription. In your professional opinion, I needed tea with honey and lemon and lots of rest."

He grinned with satisfaction and squeezed her hands. "Did my prescription help?"

"The tea is a blessing, though I couldn't manage the 'lots of rest' part."

"Can you show me around the area this weekend? Candee is good, but you're better."

She withdrew her hands and stepped backward. "I'm not a realtor."

"Doesn't matter."

"Evan is sick."

"If he continues to take the antibiotic, he'll make a full recovery by Saturday," Jacob replied. "Perhaps he can stay with your brother and sister-in-law for a bit. They live in Roses, right?"

She looked flustered. "I'm not sure. I suppose I can ask them."

"After I leave the clinic tomorrow, I'll phone you to firm up our plans."

"Phone?"

"Or I'll text you." He asked for her cell phone, texted himself, then handed the phone back to her. "Afterwards, we can go for dinner."

"You mean to eat?"

"You aren't on a diet, are you?"

"I'm trying to choose healthy. Look, this probably isn't a suitable idea."

"Order a salad."

She shook her head. "You're Evan's doctor."

"Are you dating anyone?"

"I told you." Her gaze sharpened. "I gave up dating."

"No pizzerias. I promise."

Her cell phone pinged, and she read the text with a concerned frown. "Sorry, Jacob, I need to contact the supervisor at our Roses location." She tapped a number into her phone. "A shipment is delayed because of stormy weather in New York, and the delay is causing repercussions to our stores along the East Coast. With the holidays approaching soon—"

"No worries. I'll let myself out." As she put the phone to her ear and began instructing the supervisor, Jacob mouthed, "I'll call you."

He closed the front door behind him before she could protest.

Penelope Reid was a remarkable woman. Despite her rather slapdash appearance on the plane, and the untidy state of her house, she was quick, conscientious, and decisive at her job. Too bad it was a job she hated.

CHAPTER 4

$\mathcal{P}$enelope didn't know why she'd agreed to Jacob's request, and she dissected their conversation as she pulled into the driveway of Lincoln and Shanice's farmhouse on Saturday.

Shanice had inherited the farmhouse from her grandmother, Jasmine, and the house even had a name—Jasmine's Joy.

Evan had missed the entire week at school, declaring he wasn't feeling well enough to attend, and his accommodating teachers had sent online assignments to him. Penelope hovered over his shoulder, offering to help.

"What a great idea, Mom," Evan said. "As if the teachers won't realize it's your work and not mine."

"I didn't say I would do the work." She reached for the homework papers her son had printed.

"I've got this covered, okay? Science is my favorite subject."

Science had always been her worst subject, so she agreed. She could only trust that he'd completed the assignments.

"I'm showing Jacob Williams the town of Roses and

prospective houses for sale," Penelope began, after Lincoln opened the front door and welcomed her and Evan inside the farmhouse.

Evan disappeared into the living room and dropped his backpack onto the floor. He clicked on the television set, and Penelope heard a delighted squeal when Shanice's cat and Lincoln's dog jumped on the couch beside him.

The couple had no children and frequently discussed adoption. Currently, they devoted their free time to expanding New Beginnings Toys and renovating the rambling farmhouse.

"I think showing him the town is a wonderful idea," Shanice remarked when Penelope stepped into the kitchen.

"He trapped me into this," Penelope replied.

"Trapped is when you're stuck inside for days after a snowstorm. Hanging out with Dr. Handsome is exciting."

"I'm not his realtor," Penelope said. "Besides, I can't choose the right house for him."

Shanice tucked a stand of thick ebony hair behind her ear, then grabbed plates from the glass-fronted cabinet. "For some reason, he prefers you. I wonder why?"

"Short explanation. I'm a native of Roses."

"Honestly, Penny." Shanice referred to Penelope by her nickname. "Jacob is a dream come true. Rumor has it that he's single and in his early fifties. If he wants to spend time with you, don't fight it."

Because you're married to Lincoln, who clearly loves you. You have no fears of denials and infidelity and heartbreak, Penelope thought.

Shanice plated oversized portions of sweet potato pie and carried the plates to the table.

"Jacob Williams moved into town only a short time ago and has already established a free clinic," Shanice said. "He's committed to helping the community and is an exceptional doctor."

"He's interested in his patients," Penelope said. "How many doctors make house calls anymore?"

Shanice smiled conspiratorially at Lincoln, then beamed at Penelope. "None, and certainly not for a case of strep throat. Any ideas on what drew him to visit you?"

"He is new in town."

"We've established that," Shanice replied.

"Okay, he is admired." At her sister-in-law's obvious delight at her statement, Penelope amended, "I like him as a friend."

"He's an eligible bachelor."

"I see where you're headed, and the answer is, I'm not interested. After my nasty divorce, dating is no longer in the cards for me." Penelope forked a piece of pie and smirked at Lincoln. "Are you aware your wife has already married me off to this guy?"

"She's a cheerleader for your happiness. We're both thrilled you opened your life to a man. Give him a chance. You're finally excited about dating someone. With the holidays approaching—"

"Lincoln, we're not dating. You're envisioning Jacob and I under a mistletoe, kissing, and married by New Year's Day." She peered around the expansive kitchen. "You've started to decorate for Christmas. I love the reindeer salt and pepper shakers. And the poinsettias from the garden center are gorgeous, especially the red and pink ones. I noticed them by the fireplace when I walked in."

"And we celebrate Kwanzaa, too." He looked fondly at his wife, then back at Penelope. "Don't you want to spend the holidays with a special someone? You've been alone too long."

"Maybe, sometimes."

"That special someone may be right under your nose." He studied her intently. "You blush whenever his name is mentioned."

Her warm face gave her away. "Jacob is originally from Australia."

"Ooh, I love an Australian man's accent," Shanice said.

Lincoln's eyebrows furrowed. "More than mine?"

"You don't have an accent."

He drummed his fingers on the table. "I have a Southern accent."

"So do I, and that doesn't count because a Southern accent isn't exotic. I've heard it my whole life. However, I love you anyway." Shanice leaned over and kissed him on the cheek. He placed his fork on his plate, pulled her closer, and kissed her back.

Penelope grinned when Shanice broke the kiss. "You two are an inspiration."

Their infectious laughter wafted throughout the kitchen.

Lincoln was Penelope's younger brother—square-jawed, considerate, and generous, and he and Shanice had been granted a second chance when he'd returned to Roses. He'd pursued her, married her, and they planned to raise a family.

When Penelope regarded them, a twinge of longing went through her chest. They'd found each other and enjoyed a loving marriage.

Meanwhile, her ex had cheated on her with another woman—someone decades younger and much prettier.

Jealousy knocked, though not followed by grief. Penelope refused to jump into the courting game again, and she'd declared her decision to everyone who would listen. In her defense, she'd tried dating, both online and in person, and both were unsuccessful.

Shanice shifted her gaze to Penelope. "I can't wait to meet Dr. Williams."

"He's a pediatrician, so I doubt you'll have the opportunity for a while."

"Oh, you'll introduce us well before that." Shanice wiggled her eyebrows. "Seems as if you two are spending oodles of time getting better acquainted."

Penelope leaned back in her chair. "We only spent a few hours together because his visit to my house was a—"

"House call," the husband and wife chorused in unison. "And don't forget the plane. Remember, you told us all about it."

Penelope noted the glints in their eyes and laughed.

"Did the good doctor examine Evan while he was at your house?" Shanice asked. "Water, anyone?" At their nods, she stepped to the refrigerator and grabbed several bottles.

"No, although Jacob inquired about him," Penelope replied, accepting a bottle from Shanice. "We didn't want to bother Evan because he was in his room playing video games."

"Makes perfect sense. Not." Lincoln chuckled. "Either way, we're delighted. Your divorce was difficult, and I … we … Shay and I, are pleased you're interested in a good man."

Any mention of Penelope's ex set off a chain of reactions, and she sternly fought to keep her sadness under control. She sliced her pie portion in half and slid the pie onto Lincoln's plate. "My birthday is coming soon," she explained at his quizzical expression. "I've been eyeing a lovely dress, though it's quite short and clingy. My figure could use a remodel."

"Don't shortchange yourself." Shanice placed her hand on Penelope's forearm. "You are beautiful."

"I appreciate you handling the snafu with the shipping problem the other day." Lincoln took a swig of water. "You put in a good deal of effort to solve it. I don't say it often enough, but you are vital to our company's success."

I hate my job. Penelope's words to Jacob echoed in her mind.

However, if she examined her statement, she didn't hate her job. She'd simply grown tired of doing the same tasks day after day, year after year.

Initially, she'd assumed the responsibilities of the family business to please her father. She'd worked at the toy shop throughout high school, and then slipped right back into the business after college.

When had she become indispensable? How could she ever leave when her brother depended on her? Equally important, what would she do instead? She was proficient at organizing, yet not overly adept at shaping her own life.

Her inferiority stemmed from her ex's cheating. A major hit to her self-confidence.

Old news. Old excuses. Look ahead. Refuse to dwell on the past.

"Evan assured me that he finished his science essay, though you may want to double-check," she said. "He brought his backpack, but he won't allow me anywhere near his assignments."

"He only missed a few days of school." Lincoln steepled his fingers together. "He is responsible."

She gazed out the window. A rustic barn was framed in the distance, along with a firepit, and the rolling hills of Roses beyond. "Why won't he let me help him?"

"Because he needs to learn some things by himself. Think how proud he'll feel when he turns in the assignments."

"He hates school. I wish he loved seventh grade as much as I did."

"You loved seventh grade?" Shanice smirked. "I never met anyone who loved seventh grade."

Penelope craned her neck toward the living room and observed her son. He seemed so vulnerable sitting on the couch between the dog and cat. So solitary. Her foolish fear of him failing stemmed from her own difficulties in school, she rationalized. She'd struggled and never been able to achieve the high grades her younger brother attained with ease.

Logically, she knew Lincoln was right, and she was grasping for excuses to hold on to her only child. If only time stood still, or at least slowed down.

She speculated. Had the past year flown by for Evan, as it had for her? Likely, the twelve months had been interminable.

"I want Evan to be confident in himself," she murmured.

"You're doing a fine job raising him," Lincoln said.

Then why didn't Evan have any friends?

Her thoughts tangled. When things weren't right in Evan's world, they weren't right in hers, either.

She wanted him to enjoy the childhood she never had. Her father was a taskmaster who set impossible standards. A workaholic, aiming for success at all costs.

Evan shouldn't be held back because of her—a woman who might never recover from humiliation and hurt caused by sorrow and misgivings.

"He's acting like a preteen," Lincoln said. "He's perfectly normal."

"He's down on himself," she murmured.

"He has gained weight this year," Shanice broke in, then put a hand to her mouth. "I'm sorry. I shouldn't have mentioned anything."

"It's okay." Penelope blew out a breath. "Sometimes I feel helpless. I'm trying to eliminate junk food in the house, although I'm equally guilty. Lately, I've been encouraging him to be more active. He's touchy and snappish if I mention swimming."

"He is welcome to keep us company any time. We have chickens in the barn, a dog, a cat, and more plants than we can count." He grinned at his wife. Shanice was a professional landscaper.

"Evan wants a puppy for Christmas," Penelope said.

"Get him one. He's at the perfect age, and dogs are wonderful companions."

"I work a lot. It isn't fair to the dog. Dogs love people."

"I'll give you the time off." Lincoln teased. "And Evan gets off many school holidays. It seems like the kids are hardly ever in school. Now in my day …"

"Things were exactly the same. However, it's food for thought and you're both too kind." Penelope was grateful for their welcoming invitation, though it meant she would be alone if Evan spent nights at his uncle's house. And what about the days before Christmas when he was scheduled to visit his father? The visitation stipulated every other year, and this was Evan's year to visit.

The prospect tied her stomach in a knot. Christmas was such a special season, and she would be missing those precious days with her son.

How would she cope when he left for college in a few years? Kids went to college all the time, though the possibility of Evan leaving ripped at her heart.

Then she would truly be by herself.

From across the table, Lincoln grabbed her hands. "Start living your life again."

"I'm trying. It's difficult."

Her brother's advice was sound. Why did she refute him? Perhaps the best path for Evan was to allow him room to grow.

She carried her plate to the sink. "Thanks for the pie, Shanice. I'd better run. Jacob is picking me up at two o'clock."

Shanice grinned. "You're on a first-name basis with Dr. Handsome."

Penelope stood quietly for a moment before she nodded,

recognizing the meaningful smiles exchanged between her brother and Shanice. She crossed to the living room and instructed Evan to help his aunt and uncle on the farm because the tasks were endless.

He bristled before agreeing, reminding her that Uncle Lincoln had an adorable dog *and* a cat, *and* chickens, though Evan didn't have any pets.

"You own a hamster," she reminded.

He stroked the dog beside him. The cat had settled in his lap. "Christmas is coming, right? And a puppy?"

"Let's get through this semester first." Penelope planted a kiss on top of his hair.

"Say hi to Dr. Williams," Evan called out. "Tell him I'll volunteer next Saturday morning."

"I will." She stepped to the door. She planned to meet Jacob at her house because he'd insisted on driving.

She'd told Evan she was taking Jacob house-hunting, and he hadn't remarked one way or the other. She'd wondered at the time if he'd even heard her. Apparently, he had, and didn't have a problem with it.

Dr. Williams. Jacob. She was spending the afternoon with Jacob. Her stomach tightened, full of odd flutters she couldn't define.

*A*t exactly two o'clock, Penelope peeked out the living room window just as Jacob drove up to her house in his bright-yellow Volkswagen.

She'd changed when she'd returned home, deciding on lightweight linen slacks and her favorite flowered blouse. She left the blouse untucked to cover her generous waistline.

For the next hour, she slid in and out of Jacob's car to view different areas of Roses, and soon discovered that her slacks and blouse were completely wrinkled. Fortunately, her sneakers were comfortable.

She'd worn this same outfit behind a desk in an air-conditioned office several times in the past. Today, she'd imagined driving by a few neighborhoods with Jacob, then sitting across from him at her favorite coffee shop while sipping a vanilla latte.

He, on the other hand, was dressed more appropriately in khaki shorts and a green cotton golf shirt.

"You look gorgeous," he'd said when he arrived at her front door. She'd flushed with the compliment, though now she felt plain. Her blouse had soiled when they'd peered into the grimy window of an abandoned, dilapidated house on Brook Street. Dusty sunshine filled the interior.

"I like the house," he remarked, when they were once again settled in his car and headed back to town. "I like Victorian homes."

"You're joking," she said. "I wouldn't know where to begin except to hire a bulldozer."

"I'll grant the house is in dire need of repairs. But it has good bones."

"Bones? Let's start with the roof."

"What's wrong with the roof?"

"It's caving in," she reminded. "Are you handy with tools?"

He smirked. "I don't even own a tool kit, though I guess I should put it on my Christmas list if I buy the house. However, this location is excellent."

She surveyed the street. "There are several mom-and-pop stores in the area."

"The home is big."

"Unlike your car," she observed.

He chuckled and patted the dashboard. "Can't beat compact and reliable."

He switched on the radio to a contemporary station. She recognized the holiday tune, remarking that it wasn't even Halloween yet and they were playing Christmas music. Jacob tapped the rhythm of "It's the Most Wonderful Time of the Year" on the steering wheel and sang in a deep baritone voice.

"The house has what I want most," he continued when he'd finished singing.

"Which is?" she asked.

"Besides you?"

"Get outta here."

He grinned. "I'll tell you when we arrive in town."

Despite the outfit mistake, she enjoyed the hours with

him. He was interesting, with a grand sense of humor and a clear disdain for the other homes they drove by. He seemed to gravitate to the old, rundown house.

Finally, they took a break for cups of sweet lemonade from a sidewalk stand.

"Soon, the downtown will decorate for the holidays." Penelope gestured up and down the street. "We even hold a bake-off contest."

"We?"

"Yes. I'm a resident of the town." She admonished him with amused severity.

He grinned. "Me, too."

"Keiran and Desiree, a husband-and-wife team, own O'Malley's Irish pub. Keiran bakes whiskey cakes. He usually wins the contest because his cakes are delicious, although Desiree's pistachio cake is equally delicious."

"I've never baked so much as a cupcake, but I'll patronize a good bakery any day." Jacob chuckled. "I lived in Atlanta for many years and there are several well-known bakeries specializing in smiling gingerbread men and chocolate Santas around the holidays."

"I love sweets," she admitted with a sigh. "However, I'm set on healthy eating in order to lose a few pounds."

"I agree with the healthy eating part." Jacob swept an arm around her shoulders and gave a caring squeeze. "In Atlanta, a spectacular Stone Mountain Christmas serves all sorts of food. Some might be healthy."

"You'll love the holiday events here, too," she said. "Food trucks line the streets on weekends in December. If you're up for a thirty-minute drive, an entire town lights up every house for Christmas and is utterly charming."

"I look forward to seeing it. So far, Roses reminds me of a Rockwell painting." Jacob placed a hand on the small of

Penelope's back while directing her toward a bench. "I hope you'll accompany me to Atlanta."

Her heart thumped a joyful beat. Jacob wanted to include her in his Christmas plans.

"On one condition." Penelope balanced the cup of lemonade in her hands and situated herself on the bench. "You allow me to treat."

"Nope."

She took in a breath, about to object, and he shook his head. "I'm aware you don't date, so we won't call it a date. Like today. Today isn't a date."

"Today is a house-hunting day."

"Exactly."

Good. He'd gotten the message, though she suddenly felt empty despite her firm assertions. Apparently, her emotions hadn't gotten the same message.

No, no, no. She couldn't be falling for him. Wasn't her unsuccessful marriage, her pathetic attempts at dating, evidence enough?

"Romance is off the table for me," she declared, to firm up her assertion. "My last attempt was dating a teacher at my son's school. I wanted to like him because he was a great guy. He was fun, but we always ran out of things to talk about. I wondered after I broke it off with him if it was him or me. Either way, I wasn't willing to commit to anything beyond a shared pizza."

"No dates. No pizza." Jacob saluted her. "Romance memo received, loud and clear."

She drew a long breath and groped for a subject change. "Candee mentioned you were a discriminating house buyer. Today I witnessed firsthand what she meant."

"I'm certain she used a stronger word than discriminating."

"Her description was 'picky.'"

"Completely true." His mouth twisted in amusement. "I intend to establish a practice in my home, and my choice is important both professionally and personally."

"You're looking for a house big enough to live in *and* practice medicine?"

"Yes. A neighborhood made up of both businesses and residential." He gestured up and down the block. "Similar to your area."

"Why?" she asked.

"Homey. Convenience. I'll be more available for my patients. In Atlanta, my practice was becoming more of a business. Something happened … several things, and I realized I needed to make a change."

She offered a murmur of acknowledgement when he didn't supply any additional information. "Why did you become a doctor?"

"As I mentioned, my family moved to the States, and because of the bankruptcy, all we could afford was a mobile home in an impoverished area. We had nothing at first, not even furniture. We'd sit on the living room floor and pray." At her quizzical expression, he explained, "Me, my mum, father, sister."

"And then?"

"And then God delivered. We worked odd jobs and eventually scraped up enough money to purchase several acres of farmland." He drained his lemonade, then gazed at her. "My mum wanted me to stay on the farm and help. In fact, she suggested I quit school early. She doesn't believe education is important."

"And?"

"I refused. When I graduated, I got out of town as soon as I could and never looked back."

"Your parents still live on the farm?"

"My mum does."

"Your father?"

"He disappeared several years ago. He's not the sort of guy who sticks around when the going gets rough."

"Who helps your mother with—" Penelope began.

"My sister lives in Maryland." He closed his eyes for a beat. "I understand my mum's concerns. After all, she's alone and running a farm. But I couldn't. I just couldn't stay, only to please her."

Penelope gazed back at him, giving him her full attention. "You're not a farmer?"

"Hardly. I can't even grow an herb."

"One can never have too many herbs."

He grinned, obviously appreciative of her attempt to ease the conversation, but soon sobered. "There were few doctors or dentists where I grew up. My sister married young, and her daughter, Linda, … an accident occurred when she was seven."

He breathed in a deep lungful of air. His silence, a heartfelt emotion, was so palpable she could almost taste it.

"Go on. I didn't intend to ask so many questions." But yes. Yes, she did.

She waited for his reply and scanned the park across the way, the children running and playing tag. Autumn was a magnificent season. Gold and red leaves twirled to the ground, and the landscape was splashed with color.

She acknowledged several parents as they pushed their toddlers on the swings. This was the advantage of small-town living. Some called it a downside, though she understood both sides.

"Linda didn't receive the adequate care required for her condition, at least, not in my opinion," Jacob continued. "Our community lacked quality medical doctors. Soon afterwards, I decided to become a doctor and make a difference. Somewhere along the line, I got sidetracked while climbing the ladder of success. I strove to be the best in my field."

"That's a good thing."

"Maybe I wanted to prove something."

"To whom?"

He didn't reply for a moment. "Maybe my mum. Maybe myself."

"Were you the best?"

"I accepted a position at one of the country's leading children's hospitals." He opened his cell phone and scrolled to the photos, tapping a picture of a hospital sign to make it larger.

Penelope recognized the Atlanta hospital immediately. "Impressive. Congratulations."

"Thanks. I was passed over several times when I applied for the position of public health and administrative leadership. This last time was the final straw. I was experienced, and the most qualified for the job."

"So, you quit?"

"An administrative role was my biggest dream. I worked my entire career for the opportunity. I wanted more, more, more." He met her gaze. "I sound bitter, don't I?"

"A little. You're human." She tilted her head back to view him better. His recklessly handsome features regarded her. His face was captivating, almost boyish, especially when the strong jawline and keenly carved mouth were changed by one of his devastating smiles.

Beyond them, bluebirds flew through the air, spinning and diving from tree to tree. She had the urge to slip off her shoes and relish the cool grass tickling her toes.

"I'm learning how to be content and follow my focus to help people, though I may disappoint others," he said. "Life is an interesting balance."

"Balance between what?"

"Contentment and complacency. I never want to be complacent."

"Like me?"

"You're not complacent."

"I haven't changed jobs yet," she reminded him.

"Your job is important." He tucked his cell phone back in his pocket. "Just remember not to limit yourself."

"The family business is what I know."

"All my life, I questioned my career choices and long hours," he said. "I couldn't put my finger on what needed to change. When I quit my job in Atlanta, I visited several areas in search of a medical practice to purchase. Then I learned Dr. Damian's office was available, and here I am. It's odd how things work out. I never considered a small town setting before …"

"Because a small town is beneath your big city aspirations?"

"Thanks, Penelope."

"The salary and benefits are obviously greater in Atlanta."

"No question. My job was becoming soulless, though."

"Do you … intend on settling here permanently?"

"Yes." He regarded her. His expression changed, turning thoughtful. He rubbed his thumb along her palm and raised her hand to his lips.

Her heart lurched. "Why Roses?"

"Hard-working, down-to-earth folks are the best." Lightly, he kissed her fingers, and her hand tingled. "I'm a medical man and serving in a large hospital was rewarding for two decades, but circumstances led to my change of heart, and the end result is a blessing."

Her eyes widened as she digested his remark. "What circumstances?"

"What do you mean?"

"Circumstances suggest more than one thing happened."

She slid her hand away and tucked it securely behind her back. "You mentioned being passed over for the higher hospital positions. What was the other circumstance?"

"Sad, sad story." He suddenly became absorbed with studying the brick pavement. "A family tragedy."

"Your niece?"

He didn't reply.

"Your mother?"

"She's okay. We only talk when I reach out to her."

Penelope set her cup down and touched his forearm. Whatever the tragedy, he preferred to keep the heartache to himself.

"I'm glad you chose to land in Roses," she finally said.

"Me too." His intense brown eyes locked with hers, and a quiver of attraction shot through her.

"Lucky you."

"Why?"

"You heard all my problems on the plane." A thought occurred. "I'm surprised I didn't scare you off."

"If anything, I was more intrigued." He pointed to a simple, wood-sided building. "Look. Roses has an animal shelter."

"I'm well aware. Evan reminds me every day on the way to school when we pass by."

"Have you ever stopped in?"

She nodded. "We've visited several times. The precious animals break my heart and I want to bring all of them home. Almost two months ago, the shelter took in a pregnant stray. They think she is a terrier mix, mostly Scottish."

"How soon is she due?"

"She had her puppies."

"An entire litter for Christmas?" He tried to suppress a smile. "Evan will be thrilled. How many?"

"On average, dogs have five to ten puppies. She had six." Penelope swallowed a bubble of laughter. "Good try, Jacob."

"All that pleasure in one litter and you're still deciding? Psst. Cats are easier." Playfully, he nudged her. "Let's go see for ourselves."

Penelope picked up their cups and discarded them in the trash. A few minutes later, they climbed the stairs and walked through the shelter's doors.

"Be forewarned," a volunteer teasingly wagged her finger. "You'll probably fall in love."

"I'm inquiring about the terrier mix," Penelope said. "She recently had puppies."

The volunteer bobbed her head. "The dog is out back. The vet is examining her. Are you ready to bring a sweet furry friend home today? She is on our VIP status."

"Meaning?" Jacob asked.

"She's been here a while, and we don't want her to be overlooked." The volunteer met Jacob's gaze.

"I'm interested in possibly adopting one of her puppies," Penelope said.

She and Jacob peered into the cages as they walked down the aisles. Dogs with expressive, adoring eyes stared back at them. Penelope wanted to pass her fingers through the soft fur of each dog—colors of apricot, gray, silver, brown and black. Whether the dog's characteristics resembled a pug or a husky, they all had the cutest faces.

The volunteer announced that the mother dog, named Nutcracker, had been brought back to her cage, and they all stepped over. The dog's compact build and short legs, distinctive white coat and overall sturdiness, brought a heartfelt smile to Penelope's lips.

"This dog is more precious every time I see her," she said.

"I agree. She is gorgeous." He glanced at the volunteer. "May I pet her?"

The volunteer opened the cage and the dog stepped out. "Sure. Nutcracker will sniff you until she approves."

"Right." Jacob bent down and held his hand in a fist. He averted his gaze so that he wasn't looking directly at the dog. Once he passed the sniff test, he gently petted the dog's shoulders.

Penelope crouched down with him and smiled. "You're comfortable with dogs," she said.

Nutcracker, apparently satisfied, turned and found a cozy spot in her cage.

Six squirming, wriggling puppies with pink markings on their tiny paws, playfully romped and wagged their tails. Though wobbly on their feet, their liveliness knew no bounds. All the puppies had white fur, their coats velvety and fluffy. They yipped and yelped, boisterous, and paying no attention to Penelope and Jacob.

"Two boys and four girls," the volunteer declared. She warned the puppies weren't old enough to be picked up and handled yet, as they were only approaching four weeks. Furthermore, the puppies weren't adoptable before seven to nine weeks of age.

"Which puppy are you choosing for Evan?" Jacob asked, after he thanked the volunteer. He clasped Penelope's hand and they walked back to their bench across the street.

"When the time comes, the decision will be up to him. A puppy is a huge commitment, and I'm still not certain whether Evan is up to the task," Penelope sighed. "Or if I am because I'll probably assume the brunt of the work. I'm still weighing the pros and cons."

"Tough to do."

"Depends on which side of the fence you're on. Practical, like me, or more laid-back and irresponsible, like Evan."

"I try to agree with the parent, except in this instance."

Jacob studied her for a long moment. "A puppy will teach Evan responsibility."

"You're a big help. Then I'll have a puppy and a hamster running around the house. Or six puppies, if you have your way. Please don't encourage Evan when he's at your clinic."

"I wouldn't dream of it." Jacob chuckled. "Though there's something about puppies that triggers empathy." He rested his arm along the back of the bench and turned to her, his gaze focusing on her lips.

"I can't discuss my puppy dilemma when you stare at me." She dabbed at her chin with her forefinger. "Am I dripping lemonade peel?"

He leaned toward her and rubbed his fingers along her chin. "Penelope Reid. You are lovely and I can't stop looking at you. You've successfully diverted my attention away from the puppies."

"I'm not doing anything except sitting next to you."

"Reason enough to break my concentration."

"Quit joking." She jabbed at him with her elbow.

She tried, though she couldn't tamp down the bewildering yet indisputable flurries in her chest. She felt like a teen again, all nervous and agitated and captivated by a guy.

Oh, no, she firmly reminded herself. She didn't intend to date any man, and besides, Jacob wasn't interested in her. He intended to keep things simple, if that was the correct word he used, plus he was committed to his career.

However, her impractical brain shoved the thoughts to the side.

His gaze ran along her face. "Gorgeous," he murmured, giving her an admiring smile.

She heard herself inhale but didn't move.

He bent his head. Softly, he kissed her, his lips touching hers. "You taste so sweet," he whispered.

"Lemons are sour," she teased.

"But lemonade is sweet."

"We can't begin anything, Jacob. I'm not looking for a relationship."

"Neither am I."

At least he was honest, although for some reason, his admission disappointed her. She covered her disappointment with a topic switch. "Roses needed an excellent pediatrician and all-round doctor. The residents are thrilled you're here."

"All the residents?"

"Every single one."

"Good." His lips were still close, his gaze hooded. Evidently, he wasn't self-conscious about kissing her in the middle of town. His scent was clean—the outdoors coupled with a trace of male. She pushed down the urge to wrap her arms around him, to feel the hard muscles of his forearms, his cotton shirt pressed against her cheek.

"I plan to serve the community, then I will ease up to pursue things I enjoy," he murmured. "I hope you'll do the same."

If he referred to her wooden dolls, she'd moved the craft to a back burner. "Things like what?"

"Things like—" His eyebrows drew together as his cell phone pinged. He read the message and stood. "I'm sorry, Penelope, but we'll have to forego our dinner plans for another evening. An emergency has come up at the clinic."

She stood alongside him. "Nothing serious, I hope?"

"A preteen girl swallowed a bee." He typed a response into his phone. "I recommended to the head nurse that the girl drink water, but I'll see her just in case."

"Will she be okay?"

"I look for localized swelling, though she may suffer mild pain."

Penelope matched his long strides to the car. Several times, his hands brushed against hers. When he parked at the curb of her home a few minutes later, he cracked the windows open, letting in a breeze, and apologized again.

"Such is the life of a pediatrician. I'll double my efforts to wow you by treating you to the fanciest place in town. There is an exquisite farm to table restaurant getting rave reviews." He flashed a grin before dashing around to the passenger side to open the door for her. He'd opened the door when he'd picked her up earlier, too. He was a polite, considerate man. She liked that about him.

"Please, Jacob, don't apologize, and a fancy dinner isn't required."

"It's not a date, Penelope," he said. "We'll call our time together something else."

"Like what?"

He kissed her temple, then whispered in her ear, "I'll think of something."

CHAPTER 6

Sunday mornings meant church, and this Sunday was no exception. As always, Penelope and Evan attended the eleven o'clock service. The church hadn't begun to decorate for the holidays yet, though a live nativity was planned for December.

Penelope chose a long-sleeved jersey-knit dress in sage green and topped the dress with a shawl-collared coat in a light khaki. She wore her hair loose, and when she peered at herself in the mirror, her smile was bright. She looked forward to her upcoming "undate" with Jacob.

After church, she and Evan opted for lunch at Kathleen's Tea Shop, a popular eatery.

Kathleen, the owner, had decked out her restaurant in Thanksgiving finery. Autumn-scented candles, miniature pumpkins and oranges, and golden-colored napkins created an inviting ambiance. Kathleen and her husband, Rob, were hands-on restauranteurs, and the nod was always there as a tribute to Kathleen's Irish heritage. The shamrock-green walls lent a festive flair.

As Penelope and Evan entered, the scent of yeast rolls and

fresh-brewed coffee filled the air. An Irish tenor's voice crooned a holiday tune, accompanied by a harp and fiddle.

"November is too early for Christmas music," Evan said.

"It's never too early." Penelope hummed the melody of "Holly, Jolly Christmas" along with the Irish tenor. "November is the magic time between Thanksgiving and Christmas. You can sense the spirit of anticipation. It's almost palpable."

After they were ushered to their table and seated, Evan pulled out his cell phone.

"No cell phones at the table," Penelope reminded.

With an exaggerated sigh, he tucked away the phone, perused the menu and selected pancakes, scrambled eggs, and orange juice.

"Hey, there's Dr. Williams sitting all by himself." He indicated a corner table. "Let's invite him over."

Penelope's heart skipped a beat. "I'm going out to dinner with him tonight," she replied.

"He told me when I volunteered at the clinic yesterday." Evan smiled. "He seemed excited. You do, too."

"I do?"

"Yeah. You're fun when you smile and hum Christmas songs."

She drew a quick breath. Evan was obviously more astute than she gave him credit for.

"His clinic is short-staffed," Evan said. "He wondered if you'd volunteer there in your spare time."

"He did? What spare time?"

Several days had passed since Penelope had last seen Jacob and life had marched on. He texted often, quick texts when she least expected, apologizing for his busyness. Sometimes he texted in the early morning, and she was surprised she was on his mind in the hours before dawn.

He usually began his texts with a question.

Are you awake?

Unfortunately, yes, she replied. *I hardly ever sleep.*

Same here. Once I secure more staff, I'll ease up on the hours.

Work overload. Remember why you moved here?

To help people, he typed.

From the talk in town, you've reached your goal and I'm impressed, she said. *You're an overachiever.*

How would you feel if I told you I moved here because of you?

If she were honest with herself, his question brought dreams. Dreams of a relationship. She dismissed the consideration as quickly as it surfaced. She wouldn't risk having her heart broken again.

Knock it off, she replied.

I'm looking forward to seeing you soon for our ... undate.

Is that your new favorite word?

Definitely. BTW, how is your creativity level these days?

Nonexistent.

Evan brought some of your wooden dolls to the clinic. The kids love them.

I haven't had any time for more woodcarving.

Make the time, he said.

Whenever her mind focused on him, which was often, she was touched and impressed by his story. He'd left a successful career behind to relocate to a postage-stamp community and lend a helping hand with his physician skills. In all honesty, she'd been a bit envious that he'd decided to go after what he wanted. Why couldn't she be more like him?

You're gifted, he added.

Gifted? Hardly, though she knew her cheeks flushed at his compliment.

Not easy while balancing a full-time job and raising a preteen. She stared at the phone screen. *Are you doing any more house-hunting?*

I'm fixated on the dilapidated house on Brook Street.

Why?

It's big and cheap and in an excellent location.

She sent a thinking face emoji. *Better buy that tool kit. You'll need it.*

LOL. I haven't had a chance to drive by recently. Should I make an offer? I'm pondering pros and cons and all that. Thanks again for the tour of the town.

I'm happy to assist, she said.

Truth?

Always.

The other day, I was more fixated on you than on the houses.

"How do I answer him?" she muttered to the empty room. How could she tell him *she'd* been fixated on him? Think quickly, Penelope. Start a new topic.

You seem the type of person who is quick and decisive, she typed.

Truth?

Again?

I'm decisive at work. In my personal life, not so much.

A few hours later, Jacob texted:

Good news. I've secured extra help at the clinic. I'm free on Sunday night.

For more house-hunting?

For dinner at the farm to table restaurant. Will you join me?

Somehow, he'd avoided the word date.

Sure.

See you soon, beautiful.

Please, Jacob, don't flatter me.

Why not?

I'm unaccustomed to compliments.

Get accustomed ... you are beautiful.

A smile overtook her face when she bid him a good night. He always closed his texts by calling her beautiful. He made it clear he found her attractive, and he boosted her self-esteem. She recalled the numerous instances when her father, or her ex, had muttered slighting comments about her weight. They were hurtful and hadn't helped in her effort to lead a healthier lifestyle.

She smiled. Seeing Jacob at the restaurant and thinking of his texts brought a flip of excitement she could hardly hide.

"Mom?" Evan craned his neck and waved at Jacob. "Can Dr. Williams join us?"

"Sure."

Evan jumped to his feet and hurried toward Jacob's table.

She closed the menu, deciding on coffee and toast, then looked around at the beaming couples and chatting relatives. She did love this little town. Life was slower, summer and fall had waned, and November brought a decided crispness to the air. Nearby, a toddler chortled with laughter as her father tickled her and the young mother smiled in approval.

Such a precious family, Penelope mused. Christmas will be extra special for them.

She'd always wanted more than one baby and envisioned celebrating noisy, over-the-top Christmases, but her dreaded birthday loomed, and her child-bearing years were over. The only child she had to hang onto was Evan.

She set aside her contemplations and gave her attention to Evan as he advanced with Jacob in tow. Jacob paused at a couple near them, apparently recognizing their child. He conversed with the parents and squatted beside the boy. With a broad smile, he playfully interacted, and the boy's dimples flashed. Jacob seemed genuinely interested and concerned, lingering, and chatting. He was excellent with children.

He wore navy-blue pants and a checkered button-up shirt. Again, she was struck by his athletic physique and confident manner. When he approached, he greeted her with a twinkle in his deep-brown eyes.

Sometimes, though, she detected sadness in those same eyes.

With an undisputable flutter of magnetism, she greeted him. "Hi, Jacob. Please have a seat."

"Thanks." He claimed a chair between her and Evan. "I heard a lot about this place and wanted to check it out after church this morning."

"We were at church, too. I didn't see you."

"I sat in the back."

"We sit in the front."

"Fortunately, we ended up in the same restaurant."

She lifted a brow. "What a coincidence."

He grinned. "Definitely."

He distributed the coffees and orange juice that the waitress placed on their table. "Are we still on for tonight?"

"Uh-huh."

"Two undates in one day."

Evan gulped down his orange juice. "What's an undate?"

"Private joke, mate," Jacob replied.

He poured cream into his coffee. Penelope did the same and added sugar.

"We can take a raincheck," she said.

"I wouldn't dream of it." Jacob's eyebrows furrowed, silently telling her no excuses were allowed. "I moved schedules for this evening. Sickness doesn't stop on Sundays and the clinic is well staffed. They'll do fine without me."

They placed their orders, and the waitress returned shortly and set plates of eggs, pancakes, and melted toasties on the table. A toastie was an Irish specialty sandwich, featuring cheddar cheese, ham, and onion. Complimentary Irish soda bread was also provided.

Penelope bowed her head to say grace, and Jacob and Evan followed suit.

As soon as she finished her prayer, Evan poured a gallon

of syrup on his pancakes and dove into them. When he was done, he gave her a rueful glance. "Did Dr. Williams tell you that when you finally give me permission to get a puppy, he'll go with us to the shelter to help us choose?"

"No, he never told me that."

Jacob shrugged. "I meant to."

"Dr. Williams also reminded me that Candee and Teddy Winchester raise beagle puppies." Evan finished the rest of his orange juice in one gulp. "Did you know that, Mom?"

She sighed. "I did, indeed." In a moment of weakness, she'd phoned Candee to inquire if any of her pups were available. Candee had replied that she and her husband were concentrating on their son's horses and hadn't had any time to devote to breeding or raising any more puppies.

AFTER THEIR PLATES WERE CLEARED, Evan asked to be excused and walk home.

"The tea shop is quite far from home," Penelope protested.

"Don't freak out, Mom. You encouraged me to get more exercise."

She eyed her son. Despite church that morning, he'd insisted on wearing his usual baggy jeans and an oversized T-shirt of a band she'd never heard of. Once, he'd prided himself on clean, stylish clothes, which she'd deemed remarkable for a young boy. Sometime this past year, she'd couldn't pinpoint exactly when, he'd stopped being concerned about his appearance.

Now, as he slumped back in his chair, he didn't seem surly or rebellious. He just seemed reconciled to the fact that there was no use in arguing with her.

Jacob pushed his coffee cup to the side. "How about if he walks to my clinic instead? Only a few blocks from here and two nurses are working this afternoon." He waved his cell phone in the air. "I'm on call, as usual."

Evan met Jacob's explanation with a bland expression. "Will I have to work?"

"I expect you'll make yourself useful," Jacob said. "Zack is volunteering today. You can carry out a list of phone calls together."

Evan's eyes narrowed. "You just gave me a good reason not to go."

"Why would you say such a thing?" Penelope folded her hands in her lap. "Zack is your friend."

Evan stared at the floor. "You wouldn't understand."

"Try me."

"I'm a joke to the other kids, Mom, remember? They tease me all the time."

"Treat your mum with respect, mate," Jacob said. "She asked you a question."

"Sorry, Mom."

"The other kids tease you?" Penelope leaned forward. "Even Zack?"

"Not him so much. But some of the boys at my school push me around."

A flicker of alarm added to the despair creeping up her chest. Evan was too young to defend himself. Why hadn't he confided in her? No child should be harassed, and she had a good mind to phone Zack's mother.

She brushed his arm. "Are you telling me—"

Evan flinched at her touch. His ears burned a bright red. "I don't want to talk about it anymore, okay?"

"You were bullied at school?" Penelope demanded. "When?"

"In the boy's locker room after gym practice. One of the guys pushed past me so hard I fell on the floor."

"Why didn't you tell me any of this before?"

His gaze lowered. "I'm telling you now, Mom."

Jacob regarded Evan with a quiet expression. They fastened eyes before Evan fixated his gaze on the window.

"Did Zack see any of this?" she asked.

"He was in the locker room." Evan refused to meet her gaze. "When I fell, the other kids laughed, but Zack just walked away."

"He should've defended you. You two are friends."

"Yeah, like when we were ten."

Penelope placed a hand on Evan's arm again. "I'll call the school and complain."

"Are you kidding? Everyone hates me. Let me quit and we can live on Uncle Lincoln's houseboat forever." He swiped at his eyes and shoved back his chair. "May I leave now?"

"Where are you going?" Penelope pulled her cell phone from her purse.

"I'll go to the clinic and ignore Zack."

"How will you get home? Do you want me to pick you up?"

"I'll drive him," Jacob put in.

"Thanks." Evan turned to Jacob. "I'll finish phoning more hospitals for supplies, right, Dr. Williams?"

"You're a born salesman." Jacob trapped Penelope's wrist. "Who are you calling?" he quietly asked as they watched her son leave the restaurant.

She shook off his hand and scrolled through her phone. "I might have Zack's number in my contacts. I'll talk to his mother."

"Don't." He caught her gaze and held it. "The more you try to mediate the situation, the worse his friendships and school will be. Let him and Zack work it out for themselves."

"Are you an authority on children now?"

"Kids can be cruel." He broke eye contact, his conviction flat and firm.

"Evan is an innocent child. He doesn't deserve to be picked on."

"No one does." Jacob lowered his voice. His expression was strained. "I grew up dirt-poor. I didn't wear the right clothes. I talked funny because of my Aussie accent, and not a day went by that I wasn't teased or bullied."

"You couldn't help your family's situation."

"True."

"I still feel sad for Evan."

"He'll be okay." His cell phone buzzed with an incoming text. He read the text. His dark eyebrows furrowed as he pushed back his chair. "I need to head to the hospital."

"An accident?"

"A woman was washing a glass in the sink and the glass broke. She needs stitches in her hand."

"Dr. Williams?" A striking, well-groomed woman in a figure-hugging red pantsuit, a woman Penelope recognized from Evan's school, stopped at their table. "I'm Meredith Sinclair. Do you remember me?"

Jacob inclined his head. "Of course."

"I assume I'm not interrupting anything." She flipped back her shiny blond hair and granted Penelope a quick scan. "Do you two know each other?"

"We're best friends and tell each other our deepest, darkest secrets." Jacob smiled at Penelope. His joking tone conveyed a note of fun, though his gaze was serious.

Penelope was ready to refute him, but he grabbed her hand across the table and squeezed. "Right, mate?"

His amused expression irked her. "You wish, mate," she refuted sarcastically.

Meredith cut her eyes to Penelope, then back to Jacob. "I wanted to personally thank you, Dr. Williams. My daughter, Annabelle, recovered quickly from the bee incident."

"I'm glad. How is she feeling?"

"Your quick thinking made all the difference." She gave him a flirtatious smile. "I'm speaking for the entire community when I say we're thrilled you set up a practice here in Roses."

He paused, seeming to reflect on her words. "My pleasure. Annabelle is a lovely girl."

"Thank you." Meredith turned to Penelope, finally taking more than a passing interest. "All the mothers in Annabelle's class are having a Christmas cookie exchange next month at my house. Would you like to join us? I know Evan is in her homeroom."

"If I'm free, I'll try to be there," Penelope said. "Please send me the details."

"Annabelle will give Evan the information."

Meredith Sinclair had never been one of Penelope's favorite parents. The man she'd recently divorced was a flagrant attorney, and the family had a high-class air not lost on Penelope. From what she recalled, Annabelle was pretty and popular in school.

Once she swished away, Penelope remarked, "The girl who swallowed the bee was Annabelle?"

"Yup. Do you know the family?"

"A little, though Meredith snubbed me, as usual," Penelope said. "Our kids have been in the same classes ever since I moved back here."

"She didn't snub you. She invited you to a cookie exchange."

Penelope fumbled, dumbfounded that Jacob stuck up for Meredith. She checked her watch. "Evan should be arriving at your clinic by now."

"He'll see Zack," Jacob reminded. He picked up the check. Despite her objection, he firmly shook his head and placed several bills, plus a generous tip, on the table. "I'll stop at the clinic after I finish at the hospital."

"Let me know if he and Zack talk at all."

"Please, Penelope, allow him some freedom." Jacob bent down and kissed the top of her head before she could turn away.

She stiffened.

"Is anything wrong?" he asked.

"Of course not." She'd heard a sermon once about being a stuffer and keeping her emotions inside, instead of letting them out. She'd honed that skill to a tee.

"Remember," his puzzled smile confronted her, "I know everything about you."

"Almost everything," she corrected.

"You can't hide your emotions from me."

"Try me."

"I'll pick you up at seven o'clock tonight for our undate."

"Where are we going? The farm to table restaurant?"

"Nope Dress casual." He gave a lopsided grin. "The location is a surprise."

CHAPTER 7

It was a surprise all right, because the "undate" never occurred.

Jacob phoned an hour after Penelope arrived home. She'd changed into a red sweatshirt, as a nod to the upcoming holidays, and black sweatpants for comfort. Now she stood in the kitchen and clicked her cell phone on speaker as she pulled a tray of cream cheese Christmas cookies from the oven. The recipe had been handed down from her great-grandmother, Teresa, and she baked a double batch every year, mindful to send a plate to the first responders in town. Later in the season, she'd hand-deliver a batch to the local police station, too.

"I can't apologize enough," Jacob began. "Unfortunately, I need to cancel tonight."

She lowered her head and pressed her lips tight. "Another emergency?"

"A head injury. A ten-year-old child fell off his bike and is experiencing confusion. The parents are beyond worried and a little crazy."

Sternly, she reminded herself that her disappointment stemmed from selfishness.

He'd committed himself to serving people, and his kind and concerned attitude showed. He had so many good traits, which made her care for him even more.

She tossed a dishtowel over her shoulder. "Are the parents overreacting?"

"They're sensitive, though I tried to explain the situation. The child is being transferred to the hospital to be monitored overnight. Once I finish at the clinic, I'll stop by the hospital to check on him."

She placed the tray on top of the stove. "Your patients come first."

"I appreciate your understanding. I didn't anticipate a nurse calling in sick or a child's worrisome head injury."

Juggling the difficult emergencies a pediatrician dealt with daily was difficult to imagine. He never complained. He strove for a work-life balance, though parents were emotional and easily upset when it came to the well-being of their children.

"I'll make it up to you," he said.

"Don't be ridiculous."

"Do you like flowers?"

"Everyone likes flowers."

"What's your favorite?"

"No one has asked me the question before because …"

"Don't stop now."

"Because no one ever brought me flowers." She struggled between maintaining her self-respect and answering truthfully. An irrefutable pang of sadness twisted her gut.

"You haven't answered my question."

"Roses. I love red roses."

He chuckled. "Befitting, considering the town we live in."

She grabbed a cookie off the tray and bit into it. Mmm. Delicious. She swung her arms as she made her way to the sink. Food always cheered her up.

"I'm baking Christmas cookies," she said.

"For Meredith Sinclair's cookie exchange?"

"Possibly." She bristled at the woman's name, a wave of unfounded jealousy causing her to pause. "In any event, I'll freeze the cookies for now."

"I'd be tempted to cheat and pull them out of the freezer. There wouldn't be any left by Christmas."

Slightly pacified, she laughed. "Last year, I ate a half gallon of ice cream along with the cookies I had baked," she admitted.

She flicked a glance out the kitchen bay window framing her sizable backyard. The pergola-covered patio was brick paved and the table and chairs carved from teak wood. She and Evan hardly used the outdoor space. Though she paid a landscaper to mow the lawn, the curved flower bed in the corner was sorely neglected.

In fact, her entire house was untidy.

She vacillated. Should she sit beneath the pergola devouring a tray of cookies while feeling sorry for herself because of the change of plans with Jacob, or work on her housekeeping skills?

Dappled sunshine shone through the trees, and the sun began to set.

A sudden worried thought made her stomach clench. "Is Evan at the clinic?"

"He phoned several hospitals for equipment we might be able to use, then went off with Zack and his mother to the rec center."

She wasn't certain if Jacob was teasing or serious.

Evan left the clinic without phoning her?

"Oh?" Her voice swelled.

"Oh?"

The stillness between their connection troubled her. She expected a quick, clear response and shook her head in disapproval.

"Evan didn't call or text me?" She cupped the phone to her ear and paced the kitchen. Her tone was accusatory, but she couldn't help herself.

"Does he need to ask your permission first?"

"He was supposed to ride home with you."

"I told you I'm working late. There was a change of plans."

"Without informing me? His mother?" Conflicted thoughts swept through her. She'd anticipated seeing Jacob. More importantly, her son was in a car with someone else and hadn't consulted her.

"Zack's mother is a responsible adult," Jacob continued.

Restless, she shifted and didn't immediately respond. Jacob was a pediatrician, not a parent. Therefore, he wouldn't understand.

"Is Evan headed home after the rec center?" she asked.

"I assume so," Jacob said.

"That's it? No concern?"

"Look, Penelope, let me share something with you. I overheard the two boys talking about the locker room incident. It sounded like Evan shoved the boy first. Then the boy pushed him back and Evan landed on the floor."

She slumped in a chair. "I believe my son's side of the story."

"There are usually two sides to every story."

"What should I do?"

"Be aware of the situation. Junior high is challenging for most preteens, and Evan faces a bigger hurdle because he lacks a father figure."

She bristled. Jacob made it sound like Evan's home environment was lacking, though she didn't have a choice. Roy had cheated on her. As a single parent, she strove to raise her son properly and conscientiously. However, some part of her acknowledged that Jacob's words were true. An involved, interested father figure in Evan's life might make a difference, and Roy lived too far away for more than an occasional visit. Maneuvering the tricky landscape of adolescence required Evan to sort difficult decisions, and a male brought different parenting qualities than a female. Could a man bring extra value to Evan's development?

Her job as a mother was to protect her son. After all, Evan was her only family. They were a team.

"Evan and Zack spoke at length," Jacob said. "They installed a new diving board at the pool and Zack wanted to show it to Evan. Zack's mother said it wouldn't be for long."

"Okay."

"Penelope?"

"Yes?"

"Evan won't live in a bubble forever and you can't fight every battle for him. Young people solve problems without our interference all the time and turn out just fine."

She massaged her temple with both hands. "So, you're saying I should force him to man up and tough it out?"

"No one's forcing Evan to do anything."

Isn't that exactly what you're inferring? she inwardly refuted. Jacob's statements were absurd, though she told herself not to be rude and argue with him.

Offering a stiff goodbye, she clicked off the phone, arranged the cookies on a plate, and set them on the kitchen table.

She plopped on a chair and perched her chin on her hands.

She didn't like the idea of Jacob interfering in her

parenting decisions, especially when he disagreed with her, or his judgmental inference. Surely, he meant well, but she was decidedly sensitive regarding anything to do with Evan.

In what had begun as an encouraging Sunday, discouragement washed over her. She'd looked forward to the evening with Jacob more than she'd recognized. She liked the idea of a surprise dinner. She liked the romantic idea of an "undate." And she might not like to admit it, but she was sorely disheartened she wouldn't be seeing him.

Oh, no. I'll not be getting involved in a relationship that only leads to heartache.

Jacob, whether he realized it or not, had upset her with his parenting inference.

After a deep breath, she peered at the unwashed dishes and cookie sheets cluttering the sink. The floor needed sweeping. But how could she accomplish any tasks when she lacked the drive and motivation to overcome her frustration?

She sunk deeper into her thoughts, and only one emerged.

Jacob.

Feeling emotions she could hardly rationalize, she was caring for him more and more despite their differences.

He was an earnest person. His appealing smile, his charming accent, his gentlemanly mannerisms—were all qualities she longed for in a man. He was indisputably interested in Evan and wanted to build a rapport with him. Securing a bond between them seemed important to him.

She'd tried to act like it wasn't any big deal Jacob had moved to town, but even her son had noted she smiled more often, and her brother inquired if she had spent a recent afternoon soaking up the sun because of the rosy color in her cheeks. Shanice joked that Penelope must be drinking an abundance of wine for dinner.

Though now, the reality of her life threatened to consume her.

Jacob couldn't be counted on. Her son would be leaving soon to see his father. All that added up to loneliness at the holidays. Again.

She eyed the cookies on the table and pushed the plate away. She wasn't hungry anymore.

Sure, she could stuff herself with cookies ... or ... she could be more like Jacob. He'd pressed aside his former ambitions and was pursuing a lifestyle change. He'd determined what he wanted and was going after it.

Why couldn't she be as brave?

Filled with renewed energy, she refused to brood. Instead, she'd harness her disappointment and grow.

She placed the cookies in a freezer bag and stashed them in the back of the freezer.

A scan down the hallway was a stark reminder of her untidiness. She was never the neatest person, but she wasn't a slob, either.

She peered down at her outfit. Sweatshirt and sweatpants. Before her divorce, she'd dressed stylish and sophisticated.

She fixed her hands on her hips and studied herself in the mirror over the stove. "It's time," she declared, "to begin an overhaul Penelope project."

She began with her upstairs closet and spent time organizing and tossing handfuls of drab, plain clothes into bags to donate to Goodwill. The next hour she straightened the house.

While she waited for Evan to return, she wandered to the living room and grabbed a book she'd purchased about changing careers. She sat on the plush couch and penciled in her preferences, first and foremost creating toy dolls out of wood, though she found herself writing Jacob's name on the corner pages.

Her next book choice was a romance novel she'd read several times. A woman could read these books over and over, she decided. She skimmed her favorite emotional scenes and closed the book with a happy sigh.

She glanced at her watch. Hmm. Evan still wasn't home. Should she text him?

No. She'd heed Jacob's advice and wait.

She selected another book on the coffee table she'd recently purchased: *Change Your Holiday Menu, Change Your Life.* She curled up on the couch perusing healthy, nutritious meals.

Career choices, cleaning, and cooking were all steps to confront her concerns and get a handle on poor eating habits. Inspired, she marched into the kitchen and chose fresh spinach and a bag of potatoes from the pantry.

Thirty minutes later, Evan still hadn't arrived. Surely, the center was closed by now. Her concerned thoughts were interrupted by her ringing cell phone.

Her heart jumped.

"Penelope?"

She bit down on her bottom lip. "Yes?"

"This is Zack's mother. We stopped at the rec center after the clinic."

Penelope could hardly focus. "I'm aware."

"Well, we were in an accident."

"Is everyone okay?" The terror in Penelope's throat altered her breathing. She could hardly catch her breath. "Is Evan hurt?"

"We're all fine. Evan will explain. I'm dropping him off at your house shortly."

. . .

WHEN A PINK-CHEEKED Evan arrived home a few minutes later, he greeted Penelope with a smile.

"Zack's mother phoned. Thank goodness you're all right." Penelope lunged to hug him. He seemed to tolerate her for several seconds, then moved away.

"Tell me you're okay," she said.

"I'm okay, Mom."

She flopped on a chair. "What happened?"

"Zack's mother drove into a mailbox when she was making a U-turn near the rec center."

"She should've called me sooner."

"No reason to. In a few years, I'll be driving."

"We'll see about that."

"In our state, I can drive as soon as I'm sixteen."

She held her tongue and refused to comment.

Evan had processed her divorce from his father with stoic naivety and seemed to grasp that his world would never be the same. Friends had commended his strength, and Penelope was grateful to her brother and the toy shop. They'd given her a solid purpose to return to Roses and piece her life together.

With a pang of guilt, she recognized her own strict childhood, coupled with the realization that life was tenuous, might be the reasons she was holding her son back.

With a quiet exhale, she knew there were few powers more potent than a strongminded, soon-to-be adolescent.

"Dr. Williams called to let me know where you were." She stood, telling herself not to dwell on the accident. She tossed the spinach into a salad with boiled eggs and a light vinaigrette dressing. "So, how was your afternoon with Zack?"

"It wasn't as bad as I thought." Evan placed his jacket on a chair. "You'd be surprised at the rec center's transformation. The entire place has been remodeled."

"I'd like to see it some time." She set the salad and potatoes on the table. "I haven't been there in over a year. Not since you quit swimming."

He didn't react, though he stepped farther into the kitchen and surveyed the food. "Looks good, Mom."

"Thanks. Did you guys go anywhere after the rec center?"

His face blanched. "We stayed for a while, stopped for hamburgers and milk shakes, and then Zack's mother ran into the mailbox."

You're lying, she thought. But about what? She decided not to pry and gestured to the table. "I roasted potatoes, too."

"Yeah. I'd prefer chips, though."

She grabbed the cookbook. "I'm trying out new recipes for Christmas Day."

"I'll be home by then. Don't we usually eat lasagna?"

"Different foods make life interesting, Evan." She cocked her head to the side to take in the sight of her sweet son. "I'll miss you while you're visiting your father."

"You'll only be alone a few days."

"Your father said that baby Christina weighed eight pounds and eleven ounces when she was born." Penelope's voice quavered. "Childhood is so precious. Remember when I used to read the Christmas story to you on Christmas day?"

Evan went to the sink to wash his hands, then turned to search her face. She forced a smile, although he obviously noted the sadness in her expression.

"You can read the story to me again, Mom. I like it. In the meantime, visit with Uncle Lincoln and Aunt Shanice if you miss me."

"They're flying to New York City on an extended holiday." She flipped through the pages of the cookbook and came across a recipe featuring quinoa and bell peppers. She held it up for him to see. "I'm still concerned about you flying all by yourself."

"I'm finally twelve," Evan said. "It's legal for me to fly without an adult."

"I'm still not comfortable with the idea." She flopped down on a chair. It seemed as if she was more protective of him than ever.

"What about Dr. Williams?" Evan sank into the chair across from her, whispered a prayer of grace, and scarfed down a baked potato. "You can hang out with him at the clinic. When I come back on Christmas Eve day, we'll invite him over. I bet he doesn't want to be alone, either."

"We'll see." She regarded the spinach salad. "Try some."

"Later." He eyed the salad and stood. "Aren't you and Dr. Williams going out to dinner tonight? That's why you're not eating, right?"

"He canceled. An emergency after you left."

Evan placed his dish in the sink. "What are you going to do instead?"

She had a mountain of office work to tackle. However, the living room screamed for a dusting.

An idea occurred. There was something else. Something to distract her. Something that never failed to trigger happy, nostalgic memories.

"Evan?"

"Hmm?" One foot in the hallway, he swiveled toward her.

"Let's lug our Christmas tree down from the attic."

"Mom, it's November. We always wait until after your birthday before we trim the house. Last year, we hardly decorated."

"Decorating is a lot of work," she reminded. She'd decided there wasn't much to celebrate once her family had split up.

She reined in her previous emotions. Was her resentment toward her ex-husband hurting her son? She shouldn't be going through the motions of Christmas. She should be truly appreciating the holiday.

"Lots of families decorate early." She hauled in a decisive breath. "This year, let's be one of those families."

An hour later, Penelope eyed the living room with satisfaction. Sparkling white lights twinkled from the dark-green artificial spruce. Garland, in earthy tones and decorated with pinecones, dangled from the tree branches. On her front door, she hung a cedar faux wreath adorned with red berries and gold metallic bulbs, then tied a velvet ribbon to the top.

She clasped her hands to her chest and stood back to admire the results. As she'd anticipated, the holidays brought optimism and her mood lifted.

She clicked on the stereo system she seldom used and searched for a radio station playing Christmas music. "Rockin' Around the Christmas Tree" sung by Brenda Lee, wafted through the house.

"I've never heard this version of the song," Evan noted.

She laughed. "It's one of the best, and Brenda Lee was only thirteen years old when she recorded it."

Evan foraged through a stack of boxes on the floor marked *Christmas*. "Mom, where's the ceramic nativity you painted a couple of years ago?" His voice was bubbly, his appearance relaxed.

The set, painted in a light blue, depicted Joseph, Mary, and baby Jesus.

She picked through another box. "I think I gave the set to Uncle Lincoln and Aunt Shanice."

And she remembered why. She'd intended to carve wooden dolls into a miniature nativity but never got around to it. Why couldn't time stand still? Why was she always pulled in a million directions and left the activities she enjoyed for a later time? And why did that time never come?

She surveyed the wooden dolls. They sat where Jacob had last placed them when he'd made his "house call" to check on Evan's strep throat.

A smile flickered. Jacob hadn't even seen Evan that day. He was an excellent doctor, but surely, he had come for her, and the realization brought a quiver to her heart.

Evan propped open the window seat and peered inside. "The nativity isn't in here, either." He snatched his bookbag by the stairs. "If we're done, I should go upstairs to finish my homework."

"Your hamster needs feeding," she reminded. "Tidy your room. I cleaned and straightened the house but didn't touch your room."

Audibly, he groaned. "I'm busy, Mom."

"If you want the responsibility of a puppy who requires feeding, exercise, and grooming, you must prove you're ready."

"Dr. Williams said the best time to get a dog is when a kid is eleven years old. I'm twelve, so I'm a year late already. He also said that owning a dog helps you live longer."

"You or me?"

"Both of us, I think."

"He is a fountain of information. I'm surprised either one of you gets any work done if you're chatting all the time."

"He's awesome, Mom."

Observing her son's animated expression, she knew she was running out of excuses to be upset at Jacob. Her own senseless fear of being hurt affected Evan, and he deserved the right to have a positive male role model.

Nonetheless, Jacob was a diversion, an imaginary character in her life. She'd resolved to avoid any commitments. She'd warned him that a relationship between them was out of reach. So why did thoughts of him constantly fill her mind?

In truth, he seemed hesitant, too. Sometimes, he showed more interest in Evan or the dilapidated house than in her.

She curved toward the table in the living room. Evan had homework to finish, and she had wooden dolls to carve. Another positive step in the Penelope Project. If she felt better about herself, then everything else would fall into place.

CHAPTER 8

*T*wo weeks later, Jacob drove to Penelope's house and parked at the curb. It was a special day. It was her birthday.

He hesitated, taking in a deep breath. A beat of apprehension coursed through him. He'd taken a bold move by coming to her house, but she hadn't left him any other choice.

She'd avoided him lately, and he wasn't certain why. He'd kept his texts general, inquiring about the dilapidated house and if she had heard anything. She invariably responded by advising him to contact Candee, the realtor.

He'd boasted about Evan's ability to juggle several tasks at once when he volunteered at the clinic, and how proud she must be of him. He suggested the boy pursue other activities, too, such as choosing a favorite holiday-themed book and reading to the younger children in his school or making and sending Christmas cards to troops overseas. She'd thanked him, then told him that she and Evan participated in Toys for Tots.

I appreciate your focus on my son, but I'm his mother and have things well in hand, she'd added in her text. *Oh, and I would've appreciated it if you had advised him to call me before he got into the car with Zack.*

This again? Jacob thought.

I assumed Evan would be fine, he replied. *Zack is Evan's friend, and his mother is responsible.*

Don't assume you know everything, just because you're a doctor, Penelope had countered.

Then, she had shut down the conversation.

Alrighty then. He'd nearly given up trying to get through to her. She appeared to understand the clinic's emergencies. Though how could he develop a relationship with her that had nothing to do with her son if he couldn't talk to her without her getting all offended?

Also, he'd hidden a secret, and a pain settled in the back of his throat whenever he went over his decision.

He'd opted not to tell her that he and Evan had visited the animal shelter when the clinic closed on Saturday. The shelter needed volunteers to clean cages and dog dishes, and to interact and care for the animals. Jacob and Evan also bathed and walked the dogs.

Jacob rationalized this was an important and practical first rung in Evan's learning ladder. In addition, Evan was learning more about dogs and puppies.

Well, she couldn't avoid him any longer. Fortunately, her birthday had landed on a weekday, and he figured she wouldn't celebrate until Evan arrived home from school.

He strode to the front door and rang the bell.

"Happy Birthday, beautiful," he said, when she opened the door.

Her gaze narrowed as she eyeballed the cake topper numbers on the cake he held.

"You knew I was turning fifty?" She plunked a hand on

her hip. "All I told you on the plane was that I had a birthday in November. Besides, you were sleeping."

"My eyes were half open under the sunglasses," he teased. "So how—"

"Evan mentioned it several times. By the way, where is he?" Jacob peered toward the stairway.

"In his room, where else?" She shrugged. "He should be downstairs shortly."

"May I come in?"

"Of course." She opened the door wider and ushered him inside.

"No birthday is complete without a carrot cake topped with cream cheese frosting."

"You remembered?"

"Naturally."

"I wonder if Evan did." She preceded Jacob into the kitchen. "He's been acting awfully quiet and vague."

"He knew I was bringing the cake," Jacob confessed. "We planned your celebration ahead of time."

"When?"

"Last week." He went back to the porch, returning with a bouquet of red roses he offered her, and a six-pack of ginger beer he set on the kitchen counter. "The flowers are for you. The cake too, of course. The beer is for me. Care for a cold one?"

"No thanks." She lifted a delicate eyebrow. "How?"

"I discovered the local grocery store carries ginger beer. I opted for nonalcoholic."

"Not the beer." She shook her head. "How did you—"

He winked. "You mentioned the flowers in a text. However, lately you've become almost impossible to reach." He hoped he didn't sound overly accusing.

"I've been busy."

The age-old excuse.

He sensed her winding up more excuses and changed the topic.

"Your house looks great." The ebony-black piano gleamed, and books were stacked neatly on the coffee table. He strode into the living room, perused the stack, and held up a paperback. The front cover was a bright-blue, and a couple were in a heated embrace.

"*A Tale of a Forever Heart*?" He read the title.

She followed him. "I love sweet romance novels."

"Who is the tale about?"

"A man and a woman." She snatched the book from him and set it on top of the stack.

"Have you finished it?"

"Not this one yet. I know the ending, though."

He quirked an eyebrow. "How?"

"The sweet romances I read guarantee a happily ever after. Hearts are broken, but always mended at the end."

"You like romance."

"I love romance. The novels make me happy."

Her smile, her natural vitality and exhilaration, drew him to her. His mind drifted to the upcoming holidays and spending every waking free moment together.

On a nearby table, a line of miniature wooden dolls stood straight and colorful.

"White pants, blue coats, and red detailing," he said. "The toy soldiers are ready to march in formation. What are their names? General Admiral Oregano, Private Basil …"

She poked him in the side. "You're a regular comedian these days."

His deep chuckle resounded through the room. "You name your wooden dolls after spices."

"You have a memory like an elephant."

"And your carved dolls are extraordinary, a work of art."

"Thank you."

She wore a short, clingy green dress that accented her figure. Her shiny hair fell to her shoulders in gentle, dark waves. She gazed at him with soulful blue eyes, a perfect complement to her light creamy complexion.

"Crikey." He almost forgot his words. "You are gorgeous, especially on your birthday."

She opened her mouth, and he held his palm up. "Don't disagree. A thank you is sufficient."

"It's not that. I've waited for you say the word *crikey*. The term is utterly Australian."

"A cultural assumption," he said. "The word is hardly used anymore by younger Australians. I'm part of the old guard."

"You and me both."

"At our age, we can leave our cares and worries behind. Now our job is to welcome our world and savor every moment."

Her full lips curved into a smile. Her dimples were adorable. "Wise words, Dr. Williams."

She was even more gorgeous when she smiled.

"I always imagined life would be better when I reached fifty," she admitted.

"It is."

"Is it?"

He bent closer to her. "Yes, because I'm here, your son is here, and we are all together."

"True."

There was no challenge in her tone, though her chin quivered, and she averted her gaze.

His heart lurched. Awareness of her sense of humor, her zest for life, shot through him. He didn't want her despondent, especially on her birthday. He felt a surge of something he'd yearned for and recognized the emotion for what it was.

Attraction. To her.

He'd left his ex-wife far behind when he'd learned of her infidelity. Since then, he'd harbored ambivalence about close relationships. He struggled, but with each passing day, realized that Penelope was the woman he could contentedly live the rest of his life with. Nevertheless, how could he overcome his uncertainties if she wouldn't allow him to get any closer?

"So, let's light the candles," he announced.

"Happy Birthday to you, Happy Birthday to you."

Jacob grinned at a smiling Penelope when he and Evan had finished singing.

"Time to blow out the candles," he teased. He'd debated placing fifty candles on the cake, but decided on the numbers five and zero, respectively.

She held back her hair, half-closed her eyes, and the two candles were extinguished in one blow.

"Hurray!" Jacob and Evan laughed and clapped.

"Mom, whose birthday comes next?" Evan asked.

"Well, yours is in February." She regarded Jacob as she began brewing coffee, then returned to the table to cut the cake. "When is your birthday?"

"January," Jacob replied.

"Really, Dr. Williams? Only a couple months away?" Evan blurted.

Jacob nodded.

"Truth?" Penelope asked Jacob skeptically. "Or did you just want the first slice of cake?"

"Truth." He offered a slight smile. "Although I'm happy to be served the first slice, regardless."

"And you'll be how old?"

"Fifty-one. Welcome to the fifties."

"I didn't realize you were older than me." Penelope

blinked, seeming to take several seconds to mentally regroup.

"Because I look so young," he joked.

"You and my mother are the same age for a few weeks!" Evan said. "Your birthday is next, Dr. Williams, so you can pull out the knife."

Jacob placed his palm over Penelope's delicate fingers. Surely, she felt the invisible magic shimmering between them. Otherwise, how could a woman's small hand push his heart into such a rapid beat?

"Make a wish." Penelope slid her hand away. "Keep it a secret or it won't come true."

Jacob closed his eyes for several seconds. "Secrets are difficult for me."

Especially when his secret wish stood directly in front of him. His feelings for her were shattering any final reservations. The awareness seemed sudden because he'd only met her a few short months ago.

He sat on a chair, cracked open a ginger beer, and downed half.

"No coffee?" she asked.

"I'll stick with beer."

He needed something to quell his nerves. Lately, he couldn't sleep, pondering his feelings. Could he get married again at his age? Penelope was a divorcee with a preteen boy. In the past, he'd stepped away from any conflicts. He'd attended college rather than deal with his family. Their problems and goals were too different from his. Same was true of his hospital job in Atlanta. However, he believed his decision to relocate to Roses was the right choice, and the reason was standing in the same room.

Penelope poured herself a cup of coffee and sat across from him. "Earth to Jacob Williams," she said.

"Sorry. I was thinking."

"About?"

"Your festive home." He gestured toward the living room. "The decorated tree inspires me. I wish the holidays were already here."

"I love Christmas." Despite her words, her eyes were sad.

"Me too."

"Me three," Evan chimed in. "Mom, did Dr. Williams tell you he plans to dress up as Santa Claus at the clinic next month?"

"No, he didn't." She plated a heaping slice of cake for each of them while Evan rummaged in the freezer for a carton of chocolate ice cream.

"I thought it would be fun for the kids," Jacob said, "though I haven't found a Santa costume yet."

"You will," she replied. "The children will call you Doc Christmas."

"I love Christmas," he repeated.

"Bah, humbug," she half joked. "You're Doc Christmas but sometimes I feel like I'm Mrs. Scrooge."

"Dr. Williams, did my mom mention we are spending Thanksgiving on Uncle Lincoln's houseboat on Hilton Head Island?" Evan brought the carton of ice cream to the table. "Our neighbor watches my hamster when we go away. When I get my puppy, we'll take my puppy with us."

"Oh, we will, will we?" Penelope crossed her arms.

"If my mother says it's okay, you can join us. Unless you have other plans." Evan beamed at Jacob, then glanced at Penelope.

"I don't have anything special planned." Jacob set down his fork. *Whoa. Wait. Wasn't a houseboat a boat on the ocean? Since his niece's accident, he'd avoided pools and lakes. This scenario was even scarier. This was an ocean.*

A smile flickered across Penelope's face. "Of course, you're invited, Jacob."

"Are you staying all week? I'm working until Wednesday." Inwardly, he grappled with his words. He wanted to celebrate Thanksgiving with them, but a houseboat wasn't part of the equation. Somewhere on land, a cabin, for instance, sounded infinitely better, and much safer. "I always phone my mum and my sister on holidays."

She scooped ice cream onto each plate and handed him and Evan a spoon.

"Call them from the houseboat," she replied.

"You have cell phone service?"

"The boat isn't sailing anywhere because it's not motorized. It stays in one place—docked at the marina. Water and sewer and electricity are provided by the shore power. Houseboat living is like staying at a vacation home. Do you swim?"

"Why?" He tilted his head and tried to contain his shudder. "Will I need to?"

"Not unless you want to."

"I'm not a strong swimmer."

"You won't need to wear a life jacket while you eat Thanksgiving dinner." She grinned. "The boat hardly sways."

"Hardly." He blew out a speculative breath and met her gaze. "I'll make a deal."

"What kind?"

"While I'm talking to my mum and sister, I'll introduce you and turn the phone over to you."

"Fine. I'm thrilled to chat with them both."

He gave an ironic laugh. "You're in for an adventure."

Boy, was she ever.

She wandered to the sink to wipe her hands on a dishtowel, then stepped to him. "You're completely off work for a few days?"

"I'm close enough to Roses to drive back if there is an emergency, though Dr. Hannaway, the town GP, is taking on extra shifts as we've expanded. Even though we have different specialties, the limited number of doctors here makes it possible for us to cover for each other if needed. She's excellent and no-nonsense. Plus, we use each other as a sounding board." He hesitated. "The drive from Hilton Head to Roses is what … around three hours?"

"Depending on traffic. I imagine the Thanksgiving holiday is busy at a clinic."

"Most common is a condition doctors call holiday heart." He finger quoted. At her curious expression, he explained. "It's caused by excessive drinking. The patient usually comes in pale and sweaty and smelling of alcohol."

"Is the condition serious?"

"It can be, if heart palpitations are rapid."

"Let's pray no one sees any of that," she said.

Evan piped in after he'd finished the cake and ice cream on his plate. "Can we take a ferryboat to Daufuskie Island for the day? The trip is short from Hilton Head."

"We'd have to ride on another boat to get there?" Jacob inquired.

"The ferry is small, Dr. Williams."

Jacob scraped a hand through his hair. Irrational thoughts flooded his brain. Suppose there was a strong wind and the small boat overturned?

"Not everyone is comfortable on boats," Penelope replied to Evan. "Each of us wrestle with our own fears." She nodded conspiratorially at Jacob. An understanding nod, and he tipped his head back to take in her sweet face. "My fear is planes."

He smiled. "I remember."

"Lincoln and Shanice won't be around, as they're taking an extended holiday," Penelope went on. "They hardly use the houseboat anymore. Did you know my brother is also an author?"

"What does he write?"

"Children's books. *Tuggy the Tugboat* books are his best-loved series, which is the main reason why he wants to hold on to the boat."

Jacob downed the rest of his ginger beer. "Which is?"

"Inspiration, I imagine." She sat again and sipped her coffee. "The weeks between Thanksgiving and Christmas are hectic for toy shops. I'm spending hours ordering inventory and managing invoices. Fortunately, our employees are more than capable, though with Lincoln gone, I'll be on call if anything goes wrong."

A wide grin spread across Evan's face. "We'll decorate the houseboat for Christmas. Wait till you see how we tape red stockings to the kitchen cabinets, Dr. Williams. Uncle Lincoln has an artificial pine tree in a storage unit, and we hang tinsel everywhere." Evan placed his dish in the sink and bounded toward the hall. "We also cut out paper snowflakes for the boat's windows. Don't we, Mom?"

Before Penelope answered, Evan skipped up the stairs.

"Lots of sparkle and flair." Jacob offered a bemused smile.

"This entire conversation has caught me by surprise." Penelope returned to the sink and began loading the dishwasher.

"Which part?" Jacob placed his bottle in the kitchen's recycling bin. "The paper snowflakes?"

"Not funny."

"Have I been uninvited for Thanksgiving?"

"You're still invited. A deal is a deal."

"You'll cook a turkey?"

"Roger's Diner, my favorite restaurant on the island, offers a spectacular takeout spread. The entire turkey with all the trimmings. I don't cook large meals on the boat, because the oven heats up the boat too quickly. However, there is a full kitchen, complete with a stove, refrigerator, and microwave."

Jacob strode close to her, the delicate floral whiff of lavender flooding his nostrils. The scent was calming, lightening his mood, and quelling his reservations about a sinking houseboat.

Her back was to him, and he wrapped his arms around her waist. "I missed you," he whispered in her ear.

"Yet here I am."

"I tried texting."

Her lips pursed. "Busy," she murmured.

"Are you still upset about the accident with Zack and his mother?"

"I was concerned and worried."

"I hope you don't blame me. I got caught up with patients and—"

"Don't be silly."

"However, you've avoided me."

"Busy," she repeated.

"My birthday girl has a lot of the same excuses I don't buy."

She tilted her head toward him. Her lips were slightly parted. "What don't you buy?"

The expression on her features mirrored his own, confirming his feelings. Her eyes were teasing and appraising, and his pulse thrummed a steady beat. In that moment, he realized she cared for him as much as he cared for her.

"Your excuses for avoiding me," he said. "I forgive you. Please forgive me."

"Of course." She inhaled and turned to him. "Jacob, whatever you're thinking ... this isn't a good idea."

"The best idea I've had in a long time." He cradled her face in his hands and kissed her gently and thoroughly. "In fact, I have an even better idea."

She gazed up at him. "I can only imagine."

"No more of this "undate" stuff. From now on, we're officially dating. We're a couple."

She trembled in his arms, slightly, as if he had stirred an emotion she was trying to suppress. "Promise me you'll never turn into a Roy."

He wanted to bury his lips in the curve of her neck. She brought gladness and love into his life. She was fresh and vibrant, witty, and delightful.

"I promise." He sealed his assurance with an affirming kiss.

A houseboat wasn't Jacob's idea of the ideal place to observe an American Thanksgiving. First and foremost, he was petrified of being on a boat.

Okay, not petrified. Just not totally comfortable swinging back and forth on a floating "vacation home."

The America part? He loved the country and was thrilled to celebrate the traditional holiday. After relocating, his family had become US citizens, and he appreciated having dual citizenship for both Australia and the United States.

At present, totally stuffed from Thanksgiving dinner, he placed his cloth napkin to the side and pushed back from the galley table. "Best meal I've ever had, and so much food it took two hands to carry the turkey platter to the table. My compliments to Chef Roger."

"I doubt the diner is still owned by a guy named Roger," Penelope replied.

"At least the cooks carried on Roger's legacy." Jacob patted his stomach appreciatively. "Especially the mashed potatoes with loads of butter."

Seemingly caught between laughter and agreement, she smiled and didn't protest.

"If we're done, I'll get the Christmas trimmings." Evan's face flushed with excitement. "Mom and I hauled the tree out of storage before you came on board, Dr. Williams, but there are plenty of decorations left."

Penelope gazed out the window. "The unit is on the other side of the marina."

"I know where it is, Mom. We've been here a thousand times."

"Soon, it will be dark," she said.

"Yeah, in like three hours."

"Go ahead, then." She clutched her hands together. "We'll finish cleaning, and when you return, let's start trimming the boat for Christmas."

After Evan shrugged on his leather jacket and skipped out the door, Jacob pulled her into his arms. A flow of heat passed between them, a crackle of attraction he couldn't deny. Her heady feminine fragrance called for a kiss.

"Thank you for a wonderful Thanksgiving," he said.

She licked her lips and regarded him with unabashed affection. "My pleasure."

Those lips. A rosy tint from his kisses enhanced her full mouth. He'd be thinking about those lips all evening.

He sighed and glanced at his watch. "This may be a good time to phone my mum."

Penelope brought their dishes to the sink. "Do you want some privacy?"

"No." He stepped to her, claimed her hand, and squeezed. "You're part of the deal."

"Are we video chatting with her?"

Curtly, he shook his head. "A phone call is sufficient."

Jacob peered around, admiring the boat's interior. Penelope had explained her brother had opted for white paint to make the space look bigger. The open floor plan on the upper deck featured a dining room, kitchen, and living room, and the reclaimed wooden floors were originally crafted and removed from an old school. The lower deck offered bedrooms, three bedroom, two full-sized bathrooms, and a half bath. In total, the houseboat was two thousand square feet.

The ocean views from the docked boat were jaw-dropping. Waves swished, and the cries of seagulls squawked as their wings beat through the air.

With his duffle bag slung over his shoulder, he'd admired the gorgeous wooden and rope walkway when he'd arrived. The handmade door boasted an antique porthole. "I didn't envision this type of luxury," he admitted.

"*Shay's Secret.*" He'd read the boat's name engraved over the entry and asked, "Who is Shay?"

"Shanice. Lincoln's wife," Penelope said. "Shay is his nickname for her."

"What's her secret?"

"They have a history together. They dated in college and then broke up. She left him because of our father, who didn't approve of their relationship. She never explained her reasons to Lincoln. Fortunately, they ended up finding each other again in Roses and thus, true love."

"The best kind." Jacob offered a nod of approval. "Just like your romance novels."

On Thanksgiving morning, he'd woken to a golden sunrise streaming into his bedroom window. He'd stepped outside and relaxed on the deck while savoring a cup of fresh-brewed coffee. The mouthwatering scents of roasted turkey, sweet potatoes, cranberry sauce, and warm-from-the-oven bread filled his nostrils.

"Smells like turkey day!" Evan exclaimed, and Jacob heartily concurred.

Now as he rinsed dishes, a cloud of impending doom descended over him as he anticipated the upcoming call.

"I'd prefer you're here with me when I phone my mum." He wiped his hands on a dishtowel and started toward the living room sofa with Penelope. He beckoned her to sit next to him and she complied, snuggling against his shoulder. He smiled down at her, and his breath quickened at the delightful sensation of her closeness. He drew her tighter and pressed a kiss on her lips. Her gaze lifted to meet his, and the gentle yielding in her magnificent eyes almost made him forget about the dreaded upcoming phone call altogether. He wanted to keep Penelope in his arms forever.

She'd taken extra pains with her appearance and wore a cable knit blue sweater dress. Cozy, yet casual, the dress enhanced her smooth complexion, and her dark hair shone in the afternoon sunlight.

Jacob had opted for jeans and a chambray shirt.

"Don't you want to talk to your family alone first?" Penelope asked.

"Nope." Jacob loosened his hold around her shoulders, fighting the impulse to keep her as near as possible. "My mum is … well … my mum. Our relationship is rocky, at best."

"What about your sister?"

"Kylie has had a hard go of it these past few years. She's been angry with me, though we've begun to mend our fences."

"Part of your long, tragic story?" Penelope inquired.

"The very same." He responded with a small nod. "Kylie is considering moving back to Australia."

"With your mother?"

"Possibly." He studied his cell phone, as if searching for answers. "My mum can't handle all the farm chores on her own, though my sister has frequently helped. However, now that Kylie and her husband have split, only the two women are holding onto an old, rundown farm."

"You seem to gravitate toward rundown things yourself."

"Or rush away from them. I apparently have a love-hate relationship going." He narrowed his eyes. "Are you trying to analyze me?"

"I have enough on my plate trying to analyze myself."

He hesitated. Should he phone his mother now, or wait a bit? Speaking about his mother revealed his ambivalence more than he realized.

There was no time like the present, he encouraged himself. Rubbing a hand over his jaw, he clicked on her number.

"Hello?" an elderly woman's voice answered.

"Happy Thanksgiving, Mum," Jacob began.

"Who is this?"

"Your son, Jacob."

"Nice of you to remember your mum and ring me once in a while."

"I call you every week and text whenever I can." He gave himself a small shake. "Happy Thanksgiving."

"We're not American, Jacob."

"We've lived in the States longer than Australia and we're American citizens." A familiar emptiness overwhelmed him. No matter what he achieved, he could never please her.

He peered at the stereo system in the corner. Perhaps if he was armed with relaxing music in the background, the music would subdue his anxiousness instead of being surrounded by silence. As if reading his mind, Penelope grabbed a remote. She tuned into a station of holiday classics, and "Oh Come, All Ye Faithful" sounded, sung by a male choir.

He gazed at her, curled up on the sofa beside him. She

looked the opposite of how he felt. Her features were determined and resilient.

His protector.

He smiled at that. Penelope, rising to his defense in any storm.

"Are you working today at your fancy clinic?" his mother inquired.

"Another doctor is on call, Mum. And you're confusing the clinic with the hospital in Atlanta."

"Are you all moved into your new place?"

"I'm renting an apartment. I'd love if you visited me for the holidays."

"You're a big shot doctor. You don't have time for your mother."

"I have plenty of time for you, mum." He pressed his lips tightly together.

"You didn't have time for the farm. It could've collapsed all around you and you wouldn't have cared."

"I'm not a farmer. I wanted to be a doctor and I couldn't turn down the full scholarship for being valedictorian of my class. Besides, I want to help people."

"Doesn't charity begin at home?"

His stomach churned, and he reached for the glass of water Penelope had placed next to him. "Did you receive my check this month?"

"The money was a little less than usual."

"I'm sorry. The clinic was more expensive to start up than I anticipated, and coupled with the expense of moving from Atlanta and buying another doctor's practice ..."

He rubbed his forehead, then slung an arm around Penelope's shoulders. "Look, the weather is warmer in the Carolinas than in Maryland. Roses sponsors a Christmas parade and features a holiday sing-along concert in the park."

"I like snow at Christmas."

"I haven't lived here long enough to forecast for sure." He glanced at Penelope. "I'm certain they get snow sometimes."

"Sometimes," she mouthed.

"I prefer a white Christmas," his mother said.

He sank deeper into the sofa. He'd had this type of discussion often and instructed himself to remain upbeat. Nonetheless, if he liked red, his mum would say the opposite and like blue. The past was a mere breath away, and he clearly sensed this conversation was resembling all the others.

"I'm considering purchasing a home in Roses and setting up my practice in the house." He struggled to find the right words to describe his dream. "It needs work, but the house has character."

"Our farm has character."

"Is Kylie there?" He briefly closed his eyes. "She is welcome to visit for Christmas, too."

"She's busy in the kitchen and can't talk."

"Some other time, then. Please wish her a lovely Thanksgiving." He sat still for a moment. "Mum, I'd like to introduce you to a very special someone. I'm officially dating a wonderful woman, and her name is Penelope. She wants to say hello."

"Now?" Penelope whispered.

He nodded vigorously.

She rubbed the back of her neck, then accepted his cell phone. She exchanged light pleasantries with his mother, then handed the phone to him for a final goodbye.

When he clicked off, he leaned back against the sofa. Still holding Penelope close, his body sagged.

Some conversations rendered people speechless. This conversation with his mum was one of them.

"'*Deck the halls with boughs of holly.*'" The following morning, Evan belted out the carol in a faultless tenor voice while he taped paper Christmas stockings to the kitchen cabinets. His wide beam of delight lit his entire face.

Penelope grinned. She loved seeing him happy. These were precious memories she'd tuck away and revisit forever. These were the festive times chipping away at her insecurities and resentments toward her ex. These moments brought optimism for a brilliant future.

She'd picked out a pair of linen joggers and a dazzling red sweater. She'd decided to grow out her hair, and loose brown waves framed her face. She'd parted her hair in a deep side part.

She followed Evan into the living room, where Jacob, squatting on the floor, was setting up a three-foot artificial tree. The scents of a Christmas candle, balsam pine and cedar, wafted through the air.

"Can I ask you a question, Penelope?" Jacob stood, his tall, commanding frame dwarfing the tree. He brushed silver tinsel off his jeans, though tinsel still stuck to his hair and green polo shirt.

"Sure." She smothered a giggle and reached up to pluck the tinsel from his hair. "Are you planning to turn into a Christmas tree?"

"I'm Doctor Santa, remember?" He brushed the tinsel from his shirt. "When is the soup done?"

"A few more hours. It's simmering on the stove."

Earlier in the morning, she and Jacob had picked over the turkey carcass, then sliced extra vegetables—onions, carrots, and celery—to a turkey broth. A rice cooker supplied the rice they would add later.

"Smells homey and delicious." He stepped toward the kitchen and sniffed the heavenly aroma. "All we need is a bag of sticky caramel corn to munch on while we binge watch holiday movies. I vote for *National Lampoon's Christmas Vacation*."

Evan fixed a sparkling white angel to the top of the tree. "That movie is one of my favorites. Let's stream it tonight."

Penelope stood back to admire the decorations. An eclectic mix of humorous, stylish, and handmade ornaments brought a fun, understated elegance to the boat. It was a shame, she thought, that she wouldn't be back here to enjoy the festive ambiance. However, Lincoln and Shanice declared that they would stay on the houseboat in January and celebrate the holidays then.

By late morning, red and green bulbs sparkled around the fake fireplace, and a blinking *Ho, Ho, Ho* sign hung over the corner bar. Penelope hadn't observed a true, merry Christmas since her divorce. However, she imagined the upcoming weeks with Jacob as picture-perfect opportunities to awaken her sense of joyousness in the season.

As if reading her thoughts, he reached for her hand and gave a light squeeze. His warm smile filled with love.

Love. For her. The thought brought unexpected flutters to her chest.

"Can I play video games in my bedroom?" Evan asked when he finished hanging the last strand of tinsel on the tree.

"Sure." Penelope turned to Jacob and reciprocated his smile. "Thanks for all your decorating help."

"You're very welcome," he replied. "My pleasure."

"Later I want to go swimming," Evan said. "I brought my swimsuit."

"Swimming?" She expressed her disbelief aloud. Evan hadn't asked to swim in months. "The water is cold." She hesitated to say more, though she didn't wish to discourage him, especially with Jacob staring at her.

A wistful look crossed Evan's face. "I'll just take a quick dip."

"Not in the marina," she replied. "Long gone are the days when you can jump in from the boat. This water is dangerous with electricity and fumes and operators unable to see you." Her hands gripped the chair, a myriad of accidents that might await Evan flashing through her mind. "There are *No Swimming* signs posted everywhere, and any further discussion on this subject is nonnegotiable."

"Message received, Mom. You've given me a thousand lectures about the dangers, but Pelican Beach is a short walk from here. I'm a strong swimmer. So are you. Come with me."

"I'll pass."

"What about you, Dr. Williams?" Evan asked.

Jacob's entire body stiffened. "Your mother and I will sit and chat." With that, he led her to the outdoor deck overlooking the harbor.

The view of the ocean beyond was spectacular, and she'd noted he'd taken in every detail of the houseboat, both inside and out.

"In December, the holiday lights take to the water," she said. "Hilton Head holds a twinkling boat parade."

Jacob raised a dark eyebrow. "Sounds marvelous if I can watch from the shore. However, if you invite me, then I'll be there."

They stood by the handrails, an ocean breeze cooling her cheeks.

He wrapped an arm around her. "Simply breathtaking," he breathed, as he gazed down at her face. The same breeze ruffled his dark, thick hair as he studied the sunlight glinting off the water, then contemplated the sapphire blue sky.

He looked incredibly handsome, and nothing took away from the peacefulness and pleasure of standing with this conscientious, dashing man. Earlier, he'd jogged around the marina shirtless, and she'd admired his hard chest and flat stomach as sweat pooled along his muscular arms. After returning to the houseboat and showering, he'd responded to numerous phone calls from his staff. He'd assured Penelope that Thanksgiving at the clinic had been thankfully without any alarming incidents, save for grease burns from frying a turkey, upset stomachs from overeating, and a bout of food poisoning.

"Dr. Hannaway is keeping an eye on a holiday heart patient," he said. "She's monitoring his abnormal heart rhythm."

"Is she on call the entire weekend?" Penelope asked.

"Yes. This weekend is officially my vacation. However, I'm scheduled to work at the clinic on Christmas Eve day and on Christmas Day."

"Perfect for your Santa outfit," she teased.

He chuckled. "Meanwhile, how is the toy business?"

"We fussed with our window display, and it features a lighted carousel and several handmade elf puppets. I insisted on background Christmas music to be played in the store."

"Is "Jingle Bells" the standard fare?"

"Jesus is the reason for the season, and I prefer to keep Christ in Christmas. So, "Oh, Little Town of Bethlehem" is perfect."

"I agree." He rubbed his thumb over her wrist and kissed her hand. "In addition, I like giving and receiving gifts, too."

Her hand tingled from his warm lips. "We also devoted one floor of the shop to wooden rocking horses in all shapes and sizes. There's a rocking horse convention this weekend and a couple of busloads of people are expected to tour our store."

"There's such a thing as a rocking horse convention?"

"Apparently." Penelope had checked with several of her toy shops and the holiday season was off to a promising start. Lincoln had texted from New York City and declared that he and Shay were having a splendid time seeing the famous sights.

"This is the first year Lincoln and Shanice won't be hosting a Christmas party," Penelope mused.

"I'll host a Christmas party," Jacob said.

"You will?"

"Absolutely." He searched her face. "Will you attend?"

"I'd love to."

"Good. I'm throwing a Polar Express party at the clinic and will serve hot chocolate. I requested new sleepwear donations for the children, and the outreach from the community has been overwhelming."

"Another advantage of living in Roses." Grinning, she settled on a deep-cushioned teak love seat and Jacob nestled beside her. He looped an arm around her shoulders, and her heart leapt in her chest when he nuzzled her neck. A glow of exhilaration and affection surged through her.

"This is a wonderful life," he whispered as his lips gravitated to hers. "The island is genuinely peaceful. A real corker."

"Corker?" She gave him her undivided attention. "What's that mean?"

"Australian slang for really good, mate." His eyes gleamed wickedly, and she couldn't prevent a broad smile from spreading across her face.

"This entire harbor will decorate for Christmas," she said. "Red bows on all the lanterns, and many owners will string colored lights on their boats." Her gaze roamed over the glistening water. Smooth waves followed various boats as they motored out of the harbor.

She inhaled. A whiff of salty air never failed to invigorate her.

"Why are people drawn to the water?" she mused.

"Some people," Jacob corrected with a grim smile.

She looked up at him. "What do you mean?"

"Some people are, some people aren't."

"You mentioned you aren't a strong swimmer."

He shrugged indifferently. "I can hold my own. I'm not a champion like you or your son."

"We've grown up around the water."

"Crikey, I'm an Aussie guy." He broke out in his thickest Australian accent. "My family's farm in Maryland isn't near the sea."

Penelope stood to check the soup.

"There's something I want to tell you." His gaze pinned to hers. "My story involves swimming."

Her chest tensed at his serious tone, and her voice rose in pitch. "What is it?"

"Sit for a while longer." He patted the seat and pulled her back down beside him. "I'm ready for you to hear my long, tragic tale."

By his decree, she'd assumed the subject was closed and shot him a questioning glance. "Truth?" she inquired.

"Always. You're a good listener."

"I try." He leaned back against the cushions and stretched out his long, muscular legs.

"At least when I'm not talking constantly." She managed to keep her tone joking to lighten his suddenly pensive mood.

He inhaled a lengthy breath and then released it. "My sister, Kylie, had a daughter."

Had. Penelope noted the past tense and her heart constricted.

"Linda," she said. "You mentioned she never fully recovered. What happened?"

"A swimming accident when she was young. She nearly drowned."

"How old was she?"

"She was in elementary school. The accident occurred in a friend's pool. My sister sat by the pool and looked away for a few seconds when Linda suddenly went under the water. Kylie dove in and rescued her, and her quick thinking saved her daughter. However, Linda's brain suffered from a lack of oxygen. The doctor in our little town diagnosed the injury as not severe."

Penelope reached out and patted his hand.

"The doctor was wrong." Despite Jacob's somber expression, his voice remained calm. "Linda began having seizures. A couple years ago, she took a turn for the worse and suffered from amnesia and muscle spasms before she died."

His voice cracked, bringing tears to Penelope's eyes. "Jacob, I'm so sorry."

"I miss my sweet niece. We all do." He shuddered, as if a memory from the past was ever present. "Kylie was an excellent caregiver."

Penelope's stomach twisted in a sharp knot. "The … the remembrances must be difficult for you to process and—"

"I was working in Atlanta and left as soon as my sister phoned." His gaze focused on the horizon, where the water met the sky. His voice trailed off. "I didn't arrive in Maryland on time."

"I'm certain you got there quickly."

He bit down on his bottom lip, seeming to ponder his next words. "Not quickly enough. Kylie never forgave me. She never forgave me for not being at the pool that day, either. I had visited for the weekend but had stayed back to lend a hand on the farm."

"Don't blame yourself. There was nothing you could do in either case." Penelope swallowed as the risk of tears passed and the thickness in her throat began to dissolve.

"Explain that to my sister. I'm a doctor. I should've been able to do something."

"She'll come around eventually." Penelope still reeled, and her tears flowed again. Her heart ached for Jacob and Kylie, and his family. She pictured his niece, perhaps with the same dark hair and deep-brown eyes as he had.

"Continue to reach out to your sister," she said, dabbing at her wet cheeks.

"I will. Since then, I've been uncomfortable around the water. Coupled with the difficult memories, the dangers seem more pronounced than ever." He touched one of Penelope's tears with his fingertip. "Thank you for listening. Thank you for caring."

She gazed up at him, surprised at his heartfelt thanks. She wasn't accustomed to a man who wore his feelings on his sleeve. She wasn't accustomed to the emotions he woke inside her.

They sat for several minutes, watching the hypnotic rise

and fall of the ocean, and she burrowed her face against his chest.

So that explained why his expression had paled when she'd mentioned the houseboat. He'd been leery, cautious, and a bit skittish. Now she understood why.

A while later, her cell phone buzzed, and she recognized the number immediately. *Roses Toy Shop*. The manager was capable and would only phone if an emergency arose.

She stood. "Jacob, I apologize. I have to take this call."

"We lost power on the street because a transformer went out," her manager began without preamble when she clicked on. "Two busloads of folks from the Rocking Horse event are scheduled to pull up within the next few hours."

"Are you closing the store?"

"We plan to stay open, although it's dark here with no lights. I sent the staff out for flashlights, though I anticipate cash register sales will be a challenge."

"Thankfully, it's daylight," she replied. "Do you want me to come help?"

"We're shorthanded and the rain is coming down in sheets," the manager said. "Our parking lot is tight, and someone needs to direct traffic."

Mentally, Penelope estimated the time it took to drive to Roses. Three hours. The store was open until eight o'clock, though they might close early once darkness fell. Still, she'd be able to assist for a good portion of the day.

"I should leave now," she murmured, half to herself.

"Leave?" Jacob was on his feet. "Where? Why?"

"The toy shop in Roses." She rubbed her palms across her linen joggers and irritably shook her head. Her job was interfering with a wonderful weekend, although she had no choice. Her business came first, particularly during the holidays, and especially with Lincoln out of town.

"The shop lost power because a transformer is out in the area," she said. "The staff is buying every flashlight in sight."

"What can I do?" Jacob asked.

She stared blankly out at the ocean. "Will you stay with Evan? And stir the soup?"

His lips formed a smile as he placed his hands on her shoulders. "Whatever helps."

"Thanks." She rushed inside the houseboat to grab her keys and shrug on a cotton jacket. "I'll direct cars in the toy shop's parking lot. Believe me, in the pouring rain it's the job no one else wants. I'm the owner, and I must lead by example."

"You're a professional and selfless woman and absolutely amazing."

"I hate leaving Evan."

She also hated leaving Jacob.

"Evan is fine." Jacob clasped her cold hands. "We'll play board games, walk the marina, and eat soup. Tonight, we'll watch the movie, unless you want us to wait for you."

"Don't. Sounds like a plan." She turned toward the stairs and called out. "Evan, I'm driving to Roses but should return around ten. Dr. Williams is here."

"Awesome," came the quick response.

"Drive carefully," Jacob said. Their gazes met and held. He hugged her, and she relished the solidness of his muscles, the warmth of his hands on her back heating her insides. He brought "tidings of comfort and joy," like the lyrics of her favorite Christmas carol, "God Rest Ye, Merry Gentlemen." Her breath paused for a beat at the wonder of Jacob's embrace, the wonder of *him* to make everything right.

"I'll keep your son safe," he promised, pressing a tender kiss on her lips.

He made her feel sheltered and adored, and nothing could

dampen her excitement at the upcoming weeks with him by her side.

Because nothing was as important as security and … love.

Willfully, she lifted her chin. Love was the last feeling she wanted, and contemplations along those lines only betrayed her. Still, what was more exhilarating than love, especially during the most magical season of the year?

She refused to feign indifference to him any longer. If anything, she cared for him more than she ever dreamed possible.

"No reservations about leaving Evan," she reassured herself as she withdrew from Jacob's hold. As she walked along the narrow dock to the parking lot, she scuffed at a shiny pebble in her path. "My son is in Jacob's capable hands," she said aloud. "What could possibly go wrong?"

*J*acob strode into the kitchen as soon as Penelope left. He stirred the turkey soup simmering on the stove and sipped a spoonful. Savory and delicious, and he sprinkled a dash of salt and pepper into the broth.

Penelope had placed the rice cooker, a box of rice, and a measuring cup on the counter.

He grinned. She was certainly a planner, and wow, did she look gorgeous. She was everything he could ever ask for. Efficient, brilliant, and stunning. Was that why he couldn't form a coherent thought whenever she entered a room?

"Dr. Williams, I'm going swimming," Evan announced. He emerged from his bedroom and bound into the kitchen wearing swimming trunks, sandals, and a faded T-shirt, with a towel thrown over his shoulder.

Jacob checked his watch. The time showed past noon, and Penelope had most likely driven over the bridge connecting Hilton Head Island to the mainland and was well on her way to Roses. A glance out the window promised blue skies and a clear afternoon.

"Where are you swimming?" Jacob placed the spoon on a spoon rest on top of the stove.

"Pelican Beach. It isn't far." Evan bobbed toward the window and pointed to a sandy beach beyond. "My mother said it was okay."

"I'll walk with you." Jacob covered the soup pan with a lid and turned off the stove.

"Did you bring a swimsuit, Dr. Williams?"

"No." Nor did he ever intend to swim again if he could help it, Jacob thought. He stepped to the closet and retrieved a beach towel, then two water bottles from the refrigerator. "I'll sit on the sand and watch you."

They hiked through a stretch of pine trees and a planked wooden path and soon arrived at Pelican Beach. High grass grew between silky, golden sand dunes. Waves crashed against the rocks. A field boasted yellow and pink wildflowers.

Evan paused to pick up fragments of seashells and flat stones, then shook off his sandals. Jacob followed suit, and they fell into step across the wet sand as they neared the ocean.

Jacob scanned the beach, deserted except for a young couple cuddling, and a child digging in the sand. A scattering of fishing boats anchored in the distance.

"No lifeguard?" he inquired.

"In November, not many people are at the beach," Evan replied. "Plus, this beach is hidden from the main boardwalk. Only the locals realize it isn't private and open to everyone. My mother can probably walk to every inlet blindfolded because Grandma and Grandpa lived here."

The ocean was an exceptional turquoise-blue, and the sun lit the water all a glitter. Jacob tasted the briny tang of salt and vegetation on his tongue.

Yes, this glorious island was a beaut, and his insides gave

a peculiar little lurch. Hilton Head was a second home for Penelope, and he envisioned her as a young girl, sunburned and giggling while creating castles in the sand or swimming in the ocean.

"Mom loves the beach," Evan said.

"I can see why." A cool breeze whipped across Jacob's face as he smoothed out his towel and sat. "The sea is a magical place."

"She is a champion swimmer. She swam often when we lived in Virginia."

"Not anymore?" Jacob peered upward as several seagulls circled overhead, then flew past.

"Not since we moved to Roses. In Virginia, my mother was fearless. I remember going camping with my parents and she dove into deep lakes without thinking twice." Evan set his towel on the sand beside Jacob and pulled off his T-shirt. "Now she worries all the time. Take today, for instance."

"You asked if you could swim, and she didn't argue."

"Yeah, but she always frets about the tide pulling me under the water. I remind her I'm careful and not afraid and it doesn't do any good."

Jacob feigned polite applause. "Well, I, for one, approve of your bravery."

"Can I tell you something else, Dr. Williams?"

"Certainly."

"My mom seems happier now that you two are dating. I think this Thanksgiving is the best weekend of her life. Mine too!" Evan chugged from his water bottle, set the bottle on his towel, then headed for the ocean.

"Don't go far." Jacob pulled his knees to his chest. The weather proved cooler than he'd anticipated, and he shivered, regretting not bringing a jacket.

Evan stood by the shore before taking tentative steps, then splashing in the surf. "The water is cold!" he shouted.

"I can only imagine," Jacob said. His thoughts curved to Penelope. He'd risked exposing his vulnerability, showing emotion regarding his difficult relationships with his mum and sister. The loss of his sweet niece. Penelope was kind and gracious and seemed to absorb his sadness and blame.

Were introductions between his mum and Penelope over the phone the right approach? He wanted her to meet his family, assuming they would grow to love her as much as he did. A phone chat was a start.

Whoa. Backpedal. *Love.* He'd vowed never to fall in love again. He enjoyed dating, but one heartbreaking devastation in his life was enough. When had love come into play?

His thoughts shied away from studying his feelings too intently. After his divorce, he had little confidence in his ability to judge his emotions.

You fell in love with Penelope the first day you met her on the plane, his conscience prompted. She was brave and captivating, ambitious, and loving.

Not far away, Evan waded farther into the water and then dove in. With a deliberate scissoring of his legs, he swam forward, then drifted and floated on his back.

The wind whipped up, and Jacob stood, tucking the beach towel over his shoulders. If the air was cold, the ocean in November must be bone-chilling.

"Aren't you freezing?" he shouted to Evan.

Evan turned, but apparently didn't hear Jacob. The boy paddled to a rocky shore in an inlet, found a sunny spot, and sat beneath a ledge.

"Smart kid," Jacob muttered, seeking a sunny location on the sand for himself. His cell phone buzzed, and he yanked it from his pocket, assuming Penelope might be calling.

Instead, the phone number from the clinic floated across his screen.

"Dr. Williams?" a woman inquired when he answered.

"Hello, Dr. Hannaway." He recognized the woman's voice.

"Our holiday heart patient is complaining of chest pain," she said.

"What's the patient's age?"

"The man is in his sixties."

The wind picked up and the percussive sounds of the waves hitting the shore grew louder.

"His heart rhythm hasn't stabilized?" Jacob pressed the phone closer to his ear, turned away from Evan, and focused on the sand to concentrate. He noted that the young couple and the child had disappeared.

"His heartbeat is more rapid."

Jacob gnawed his bottom lip and weighed the options. "Let's use a beta blocker to slow the heart rate."

"I agree. Thank you," Dr. Hannaway replied.

Jacob clicked off and twisted back to view Evan.

The boy waved, then climbed higher on the rocks. The kid was adventurous, and Jacob debated whether he should discourage him.

When Evan neared the top of the ledge, Jacob watched in mounting fear. "That's far enough. The peak is too high!" Panic rose in his throat. Surely the rocks were slick.

"I'm okay. I'm gonna jump. I've done this before." Evan slipped and righted himself, then swiveled toward the water and stretched out his arms.

Weighed down by dread, a knot twisted in Jacob's gut.

"Don't!"

Afterwards, Jacob couldn't remember if his shout had been loud enough to carry.

A split-second later, Evan dove in.

All was quiet.

Jacob stood stock still, frozen in horror. Surely Evan would quickly break the surface and tread water. Uneasiness poured along his spine.

Drowning. His niece. Not again.

Twice, he hadn't been there to save Linda. But he would save Evan.

He could swim. Not great, but enough.

He cast his gaze across the shore. Still no sign of Evan.

Fear spiked. Time sped up, though his movements seemed to slow down.

No. He refused to be paralyzed. He flung his towel to the sand and raced toward the ocean.

RELIEVED that the power to the toy shop had been restored, Penelope hummed the melody of "Angels We Have Heard on High." A tabernacle choir belted the carol from her truck's radio as she headed back toward Hilton Head. The manager had phoned, and everything was under control.

As she stepped into the houseboat, she was still humming the carol. "Surprise! I'm back!" she called out.

Hmm. Her smile turned to a frown of dismay when no male voices greeted her. A quick search indicated that Evan had headed to the beach and Jacob had accompanied him.

As she swapped her shoes for a pair of beach flats, her mood elevated again. A rush of happiness spread through her at her son's decision to swim. He seemed to be gaining confidence and self-assurance, and she attributed both to Jacob's excellent influence.

Jacob was responsible and caring, intent on building a careful and considerate rapport with Evan. He clearly enjoyed the boy's company, communicating and focusing on him.

She closed the distance on the short path to Pelican Beach, following sandy footprints. She paused and shaded her eyes. Head down, Jacob stood talking on his cell phone.

Her gaze riveted on Evan poised at the top of a rocky ledge.

A wave of icy, stark fear flowed through her, and her blood froze.

Her son was a good swimmer. But—

Without warning, Evan lost his balance on the rocks.

"Evan, be careful!" She trembled. Her pulse skittered.

He righted himself and stretched out his arms.

Unease spun up her spine. She broke into a run at the sight of him diving into the water and heard herself scream. A lead weight took up residence in her stomach.

From her peripheral vision, she noticed Jacob. He'd clicked off his cell phone and stood motionless for a split-second. His failure to act didn't escape her.

"Jacob!" She caught up with him and grabbed his arm as he lunged toward the water with her. "What are you waiting for?"

A roll of waves washed up to the shore, as Evan broke the water's surface.

Penelope reached him first. "Have you lost all your common sense?" Her speech was mumbled, echoing in her ears. Her mouth was dry.

Evan's wet swimming trunks were plastered to his legs. He was drenched.

"Don't have a fit, Mom. I didn't fall in if that's what you're upset about."

Despite the coolness in the air, she was sweating. "Think about how high the ledge is. What you did was nothing short of reckless." She glared at Jacob as she wrenched a towel from him. Her hands shook as she wrapped the towel around her shivering son.

The threesome returned to the houseboat without speaking, their footfalls heavy in the sand. Evan pleaded tiredness, grabbed a protein bar from the kitchen, and headed to his bedroom.

Jacob walked with her to the living room.

"Wanna talk about this?" He crossed his arms, his hip perched on the side of the sofa.

Still fuming, she snapped, "No!"

"Okay. I understand." He gazed at her, waiting several seconds. "Are you certain?"

"More than certain."

"Right. Sure." Soundlessly, he strode from the room.

She stood alone. After a few minutes, her breathing returned to normal, and she no longer gasped.

"Penelope?" Jacob's voice was elevated enough to carry from his bedroom before he reappeared in the living room.

"What?" In the charged silence, she jumped at her name being called.

"I'm leaving." His duffle bag was slung over his shoulder. He unlatched the door leading to the outside walkway.

She regarded him. "You're leaving." They both knew she wasn't asking. She was telling.

"My decision is for the best." He paused, opened the door wider, then turned to watch her.

Her heart thumped louder in her chest. She imagined he might seek forgiveness for his negligence and beg her to let him stay. But he didn't assume any wrongness for allowing her son to attempt such a dangerous stunt. He didn't speak or beg. He said nothing.

"I assumed you were here until Sunday," she finally spoke.

"No reason to extend my holiday."

"Because of what happened at the beach?" She flinched at the renewed remembrance, and the terrible dreamlike pang in her chest when she'd viewed Evan's wild dive into the sea.

Jacob shrugged. "That's part of it. But I'll never be able to get through to you."

"Evan could have drowned."

"He didn't drown. He's safe. He's an excellent swimmer and he chose to dive in. He's old enough to determine his strengths and skills."

She pushed out a breath. Jacob was a doctor, a pediatrician, and worked with children. But he didn't have any children of his own.

"You should've stopped him when he started climbing the ledge," she said.

"I wanted to allow Evan some freedom. He's a fearless kid. That's a good thing."

Goosebumps traveled up her arms at the thought of what could have happened. "Is it?"

"Yes." Jacob turned on his heel and swung toward the door.

"Fearlessness doesn't keep him from danger." She lashed out at Jacob's retreating back. "You're not a parent. You could never understand."

He twisted. His dark-brown eyes flared with emotion. "This conversation isn't only about Evan. It concerns you. You're sheltering him too much and he can't be wrapped in cotton forever. What are you afraid of?"

She cringed. Jacob's remarks hit home, but she refused to admit he was right. "You don't know my whole story."

"I know enough. I know about your divorce and your move back to Roses. I know you hate your job and—"

How could she explain her childhood and her domineering father? And her loneliness after Roy's infidelity? Or her sadness and impending dread at spending the Christmas holiday alone—without a loving partner to share each special moment? She'd sound pathetic and needy, a side of her she refused to expose. He knew enough about her already.

She supported herself by leaning against the wall. She attempted to compose her features, though she was crying.

"Hey, beautiful." He stepped toward her, his expression softening. "You're carrying too much on your shoulders. You're a single mother and work too hard."

He offered consolation, though she refused to accept. She didn't need his pity. She was a competent woman who had learned to rely on herself.

"When Evan was young, he was afraid of heights." A tear trickled down her cheek. "Ironic, isn't it?"

Jacob caught her rebellious tear with his forefinger. Gentleness filled his eyes. "He overcame his fear."

"He was overly cautious. I was mindful and tried to encourage him."

"You obviously did a good job."

She inhaled and stepped back, eyeing the open doorway. The sun was beginning to set, and its fiery golden glow lit the harbor. Several boat lights flashed. A seagull perched on one leg on the handrail of the roped walkway. The bird seemed undecided whether to dive into the water or fly away.

"Evan is all I have," she said quietly.

"You have me."

She let out a sob as the bird flew up into the sky. "Do I?"

His gaze never left her face. "I'm here, aren't I?"

She took in his handsome features, those soulful eyes, and his firm, chiseled mouth. He was the epitome of maleness, and all she'd dreamed about since they'd met.

But then another thought forced its way in. She couldn't endure any more heartbreak.

Jacob moved forward. She moved backward. The gap between them stretched a few feet, though figuratively the distance could be measured in miles.

"Evan is a smart, intuitive kid," Jacob said. "He recognizes even more about you than I do."

"Like what?"

"He realizes you've never gotten over your divorce and your ex's betrayal. Evan worries about you because you worry about him. And too much worry isn't good for a kid."

"What you're saying isn't logical."

"Think about it, Penelope. I'm perfectly logical." The edge in Jacob's tone caused her defenses to rise. "And there's something else that drives me bloody insane."

"What?"

"I get that your marriage ended unhappily, and you felt betrayed." He stiffened; his entire body strained in an unbending line. "But why won't you give us a chance?"

"You're spouting opinions as if you were a psychologist." Words caught in her throat. "You're a pediatrician, Jacob."

Oh, but he was right. He'd scored a bullseye. She didn't allow any man to get too close.

"Why are you so frightened of a second opportunity for happiness?" he asked.

Why? Maybe because she was afraid her intense love for him might consume her. If something happened ... if he broke her heart, he'd break Evan's heart, too. And Evan was too vulnerable.

"I appreciate your concern, but I'm well, and so is Evan." Her tone raised and her eyes smarted with tears she refused to shed. "Safe travels, and please don't try to contact me."

He paused, unmoving, forcing her to stare into his fathomless eyes. This wasn't the moment to remember his tender kisses, the upcoming festive celebrations she'd anticipated sharing with him. A happy Christmas, brimming with gladness and miracles.

He fished in his duffle bag and pulled out a gift, meticulously wrapped in red and green foil paper, and handed the package to her.

"I planned to give you this tomorrow. I envisioned us sitting under the tree with mugs of soup. Well, I'm some kind of fool, aren't I?" The sharp tone of his voice was tempered, though his words were weighty and significant. "In any event, Penelope, Merry Christmas."

CHAPTER 12

*B*ack in Roses on the Monday after Thanksgiving, Penelope found that she could hardly concentrate. Although Jacob texted often, her replies were short.

Can we talk? he asked.

Nothing to say, she replied.

I'm sorry about what happened at the beach. I panicked. No excuses. I shouldn't have hesitated.

Apology accepted.

Wanna take a trip to Stone Mountain in Georgia? he inquired the following day. *I'll ask Dr. Hannaway to fill in for me. You and Evan will love it. There are millions of dazzling holiday lights and spectacular shows.*

Sounds like you're reading a pamphlet about the place.

LOL. I am.

No, thank you.

Are you busy?

Always.

What about the Christmas town you mentioned that's about thirty minutes away from Roses?

I can't, she responded.

He reverted to: *Can we talk?*

Nothing to say, she repeated.

Have dinner with me. You choose the restaurant.

Her fingers hovered over the phone's keyboard. She wanted to accept his invitation.

But no, she couldn't.

Not possible, she typed. *Please. Leave me alone.*

When one week turned to two, then three, and the calendar dutifully inched closer to Christmas, she came to terms with a cold, hard fact.

After several days of similar texts, Jacob had stopped contacting her. Since then, she hadn't heard a word from him. She drew her arms close to her body and stared down at her empty hands. Good. He was finally doing what she asked.

Then why did her chest ache, and why did she need to gulp air at every turn?

She cried herself to sleep at night and awoke to red eyes and a splotchy face.

When she casually inquired about Jacob after Evan's volunteering sessions at the clinic, Evan ran a hand through his shaggy hair, then tilted his head to study the ceiling, as if to deter her from asking any more questions.

Shanice phoned and confided that Evan had told her that his mother had fallen in love with Jacob, and then she'd sent Jacob packing after a big argument.

"Mom pretends she isn't interested in Dr. Williams," Evan stated. "Though it's obvious, she cares about him a lot." He also added that their disagreement was all his fault.

"Oh, no." Penelope gasped and denied, while a cold weight settled on her chest. "Evan made a reckless choice, but the argument wasn't because of him."

Or was it?

"Evan hasn't told you the entire story," she continued.

"Do tell," Shanice said.

"I left my son in Jacob's care, and Jacob was negligent." Penelope's voice thickened. "However, Jacob did apologize. Several times, in fact."

"Then all is well."

Yet there was more to the story. Penelope's every thought was of Jacob, and, because of her decision to end their relationship, she was forced to shoulder her hurt alone. Perhaps she should have asked him to stay on the houseboat and talk things out as he'd requested. Perhaps she should have answered his texts differently.

He should have persisted.

However, he was too much of a gentleman. He'd listened to her and eventually heeded her instructions. She wondered how long it would take for a handsome, eligible doctor to find someone new—just in time to celebrate the holidays.

Tears trickled down her cheeks, and she furiously brushed them away.

With inner regret, she recognized that Jacob was everything a man should be. He was intelligent, he made her laugh, he was ambitious, and supportive of her business and hobbies. He was dependable, and equally important, an excellent role model for Evan.

Though now he was no longer in her life because she'd pushed him out.

Seasons had changed for her once again, and slowly, her spinning world began to slow down. When she looked around, she realized she was blessed.

Through renewed determination, she threw herself into wood carving, and finished a dozen delightful dolls for Christmas. The dolls were unique, endearing, and no two were the same. The craft kept her mind and hands occupied, and she was grateful for the distraction.

She donated the dolls to the homeless shelter, and Evan brought several to the clinic.

Her toy shop was frenetic with activity, and whenever Penelope lent a hand during a shift, she couldn't help but compare the atmosphere in the shop to a jubilant party. Children were excited. Parents were thrilled. Everyone was kinder at Christmas.

She was busy beyond words.

And she was heartbroken.

Occasionally, Evan mentioned Jacob. She tried to act nonchalant, though her insides cracked. She avoided driving by Jacob's office or the clinic, fearful of encountering him. She never saw him anywhere.

Several days before Christmas, she paused in her kitchen and opened the window, allowing a light winter breeze to freshen the room. December brought unusually warm temperatures to the Carolinas, and, according to the forecast, the prospect of snow grew less promising by the day. Instead, the weather proved mild and wet.

She stood by her granite countertop, sorting two dozen frozen Christmas cookies. True to her word, Meredith Sinclair's daughter had given an invitation to Evan, and Penelope was invited to a cookie exchange on Sunday.

She pondered how to gracefully decline. The toy stores were demanding, but on Sunday every shop was closed, a decision she and Lincoln had made years ago. They gave their employees a break from the workweek to rest and worship God as they chose.

Her mind returned to the cookie exchange. The prospect of conversing with all the other mothers from Evan's class was awkward. They were an elite clique, and she didn't have much in common with them.

Except for one important point. They all had kids the same age and were struggling with the onset of their children's difficult adolescences.

.   .   .

"Let's go Christmas shopping!" Candee phoned Penelope on a gloomy morning a couple of days later. "I'm looking for another gift to put under the tree for my son, preferably something with horses, and it finally stopped raining. Come with me. No excuses allowed."

Penelope cupped her cell phone to her ear. "I'm working at home today and drowning in paperwork."

"Take a lunch break. I insist. I'll pick you up at noon."

Quickly, Penelope changed her sweat suit for tailored black slacks and a green embroidered *Merry Christmas* sweater. She topped the outfit with a woolen coat in a light tan. She cast a quick appraisal of herself in the mirror and pulled her hair back at the crown, allowing a spring of curls to cascade around her face.

At precisely noon, Candee arrived. Candee welcomed the holidays and dressed appropriately in white slacks and a heavy knit red sweater.

"Nothing compares to the thrill of seeing Roses decorated for Christmas," she announced, when Penelope slid into the passenger seat of her car. "The tree in the square is gorgeous at night when it's lit up."

"I read online that the town is encouraging white lights for all the shops, to keep an old-fashioned holiday look," Penelope replied.

"Read? Haven't you seen any of the displays?"

"Not yet." Penelope batted a hand through the air. Her chest tightened around the ever-present heaviness. "The holidays aren't the same for me anymore."

"Make this a magical Christmas. You're the one in control." Candee's tone was confident, though her gaze was anxious as she scanned Penelope's features. "You look pale. Retail therapy will cheer you up."

"My shopping is done. Evan has everything a boy his age needs. Besides, he hardly ever asks for anything."

Except a puppy.

A few minutes later, Candee parked her car, and the two women jostled through the crowds and headed down the main street arm in arm.

Penelope sniffed a temptingly decadent aroma of dark chocolate, along with roasting chestnuts from a sidewalk vendor. The streets hummed with excitement, and Christmas was in the air. Each shop hung wreaths on their front windows, embellished with red and white ticking stripe ribbons. Several vintage wooden sleds stood propped by the doors. The women paused to admire bundles of fragrant garland adorning a clothing boutique's green window boxes.

A smart, fancy French poodle trotted alongside its owner. The poodle's curly-black coat was groomed in the traditional poodle style.

"Dogs are precious." Candee stopped to compliment the dog, then curved to Penelope. "Are you still adopting a puppy from the shelter for Evan?"

"Definitely. The terrier mix had her puppies, and one will be a surprise Christmas gift for Evan." Penelope brightened. "I've checked on the puppies often, and they're all so lovable. Their fur is mostly white, and they have the cutest expressive eyes and ears. Four puppies are still available from the litter and the shelter told me that Evan can choose his favorite."

"When is he flying to Florida?"

"As soon as school lets out. He'll return home on the morning of Christmas Eve."

"His visit is short," Candee said.

"I'll drive him to the airport. He's flying direct, and this is the first time he'll be alone."

"He'll be fine."

Penelope regarded her friend with a level look. "You sound exactly like Jacob."

The women ducked into a candy store, weaved through a

knot of people, and selected slabs of milk chocolate fudge. They claimed two wooden rocking chairs on the store's wide front porch, and remarked on the shoppers as they passed.

Candee bit into a piece of fudge, leaned back in her chair, and closed her eyes. "Heavenly," she moaned. "Now, speaking of Jacob …"

Penelope's stomach lurched. In the weeks since she'd last seen him, she'd considered texting him. Then she wondered why he'd stopped texting her.

She longed to share the incident on Hilton Head Island with her friend. Yet, she was hesitant to burden Candee with her problems.

"When is the last time you saw Jacob?" Candee asked.

"Thanksgiving weekend."

Exactly three weeks, four days, and twenty hours ago, Penelope thought. Not that she was keeping track, of course.

"Jacob bought the dilapidated house on Brook Street that you looked at together. He was able to snag the house for a steal."

"He did?" Infuriated because he hadn't texted to inform her, Penelope sat straighter and placed the fudge on her lap. "When is the closing?"

"The beginning of January. The house needs a tremendous amount of elbow grease, but he is thrilled and intends to set up his physician's practice there."

Penelope's next reaction was an inward burst of pride. Hurray for Jacob for pursuing his dreams. Nonetheless, he hadn't reached out to tell her the exciting news. And she'd been the person who had first showed him the house.

"He asked about you." Candee's quiet voice checked Penelope's thoughts.

"Oh?" Penelope felt her forehead knit into a frown. "What did he say?"

"He said he missed you. Very much."

Penelope shot up from the chair. Her fudge fell from her lap. "Not enough to phone me, though."

"If my opinion will make it easier to admit your feelings for him …"

Feelings? The fact that she couldn't stop thinking about him? The fact she often played out their argument in her mind, and wished things had turned out differently?

Penelope picked up the fudge, threw it in the trash, and sat back down. How did a woman recover from a broken heart?

You're a professional and selfless woman and absolutely amazing, he had said.

You are beautiful.

No more thinking about him, she scolded herself, yet the memory of his attentiveness, his tender kisses, his kindness, lay suspended in the air.

"Knock, knock, my friend. Come back." Candee reached over and tapped Penelope's shoulder. "That man genuinely cares about you, and I believe you care equally for him. His feelings for you are so intense, it would astonish him if he stopped to examine them. Whatever your differences, please give him a chance."

"He was wrong. He needs to reach out to me again."

"Forgiveness is a powerful gift, especially at Christmas. Accept this gift, for it promises peace. Isn't the holiday all about reconciliation and good will toward men?"

Piped in music from the candy store spilled onto the porch, lyrics of "Tidings of comfort and joy, comfort and joy, oh, tidings of comfort and joy."

"God Rest Ye Merry, Gentlemen." Penelope's beloved Christmas carol. She rocked on the chair as optimism bloomed. Perhaps there was a chance for her and Jacob, after all.

Candee finished her fudge, and the women continued

perusing the shops. Candee spotted an oil painting of a horse for her son's room, while Penelope skirted into a local hardware store.

"Are you handy with tools?" she'd questioned Jacob after they viewed the dilapidated house.

"I don't even own a tool kit," he'd replied.

She didn't understand why she considered buying him a Christmas gift and couldn't imagine when she might give it to him. Nonetheless, she purchased a kit featuring pliers, a hammer, and a screwdriver. It was a start at reconciliation, although later she would wonder what madness had possessed her to buy such a thing, especially when she requested the merchant to wrap the gift in winter wonderland foil paper.

"Did you need some tools?" Candee inquired with a laugh when the women met outside their respective shops. Her gentle prodding made Penelope feel churlish for questioning her purchase. Jacob's smile warmed her heart, and his thoughtfulness toward the community knew no bounds. He was level-headed and tuned into her emotions. Plus, he respected the boundaries she'd set. She couldn't fault him for that.

On the houseboat, he'd looked breathlessly handsome in casual jeans, and his polo shirt had fit his broad shoulders to perfection. She well remembered the thrill of gazing into his dark eyes when they'd captured and held hers.

"I promise," he'd replied when she'd asked him to never turn into her ex, and tenderness had swelled in her heart at his earnest response.

He'd sealed his words with a deep, toe-curling kiss that had left her breathless.

She wasn't certain he loved her, but he did care for her. And after all, it was Christmas. She'd write out a card and congratulate him on his home purchase, then send the gift to the clinic with Evan. She smiled, imagining Jacob unwrapping the gift and then texting her.

She clutched his gift close and strolled the sidewalk with Candee. She flashed her friend a smile when she kept inquiring about Penelope's "secret" from the hardware store, because Penelope refused to divulge the details. Some things, she decided, required a privacy of the heart.

A jarring note of laughter echoed from the steps of a nearby shop. Meredith Sinclair stood with a group of women, her stunning blond hair and slim figure reminding Penelope of a runway model.

"Dr. Williams is coming over for dinner soon," she told the women. "I didn't want the poor man to be alone during the holidays. I'm making my famous baked ham with pineapple and all the trimmings."

"Did he accept?" one of the women asked.

"He said it all depends on his work schedule, but he seemed more than a little interested." With a twitch of her checkered pencil skirt, she reminded that she'd see them all at her cookie exchange on Sunday.

Jacob's social life is none of my business, Penelope thought. She rubbed her forehead and closed her eyes. He was free to date whomever he chose. Besides, she shouldn't have been eavesdropping, though Meredith had spoken loud enough for the entire town to hear.

Penelope had listened to the conversation with annoyed sadness, wondering if Jacob would accept the woman's invitation. In that instant, Penelope resented the town, and all the women's gazes who now seemed focused solely on her.

Her thoughts scrambled. Perhaps she should return to Hilton Head with Evan and live peacefully on the houseboat.

With a look of feigned naiveness, Meredith sidled over. "Penelope, I didn't see you at first. Are you free to attend my cookie exchange on Sunday?"

While Candee looked on, Penelope met Meredith's gaze with measured composure. She took a brief mental pause and focused on the positive things in her life. She'd created an uncluttered, relaxing atmosphere at home. She and Evan were eating healthier, and she was looking forward to spending Christmas Eve with Evan and his new puppy. She was better than jealousy or ill will.

She straightened her shoulders. "Evan is leaving for Florida soon, and we'll be attending to last-minute details," she replied. "I'll donate my cookies to the first responders in town. Thank you for the invite, and I wish you and your family a Merry Christmas."

A couple of days later, Penelope found her son in his bedroom, a half-empty, open suitcase on his bed. His phone was propped beside him, tuned to a pop station playing a rock version of "Jingle Bells."

"You haven't finished packing for your trip yet?" she asked.

"Florida is hot, and I won't need much."

"We leave in an hour," Penelope reminded, handing Evan a box wrapped in pink and white paper. "Please give this gift to your father and stepmother for the new baby. I carved a wooden doll for Christina."

"That was nice, Mom. She can't play with it yet."

"Someday." Penelope leaned over and smoothed Evan's dark hair. He sat on the bed with his legs stretched out. Lately, he'd been swimming at the rec center, perfecting his butterfly stroke, and training with the swim coach. He and Zack hung out after school, and Evan looked calmer and happier. He was coming into his own and finding his way.

He scanned her features. "I'll miss you, Mom."

"I'll miss you, too." She regarded her fine-looking son,

and her heart burst with pride. She reached out and gave him a quick hug, envisioning his thrill at the surprise puppy waiting for him when he returned.

"Dr. Williams is working overtime at the clinic." Evan adjusted the volume on his cell phone and the music muted. "You should see his Santa Claus costume. It's too big, and he holds up the pants with a wide black belt. He couldn't find a white beard, but he wears a red velvet hat. Everyone thinks he looks funny. Dr. Hannaway is always serious, but even she laughed when she saw him."

Penelope nodded. "I bet."

"He liked the Christmas cookies you sent, especially the ones with the chocolate filling. He snuck a few while I gave them out to the kids and he said you're an excellent baker. He's working eighteen hours every day between his private practice and the clinic."

They sat in silence for a minute, listening to the next selection on his phone.

"Silent Night." A quiet, peaceful song. Simple.

I'm learning that simple is best, Jacob had mentioned.

"What are we doing on Christmas Eve?" Evan asked. "Uncle Lincoln and Aunt Shanice aren't here."

"I'll pick you up at the airport and in the afternoon, we'll attend church service."

"What will you do when I'm in Florida with Dad?"

"There is plenty of work at the toy shop to keep me busy. Don't worry."

Evan worries about you because you worry about him, Jacob had said. *And too much worry isn't good for a kid.*

She squeezed Evan's hand. "I love you, and you've made me infinitely proud. When your father and I divorced, I was stuck, but you're here, we're together, and I'm happy it's Christmas."

"Okay, Mom, okay." His smile was affectionate. "Can I tell you something?"

"Of course."

He darted a glance at her and took a deep breath. "Remember when Zack's mother got into an accident?"

Her heart stilled. "How could I forget?"

"I told you she backed into a mailbox near the rec center."

"Right."

"I have a confession." He pulled at the collar of his T-shirt and shifted on the bed. "I lied to you, and I'm sorry. After we stopped for milk shakes that day, I asked Zack's mother to drive us to the animal shelter to see the dogs. I didn't want to get you upset and tell you. I knew we were already late, but I couldn't resist."

"You're forgiven for lying." Penelope fought against the impulse to reprimand him. Lecturing wasn't helpful, and she understood his underlying reason. "I love dogs, too."

"So does Dr. Williams."

Her emotions swung back and forth between desire and despondency at the mention of Jacob's name.

"If you're geared to homeschool next semester, we can live on Hilton Head Island," she offered.

"Are you kidding? I'm trying out for the swim team, and we practice every day after school." Evan drew his legs up and rested his chin on his knees. "Someday, when I go to college, I'd like to study abroad. Maybe I'll win a scholarship. My coach said there are loads of opportunities if I practice real hard."

The idea of Evan leaving and going to another country brought tears to her eyes and a discreet sniff she hoped he didn't hear.

"Not forever," Evan assured. "I'll come back often. I promise. Especially for Christmas."

"All kids should travel abroad." Her voice broke as she

pulled him into another hug. "Your experiences there will frame the rest of your life."

"You're a cool mother," Evan said. "Now I need to finish packing."

AFTER PENELOPE DROPPED Evan off at the airport with a tearful goodbye, she hurried home. Obsessing over the details, she'd set up a puppy checklist and purchased water bowls, a crate, puppy food, a dog bed, toys, and a leash. She'd hid all the items in the garage.

Satisfied the house was prepped and ready for the precious, cute addition, the next few days passed quickly. Evan texted when he'd landed in Florida. He assured he was having a good time and that baby Christina was adorable, although she cried a lot.

Occasionally, when Penelope passed the decorated Christmas tree in the living room, she glanced under it. Several bundled packages topped with gold ribbon were from Lincoln and Shanice, plus an assortment of gifts from her ex that he'd sent ahead for Evan.

Jacob's tool kit sat wrapped in the winter wonderland paper, and she pondered when she'd ever give it to him. Alongside was the gift he'd given her, packaged in red and green paper. She hadn't opened his gift. Obviously, he hadn't opened hers.

The realization made her want to pour out her sorrow, the pang of longing so strong, she felt weak. She wrapped her arms around her stomach and hunched over, overcome with sadness. Jacob was so impressive, so kind, so remarkably good-looking. If he'd only text her again, she'd agree to see him.

No, no. She couldn't waste her emotions on a man who didn't care. She deserved more from him. And he deserved more from her. Regardless, they couldn't give each other what they both needed because pride stood in the way.

Lincoln phoned and requested she fly to Virginia to tidy up loose ends from the recent acquisition. Though reluctant, she asked pointed questions and eventually agreed. Dismissing her negative thoughts, she pushed up the sleeves of her wool blazer and flew the short, round trip to Virginia the following day.

As PLANNED, Penelope picked Evan up at the airport on Christmas Eve day.

They stopped home to change and unpack. Mindful they were picking up his puppy after the afternoon church service, she dressed in gray slacks and a silvery sweater adorned with snowflakes. Lately, her clothes fit better, and she attributed her success to healthier eating. She had also initiated an exercise routine, which included a thirty-minute daily walk.

A Scottish plaid scarf, red quilted vest, and high leather boots completed her ensemble. Tasteful, yet casual enough to handle a wriggling puppy.

She paused to study her reflection in the hallway mirror before they left for church. When she tucked an errant tendril behind her ear, her faux diamond stud earrings flashed back at her. She'd styled her hair in a loose bun, adorned with a pearl clip.

Evan wore tan-colored chinos, a polo shirt, and his black leather jacket.

The rain had cleared out, and the forecast had changed. There was a possibility of snow for Christmas Day, the weatherman declared, which was a huge event for the Southern residents of Roses.

After pausing to speak with the pastor and admire the

live nativity after church, she drove to the animal shelter as early evening neared. A star-spangled sky promised clear weather, at least for now.

She'd checked ahead to be certain the shelter was open, and the volunteer assured two puppies were available for adoption.

"Mom, this isn't the way to our house," Evan reminded.

Hardly able to contain her excitement, she parked in front of the shelter. The interior lights blazed, cordial and welcoming.

She swallowed a laugh. "Are you ready to take your new puppy home?"

His eyes rounded. He clutched the door handle, then swiveled to her, his face beaming with elation. "You mean it?"

"Absolutely." She embraced him, envisioning his joy at seeing the puppies. "Merry Christmas!"

He burst into tears. "Don't mind me, Mom." He wiped his wet cheeks with a chagrined smile. "I'm just so happy."

A car pulled up and parked behind them. She stole a glance in the rearview mirror, and her hand went to her throat. A very yellow, very recognizable Volkswagen.

"Yay, it's Santa Claus." Evan threw a fist pump, then flung open the door and dashed from the truck.

Penelope got out and leaned against her truck. Her heart raced.

A tall, broad-shouldered man, carrying a bouquet of roses, strode toward her. A whisper of moonlight lit his path.

And he wasn't Santa.

"Hi, Evan." Jacob pulled off his red velvet hat and shoved it in the pocket of his rumpled Santa suit. "Hello, Penelope."

"Jacob." Incredulous, Penelope hung back in surprise. She searched for her voice and couldn't find it. "Are you here for a puppy?"

"I'm here for you, Penelope." He laid the bouquet on the hood of the truck. "Merry Christmas."

Breathe, Penelope, breathe. The fragrant scent of a dozen red roses wafted in the night air. "You're not working at the clinic?"

"I've seen patients all day. Dr. Hannaway stepped in for me."

"Mom is getting me a puppy, Dr. Williams!" Evan's eyes sparkled.

She gave Evan a radiant smile and nodded toward the animal shelter. "The volunteer is waiting for you. There are two puppies left to be adopted."

Evan broke into a run and took the stairs to the shelter three at a time. With a decided wave, he hurried inside.

"I'll meet you in a minute," she called out to him.

Jacob's posture was still. He released a sigh and stared at her. "Penelope, you are amazing."

"I planned this ahead."

"You're a planner."

He resembled a man who had just stepped out of her favorite romance novel, a handsome hero, though he had a full day's growth of a dark beard. He looked thinner, yet perhaps she imagined it.

"Why are you here?" Her voice shook.

"You ignored me. I waited like you asked, but when I didn't hear from you, I resorted to Plan B."

A thought niggled, then broke free. He'd done the gentlemanly thing, abiding by her wishes. And then he hadn't.

Curious, she tilted her head up. "What is Plan B?"

"It's my twofold puppy plan. Evan and I volunteered at the shelter, and I got friendly with everyone." His deep voice strengthened. "Sure enough, they mentioned you planned to surprise Evan on Christmas Eve."

He stepped forward. Curtains stirred in the windows of

nearby residents. Twinkling white lights shone from inside. The smell of wood-burning fireplaces permeated the air.

She gestured toward the homes. "There's the disadvantage of small-town living. Everyone knows everybody else's business."

"The advantages are a close-knit community and slower pace." Jacob's lips curved into a smile. "Oh, let's see, and a quaint, idyllic community, and a beautiful woman. A woman I'd really like to date again."

Tears swelled in her eyes. "You're working nonstop."

"I'm changing my schedule. Along with several other aspects of my life."

"You bought the house we looked at. Candee told me."

He chuckled. "A cheap house will allow me to work less, plus I'll be able to have an office there and see patients. The home is a start, but I need more."

"What do you need?"

"You." He caught a stray tear that trickled down her cheek. "Even though you broke my heart."

She inhaled, drawing a sharp breath. "I did? I didn't realize—"

"That I loved you? Well, I do. And I apologize for what happened at Pelican Beach. If you give me a second chance to prove myself ..." He quirked an eyebrow and smiled. "After all, it is Christmas."

"Jacob, please don't apologize. You did nothing wrong. You care. That's not a fault."

The chemistry between them crackled. There was magic in the air. The magic that came with Christmas. The magic that came with love.

Her anger at him had been foolish and juvenile. She'd lashed out at him, though Roy had been the source of her hurt and insecurities.

"My mum and sister are moving back to Melbourne," Jacob said. "I told them I'd visit."

"Good."

"Will you join me? With Evan?" His words rushed together. "You can talk to me nonstop on the plane. I realize flying is involved unless—"

"Jacob, I … I need a second … I wanted to tell you I flew to Virginia recently." She dragged air into her lungs. "I was afraid at first, but then I realized there was something else I was even more afraid of than flying."

He gathered her in his arms and drew her close. Nearer, tighter. "What?"

She pressed a hand to his heart. "I was afraid I had lost you because I pushed you away. I love you, too."

"You'll never lose me. Roses is where I intend to stay." He traced her lips with his fingers. "Will you give me another chance?"

"I have a son."

"An amazing son. As amazing as his mother."

She ran her fingers along his strong cheekbones. She loved his good-looking features, his nearness, his solid hold. She turned her face into his chest and listened to the steady thud of his heart.

He lifted her chin and cupped her face in his hands. He kissed her, slowly at first, warm and emotional, then more intensely as his mouth captured hers. "I love you, Penelope. You're special, and when I lost you from my life, I knew I needed to find a way to bring us together."

She grinned. "Plan B?"

"The twofold puppy plan."

"Wait." Her grin widened. "What do you mean by twofold?"

A shout from the shelter's entrance startled her, and she pulled back from Jacob's embrace.

"Mom, are you coming inside?" Evan cuddled two fluffy, cream-colored puppies in his arms. "I chose my puppies!"

She shuffled back a step. "Puppies? As in, more than one?"

"They're brother and sister. They can't be separated because I named them." Evan's face was flushed and radiant. "Come and meet Kris and Kringle. Kris is the boy and Kringle is the girl. You'll fall in love. I promise."

"We're already in love," Jacob whispered. He twined his fingers around hers and led her toward the entrance.

"All this love at Christmas." She smiled and affectionately nudged him. She was at ease with her world.

"Doctor Williams, your dog is waiting for you," Evan declared as they approached.

Penelope touched her throat. Her breath stalled. "Jacob, you're adopting a dog, too?"

"Truth?" He grinned and kissed her temple.

"Uh-huh."

"I'm adopting Nutcracker." His dark eyes lit with an inner glow. "What better way to celebrate Christmas than with two puppies, a mother dog, a stepson, and a beautiful wife?"

"Stepson? And wife?"

"A fantastic stepson and a *beautiful* wife. Penelope Reid, will you marry me?"

She answered without hesitation. Her smile filled with love as she rested her trembling hand on his cheek. "My answer is yes. Yes, yes."

EPILOGUE

ne Year Later

"Who eats quinoa and red peppers during the holidays?" Evan asked.

"We do." Penelope held up her *Change Your Holiday Menu, Change Your Life* cookbook. "Don't you want to continue to eat healthy?"

"This year I vote for cream cheese cookies." Evan looked to Jacob for backup.

Jacob chuckled and raised his hand. "I second the cookie vote."

His wife stood at the stainless-steel sink. The sink at his new house on Brook Street, Jacob thought with a satisfied smile.

Penelope drummed her fingers on the counter and grinned at them both. "Don't either of you like quinoa?"

"I tried it last year," Jacob replied.

"And?"

"I agree with my stepson. Cookies are better." Jacob strode to her and wrapped his arms around her waist. Strains of "It's Beginning to Look a Lot Like Christmas" wafted from the living room stereo.

She gazed at him over her shoulder. "I'm not baking any more cookies, because we're flying to Australia in a few days."

He pressed a kiss on her fragrant hair. Today, she held it back with a silver spangled clip.

"Fortunately, you froze two bags of your chocolate cream cheese cookies in November," he said. "They're my favorite."

She pulled from his embrace, stepped to the refrigerator, and rummaged in the freezer. "Then why is there only one bag of cookies left?"

Jacob and Evan pointed at each other, winked conspiratorially, then burst out laughing. "Recently, we had a late-night cookie festival," Jacob confessed.

She laughed, revealing her adorable dimples. She was gorgeous when she laughed. Her eyes were soft and shiny.

"I'm outnumbered by animals in this house." She gazed at the two sleeping dogs in the corner: Kris and Kringle. They weren't considered puppies anymore, though Kris still had puppy energy, and Kringle continued to chew on everything in sight. True to their breed, the dogs were willful, independent, and more than a little stubborn. However, they'd settled into the routine of life at the Williams' new home.

"What do Australians eat at Christmas, Dad?" Evan swiped three cookies from the freezer bag and placed them in the microwave to thaw.

Dad. Jacob took the word to heart. His stepson's acceptance and love meant the world.

"We usually begin with prawns at lunchtime. Lots and lots of prawns and they are massive. My sister is making lasagna, so at least we'll get our lasagna." Jacob gave a thumbs-up to Evan. "And my mum is serving a cold roasted chicken."

"Why cold?"

"It's too hot in Australia in December to cook a lot. Fortunately, my mum and sister bought a home with a pool, and you'll still be able to keep up with your swim practice."

Penelope caught Jacob's gaze and smiled. "Melbourne. Your hometown."

"Yea. I'm looking forward to showing you and Evan the sights." His chest expanded with each breath. "I remember restaurants by the Yarra River, and my mum is excited about the performing arts complex."

His mum had sold the farm at a profit, and she insisted that he no longer needed to send her money. Along with the savings on the inexpensive home purchase, he'd curtailed his hours at the clinic and hired another doctor. Seeing patients at his home office enabled him to spend more time with Penelope and Evan, the two loves of his life.

Spurred by Penelope's encouragement, Jacob had phoned and spoken with his mum and sister for hours. They'd shared stories about his niece, Linda, and grieved, while continuing to cope with the devastating loss. They sought comfort in their memories and had resolved to stick together.

"Australia is far away." Evan glanced at his two dogs. No longer puppies, Kris and Kringle resembled their mother, with white coats and almond-shaped eyes. Their paws turned out, and the distinctive pink markings they once had on their nose and paws had changed to black. "I'll miss them."

"Uncle Lincoln and Aunt Shanice will take excellent care of our animals," Penelope assured him.

"Nutcracker, Kris, Kringle, and Giblet." Evan grabbed the cookies from the microwave, shouldered his swim bag, and started for the door. "Gotta go. Practice begins in an hour and Zack's mother is picking me up."

"Have fun," Jacob and Penelope chimed.

Once Evan left, Jacob grabbed Penelope's hand and led her to the living room. Nutcracker, never far behind Jacob, took up her favorite spot by the fireplace.

They'd positioned Penelope's faux fir tree by the front window, and decorated it for Christmas in a tasteful, subdued flair. His tool kit sat under the tree. A thoughtful gift. Last year, they'd chuckled with the realization that it would take more than a tool kit to renovate a fixer upper on Jacob's limited budget. Together as a family, they'd painted floorboards, discarded the ancient front door for a new red one, and hung curtains. They'd left carpet, bathrooms, and kitchen appliance installation and remodeling to the professionals.

But renovate they had. Room by room, until the Victorian shone shiny and preserved. Jacob adored the home's character, the quirky light fixtures, and the unique woodwork and intricate moldings.

Penelope elected to place his Christmas gift to her from last year, the photo he'd taken of her when they'd first met at the airport, on the coffee table.

He smiled as he regarded the photo. His beautiful wife, wearing a cream-colored crepe blouse and brown slacks. Her dark hair, shaped in a short bob style, had grown longer this past year. Silver highlights still framed her lovely face.

The photo was placed in a glass frame alongside a stack of romance books. A row of carved wooden dolls, all named for various spices, were ready to be transported to the nearest hospital or shelter for children of all ages to enjoy.

After Penelope and Jacob had wed six months earlier, and his house was finally livable, she and Evan had moved in. Candee had secured a buyer for Penelope's house the first day she'd put it on the market. Success all around.

"I'm glad you decided to cut back your hours at the toy shop," he said, pulling her beside him on the sofa.

"Me too, yet the decision was difficult." She offered a tremulous smile that touched his heart. "I love my craft. Woodworking is infinitely rewarding."

"You're amazing and talented, beautiful." He brought her fingers to his lips for a kiss. "Do you know how much I love you?" His heart filled with more emotion than he thought it could hold—happiness, appreciation, and love.

"I hope looking after all our animals isn't asking too much from Lincoln and Shanice," she said. "They were out of town last Christmas—"

"And we'll be out of town this Christmas," Jacob finished.

She gazed up at him. "Are you certain the only flight you were able to book leaves on Christmas Day?"

"Yea. The trip takes about twenty hours, with two stopovers."

She shuddered and threw him an accusing stare. "Crikey."

He laughed. "Just sleep, eat, watch movies, and, most importantly, talk."

"Okay." She sighed and snuggled nearer him.

He gazed around his home. A beaut. His dream for a simple, rewarding life had come true. What a wonderful road he and Penelope had traveled. Eighteen months ago, he'd never have imagined a Christmas like this.

Though here he was, in this Americana town he called home, with a woman he loved more than anything in the world. When he'd surprised her at the animal shelter on Christmas Eve almost a year ago and declared his love, she'd cast aside her pride because she loved him, too. And that remembrance would remain in his heart forever.

He'd changed his lifestyle to accommodate his beliefs and found love in the bargain. Finally, he was at ease with his world.

"Jacob?" Penelope asked.

He gazed into her compelling eyes and outlined the curve of her jaw and cheeks. "Hmm?"

"How will we celebrate Christmas if we're not in Roses, or even in Australia yet?"

"Simple." He drew her close and kissed her. "We'll celebrate Christmas in the air."

THE END

ABOUT THE AUTHOR

Josie Riviera is a *USA TODAY* bestselling author of contemporary, inspirational, and historical sweet romances that read like Hallmark movies. She lives in the Charlotte, NC, area with her wonderfully supportive husband. They share their home with an adorable shih tzu, who constantly needs grooming, and live in an old house forever needing renovations.

Become a member of my Read and Review VIP Facebook group for exclusive giveaways and ARCs.

To connect with Josie, visit her webpage and subscribe to her newsletter. As a thank-you, she'll send you a free sweet romance novella directly to your inbox.

A Christmas Puppy To Cherish
A Homecoming To Cherish
A Summer To Cherish
Romance Stories To Cherish
Romance Stories To Cherish Volume Two
Cherished Hearts Six Book Volume
Aloha To Love
Sweet Peppermint Kisses
Valentine Hearts Boxed Set
1-800-CUPID
1-800-CHRISTMAS
1-800-IRELAND
1-800-SUMMER
1-800-NEW YEAR
The 1-800-Series Sweet Contemporary Romance Bundle
The 1-800-Series Romance Bundle Volume Two
The 1-800-Series Complete Collection
Irish Hearts Sweet Romance Bundle
Holly's Gift
A Chocolate-Box Christmas
A Chocolate-Box New Years
A Chocolate-Box Valentine
A Chocolate-Box Summer Breeze
A Chocolate-Box Christmas Wish
A Chocolate-Box Irish Wedding
Chocolate-Box Hearts
Chocolate-Box Hearts Volume Two
Chocolate-Box Double Hearts
Recipes From The Heart
Leading Hearts
New Year Hearts
SENIOR HEARTS
Summer Hearts

Christmas in the Air (1-800-Book)
A Very Christian Christmas

Most books are available in ebook, audiobook, paperback,
Large Print paperback and Hardcover.
Many are FREE on Kindle Unlimited!